Early Warning

By Jane Smiley

Early Warning

JANE SMILEY

MANTLE

First published 2015 in the United States by Alfred A. Knopf,
a division of Random House LLC, New York,
and in Canada by Random House of Canada Limited, Toronto,
Penguin Random House companies.

First published in the UK 2015 by Mantle
an imprint of Pan Macmillan, a division of Macmillan Publishers Limited
Pan Macmillan, 20 New Wharf Road, London N1 9RR
Basingstoke and Oxford
Associated companies throughout the world
www.panmacmillan.com

ISBN 978-1-4472-7564-0

1 3 5 7 9 8 6 4 2

A CIP catalogue record for this book is available from the British Library.

Typeset by Scribe, Philadelphia, Pennsylvania
Printed and bound by CPI Group (UK) Ltd, Croydon, CR0 4YY

Visit **www.panmacmillan.com** to read more about all our books
and to buy them. You will also find features, author interviews
and news of any author events, and you can sign up for e-newsletters
so that you're always first to hear about our new releases.

*This trilogy is dedicated to John Whiston,
Bill Silag, Steve Mortensen, and Jack Canning,
with many thanks for decades of patience, laughter,
insight, information, and assistance.*

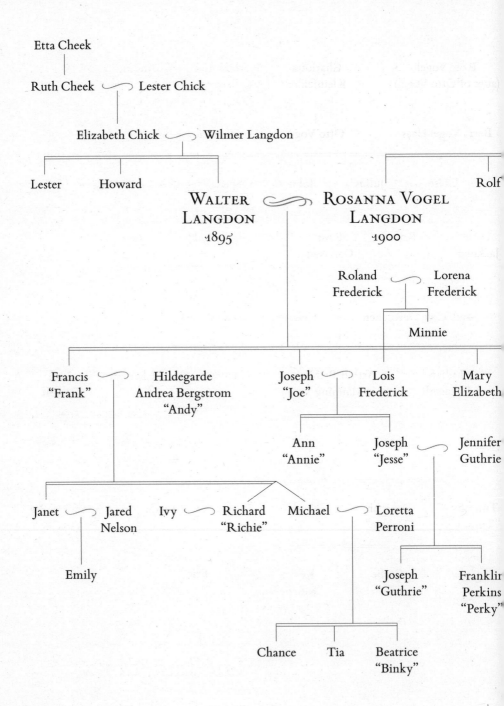

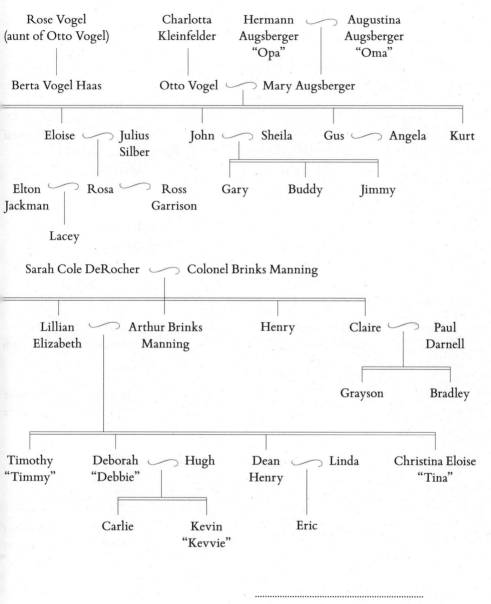

The Langdons

Early Warning

1953

THE FUNERAL WAS a riot of floral exuberance—not just lilies, but daffodils and tulips and sprays of apple and pear blossom. Frank Langdon sat with his daughter, Janny, about six pews back on the right; his wife, Andy, and their month-old twins, of course, couldn't come all the way to Iowa. Janny, two and a half, was behaving herself. Frank took his hand off her knee, and she stayed quiet. The broken sounds of tears being suppressed rose all around him. Frank's sister Lillian, her husband, Arthur, and their four kids were two pews ahead on the left. Mama was sitting in the front pew, staring straight ahead. Granny Elizabeth was sitting next to her, alone now—Grandpa Wilmer had died in the summer; in the intervening nine months, Granny had traveled to Kansas City, St. Louis, and Minneapolis. His mother liked to cluck knowingly and say, "She's blossomed, hasn't she?"

His brother Joe's baby, the same age as his twins, looked like she weighed what they did together. Joe's wife, Lois, and her sister, Minnie, passed the baby back and forth to keep her quiet. Frank stared at Minnie for a moment. He had known her his whole life, walked to school with her for years, known always that she was on his side. Maybe she loved him still. Frank cleared his throat. Annie, the child's name was. Janny couldn't get enough of her—she talked to her and stroked her head if she got a chance. Across the aisle from Minnie were Frank's brother Henry, his communist aunt Eloise, and Eloise's daughter, Rosa. His sister Claire—fourteen, nineteen years to the day younger than Frank himself—kept turning her head and looking at Rosa, and why not? The girl was at her peak at twenty, severe and slender, with the look of a French actress. She made Henry, who was only months older, look like a girl, Claire look like a sheep, Andy, even glamorous Andy, look like a frump. Rosa was much more alluring than his aunt Eloise had ever been. Frank looked away. It was his father's funeral.

After the interment (where Janny wanted to walk from grave to grave, smelling the daffodils in full bloom; Frank didn't stop her), Frank calculated that he'd kept that sad smile on his face for eight solid hours. He held his drink, Scotch and soda—supplied by Minnie, who was now assistant principal at the high school and lived here, apparently comfortably, with Lois and Joe. Frank watched the neighbors come and go. This house, much grander than the house they'd grown up in, was industriously clean. The famous dining room with the sliding French doors that had been the envy of farmers around Denby, Iowa, all through Frank's childhood, still had flowered wallpaper and heavy moldings. While he was pondering the double-hung windows, Arthur Manning came up to him, as if they were merely brothers-in-law who just happened to see each other at a family funeral. Frank often wondered if his sister Lillian had any idea of what her husband talked to Frank about, or the uses he put him to.

Arthur held Tina against his shoulder. She was three months now, wiry and active, as if she planned to head out the door any moment. Arthur's tweed jacket was festooned with a folded diaper. Arthur jiggled and comforted a baby the way a great athlete hit a ball, as if his adept grace and evident reproductive success were the easiest thing in the world. Tina burbled and muttered, wide awake and not crying. Frank admired this.

Arthur said, "How are Richie and Michael doing?"

"Coming along," said Frank.

"What are they now?"

"A month. But they were four and a half weeks early, so let's call them newborns."

"Precocious, then," said Arthur, with a straight face, and Frank smiled a real smile. He said, "It's a good thing Mama hasn't seen them. She might suggest putting them down."

Arthur's eyebrows lifted.

"Mama's strict about babies. If you aren't good-looking, you could be carrying something contagious."

Arthur kissed Tina on the forehead.

"Don't worry, Arthur," said Frank. "Tina would pass."

Arthur laughed. But Frank could see it—even at his father's funeral, Mama doled out words and smiles like stock options. Annie and Lillian were the preferred stock; Timmy, Arthur's oldest at six, the class-A common stock; Debbie, five, Dean and Janny, both two and a half, the class-B common stock—not much of a risk, but not much of a dividend, either. Tina, who could still turn out to be blond, could rise in value or decline. As for Frank himself, well, he had taken his company private, and Mama didn't have much of an investment there at all—a peck on the cheek, a reassurance that everything was going to turn out fine. Frank lowered his voice: "Have you talked with Eloise?"

Arthur jiggled Tina again. His voice was low, too. "We clinked glasses, but we haven't exchanged actual words."

"Were you congratulating each other on the death of old Joe?" Stalin had been dead about two weeks.

"I think we were."

"Did your organization have anything to do with it?"

"Not that I know of," said Arthur, seriously. "Just dumb luck, I suspect. But we will take the credit if it is offered to us." He shifted Tina to the other shoulder. "Maybe he doesn't matter, though. There's no sign that things have changed or that their ambitions have waned."

Frank nodded, then said, "You know what we said in the war? Two Russkies die, four more pop up. Why would Stalin be different?"

"You know that, when Hitler and Stalin were playing footsie, Hitler promised him Iran, right?"

"I didn't know that."

"He did. Now Mossadegh hates the Brits so much that he's heading that way, too. However Iran goes, so go the rest of them."

"Truman would have let them have it," said Frank. "He let them have Eastern Europe. Maybe Ike has more balls."

"Zorin is in Tehran now. He was in Prague in '48. Coups are what he does."

Frank half expected Arthur to ask him to do something, but he couldn't imagine what that would be. Jim Upjohn, the savviest investor Frank knew, had recently put a lot of money into Getty, but Getty was based in Kuwait and Arabia—nothing in Iran. Arthur said, "I'm ready for bedtime. How about you?"

Frank said, "Always."

But dinner was served. Once they were seated, Janny between himself and Minnie, who kept putting bits of food on her plate, Janny seemed to cheer up. She ate everything Minnie gave her, and asked for more of the canned corn. There was plenty, as always—beef stew, beans, rolls, the newest possible potatoes, an angel-food cake. When everyone had eaten their fill, Joe told a story—the kind people tell at family dinners after a funeral, about the person who died. "One time, Papa sat me on our horse Jake, and then led me to the apple tree and had me pick apples. I would hand them to him, and he would put them in an old feed sack."

"Oh, that was the Arkansas Black," said Rosanna. "So good. Only cropped every two years, though."

"When Walter showed up to propose to you, Rosanna," said Eloise, "I remember he wore the strangest hat."

"It was a derby!" exclaimed Rosanna. "Very stylish."

"I was looking out the window. I thought he was wearing a turban."

"How did that look like a turban?" said Rosanna.

"I didn't know! I'd never seen a turban, either."

Everyone laughed.

Minnie said, "What about the rattlesnake?"

"What rattlesnake?" said Joe.

Frank suddenly remembered this.

Minnie said, "Frankie and I were picking pole beans. We were maybe seven. There was a snake under the bottom of the fence, a step from where we were. Walter must have been watching us, because, as soon as I screamed, this long, forked stick came down and pinned the snake's head right to the ground. We ran away. I don't know what Walter did with the snake."

Frank said, "He cut off the head with a hoe. I remember him saying that the cut-off head could still bite."

Debbie said, "What do you remember, Mommy?"

"Well," said Lillian, "one time when I was working at the drugstore, I was at the counter late at night, adding up what I had sold for the day, and someone sat next to me, and kind of leaned into me, so I moved over without looking up from my figures, and he leaned into me a little more, so I moved over a little more, and he elbowed me in the side, so I whipped around to tell that guy to get away from me, and it was my papa, grinning like mad that he had played a trick on me. We laughed all the way home."

Debbie nodded. Frank had never thought of Walter as playful.

Henry said, "When I was about nine, we came out the back door in the morning, and Papa said, 'Look at that.' He was pointing at something. Then he moved his finger in a curve and said, 'See that sheen?' and it was a huge spiderweb covered with dew. It must have been ten feet across, and perfect."

Claire started crying. Rosanna said, "We could have lost him long ago." She dabbed at her eyes with the hem of her apron.

Everyone sat up.

She nodded. "Papa fell into the well. He was standing on the cover of it—the old well—and it broke away. He flung out his arms to the sides and caught himself. That well out by the barn—that's a deep one. He climbed out and never said a word about it until a couple of years ago. He told me he hung there, trying to decide. I asked him, 'Walter, what were you trying to decide?' He said he was trying to decide how to get out, but I'm sure he was trying to decide whether to get out, because I'm telling you, back in the Depression, it seemed like either a slow death or a quick one were the only choices." She shook her head. "So—I tell myself we had twenty extra years. That's what I tell myself."

The memory of his father that came to Frank was of having his pants pulled down and being beaten with the belt—no memory of pain, only of Walter looming over him, the muscles of his forearm twitching and bulging, the words matching the rhythm of the blows, Frank's close-up view of the hairs on the back of Walter's hand.

LOUIS MACINTOSH LOOKED LIKE about ten people that Frank knew—that was, he was not tall, not fat, not thin, not handsome, not ugly, not dark, not light. He was not surprised to see Frank and Arthur when they showed up at dusk at Stewart Air Force Base, so Frank wondered what MacIntosh's handler had told him. They boarded the plane, a De Havilland Comet, a sleek-looking airplane (Frank considered himself somewhat of an amateur expert—he worked for Grumman, and he had been taking flying lessons for a year). A simple blue stripe was painted along the fuselage, but no other identification mark. There were ten seats to each side of the aisle, and an unmarked canvas bag sat on each seat, belted in. Frank's and Louis's seats were behind the bags; the toilet was behind their seats. Frank did not have a suitcase, nor did Louis. After Arthur left, someone closed up the plane and someone flew it, but Frank didn't meet or even glimpse the crew. When they took off, Frank saw only the edge of a dreary sunset over the dark lumps of the Catskill Mountains to the west.

Unusually for him, Frank got no feel for MacIntosh, but maybe that was because Frank was better at picking up details at a distance. They both sat quietly, the narrow aisle between them. The canvas sacks of money were uniform—clasps turned and locked, tops folded over, the outline of the square corners within just barely visible. Whoever had packed up what Arthur had said was ten million dollars, Frank thought, was an orderly person. Louis dozed off.

They flew east. The Comet was a quiet plane. Frank was interested to note how they'd installed the engines—not under the wings, which was what he was used to, but within them. And the wings themselves reminded him of some sort of swooping bird—a barn swallow, maybe.

When Louis woke up, he shook his head and looked around, then shifted in his seat with a groan. After a moment, he stood and went into the toilet. As soon as Frank heard the door lock, he was on his feet. He felt all the pockets of Louis's jacket, which was draped over the back of his seat, and all the pockets of his coat, which was folded into the open compartment above their heads. No wallet—that would be in Louis's pants. No briefcase. He looked in the pocket of the seat in front of Louis, and he felt under Louis's seat. Nothing. He sat down again as the lock turned in the door of the toilet, and stared out the window. Below them, the vast Atlantic, black under the moonless cascades of stars.

Frank had intended to beg off this time. Arthur's earlier "assignments" for Frank had been convenient and interesting, and getting to know Jim Upjohn might have been the best thing that had ever happened to him—Jim Upjohn was not only a good friend and a great connection, he was also endlessly eccentric, and fascinating as only a wealthy man at the center of what Aunt Eloise always called "the ruling class" could be. This job—making a very long-distance delivery—had no evident purpose (at least, evident to Frank) and seriously interfered with his day-to-day routine. As usual, the only payoff was giving Arthur what he wanted, and getting Arthur's gratitude in return, and once Arthur got your attention, he could be very compelling.

But Frank's resistance had been momentary. All he had to do was think of spending yet another evening at home with Andy, Janny, and the twins (not yet six months old, but six months felt like an eternity, and twins seemed like quintuplets if you never thought, waking or sleeping, about anything besides feeding, diapers, bathing, burping, crying). Andy was always either tending to one of them or out on the back deck, smoking a cigarette. She had risen to the occasion, no two ways about it—the nurses they'd hired for two months had taught her to order her every moment and the twins' every moment; the boys were thriving, but at the expense of all that was idle or easy. After much hemming and hawing, he and Andy had bought a house in the winter. It was an airy, modern split-level with plenty of windows, contemporary furniture, and wall-to-wall carpet. It felt as bleak in the summer and the spring as it had in January, when they moved in. Doing this job for Arthur felt like playing hooky—returning to his younger, sharper, brighter, and more restless self. If only Andy—the Andy of two years ago—could have come along.

When they stopped to refuel in Sardinia, he wanted to walk around, smell the air. What was her name, that girl, the love of his life? Joan, it was. Joan Fontaine, he had called her. A whore. But it was foolish to daydream about a woman who was lost; instead, he sat quietly and waited for Louis to make a move. When the door opened, Louis stood up and scuttled forward. It was, indeed, Mediterranean light here. Hard to believe that he hadn't been to Italy or France since the war. It was as if he had no idea that Italy would have changed or recovered since he last reconnoitered this cratered city or that blown-up house, looking for Jerries. He had treated stories of postwar renewal in newspapers as unsubstantiated rumors without even realizing it. The airfield was barren, just a long stretch of concrete with a rudimentary tower at one end, not far from the fuel tanks.

Louis hunched down the steps. Frank went into the toilet and pissed without flushing—flushing would release onto the tarmac. He went back to his seat and ate half of his sandwich. When Louis returned, he brought a couple of Cokes. Frank took one.

Louis sat down and buckled his seat belt. Frank said, "This reminds me of the war."

"You in the European theater?"

Frank said, "Africa first, then Italy." Someone closed the hatch. Frank could hear the crew shouting something.

"Pacific for me. Midway. Philippines. Nimitz was a great man."

"Not so many cats to herd," said Frank. "At the time, I was a big fan of Devers, and I couldn't figure out why Ike stopped us at Strasbourg, but now I understand a little more about outrunning your fuel supply."

Louis nodded, then said, "I think you had the prima donnas with you. Montgomery was a fool."

They sniffed simultaneously. The plane began taxiing down the runway, and Frank turned to stare at the beach and then the ocean, so much paler here. Louis said, "Can't say I'm all that comfortable in this aircraft."

Frank turned and looked at him. "Why not?"

"That BOAC Calcutta crash."

"I didn't hear about a Calcutta crash."

"No? Last May sometime. Everyone killed—crew, passengers, everyone."

Frank again glanced out the window at the engine.

Louis said, "Here's the creepy part, you ask me. Witnesses say, when the plane went into the Indian Ocean, it was on fire"—Frank couldn't help looking at him now—"and the wings were gone. Just say this: let's hope we don't encounter a hurricane."

"Let's hope that," said Frank. They were quiet. And it was odd that they were using an English plane, given the antipathy the Iranians were supposed to feel toward the Brits. On the other hand, it was the fastest plane Frank had ever been in—twice as fast, if you included takeoff and landing, as a DC-6. Frank looked out the window past the wings this time, and imagined a hundred thousand hundred-dollar bills fluttering in the air.

THE SUN WAS GOING down again—Frank checked his watch. For him it was about nine or ten in the morning, but here, where the Mediterranean ended and Asia began, it was darkening and reddening toward nightfall.

He had dropped off, but it had been a restful if alert sort of doze that not only reminded him of his time in North Africa but made him remember what it felt like to be twenty-one rather than thirty-three. He undid his seat belt and stood up, allowing himself to yawn. He cocked his head to the side and slid toward the bathroom, opened the door, went in. He gave himself a bit of time, but not too long, and then he stood up, flushed, waited another moment. He unlocked the door. Louis was sitting just as he had been most of the trip, rereading his copy of *The Saturday Evening Post*. Frank saw at once that the angle of the folded top of the third bag forward on the right—Frank's side—was slightly different. And the middle of the three clasps had not been twisted as tightly as before. The other clasps were unchanged. This was why Arthur had hired him—to notice things. Frank sat down again. Louis paid no attention to him. Frank had no idea what Louis's self-defense skills were. Frank also had no idea how his own skills might have deteriorated since he was actually twenty-one and could grab some guy's fist almost before the guy decided to pop him one.

The Comet landed in a different kind of dark from American dark—much deeper, no glow of nearby cities or streetlights or even headlights making their way from one empty spot to another. Wherever they landed—it was August 13 here, almost the 14th—Frank knew they were somewhere in Iran, but it was not a base or an oil field. It was a quiet place, dry-smelling. The door opened. Three men came up the stairs and began carrying away the sacks. When the man picked up the last two of the ten sacks, Louis stood up to follow him. Frank stood up to follow Louis. Louis had his jacket on, and when he came to the top of the stairs, he slipped into his coat, but that didn't stop Frank from noting the rectangular outline just barely discernible against Louis's chest.

At the bottom of the stairs, Louis broke into an easy trot. The three men with bags were dim in the dark, almost out of sight. Frank was on Louis in a moment, grabbing his wrist and pinning it high and tight behind his back. Louis grunted. Frank said, "I can break your arm, Louis, easy as pie." Louis twisted, and Frank lifted the arm even higher. Louis bent over, and Frank reached around with his left hand and slipped it inside Louis's coat and jacket. He felt the stiff rectangle and pulled it out. There was only one. He stepped away from Louis and flipped through the packet. Louis stumbled forward, caught himself, but didn't do anything other than press and rub his right shoulder with his left hand. He said, "You dislocated it."

"Want me to put it back in?"

"What the fuck do you care, Freeman? It's not your dough."

Frank smiled. Arthur had rebaptized him yet again.

A car pulled up—something nondescript and old, but heavy. The driver got out and opened the trunk, and the ten bags of money were piled in it. The trunk was closed. The driver then opened the back door on the passenger's side, and Louis got in. The driver closed the door. The driver had a beard. He didn't say anything. The three men who had transferred the bags came over and stood rather close to Frank—as close, say, as New Yorkers would stand, closer than Iowans would stand. He felt mildly uncomfortable. After about two minutes, the passenger door of the car opened again, and Louis got out. The man to Frank's left gestured for him to get in. Frank got in. The door closed with a thud.

The fellow in the car was wearing a U.S. Army uniform, two stars on his collar. He held out his hand, and Frank shook it. "Mr. Freeman. Thanks for your help. Arthur speaks highly of you, and, my Lord, we couldn't do a thing or take a step without Arthur. If this shebang goes over, we have Arthur to thank, once again." He cleared his throat. "Looking iffy at this point, I must say. Why this had to come to a head in August is a mystery to me. Must be the hidden hand of the Soviet menace. You got anything to report?"

Frank shook his head.

The man stared at him, the hardness of his gaze belying his casual tone. But how long had Frank been telling lies? As long as he could talk. Finally, Frank said, "Routine operation, sir."

The man nodded. His jacket strained over the pistol in his armpit.

Frank waited for him to hold out his hand for the packet of bills, but he didn't. He rubbed his forehead, as if he had a headache. He said, "Well, then. MacIntosh is staying with me here. I believe you are going back via Majorca. To Cuba? I can't remember. I had some food put on the plane. Good luck to you."

The man knocked on the ceiling of the car, and the passenger door opened. When Frank got out, he was alone beside the plane. Louis and the three men had been taken away, and now the big car drove off, too. It was dead quiet. Even the air was still. The only movement was the flight of two huge birds, probably some kind of vulture—they landed maybe thirty yards away and picked over a carcass for a minute, then lumbered into the air again. Frank had seen vultures before, but as he watched, something about the air and the light entered him and terrified him. The crew of the plane could easily shoot him and leave him here; he would be bones in a day or two. But that wasn't it, exactly. He looked upward, at the endless stars across the flat sky, and recognized nothing—not the Milky Way or the Big Dipper or even, for a moment, that dishlike sliver that was the moon. For thirty-three years he had thought that the unknown was a friendly thing. Now that idea vanished in a millisecond. He swallowed hard, then ran his hand down the side of his trousers and felt the packet of money in his pocket. His assignment. It was reassuring.

By the time they landed at Stewart, his watch had run down. Arthur was there, as if he had never left, at the bottom of the stairs.

"Nice plane," said Frank.

"Something borrowed," said Arthur. Frank took Arthur's right hand and slapped the packet of hundred-dollar bills into it. Arthur barely glanced at them, just put them in his pocket. He said, "You met McClure?"

"Two-star general?"

Arthur nodded. "Tell me everything he said."

"Well, he thanked me for coming, and—"

"No, I mean his exact words."

Frank repeated all of what the general had said to him, understanding at once that this was why Arthur had sent him—his eidetic memory. What else any of it meant to the government, he had no idea and knew Arthur wouldn't tell him. Nevertheless, he did ask, "What's the money for?"

Arthur said, "Popular uprising." Frank thought he saw the ghost of a smile, but only that.

Arthur dropped him outside the split-level just at dawn. He picked up the newspaper, eased in through the lower entrance, then went up to the kitchen. All was quiet for once. On page two, the paper announced that Mossadegh had won the election in Iran. There was no mention of unrest, but as he watched the coup unfold—Mossadegh was out by the end of the week—Frank couldn't stop thinking of that human cipher Louis MacIntosh, who was exactly the sort of person Frank would never have entrusted with buying a gallon of milk at the grocery store.

WHEN HE GOT BACK to Iowa City for the fall semester, Henry Langdon went to a place on Iowa Avenue that sold old things and looked and looked until he found a wooden box with a lock (and a key) for storing his letters from his cousin Rosa (at Berkeley) and carbon copies of his own to her. His were typed, but hers were handwritten. The question of typing had posed a real dilemma— you wanted your personal papers to be handwritten, because they were more, well, personal that way, and also because future literary scholars (the career Henry was preparing himself for) would be able to get a better sense of your personality and character from your handwriting than they would from typing. But it was almost impossible to make a good carbon copy by hand, and it was easy with the typewriter. The box was cheap but roomy. In it, he placed the letters as they had been written—his, hers, his, hers—then, on top of them, that Indian-head gold dollar his father had given him, eleven years ago now. The date on the dollar was 1888. Looking at the dollar, Henry wondered if his joy at being back in Iowa City was some kind of betrayal, especially since here he didn't think of his father or the farm more than once or twice a day. ("And a good thing, for heaven's sake," his mother would say.) He thought of "The Anglo-Saxon Chronicle," he thought of the Venerable Bede, he thought of Defoe, he thought of Rosa Rosa Rosa.

He hadn't seen Rosa since his father's funeral in the spring, but they wrote twice a week. He hadn't counted on Rosa's visiting Denby (meaning "village of the Danes"—it gave him a bona-fide sense of pleasure to know that), or on himself traveling from Iowa to California, so he couldn't say that he was disappointed, exactly, not to have seen her.

The tone of her letters was satirical but good-natured, always affectionate. She now referred to her mother, his aunt Eloise, as "Heloise," never "Mom," and "Heloise's" adventures were a source of amusement—"Tuesday, Heloise ran out of gas on the Bay Bridge, and lo and behold, she had left her purse on the kitchen table, so she waited in traffic with a piece of paper in her hand ('OUT OF GAS PLEASE HELP') and who should stop to pick her up but Gary Snyder, who is a poet, maybe our age. He was riding a motorcycle, and Heloise got on the back and rode to the gas station! She told me he was darling. I am guessing she is going to fix me up with him any day now."

Henry's own letters left something to be desired, he thought. They were detailed and earnest, and quite often he found himself going on too long about things that excited him, like how the system of Roman roads in England dictated subsequent linguistic boundaries, even a thousand years after the end of the Roman Empire (another difficulty with carbon copies—no erasing). But she wrote faithfully; her letters were as long as his and as frequent, and though she often talked about meeting various guys at coffee shops or poetry readings (everything free—no Hollywood trash movies), she never mentioned any name in more than two letters.

Henry knew that Rosa knew that Henry loved her. He signed his letters, "Love, Henry." She signed her letters, "Yours, Rosa." For six weeks, he dreaded Thanksgiving, when she and Aunt Eloise would be coming to the farm and he would have to see her.

On the Wednesday he left for Denby, he spent the whole morning deciding what clothes to take, aware all the while of his roommate's bag beside the door, full of dirty undershorts heading back to Dubuque for their once-a-semester laundering.

Rosa was wearing what she always did—black shoes, black pants, black sweater—though her dark hair was cut in a different style, shorter than Henry's now, showing the nape of her neck. Her neck was long—he hadn't noticed that before. Or the mole on her cheekbone, or that her fingernails were bitten, or that her eyes were brown. They had exchanged 160 letters, counting both hers and his, and he might not have recognized her on the street. She hugged him and kissed him on both cheeks, and he stood stiffly. I'm such an Iowan, he thought miserably.

Thanksgiving Day itself was like the funeral had been—everyone on their best behavior, sitting at the dining-room table for a long time, and lots of talk about his father. Papa was in every room, every sentence, every holiday dish. In an odd way, he was in everyone's face, even the faces of those who had never been said to look like him. Every face except Rosa's. Maybe that was why Henry kept staring at her.

Henry hadn't expected to hold Rosa's hand, or to sit next to her; he'd imagined a conversation about *Waiting for Godot,* which Rosa was reading, or *Paradise Lost,* which Henry was reading. That hadn't happened by Friday morning, which was maybe why Henry was still lolling in bed when Aunt Eloise came over from Granny Mary's by herself for breakfast. Since his supremely orderly, book-filled room was off the kitchen, he could hear them quite well. Almost the first thing his mom said was "How does she expect to find a husband, dressed like that? And with that hair. Look at it, it is so short." His aunt Eloise was seven years younger than his mother, but it could have been twenty, given Rosanna's bossy tone. Henry covered his mouth with his hand so as not to make any noise.

Aunt Eloise said, "Come on, Rosanna. She's twenty. I'm not worried. And anyway, you know who Audrey Hepburn is, don't you? That look is all the rage."

"I'd had Frank by the time I was twenty."

"Look how that turned out." Eloise coughed. Henry knew she was joking, and could imagine his mother waving her hand. "Anyway, I was almost twenty-five when I met Julius. You don't take the first one who comes along anymore." Point to Eloise, thought Henry.

Now there was a silence, and Henry eased himself upward on his bed to hear better. Eloise went on. "In a big city, you have to . . . well, you can, pick and choose."

"You picked and chose Julius?" Point to Rosanna. Henry bit his lip. He didn't remember his uncle Julius very well, except as having that delightful English accent and imposing, articulate English manner. Henry would have picked him, too, he thought. But Julius had died in the war, early, in the failed invasion of Dieppe, when Henry wasn't quite ten.

"I did," said Eloise. "If you want to know, yes, I pursued Julius, not the other way around. You thought Julius was strange, but I thought he was elegant. From the first time I saw him."

Their voices were still good-natured, or at least level.

"Well," said Rosanna, after a moment, "he was argumentative."

"I know that," said Eloise. "But, then, that was what I was used to—growing up with Mama and Papa, and living here."

Point to Eloise, thought Henry.

A chair got pushed back, and then, a moment later, the spigot turned on, so it was his mother who'd gone to the sink. Henry picked up his book, and then Eloise said, "Ma knew I had another friend. I'm surprised she never told you."

The sound of the water stopped. Rosanna said, "No, she didn't. What happened to him?"

And Eloise said, "He went back to his wife."

Henry thought he might really have to wander into the kitchen just to see the looks on their faces.

"Did Ma know about that?"

"She knew everything. She gave me advice."

After a moment, Rosanna said, "What in the world was Ma's advice?"

"Did I know where to find some Queen Anne's lace? And did I know the difference between that and poison hemlock?"

"Everyone knows the difference who was raised on a farm."

Now there was a silence, and Henry thought about the fact that maybe he did not know the difference. Finally, Rosanna said, "Did you ever have to act on Ma's advice?"

Eloise said nothing; maybe she shook her head, or nodded, but her answer was not for Henry to know.

In the end, Henry had to settle for mostly admiring Rosa from afar. Every so often she gave him a look or a smile. She laughed when he laughed, and teased him once or twice. To Eloise, she said, "Don't you like Henry's sweater? It's so classic." She called him "Cousin Henry" a few times, as a joke, and then it turned out she was reading a book of that name, by Anthony Trollope, so they did have one tête-à-tête, though the only Trollope Henry had read was *Orley Farm*, extra-credit for his Victorian-literature class. The best thing was that, the day after he got back to Iowa City, there was a letter in his mailbox, postmarked Denby, from Rosa. She wrote, "Dear Henry, I'm sitting at the dining-room table, here at Uncle Joe's. Baby crying. You think I am doing calculus problems but really, I'm watching you. You are reading something with gold lettering on the spine. Every so often you look at Heloise. I wonder what you're thinking. . . ." It went on for three pages, and it was signed, "Love, Rosa."

1954

∽

TINA MANNING WAS HAVING her first-birthday party. Debbie
Manning had drawn the invitations with crayons on cards, and
then she and Timmy walked all over the neighborhood by themselves to deliver them. Timmy was a good boy, for once. He stood
while they looked both ways when they crossed the street, and did
not pretend to run in front of cars. He had never actually run in
front of a car, but sometimes he would stand on the curb, jumping up
and down, and then jerk his body like he was going to do it. In the
summer, a lady who was passing screamed when she saw him, and
then Debbie herself screamed, and then Timmy fell down laughing.
Debbie hoped that the lady would stop the car and get out and smack
him, but she just shook her head and drove on.

Fifteen invitations had taken Debbie three days of hard work.
Mommy had had to give her Oreos to "keep up her strength," but
Debbie was happy to do it, because Tina was a wonderful child. She
had walked at ten months, could already say "Debbie," and would
stick out her foot and let Debbie put her sock on or take it off again
and again. Very soon, Debbie thought, she and Tina were going to
have a horse, which they would keep in a silver spring. Debbie had a
picture of this silver spring hanging above her bed—she'd used almost
her entire gold crayon for the horse and her entire silver crayon for
the spring. Debbie made sure that the gates at the top and the bottom

of the stairs were always closed, so that Tina would never tumble down them.

Debbie put on her red velvet Christmas dress for the party and zipped it up the side all by herself. Then she put on her white socks with the lace around the tops, and her black Mary Janes. She looked in the mirror. She looked very good. She opened the stair gate and closed it and locked it, then went down, holding the railing just in case Timmy came along and pushed her. At the bottom of the stairs, she opened the gate and closed it. The clock on the mantel said six o'clock. She was the only girl in her kindergarten who could tell the time every time the teacher asked. Even though he was a year and a half older than Debbie, Timmy said that he could not tell the time or recite the alphabet, but Debbie knew that he could.

When the doorbell rang, Daddy came in from the dining room, called out, "Just a minute," then kissed her on the forehead. She gave him her hand, and they went to the door. Daddy opened it. Outside, in the cold, the Meyers were standing on the step, the two boys behind them, their mom and dad. Their mom said, "Oh, Arthur! You look ready to have a good time!"

Daddy said, "Mary! Darling girl! Step right in! Hi, boys! Lillian and Tina are holding court in the dining room so that you warriors can use the living room for your battles." Debbie mouthed the name "Mary." Four girls in her first-grade class were called Mary.

This was how it went for a long time. The doorbell rang and they went to the door, and people came in, and most of the time they handed Daddy a bottle and handed Debbie a wrapped present, and said, "So—where's the birthday girl?"

The birthday girl was standing in her playpen, and as each set of guests brought in their present, Debbie arranged the stack in front of her.

Soon, all the parents were laughing and talking very loudly, and the other kids were running from room to room, playing tag. Timmy loved tag—he was always It. If he tagged you, you had to sit down in the nearest chair and pretend you were dead. The last child to get tagged would get a prize, but the prize was just an old toy cowboy or something like that.

Finally, Mommy came over and said, "Deb, I need your help with the cake." Debbie followed her to the back hall, and then Mommy told her to hold out her hands, and into them she placed the yellow cake with pink frosting they had made the night before. "Happy Birthday Tina" was written across the cake in green letters. The cake was only one layer, and not heavy. Debbie carried it carefully on its silver platter into the dining room, and all the children and parents started clapping.

Daddy had gotten Tina out of the playpen and stood her on a chair at the head of the table. She had a big white napkin tied around her neck, and her hair was sticking out all over her head. Debbie set the cake in front of her on the table. Everyone sang "Happy Birthday," and Tina stared all around for a moment, and then, right when they got to "dear Tina," she flopped forward like a rag doll and put her face in the cake. When she stood up again, she had cake in her hair and on her chin. Mommy said, "What a clown!" and everybody laughed much more than Debbie thought they should.

At that very moment, Debbie decided that she did not want any of the pigs-in-a-blanket she had helped make, or the carrot-raisin salad, or the other cake, the two-layer one meant for eating. She backed away, slipped through the living room, unlocked the gate, locked it again, and tiptoed up the stairs. In her room, her dolls were quiet on her bed. She got out of her red velvet dress and put on her Minnie Mouse pajamas.

In the morning, the whole downstairs was a mess—all of the ashtrays were full of cigarette butts, and where the glasses were not tipped over, they, too, had butts dropped into them. Tina's presents had been unwrapped and piled in a stack in the playpen. Mommy and Daddy were at the kitchen table with Tina, who was eating zwieback. Daddy said, "Here she is!"

Mommy said, "Oh, my head hurts. How did so many people get here?"

Debbie said, "I didn't like that party."

"Out of the mouths of babes," said Daddy.

"I'm surprised there are any secrets at all," said Mommy, "given the level of the drinking."

"There aren't any secrets," said Daddy, "but, thankfully, no one can remember what they heard once they're sober again."

Debbie went to the refrigerator and found an egg in the door. Mommy groaned, but she did get up and find a pot. Poached were Debbie's favorite.

ROSANNA, who was watching Annie while Joe was out plowing and Lois was in town, saw him sitting on the front porch railing. His stoop and his sidelong glance told her it was Roland Frederick, looking about a hundred years old. She opened the door and said, "Roland! We thought you were dead!" His eyes bloodshot the way they always got when a man had given himself over to drink.

He said, "Well, I ain't."

How long had he been gone? Years, anyway. He was Minnie and Lois's father. Maybe they had all assumed he was dead. But this was his house, wasn't it? Annie was upstairs, napping. Rosanna picked up the sock she was knitting. Four needles, eight points; she grasped them tightly and kept her hand beside her waist. You never knew with a drunk. An angry drunk especially, of course. She said, "So you must have some travels to tell about."

"Could be," said Roland.

His mouth dropped open a little as he looked around, and there were plenty of teeth missing. Roland Frederick had been a handsome man and a handsomer boy—he and his father, Grafton, had driven around town with a matched pair of grays when Rosanna was—what?—twelve or fourteen, and they sat up square every moment—never rolled about on the seat, laughing and making fools of themselves, like her own Augsberger uncles. Roland had disappeared during the war—too overwhelmed by his wife, Lorene's, terrible stroke to stick around and do his job. No one had been surprised, maybe least of all Minnie, though she hadn't talked about it. Rosanna said, "Would you like a glass of water, Roland, or a cup of tea?"

He stared at her, then said, "Your Frank married into this house here?"

Rosanna laughed. "Heavens, no. Frank's off making a million somewhere. Joe is married to Lois. They have a little girl. Let me get you something. Lois made some biscuits just this morning, and there are shortbread cookies, too. Come on into the kitchen, and tell me what you've been up to."

He allowed himself to be led, but kept looking around, as if he found the place strange. He said, "What are you doing here?"

"Oh, I come over. My house is a little lonely now. Since Walter died." She didn't think it was a good idea to mention Annie.

"When was that?" He spoke abruptly, as if insulted.

"Just over a year ago. Heart."

She set a plate in front of him on the table, a biscuit with some butter and cherry jam, two little square cookies. She had left her knitting on the dining-room table, but she knew where the knives were. However, inside the house, Roland seemed harmless.

"Walter always thought he knew everything."

Rosanna felt herself prickle. "Well, I don't know about that, but he always admired this farm you had, Roland."

"Wanted to get his hands on it, I'll be bound."

"I think Walter knew his hands were full."

"Who planted that north field out there?"

"My son Joe, and also my brother John." She made her voice clear and bright. You never knew what a drunk could remember. She went into the pantry to find the tea.

She hadn't thought of Roland Frederick as having a point of view. He was an efficient farmer with a beautiful farm, and then he wasn't. He had the most beautiful house and the most admirable wife; everyone in the neighborhood had thought of them as Mr. and Mrs. Frederick, never Roland and Lorene. When Mrs. Frederick had her stroke it had been an impersonal drama, tragic but wordless, the sort of drama that farm country abounded in. Now, looking at Roland, Rosanna knew that he had a story, too, something howling and painful that could make a claim on her, on Joe, on Lois, on Minnie. On Annie. Whatever Minnie said, this was his farm. Rosanna poured out a cup of tea and pushed it toward him, but he stopped it with his hand, so she took it back and folded her own hands around it. She said, "Well, I wish you'd tell me some of the places you've visited."

He ate one cookie and half the biscuit, rolling bits around in his mouth and then swallowing them.

Finally, she said, "Are you working now?"

"At the stockyards. Omaha."

"That's steady work."

"I shoulda left this place when I first had the chance."

"When was that, Roland?"

"Was all set up I was going to Chicago to work for a man my father knew in the shoe business. Before the first war. Start by doing the books, then go on the road, selling shoes. Well, my dad died right then, and my uncles hated to see me go, so they made it real easy to get going on the farm. Lorene was my second cousin, you know. From over around Grundy Center, where three of the uncles lived. Oh, they suckered me. Everyone was just scared to death of the sins of the world. Lorene was a good girl—she would watch over my spirit." And then he put his head down on the table, his old, dirty gray hair right on the little plate, and he started bawling. Rosanna moved the plate. She said, "I'm sure they thought they were acting for the best."

"They never had any doubt about it. Or about anything else."

"You were a good farmer. Walter respected you. And Minnie and Lois are both such good girls. There's more to everyone than meets the eye. But there is what meets the eye, too."

Roland took a deep snort and sat up, then pulled a dirty bandanna out of his pocket and wiped his nose. Rosanna picked up the plate, carried that and the teapot to the sink. He was out of the room just like that, and she skittered after him, not quite knowing what she would do if he headed up the stairs, but he didn't. He went straight to the front door and left without another word. Rosanna closed the door behind him.

Through the window, she saw him go down the steps, look around, and make his way to the car parked there—a Ford, maybe a '48. He sat in it for a long while, and then drove away. The car was gray. She wrote that down on a scrap of paper.

It took her two days to tell Minnie. Really, it was that she didn't want to see the very thing she saw when she related the incident—Minnie's nostrils flaring and her eyes hardening.

Minnie said, "He'd better not come back."

"He might not."

Rosanna didn't ask who owned the farm, where the papers were. Worse came to worst, they could vacate the house for a few years, the few years that Roland had to live. She said, "Your father is pretty far down the road now, Minnie."

"That's the good news, then."

"I suppose it is, yes."

Rosanna never knew if Minnie told Lois or Joe. As for herself, Rosanna thought of telling Granny Elizabeth about it, maybe just as a way of hearing more about Roland's uncles—she would have a thing or three to say. But in the end she said nothing, feeling each time she opened her mouth that there was some species of betrayal in it.

THE TWINS WERE eighteen months old now, walking (and standing and staring and screaming and sitting) just like other children more or less their age, and Andy found herself increasingly preoccupied with those baby scrapbooks her brother's wife had sent when they were born. Andy had gotten Janny's to the six-month mark—the last photo was of her sitting up in the baby bath with her fingers in her mouth. Richie's and Michael's—not even birth pictures. Birth pictures of the twins existed, but they reminded Andy more of mug shots than of baby photos, naked in incubators, little skinny limbs and odd heads, no hair except where it shouldn't be, on arms and back, like monkeys. She had stuffed the scrapbooks onto the upper shelf in the closet in Richie and Michael's room, and every time she slid open that door, she would see their spines, white, pink, and blue, the silliest objects in her very modern house, ready to get thrown out.

But she couldn't do it. Throwing them out would be giving up forever, acknowledging that her maternal instincts didn't exist, had never existed, would never exist, no matter how affectionately she spoke to her children, or spoke *of* her children, no matter that she touched them gently, petting them as if they were cats, smiled at them, nattered on in baby talk like the book said to do, no matter that she followed all of Dr. Spock's suggestions religiously, the way she had followed rules her whole life. Her mother still laughed about the time when she was eight and they had had a screaming argument about Andy's cleaning up her room. Her father walked through the kitchen, picked up a piece of stationery, and wrote down the rules (in Norwegian), then tacked them to her door:

1. Elske Gud
2. Adlyd din eldeste
3. Elske din neste
4. Bo ren i kropp og sinn

5. Alltid fortelle sanheten
6. Sett bort sinne

"Love God, respect your elders, love your neighbors, be clean in body and mind, always tell the truth, put away anger." The joke was that, as soon as they were written down, she followed them to the letter. That paper fluttered on the door of her room for years, a joke to them and a burden to her.

There was so much that she did not know about her children. She could run down the list right now, sitting in the living room with her cigarette in one hand and her ashtray in the other (she always emptied her ashtray after one smoke; she stubbed out the butt over and over until it was cold and flat—what if an ash leapt for the curtains and burned the house down?). She did not know if they were cute. She did not know if they were smart. She did not know if they liked her or each other or Frank. (And what did they really see of Frank? Not much.) She did not know if they were happy or difficult or spoiled or behaving appropriately for their ages. Take this example: Michael, who now weighed twenty-three pounds, twelve ounces, walked past Richie, who weighed twenty-three pounds, eight ounces, and knocked him down. Richie sat suddenly on his bottom and began crying, then threw himself on his back and started kicking his legs. Did Michael mean to knock Richie down? Did he intend Richie to feel pain? Did Richie feel real pain, or was he just angry? When Michael started to cry a few moments later, was he responding to Richie's tears? Then, when Janny's door, up the stairs of the half-landing, slammed, was that because she had slammed it? Could a three-year-old slam a door in anger? Andy never had, she was sure. Was Janny angry about something? If there were less crying in this room, would she be able to hear whether Janny slammed her fingers in the door?

Andy stood up from the couch and walked to the bottom of the stairs. She could not hear crying, so probably Janny was all right. She had already asked Janny if she was all right three times since lunch.

She walked over to Richie and set him on his feet. She took him by the hand and led him to the toy box, where she found his favorite book (this she did know—it was *The Night Before Christmas*). She opened it to the page where Ma in Her Kerchief and I in My Cap were lying in bed. Richie sat down with a bump and stared at the picture. She could take the boys outside and strip them down and sit them in their little pool—it was a hot day—and she could make sure that there were only two inches of water in the bottom and that she was looking at them every single moment, in case one of them fell over.

The doorbell rang, and Andy leaned forward. She saw Alice Rosen shade her eyes and press her nose and chin to the window beside the door. The bell rang again. The garage door was open, and the Rambler was parked there, so Alice knew she was somewhere nearby. Alice was funny and kind. Maybe it would be good to have Alice come in the back, find her where she was standing, and dose her with a box of cannoli—that was something she often wanted to share. But Andy did not move, and so Alice disappeared. There was the sound of a car leaving. Andy felt the oddest thing: something in her body draining away, as if she had been feeling pleasure or antici-pation without knowing it, and now she was disappointed.

Michael had heard the doorbell, too, and he knew what it meant. He walked toward the stairs, and when he came to the top, he stood there looking down and said, "Daddy!" (Maybe they saw more of Frank than she gave Frank credit for?) Then Michael turned and knelt, putting his hands on the top step, and made his way backward down the five carpeted steps. Frank didn't believe in gates—why live in a split-level if you were going to restrict their freedom? Any kid could fall down five or six steps and live to try again. Michael turned, sat on the second step from the bottom, and kicked his feet. Richie pushed his book aside and stood up. Whatever Michael was doing, Richie had to do, too. His diaper was full, but she wasn't quite ready to change it. Instead, she went over to the table and got her ashtray and her pack of Luckies.

1955

❦

ON A QUITE SNOWY DAY (for D.C.) at the end of February, Lillian Manning found Lucy Roberts, only four, sitting on the couch in the playroom at seven-thirty in the morning, waiting for the cartoons to begin. Lillian felt the little woolly feet of Lucy's sleeper; they were cold and wet. She found some of Deanie's PJs in the laundry (Dean and Arthur had gone to Dean's third skating lesson), then called Betsey Roberts, who was sound asleep and hadn't realized that the front door to her house was unlocked and wide open. Fortunately, the Robertses lived across the street and down one: not much harm done. Betsey said Lucy could stay, so Lillian gave her a couple of pancakes and some orange slices. While Timmy and Debbie were eating their cereal, the knocks on the front door began. By the time *Bugs Bunny* came on, there were twelve children cross-legged on the floor staring up at the TV. They sat quietly for *Roy Rogers* and *Sky King*; then some of the girls went up to Debbie's room, taking Tina with them, and a couple of the boys went out to the backyard with Timmy to slide down the "ski slope" Arthur had made.

Lillian carried Lucy home in her dried-out sleeper. Betsey seemed a little embarrassed—Lucy, she said, was such an active child, and she talked about Debbie every day—where was Debbie, was Debbie coming, what was the name of Debbie's teddy bear? Lillian and Betsey laughed together.

When she got home, one of the boys had a scrape on his elbow. Lillian washed it off and put some mercurochrome on it, and though Lillian could see tears frozen on his cheeks, he dashed out to play some more. They were standing on their sleds now, teetering at the top of the tiny slope, and then raising their hands and yelling as they slid down. Five inches of snow—no more—but Arthur had sprayed it with water and let it freeze overnight. Lillian watched out the window while she did the dishes. Arthur had installed a Dishmaster on the spigot of the kitchen sink; the water ran through a hose to a brush with a button on it—when you wanted to scrub, you pushed the button for suds, and when you wanted to rinse, you stopped pressing the button.

Dishes done, Lillian went to the bottom of the stairs and listened. All was quiet. Maybe they were dressing up, which was fine with Lillian, who threw all of her old heels and slips and blouses and skirts into Debbie's dress-up box. She decided to check on Tina, though really she was checking to see if the girls were fighting yet.

Tina was lying on her back at the top of the stairs, her blanket in her hand and her thumb in her mouth, sleeping. Lillian opened the gate without a squeak and gently picked up the toddler. Tina awoke only long enough to snuggle against Lillian while she carried her into her crib. It was one-thirty-five. She would sleep until three, Lillian guessed. Tina had such thick hair now, it was down past her shoulders and dark, like Arthur's. In fact, she looked so much like Arthur, and had so many of his mannerisms, it was almost uncanny to watch her. Arthur hardly ever disapproved of anything, but when Timmy did intentionally hit a tennis ball into the front picture window just to see if it would bounce ("It wasn't a baseball! I thought the tennis ball would, I really did!"), Arthur's eyebrows made a V-shape over his nose, and the corners of his mouth turned down. Tina made the same face when she saw green beans on the tray of her high chair.

The four girls were playing nicely—Debbie in charge, as usual. Lillian watched them from the doorway, smiling when anyone looked at her. Debbie was a strict child, but fair. Once, Lillian had pointed out that maybe her friends, unlike Timmy, did not know the rules to some game and were not actually flouting them; Debbie was amazed. When Lillian then suggested that if Debbie knew more than other children it was her job to be patient and teach them,

Debbie understood immediately. She was a good girl. No one in this room reminded Lillian of herself or of Jane, her first friend. These girls had always been in neighborhoods populous with children who were not cousins. Mama had pitied the children Lillian knew, and why not? During Lillian's Depression childhood, there had been plenty of kids in rags or in shoes with flapping soles—Jane's parents ordered the family shoes out of a catalogue once a year, and when the children grew out of them, they wore them anyway. Children had disappeared—the farm was lost, said Papa. Lillian had hated those words, imagining that a farm could be lost in the woods, like Hansel and Gretel. Now Margie Widger marched her third piece up the last tunnel into the Sorry! home base (which looked rather like a bomb shelter for the four members of the Yellow family), then glanced at Lillian. Lillian said, "When you girls are hungry, I've got peanut butter, salami, and chicken-rice soup."

But there was no peanut butter—Timmy and the boys had found it and eaten it, digging it out with carrot sticks and celery. While she was cleaning their mess up, Arthur came in with Dean. Dean was larger and stronger than Timmy had been at the same age, though not as daring, so Arthur had decided Dean would start at four and soon be playing hockey for, as Arthur always called them, "Les Canadiens." Arthur had not actually been to Montreal, but he also declared that Dean would begin his French classes in the summer. He called him Doyen and sang to him in French—"Alouette," "La Vie en rose." Arthur now also went about asking people if he himself didn't look very much like Yves Montand, but younger.

Lillian said, "How did he do?"

Arthur said, "How did you do, Doyenny, *mon fils*?"

Dean looked up at Arthur and said, very carefully, *"Tray bun, papaaah."*

Arthur grinned, then came over and hugged Lillian and said, "You are such an exceptional broodmare, *ma chère*." He kissed her on both sides of her neck while Deanie stared. Lillian extricated herself and said, "You must be hungry, Dean."

Dean said, "Is there ham?"

"Jambon!" said Arthur.

Lillian said, "Please go out back and check the boys for broken bones and missing teeth."

"They've been having that much fun, huh?" He went out the back door. Dean went to the table and climbed into his chair. Lillian knew what that broodmare remark meant—he was in the mood for another. Bob and Bev D'Onofrio, at the end of the street, were about to produce number eight, and the Porters, three streets away, had a child in every grade at the elementary school. Lillian knew more about how babies were made now, and at a certain time of the month, she did a little more late-night sewing or pretended every so often to have fallen into a deep, deep sleep. Four was enough, she thought. If he got really importunate, she would give Arthur a puppy—he was a big fan of *Rin Tin Tin*.

Lillian put Dean's plate in front of him, then sat there, chin in hand, smiling, as he ate. He was methodical but thorough—she put her hand out and stopped him when he picked up the plate to lick it. She asked, "Did you skate well?"

"I let go of Daddy's hands two times."

"Good boy!"

"I was strong."

"I know you are. Do you like it?"

Deanie nodded. Then he said, *"Je swiss un bun garsson."*

Lillian said, *"Oui!"*

"Can I watch something?"

"You can go see what's on."

He got down from his chair and went into the playroom. Lillian took his plate to the sink. Outside, there were six boys now. Arthur formed them into two teams. The team to his left had to pat their stomachs with their right hands and rub their heads with their left hands. The team on the right had to pat their heads with their right hands and rub their stomachs with their left hands. It took about one minute to get everyone laughing and falling in the snow. Lillian laughed, too.

AFTER LESS THAN a semester at Berkeley, Henry decided that he hated the place. He did not want to believe that he was so shallow it bothered him that his clothes were slightly off, though how he experienced it was that everyone else's clothes were slightly off—too aggressively casual, or dirty, or black, black, black. But perhaps they wore black because it was so cold all the time? Colder than Iowa—clammy, moldy, creeping into your joints, and the sunlight just for color. The landscape irritated him, too: up, down; up, down. The sky was very closed in, almost trapped. He kept his eyes on his feet.

The teachers and his fellow students always smiled after he told them where he'd done his undergraduate work. Henry knew what they were thinking: wasn't it a relief to be here, in Berkeley, the promised land? He even had one teacher who spoke more slowly and clearly to him than to the other students—Professor Pradet, a man who had never heard of "Iowa." And when he did well in Old English, that teacher always gave him extra praise, as if he were consistently exceeding expectations. In that class, two students had come from Harvard and one from Stanford; the only public-university graduate was from UCLA. In his Chaucer seminar, there was another outcast, Pat Clayton from Ohio State. But Pat wore the same clothes every day, was about to become a father, and talked only about rents, food prices, and the scarcity of jobs in medieval lit. Henry had nothing in common with him, either.

It didn't help that, before Christmas, Rosa embarked upon a highly volatile romance with an older man (well, he was almost thirty to her twenty-two), named Neal Cassady, who was very handsome but also the sort of person whose life was a performance—or, you might say, a mess, Henry thought. Aunt Eloise disapproved, too, which may or may not have egged Rosa on. Henry said a small thing ("I see what you see in him, but what do you see in him?") in an almost sincerely inquisitive tone of voice. Rosa slammed down the phone and didn't speak to him for a month. Then Cassady went back to his wife, and Rosa called Henry to insist that Neal Cassady was *nothing* like her father, and if Heloise said one more Freudian word, Rosa would wring her neck. When Henry said, "That's very Greek of you" (he was thinking of Electra, Orestes, etc.), she suddenly laughed, and then started crying and asked if he would go away for the weekend with her, because she couldn't "stand it anymore." He made himself pause as if hesitating before saying yes.

He thought he accepted that he and Rosa were not going to advance their own relationship past the epistolary stage. He had accepted that they were cousins, that there was scandal awaiting them if they went any further, and he had decided to see it as his particular fate that he should fall hopelessly in love with his cousin (but there was plenty of precedent in Romance literature for forbidden love, and maybe it was the least inconvenient kind). Once he moved from Iowa to California to be in the same city as Rosa, and had even moved to Rosa's neighborhood, off Shattuck, he was forced to admit that she was hot-tempered, selfish, and not terribly neat. But he loved her even more, and could not sincerely turn down a chance to be with her. She said she would pick him up in twenty minutes.

Rosa was driving Eloise's car, a gray Deux Chevaux that normally she laughed at. Henry had expected Rosa to look rumpled and distraught, but she looked normal. She leaned over to give him a peck on the cheek and peeled away from the curb, then zipped to Telegraph Avenue. When they turned south on Route 27, he remembered to ask where they were going. She said, "Carmel." Henry perked up. Maybe his hatred of Berkeley was specific. California was as big as France, and, everyone said, as various. It was his own fault that he had not even gotten on a bus or a train and gone somewhere.

And, sure enough, soon he observed that the lie of the land south of the Peninsula was different from San Francisco, and the weather was warmer, too, brighter and drier. Beyond that, though, he could take no interest in the local language, history, geology, or products—he only had eyes for Rosa. The more normal she seemed (Did she usually smoke three cigarettes in an hour, or was he only noticing that now? Was she looking thinner? When he said something about Francis Drake repairing his ships in California, was she making a face?), the more he focused only on her. They walked Carmel Beach, a flat, golden expanse at the foot of a pleasant, clean town that was much more Spanish-looking than San Francisco; he stared so deeply into her face that he fell into a hole some child or dog had dug in the sand, and went to his knees. Rosa laughed for the first time in hours as she held out her hand to him. Maybe he was good for something, then, he thought.

She had money. They ate sole caught nearby for supper and went to a movie in downtown Monterey. Henry watched Rosa's profile as she gazed at the screen. She seemed to follow the plot, but Henry only noticed that it was about Grace Kelly somewhere in South America.

The rooms at the hotel Rosa found in Carmel were small, fake adobe. Without commenting or seeming to notice that this was unusual, Rosa put on her pajamas and got into bed with Henry. She was so businesslike and quick that he hardly got a look at her breasts, her thighs, her derriere, but he tried to think that this was his dream come true. She pressed herself into his arms and fell asleep. But it was like nothing—worse than that, uncomfortable. Even though he felt the breeze from the open window on his forehead, he couldn't disentangle himself from Rosa to get up and close it. It was strange to feel her breath on his neck, strange to sense the weight of her head pressing his arm into the unforgiving mattress, strange to feel her knee push between his legs, strange to take in her scent (she hadn't bathed before getting into bed), a combination of salt and sweat and the detergent her pajamas had been laundered in. She slept like a rock—an unconscious weight tilting the bed, so that finally he had to ease backward, toward the wall, and contain and balance himself there all night, until Rosa woke up, sat up, and said that she had just been dreaming of waffles. After breakfast, Rosa said that she thought they should drive down the coast, but Henry said that he had an exam the next day and absolutely had to get back to school, to the library, and to something (he kept this part to himself) that he understood.

He did not look at her on the drive home, only out the window, and he decided that maybe California was as interesting in its way as everyone said it was.

LATELY, Joe Langdon kept wishing that he had a photograph of his father when Walter was thirty-three, the age Joe was now. What he would look at was not the hairline or the wrinkles, but the belly. When had Joe's come on? He could not remember. His mother said he was getting to look more like Walter every year, but she was talking about worry lines between his eyebrows. She said, "Well, you had to be a farmer, didn't you?" And he always said, "You could have married more commercial bloodlines," and that shut her up for a day or two. He knew she knew he was referring to the Crests, who had the grocery store in town. Dan Crest was rumored to have had a crush on Rosanna, which was why he gave her more for her eggs and butter all through the Depression than he gave anyone else. Maybe the farming came from the Vogels—his grandmother Langdon cared so little about farming now that she had plowed under her rosebushes in case she got the money to go to Europe all of a sudden. His mother's brothers, alive and dead, were as wedded to the land as Joe was, so who was Rosanna to talk?

He might pat his belly with regret, but when he stepped into the kitchen after kicking off his boots on the back porch, the Parker-house rolls cooling on the table looked damn good, buttery little half-circles, crispy on the bottom and the top. You didn't have to put another dab of butter on them. He shouted, "Lois?" But there was no answer, so he went through to the living room and looked out the window. Lois had set Annie's playpen on the porch, in the middle of a patch of sunlight. Poppy, the six-month-old spaniel puppy, was in there with Annie, sort of flopped on the toddler's legs, with her head back and her tongue hanging out. Annie was stroking Poppy on the chest with both her hands—nicely, as Joe had taught her. Annie seemed to be a real dog-lover—if there was a dog in the room, she wanted to be with it.

Lois got good cream from the Whiteheads, who had several Jerseys. She thought chickens were disgusting, but eggs were divine, and she didn't waste her egg whites on angel-food cake—she preferred meringues and soufflés. As for the yolks, well, nothing like a smooth hollandaise or some vanilla ice cream. When Rosanna came over on her birthday, and Lois served chocolate mousse with whipped cream instead of angel-food cake, Rosanna didn't say a disapproving word, ate every last bite. Lois's *Joy of Cooking* had already fallen to pieces; Minnie had bought her *Betty Crocker,* which Lois read after dinner as if it were a novel. Then Minnie brought home a copy of a magazine for gourmets, which were people who liked to eat, and Lois pondered these recipes, whispering words to herself—"mortadella," "tagliatelle," "scaloppini." She made one recipe, noodles with a fancy sauce. They had all the ingredients (beef, pork, veal, bacon, onion, carrots, celery), except for something called a truffle, which Minnie maintained was like a mushroom. At the end, she stirred in some Jersey cream. It was good.

Now Joe saw her looking up into the butternut trees, though they wouldn't blossom for another month. Her mother had baked with butternuts all the time, and so, last fall, she had done it herself, and Joe had to admit that the cookies were delicious. Rosanna wouldn't taste one; she had said, "Is there poison ivy in the salad, then?"

Lois saw him and called out, "Did you see my rolls? I think they turned out fine."

To go with the Parkerhouse rolls, she had warmed up the pot roast from the night before with the last of the spinach. There was less than a cup of peas—the first of the season—but they were sweet, light, and delicious. For dessert (how could Lois serve a meal without dessert?), there were some shortbread cookies. Joe took only one of those. Annie ate happily—a serving of pot roast, a spoonful of peas, half a roll, half a cookie, a cup of milk. Like Lois, she was lean and tall. Lois herself ate only a roll, a bite of pot roast, and some peas.

Joe said, "Are you feeling okay, Lo?"

Lois shrugged, then said, "Okay enough. Just not hungry." She reached over and wiped Annie's mouth. Then she said, "I have something to tell you." She said it in her normal way, calmly and straightforwardly.

Joe waited.

Annie wiggled, and said, "Down!"

"Down, please!" said Lois.

"Please!" said Annie.

Joe stood up and removed the tray of the high chair and set Annie on her feet. She ran into the living room. Lois said, "I'm pregnant."

Joe sat down again, and pushed away his plate. Then he said, "How long?"

"Couple months."

"So . . . due in November?"

"Mid-November."

Joe nodded, got up from his chair, and carried his plate into the kitchen, where he set it on the drainboard. He went out the back door. The weather was warming up—a nice breeze from the west was fluttering through the daffodils and the apple blossoms. He stepped into his boots. He thought about putting his jacket back on, but decided he wasn't going to be needing it. Two more days of warm weather and he could plant the long field north of the house that had been in beans last year. Corn this year. Not seed corn, but field corn. Mid-November. Well, that was a good time. All the fall work would be done by then. Annie would be almost three. Joe had heard that three years was a good space between two kids. Close enough to be friends (eventually), but far enough apart not to be in each other's business every minute of the day. On balance, the news was good. Joe pushed his cap back and headed for the barn, trying not to be too happy, trying to remember a farmer's first principle, that many things could go wrong, to focus on the fact that there were a few things that he could stand to fix on the planter—little things, nothing major. But he skipped a few strides, just because he couldn't contain himself.

THIS YEAR, Frances Upjohn had talked Andy into spending August on Long Island—the Upjohns had a big place on Gin Lane in Southampton—but Andy had refused to be a guest for thirty-one days, so, because they were late getting started, all they could find was a house in Sag Harbor, and nowhere near the beach, which was fine, said Andy, because she hated the beach. It was a dark place, facing north, with beat-up summer-house furniture. Frank came Friday nights, went home Sunday nights; today he was looking after the boys while Andy and Janny went shopping.

Frank sat about halfway up the stairs, nursing a beer, watching them. They had eaten lunch, and now they were watching TV, Richie rolled up in his blanket and Michael sitting cross-legged. Neither was quite as far along as their cousins Timmy and Deanie had been at their age—Frank had to admit that Timmy was a phenomenon in some ways, the son Frank would never have. When Timmy was two and a half, which was what Richie and Michael were now, he had liked to get up on the back of the couch and walk along, pretending he was on a tightrope, his hands above his head. Richie and Michael ran around, but Richie sometimes stumbled and fell for no reason, and Michael had a sort of rolling gait—nothing efficient. Andy told him he was too critical of them, but he liked them better than he liked Janny, who was stiff and remote, the spit and image of his father right down to the tip of her rather large nose. She had started kindergarten early, though, and could now read "at fourth-grade level," and that would serve her well. He could send her off to Rosemary Hall for high school, then Radcliffe, and then her equally boring uncle Henry could find her something to do.

No, it was true, Frank thought. You didn't have to be a farmer or the son of a farmer to know that breeding was always a gamble. He and Andy should have begotten a race of gods and goddesses. He finished his beer and called down to the boys, "Wanta have a contest?" Richie, with rounded, placid eyes, looked up the stairs.

Frank moved a couple of armchairs, then pushed most of the dining-room chairs against the wall. He took one of them and set it in the middle of the kitchen. The boys were still lolling. He turned off the TV—it was one he hadn't seen before coming to this house, a portable GE with a clock. He took each of the boys by the hand and stood them up. Richie knew better than to cry when Frank took his blanket away from him and tossed it toward the stairs.

Frank said, "Okay, fellas, here's the course. You start here, at the bookcase, and then you run to the green chair—that's the green chair—turn right—this way"—he demonstrated right—"and then run straight into the kitchen and go around the chair, and come back to this spot." With his toe, he pointed out the threshold between the dining room and the living room. He said, "Let's try it."

Still grasping the boys, he led Michael and half dragged Richie over to the bookcase. Then he trotted them (slowly) toward the center of the room, turned right at the green chair, and trotted them (even more slowly) through the dining room into the kitchen. Michael stumbled as they went around that chair, but regained his feet right away. Frank exclaimed, "Come on, boys! This is the home stretch! Put on some speed!" He dropped their hands, and they half ran across the "finish line."

"Okay!" said Frank. "That was the warm-up!"

He walked them back to the base of the bookcase and stood them about a foot apart, both facing ahead. Now he whispered in Michael's ear, "Keep your feet—you can beat him easy! Got me?" He backed away, made eye contact, and stared at Michael until Michael nodded. Then he whispered in Richie's ear, "If he stumbles, Rich, you just keep going. Slow and steady wins the race. You listening?" Richie nodded.

Frank stepped back and held out his arm, then he said, "Ready? Set? Go!" He dropped his arm, and the two boys took off. Richie understood the course better than Michael—he did make the right turn and head into the dining room while Michael was still wondering what to do—but then Michael spun around and overtook him at the chair in the kitchen, and, in fact, poked him in the side with his elbow, causing Richie to stumble. When they got to the finish line, they were about a step apart, Michael in the lead. Frank stood in the middle of the living room, scowling and shaking his head. He said, "What a pair of slowpokes! This race is going to have three heats. That was number one. Go back to the start." He pointed to the bookcase.

He sent them off again. This time, Michael had learned something—he turned at the proper spot and headed for the kitchen with Richie on his heels. But Richie had learned something, too, and when they came to the chair, he turned his hip and popped Michael, sending him sprawling. He crossed the threshold by himself, grinning, and said, "I won! I won!"

"You did!" said Frank. "You won! Can you beat him again?"

Richie nodded emphatically.

Frank said, "Okay, then. You each had one win. Richard, you go stand by the bookcase and wait."

He went into the kitchen, where Michael was sitting on the floor, his face hot and flushed. Frank squatted down and said, "Michael? You mad?"

Michael nodded.

"Are you really, really mad?"

Michael nodded again.

Frank said, "Okay, then, you go beat him. You are faster, and you can do it. You got that?"

Michael nodded and clambered to his feet. When he arrived at the bookcase, he stuck his tongue out at Richie, who responded in kind. Frank said, "Save it, boys. Just run fast!" Then, "Ready? Set? Go!" This time, the squabbling commenced almost immediately—Michael bounced Richie into the green chair, but Richie kept his feet, followed Michael, and grabbed his shirt. Frank said nothing. Michael smacked Richie on the arm and then pushed him, but they both kept running through the dining room and into the kitchen. At the kitchen chair, Richie did a smart thing—he pushed the chair a couple of inches, so that Michael had to duck to one side to avoid it. In the meantime, Richie, having shortened his own course, was two steps into the dining room while Michael was still going around the chair. But Michael was faster, and when he caught up to Richie, he reached out and grabbed his hair and pulled him down. Frank barked out a single laugh. He had to give Richie credit, though—instead of crying, he crawled forward as fast as he could and grabbed Michael's pant leg and brought him down. Then he crawled over the finish line first. Frank now laughed out loud, and both boys turned and stared up at him. Frank said, "I guess Richie wins. Richie wins by a neck." Richie started laughing, too, but Michael's face began to crumple, so Frank said, "What's the prize, boys? What does the winner get?"

Both boys looked at him. He said, "The winner gets tickled!" He fell upon Richie and played his fingers over the tiny ribs until Richie was squirming away and laughing. After a moment, Frank stood them up. He wiped tears off Richie's face with the tail of his shirt—he didn't want Andy to see those—and then he got a Kleenex and wiped both their noses. "You boys tough?"

Both boys nodded.

"Are you really tough?"

They nodded again.

"All right!"

But they were still angry at one another; when they went back to watching TV, Frank had to sit them on cushions a couple of feet apart so they wouldn't continue the argument. By the time Janny walked in, and then Andy, they were quiet enough. Andy said, "Whew! It's nice and shady in here. We could have stayed home, it's so hot. You guys have a nice afternoon?"

"We did," said Frank. The boys nodded; undoubtedly, "nice" was not the word to describe the particular pleasures of their time together. But "nice" was not for boys, Frank thought. "Educational," "stimulating," "active." Right out of Dr. Spock, Frank was sure.

1956

GRANNY ELIZABETH WAS BOUND and determined to go visit Henry in California (and Eloise, too—ever since Eloise had lived with Rosanna and Walter back in the old days, helping with Frank and Joe, Granny Elizabeth had had a special fondness for her), and so Claire found herself on New Year's Day, her seventeenth birthday, helping Granny down the steps at the station in Oakland or Berkeley or somewhere damp, dark, and chilly. Granny had on her furs—a set of four minks with heads and tails, biting each other around her neck. The thing was ten years out of style, but she was enormously proud of it—"It's the dog she never got to have," said Joe. Claire, carrying both the suitcases, had to hurry to keep up with her grandmother as she clicked down the platform toward the waiting room. "California!" she exclaimed. "You know, Claire, in a day or two, I will stand on these eighty-year-old feet and stare out over the Pacific Ocean, and that is a thing no Chick or Cheek has ever seen before! Stuck in the mud as always, just like hornbeams on the riverbank, looking at the lucky creatures drifting by! There he is!"

The Chicks and the Cheeks were Granny's ancestors back in England. Secretly, Claire always thought maybe the names were a joke, that they were really "Smiths" and "Johnsons."

Henry was laughing as he took the bags from Claire. Then Eloise was hugging her, and Rosa kissing her, and Henry was saying, "How was your trip, Granny?"

"Not long enough by half," she said, "but I hear this is as far as you can go."

The next morning, Henry showed up at Eloise's. As soon as they finished their coffee, they piled into Eloise's car, and Henry exclaimed, "Westward ho!" Two hours later, they were standing in the brilliant sunshine, at a place called Drakes Bay. The weather was not hot but, compared with Oakland, almost heavenly.

Claire kept her eye on Rosa, who slipped off her shoes and socks and set them beside an oddly shaped rock—they would pass it going back to the car. They were the only people on the beach. Rosa was five months younger than Henry, almost twenty-three, but years more mature. "Ah, the beach!" exclaimed Granny, with joy. But to Claire it was a stark, strange thing: flat, cool sand running under flat, cold water, the brilliance of the clouds and the sea and the sun almost too much to look at. Granny Elizabeth stood up straight, her arms thrown in the air. Henry touched something in the sand with his toe and bent down. It was a shell—concave, pearly on the inside, and rough gray on the outside. Claire said, "What's that?"

"Only an oyster shell. But you know how they know that Francis Drake stopped here? Shards of broken porcelain from vessels he would have been carrying on the ship. By the time he got here, he had one ship, the *Golden Hind*. He started out with five. These cliffs here"—he swept his arm around, and Claire noticed the tall, pale cliffs looming over the grayish-yellow sand—"reminded him of Dover, England, where there are also cliffs, so he called this 'Nova Albion,' which basically means 'New England,' and claimed all this coast for Queen Elizabeth."

"Was that before the Pilgrims?" said Claire.

"Forty-one years before." Henry scraped his toe through the sand again.

Since moving into Henry's old room at home, Claire had looked through some of his books. She couldn't believe how boring they were. She thought it was really too bad that Henry should be so good-looking—he was twenty-three and looked like a blond James Dean, except he didn't—James Dean walked around like he had a plan, and Henry walked around like he was going to the library, which he was.

He did everything Rosa said. Rosa had her nose in the air, Claire thought, and when she smiled, it was only to laugh at you, or even less than that—she smiled to herself because it wasn't worth it to notice you. Right now, she was walking ahead of all of them, her hands in her pockets, sometimes shaking her head to make her hair blow, and then gazing out to sea as if she saw something that she was going to go write a poem about. Aunt Eloise might look a mess, but she was nice. How did her daughter turn out not to be? Claire wondered.

Granny Elizabeth came up beside Claire and took her hand. "Claire, honey," she said, "I do think this is the most beautiful place that I have ever seen. You are a sweetheart for bringing your granny all the way out here."

Claire said, "It was fun. It is fun, I mean."

"Albion means 'white,' you know. I don't know why that means England, too," said Granny Elizabeth. And then she sat down in the sand and burst into tears.

Claire stopped dead and squatted down. After a moment, she put her hand on Granny's knee and pulled the hem of her blue crepe dress down a little. Granny's crying sounded to Claire like something falling—dishes out of the cupboard, or ice down a frozen slope. Claire didn't like crying at all; she hadn't cried since the day her father died under the Osage-orange hedge.

"You know what I did when I was your age, Clary?" said Granny Elizabeth. "I played the piano. We had this old-style parlor piano, not even eighty-eight keys, but I played it every day. I played it for your grandpa, and I thought he liked it, and then, when we were married for about six months, he said it was irritating. He didn't ask me to, but I did stop, because I didn't want him to hear me, even through the window." Then she cried again, and said, "Oh, Wilmer!" Claire knew that there was more to the story—her father's two brothers, men she'd never met, had died young, which was strange to think of. Claire took Granny Elizabeth's hand.

"Walter was such a good little boy. I thought the worst day of my life was the day your father went away to the army in 1917, even worse than when little Lester died. I was only nineteen when that happened." She fell silent. "Then, of course, Howard went in the influenza after the war." She pulled her handkerchief out of her sleeve and blotted her eyes, then said, "Oh me. How many times did I wish that it had been me to go? I had that flu, too." Claire dreaded what might start now—Granny Elizabeth had outlived all of her children, and if they were to talk about that, and then get on to Claire's own feelings about the death of her father, she didn't know if she could stand it. She felt Granny's hand tighten around hers. But then Eloise noticed them. A look of alarm suffused Eloise's face as her lips formed the words "Henry! Rosa!" The other two turned around abruptly.

Granny Elizabeth saw them coming, and she leaned in toward Claire, speaking right in her ear. She said nothing about her father after all, only something that Claire would never forget: "The best that can happen to a girl, Claire, is to be a bit plain, like you. You think I'm being unkind, but I am telling you a truth. A plain girl has a longer time to herself, and when a man falls in love with her, he loves her for herself, for who she is."

Eloise hurried up and knelt down. "Are you all right? Did you fall? Beaches are so treacherous."

"Oh no, Eloise, dear. I didn't fall. I'm fine. I just had a weak moment. Weak in the brain. Oh my. Why is it that beautiful places give you sad thoughts?" Claire held out her hand. Eloise took Granny Elizabeth's elbow and said, "Do you want to go back? I'm sure you must be tired." Henry stepped forward and offered Granny Elizabeth his arm. After everyone helped her up, they continued down the beach, Rosa first, Eloise right behind her, Henry, Claire, and Granny Elizabeth behind them.

CLAIRE KNEW she was a quiet girl. Supposedly, she didn't say "Mama" until she was nearly two. "It wasn't that she couldn't," said Rosanna, "it was that she didn't care to."

But what, thought Claire, was the use of talking when no one was listening? You could see it right here in Eloise's apartment. Some people talked all the time—Eloise and Granny Elizabeth. Henry yakked, but in spurts—Sir Francis Drake was the eldest of twelve children, he fought the Spanish Armada, and on and on. Rosa said little, but whenever Rosa said something ("We should put some mushrooms in it"), the others fell silent, smiled, and nodded. Henry was in love with her and watched her every move. Eloise didn't notice, because she did the same thing. Rosa was a perfect example of an only child, thought Claire—she behaved herself, but it was because she was always on the stage and the lights were always up.

In the five days they spent in Berkeley, Rosa didn't introduce them to a single girl. Plenty of boys came over—they were kind of stinky and not good-looking, and they wore messy clothes. Everyone smoked and sat around, talking and talking. They watched out to see if you were listening, but they didn't say anything right to you, they just went on and on about being and nothingness while thinking that they were talking about something. In the end, pigs were more interesting. If Claire had been asked her opinion, she would have described how pigs look for their favorite foods in the slop, how they push the orange rinds to one side and eat the potato skins first, then come back to the orange rinds and nibble them, and she had even seen a pig eat a lemon rind and wrinkle its nose. Also, pigs had friends, and they grouped together; quite often, they liked the pigs who looked more or less like they themselves did. There were a couple of pigs in every litter whom the other pigs stayed away from. Claire had plenty to say, but not anything that anyone wanted to hear.

Eloise took them to see the Golden Gate Bridge, which they drove over one way, and then they turned around and drove back over it the other way. They went to Chinatown in San Francisco. Granny Elizabeth wanted to buy a doll, and she had the money, but Eloise insisted on bargaining for it, and then, when the price got down to two dollars, Granny Elizabeth walked right up to the woman and paid her four dollars anyway. The night before they went home, they had dinner in a restaurant where, in her show-offy way, Rosa ate only vegetables. They had ice cream for dessert. Henry told a story about his adviser, who had divorced his wife because she kept mispronouncing the word "album." She could not stop herself from saying "alblum." Henry said, "He corrected her, but she was really stubborn."

"Why don't you go digging in Mexico or somewhere?" said Rosa. "New Mexico. There's plenty of interesting archeological stuff there."

"There is." Henry's voice was sharp. "But I didn't start with that culture. I started with Indo-European, and it's too late to change now." His lips snapped shut, and Aunt Eloise looked from him to

Rosa. Rosa shrugged. It was a careful shrug—she knew Henry was looking at her, and she wanted him to understand that, whatever he did, she, Rosa didn't care.

"How many languages do you speak, Henry?" said Granny Elizabeth, oblivious.

"English. German. I can read French and Italian. If you can read Italian, you can work out Spanish. I can read Latin, Middle English, Old English. There aren't many texts, but I can make it through the Gothic version of the Bible. I'm taking Greek this semester." Henry's voice rose.

Rosa turned her head slowly, toward him, and then away from him, across the room. Aunt Eloise took another sip of her wine. Claire saw then that she and Rosa did have something in common, and that it was keeping secrets. Claire's secrets might be about the family life of pigs, but Rosa's were more interesting, and maybe sadder than that.

Granny Elizabeth wiped her mouth and said, "Well, I am sorry to go home! And the penny jar is empty, upside down, drained dry, but this trip was worth it!"

"What's next?" said Henry. "You should go to England, Gran." He dragged his gaze away from Rosa.

"I think Hawaii!" said Granny Elizabeth.

WHEN JOE CAME IN from cultivating the field that ran behind the house, the first thing he did was splash water on his face at the outdoor sink. Then he kicked off his boots. It was hot and he was thirsty, and although later he remembered that the door was ajar, at the time he just closed it behind him. He was hungry. He shouted for Lois, but there was no answer, and then he glanced out the kitchen window and saw that the car was gone. Minnie, of course, was at the high school, administering something or other—even in the summer she was gone most of the day. He opened the refrigerator. The plate of leftover ribs, right next to a dish a strawberries, had a little note— "Took Jesse to his six-month checkup. Annie is with your mother. Eat them all, Lois."

He did eat them all. They were cold and delicious. He ate them standing by the kitchen counter, and with the strawberries, he did a thing slightly frowned upon, at least by his mother—he dipped each one into the sugar bowl before sucking it off the stem. Then he scraped and rinsed the plates, washed his hands, and went back out. He had at least four more hours, he thought, but he didn't mind cultivating. It was precise work; he liked seeing the weeds uprooted and covered by the soil, but the rows of corn plants still standing—small, neat sown seams.

Sometime later, he saw Lois waving to him. He finished his row, made his turn, tried to ignore her. He hated turning the tractor off and on unless he had to. She went inside. He continued his task, but he watched, promising himself that if she came out and waved again, he would go see what she wanted. She didn't come out. Joe finished the field, once in a while glancing toward the house. Nothing.

On the porch, Joe heard Minnie say, "Do we call the sheriff?"

Through the screen, Joe said, "What about?"

Minnie's face turned toward him, blanched but blank. She said, "My father is at the bottom of the basement stairs."

Joe didn't understand at first, then, when he registered how pale and how angry Minnie looked, it finally clicked. "Is he dead?"

Lois said, "He's really cold. As though he's been down there a long time. I saw him when I opened the door to go down for a jar of peaches. What was that, an hour ago." Her voice was flat, matter-of-fact.

Joe peered down the stairwell. There wasn't much light, but he could see the old man staring upward, his neck twisted to the right and backward. His hands were above his head, as if he had been reaching for something on his way down. He was wearing a dirty shirt with long sleeves, and overalls.

Sheriff Dee arrived just then with his deputy. After they spent maybe fifteen minutes in the cellar, they sat everyone at the kitchen table for the questions, which Sheriff Dee asked as if he were reading them from a piece of paper, though he wasn't. Lois bounced Jesse on her knee. Minnie looked half upset, half angry, but Lois looked blank. The deputy, Carson, wrote everything down. Joe told about the back door being ajar when he came in the first time. Lois told about noticing a car by the side of the road when she went into town, but she didn't recognize it, it was partly in the ditch, there was no one in it—she'd thought maybe someone had run out of gas. They never used the front door, but, no, neither of the doors was locked. No one locked their doors around here. And what had they all been doing today? Rosanna had been at her house with Annie, Minnie had been at school, Joe had been out cultivating the corn, Lois had been away for about four hours, taking Jesse for a checkup, then shopping, mailing some letters, visiting with Dave Crest at the store, and browsing at the Denby library. Witnesses? Joe didn't say anything at first; then: "I guess my only witness is the cultivated field."

The deputy nodded, but Sheriff Dee remained serious and still.

Rosanna said that, yes, Roland Frederick had appeared—when was that?—two years ago now, came and went, said he was working in Omaha, seemed like he'd been drinking steadily for eight years, hardly coherent, but, no, he hadn't seemed threatening, exactly, and he'd gone away as quickly as he came. She had told Minnie about it. Joe's head snapped toward Minnie; then, under the table, he took Lois's hand.

Minnie said, "I thought I mentioned it to you, Lois." She cleared her throat.

Once they had been "questioned," Joe and Minnie sat there while Sheriff Dee and Deputy Carson—oh, Seth, his name was, Rodney's kid—walked around the house, looking at this and that, going out on both of the porches, then coming in, staring at the floor, checking doorknobs. They went back down into the cellar, but this time only stayed for under five minutes. It was now after six. Sheriff Dee went to the phone and called the undertaker. Lois asked if they were free to go over to Rosanna's for the rest of the evening, and that's where Minnie, Lois, Jesse, Rosanna, and Annie did go, taking Poppy along. But Joe stayed, sitting quietly at the table, making sure that Nat sat next to his leg while the undertaker and his two assistants carried the shrouded corpse up the stairs, through the kitchen, and out the front door. Nat growled once or twice, but he knew better than to bark. Joe gazed at him, wondering what he knew—he would not have been in the house, but he might have seen something. Joe felt ashamed and somehow suspected, though he didn't know why or of what. Maybe because he really was an interloper in the Frederick house? Maybe because at last the farm was his?

DR. KATZ SAID, "How about dreams?"

Andy was lying on his couch, though it was more like a daybed.
He was behind her. This was her thirty-second appointment. She had
started in the summer, after reading about how H-bombs had potential as usable conventional weapons. She realized that she could not
get the word "fallout" out of her mind—it was planted in there like
a black pea that sometimes sprouted and sometimes did not—but Dr.
Katz didn't seem interested or impressed by her worries. He said he
wanted something "deeper." She was up to five days a week now, as
of September 1, when they both returned from their August vaca-
tions. It had been fifteen dollars a session, but since she was seeing
him every morning, like a regular job, he was doing it for $12.50.
Frank didn't mind. This year he stood to earn fifty thousand dollars
at Grumman, and that did not include their investments in what they
called their "Uncle Jens Fund," named after that strange great-great-
uncle of hers who had left all his money to be divided up among
his descendants, but only after those who were living when he was
still alive had themselves died—a grouchy, Nordic legacy that Andy
hadn't yet mentioned to Dr. Katz. She said, "Not much. Well, one
sticks in my mind."

It was part of her job to offer the dream. She lay there for a minute or two, allowing the silence to build around her, then said, "Two
mornings ago. I'd sort of forgot it, but it's coming back to me."

She closed her eyes and continued. "There were hills, but no trees.
I am on a hillside, and a river is running below me, fast and frothy. I
am supposed to go down there. I'm a little afraid. I also know that I'm
a very beautiful girl—say, fifteen. But I'm not me. I have silky blond
hair to below my waist. I'm sitting on the hillside, twisting my hair
between my hands."

Actually, the dream was not a dream, but a story she had read.
Andy, as far as she knew, didn't have any dreams. But Dr. Katz seemed
to like the dream stories she told him, and to find them revealing.

She went on, "I've been married twice already. So maybe I'm not
fifteen. But it seems like both those things are true. The main thing is
the feel of the grass on the hillside—rough and full of burrs."

"Hmm," said Dr. Katz.

"Then a man comes up to me, and I know that this is my new husband, and I really like him best." She paused, then said, "He smiles more than the others did. He's not Frank. Anyway, we walk along the hillside, which is steep, and then, all of a sudden, he has a bow in his hand, and he's shooting arrows at some people. And his bowstring breaks, and he asks me for some of my hair. I say no."

"Explain, please," said Dr. Katz.

"I can't explain. I just say no. So he stands there with the broken bowstring, and then he is shot through the neck, and I woke up. I guess I looked over at Frank, and he was lying on his back, but he was fine. So I lay there for a few minutes, and then went back to sleep." In fact, Frank was not next to her. But, then, she hadn't had the dream, either.

Dr. Katz said, "Do you feel that you withheld something from your husband, and it killed him?"

"Well," said Andy, "he was outnumbered."

"Is that what you feel, that he was outnumbered?"

"Why would he think that he could use hair as a bowstring? It makes no sense."

"Did you feel that in the dream, that his idea was a foolish one?"

"I felt nothing. I just said no."

"Did you feel in mortal danger?"

"No."

Andy was beginning to regret that she had told this story. Finally, she said, "People die in my dreams all the time." From, she thought, fallout. Dr. Katz said, "Yes, they do," which surprised her. She said, "But it seems like, in the dream, I always know that it's a dream, and that the person is not really dying, or that the person is not really a person. One or the other."

"You do not grieve for them."

Andy said, "No." A question offered itself: was she a heartless person? When Lillian told her over the phone the night before that the son of a friend of hers, nine years old, also named Michael, had been hit by a car crossing the road by the house, killed instantly, Lillian wept in sympathy, but Andy felt cold, stared at the ash of her cigarette, had nothing to say. Was she the most heartless client he had? But you weren't supposed to ask questions, you were supposed to arrive at answers.

There was an extra-long silence. Andy thought of being honest and telling him that she had related a story, not a dream. But then he would ask her what the difference was, and she would have to say that she didn't know.

1957

〜∞〜

WHEN DID LILLIAN HAVE TIME to read the papers, or to watch the news on TV? And yet things filtered through—Hungary in November, the Suez crisis at the same time, both of them crushing. Even so, though Arthur came home a little late, he did come home in the usual way, full of fun and with a big appetite, two helpings of everything, though you couldn't tell that to look at him. He didn't lose his sex drive until February, which Lillian thought, secretly, was a bit of a relief. Then, one night, she got up to go to the bathroom, and when she got back to bed, in the moonlight the tears were glistening on his cheeks and his eyes were wide open, even though he was lying still and not saying a word. It was like getting in bed with a stranger. She said, "Arthur?"

He rolled onto his side, his back to her, and she slipped under the covers. She put her hand on his head and scratched, just very lightly, and it put her right to sleep. Sometime after that, he slipped his arms around her sleeping body and woke her up, sobbing on her shoulder. He hadn't been like this for years, not since Timmy was born alive and healthy. Even when his father died, his eyes had remained dry and his back straight.

She did what she did with Debbie and Deanie, just let him sob, patting him lightly on the leg. She could see the phosphorescent hands of the clock glowing from where she lay—a quarter after three, march-

ing on to a quarter to four. Finally, he heaved a big sigh, pulled his
one arm from underneath her, and sat up. She said, "You okay?"

He wiped his face with the corner of the sheet and sighed again.
He said, "Well, if this room is bugged, I'm probably out of a job."

"Is this room bugged?"

"I've checked. I don't think so."

Lillian said, "You're kidding me."

"I hope I am."

He stood up and went down the hall to the bathroom. She heard
him open and close doors—peeping in on the boys and the girls.
Then he sat down in the armchair and said, "Did we say Dean could
sleep on the floor?"

"For now."

"Okay. I just wanted to make sure Timmy is not imposing some
cruel and unusual punishment."

"No, Deanie's agitating for a tent. He wants me to tack one side of
his blanket to the wall."

Arthur said, "Please tell me that we've been married less than a
hundred years."

"We've been married eleven years and three months."

Arthur let his head drop onto the back of the chair and inhaled
deeply. Lillian was sure right then that he had found another
woman—someone who had no children, or whose figure was holding up better. She, who had once worn a 4, now wore an 8. What
had ever made her think that such a dashing man as Arthur would
be satisfied with her? Georgetown was a hotbed of infidelity—the
women who didn't talk about it all the time were those who sleeping
with their friends' husbands, and so you could always tell who had
just commenced an affair.

He said, "I don't know how I'm going to take it anymore, and
now—"

"Now what, Arthur?"

He leaned forward and put his face in his hands, and mumbled
something. Lillian realized that he was not talking about their marriage. She knelt down in front of him, took his hands away from his
face, and said quietly, "Say that again, Arthur."

"Eighty percent of our budget goes for absolute crap."

She waited.

"I hate Frank Wisner. I hate every stupid idea that he ever had, starting with parachuting blockheads into Poland at the end of the war. Direct action! Sabotage! Subversion! His operations are the definition of 'half cocked'! And I like Ike. I do like Ike! But thirty thousand got killed in Budapest, just mowed down, and it was because Ike wouldn't lift a finger, and the Russians just rolled over them. Wisner hated Nagy, he'd once been a commiebastard—that's how he talks—there is no redemption for commiebastards. We had two guys translating from the Hungarian—two, just two—but everything they translated indicated that Nagy was going to go our way, and everything we broadcasted said, 'Go, go, go, we're right behind you,' but they didn't actually look around, because if they had they would have seen us running the other direction, because Ike has some other plan, God knows what it is."

"The Hungarians knew it was risky, Arthur. . . ."

He took her hands and peered into her face. He said, "You know what I do every day, Lillian? I exaggerate the Soviet threat. I say they have a hundred new bombers when they only have ten. I say that there are twenty divisions when there are ten divisions. I say that they are thirty percent closer to thermonuclear-tipped ICBMs than they are."

"Why do you do that, darling?"

"Because maybe the Soviets are lying and our sources are wrong and we have to be on the safe side, and eighty percent of the budget that goes to doing crap is taken away from finding out crap. Because I've become a jerk. Because that's what they want to hear. I do feel like I've been doing this for a hundred years and that I can't do it anymore."

"Then quit," said Lillian. You have four children and a mortgage. But she didn't say this.

"Who takes over from me when I quit? Some kid from Yale who looks at the figures and stretches them even further. Some kid from Yale who can't wait to be sent to El Salvador or Vietnam and is only wiping his shoes on the doormat of analysis."

"But you've been thinking like this for a while, Arthur. What's bothering you right now?"

"We didn't know! We didn't know a thing about either the Hungarians or the Suez attack before they happened. Were you surprised when you read that in the paper?"

"Well, yes, but—"

"I was just as surprised as you, Lillian. I nearly fell down the steps. I picked up the paper out on the front porch, and I opened it and I read the headline, and I grabbed the railing, and it was a good thing I did, because I had reeled backward and a moment later I lost my balance."

"That's six steps," said Lillian.

"It would have been a mess," said Arthur.

"Did you get in trouble for not knowing?"

"No! I had my excuses all lined up, and no one said a word. They don't care! The White House doesn't know what we know or when we know it, and Dulles and Wisner just cover up, because, if people started wondering what we know, then they would start wondering why we do crap, and our funding would be in danger, and we can't have that."

"Why not?"

"Well, the charitable way of looking at it is that we might actually need it for something worthwhile in the future."

"But why were you crying? I mean, tonight rather than last night or last November?" She ran the tip of her finger along the angle of his cheekbone, an angle that she loved in him, in Timmy, in Dean, in Tina, and then she touched her fingertip to her lips.

He said, "We're already on to the next mess."

Lillian said, "What is that?"

"Deposing Sukarno. Wisner swears he's a closetcommie. The Indonesian ambassador says Sukarno loves Ike like a father. What am I going to do?"

Lillian said, "I don't know."

It was now almost five. The alarm was set for seven. They got back under the covers, and Lillian pressed herself into Arthur's arms. He held her at first loosely and then tightly. What would her mother say? Lillian thought. When Rosanna was thirty, Mary Elizabeth had already died, and then, not much later, Henry was born right there in the downstairs bedroom, in a howling wind, with Joe looking on. Probably, her mother would have considered worries like Arthur's abstract and even unimportant. Lillian could not tell Arthur what to do. But she knew there had been a shift, as slow but as inexorable as the movement of an hour hand—the cocoon she had made herself in this house was beginning to crack, and something quite different from the caterpillar inside it was about to emerge. Her mother would toss her hand, roll her eyes, and say that you had to grow up sometime. She would also probably say that such a thing was never good.

JIM UPJOHN HAD a theory about women: there were those younger and prettier than your wife, but cut from the same cloth—say, they had gone to Vassar, as your wife had, if only for a year. Alex Rubino had a theory, too: you found women who were as unlike your wife as they could possibly be, and made sure that these women never crossed your path again. For a long time, Frank laughed at both of these theories, because he kept expecting the return of a certain tide—that rush of feeling for Andy that he had felt just before and after they were married, before the twins siphoned every mote of energy in their own direction. But the twins were just kids now, not enormous representations of obligation and fatigue, and Andy had made up her mind that something about her own childhood was lingering around her, a shroud, a ghost, a bearskin rug. She, of course, wasn't the only woman they knew in psychotherapy—Frances Upjohn was quite fond of her Jungian. Both Frank and Jim thought that therapy was a luxury women could afford because they didn't have much to regret; without mentioning it, they both knew they were talking about the war, and the only way you were supposed to talk about the war was as an adventure. They let the subject drop.

When Frank got picked up in the Waldorf, he was sitting at the bar, nursing a gin and tonic. He was wasting time, not going home, because the twins, then a year old, were a riot of screaming and upset. When she passed him, murmuring, "That looks good. Buy me one?" he didn't even realize she was a whore. What a hick, he thought. Once a hick, always a hick. She was a nice-looking girl, dark, slender, wearing a pair of shoes Andy would have admired. But he wasn't a guest in the hotel, and so didn't have a room. After an hour, they left the Waldorf, and he kissed her by the front door, before she went uptown and he headed for Penn Station and home. Why had he kissed her? Because she opened his eyes. Of course, he paid her, too.

He tried it a month or so later at the Waldorf, taking a room for the night, then watching the girls work the bar. That time, the girl had been slightly younger—maybe twenty-five, and blonde, from Los Angeles, she said, looking for a job on Broadway. But she, too, wore shoes that Andy would have admired, and she carried an expensive handbag. He gave her a twenty, told the man at the desk he was called away. The next hotel he tried was the Plaza—the wrong direction. Farther south, he thought, would suit him better. The Roosevelt seemed perfect—you could walk from there to Grand Central, and the ambience was not quite as stuffy as at the Waldorf. It was winter by then; the first girl he found had a nice Sandra Dee hairdo, headband and all, and her coat was from Macy's, not Bergdorf's. She talked with a little whine in her voice, like the wife in a movie he'd seen, *The Killing*. The second girl was from the South somewhere, and maybe this had been her first time, because when he took her up to the room, she walked around, touching things like the windowsills and the wallpaper.

The third time, he paid for his room at the Roosevelt (twenty-eight bucks), then left because he was too bored to stay. The Mansfield, a little farther south, looked right, but he decided to try the West Side. The Algonquin amused him for a month or two—the rooms were not terribly expensive, and the girls more experienced, as if they had tried out for the Plaza and the Waldorf but hadn't made the cut. Four girls there—Leslie, Peachy, Zandra (really?), and Honey. He was ready for someplace new.

He got as far south as the Chelsea Hotel, and he liked that—there were girls coming out of every door and leaning out of every window. But he didn't fit there, with his clean suit, nice shoes, and carefully cut hair. Better to observe the Chelsea Hotel from a distance. Three blocks away, he happened upon a ramshackle, narrow building on West Twentieth Street that faced north. The bar was called the Grand Canyon, and it had two entrances and a large window looking out onto the street. He walked through twice, looked around, greeted the desk clerk in a friendly way and reserved a room, then returned to the Grand Canyon. Three people sitting at the bar. The tables empty. Frank sat by the window. Because it was late May, the light was fairly bright. None of the regulars wanted to sit in the glare.

Frank asked the bartender for a gin and tonic. He took his drink to the sunny table and sat down. A new mixer, Bitter Lemon, masked the flavor of the gin almost entirely. He formed the name with his lips, and made up his mind to look for some. The first girl through the door caught his eye, gave him a big smile. She went to the bar, ordered a Scotch and soda, and made an elaborate show of walking past him, looking for a table, then walking past him again. When she finally settled herself, he looked over at her, lifted his eyebrow, and smiled. His smile, he knew, was irresistible. He was no less good-looking than he had always been, just sharper and harder.

This one was wearing a mouton jacket. The waist of her dress was cinched tight, and she had Jayne Mansfield tits, but Frank estimated that she had ten years on Jayne Mansfield. She got up and came over to him, not forgetting to sway her hips and let her eyelids droop. She said, "You from around here?"

Frank cocked his head, neither shaking it nor nodding. He gestured for her to sit down. She said, "You staying at this hotel?" She waved her hand to indicate the building they were sitting in. Frank kept smiling.

She said, "Yeah, well. Fine." She smiled and took a sip of her drink. Frank felt himself get a little excited. There was a kind of run-down quality about her that he hadn't seen much of lately. He took his room key out of his pocket and set it on the table. She nodded, then smiled and said, "So I guess you aren't from around here. By the looks of you, you must be from Germany, maybe, but that's okay with me. I was just a kid in the war. Worse now, in a way, at least where I'm from—Allentown, that is, a little ways west of here." She babbled on, confident that he didn't understand a word of what she was saying. She smiled at odd places in her discourse, he supposed to keep him interested. "So, anyway, they say New York's a big city and all, but it's just another small town. Me, I would like to go somewhere else, but I can never get together the dough." Frank noticed that her right cheekbone was a little bruised, carefully made up. What got him a little more excited—the bruise itself or the care in hiding it—he didn't know. He moved to stand up. She said, "Okay, then, Mr. Schulz, yes, let's get it over with, since you ain't got much to say."

They went out of the bar and through the lobby; he put his hand on the back of her waist and guided her away from the elevator and toward the staircase, which was shabbily elaborate, with a faded green silk rope and tassels looped along the pink-satin-papered wall. He pressed her up the stairs. He heard her say, "I guess it isn't enough to work all day, can't even take the elevator." She probably didn't know that she had a magnificent ass, perfectly heart-shaped and outlined by the shiny material of her burgundy-colored skirt. He kept her in front of him, and handed her the key. When she unlocked the door, he pushed it open and pushed her through so that she stumbled, though she didn't fall. She said, "Hey! *Nein! Nein* with the rough stuff, Herr Schulz!"

Frank smiled and nodded.

He was gentle after that, but quick—he had a huge erection, hard and upright, throbbing against the belt of his pants. As soon as he was inside the room with the door shut, he stepped out of his shoes and dropped his trousers. Her eyes widened.

She set down her purse, stepped out of her own shoes. Her skirt had a side zipper, and it took her a moment to get out of it. She was wearing a pretty tight girdle, which was arousing, and after she took off her stockings (carefully, so as not to run them), it took her some effort to slip out of it. She kept her eyes on him, though—alternating between looking at his cock, which he was stroking and then slipping into the condom he had brought along, and his face.

He didn't give her time to take off her blouse, just sat her firmly on the end of the bed and then pushed her back. He was so excited that he had to close his eyes as soon as he entered her and think of Andy to calm himself down, Andy smoothing Pond's cold cream all over her face. Then he opened his eyes, and his face was right beside the face of this whore; her eyes were greenish gray, and you could see the bottom arc of the pupils above her darkly mascaraed lower lids. He had his hands on her perfect ass and he was tearing her apart.

Or so it seemed, but of course not. He finished thrusting and she gave an unconscious little sigh, waited a polite few moments, and then eased him off her and went into the bathroom.

When she came out, he almost forgot that he couldn't speak English, but he remembered at the last moment, and just took two twenties out of his billfold and held them out to her. He threw the twenties on the bed and shrugged. She paused, then reached out and took them, putting them in her handbag without finding her own wallet. Then she pulled out a pack of Kents and a Zippo lighter and went over to the window, which she opened three inches. She said, "You know, stupid me, I gotta have a smoke first, even before I put my clothes back on. I been smoking since I was thirteen—can you believe that?—my brother got me going. He used to swipe my dad's Viceroys. My dad thought he was smoking four packs a day!" She laughed.

Frank couldn't stand this woman. She was perfect.

He was out of there by six and home by six-forty-five. It was still light, and Janny was playing with another girl from down the street—what was her name?—they were tossing Janny's Pluto Platter back and forth. Frank was in a good mood, so he didn't let their clumsiness bother him. He went through the gate, set down his briefcase, and said, "Hey, girls. Let me show you a trick."

Janny approached him more suspiciously than the neighbor girl, who walked right over and handed him the disc. Janny stood off a step or two. He knelt on one knee and put the girl's hand on the front of the disc, then put his head next to hers and his hand over hers. Then he said, "Okay, now, you keep your hand flat and your thumb up and you watch the top of the Pluto Platter the whole time you're throwing it. You look at where you want to throw it until you let go. You want to throw it right where your thumb is, okay?" Then they tossed it toward the gate, and it landed on the walk right there, in front of the gate. The girl jumped away from him and said, "That was good!" She ran to get it.

Janny said, "I want to try it."

"Okay, then. Come over here." She nestled against him suddenly, as if her usual reserve had collapsed. The neighbor girl brought them the Pluto Platter. He kept his mouth shut, but Janny had been listening, and she arranged herself the way the other girl had and tossed the disc. It went right over the gate and into the street. He squeezed her shoulder and said, "Good for you, Janny," then gently, ever so gently, pushed her away.

SPUTNIK HAD BEEN DISCOVERED up there in the sky in early October. Now that Joe was beginning the corn harvest with his uncle John and John's son Gary, he had plenty of time to stare west, imagining a just barely visible glowing plume rising over the horizon, and plenty of time to look east, wondering what was happening behind him. Of course, no farmers discussed this. The real mystery was that they hadn't thought about it in this way before. Yes, the Russkies had had the bomb for years now, but bombers took a while and could be shot out of the sky somewhere over, say, Canada. But missiles, like the one that launched Sputnik, took less than half an hour, it was said. Faster than a tornado, hardly time to head for the storm cellar. This year had been a good one for tornadoes, too—nine in May alone, and five more in the summer—though none had touched down as close as the one in '51, which took out most of that church up in Randolph and stayed on the ground for almost an hour, people up there said. Joe himself hadn't seen a thing that day—just been standing in the barn, fixing something, and looked up to see how green the sky was. Well, bombs and missiles would be worse.

These were not thoughts he shared with Lois or Minnie. It might be that Lois, who read only cookbooks and was bored by the news, didn't know what Sputnik was, though Minnie, because of her position at the high school, of course did. One of the first things she'd said about it was "Look out. More homework." And she was right. A big deal was being made in the paper every day about whether American children were wasting their time in school reading *Dick and Jane* and learning addition tables—maybe they should be reading something more challenging and learning how to use a slide rule in second grade. According to Minnie, who did keep her ears open, they were going to put "missile silos" out west, in the Dakotas and Nebraska. Those would be targets, too.

The funny thing was, and he was reminded of this every day he harvested the corn, he had just bought a new tractor in the spring, an International Harvester 400, a huge thing, 48 horsepower, and he had spent the whole summer worrying about how and when he was going to pay it off. That Sputnik satellite got into his mind (they said you could see it passing over, but he hadn't), and he forgot to worry about the tractor, even though it was red, like the bull's-eye in a target.

They finished the row they were harvesting, at the far end of the north field behind his house, and he jumped down off the tractor. As they walked toward the back door, John, who was seven years older than Joe but looked the same age, started talking about a combine he'd heard about that propelled itself. The tractor could be off doing something else. Gary said, "Like what, grocery shopping?" and they all laughed.

"No," said John, "it's got these snap rolls to get rid of the stalks and the leaves. Then the ears go through the cylinder, and out come the kernels. You got good bins, you can let the kernels dry out right on the farm."

"What would we do all winter, then?" said Joe.

Before John could answer, Gary said, "Fix the combine."

They kicked off their boots, took off their jackets, stomped around, and brushed themselves down. Even though not much in the way of dust was rubbed away, they were only going into the kitchen. Lois wouldn't complain about that. As soon as they were inside and pulling out their chairs, she started taking dishes out of the oven. First came the green beans, then the roast potatoes and carrots, then the rib roast. This extremely appetizing piece of beef was from one of John's steers—he still kept five or six head in the hillside pasture he had up there, not a slope he wanted to plow, up, down, or sideways.

Joe said, "Where're the kids?"

"Jesse's napping, and Minnie took Annie into Usherton for the afternoon. I think she is taking her to a matinee of some movie about a squirrel."

Joe said, "I hope it doesn't scare her to death."

But, really, what was the use of talking, when there was all this food to eat? He, John, and Gary dove in.

Joe said, "Granny Mary loves Burt Lancaster. She says he reminds her of a boy she once knew."

Gary stared at him. Joe shrugged. Gary was twenty now. He was the only one of John's three to stay on the farm—and why wouldn't he? With John, they all farmed seven hundred acres between them, and no other relative—not Frank or Henry or Buddy or Jimmy or Kurt—had the slightest interest. Even Gary was iffy—he talked sometimes about joining the army. But someday he could have this, if he wanted it.

Lois sat in her chair with her elbow on the table and a smile on her face. In the summer, she'd won the pie contest at the county fair for the second year in a row. Dave Crest found some old variety of apples called Spitzenbergs, and she made a pie layering thin slices of those with blueberries. But when she was trying out her recipe (ten pies altogether), she ate just a sliver of each. Joe knew Lois didn't love him anymore, and probably his love of her had flowered and faded, too, something not deeply rooted or lasting, like his old love of Minnie, but they all got along; on a farm, practicality ruled.

Love was for the children—Lois was especially good at that. She was responsible and affectionate, and she had a remarkable way of teaching them things. When she had to tell them something, she squatted down, took hold of a little hand, and looked the child in the eye. Then she explained, and they nodded, and they really did understand. How many times when he was a kid had Joe himself sworn up and down that he understood, just to get Walter or Rosanna to go away and leave him alone? How many times had he seen Frank nod agreement, flash his brilliant smile, and then go right back to making trouble once Walter was out of hearing? Joe let the kids crawl all over him, and he carried them on his shoulders, and he bounced Jesse on his knee. He mimicked animal sounds and bird sounds for them. When he told Lois how Lillian had once read books to Claire while Joe made the animal noises in the background, Lois loved that anecdote, so they tried it, and their kids loved it, too. He wasn't a good disciplinarian, but Minnie's expressed opinion was that strict fathers were too scary for small children. If there was spanking to be done, well, Aunt Minnie could do it, and Joe could stand in the background, frowning and shaking his head, and then Mommy Lois could hand out a cookie afterward and sit with the child, petting Poppy. Minnie had lots of opinions about kids and their families, as well she should, given the parade of kids through her office every school year.

Between them, Joe, John, and Gary ate almost everything on the table, and then John pretended to need Gary to pull him out of his chair. Joe said, "Say, John, what did you feed that steer? Meat's delicious!"

"Clover all up and down that slope."

Nat and Poppy were sitting on the back porch when they came out, and full of burrs. Joe would have some brushing to do that evening, and probably there were ticks on the dogs, too, if they'd been in the burrs. In front of him, John said something that floated away in the wind. Joe smiled. Yes, he was. He was a happy man.

1958

~

WHEN HIS DAD and his mom were going back and forth all winter about whether to move out of D.C. and if so where to go, Tim was against it. He had a group of friends, and he was the boss of those six guys, who ran with him on the playground and roamed with him in the neighborhood. Three streets in any direction, there were stores, parks, playgrounds, anything you wanted. But it was also true that, if he was going to get rid of Dean and all his crap, then they needed a bigger house. Somehow, no one was in favor of Tim's preferred plan, putting Dean and his stuff in the cellar, or his alternate plan, taking over the cellar himself. You got out of the cellar by going up a few steps and pushing open a metal door, and there you were in the side yard. That was a possibility until he and Brad Widger laid some boards around the floor of the cellar and then ran a line of DuPont Cement along the boards to a cherry bomb inside a tin can (he had poked a hole in the side of the can for the fuse to stick out of). When the bomb exploded, the bang was pretty loud. Debbie, who was reading on the couch, said that she was lifted into the air, and Mom almost fainted, because she knew that Tim and Brad were in the cellar, and she thought the furnace had exploded. The tin can had gone up the stairs, bounced against the door, and unraveled along its seams. Mr. Widger whipped Brad with his belt, and Dad had made Tim clean the walls of the cellar with a scrub brush.

All of a sudden they found the perfect place—open house on Sunday, purchase agreement on Monday, then moving in two weeks later, March 1. It was expensive—forty thousand dollars (though Mom and Dad didn't know that he leafed through the papers on Dad's desk one day and discovered that). He also knew, from listening to them whispering in the kitchen, that Colonel Grandfather Manning Sir had left just about that amount in his will. The new house was on five acres, all on one floor, and had six doors to the outside, any of which Tim could get out of anytime, day or night, that he cared to.

He remained grumpy. There were only twenty kids in his new sixth-grade class, and as if that wasn't bad enough, the junior high was small, too—forty kids in that class. He felt stuck in the middle of nowhere. Until he met the Sloans.

Steve and Stanley were the oldest of eight. Steve was three months older than Tim, and Stanley was ten months younger. The Sloans knew the entire area like the back of their hand (or hands). Their dad was an electrician. Electricity was interesting, and by smiling at Mr. Sloan and paying attention, Tim got himself taken along when the Sloan boys had to work Saturdays, which was fine with everyone at home—Dad thought he was learning something practical, Mom thought he was making new friends, Debbie thought he was not pestering her, Dean thought he was not tormenting him, and who knew what Tina thought; she was always staring at him with her thumb in her mouth, even when it was painted red with iodine.

The Sloan boys were not exactly troublemakers, but that was because the Sloan parents' definition of trouble was a narrow one. Roaming far and wide, catching a fish or two, stealing strawberries or raspberries, swimming in the creek, swinging on branches back and forth across the creek—none of these activities were considered troublemaking. If there was a surplus of something, you could have some even if it didn't quite belong to you.

On their bikes, it took Tim, Steve, and Stanley about fifteen minutes to get to the new development, a string of one-acre lots where some contractors were building big houses. The house and the barn were way up a hill behind these lots; Steve said the people in that house sold the land because they were old and running out of money. All the lots fronted on Quantock Road, formerly dirt, now paved. A street went up the hill between the fifth lot and the sixth lot. This was a new street, called "Harkaway Street." There was a pond up by the old house, and a little creek ran from it down Harkaway Street and into a big pipe, carrying the water past Quantock Road, where it went back into the regular creek bed and down the valley. The pipe was fun to play in. Steve said that if you were in the pipe and there was a sudden flash flood, it would carry you out of the pipe in less than ten seconds, so it would be fun and not dangerous. Stanley said that this had never actually happened.

The other interesting thing about Harkaway Street was that big kids in cars parked there with their girlfriends and made out—sometimes, according to Steve, all night.

It was a Friday, after supper, not even very dark. Tim had eaten and then eased out the back door and found Steve and Stanley, who were on their own because their parents had taken all the other kids to see *Old Yeller*. Steve and Stanley had noticed a Thunderbird up there, facing into the valley, top down, lights off. Tim didn't know what they were going to do, but Steve and Stanley did. They rode their bikes past Harkaway Road to where the house was almost finished being built on the eighth lot. They left their bikes behind the house, then walked back to the corner of Quantock and Harkaway, went down the bank, and into the pipe. The pipe was dark, but Steve had a flashlight. They followed the pipe almost to the end, and when they got to the iron ladder built into the pipe, Stanley climbed it. He was so far above them that Tim couldn't see his feet, but Steve then climbed up three rungs. He braced himself against the rungs; way at the top, Tim could see a sliver of light where Stanley had pushed open the manhole cover.

Now there was a flash of a match when Steve lit a cherry bomb, which he passed carefully to Stanley, who tossed it or rolled it under the Thunderbird. Then he let down the manhole cover and he and Steve climbed down the ladder. Tim heard the bang of the cherry bomb going off. Then there was a faint scream, and after a few minutes, the Thunderbird roared away. Steve, Stanley, and Tim could not stop laughing. "We did it at midnight a few weeks ago," said Steve. "Those guys were really surprised."

"Why doesn't it blow the car up?" said Tim.

Steve said, "Just doesn't. A blockbuster might. We got a couple of those, but we just use cherry bombs for this, because they roll."

When he sneaked back in the house later, his dad was in the kitchen. He spun around when Tim came in from the back, and said, "What are you doing? I thought you were in your room!"

Tim said, "I was getting a Coke in the garage," and Dad said, "So where is it?" and Tim realized that he should actually have a Coke in his hand if that was his excuse, but he said, "I changed my mind."

Dad stared at him, but let it pass.

Then Debbie came into the kitchen and said, "He was out on his bike. He's been out on his bike for an hour."

Dad said, "Were you lying to me?"

And Tim said, "No, because you didn't ask me if I was out on my bike, you asked me what I was doing."

And then Dad did the thing he always did, which was to laugh, and Debbie said, "He goes out on his bike at night a lot."

And Dad said, "Maybe that's my business rather than yours, young lady."

Debbie set her bowl, which had greasy unpopped popcorn kernels in the bottom, in the kitchen sink, then turned on the water, elaborately washed and dried it, and wiped down the sink. Tim knew she was doing this to him, showing off. She often informed Mom that things were out of control, and Mom always said, "Goodness, you are just like your grandmother, right down to the ground."

Tim said, "Hey, Dad. Did you hear the one about the two morons who were building a house?"

His dad smiled.

Tim said, "So—the one moron, he would take a nail out of his pocket and look at it, then sometimes he would nail it to the house, and sometimes he would throw it away. So the other moron says, 'Hey, you moron! Why are you throwing away all those nails?'

" 'Because, you moron, they point the wrong direction!'

"And the second moron starts laughing and laughing, and says, 'What a moron you are! The ones that point the wrong direction go on the other side of the house!' "

His dad laughed and ruffled his hair. They walked toward the TV room, and his dad said, "Stay in at night, Tim, okay?"

But Tim knew that he didn't really mean it.

....

LILLIAN FELT THAT she had the place pretty well organized. What had it taken, two months? The living room, which was off limits for the kids, had beige wall-to-wall, pale-green armchairs, a pinkish sofa, and their Chinese prints from the old house. The family room had sturdy rattan furniture, and sort of an oceanic air—it faced right onto the swimming pool; since it was May and hot, the sliding glass door was always open, and towels and face masks and snorkels dribbled in, along with trails of pool water. Tina had spent three months—from the first day they knew they would be moving here—learning to swim at the Y. Lillian had been so nervous that she checked the gates to the pool area twenty times a day, but now Tina was swimming— well, dog-paddling—all the way across the width of the pool, and Lillian was no longer waking up nightly (in their own pale-gold bedroom with pale-olive drapes) listening for tiny splashes.

The new kitchen was big; Lillian bought a range and a new refrigerator. There were two windows in the kitchen that looked out onto the pool, so she could cook, talk on the phone, wash up, and still see everything. She had given up on supervising Timmy—he was out of the house and gone before breakfast. Debbie had a sixth sense of what trouble he was into and always reported, so she let herself rely on that. Deanie, for all his size and hockey ability, was just as happy reading a book (so like Arthur!)—she didn't worry about him. And Tina was a cautious child; the kindergarten teacher reported that she watched the other children and did what they did, which was not surprising in a fourth-born.

If there was someone to be worried about, Lillian knew that it wasn't herself—she was as pleased with the new house and the new neighborhood as she had thought she would be the first time they went through the place. But the new house was closer to Arthur's office, and no matter how secretive he had been at first about the address, colleagues from the office had begun to stop by for a drink on their way home and keep on talking about business. Five acres in the country and a child-free overstuffed living room were perfect for quietly deploring this and that subversion, coup, mistake, and then falling silent if anyone (like Lillian herself) came into the room.

There were five of them, most of the time—Arthur, Larry, Burt, Jack, and Finn. They entered through the front door and went to the liquor cabinet and helped themselves. Lillian, who was the one who stocked the liquor cabinet, noted they they liked Grant's Stand Fast the best, though the levels of the Gilbey's and the Noilly Prat steadily diminished also. Arthur's business was full of partiers; for one thing, most of them knew each other from Yale or St. Paul's. Lillian had been to her share of parties, given her share of parties, and she got along with the Vassar girls well enough (though, while she was navigating this world, the ups and downs of North Usherton High School were never far from her mind). But these get-togethers were not parties. All through Spring Training they talked about baseball, and Arthur pretended to be a Braves fan, but when they were talking about the office, there were a lot of long faces and meditative sips. Lillian came to understand that the days they gathered in her living room were bad days. Arthur told her almost nothing about why they were bad days.

Arthur got everyone out by seven, and he was good about sitting at the dinner table and asking the kids what they had been doing all day, but on the bad days, he just pushed his food around on his plate, even if it was sirloin steak, his favorite. Then, after he had joked with Timmy, listened to Debbie tell him everything she had done (by the minute, it seemed), spoken some French with Dean, and asked Tina about words that started with "b" or "t" or "n," he would get up, veer ever closer to his office, then, finally, close himself in there while she did the dishes and watched TV and put the kids to bed. He reserved his one hour's worth of high spirits for the dinner table.

She went to a kaffeeklatsch on Thursdays, after dropping Tina at her three-day-per-week nursery school—seven women who lived in the area and who were friendly and sociable. Lillian said nothing about Arthur, but what they said about their own husbands made her ears burn: everything from how hairy they were to how one of them picked his teeth at the dinner table and then threw the toothpick over his shoulder for the wife to find. Black eyes were discussed, and grabbed wrists, and yelling in front of the children. The three women who seemed happily married preened a bit. They complained about opportunities they had missed to work for a newspaper, or sing on Broadway (Really? thought Lillian—Rosanna would have called this woman "about as attractive as a shoe, if you ask me"). One of them swore that Ann Landers said that if you walked by your husband's trousers hanging over a chair, and you bumped into them and his wallet fell out, then you could pick it up and remove necessary funds if you had to. Another woman said that her husband never stooped to pick up his change—he just left it on the floor of the closet. Ten or twelve dollars a week, it came to.

The day after Arthur had seemed especially blue, one woman said that she suspected her husband of stepping out on her, because he "had to work late" three Fridays in a row. She plied him with drink until he passed out on the couch, prodded him into bed, and then, when he was sound asleep and comfortable, stroked his forehead and whispered questions into his ear. He had come up with several endearments, and a name, "Liza," and then she had whispered over and over, "Liza who, Liza who?" Liza Rakoff! Lo and behold, there was a secretary at his office, Elizabeth Rakoff, and when confronted, he admitted that he had taken her out and was attracted to her, but he *swore* he hadn't gone to bed with her. He was in the doghouse now.

Four evenings later, on an especially troubling Monday, all the sad-sack men gathered, the Gilbey's and the Grant's were drained dry, and Arthur said so little over his pork chops that night at supper that Debbie afterward asked her, very seriously, if Daddy was all right. Lillian made Arthur a hot toddy, which she took to his office door around bedtime.

Arthur was sitting at his bare desk, glowering out the window. His office was on the opposite side from the pool, and his nice large window looked over a long slope to the woods. It was so dark that the only thing visible in the glass was Arthur's own reflection.

She said, "I brought you something soothing."

"Your voice is soothing."

"Drink up. Come to bed." She led him down the hall. He drank in a preoccupied way and fell asleep while she was doing her face in the bathroom.

Normally, Arthur did the last check of the night. Lillian did the best she could—she covered Tina, turned out Dean's light, told Timmy he had to get up early, and smoothed Debbie's always unruly hair. She made sure the garage was closed, locked the pool gates and the six doors. She wished for a nice big watchdog, turned out the porch lights, and walked down the dark hall to her bedroom. Arthur hadn't moved.

She knelt on her side of the bed and leaned over him. His breathing was even, steady. After hesitating, she whispered, "What's wrong, Arthur? What's wrong, darling?" She felt like a fool. "What happened?"

Arthur groaned and shook his head. Lillian sat very still and watched his eyelids, but they didn't open. He got quiet, and she tried again. "Just tell me, Arthur. I need to know. I won't tell." Her voice was almost inaudible, even to herself. "Just tell me a little little bit." Arthur turned on his side and put the pillow over his head. Lillian waited, listening to an owl hoot in the distance, and then another call—a fox, she thought, which made her think of Frank. The house creaked. She sighed and eased under the covers.

The next thing she heard was "Wissszzzzzner."

She opened her eyes. Arthur was kneeling above her, scratching under his arm, and smiling. When he saw she was awake, he said, "A little birdie was whispering in my ear."

Lillian said, "Oh. Were you awake?"

Arthur nodded.

"Now I feel silly."

Arthur lay down next to her and arranged his arm for her to roll up against him. Just when she was relaxing, he whispered deep in her ear, "It isn't good."

She waited.

"We've been bombing and bombing and bombing the Indonesians, pretending that the bombers are Indonesian rebel bombers. But they are our bombers. If there's a fucking commie anywhere out there, I will shit in my own hat. The whole operation has been such a failure that we are about to switch sides, and congratulate Sukarno on suppressing the commies. It's our planes he's shot down."

Lillian didn't move.

Arthur was silent for a long moment, then said, "It's Finn and I who have to rewrite the reports headed to the White House. Lots of civilian deaths."

Then he said, "And the reports about Frank Wisner. Everyone in Indonesia says that he's crazy as a bedbug." Arthur's tone hardened. He moved away from her, said, "I wish I could say I feel any pity or compassion. It was just that today we were all whispering about Wisner, and when I was sitting in my office, thinking about him, my heart started pounding, and I was just so angry I could have burst into tears. Believe me, I was not thinking, Oh, you poor guy—I was thinking, Why go crazy now, why not years ago?"

She said, "Faye Purvis got her husband to admit he was in love with his secretary that way."

And now Arthur really laughed.

She didn't suggest that he quit his job.

TIM KNEW Janny loved him best. Uncle Frank had flown her down for a visit on his new plane, and then taken all of them up for a ride. There were only four seats, so Tim sat in the copilot's seat, and Mom and Dad sat behind him. Dad kept saying, "Lil! Take your hands down! It's beautiful!" Tim liked it, but he got a little sick, so he didn't like it as much as he told Uncle Frank he did. The best part was flying over their own house, a long L with a gray roof, set flat into the rectangle that was their "property," the oval of the swimming pool tucked into the L. He hadn't realized they had so many trees.

After Uncle Frank left, Janny stayed for six weeks, and went to day camp with Debbie and Deanie. Tim roamed the neighborhood with the Sloan brothers.

Janny had five matching outfits, a different one for every day of camp. Mom said, "That makes it easy," because they were always waiting for Debbie to decide what she was going to wear. One day she wore a ballet outfit. Tim thought she was a birdbrain.

Janny asked Tim questions: Did he have a baseball bat? Did he have a ball? Would he teach her to hit the ball? Would he throw the ball twenty-five times? How deep was the deep end of their pool? Did he ever dive into it? Did he know how to do a jackknife? How about a cannonball? Can you show me a can opener? Tim showed her how to hit the ball, pitched the ball not twenty-five but thirty-two times, tried a jackknife, demonstrated a cannonball and a can opener (on this one he really rocked back and made a big splash). Janny watched him intently, her hair plastered to her tiny head and her swimming suit drooping on her skinny body. She was only eight. When he did something funny, she laughed and laughed.

She also played with Debbie, of course, endless games of War, Slapjack, and Crazy Eights, and she even played with Deanie—Old

Maid and pickup sticks. Debbie's friends came over, and they played blindman's bluff, hide and seek, and spud (Tim and the Sloan boys were allowed to join this game if they didn't aim the ball straight at the girls). Since it was summer, Mom and Dad let them stay up until ten-thirty or eleven every night.

Every morning, Janny came into his room before he was awake, sat on his bed, and asked him what he was going to do that day. He told her—build a fort with the Sloan boys, bike into town, swing on the rope that hung over Wilkins Creek (which was way wider than Harkaway Creek), build a glider, solve a murder mystery, jump off the roof of the house into the pool when Mom wasn't looking. At the end of the day, she sat on his bed and he told her what he had done: the glider sailed for twenty miles, the water from his jump had splashed all the way into the living room. None of it was true—he had just biked around, and the fort was four hay bales and an old tarp. But she didn't care one way or the other. She said she never, ever, ever wanted to go home. She hated Uncle Frank, Aunt Andy, Richie, Michael, and Nedra, the housekeeper, all equally. Mom stroked her head and said, "Everyone feels that way once in a while, sweetie," but Tim was twelve and had never felt that way. And then, two days before Uncle Frank was to come pick her up, she really did cry and cry and beg Mom to adopt her and keep her—she would always be good, every day, and help around the house. She got straight A's and was reading at ninth-grade level—the last book she read was *Jo's Boys*—and Mom had to keep patting her but shaking her head and saying, "No, Janny, we can't do that. Frank and Andy love you and miss you. We were lucky to get you this long."

Everyone was in bed, and quiet, and Tim was almost asleep, when Janny tiptoed into his room in her pajamas and lay down on his bed. Tim didn't say anything; in fact, he let out a tentative little snore, to see if she would believe it, and she did believe it—she shook his shoulder to wake him up. He said, "Huh?"

Janny said, "Are you going to miss me?"

Tim said yes. Whether he meant this, he had no idea.

Janny said, "Can I sleep here? It's hot, and I don't need covers."

Tim moved over toward the wall. Janny moved a little bit, too, away from the edge of the bed, so that she wouldn't fall. He said, "When is Uncle Frank getting here?" He was hoping for another ride in the plane. Steve Sloan said that if you stared at something still, like the horizon, you wouldn't get sick.

"He told Aunt Lillian on the phone. I don't remember."

Now she took a deep breath, but she didn't cry. Tim thought that was sadder in a way. Then she said, "Maybe you could come visit me. In Southampton. We could go to the beach."

"Maybe," said Tim. Then, "But I would have to bring Debbie. She would never let me go there without her."

They didn't say any more. She fell asleep on her back, and Tim lay awake for a little while, looking at the ceiling, and then looking at her face two times. Was she pretty? Tim didn't know. He fell asleep. Someone, Mom or Dad, came in before he woke up and carried her out. They had pancakes and applesauce for breakfast. When they took her to the little airport, Uncle Frank didn't offer to take them for another ride. Janny did run up to Uncle Frank, and did hug him, and he did pick her up and kiss her on the cheek. And every so often after she left, Tim missed her. He decided that she was pretty, but he didn't say anything about that to Steve or Stanley.

ANDY PUT HER HAND over her eyes. It was interesting that the story was as familiar to her as an old sweater—admittedly a Norwegian sweater—because it was a farmer's story. She couldn't remember where she'd read it. Two brothers, Kristjan and his brother Erik, and the mad wife, in this case Signy. Kristjan would have been thirty-five, and Signy would have been no more than twenty. Kristjan and Signy were married three years before they had a child—maybe there were a couple of miscarriages—but then a girl was born alive, and Signy insisted on giving her an American name, Fanny. Fanny was much doted upon, and Signy was very careful of her, but her care didn't matter in the end, because Fanny sickened anyway, and died on her first birthday. This event took place in the spring, and shortly afterward, Kristjan and Erik had to go away overnight to buy a team of horses they needed for spring plowing. When they got back, Signy had gone mad.

"What did that mean?" said Dr. Katz.

"She looked for the child, who had been buried in the graveyard, all over the farm. She ripped open her featherbed and pulled all of the feathers out, looking there. She thought she might be in the wood box, or in some trunk or other. Wrapped in a blanket. Whenever she saw a pile of something, or something rolled up, she imagined that the child was in there, trying to get out. She was always whipping around to look behind herself. Finally, she took to wandering the farm with a spade in her hand, digging here and there. It was a full-time job."

Andy wondered if she would have the same reaction if Janny or Michael or Richie died, and if so, whether it would prove to her that she truly loved that child.

"The death of a child often leads to some form of hysteria," said Dr. Katz.

Andy cleared her throat. "Kristjan and Erik kept her in the barn for the rest of her life, in a stall, next to the horses. They had gone to the asylum, which wasn't far away—Mendota, I think—and they didn't like the idea that all those people would see Signy and talk about her, so they took care of her as if she were one of the animals. I think she lived about five years after the baby."

Dr. Katz said, "And yet?"

Andy said, "And yet?"

"I mean, this story sticks in your mind. You say you think about it frequently, and yet you tell it with great equanimity. I am, if I might say so, struck by your tone."

"My tone?"

"Yes."

For the first time ever, Dr. Katz leaned around and caught her gaze. He said, "To me, this story seems to be one of great injustice. But you seem not to delve into the feeling of it."

Andy said, "But what about the time Uncle Freddy, who was the second child of the oldest brother, went out in the evening to bring in the cows, and fell into the pond, and it was so cold that he couldn't make it back to the house before he froze to death? He was fourteen. They found him before bedtime, but only because his mother happened to look out the window and ask why there was a cow in the front yard."

But Dr. Katz only sighed again. Andy wondered what she could come up with that would move him, actually move him, and then, maybe, make her feel something, anything.

1959

R UTH BAXTER WON Claire over the first day of secretarial school
when she said, "You're from Usherton? Aren't you lucky! I had
to come from Buffalo Center," and without even pausing to think,
Claire exclaimed, "Oh, you poor thing!" Ruth had a plan for every
hour of every day. She was twenty now. She would dress perfectly,
cultivating verve and style, until she was well out of the secretarial
pool, and then she would cast about among the younger men in
the lower reaches of management, and attain herself an ambitious
husband exactly five years older than she was. By the time she was
twenty-eight, she would have a house in West Des Moines, two children, a dog, and a charge account at Younkers. The ultimate goal was
a membership in the Wakonda Country Club. If she and the future
husband had to be transferred (sometimes that happened), Kansas
City was preferable, St. Louis acceptable. The first step, getting a job,
was easy as pie—they both ended up at Midwest Assurance.

Ruth, Claire had to admit, was even plainer than she was, or,
rather, she had begun with fewer evident assets, though she didn't
have to wear glasses. But once she had shaved and plucked and dyed
and girdled and curled and sprayed, once she had modified her accent
to make it less Minnesotan and more unidentifiable, once she had
taught herself to react to everything any boss said as if it were elec-
trifying, she seemed to be on her way, so Claire duly plucked and

painted and cultivated. She also took Ruth to her optometrist and had her choose Claire's new frames: "cat eyes," black with gold along the upper curve. Claire's manner was not as arch and vivacious as Ruth's—she could not manage that—but by thinking of Henry and Rosa, she could manage some good-natured irony and a few amused observations.

The first reason for turning down the proposal she had from Wayne Gifford, who was twenty-seven and worked in Claims, was not, oddly enough, that she didn't especially like him; it was that she didn't want to tell Ruth that she had attained their common goal first. But the second reason, that she didn't especially like him, was good enough, too. For years she had thought that her main goal in choosing a spouse was that he not remind her of Frank, Joe, or Henry, that he remind her of her father, but not be a farmer. Wayne did not remind her of Frank, Joe, Henry, or her father—he was not good-looking, not nice, not smart, and he didn't seem to enjoy her company all that much. While she was ridding herself of Wayne, the fellow Ruth had her eye on, Ed Gersh, introduced her to Paul Darnell.

Paul Darnell was more than thirty, and he was a doctor. He had just opened an ear, nose, and throat practice. He was scowling, abrupt, and from Philadelphia. He hated Des Moines, hated Iowa, hated humidity, hated the Midwest, didn't much like being a doctor, and was vocally glad that ears, noses, and throats only rarely led to sudden death (influenza and scarlet fever he sent to the hospital, and throat cancer he sent to the oncologist). He planned to treat ear infections by day and pursue the passion that his father, also a doctor, had forbidden, by night—playwriting. He thought Claire was not at all plain. Her eyes were diamond-shaped; he took her glasses off and gazed at them. Her hands were slim and graceful. She had great ankles, and a twenty-two-inch waist, and she was funny. On their third date (for dinner, then *The Big Country*) he said, "I am perfect for you," and thereafter proceeded as if she had said yes to an official proposal. He did not remind her of anyone she had ever met. Ruth said he was "a catch."

Paul told her that, in the quiet backwaters of Des Moines, he could write in peace and comfort for ten years, then explode onto the New York scene (though not Broadway—never Broadway, which was far too corrupt to produce anything really meaningful). He talked in a way no one else she had known talked—he ranted, argued, joked, and gave her compliments. He responded to each of her facial expressions as if she had said something. Claire thought that if he just wrote down half of what he said while he was saying it, he would have a play.

Ruth's idea was that you could tell your intended was getting closer and closer to proposing each time he added a regular date to his schedule. She had gotten Howie Schlegel, and now Ed, from Friday, to Saturday, all the way up to Sunday. Howie had dropped out after about three months, not ready for the pressure. Ed seemed to be holding up, though his family were not already members of the Wakonda Country Club, but over there in Davenport, where they were from, his father and his uncle did play plenty of golf on the public course.

Claire did not want to be spending her Sunday afternoons, or even every Friday evening, with anyone, so she and Paul suited one another, since he liked to have a lot of time to himself, but also to call her at the last minute and ask her out. He did everything abruptly. All of this Claire kept to herself. When Rosanna asked her whether she had any special "beaux," she said she did not, and Rosanna just put her hands on her hips and got a look that said that she had expected this all along. But Rosanna had been married at nineteen and a mother at twenty, and Lillian was just the same, and even though Granny Elizabeth had been very cruel that day on the beach, well, in the end, was she any crueler than Ruth, who was always suggesting hairstyles and lipsticks? As long as Paul was sure they were going to get married, then Claire's job was to make best use of her present freedom. No, Paul was not a farmer, and did not remind her of her father, but he was attentive, and her goal was attained: since he was not like Frank, Joe, or Henry, she would not be like Andy, Lillian, or Lois.

ONE DAY TOWARD the middle of May, Jim Upjohn called Frank at the office and told him to come after work to the Plaza. There was a man he wanted Frank to meet. Andy was in Iowa, visiting her parents, and Nedra was staying through the weekend, so Frank had been planning a rendezvous at the Grand Canyon with a girl named "Ionia" (really Effie, though Effie didn't know that Frank had looked through her purse when she went to clean up the last time), but Jim pressed him, and so he went.

The man was an oddball, in the sense that he was wearing a very expensive suit, certainly made for him, but he was so impossible to fit that he looked terrible anyway. When he went to shake Frank's hand, his hand enveloped Frank's in a horny clamp even though he was six inches shorter. His hair marched around his red, shiny head in patches, and there was a quality of scaliness to his bald parts. His eyes were bright and suspicious. Jim said, "Dave, I want you to meet Frank Langdon. He might be the man you're looking for."

"Not looking for a man," said Dave (Dave Courtland, it was; Frank had heard of him, though he wasn't sure where).

"Are you looking for a woman?" said Frank.

"Not looking," said Dave Courtland.

And Jim Upjohn said, "Well, you better be; otherwise, your kids are going to ease you out of there before you know it."

Frank pretended this was not interesting. The Oak Bar had a self-conscious quality, Frank thought, as if it knew it was in a hotel and really wanted to be off on its own, not so accessible to out-of-towners. Jim ordered drinks for all of them—a martini for himself, a whiskey and soda for Dave Courtland, and a beer for Frank. If Frank was thirty-nine now, then Jim Upjohn was forty-four or -five, on a kind of plateau of self-assurance that came not only from wealth and not only from his war experiences, but also from considering himself a free thinker and a charitable man (who still sent money to the *Daily Worker*—try and stop him). Oh, and there was the fact that his fortunes, always prosperous, had risen on the postwar economy like a cork on a flood. He frequently made "wealthiest in America" lists, and only Frances Upjohn knew what the exact amount was. Probably because of Jim, Frank had had a very good year, promoted to VP in charge of development at Grumman, making a nice sum, and, thanks to Jim's tips, though he and Andy were not on any "ten most" lists, Uncle Jens was spinning in his grave. Every time Andy opened a brokerage statement, she said, "Do you think this is real money?"

Jim said, "Dave and I were just talking. I serve on the board of Dave's company, that's Fremont Oil—you know them, Frank—and I told him he needs to talk to you. He needs to talk to someone entirely outside of that world."

"So you say," said Dave.

Jim said, "This is what makes Dave such a great oilman. He is stubborn as a doorpost. It's a medical condition brought on by petroleum fumes."

Frank said, "I know you recently discovered a big field in Venezuela."

"How'd you know that?" Dave looked as though he might punch him.

Jim said, "I told you, Frank Langdon is a scout. He's got his eyes open twenty-four hours a day. Even when he's asleep. He was an army sniper in Italy during the war."

"I thought the marines in the Pacific did that."

"There were a few of us in Europe."

"How many kills you get?"

"Twenty-six," said Frank, "but one was a Jerry who asked me to do it."

Now Dave actually looked at him, and Jim did, too—Frank had never told him this story. He said, "It was in Sicily. A German officer was being driven up the mountain, and they went over the edge. The driver was impaled on the steering wheel. The officer got himself out, and when we came up to him, he was just lying there. He tried to shoot himself and failed. When he saw us, he asked us to do it for him. He was the only one I ever saw up close. Seemed more like a murder in a way." Frank spoke coolly.

"Missed both wars," said Dave Courtland. "Too young for the first one and too old for the second one." That would make him fifty or so, but he looked twenty years older than that. Frank said, "You start out in Texas?"

"Nah, Oklahoma first, then Texas. But the war effort drained those fields. Mexico looked good for about a minute, but I knew that Red, Cárdenas, was trouble before the big boys did. I had a feeling about Venezuela from the beginning. No roads, no nothing. We used to explore on foot, donkey if we were lucky. When that fellow who worked for Jersey was killed by an arrow while eating his eggs and bacon one morning, I just thought it was exciting."

Frank nodded, then said, "And these days?"

"'Bout ten percent more civilized, but better than butting up against the Russkies."

"That seems to be the problem," said Jim Upjohn. "Dave's sons want to make a big investment in Saudi. Dave says better the devil you know."

"Your sons are Hal Courtland and Friskie Courtland?"

"Friskie, yeah. Christened William Flinders." Dave made a low, rough, loud sound in his throat that Frank decided was a cough, then said, "You know anything about the oil business?"

"Only what I read in the papers," said Frank.

"See," said Jim, "this is where you're making your mistake, Dave. You think that the oil business is different from any other business, and it's not. Real estate, airplanes, bombs, cookies, rutabagas—all the same. You identify the customers, you identify the product, and you bring the two together."

Dave looked Frank up and down, then said, "The thing I'm not good at is getting along with people. I just seem to blow my top. You good at getting along with people?"

Jim said, "Frank gets along with everyone."

Frank thought, Or with no one. And that was a pleasant thought.

The conversation ambled forward, Dave Courtland taking an intermittent interest in it, but also looking around the bar, staring at this customer and that one, and not always the females. Frank saw why Jim was after him to run Fremont: Dave was a kind of farmer, with oil as his crop. Proud that he hadn't gone to school after the age of twelve, proud that he'd taught himself everything he knew, but now confused at how often he felt adrift. Hal and Friskie (Harvard and Yale? Princeton and Dartmouth?) would have perfected their slightly condescending manner, and of course they wanted to invest in Saudi—they could hobnob with Europeans and Rockefellers and art collectors. Frank agreed with Dave Courtland that it was better to drill on your own side of the Atlantic.

Jim sat on any number of boards of directors, including Pan Am and Douglas Aircraft—he had taken Frank on the maiden run of the DC-8 a year ago May, and Frank had been impressed. He knew that Jim loved the DC-8, and suspected that he was behind Pan Am's big order of those planes when everyone else assumed they were going to go with Boeing. Now he was up to something, but when had Frank ever not gone along with Jim Upjohn? It was like that first time he had taken Frank for a ride in his—what was that?—a Fairchild something—an Argus. You could see through the roof of the plane. It had been a revelation.

All of a sudden, Dave Courtland balked. He bucked, he reared, he backed away. He said, "I've had it for today. I'm going up to my room and having supper, then turning in for the night."

Jim Upjohn was as smooth as could be. He said, "Good idea, Dave. They serve quite a good filet here; you should try it."

Dave Courtland was already gone, leaving Jim to pay for the drinks. All Jim said was "That man's got forty million bucks, and those boys are siphoning it out of his pocket."

Frank said, "You ever siphon gas?"

Jim Upjohn shook his head.

Frank said, "Well, it tastes like hell, and it gives you a hell of a headache."

"Something Hal and Risky Friskie truly deserve."

Frank said, "I don't understand what you want from me, though."

"We'll see. My idea at this point, though, is: Dave hires you to replace himself as COO. You walk around beside him, you sit down next to him, you stand a little off to the side, and you say not a single word, and those little boys will be shitting their pants."

"I have a job," said Frank.

"Oil pays very well," said Jim.

They parted at the door, and Frank headed into the park.

FIRST, ROSANNA SAID what she always said: "How's the weather?"

Lillian had long since learned that her mother wanted to know in detail and could not be put off, so she said, "Not bad. Warmish—maybe in the high forties. Sunny."

Rosanna said, "Well, that cold snap here is over, but it's still below zero every night. You know it got down to fifteen below. In November. I am not looking forward to actual winter."

"Brr," said Lillian.

Rosanna said, "How did those boys behave themselves?"

"They were fine," said Lillian. Frank, Andy, and their three kids had flown down Wednesday for Thanksgiving and left that morning. Rosanna waited. Lillian said, "Really, they had one fight with each other. They were fine with Tina. She had some toy—oh, the Mr.

Potato Head—and Michael asked her for it very nicely. That doesn't mean that he's as nice with his brother, Richie. . . ."

"I never saw anyone for taking what the other child had just to get it like Frankie was. Whatever Joe had, Frankie swiped it, and then, as soon as Joe was out of the room, he lost interest and dropped it. Didn't matter what it was. It could be a piece of lint."

"They argued over pieces of lint?" Lillian was always amazed at what Rosanna said they had played with during the Depression.

"You know what I mean," said Rosanna.

"Janny stuck to Timmy like glue, so they went bike riding, and the twins couldn't get enough of Dean. There was one hair-pulling incident, and then Dean got them to run around the yard with him, trying to keep the paddleball going. They were laughing." Lillian waited for Rosanna to ask about Andy's drinking. She had her reply all ready—"Hardly anything, Arthur was the one who . . ."—but Rosanna said, "Well, good for Dean. Those little boys always strike me as deadly serious."

Now it was Lillian's turn to cluck. "Well, Janny is serious, too. It's just their temperament. I mean . . ." Lillian hesitated, then went on: "When have you seen Andy laugh out loud? She smiles, and she chuckles once in a blue moon, but I've never seen even Arthur get a real laugh out of her."

Rosanna said, "Dear me."

Lillian decided to change the subject. "Did you have anyone besides Claire?" They both knew what that meant.

"He's a doctor. Ears, noses." Rosanna said this rather dismissively.

Lillian smiled, but said, "Was she wearing a ring?"

"No ring," said Rosanna.

"How did they act?"

"Like good friends."

"No hand holding?"

"In front of me?"

"You can tell if there has been hand holding in the last minute or two."

"Didn't see any of that. He talked mostly to Joe and Lois, as a matter of fact."

"What about?"

"Crop prices with Joe, and ear infections with Lois."

"How is Henry?"

Rosanna clucked again. Lillian waited. Rosanna said, "I thought Henry was going to bring home this girl, what was her name, Sandra. But he said that was all over."

"Really?" said Lillian. "He seemed to like her."

"Did he bring her there?"

"He was going to, but she got the flu or something. She sent along a tin of cookies with him. In the spring sometime. I did think they were serious. She has her Ph.D. from the University of Manchester." Then she said, helpfully, "In England. I thought she was kind of his dream girl. Her last name is Boulstridge. He said it was very rare."

"He would know," said Rosanna. "But you never saw her."

"I saw a picture of them. She was cute. He had a picture when he visited."

Rosanna clucked, then said, "Same thing happened with that other girl, the Canadian girl. He talked all about her for months and months, said she couldn't wait to come visit, and then she was gone with the wind."

"He's picky," said Lillian.

"Where does that get you?" said Rosanna. "He's too good-looking. He's smart, he's got himself a good job at Northwestern, teaching crazy old languages; he goes to Europe every summer and has a ball digging up old junk, if you can believe that." Lillian could almost see her mother's eyes rolling. Then, "How is Arthur?" Rosanna spoke suddenly and sharply, in order, Lillian thought, to take her by surprise and trap her into saying some revealing word. But all words were revealing—"fine," "better," "okay," "not bad," "the same," "eating well," "sleeping sometimes," "roaming the house and the yard," "sitting in the car without doing anything." Losing his mind. When they were having just one drink before dinner (beer for Lillian and Frank, martini for Andy and Arthur), Arthur had asked Andy what she thought of psychoanalysis, and when she answered that she enjoyed it, that, yes, it was worth the money (she and her analyst, Dr. Grossman, were learning a lot of things), he had stared at her almost, Lillian thought, in pain. She said, "Arthur is working hard."

"I never met anyone like Arthur," said Rosanna.

"There is no one like Arthur," said Lillian.

There was a pause; then Lillian said, "Did you make the gravy?"

"Always do," said Rosanna.

"I made mine just like you make yours," said Lillian. "When dinner was over and we were all just so full, Arthur took the gravy boat and poured the last few tablespoons right into his mouth. Then he licked his lips and rubbed his stomach. I thought Debbie was going to disinherit herself, but the other kids were laughing."

"Oh yes, your Arthur is one of a kind," said Rosanna.

DR. GROSSMAN'S OFFICE was farther up Riverside Drive, at Seventy-eighth Street. It was easy to get to, there was plenty of parking, and Andy could imagine herself and Dr. Grossman as friends rather than doctor and patient. It wasn't just that Dr. Grossman was a woman, it was that she seemed to have a naturally sunny disposition, and also that she was nicely dressed—not only expensively, but with thought as well as taste. It was sort of a perverse victory, Andy thought, that Dr. Katz had fired her, or, rather, kicked her up the ladder to someone more expensive, and less accommodating. Dr. Grossman didn't let her get away with telling stories as dreams, or lying silently on the couch for more than a minute or two. Sometimes Dr. Grossman even argued with her. Now Andy felt that she was truly brave, forging ahead as Dr. Grossman uttered one skeptical noise after another.

"Considering what has happened to Eunice since, I don't feel terribly bitter, and I know she was, we were, very young." Dr. Grossman did not rise to this bait, so Andy went on. "She set out to seduce Frank—I knew that at the time, because she told me she wanted to. You know how girls are. Some of them, like me, just go around a bit underwater, and everything comes so slowly. So, oh, I guess it was the summer, six months after our friend Lawrence died, that Eunice just came out with it in a letter. She was going to lose her virginity anyway—it was as inevitable as the war—she didn't believe for a moment that Roosevelt would leave the English in the lurch—so why not lose it to someone like Frank Langdon, the best-looking guy you'd ever seen? It was such a small thing compared to, say, the collapse of France. I mean, she wrote that." Andy fell silent; Dr. Grossman cleared her throat. Andy added, "Small compared to other things, too." It was true that seeing Dr. Katz and then Dr. Grossman every day, the only Jewish people she had ever known, really, made her think of the concentration camps, then atom bombs—she could hardly remember the war itself through the smokescreen of hydrogen and atom bombs. And there was no remembering with Frank. He never said a word about what he had done or not done. "Of course, at that time, I didn't know that she had already lost her virginity years before, and not in a very nice way, to an uncle, I believe, though he was fairly close in age—I think she was fourteen and he was seventeen." Dr. Grossman made a low noise, maybe disbelieving, maybe disapproving, but, as far as Andy knew, this tale of Eunice's was as true as any other. "Of course, I didn't tell Frank what she wrote. I never talked about sex to Frank, and to be honest, he seemed a little shy about that sort of thing." She paused for a long time and waited for Dr. Grossman to prompt her, but Dr. Grossman said nothing, just uncrossed and recrossed her legs.

"When school started up again and Eunice returned from vacation, I saw that she meant it. Her eyes were all over Frank. The three of us weren't together very often, because why would we be? The person that linked us was gone."

"Please tell me again how he died?" said Dr. Grossman.

"Infected tooth," said Andy. "Utterly needless." She cleared her throat. The sun poured in the window, and Andy could easily sense the Hudson River below in the quality of the light. "However, in the Union or walking across campus, if I was with either of them and the other one appeared, no one had to tell me a thing. It was like magnets. It hurt my feelings at first, but then it didn't. Whatever was going on between them just squeezed some other things out of him that I actually preferred—'I love you,' stuff about his family, his brother Joe. Joe is a wonderful person. The sense of sin did it. You know, that is the one time in my life with Frank that I ever saw him be sorry for anything, anything at all. His usual attitude is very fatalistic. If Michael hits Richie and blackens his eye, or Janny gets bullied at school, then it was just what was meant to be. I mean, when I showed him that article in the *Times* that said that the Russians have a hundred missile bases, and said what would we do if . . . , well, he said, 'Just sit right here.'"

"So—go on with your story."

"Frank thought it was a dead secret, but Eunice gave me the blow-by-blow. How he kissed her, where he touched her, which item of clothing he took off first, how one time he ripped her stocking. Believe me, I was not envious. Sometimes I thought she was crazy, and she was doing it not with Frank but with someone she thought was Frank or she was telling me was Frank, but wasn't really. I mean, Frank was nicer to me every single day, and rougher with Eunice, apparently. It was like I had to choose—there were two of him, or there were two of her, or it just wasn't my business. Like I say, I was so young."

"Have you seen this kind of split personality since in him?"

Of course the answer was yes. Or no. Andy thought about Frank, the Frank she had sat with at dinner the night before, silent for a while, then irritable with Janny, then laughing at the boys, then seeming to enjoy his au-gratin potatoes (Nedra's were indeed delicious), then telling her a joke, then asking her what a dress she bought for one of Jim Upjohn's cocktail parties had cost ($230), scowling only for a moment, then laughing. She said, "I would say that my sense of what is in a personality has gotten larger since then. His or anyone else's."

Dr. Grossman said, "Hmm." That was a sign of approval.

Andy said, "Anyway, he ran off to the war. That's how he put it back together again. It was Eunice who suffered."

"And how did your friend suffer?"

"Well, the fellow she married beat her senseless more than once."

"Do you mean that literally?"

Andy said, "Yes."

"How do you feel about that?"

Andy said, "I feel nothing about that."

Now there was a long silence, and Andy knew that Dr. Grossman believed her.

1960

〜

HENRY DIDN'T THINK about Rosa much. Sometimes he identified her to himself as his "first love," rather like Flora in *Little Dorrit*—the wrong girl, fortunately escaped, though she wasn't silly, like Flora—she was argumentative, resentful, beautiful, and severe. And yet, when he got to the part in Eloise's letter where Eloise said that Rosa had gotten married and seemed to be having a baby, he felt his mood darken. He read it over: "I don't know if you met Elton Jackman when you were here. He is friends of friends. Anyway, Rosa has told me that she and Elton had decided to get married in a simple ceremony down in Big Sur (to which I was not invited, also not surprised) and they will now live down there with some friends until their baby is born (I guess it's due in June)." Then she went on to write about some organizing she was doing in Oakland.

Henry had met Elton Jackman once—a small, wiry fellow whose real name, it was said, was O'Connell, and whose real game, it was said, was fencing stolen goods, though when the horses were running at Golden Gate, Bay Meadows, or Tanforan, he spent most of his time there. Jackman would take Rosa's literary friends to the races and induce them to bet (and to fund his betting); he would give them a decent tip often enough so that they felt flush. Jackman, talkative and funny, was a bona-fide member of the Lumpenproletariat. Henry thought he was maybe forty-five or so by this time. He himself was twenty-seven, Rosa nearly twenty-six; when he broke up with Sandra, this seemed old, but now it seemed almost virginal. He had thought that failed romances were Rosa's vocation, along with mourning the father she lost in the war. Obviously to everyone, including Rosa, these two activities were deeply and meaningfully intertwined, and getting knocked up by Eddie O'Connell could easily be the culmination of them.

There was a letter from Sandra, too, not in today's mail, but in Friday's, now four days old, which he hadn't read, much less responded to. He sincerely hoped that Sandra was full of the same news—she was marrying an older man, she was pregnant, she was happy, she was defiant, she was thrilled beyond words to have escaped their hasty engagement, which Henry had attributed to the excitement of finding not one but two Roman coins in the same day on their dig in Colchester ("Camulodunon," then "Camulodunum," then, perhaps, "Camelot"?).

Henry went into his perfectly neat bedroom and opened his perfectly neat closet. Stacked on the shelf, perfectly folded, were three sweater vests in shades of brown—he called them "tobacco" (an Arawakian/Caribbean word apparently related to Arabic *tabaq* for "herbs," describing in its very being the colonization of the Western Hemisphere by the Spanish), "rust" (from the Old English root, *rudu,* for "redness," and obviously related to "red," but also to *erythros,* Greek, and *rudhira,* Sanskrit, and the only color with such broad provenance, and what did that mean?), and "shit," the darkest one, from Old English *scitan,* to "shed," "separate," or "purge," also the root for "science"). Henry chose the rust, and then a nice Harris-tweed jacket with a bluish green cast, and a navy blue scarf.

The idea that his class would be starting on *Beowulf* in two hours reminded him that he should drop a note to Professor McGalliard, that man of infinite patience who had taught him everything he knew—or, rather, everything that Henry had been capable of learning at the time, which right now didn't seem like much—and who had recommended him for this position. Henry had a couple of chapters to go on his dissertation, but when the department had gone to McGalliard for advice right after Professor Atlee dropped dead of a heart attack in August, he had recommended Henry most highly, so here he was. Professor McGalliard had never married. Now that

Henry was rid of Sandra, never marrying seemed like the purest option.

Henry put on his coat, picked up his briefcase, went out the door to his apartment, closed the door behind him, made sure it was locked, put on his rubbers, wrapped his scarf around his neck, and went down the three steps to the outside door. Several kids had come home for lunch from the nearby elementary school, and were making snowballs in front of the apartment building next door. Henry waved to them. It was January. There had been four snowstorms before this, and all three of the boys knew that Henry had good aim, so they smiled, shouted hello, and kept their hands down.

Henry swore that he would open Sandra's letter when he got home that evening.

He had five students. Whether they would get through all thirty-two hundred lines of *Beowulf* by May, Henry had no idea—that was sixteen weeks. Two hundred lines a week might be a lot. But anything was better than nothing. They looked at him expectantly, and so he opened a large book to a marked page and pushed it to the center of the seminar table. He said, "See that mound? I wish the picture were in color. It's a beautiful grassy green. It is Eadgils Mound, in Uppsala, in Sweden. When it was excavated in 1874, it contained a corpse lying on a bearskin, with his sword and other precious possessions, indicating that he was a king. He seems to have died in the middle of the sixth century. When you are translating this poem, I want you to think of it as not only a monster tale, but also a historical record. This poem is considered to be about Eadgils, the king in the grave." The students' heads went up and down.

Class lasted two hours. They got twenty-five lines translated—from *"Hwaet! We Gardena"* to *"man geptheon"* ("What! We learn of the Danes of the Spear . . ." to "a man shall thrive"). It did not make much sense, but the students seemed to enjoy the puzzle. That's what Henry said at the end of the class: "Think of the poem as a puzzle, not only a translation, but a jigsaw puzzle that will only become a meaningful picture when you've put all the pieces together. That means we have to be patient."

He ate his supper at a café near the campus, then trotted all the way home, which took a single invigorating hour. Once home, he put off reading Sandra's letter by working on his last chapter, a consideration of "The Battle of Maldon" and the monk Byrhtferth.

Finally, he picked up Sandra's letter, slit it open, and got into bed with it. He was so sleepy that he hoped he wouldn't really understand a thing that she wrote. The letter was surprisingly short. It read, "Dear Henry, I have only one thing to say. I no longer think that our engagement failed because you are American and I am English. I know I said that, and it made sense at the time, as Americans are known for their enthusiasm which then falters as novelty and amusement give way to commitment and familiarity. My sister told me about a fellow she went for at University who treated her as you treated me—always kind and more and more distant. He came up queer as a nine bob note. You might think about it. Yours truly, Sandra Boulstridge."

The interesting thing to Henry was that he wasn't offended. But he also decided to complete his dissertation before thinking any more about it.

HER MOTHER AND FATHER could not afford to buy her a horse. No plan or scheme that Debbie had managed to come up with (including sending Uncle Frank and Aunt Andy a letter, asking very respectfully for a loan of a thousand dollars, to be paid back in ten years, at 5 percent interest) had worked. But now that Debbie had met Fiona Cannon, who was a year ahead of her at school, she didn't care about a horse of her own. Fiona had two horses—or, rather, a horse (Prince) and a pony (Rufus)—and riding with Fiona was far more fun than any camp or lesson she had ever experienced. She rode Rufus, who was a pinto and very low to the ground. She had fallen off Rufus dozens of times—she was expected to fall off Rufus. She was also expected to watch Fiona, who rode Prince. Debbie knew the expression "He rode rings around her," but she had no idea that it was so much fun to have rings ridden around her.

Fiona lived three stops farther on the school bus. She was an only child, and she kept Rufus and Prince at home, but home was not a fancy place with a stable and a riding ring—home was a two-story house with a wraparound porch down by the road, and a big fenced field that dipped, ran up the hillside, and ended at the trees. Rufus and Prince lived together in the field, and all of Fiona's equipment and tack was stored in the garage. Fiona's mom was a teacher at the high school, and her dad had a diner in town that served breakfast and lunch but not dinner. Debbie had been there; she liked the waffles.

When Fiona invited her—not every day, but lots of days—Timmy was supposed to tell Mom that she was going to Fiona's, and most times he did. They dropped their books inside the house, changed clothes (she was just a little shorter and thinner than Fiona), and went out back, where Fiona stood at the gate with a bucket of oats and a lead rope, smacking the chain of the lead rope against the bucket and shouting, "Come in, come in!" And then the best thing happened— Prince and Rufus came galloping down the hill, exactly as if they were happy to see them, Fiona of course, but also Debbie, it seemed. While Prince ate from the bucket, Debbie fed a couple of handfuls to Rufus. Then they brushed them and picked their hooves.

Debbie stood Rufus up next to the fence and clambered on bareback. He was slick beneath her, so she entwined the fingers of one hand in his mane and gripped the lead rope with the other. Fiona eased onto Prince, and sat there, limber and relaxed, until Debbie felt secure; then Fiona clapped her legs against Prince's sides and headed diagonally up the hill in a big walk. Rufus jogged a little to keep up. Prince was a beautiful horse, a Thoroughbred who had raced at Pimlico. He was a chestnut (Debbie mouthed the word "chestnut") with a blaze and two white feet.

As far as Debbie could tell, Fiona could do anything on a horse. It was not only jumping and fox hunting—in Virginia, lots of people did that. Fiona loved riding bareback, and she could do some things that you only saw in movies, like slide to one side and show her face under Prince's neck at a canter, and then pull herself upright again. She could also ride backward, jump off at a trot and a canter, and get Prince to turn, stop, and back up without any bridle or halter at all, just voice commands and the weight of her body.

Debbie wasn't sure what Fiona saw in her—they weren't special friends at school. Debbie was in a group of seventh-graders who took Latin instead of French and thought serving on the Student Council was important. Most of them didn't know who Fiona was, but in the fall, at the bus stand, Fiona had overheard Debbie say to one girl that she was going to have a set of riding lessons, and then she had started talking to her that afternoon. The next day, she had invited Debbie to meet Rufus and Prince, which was, of course, fine with Mom, who thought that Debbie did not need to copy her homework over twice just to make sure every word was perfect.

The horses ambled along nicely, until the dip was below them and the hillside stretched damp and green before them. All along the fence to their left, the dogwoods were blooming against the darker background of the not-yet-leafy trees, and there were a few bluebells. In the fall, they had picked blackberries at the top of the hill, right from the backs of their horses, while the horses ate grass. Now they walked along the fence about halfway up the slope; then Fiona said, "Stop a minute and watch this." Debbie pulled on Rufus's lead rope, and Rufus halted. Fiona trotted on up the hillside for another ten or fifteen feet and turned Prince, still trotting; as he trotted down the slope, she squatted on his bare back, and then stood up. After a few strides, she dropped the lead rope and jumped into the air, bending her knees. He trotted out from under her. She landed on her feet. Debbie clapped, and Fiona gave a little bow. She pulled a piece of carrot out of her pocket and called, "Prince! Come in!" Prince looped a lazy circle and took some bites of grass, but after thinking about it for a moment, he came up the hill and received his carrot. Rufus wanted a piece, too. When Fiona had given him a tiny bit, she said, "I started doing that over the weekend. I want to try it at a canter."

Debbie had learned to sit calmly on Rufus and say, no matter what Fiona proposed, "That would be fun." What Fiona saw in her was a mystery, unless it was that whatever she wanted to say about the horses Debbie was happy to listen to: Prince had won three races, his racing name was Ball Four, he was by Shut Out, which meant Shut Out was his sire. One day, out fox hunting, Fiona had stayed in the front, and when they had a kill she got a pad; a pad was the fox's foot; only grown-ups got the brush, which was the tail, or the mask, which was the head. Her boots had cost sixty dollars; her saddle had cost seventy-five dollars; it was from England. Someday she was going to hunt in England; the best hunt there was the Belvoir; she could grow up to be a whipper-in. Now she said, "Okay, I'm going to do it again. You go down the hill and wait on the flat part." Debbie turned Rufus and went down at a walk while Fiona went up at a canter. By the time Debbie had Rufus right in the middle of the flat part, Fiona and Prince were at the top, pointed downward. Debbie waved. Fiona clapped her legs against Prince's sides, and he started to canter. Fiona leaned back, and then she was squatting on Prince's back, her hand still clutching the lead rope, and then Prince was galloping right at Debbie and Rufus. Fiona stood up. Debbie held the pony's mane, bit her lip.

Prince kept coming. Fiona stood like someone in the circus, her knees slightly bent, holding the lead rope with both hands—maybe she had decided she was going too fast this time to jump off. But she didn't look scared; she looked surprised and excited. They came on. Debbie had no idea what Rufus would do. The hoofbeats sounded loud to her, even though they were muffled by the grass and the dirt, and Prince looked enormous. They came on. Debbie tightened her legs around Rufus's fat sides. She could see Fiona's mouth open as she raised her right hand and straightened her shoulders, still standing on Prince's back. Debbie's heart was pounding. At the last moment, Rufus jumped to one side, and Prince skipped to the other. Debbie slid but hung on. Fiona flexed and kept her balance. Two strides later, she squatted down again, with Prince still galloping, put her hands in his mane, and dropped to his back. At the lower fence, Fiona brought him around in a big trot circle, then came back up the hill. Debbie fell forward onto Rufus's neck, her face in his bushy pony mane. She did not want to be the one to faint and fall off. She closed her eyes.

Fiona's face was flushed, but she was nonchalant about the whole thing by the time she and Prince got back to Debbie and Rufus. Rufus was nonchalant, too, but Prince was delighted with himself—he arched his neck and picked up his feet and took deep breaths. Fiona said, "Horses are really good at knowing where they are." Then, "I'm sorry if I scared you."

Debbie said, "You didn't."

But for the rest of their ride, all they did was wander around the field. Fiona made Debbie trot in a circle both ways for a few minutes, just to practice. And, of course, when the horses were cooled out and they went in the house for a snack, Mr. Cannon was home, and he said, "You girls having a good time?" Fiona shrugged. Debbie said, "Yes. I love Rufus."

"He's a good pony."

After they looked at Fiona's latest issue of *The Chronicle of the Horse,* Mr. Cannon drove Debbie home while Fiona took the horses their hay. All Mom said when she walked in the house was "Hi, honey. The fresh air is doing you good."

JIM UPJOHN HAD his way, of course, and Frank was brought in by the board of Fremont Oil to "reorganize and redirect operations." Frank's "objectivity" was secured by means of a very large salary and no stock in the company. Uncle Jens had some proportion of his assets in oil, but none in Fremont. Fortunately for Frank, Hal and Friskie had already moved the corporate offices from Tulsa to Manhattan, so, when Andy and Janny went looking for a new house the better to accommodate Frank's new position, they didn't have to look far. Andy liked Englewood Cliffs, because she could get to the Upper West Side quite easily, and the schools, the private schools, were said to be excellent.

Frank was quite friendly with Hal and Friskie. Hal was thirty-one and Friskie was twenty-eight. Frank alternated between treating them like kid brothers and like experts. Every time Hal told him what to do, Frank smiled cheerfully and said, "I think that's a great idea." Friskie wasn't much of a suggester, more of a complainer, so when Friskie came charging into his office, upset about something, Frank was sympathetic, offered him a drink (Friskie liked a straight shot of The Glenlivet). He also listened to their views about their father— that he was over the hill, that he didn't understand the modern world, that he always acted on impulse. When push came to shove, that's what he did—shoved them around with those big hands of his. Frank nodded and shook his head with all kinds of sympathy and said that his father had been just the same way, a farmer who had his belt off at least once a day, "The only question was, buckle end or not buckle end?" This made them laugh. They thought Frank was on their side.

Jim Upjohn had led him to believe that Dave Courtland would be buying property somewhere nearby—if not Manhattan or New Jersey, then a place in Southampton. But Dave Courtland hated the East as much as he hated the North. His favorite places were Caracas and Galveston. Frank did not mind not seeing him, because he and Jim Upjohn were in complete agreement about developing the Venezuelan oil fields to their most attractive potential, and then allowing a hostile takeover by Jersey or Getty. When Frank expressed a bit of nervousness about Dave Courtland's reaction, Jim laughed and said, "Oh hell. Millions of bucks are a good tranquilizer. He'll have a tantrum and then, no doubt, decide to use that money to do a little more exploring. And that will rejuvenate the old coot. We'll buy him a nice donkey. The fellow who started a company can't run it when it's going strong. They get bored and cranky, so you have to send them out to start something new. Maybe he'll get remorse, like Carnegie did, and build something for the workers." Jim Upjohn was the only man Frank regularly spoke with who pronounced it like Eloise did, "the workers."

Frank said, "What about Hal and Friskie?"

"They're both engaged, as you know. Hal's marrying into the Corneliuses, and Friskie's got himself a Sulzberger cousin. First cousin. The fate of the company is a problem for them, not a project. The way I see it, we're pointing them all toward a form of family happiness they've never experienced before." Then he laughed. Jim Upjohn was the most casually self-confident person Frank had ever met.

BILLY WESTON, who lived down the street from Richie and Michael (for now, but Mommy said that they would be moving soon, and to a much nicer neighborhood), had gotten a tent for his eighth birthday, and had invited Richie and Michael to help him set it up; Billy's dad had shown him how to pound in the stakes and said that he could work on it on his own. As far as Richie was concerned, there was only one thing wrong with Billy Weston, and that was that he didn't have a twin. Richie had to watch very carefully to see whether Billy, who had lots of good stuff, seemed to be playing more with Michael or with him. If Billy had had a twin, then he and Michael would each have had a friend, but Billy had four sisters, who ran into the house every time Richie and Michael came over.

The tent was not a tepee. It was long, and each end was a triangle with flaps that hung down, and the flaps had four ties. There was a floor in the tent, and Billy said that you could take it into the woods when it was cold or rainy and zip up the flaps and have a lantern inside and sleep all night, even if a bear showed up. They were not taking it into the woods; they were setting it up in Billy's backyard.

What you did was, you spread the tent out on the grass, and made sure that the floor was smooth and that the edges were straight. Then Billy, who was inside the tent, gave Richie four stakes and Michael four stakes. A stake was a pointed piece of iron with an L-shaped bend at the top. Richie did what he was told, which was to go along the long edge of the tent on one side and pull out the loops, then set a stake beside each loop. Michael did the same thing on the other side.

Billy had one hammer. The three of them took turns. Billy pounded a stake on Richie's side and a stake on Michael's side; then he gave the hammer to Richie, and Richie started to pound the stake. It was easier than a nail, because the L-shape wasn't as small as the head of a nail. Richie hit the L-shape twice, and it went in a little. Michael said, "I want to do it." Richie didn't pay any attention to him, and pounded twice more. It got in a little ways farther, but still not halfway. Richie stopped and took a deep breath. Michael stuck out his tongue. Richie hit the stake twice more.

When the stake was finally in, with two hits from Billy, they took the hammer around the tent, and Michael did his first one. He got it in on four hits. Pretty deep, too. This made Richie mad. It always made him mad that he was older but Michael was bigger and stronger. Michael never let him forget it. His dad said that that should make Richie fight harder and smarter, but that didn't work every time. Billy brought the hammer around, and the other two boys watched Richie do his second stake. Because he'd had some practice in aiming this time, he got it in on four hits, so he felt not as mad. It went like that. After all the stakes were in, they walked around the tent and crawled into it and sat and lay down, then crawled out of it. It smelled bad, but Richie thought it was neat—a little dark, like you could hear a ghost story in there. Billy must have felt the same way, so he went into the house to get a blanket and some comic books. He was still talking more to Michael than to him, and Michael kept giving Richie that look. The thing about Michael was that he didn't have to say a word to get Richie—his every look and movement rippled through Richie, no matter whether he wanted them to or not.

Once they had the blanket and the comics, Billy decided they needed 7-Ups because they had worked hard, so he headed back to the house. Michael took the blanket into the tent to spread it out. He said, "Leave the comics alone. I get first dibs." Richie didn't say anything. He most of the time didn't say anything.

Squatting there by the side of the tent, Richie saw that one of the stakes might be coming out, so he picked up the hammer where they'd dropped it in the grass and hit the stake. It went in a little, so he hit it again. It was after the second hit that he saw the bump moving along the roof of the tent. Of course he knew it was Michael's head—he wasn't an idiot. The bump pushed out, then slipped to the right, then pushed out, then slipped to the right, and he lifted the hammer and hit it. There was a loud groan. The bump went away, and there was a sound of rustling. He went around and looked between the flaps. Michael was lying on his side.

Just then, Billy showed up with the 7-Ups and said, "What happened?" And Richie said, "I hit him with the hammer."

Billy ran for the house.

That was when it got scary, because Mrs. Weston came screaming out the door and the girls were behind her, and all the girls gave him mean looks. Billy looked worried, too. Michael was still lying there; "out cold" was an expression they said on TV. This must be it, Richie thought.

Mrs. Weston dragged Michael out of the tent and laid him on the grass, and the oldest girl, Randy, ran into the house to call Nedra; as quick as could be, Nedra came running down the street and through the gate, shouting, "Oh my Lord, oh my Lord! What a pair of boys, it's always something." She smacked Richie on the head and said, "This time maybe you killed him and got your wish, you naughty child. I will deal with you later."

Nedra had a stick of butter in her hand, and as she started to open the paper wrapping, Michael groaned and moved. Nedra held him down and said, "Now, don't move, Michael; that a boy." Mrs. Weston patted Michael on the arm. Nedra felt around on Michael's head and said, "Well, here's the goose egg—heavens to Betsy—big as my fist," and she put the butter on it and made him lie there. The girls went back inside. Then Nedra said, "What in the world did you do this for? Two days ago, they were pushing each other on the stairs. They said it was just a game, but it looks like all-out war to me."

Richie said, "It was just a game."

Mrs. Weston started shaking her head. "Well, boys don't know the difference half the time. And girls! Well, I don't know which is worse. He's coming around." Michael sat up. Richie wondered if Nedra was going to tell on him. Nedra said, "Maybe I should take him to the doctor. Mr. Langdon is in Venezuela again, and the missus is over the river."

"Oh, I don't think so," said Mrs. Weston. "He's fine. Let's have a cup of coffee. Look at him. Michael, you okay?"

Michael nodded.

"Do you feel like you need to go to the doctor?"

Michael said, "I don't want to go to the doctor." He felt his bump, then sniffed, but he didn't cry. He didn't have a single tear. "Can we go in the tent and read some comics?"

"Sure," said Mrs. Weston. "But if you feel like you are going to pass out, you send Billy to get me, okay?"

Michael nodded.

Nedra said, "I need a smoke."

Mrs. Weston said, "Me, too."

The two women stood up, and after a moment, Michael crawled into the tent, then Billy. Richie crawled in after them. They settled themselves, and Billy handed each one a comic book and a 7-Up. That was that, thought Richie. For now. But he was going to have to watch out, and not for Nedra. He looked around Billy at Michael, who was reading and touching the bump in the back of his head with his finger. No, Richie thought, he wasn't sorry. It was a good thing he hadn't been made to say he was.

THE NEW HOUSE HAD a long driveway, but Andy had already foreseen the blizzard and left the car at the end of it—all she had to do was wait for the plow and shovel it out. As soon as she got up, she pulled on her warm clothes and went out to check. The snow, still quietly balanced just where it had fallen, undisturbed as yet by wind or movement, was a work of art. She stood beside the car, staring around. Though she had never been one to make use of snow, like her brother, Sven, and the other Norwegian relatives, she had always appreciated it as a type of raiment, hiding, smoothing, brightening.

Inside, the call had come—no school. She prevented herself from mentioning snowstorms in Decorah—that time they were walking home, which normally took fifteen minutes, and so much snow fell just in that struggling half-hour that she and Sven had to take refuge in the house at the foot of their block, and be taken home an hour later by that neighbor boy—what was his name?—who pulled them on a sled. She said, "What are you going to do today, then?"

Janny looked up at her. "Can anyone come over?"

"In this weather? I doubt it," said Andy.

"I think we should bake some Christmas cookies," said Nedra.

"Spritz would be nice," said Andy.

"I like those best," said Janny.

"What about the boys?" said Andy.

"They will do what they do," said Nedra.

"At least they have their own rooms now," said Andy.

"When they need solitary confinement," said Nedra.

Andy laughed.

Frank was somewhere. Andy couldn't remember where. All she knew was that after Christmas she was expected to go with him to Caracas, take kisses on each cheek, and speak a little Spanish. And after that, he had told her, now that they were moved in and the decorators had finished their work, she would be expected to have parties, at least cocktail parties—catered, it was true, but still busy and invasive. Possibly she would talk to Dr. Grossman about that very thing today.

The plow had gone by when she came out again, and done an excellent, quiet job. It took her no time to shovel out the car, and quite soon, she was heading toward East Palisades, carefully but smoothly. Most of her neighbors were snowed in. East Palisades was fine, and when she turned south on the Parkway, she saw that everyone was moving along. The jam on the GW Bridge was a pleasant jam—the sun was shining now, and the Hudson, not frozen, sported glinting lozenges of thin, floating ice. Then she turned south on the West Side Highway, and from there, only five miles, however long it took. Since she had given herself an hour, she could take her time. Riverside Park was as beautiful as her own road had been, but in a bright, urban way, and plenty of people were out, walking in their furs and boots, smiling, enjoying the novel cleanliness.

When Dr. Grossman opened the door to Andy, she looked a little surprised—how had Andy made the trip on such a day? So Andy thought of telling her that old story about the snow: six inches in half an hour, an avalanche. Had they been frightened? She couldn't remember, and Sven would not have admitted it if they had. She could say that they were layered and piled with bright-colored knitted hats and sweaters and mittens and vests and leggings and stockings— imagining it made her feel happy as she settled down on the couch.

But there, there she was again, and what she did tell was the story of Uncle Jens and Aunt Eva, the immigrants, the first to come, who tried Minnesota, or was it North Dakota? Wherever the most Norskies had gone and the land was cheapest. They had no luck, though: Aunt Eva went mad with the endless horizon and took refuge on a wooden trunk they had brought with them from Stavanger, and then Uncle Jens got caught in a blizzard, skiing from town with provisions. He took refuge on the leeside of a haystack, and was found frozen there days later. Dr. Grossman said not a word as she told this story, and why was she back to doing this, telling stories? It had nothing to do with her family. Uncle Jens had made a fortune, for his time, and Aunt Eva had been a well-read and well-respected matron, who spoke not only Norwegian and English but French, and had traveled to Copenhagen and then to Paris as a girl, before coming to America. She'd thought that Dr. Grossman was immune to this, and had refrained for months, but then Dr. Grossman had made the mistake of saying that every story, every dream, everything that you were moved to relate had meaning, and often those things that seemed most meaningless had the most hidden meanings. Andy didn't know whether to believe her, but she had succumbed to temptation. Now there was a long silence, and Andy brought into her mind once again the way the lattice of snow had lain so gently upon the tree branches that morning, how fluffy it was, how beautiful and transient.

1961

 ~

AT FIRST Joe and Minnie had laughed about Rosanna's opinions of the new President and the new First Lady. Since Rosanna was Catholic by baptism, Joe thought she would be proud that a Catholic had gotten to the White House. All Rosanna said was "Irish Catholics and German Catholics do not see eye to eye." But, really, she didn't mind the President himself—he was a good-looking boy and had a pleasant speaking voice, if you could get over the Boston twang. It was the wife who got her goat.

"Jacqueline!" exclaimed Rosanna as they watched the Inauguration. "What a name for a First Lady! What happened to 'Eleanor,' or 'Mamie,' or 'Ethel'?"

"The sister-in-law is Ethel, as you know," said Minnie, who was home with a flu, a fever of 102.

"She's younger than Lillian! And old man Kennedy is a crook—everyone knows that—and hand in glove with Daley and worse."

"I didn't know you cared," said Minnie.

"What do I do? I sit and watch TV. And you can't have the late movie all day, which I wish you could, then I wouldn't bother with the *Today* show, the *Five O'Clock News,* or the *Ten O'Clock News.* Goodness me. Look at her mouth. She has the strangest mouth. That's what I don't like about her. Her fake smile."

Minnie never forgot that Rosanna herself had been quite a beauty

in her day, though her day hadn't lasted very long. The final thing to
go had been her smile—open, sudden, and bright. Even when Minnie
was a teen-ager, she had noticed that about Rosanna—always cloudy,
always serious, and then the smile piercing the darkness. Her teeth
had been good, too, large and straight, not like Minnie's mother's
teeth, which she usually hid behind her hand. Ah well. Every thought
of her mother still made Minnie sad. Almost fifteen years now since
her passing.

Rosanna said, "You want some more tea? The chamomile pot is
warm. You need it."

Minnie slid her cup across the table, and Rosanna poured more of
the pale-green liquid into it. She inhaled as she did so and said, "My
favorite. The fragrance of June, right here in January."

"It is nice," said Minnie. "Which reminds me, I found a last jar of
spiced peaches down in the cellar. Lois must have hidden it." The cellar where her father had died. Minnie contained a sigh. If you lived in
the same place long enough, everything reminded you of everything
else.

"Well," said Rosanna, "we'll let her present it to us. I'm sure she
has a plan."

"Doesn't she usually?" said Minnie.

"The second child always does," said Rosanna.

They went back to watching the TV.

"You see?" said Rosanna. "She can't take the cold. She looks very
uncomfortable. Those French clothes aren't made for warmth, that's
for sure."

The new President began his Inaugural Address, and Minnie, who
had voted for him (without telling Rosanna), was impressed. It was
just the sort of thing she would wish her students to hear (and since
she had purchased five televisions for the high school, she knew that
they were, indeed, hearing it). It was a war hero's speech, recalling
younger days, glorying in dangers survived. He made Eisenhower
seem dreadfully boring and old. Wrinkled, too. It was strange, Minnie thought, to have a president her own age. She had always thought
of presidents as old old men.

Rosanna was shaking her head from side to side, but not saying
anything.

Minnie said, "When does Lois get home on Tuesdays?"

"About three-thirty. On Tuesdays and Thursdays, she picks up Jesse at the kindergarten." Rosanna's voice had warmed up. Everyone's voice warmed up at the thought of Jesse (really Joe Jr., but his own charming self already). Lois was working at Dave Crest's store part-time now. Rosanna said, "If there was ever a mother who needed more children, it is Lois. She was born to raise a brood."

"I think she's decided to quit while she's ahead," said Minnie.

Rosanna laughed and said, "Well, no matter how long this brouhaha takes, I will sit around making myself comfortable until she brings that darling child home, just to get a hug from him."

"She can drop you, if you want."

"I do not want. I am not *Jahque*leen Kennedy, afraid of a little snow, sleet, wind, or subzero temperatures."

Minnie said, "Did you ever not have an opinion, Rosanna?"

Rosanna said, "Never."

THE EVENING AFTER Arthur had his first meeting with a man named McGeorge Bundy, Lillian was surprised at his mood. Arthur was not impressed by the Kennedys, either Jack or Bobby. Both were hot-headed know-it-alls; the only difference between them was that one had a modicum of tact and the other didn't. But when Lillian chuckled at Bundy's name, Arthur frowned, though only a little—he never frowned at Lillian as if he were angry at her. She kissed him to make up, and Arthur started talking at once, leaning against the sink with his whiskey and soda in his hand while Lillian stirred the spaghetti sauce and watched Tina coloring at the kitchen table. She did it in her own way—every figure was done in different shades of the same color. Arthur said, "Well, how long have I been aware of him? I know he was working with Kennan and Dulles as long as ten years ago. On our side of the Marshall Plan."

"What side was that?" said Lillian.

"Funding anti-communist groups in France and Italy."

"Oh," said Lillian.

"But I never met him. What is he—about my age, I guess. But he looks younger. He's a hopper."

Arthur hadn't seemed this impressed in years. "Everyone knows he's Mr. Smart." Arthur snorted, then downed his drink and turned toward her. He said, "But listen, Lil, here's the thing. He looks you in the eye. He listens."

"What did he say?"

"Only 'Oh, you're Manning, I think we need to have a cup of coffee sometime soon. Call me.'"

"Maybe he says that to all the boys," said Lillian, but with a smile.

Arthur said, "He should say that to all the boys. You know how I think. The servants know what is going on. The prince who consorts with the paupers ends up learning how the world operates."

At the dinner table, he was in such a good mood that he did something he hadn't done in ages, which was to tell a story. They were almost done with supper (though Arthur made them say "finished with dinner"), and Debbie was just picking up her plate to carry it to the sink, when Arthur said, "Guess what?"

Debbie's head turned, and Dean said, "What?" Timmy and Tina looked up. Even at almost fifteen, Timmy (Tim, he insisted) couldn't resist his father.

Arthur said, "I saw the funniest thing in town today. I was walking back to the office after lunch, and there was a dog—you know, a big dog, like a greyhound—and it was walking along. It had a wool coat on and a little hat."

Tina said, "We should have a dog."

"We should have this dog," said Arthur. "It was walking on its hind legs, easy as you please, and almost as tall as I was."

Tina laughed.

Tim said, "Was it wearing high heels?"

"No shoes," said Arthur, "and it wasn't a female. That much was evident."

Now Tim laughed, and Lillian did the obligatory "Goodness, Arthur."

"So," said Arthur, "I can't tell you how many people were ignoring this dog. I don't know why that was. Embarrassment, maybe. But I was staring at him, and he saw that, so he came striding over to me and said, 'How do you do?' I shook his paw. His nails were very neatly trimmed."

"He could talk?" said Tina.

"He could," said Arthur. "Though obviously he was not fluent in English. He said, 'Purrrrhaapppss yew cn tll I are new in tawnnnn.'"

Lillian tried not to think about why Arthur had stopped telling stories.

"I said, 'You seem to fit in well enough. Are you looking for a particular office building?' He reached into his pocket and pulled out a little note. I couldn't read it, though—it was in code, scratches and pokes in the paper. But he said, 'Depppertmnt if Stet.' We weren't far from that building." Now he fell silent, and went back to eating, as if this were all he had to tell. Debbie gazed at him for a moment, then took her plate to the sink, but Dean wasn't going to give up. He said, "That's all, Dad? What happened?"

"Oh, nothing much," said Arthur. "I accompanied him to the entrance of the building. I could hardly keep up with him. We chatted. He was from Boston, gone to Yale, worked at Harvard. Very ambitious for a dog, I thought. I decided that it was just the Boston accent that was putting me off. When we arrived, I could see immediately that they knew him perfectly well at the Department of State."

Long pause.

"What did they do?" said Lillian.

"Well, the Great Dane came out—the fawn one, you know, the brother of the black one—and the two of them sniffed each other's front ends and back ends, then they went around, pissing on all the bushes. And then the greyhound mounted the Great Dane, and the Great Dane lay down and put both paws over his eyes, and the whole world was saved."

Debbie said, "Oh, Dad!" and rolled her eyes, Tina looked a little confused but willing, and Tim and Dean laughed.

But it didn't last. Only a week or two later, Arthur was getting up in the night and roaming the house again. Lillian knew it was because of what happened at the Bay of Pigs. She also knew his pattern now. He would sit in his study after work and stare out the window; then he would summon some sort of strength to get through an hour or so before going back into his study until bedtime. He would sleep for two or three hours and roam the house. After a while—this time it took two weeks—he would tell her something. He said, "We sprang it on them!"

"On who, Arthur?" They were sitting up in bed, half whispering in the darkness.

"On Bundy! On Kennedy!"

"I thought you meant Castro."

"That's the problem right there. Didn't spring a thing on Castro! The Soviets had warned him. He knew more about it than I did. Dulles just went in to Kennedy and said, The operation is ready, it's going to work, let's do it—and he fell for it. It's only April, for God's sake. Half his staff is still looking for a place to hang their hats!"

"What now?"

"Well, I won't be surprised if they disband the agency. The President is fit to be tied, and I don't know what all." He said this rather calmly, as if his whole career would not be destroyed, and so Lillian held her tongue, just to see what he would say next, if his first thought would be about herself and the children or about that other world he lived in. He blew out some air and groaned. Then he said, "Lillian, my darling, my dear, I want to tell you a story."

Lillian felt herself get a little nervous, but she took his hand in hers and said, "Please do." The closet door was open. She really wanted to get up and slide it closed, but she stayed put.

"Once upon a time," said Arthur, "there was a woman named Sarah Cole DeRocher, and she was given in marriage to Second Lieutenant Brinks Manning not long after he graduated from the U.S. Military Academy at West Point."

"Your mother and father," said Lillian.

"Sarah Cole was an only child of older parents. Her family had long resided in Macon, Georgia, and most of the uncles and aunts were ancient and unreconstructed loyalists to the Confederacy. They referred to the Civil War as the War of Northern Aggression. Marrying Lieutenant Brinks Manning in 1915, as he was preparing himself mentally for the probable American entry into the Great War, was an act of the highest rebellion for Sarah, and when he took her away to the North, her parents disinherited her—though from what, you have to ask yourself, since they had nothing. She was nineteen. But, darling, she was not Lillian Langdon, a girl with a job and some money and a large fund of vitality. She was a child, and within a year, she bore another child—not me, I am not suddenly forty-four years old, but a girl child that she named Sarah, after herself, a very unwise thing to do. And in the influenza epidemic of 1918, when my father was still far away in Europe, Sari, as my mother called her baby, died in the course of twenty-four hours. Life to death, breakfast to breakfast, here today and gone tomorrow."

Lillian felt tears come to her eyes.

"When my father got back from the war, he was disappointed in his bride. He had grown up, and she had not. But, of course, that was then, and he made the best of it, and in due course, another child was born, little Arthur. I looked just like a Manning, and my father was deeply relieved. He was a military man. His specialty was equipment. He was proud of everything he knew about equipment, whether it was a machine or a horse. He could deploy a flock of pigeons, fix an engine. He was just like me—he despaired of the glamour boys who always had to run out ahead of the supply line because they were too impatient to wait. But he liked the army, the order of it, and he was a great patriot. Just like me."

"Just like you, Arthur."

"One day, my mother put me down for my nap. I was two and a half, and a good sleeper. She rocked me, held me, carried me to my bed, and then she covered me and told me to have a nice long sleep, that we would have cake for dinner. I remember every word."

Lillian felt her heart start pounding.

"Then she went into her room and got the belt of her dressing gown and she tied it to the bottom of a fat newel post, and then she hanged herself. When my father came home for his dinner, he saw her there. I was screaming from my room."

Lillian started shaking.

"My father never hid any of this from me. He told me what I asked to hear, and he told it honestly. The woman he found to take care of me was a kind and loving woman, and when he sent me to boarding school, he sent me to a pleasant place with lots of animals and playing fields, and he made sure I was big enough and strong enough to defend myself, which I was. He never said an unloving word about my mother, but he would look hard into my eyes, Lil, and what he was looking for was that weakness, that failure of spirit. That fatal inability to take it, whatever it is."

Lillian said, "You can take it, Arthur." She was sure of this—he looked intent and perplexed, not broken, or breaking. But he said, "Wisner couldn't."

"You hated Frank Wisner."

"Why do you think that is?"

"Because he was wrong and foolish all the time?" Then she said, "There is no one like you, Arthur. You make Frankie look dull and Henry look stupid and Timmy look shy. You make Joe look weak. I cannot live without you."

And they both knew what that meant.

BY THE SUMMER before ninth grade, Debbie had become a pretty good rider, and she was too big for the pony, which was fine, because Fiona had a new horse, another old racehorse but more elegant than Prince, a bay with a star named Rocky (racing name Roquefort, with French bloodlines). Fiona loved him. He was a jumper; though he could not be hunted, he could jump six feet, and had done so. Oddly enough, he wasn't bad on the trail—his problem was not spookiness, said Fiona, it was bossiness. He would go on the trail with Prince if he could go first. That was fine with Prince.

Fiona didn't scare Debbie anymore—she was used to Fiona. Everyone at school thought Debbie was lucky to be friends with her.

In the hot weather, they rode trails every day. The first time they stole a watermelon, Debbie was nervous. But it was easy. They walked Rocky and Prince along a trail that ran along the far edge of a sandy watermelon patch that was hidden from the house and barn by both a line of trees and a stand of weeds. Fiona stared at the watermelons as they walked slowly past, and when she saw a ripe one, she slid off Rocky, handed the reins to Debbie, and skittered over to it, bright and oblong in the sun. Then she stood up, looked around, hoisted it (it was heavy), and dropped it. It burst open in a glory of reddish pink. Because she was Fiona, she offered pieces to the horses first, and Debbie saw that they knew what they were getting. Rocky stuck his nose into the wet sweetness and sort of slurped it up, licking and chewing at the same time. Fiona said, "We have to remember to wash their bits." Prince had his turn, and then Fiona ran over and got pieces for Debbie and herself. After they were finished, Fiona took a dollar out of her pocket and secured it under the broken melon.

The second time, Debbie and Fiona were talking about a show Fiona had entered and didn't notice the horses' ears flicking. They took the exact same path to the melons, and Fiona jumped off Rocky and handed his reins to Debbie. Debbie was looking into the woods, not toward the farmhouse, because she was just a little afraid of having a deer jump out and spook Prince. Fiona broke the watermelon and brought some over, then went back for more. It was then that they heard the shout, and about a moment after that that they heard the other thing, the shot. Debbie had never heard a shot before, that she knew of. But the horses threw their heads, Fiona dropped the pieces of melon, and she jumped onto Rocky as fast as Debbie had ever seen her. They took off down the trail that ran past the edge of the melon field, Rocky in the lead, Prince right behind him, and there was another shot. Fiona, who was bending over Rocky's neck, yelled, "Ouch!" and her hand came around and touched her behind. Then Prince shied to one side and almost lost Debbie, but she stayed on. They galloped. Debbie did not see a trail; she had to keep her head low and let Prince figure it out, because she had no idea where they were going.

They ended up near the top of the hill behind the farm, and when they came out into a little clearing, Debbie could see the farmer. He had his shotgun over his arm. The horses were breathing hard—the run up the hill had taken the wind out of them. Fiona dismounted and ran her hand over her behind and then over her right arm. There were marks—tiny red dots. She licked them. She said, "That's salt. He fills the shells with rock salt and shoots them."

"He's done that before?"

"He shot me twice last year, but he didn't hit me." She ran her hand over her behind again. "It stung. Did it go through my breeches?"

"No. There aren't any holes."

"Okay. Well, I guess we'll stay away from him for a while."

"Maybe Prince got hit. He spooked."

But there was no blood on Prince. Once again, when they got back to Fiona's, a half-hour ride from the top of the hill, and the horses were cool and calm, Fiona kept her adventures to herself. It was summer, so her mom was home, sewing in the dining room. She said, "Oh, hello, girls. Beautiful day—not too hot, for once. You having a good day?"

And Fiona kissed her on the cheek, easy as you please, and said, "Not much going on."

"Oh, that's the good old summertime." When Friday came, and Debbie had her slumber party with her other friends, the good girls, she had to admit that she found them a little numerous and irritating.

SHE WAS AHEAD of him, walking down Maiden Lane, almost to Front Street. Frank recognized her from the back, just the way her hips shifted from side to side. He sped up, and came up to her right at the corner, and they stood there, waiting on the traffic. He pretended not to look at her; he was adept at that. She was wearing a black wool coat, nicely cut, cheap. Of course, her face was much older— she would have been almost the same age as Frank in '44, so in her early twenties. That would make her at least thirty-eight or so. Frank gave her a little smile, somewhere between friendly-on-a-deserted-street and would-you-like-to-get-a-drink. She glanced at him and looked away. Of course, she didn't recognize him—he was no longer a GI, his hair had darkened, he was wearing a very expensive suit and custom-made shoes. He dropped back and let her go ahead. He slowed his steps and watched her, and the farther she got away from him the more certain he was that he was right—it was she, "Joan Fontaine," the love of his life, the prostitute (but so unprofessional) that he had spent—what?—four, five hours with on Corsica after the Italian campaign. He watched her walk toward the entrance of a pleasant-looking red brick building on the corner. When she had closed the door behind herself, he walked that way and passed the door. He did not stop, but he noted the address: 158 Front Street, between Maiden and Fletcher.

He kept walking up Front until he found the subway station at Fulton Street, and went home. Once he got there, he was in such a good mood that he sat with Janny for half an hour, listening about the Halloween party at school (Mary Kemp had real wings—well, not real, but see-through—and Doug Lester came as Satan and the teacher sent him home). Richie and Michael had gone out dressed as a pirate and a cowboy. They were now fighting over the sword and the gun.

Frank had a long history of knowing exactly what he was doing. He looked at a thing, there was a click, and he was right. All he had to do was act on that thing. It hadn't started in the war, but he had noticed it in the war—he always knew before he fired his weapon whether he was going to get a kill or not. The other snipers in his squad had talked a little about the same feeling. Lyman Hill, the best of them, thought it was a predatory instinct—not the instinct of a wolf, but that of a hawk or an owl, a sightline followed by a swoop. Frank pictured the woman again in his mind. He tried to imagine what she had been doing in the last seventeen years that had brought her to this street corner in New York City. He couldn't imagine it, but he knew that he would find out.

1962

~ ∾ ~

STEVE SLOAN DECIDED that he was going to learn to play the guitar, and Stanley Sloan went along with this—he chose bass. Tim
didn't know anything about music except that he liked everything
but Ricky Nelson. The Sloan boys had been up to Philly and gone
to *American Bandstand*. Tim liked the Marvelettes, and who did not
like "The Duke of Earl"? But he had never thought about actually
making music.

Steve Sloan never saw anything that he didn't think he could
do, and anyway, his uncle on his mother's side was a piano player
in various musical establishments up and down the Jersey Shore. He
bopped around the halls at school muttering "Stand by Me" under his
breath, just, Tim knew, to be showing off. But the girls smiled fondly
as he walked by. Tim had been trying to cultivate a more reserved
demeanor, interesting but distant. It wasn't working. So he chose
rhythm guitar.

When he asked his mom for a guitar, she looked at him and said,
"Oh, that would be fun. Your uncle Frank had a lovely voice as a boy,
and, of course, Granny Elizabeth quite enjoyed playing the piano."
She walked away, humming. This was not quite the response he was
looking for. At least, Mrs. Sloan would throw up her hands and say,
"Not again! I wish you boys would quit bothering me!"

They played in the Sloan brothers' room. Steve said that they would learn three chords—that was all you needed at first—then they would work on rhythm, and in the meantime, they would find a drummer of some sort, but he had to be steady. It didn't matter if he was their friend; in fact, it was better if he wasn't. He would be their employee.

In the years he had known Steve and Stanley, they had gotten in a fair amount of trouble. Steve had started Tim smoking, Steve was the one who had the beers, and the one who didn't mind driving without a license if it had to be done; that time they hitchhiked to Norfolk had been his idea (Mom and Dad had never even heard about that one). His way had always been, I'm doing this, and you can come along if you want. But now he stood over Tim and Stanley, showing them the chords, how to place the fingers of the left hand and how to strum with the right, and he counted and stopped them and started them and counted again. He wasn't terribly patient, especially with Stanley, but at the end of two and a half weeks, they could play "Tom Dooley," which only had two chords, D and G, and "This Train," which carried no gamblers, no crap shooters or midnight ramblers. Steve and Stanley's mom taught them "Follow the Drinking Gourd," which she said was about slaves heading north to freedom before the Civil War—the Drinking Gourd was the Big Dipper, which pointed to the North Star. Steve sang the lyrics, and Stanley sang the harmony. Tim sang "hey hey hey," or "woo woo," and sometimes came in on the refrain. About three-quarters of the time, they finished together.

Steve now began looking for a "gig," which was a chance to play together in public, and Tim sincerely hoped that he would fail in this attempt. Over the next two weeks, they added "Frankie and Johnnie" and "Good Night, Irene" to their "repertoire." But three girls came up to him on three consecutive days and said, "Hey, Tim. I hear you guys have a band," and all he had to do was kind of cock his head and shrug and say, "Just getting started, really." Then he would lean back against the wall and rest his right foot behind his left foot and act as if he had all the time in the world, and the girls would giggle and smile and hug their books to their chests and look up at him, and this made him realize that he was getting pretty tall.

"WELL, THEY AREN'T my nightmares," said Andy, "but I think they're interesting and important, and since she's screaming almost every night, maybe we should talk about them."

"Maybe we should," said Dr. Grossman.

Andy sat up. She and Dr. Grossman exchanged a glance that indicated to Andy that their usual relationship was taking a little break, and they gave each other that feminine once-over—hair, necklace, stockings, shoes. Then Andy said, "Last night, it was pretty obvious. I mean, no hidden meanings here. It was a boom and a mushroom cloud."

"Janny is how old now?"

"Eleven. She'll be twelve in the fall."

"How do you think she knows about these things?"

"How would she not?" said Andy. "My neighbor two doors down is building a bomb shelter behind his house, down below the kitchen. The workmen have been there for two weeks, putting in the angled air pipes. Their little girl—her name is Melissa—told Janny last week that if she happened to be spending the night when the bomb came she could go into the shelter, but if she was at our house they wouldn't let her in. Or us, either. Now Janny wants to build a bomb shelter."

"What do you think about that?" said Dr. Grossman.

"About building a bomb shelter?"

"No, about what the child said to her."

"It sounds fair," said Andy. Then she sighed. "If we have the news on, she puts her fingers in her ears, and she really presses them hard so she can't hear. Sometimes she goes into the kitchen and I can hear her humming all through the news to drown it out."

"Have you and your husband tried to explain to her—"

"What is there to explain?" said Andy. "Frank would never build a bomb shelter."

Dr. Grossman fell silent.

Andy imagined Dr. Grossman sitting, quietly reading intellectual books in German—not only Freud, but *The Sorrows of Young Werther.* Dr. Grossman and Mr. Grossman would be sitting in matching armchairs, and somehow their reading or their experience had taught them to accept what must be accepted, rather than to fear it. Normally, Dr. Grossman's office, neat and tastefully decorated, was calming. But today the very light said, "No hope." Andy didn't terribly mind if the failure of hope was hers—she was used to that—but she did mind if the failure of hope was Dr. Grossman's. She felt herself become a little angry.

She flashed out, *"Nordmennene vise seg å være rett allikevel, ikke sant?"*

"Excuse me?" said Dr. Grossman.

"Admit it!"

"Admit what?"

"There is no salvation."

"I never said that there was," said Dr. Grossman.

There was another long silence, and then Andy said, "Is there something I can do for her?" For me?

"I have a colleague," said Dr. Grossman. "She might benefit from seeing him."

But as she left the office, Andy thought, it was nature over nurture, wasn't it? Ragnarök or nuclear exchange, what was the difference? How appropriate that the DEW Line (the "Distant Early Warning Line"—Andy mouthed the words) ran across Greenland, Iceland, and no doubt Norway. What was his name again—Loki—the one bound to the rocks with chains and ropes made of the entrails of his own son. Loki, the god of the moving earth, of crevasses opening up and caverns collapsing, was the one who had always frightened her, not Surt, the fiery one. When she was Janny's age, any trembling, even of the branch her swing was anchored to, had put her in a fright. In the last ten years, she had considered and put away her fears—thermonuclear, fallout, Mutually Assured Destruction—one by one. Now they were back, and Janny seemed to sense them. The thing not to tell Janny was that there would be just two survivors, a couple named Líf and Lífþrasir, say Adam and Eve. But not Janny, not Richie, not Michael. Not Andy, not Frank.

FRANK DID NOT HAUNT Front Street and Maiden Lane; he circled it, wending here and there, his eye always peeled. He had the time— he'd given up the whoring and the flying and practically everything else. He told Andy that he had taken up golf, and was planning to join a country club but hadn't decided which one, so he was visiting all of them. He even bought a set of clubs and kept them in the trunk of his Chrysler. But he didn't drive the Chrysler anywhere near the Knickerbocker. He zipped over the GW Bridge, down the West Side Highway, then left on Canal Street. Then he parked in a lot near Chinatown, and started walking. Sometimes he walked first toward the river and then south (southwest—his inner compass was still accurate). Other times, he walked down Pearl Street or Gold Street, scanning the passing women.

He saw her twice in the first week in March. Both times, she was wearing the black coat. He followed her at a distance, taking note not only of where she went and which buildings she frequented, but also of whom she spoke to, whether any men walked along with her or picked her up (they did not), and whom she greeted. The first afternoon, he followed her for an hour and never got closer than half a block. The second time, she went into that same brick building after thirty-seven minutes. He needed a plan.

Events at the office interfered for a while. Friskie got drunk and slapped the Sulzberger cousin in the street outside the Waldorf after a dance—it got into the papers; the girl broke the engagement; Dave Courtland said high time, she was a Jew; and Frank had to fly down to Galveston and talk not only to Dave, but to the wife, Anna. It took seventeen days to work out a reconciliation, and the Sulzberger parents were not happy, but, on the other hand, they had not heard the "Jew" comment, and Friskie was a very, very handsome young man. Then the head of the Venezuela office, Jesús De La Garza, came for a visit, and he was in New York for seven days and out in Southampton for a long weekend. After he left, Jim Upjohn told Frank, he tacked a note to the door of the room Jesús stayed in that read, "Mine eyes have seen the glory of the going of the Lord."

The gift was that Frank was sitting at a table in the White Horse Tavern, and he saw her through the window. She passed the outside tables, came in, sat down nearby, and pulled out a copy of *The Atlantic Monthly*. Her coat was a slender trench, two years out of style. When she pushed her scarf back, he saw she had short, thick hair now, dark with scattered gray streaks, but neatly cut. She was fuller in the bust than she'd been during the war, and had just the beginnings of a belly, though she was neatly girdled. As she read, two wrinkles formed between her eyebrows, and her mouth thinned a bit, though her lips were still fuller than most women's. She ordered a sherry and kept reading. He squinted: it was an article entitled "Anyone Can Play the

Harmonica." This was true, in Frank's experience, so he was surprised that there would be an article about it.

She must have sensed him looking over her shoulder, because she glanced in his direction and gave him one of those little smiles. He said, "Do I know you?"

"I don't think so." Her accent was very good, just an underlying melody of the Mediterranean.

Then he said, "May I know you?"

This time she laughed, and it was the same laugh he remembered, merry and deep, the laugh of a woman with plenty of experience.

"I come from a long line of harmonica players."

"Is that possible?" said the woman.

Right then, Frank knew that his fate depended upon pretending that he had never met her before, to collude in the idea that he believed she was from Queens or Rome or wherever she wanted to be from. What people had done to survive the war was their own business, was it not? He smiled, knowing that his smile was still hypnotic if he really meant it. "My brother is a farmer in Iowa who makes harmonicas by hand, from roots and branches."

She did laugh. She did.

They chatted for an hour, exchanging only names—hers was Lydia Forêt—but nothing about occupations or background. Button by button, she removed her coat. He took it from her and hung it on the coat rack. She was wearing a navy-blue sheath with a slender red belt. Frank took off his own jacket and loosened his tie. They discussed whether the humidity had gotten worse and the likelihood of a storm. Others were talking about Carol Burnett, who had won an Emmy the night before, so they did, too. "She's funny," said Frank. The woman said, "She'll do anything. I like that." Then she reddened a little and said, "For a laugh, I mean. I saw her do a show a few years ago somewhere around here, I think." Frank said that he had seen Nichols and May on Broadway the previous year. The woman said that she had a ticket for *My Fair Lady,* and she was looking forward to seeing it. Frank said that he knew some people who had gone to the opening night of that. There was a pause in the conversation, and Frank said, "So—can anyone play the harmonica?"

"I guess this gentleman did." She glanced at the page. "Herbert Kupferberg. In between watching *Tannhäuser* and Mozart, he taught himself to play 'Taps.'" She glanced at her wristwatch and moved her feet. Frank stood up and fetched her coat. Then she stood, and he held it for her. He said, "I would like to talk with you again."

She smiled. It was that same smile from eighteen years ago, sunny, retreating. She said, "Perhaps we shall run into each other." She shook his hand, then turned and walked briskly through the White Horse Tavern door and click-click down Hudson Street. When she turned her head to look at something, Frank felt ravished and limp.

RUTH BAXTER'S CONSIDERED OPINION was that an autumn wedding was more unusual and therefore smarter than a June wedding or even a Christmas wedding, though you had more freedom with a Christmas wedding in choosing the colors of the bridesmaids' dresses; but if, as Claire insisted, there were only going to be three bridal attendants (you could not say "bridesmaids," because Lillian was not a "maid"), and four junior bridesmaids (Debbie, Janny, Tina, and Annie), then the color problem was easily solved—autumnal yellows and golds, with a touch of red here and there to go with autumn flowers ("Not the brightest of the year, but very classy," said Ruth). Ruth's own marital plans remained unclear, but Claire had become firmer in her identity as the future wife of Dr. Paul Darnell. For one thing, she had gotten fairly adept at her secretarial job, and it seemed silly for Paul to employ his current secretary when Claire could do the work for free; for another, she was almost twenty-four. Even if she got pregnant right away, she would be almost twenty-five when the baby was born, which meant that it might be rather difficult to regain her current figure afterward.

She went in and out of Paul's house, installing her cookbooks on a shelf in the kitchen, even cleaning the frozen remains of unidentifiable leftovers out of his freezer for when they got back from their Point Clear, Alabama, honeymoon. She spent a morning clearing shelves in his garage, and then went to his bedroom—she just stood in the doorway and looked around, knowing that, in a few weeks, folding, washing, and hanging up all of these articles of clothing that were so redolent of Dr. Paul Darnell would be her job.

She loved him. Her mother was proud of the way she had come around to that—not by means of romance or being swept off her feet, but by means of patience and friendship. After Claire made it clear that she was going to marry Paul, Rosanna said, "Well, he is a diamond in the rough, a very good man deep down, and the children will smooth off the edges." These days, Rosanna recalled Walter as the opinionated one, the hard-to-please one; though neither Claire nor anyone else remembered the two of them in this way, Claire thought it reassuring that Paul reminded Rosanna of her father. The wedding was set for October 14. Minnie and Lois were putting together the reception, to be held at Joe and Lois's house, and Annie was training Jesse to carry the rings on a pillow.

Around the first of October, the crying started. Claire and Ruth went to a movie called *I Thank a Fool,* expecting that Susan Hayward was going to be good, but the movie was irritating and confusing, not sad. Nevertheless, at the point when the villain broke through the fence he was leaning against and fell over the cliff, Claire felt herself seize up, and then there were tears off and on all the way back to the apartment she and Ruth were sharing. They made popcorn, and she forgot about it. In the morning, more tears came when she ran her stocking, and then tears again when, after lunch break, her boss told her that she had to retype a letter she had given him, because she had misspelled "receipt" three times. Two days later, she froze in that weird way again and cried over a chicken sandwich in the commissary, and the day after that, Paul called her late at night, and when he hung up without saying, "I love you," she cried again, even though he had called her "honey" three times and "sweetheart" once.

Crying was a little time-consuming when you were going to the florist and the bakery and calling the justice of the peace on the phone about last-minute arrangements and reading Lois's list of what she was making (finger sandwiches with tiny shrimp and rémoulade sauce, Swedish meatballs, sliced apples smeared with blue cheese from Kalona). She cried on the phone with Rosanna while they were talking about where the Darnells were going to stay the weekend; Rosanna was suspicious and reluctant to drop the subject of why she was crying.

Ruth thought the crying was charming and appropriate—she was getting married! She would be with Paul for the rest of her life! That could be fifty or sixty or seventy years, and much sadder if it were not that long than if it was! Obviously, it was sad to leave Ruth herself behind, but Ruth had hope, because there were three men she knew now, and one had gone to Grinnell.

After five days of the crying, she decided that it was just another thing to organize, so she equipped herself with plenty of Kleenex and continued about her business. October 14 barreled toward her; soon enough, Lillian and Arthur and Tim and Debbie and Dean and Tina and Frank and Andy and Janny and Richie and Michael and that woman Nedra, who had to come along, and Henry (no girlfriend) were wandering in and out of Rosanna's house and Joe and Lois's house, and there were two boys from the high school, too, whom Minnie had hired to hand around trays, put out chairs, and empty ashtrays. Eloise couldn't come, but she'd sent a set of dessert plates with seashells painted around the rim that were Claire's favorite present, and reminded her of that New Year's trip to California with Granny Elizabeth, who had died this past spring (and the only thing sad about her passing, at almost ninety, was that she had never made it to Hawaii). Claire thought Granny Elizabeth would have said that she had done a good job—just what she herself advised, waiting this long, and choosing Paul.

Debbie got the younger girls dressed, and when they stood up in a row to have their picture taken, Claire thought that the way their velvet dresses shaded in color from green to gold made a beautiful effect. Lillian, Ruth, and Paul's sister, Irene, looked nice, too, and Lillian, of course, made much of Claire's own dress—how lovely it looked on Claire; the one thing she, Lillian, would never have in this lifetime was a wedding; of course, the war had made everything different, but what a luxury, and Claire had done such a good job planning all of this—Lillian just kept talking, in spite of the hairpins between her lips, as she buttoned all of the buttons down Claire's back, and secured her bun and pulled out the curls on either side of her forehead so that they framed her face for when Paul would lift the veil and kiss her. Lillian had never understood the idea of a morning wedding—late-afternoon weddings, like this one, gave you such a warm, cozy feeling.

Joe gave her away. He looked very handsome—Lois had basted some alterations into his rented tux, and he had gotten a good haircut. When they were standing in the vestibule, watching the girls follow Jesse (who did succeed in balancing the rings on the pillow all the way down), he put his hand on her shoulder and kissed her on the cheek and said that he was very proud of her, and then he squared up and off they went, and tears leapt into her eyes when Paul turned and watched her come, smiling happily. Then he grabbed her hand when she got there, as if he might have missed her at the last moment, and so, when it came time to say, "I do," she said it a little loudly. On the way back up the aisle, she saw that her new in-laws were smiling at her as if they meant it, even Dr. Evan. Then Arthur had to leave, rush back to Washington all of a sudden, but Lillian said that was the Kennedys for you—they always wanted everything right now, no matter how unimportant it was. "If people only knew what they are really like. Shocking." But then she made a lip-zipping gesture and rolled her eyes.

Lois managed the reception perfectly—the whole house was lit with candles, and there were plates of food everywhere, all of it delicious. And when Claire stood on the landing of Lois and Joe's staircase, and tossed her bouquet, Debbie made sure to catch it. Moments later, they were off in Paul's cream-colored Oldsmobile, Dr. and Mrs. Paul Darnell, 1209 Ashworth Road, West Des Moines, Iowa.

1963

EVEN THOUGH Richie had said several times that he would like to move back to the old house, Mommy and Daddy either laughed at him or didn't say anything, and finally Janny came into his room one afternoon and said, "Stop talking about it. They are never moving back to the old house. This house cost sixty-two thousand dollars!" Now it was better, and Richie was willing to admit that he liked his room—having it to himself, and also that he could keep his train set up all the time. And it was his train set. All of the engines had been given to Richie, and if you owned the engines, then you were the boss.

Donna Fitzgerald's house was on the way to a pond they liked, so they had to pass it if they were going to play at the pond. The pond had plenty of frogs and also lots of fish, and the most fun was to throw stones at the frogs. Richie had hit a frog three times in the fall (Michael had hit four). Throwing stones at the fish was fun, too, but because of *refraction,* you could not actually hit one. Nedra had said that they should have a fishing pole or two if they promised not to poke each other's eyes out, but they didn't get any fishing poles, and now the pond was frozen, and so it was much more fun to run and slide from one side of the pond to the other.

Donna Fitzgerald had skates, and one day she yelled at Michael and said that the pond was her very own. But there was a fence between her house and the pond, and the next day, Michael had watched in secret as Donna came out of her front door, walked to the road, turned right, and went toward the pond, her skates slung over her shoulder. If the pond were hers, she would not have walked there by the road. So the pond was not hers, according to Michael.

Richie said, "Well, it's not ours, either."

"But she can't stop us, and we can go there whenever we like."

She was a big girl. The other kids said she was eleven, or maybe twelve, but she was heavy-shouldered and she had breasts, and she also had big feet. She went to the public school, and the other kids also said that she should be in seventh grade but she had been held back twice, and she was still in fifth grade. Michael grabbed Richie and pushed him through the opening in the fence, and then kind of poked him so that he would walk along ahead. By this time, Donna was on the far side of the pond, lacing up her skates. The ice was a foot thick. It was pure white, with lines of cracks in it that had frozen over, and it ran smoothly into the snow on every side. There were two places where you could climb to the top of a little hill and run down through the snow, then launch yourself, sort of leaning back, and slide to the middle of the pond. Richie had gotten most of the way to the other side once.

Now Donna stood up and made twisty steps to the edge, then lifted her arms and one leg and slid onto the ice. It was not like that girl in *Snow White and the Three Stooges,* though, because Donna Fitzgerald was so fat.

The pond was tear-shaped, and the tip of the tear was long and curved. Donna headed in that direction. Richie could hear the sound of her skates scraping on the ice—it was that still today. Nedra said more snow was coming. Donna disappeared.

Michael had picked up a piece of a branch, rather thick, and was bending over the edge of the pond, smashing the end of the branch into the rim of the ice, breaking it into little pieces. Richie scrambled to the top of the hill and ran down as fast as he could, and when he passed Michael, he smacked his brother and knocked him down. He then slid a long ways without even trying. He could almost, he thought, have spread his arms and taken off. When he came back to the hill, Michael punched him in the stomach, and then they both ran down the hill and slid. Michael slid two feet farther than Richie. They slid four more times.

Richie said, "We should learn to skate."

"Nedra said you can go to a rink in Englewood and take lessons."

They both sighed. They had been kicked out of swimming lessons and out of tennis lessons for fighting. The tennis coach had even given them a second chance, but they had then been kicked out again when Michael smacked Richie with the rim of his racket, and not just the strings.

"Dad said you just put the skates on and skate. The faster you go, the less you fall down."

Michael punched him in the stomach again, but he could hardly feel it with his heavy coat. He pulled Michael's hat down over his eyes, and then pushed both of his shoulders until he sat in the snow, got around behind him, and pushed his face in the snow. Michael came up gasping, his face all red and icy, grabbed Richie's mittens right off his hands, jumped to his feet, and ran. Richie laughed and fell backward, then lay on his back in the middle of the pond, looking up at the clouds; Michael returned and dropped the mittens on his face. Michael was laughing, too.

At the edge of the pond, a little hidden under a wooden box, were Donna Fitzgerald's galoshes. They were large and black, with buckles. Inside them were some thick wool socks. They removed the socks, then filled the boots with snow and a few pebbles that were lying around, and some sticks. The socks were red. Michael picked them up and headed down to the tear-shaped part of the pond, where the water came in. Donna was practicing spinning around or something, and he ran past her, waving her socks, to where the ice was pretty thin. He got down on his knees. When he started soaking her socks in the cold water, she shouted, "Hey, you little brat!" and skated at him as fast as she could. He stepped gingerly toward the even thinner ice and stood there, waving the socks.

She got closer and closer, and then she went right through the ice. Michael shouted, "Fatso, fatso, fatso!" and ran past her, throwing the wet socks at her. He turned around once and saw that she had dropped into the pond up to her thighs. She started screaming and waving her arms. Michael kept running.

Michael passed Richie and said, "Come on, let's go home," and Richie followed him. He did not stop or turn around to look at Donna. They came to the edge of the pond, ran up the hill, got out to the road, and ran home. When they got there, Nedra was making a meatloaf. She said that Mommy and Daddy were going out for dinner, and they would be eating early. Michael followed Richie into his room and said, "There are two of us and one of her, and if you ever say that we were even at the pond, I will break your arm."

"What did you do to her?"

"I think I killed her."

Richie didn't answer, and Michael went back into his own room.

Richie thought it was interesting, a few days later, to discover that Donna was fine and Michael hadn't killed her. Life wasn't like in the movies, then.

ARTHUR HAD ALREADY ACCEPTED the Grumman job, and Lillian had gone around Bethpage and a few other towns on Long Island with Andy, and Andy had helped her put a bid on a house—much smaller than the one they had in McLean, but big enough. Tim had persuaded her to let him stay with the Sloans for the rest of the school year, and Dean had found a hockey team not far from Bethpage that looked pretty good. Debbie wasn't saying anything, and all Tina wanted to know was whether she would have a bigger room in the new house. The day before the Realtor came and went over the McLean place, she got a cleaning crew in and made it look as good as she could. The Realtor hummed here and smiled there and stared at the pool and admired the view from Arthur's office, and all in all, Lillian decided that getting Arthur out of the agency was the less evil alternative.

Arthur now professed to be glad of the Cuban Missile Crisis. The only time he'd been really worried, he said, was when he was getting on the plane in Des Moines right after Claire's wedding—the U-2s had photographed the equipment in Cuba, and Arthur, not having yet seen the photographs, had imagined such powerful missiles and warheads that when he saw the medium-range R-12s that were there, he was almost relieved. He said to Lillian, "So they kill us in Washington. They can't get everyone with that crap." And, yes, maybe it had been touch and go there for a moment—no one would ever know the truth about that, would they? Even the Kennedy brothers, even Khrushchev, even General LeMay probably would never know—all of their memories of those moments would be filtered through a mix of relief and regret. At least no irretrievable impulse or accident had intervened. And so, Arthur told her, in the end, it did everyone good to have to face up to the implications of ten years of posturing, and when Khrushchev decided that he wasn't Stalin after all, and Kennedy decided that he wasn't Churchill, the subsequent clearing of the air was worth the shock. Not to mention that Kennedy had decided to dismantle the Thor missiles in England and the Jupiters in Italy and Turkey—he had turned out to understand the Golden Rule, and LeMay had turned out to understand that Kennedy was indeed commander-in-chief.

But Arthur was drinking more—four times since Christmas, Lillian had had to put him to bed, and another time she had found him passed out on a lounge chair by the pool. And hadn't the idea crossed her mind that he stopped at the lounge chair because he couldn't make it to his real goal, the deep end, nine feet of prospective release from every argument, every uncertainty, every dilemma? How long had it been since he wanted to make love? Valentine's Day he made a game of it, with chocolates and a new peignoir, but the old ardor, that combination of lust and paternal yearning, had been absent.

She stood at the door with the Realtor, nodding. The Realtor's instinct was that the place would show beautifully. She held both of Lillian's hands between hers and moved them up and down. Then the Realtor turned her head and said, "Oh, I think you have a visitor. Well, Mrs. Manning, I really look forward to this! How are you, sir?" And she clickety-clacked down the walk and got into her Lincoln. The man nodded to the Realtor and hurried up the walk, hunched over but smiling. Lillian's gaze flicked to his car—only a Ford, a Country Squire. And then Lillian was shaking his hand, and he was saying, "Mrs. Manning! We haven't met before, but your name is always on Arthur's lips. I gather you are a font of wisdom!" And Lillian said, "Would you like to come in, Mr. Bundy? I'm afraid Arthur isn't here at the moment."

He said, "Thank you, I would like to chat with you for a moment or two. I won't take much of your time." He did have that gaze that sought hers out. While he was shaking her right hand, his left hand went to her elbow and then to the small of her back, and she was given to understand that she would do whatever he asked.

They went into the living room, and he sat on the pinkish sofa, leaning forward, his hands clasped between his knees, and his shoulders hunched. He said, "Now, Mrs. Manning—but I think of you as Lillian. May I call you Lillian?"

Lillian nodded.

"I just heard of Arthur's plans this morning, at breakfast, and I jumped in my wife's car because it was right outside the door with her keys in it. That's how worried I am about Arthur."

Lillian said, "I think Arthur will be fine once he's got a different job."

He smiled. "Ah. Maybe. What I'm worried about is Arthur abandoning me. Every day, I say to the President, 'Mr. President, Arthur Manning says this, or Arthur Manning says that,' and if I can't say that to the President, I don't know what I *will* say."

Lillian felt herself staring. Then she said, "I don't think Arthur realizes he has such influence. He's never even met the President."

"That's the point, isn't it? The President is very, very good at ignoring everyone in the room. It's the ones outside of the room that make him nervous." He smiled. Lillian realized that she was supposed to smile also, and did.

"What does Arthur say?"

"Arthur is very cautious," said Mr. Bundy. "And I have to say, when we got the news of Ap Bac, it impressed me, and it impressed the President, that Arthur wasn't in the least surprised." Arthur had told Lillian about Ap Bac—a battle in a village in South Vietnam where the Viet Cong had made the South Vietnamese and the American reinforcements look like fools. Bundy shook his head. "Terrible rout, that was, and about as far from Saigon as from here to Baltimore— less even." He wrung his hands and shook his head.

Lillian said, "I didn't hear about that." It was the job of all the wives never to hear about anything.

"January 2, and that was part of the problem. The South Vietnamese forces had to wait for the Americans to sober up after New Year's, so they let the enemy get the jump on them."

"They knew you were coming."

"They baked us quite a cake." He didn't smile.

"Well, sir, I suppose, since you bring it up," said Lillian, "that's Arthur's problem. No one is surprised at any given action except our side."

"Yes! That is so true! A perennial frustration. Perennial!"

Lillian said, "I think Arthur has made up his mind."

"Oh, he has. Indeed, he has. I know that. But have you made up your mind?"

"Excuse me?" said Lillian.

He stood up and went over to the window. "What a wonderful place this is, ideal for children, adolescents. A very welcoming and comfortable place. Lovely landscape. Nothing like this even exists around Bethpage."

"You know we're going to Bethpage?"

He smiled. Of course he did.

"Arthur is a figure around here! Respected for his conscience and his wit, not to mention his belief in our country. Arthur is irreplaceable, and I shudder at the thought of doing without him."

He came back to the sofa and sat down again, but this time he leaned forward and took Lillian's hands in his own. "Lillian. Do you know what my job is?"

Lillian shook her head.

He said, "I am the national security adviser. My job is to apply the brakes. I recognize as well as anyone that the road leads downhill, a steep hill. There are plenty of people that I see and talk to every day who want to step on the gas and drive the car straight over the cliff. There are a few who want to turn off the road and stop. They don't have a chance, no matter what the President truly thinks—and, between you and me, even I don't know what the President truly thinks. But I can apply the brakes, with Arthur's help. I can and I do, and I will."

He was hypnotic, the way he cocked his head and caught her eye, and then nodded ever so slightly until she was nodding with him. And then the brilliant smile—the smile that told her that she agreed with him, Arthur was essential, they couldn't do without Arthur.

It was on the tip of her tongue to say that she wasn't sure that Arthur could take the pressure any longer, but she didn't say it, because she knew, as soon as she thought it, that to say it, or even imply it, would be the greatest betrayal of all, would be a kind of catalyst. Instead, she said, "I think Arthur will certainly appreciate your desire, sir."

"Please don't call me 'sir,'" he said. "Makes me feel about eighty. I know he's kept quiet about this in order to avoid having me plead with him."

"Arthur is a secretive person anyway," said Lillian.

He knew he had won. He glanced at his watch, and stood up from the pinkish sofa.

At the door, he took both her hands, just the way the Realtor had done, and shook them up and down. He said, "You must do what's best."

She knew what that was.

Arthur, of course, knew that he had been there. After the kids left the dinner table, he said, "Persuasive, isn't he?"

"He is, Arthur. But I am not going to try to persuade you. He thought I would, but I won't."

"I have been at this for seventeen years—twenty if you count the war, Lil."

"I know."

"The Grumman people Frank knows have interviewed me three times."

"I know."

"There's a fortune to be made there."

"Is there?"

Arthur didn't say anything, but, yes, there was. "However."

Lillian turned her fork over on her plate.

"I can't say I liked my prospective new colleagues terribly much. Very serious, serious people."

"Aren't your present colleagues very serious people?"

"They have been whittled and honed and pared and polished. At the bottom they have a few qualities left."

"Which ones?" said Lillian.

"Wit. Dread. Hope. Not always in that order."

"I don't really like the new house."

Arthur said, "Shall we do the easy thing, then?"

And once again that day, Lillian just nodded.

JOE AND HIS UNCLE JOHN kept arguing about what to plant, how much to plant, whether to leave some acreage fallow. Joe had seen a picture of stored corn reserves in a *Time* magazine, and the picture spooked him—hills and billows of grain just sitting there. The article said there were something like a billion bushels in storage, and no market—maybe no future market until 1980, not for seventeen years. Joe remembered the old saying "The best place to store corn is hogs, and the second best is whiskey." His dad had made use of the first option, though not the second. However, Joe didn't have hogs anymore—they were too much work for one man with no one to help him. Yes, the government had bought the surplus corn in the winter; a few of those billion bushels no doubt had belonged to Joe Langdon and John Vogel. John had no doubt that the government would pay for it again this year, store it again, and come up with something to do with it—rocket fuel, maybe. In the fall, the Canadians had sold almost seven million tons of wheat to the Russians—a first, as far as anyone knew, but secret deals happened all the time, didn't they? Wheat wasn't corn, however, and Joe hadn't paid too much attention, though everyone sitting in the Denby café had been pretty hot under the collar, half of them wondering why the Canadians would feed the enemy ("Well, the Cuban missiles weren't pointed at Montreal, were they?" said Bobby Dugan. "Every man for himself, and why not?"), the other half wondering how the American government had been so stupid as not to get in on the deal ("Food is food; if they're starving, we're no better than Stalin was, not to sell it to them"). At least the government was consistent, thought Joe. It would be a sign of craziness to feed them with one hand and blow them up with the other.

But that didn't solve his problem about what to plant. He found himself longing for oats, but there wasn't even a pretend market for those, and how would he harvest them? Corn was the tall, golden darling. Those broad leaves rose, stretched out, and soaked up the sunshine, and one kernel planted turned into hundreds harvested—and there was your problem. Plenty of soybeans in those storage bins, no two ways about that, but Joe decided in the end to plant more beans this year than corn. They were starting to make stuff out of beans—not just oil and feed, but paint, plastic, and fiber. John thought beans were a passing fad, though the fad hadn't passed in fifteen years. Joe knew he could press the point, and John would yield.

AS SOON AS she came back from Caracas, Andy made her first appointment with Dr. Smith, whose office was in Princeton. Dr. Smith's house on Green Street in Princeton was much more difficult to get to from Englewood Cliffs than Dr. Grossman's office on West Seventy-eighth Street, but the inconvenience of the trip was part of its appeal.

Dr. Smith was taller than Andy, with eyes so blue that they were used-up-looking, as if Dr. Smith were on his way to becoming an albino, but his gaze was keen, and he had a beaky nose and muscular wrists. He shook her hand and looked her up and down, then led her to his therapy room. His fee was twice Dr. Grossman's. She had not fired Dr. Grossman, or vice versa. Dr. Grossman thought that her issues with her father were on the verge of being resolved. Lars Bergstrom had always been a quiet man, but powerful in his way. If they could get to the heart of Lars's pattern of withholding affection and approval from Hildy (the child Andy) and Sven, there would be real improvement.

Dr. Smith said, "You may notice that I don't have a couch. Adults should sit up. If you need to lie down, or wrestle with some objects, or hit things, that's what those two mats in the corner are for. This room has been soundproofed. You are free to misbehave, and also to behave." Andy looked around. The office could as easily have been a public bathroom—that was the thought that came to her. He asked her if she had ever seen a psychoanalyst or a therapist before. She shook her head no. He asked her how she had found him. She said in the phone book. That struck him so that he barked out a laugh. He said, "Well, I'm in there, but no one ever admitted finding me there before."

Dr. Smith said, "Here is a piece of paper. I want you to write the first five words that come into your mind. I will give you thirty seconds." Andy wrote "fallout, contamination, beautiful, screaming, maple." The first two were obvious; the third was about Princeton; the fourth was about the boys; and the last word was about the trees she had noticed on the way into town. Dr. Smith said, "Can you make a single sentence that uses all of these words?" Andy shook her head, but Dr. Smith said, "Just try." The sentence she came up with was

"Because of the fallout and contamination, the beautiful woman was screaming underneath the golden maple tree." As soon as she said this sentence, she could see it, a blonde in a ski outfit, standing halfway up a wooded hillside, rubbing her hands madly down her arms, over her face, and the glittering particles of plutonium and uranium, rising up and falling back, dancing around like sprays of water as she attempted to brush them off. Every time she screamed, the particles would form a little tornado around her mouth and get sucked in.

"Your automatic response, Mrs. Langdon, would seem to be awe. You speak of fearful things, but they don't frighten you, they impress you. I would go so far as to say that they stun you, and slow your reflexes in some way. They preoccupy you, and you don't mind that. You gain nourishment from them, even at the expense of some sort of imagined negation of the self." Andy stared at the doctor. He sounded like an ass.

"Mrs. Langdon," said Dr. Smith, "it may simply be that your capacity for spiritual experience hasn't yet been realized. That what you perceive as ennui or even indifference is simply your search for meaning in a life that strikes you as false and superficial." Andy nodded. "You may or may not ever return to this office. I don't suggest that you do. Part of the reason that my fees are so high is that I want them to mean something to my patients—and the thing I want them to mean is sacrifice. Are these fees, should you come three or four times a week, difficult for you to meet?" Andy nodded, though they weren't—Uncle Jens's investments were up to several millions. Everything she had spent on Dr. Katz and Dr. Grossman had been mere fiscal effervescence. But "yes" was the right answer, of course. "What I show you, the paths down which I lead you, might well be frightening, but that is what enlightenment entails." Andy nodded again. "No, please don't nod or say yes right now. Go away. Think about it for a long time. Look at your children and your husband and your life, and make up your mind. The journey you will embark upon is a journey into the unknown." Andy prevented herself from nodding again. They stood up. He walked her to her car.

AT EXACTLY the same time that Andy was turning from Nassau onto Witherspoon, Frank was standing on the corner of Forty-eighth and

Eighth Avenue, scanning the crowd for Lydia Forêt, Joan Fontaine, the love of his life. They had chosen the Belvedere as just the sort of hotel that no one at Fremont Oil or *The New York Times* would ever frequent, and also a place too expensive for Lydia's husband, Olivier Forêt, from Calais, France. Olivier managed construction sites. He found the beams and the boards, the teamsters and the plumbers, the painters and the Mohawk construction workers. Olivier did not believe in fashion; he believed in utility. When Frank expressed disbelief that a Frenchman could feel this way, Lydia said, "Not only is he not like a Parisian, he's never once been to Paris. The French from the countryside aren't like Parisians at all." There she was. He saw her at least a minute and a half before she saw him, and so he had time to admire the way, as she turned her head to check the traffic, her jawline sharpened and her cheekbone accented itself. She smiled. Frank hoped it was because she was thinking of him.

Moments later, they were sitting at separate tables in the bar of the Belvedere. As soon as they had their drinks, Lydia's gaze began to drift toward his, at first shyly, but then more boldly. Frank did the same: he pretended not to know her, then not to be interested in her, then to feel a dawning of desire. Their gazes locked; she took a deep breath and put her hand to her bust. Frank licked his lips and took another sip of his gin and tonic.

They both had keys to the hotel room, of course. It was their usual room, 312. Frank went up the stairs while Lydia went up in the elevator. They met at the door, still behaving as if they were strangers, and then Frank unlocked the door, and once they were inside, she pressed herself into his arms, and he carried her to the bed. In every conversation they had had since he first saw her, in the course of every lovemaking, in every hour they had spent after making love, lying tight against one another, she had never alluded to her early life as a prostitute, had never admitted living in Corsica, had never admitted meeting Frank, taking his packet of cigarettes. She admitted only that she was from Milan, was married to Olivier, had come to the United States in 1952, that she was thirty-nine years old. For his part, Frank never said a word about Andy or the kids, about Dave Courtland, or Hal, or Friskie. When he had to go on business to Texas or Caracas, he simply disappeared, and she asked no questions.

If he had doubted that he recognized Lydia's face (but he never really did) or her posture or the back of her head, Frank knew that he did recognize her crotch, the texture of her pubic hair, the shape and prominence of her labia, the exact way she took him in and held him, the recesses of her vagina. He always preferred the way they had done it that first time, him lying on his back on the bed, so sleepy from the war, and her sitting on him. But they tried different things, just so he could pretend that he wasn't that boy anymore, that he had had experiences and learned from them. However Olivier Forêt treated her, and she said nothing about that, she seemed to enjoy Frank's ardor, and his kindness. He never told her that, outside this room, he was not known for kindness.

1964

～

AFTER HE WATCHED the Beatles on TV, and then got himself into the performance at the Coliseum, Steve Sloan made Stanley and Tim watch the second Ed Sullivan performance together. They were absolutely quiet; Steve watched George Harrison's guitar playing as closely as he could. The next day, he threw out all of their songs and fired the drummer. Enough "Tom Dooley." Enough "Banks of the Ohio." If you wanted girls to scream, then hangings and drownings were not the way. Steve had to admit that when he'd heard "I Want to Hold Your Hand," he hadn't been impressed. But the song had a beat, the Beatles had a look, and the girls in the audience were weeping and clawing their faces. Steve's goal was that they would play at least one set at their senior prom, in June. Between now and then, they had to come up with new songs and a new look—not imitation Beatles, but themselves renovated and renamed: The Sleepless Knights? The Knight Riders? The Colts?

Debbie watched the Beatles at home, with Mom, Dad, Dean, and Tina, and two days later, she came home with a Beatles magazine. Tim laughed at her, but when she wasn't looking, he glanced through it. He decided that he looked most like John. At school, he noticed that the girls quickly formed into groups—those who preferred John, Paul, etc. The mommy types, like Debbie, preferred George; otherwise, he couldn't detect a pattern.

Tim had applied to Williams, Amherst, and U.Va. His father had gone to Williams, Amherst was down the road from Williams, and his great-uncle had gone to the University of Virginia two years before his grandfather had gone to West Point. Steve Sloan hadn't applied anywhere. His plan was to leave home the day after graduation (his eighteenth birthday was in May) and head for New York, guitar in hand. Stanley was a year younger, so he would be working for his father all summer. The prom would be their farewell gig.

They all spent the last two weeks of March writing songs, and, Steve said, the stupider the better. "I Want to Hold Your Hand"? "I Saw Her Standing There"? Not a word about fucking. No wonder the ninth-graders were going bananas. Tim came up with "Come here to me, yeah yeah. Baby, I see you now. Come here to me, yeah yeah, and say hello. Hellooooo. Helloooo. Come here and say hello. Baby, I see you now, please don't go." They did it in G, with Tim singing the harmonies. Once they had mastered the first verse, he came up with a second verse: "Walk me down the street, yeah yeah. Baby, take my hand. Stand next to me, yeah yeah, and please don't go. Don't gooooo! Don't gooooo! Walk me down the street, sweep me off my feet, please don't say no!" Then the first verse again. He was pretty proud of it.

He was sitting in his car in the parking lot of the high school at the end of the day, with the windows closed, practicing this song at the top of his lungs, when Fiona Cannon walked up, opened the passenger's side door, and got in. She said, "No, sing it. I want to hear." So, though he warbled and went off key for a note or two, he finished the song.

She said, "Could be worse."

"The song or the voice?"

She laughed.

Fiona Cannon had had one boyfriend, Allen Giacomini, who rode a motorcycle. The other boys were afraid of her. She said, "You want to drive me home?"

"Where's your car?"

"In the shop. They're replacing the brake pads."

"How many miles does that thing have on it?" Fiona drove a '56 Chevy, blue and white.

"A hundred and four thousand." She leaned across him and looked at his odometer. He was driving his dad's old Mercury Comet, '60 station wagon. It was useful for hauling the Colts and all their instruments around, but he wasn't proud of it. The odometer said 54568. She didn't remark upon it. He said, "Sure, I'll drive you home."

After that, he didn't drive her home every day, but sometimes he did, and sometimes at lunch she would come out to the parking lot and say, "Want to go get a Coke?" Or she would get in, lift her hair from her collar, and say, "Want to see a movie Friday night?" (Never Saturday at first, because the fox hunting was on Sunday until the end of March.) Even when her car was there in the parking lot, she would leave it behind; that meant he had to pick her up in the morning and bring her to school.

He took other girls out—Allison Carter and Janie Finch, on regular dates to movies and parties when he wasn't practicing with the other Fire-Eaters, Dragons, Camerons. "The Camerons?" he said to Steve. "What is that?"

"A famous highland clan. The Camerons are coming."

Stanley said, "Those were the Campbells."

For two weeks, they were Steve and the Rattlers. When *The Beatles' Second Album* came out, and Steve saw that it had "Long Tall Sally" and "Roll Over Beethoven," which were by Little Richard and Chuck Berry, he relaxed a bit, and said that they didn't have to write all their own songs, but the ones they didn't write had to be by black people. They started practicing "What'd I Say."

Then the skinny envelopes arrived from Amherst and Williams, the ones that said, "Thank you for applying." The fat one was from U.Va., but Tim had known he would get in there. Tim wasn't disappointed. His *dad* was disappointed, but Tim wasn't. There was nothing wrong with U.Va. And it was cheap, which was what he said to his mom. Amherst was thirty-two hundred dollars a year, and Williams was thirty-six hundred. His mom said they would have found it, it was worth it. But U.Va. was fine with Tim, not such a change from everything he knew.

With his fate decided and Fiona showing up now and then, Tim maybe felt better than he had his whole life. She started saying, "Ever driven ninety? Ever gotten over a hundred? How fast will this thing go, really? Ever spun out?" Once, at seventy-five, she put her hands over his eyes and laughed. That evening, she showed him a spot on the hill above her house, looking west, toward the Blue Ridge, and while he was kissing her, she unzipped his khakis and put her hand in there. He felt her hand through his shorts, and then she eased his cock out of his shorts, too. He said, "You're the only person I ever met who is crazier than I am."

"How crazy are you?"

"Ninety-five, but not a hundred."

She unbuttoned his shirt, and slid her cold hands across his bare skin and lay her head on his chest. His cock pressed into the rough fabric of her Levis. But that was as far as he got that night.

A week later—it was now May—they were driving in the Comet to Arlington to see *The Last Man on Earth,* and she kept reaching over and tickling him. For a while he laughed and pushed her away, but she kept at it, so finally he lost his temper, which he had never done before, and shouted, "Quit it! Fuck you!" They stopped at the next light; she opened the door and jumped out. When she slammed the door, he reached over and locked it, and then the light turned green, and as he was pulling away, she vaulted onto the roof of the Comet. He drove. She started pounding. He sped up, but she stayed up there, pounding, and when he pulled over, maybe a mile down the road, and unlocked the door, she jumped down, pulled it open, and threw herself across the front seat. She was laughing. She took his hand, and they went to the movie, which was about vampires. That night, she showed him a way to get into her room—he had to climb a tree, cross a roof, and go through the window she opened. It was worth it.

ANDY DIDN'T GO back to Dr. Smith right away. After that first appointment, she decided that he made her nervous—not exactly what he said, but the eyes, the posture, and the hands. After JFK's assassination (there were only two time periods in the world now, before and after that event), she had started reading a book about frontal lobotomies. As far as Andy could understand it, the doctor lifted the patient's eyelid, pressed the point of an ice pick against the top of the eye socket, and drove it into the patient's brain with a hammer. Then he did it on the other side. Dr. Smith struck her as the sort of person who could comfortably do such a thing. But Dr. Grossman was giving up on her—Dr. Grossman had consulted her mentor about

Andy's "lack of affect." Their only really good session had been as friends, deploring the assassination, expressing a fear they shared that much more was going on in Washington and in the world than most people suspected. After that one, though, Dr. Grossman had gone back to being a professional, and Andy had begun to run out of tales to tell, either as dreams or as childhood experiences. She read about Freud's patient Dora, and made the mistake of telling one of Dora's dreams as her own. Dr. Grossman seemed to recognize it, though as a dream Andy thought it was fairly common—returning home after the death of her father, then getting lost, not nearly so interesting as dreaming that a guest came for dinner, ate more than his share, and then went out to the outhouse to relieve himself. When he was halfway to the outhouse, he suddenly swelled up to a monstrous size, jumped onto the roof of the house, and began riding the house like a horse, screaming and shaking the whole place. This dream Dr. Grossman found trivial and without meaning.

And so she returned to Dr. Smith. With the spring, he seemed healthier and not as depressed as he had in the fall. She wrote him a check for five hundred dollars, ten appointments in advance. The next thing she had to do was stand up against the wall in his office so that he could draw pictures of her—front, back, left side, right side. This took the whole of the first fifty minutes. At her next appointment, he laid the pictures on the table in his office. Over each of them, he had superimposed a grid, and by means of this grid, he diagnosed where and to what degree she was out of balance. For example, if she had had disproportionately large hips, he would have diagnosed a blockage between her lower body and her upper body. For these women, the first step to a cure was to lift their shoulders and open their mouths wide, and to make a habit of taking deeper and deeper breaths. As a result, they would eventually speak the truth about themselves.

In Andy, the disproportion went the other way—she had broad shoulders and a prominent bust, but narrow hips, slender legs, and slender feet. She was barely, he said, connected to the earth, and, more important, to her sexuality. How often did she and her husband have sexual relations?

"Almost never," said Andy.

And did she have sexual relations with other men?

"No," said Andy.

"Women?"

Andy shook her head.

He took her over to the mats and had her sit cross-legged and close her eyes. He straightened her here and adjusted her there. It hurt. Then he had her think of sex and say five words. The five words she said were "shoe, earth, automobile, bath, and Kennedy." But she wasn't thinking of sex—those were just the first words that came into her mind as she looked around his office and out the window. There was a long silence.

She opened her eyes. The position was getting slightly more comfortable, and she took a deep breath. Just then, Dr. Smith sat down on the mat right in front of her, crossing his legs in an Oriental position, with his feet turned upward on his thighs and his knees flat on the mat. After a moment of silence, he leaned forward until their faces were almost touching, and he enunciated the words "Don't bullshit me, Andrea Langdon. I don't like it."

His breath was sour. Andy jerked backward, but then she said, "All right."

They agreed to meet on Mondays, Wednesdays, and Fridays.

JESSE WANTED to learn to drive the tractor. He was very sober about this, undeterred by Joe's previous reactions. "When?"

Joe said, with pretend seriousness, "I don't know."

"Did you think about it, Dad?"

"Since when? Since yesterday, when you asked before?"

He nodded.

"No, Jesse, I haven't thought about it since then. You are eight."

"Uncle Frank drove Grandpa's car to Usherton when he was my age."

"Who told you that?"

"Granny Rosanna."

"She must be remembering wrong." He didn't say that Frank had been thirteen at the time, which was bad enough.

"How old was he?"

"Laws were different then."

"How old was he?"

"Tell me, is your name Walter?"

"Why do you ask that?"

"Because your grandfather Walter drove his mom and dad crazy asking questions."

"Really?"

Joe looked at Jesse, said, "Get down off the seat of the tractor."

He got down. Then he said, "Really? Crazy? Like they went to a mental asylum?"

"No, like they whipped him."

"Are you going to whip me?"

"Have I ever whipped you?"

"No."

"Am I going to whip you?"

"No."

Then there was a silence, and Jesse said, "When can I learn to drive the tractor?"

Joe laughed and said, "When you're thirteen. Let's see. That was summer, so Frank was thirteen and a half when he drove that car. You are eight and a half. So you have a while."

"Five years."

Joe allowed himself a smile, then said, "Good subtraction. You must be a smarty-pants."

Jesse didn't smile, only said, "When is it going to stop raining?"

"The weatherman says later in the week."

"Is the corn ruined?"

"Not yet."

"Are you worried?"

"I'm never worried."

"Why not?"

"Because," Joe said, "something always works out on a farm."

IT WAS Henry's idea that Claire and Paul would take their two weeks' vacation in England, where he was helping at a dig not far from York—he wasn't an archeologist, but he thought all medieval-lit professors should get out of the library and into the dirt or the bog. He wrote to Claire that it was a beautiful spot—there was plenty to see, not only York Minster, but the Shambles, an old street still left from the Middle Ages, as well as a castle and several museums. She and Paul could also go for walks nearby, in the Vale of York, or a little farther away, in the Lake District.

Rosanna said, "Well, Granny Elizabeth would have loved that, though the Chicks and the Cheeks, as she never forgot to tell me, were from Wessex, which is way at the other end of England." This reminded Rosanna of something, and three days later, in Claire's mail came a little box, wrapped in white paper. When Claire opened it, inside there was a tiny lace handkerchief, quite discolored but lovely, of handmade crochet lace in a scalloped pattern. There was a note attached. Claire opened it carefully. There was her father's handwriting: "Made by my great-grandmother, Etta Cheek, sometime around 1830. Saved for Claire, March, 1942." She had never seen the box, the handkerchief, or the note. She was three years old in 1942. She burst into tears. She thought she could smell the scent of his clothes rising around her.

When she called the next day and asked, her mother said, "Oh goodness. That year, Frank was in Europe. We simply forgot your father's birthday, so here is what Walter did. He went and found a box of different things, one for each of you children. He let everyone choose from the box what you would most like to have. Lillian chose a feather. Joe chose a sprig of something, thyme? Lavender it was. Henry chose a coin. And we put away a photo of your father and a couple of army buddies for Frank. This handkerchief went to you. We set it aside for safekeeping, and you know what happens when I do that. When you said you might go to England, it struck me that that was what was in that little box in my dresser drawer. I'm sorry it has taken me so long to . . . Oh, Claire, honey, don't cry."

But it was no use—Claire cried and cried. She wrote to Henry, did he remember that coin, but of course he did. It was an Indian-head gold dollar, he replied in a letter back. He wrote that he kept it with the Marcus Aurelius coin he'd found loose in a muck pit in Winchester. Once again, she opened out the tiny handkerchief. The very thin linen was four inches by four inches, and the crocheted border looked as if it had been made out of sewing thread in a pattern of leaves, like elm leaves. She smoothed them under her finger. That very afternoon, she took it to a picture framer to preserve.

Paul did not like the fact that their bed-and-breakfast had twin beds with footboards. He was too tall for footboards—he had to sleep on his back with his legs spread and his feet to either side of the foot-board, or else on his side, curled up, and one time he stretched out and bumped his head on the headboard. And then, for breakfast, they served the toast cold, in a rack, unbuttered, and when you buttered it, it fell apart. Henry showed them around; Paul could not help correcting him—surely York Minster was York Cathedral? Were those really kings in the choir screen (though Claire could see that they had crowns on)? Was that window really about the War of the Roses? Had Henry ever read *Richard III*? Henry was polite every moment.

The third night, sitting across from her in his pajamas, on the other twin bed, Paul said, "I sound like an ass, don't I?"

"I don't think Henry is ever wrong about this sort of thing."

Paul said, "He's been very decent."

"He likes you."

"I can't imagine why."

She sat down next to him. The bed dipped almost to the floor. She said, "I can't imagine why not."

"I know I can be a jerk."

"You don't try to be a jerk. The jerkiness just pops out once in a while."

Paul put his arm around her, and they lay back on the twin bed. The next morning, Paul asked for a room with a double bed, and as it happened, someone was checking out that very day, and the owner of the bed-and-breakfast would move their things. That day, Henry had to work, and so they went back to York Minster, bought a nice simple guidebook with large pictures and short explanations, and enjoyed their morning very much. The best part of the day, besides "tea," was the hour she spent in a small bookstore, uneven floors on three levels, books piled everywhere willy-nilly. On the shelves marked "Local Interest, Yorkshire," she saw *Wuthering Heights,* which she had been supposed to read in ninth grade and had never even started. She bought it for a half-crown.

Henry took them to supper in an Indian restaurant with eight of the other diggers, all of whom were about her age or younger, enrolled in colleges and graduate schools in the United States and England. Four of the boys had beards, which Claire thought was interesting. One couple lived in a tent not far from the dig. That day, Henry had let them take a shower in his room, because they had spent the last three days digging up the tanning pit to see if there was anything in there. The girl gaily related how the boy had had to hold her by the ankles for the last bits, as she scraped the bottom of the pit with her trowel. "Up and down, in and out, and stinking to high heaven."

Henry turned to her. "In the Middle Ages, they tanned leather with manure."

The boy said, "It was pointless to bathe, since we had to do the whole thing. So we just slept outside the tent. Thank goodness, it hasn't rained."

Claire looked them up and down. They seemed clean enough now. One of the boys was a Negro man. He was about Claire's age, and had gone to school in New York. His name was Jacob Palmer. He didn't seem to realize that he was the only Negro in the restaurant. He chatted and laughed at Henry's jokes just as the others did. Claire noticed that she glanced at him more often than Paul did, but Paul was from Philadelphia, not Des Moines. Claire was in favor of civil rights. She'd thought it was shocking when that church was bombed in Alabama the year before, but everyone forgot about that when Kennedy was assassinated. Then those three boys, just about her age, were murdered in Mississippi, and their bodies were discovered four days before she and Paul left for England—eight or nine days ago now. She hadn't heard any news about them since coming here, but looking at Jacob Palmer in this sea of white people made her think of them. However, it was easy to be in favor of civil rights when she spent all day sitting in Paul's office, listening to his patients (or their mothers, actually, since many of his patients were children with ear infections) babble on about whether now, since President Johnson signed the Civil Rights Act, they were going to let Negroes into the Wakonda Country Club. And why not? thought Claire, who had been there twice. There were plenty of Negroes there already—caddies, waiters, groundskeepers. Jacob Palmer talked just like the other students— about the excavations, the grid, the sherds, the artifacts.

That night, she began reading *Wuthering Heights*. She didn't put the book down for two hours—Paul was sound asleep. Heathcliff was said to be dark-haired, but when she read about him, the face in her mind was Frank's, not Joe's. Two days later, when Henry took them to a town called Otley for just a little walk, and not into very steep countryside, that was where she imagined everything in the book to take place. It was a shocking book, but when she finished it, she turned back to the first page and started over.

AFTER HE DELIVERED his trunk and his suitcase and met his two roommates, Tim drove back to McLean. He did not drive Wednesday to his house, where they were expecting him for a last lunch before Lillian took him back to school and left him there; he drove Tuesday, late, to Fiona's, and parked on the road up beside the horse pasture. It was nearly midnight. The weather had been hot and humid, and there were flies and midges everywhere. Fiona was leaving for Missouri in two days, for a college that was known, from what Tim had heard, solely for its horse-riding program. Rocky, who had been some kind of champion for 1963, had been sent ahead. Debbie had earned enough money working for a summer day camp to take over Prince's expenses for the school year. The only one who got nothing in all of this, as far as he could tell, was himself.

Tim jumped the little ditch and crossed the Cannons' yard to his tree. He chinned himself on the lowest branch, then caught his foot on a little knob maybe four feet off the ground, and swung onto the branch. Then he stood up, stepped onto the next branch and the one above that. From there, he jumped lightly to the roof of the back porch, squatted down, and duck-walked to Fiona's window. The other window looking over the roof of the porch was a bathroom, so the curtains were usually closed. Only once, sometime in May, had the curtain been flung wide, and a face, the face of Mr. Cannon, stared out over the roof. But Tim had frozen outside the triangle of light, and the curtain closed again. Fiona remembered that particular night as their most romantic. The window was up and the screen unlatched. When he put his hand on the sill, Fiona said, "Who's there?" in a soft, trilling voice. Tim said, "I don't know," also in a soft voice. This exchange made them laugh. He pulled the screen out and slid through the opening, then turned and secured the screen in the window frame. The light of the full moon, which had been obscured by the thick foliage of the tree, shone on the bare floor of her room and the end of her bed. He saw that she was totally naked. He said, "Hot, huh?"

She laughed again.

Tim began to take off his clothes.

She had a rule that he couldn't come during horse shows (and there were lots of horse shows in the summer). Two nights she had been sick, and he had stayed away for a week after spraining his ankle playing baseball. What with taking all his stuff to the university and then some orientation classes, he hadn't been here for six nights. He lifted the elastic of his shorts over his erection, dropped them to the floor, and slid in next to her, partly under the sheet. She kissed him. Her lips were always sort of flat and hard to begin with, then they softened and warmed. He pressed his erection against her stomach, and her leg came over his, drawing him closer; then she put her hands on either side of his head and slipped her tongue into his mouth. His cock got harder—too hard, he thought. If he entered her now, he knew he would come quickly. He decided to think of something, and then he thought of burning his tongue on hot soup. He thrust once, and then another time, and then he stopped. Her eyes were closed. She turned him over on his back and rose above him, smiling, in the moonlight.

She moved slightly, smoothly. The bedsprings creaked one time, and she stopped. Crazy as she was, she had never done anything that might disclose to her parents (fortunately, upstairs and at the other end of the hall) what was taking place in her bedroom. She said that they were sure she was still a virgin and "occupied her time" so thoroughly with the horses that she didn't have a moment for boys. It was true that, since the beginning of the summer show season, they hadn't gone on a single actual date—not eaten a bite together, seen a movie, been to a party. Did anyone know they were even friends? Tim had said nothing to Steve or Stanley Sloan. Thinking of this secrecy made another thrust irresistible. She groaned, hardly louder than a breath.

She smiled a beautiful smile that he almost never saw, except in the framed picture on her desk of her on a horse, seven years old, her hair sticking up and her grin delirious with pleasure. Her smile made her eyes crinkle upward and revealed her inner mischievousness. He pulled her down and kissed her again, two or three times. Burning soup. Burning soup. His cock, just for a moment, stopped throbbing, but his balls made themselves felt, hard between his legs, ready to ache.

She froze, put her hands on his shoulders, and looked toward the door of her room. Then he could hear it—a footstep in the hall. Her father's voice said, "Fiona?" Then, "Fiona?"

Fiona's head turned and she stared down at him, made an O with her mouth, and said, as if she were just waking up, "Huh? Everything okay, Daddy?"

"I thought I heard you."

"What?" Just exactly as if she had been asleep.

Then, because he moved, because she moved, Tim ejaculated. His back arched, his entire lower body shook and throbbed, and his mouth opened. At the very moment that he felt the usual scintillating thrill run into his brain, her hand, a large hand, covered his mouth. He opened his eyes and put his own hand on top of hers. As best he could, he stilled all movement. She said, "I'm fine, Daddy. I must have fallen asleep reading my book."

"Your door is locked."

His muscles seemed to vibrate, but he wasn't moving.

"Oh, I did that by mistake. I'll unlock it in the morning." She yawned loudly. "I'm just so tired. Night-night."

"Night-night, honey. Just as long as you're okay."

"I'm fine, Daddy."

Tim realized that he hadn't pulled out.

Now they were absolutely still, listening to the retreating footsteps—three, four, then up the stairs. Tim felt a belated urge to flee, but she had him pinned. Her strawberry-blond hair was in her face, and she was looking down at him with, it must be said, an adoring look in her eyes.

They slept until dawn. Tim woke up when he felt her move beside him. It was the first time he had ever spent the night with her. She looked good even in the early light, even as she whispered, "It's after six-thirty. When I go down to breakfast, you need to leave."

He nodded.

She dressed methodically. She made a fat ponytail and wound a rubber band around it. She kissed him on the forehead, then on the lips. She went out the door; he waited until all footsteps had quieted, and slipped out the window, down the tree, across the ditch, and up the road, without looking back. If someone saw him, he figured he would hear about it soon enough.

AT THE MADEIRA SCHOOL, not four miles from Aunt Lillian and Uncle Arthur's (though she could only go there once in a while), Janny informed the other girls that her name was Janet, and after that, she felt older, smarter, and prettier. It didn't matter that Tim was gone to the university and Debbie was busy with her last push before college applications, or that Aunt Lillian herself seemed a little distracted. Whenever Janet got leave, there was so much going on— all of Dean's friends splashing in the pool; Tina at the easel in her room, or wandering around talking to herself (when Janet asked her what she was talking about, she said she was telling a story); Aunt Lillian cooking enough for ten, adding plates for friends until some- one had to sit at the counter, with Uncle Arthur's colleagues in and out (once, she opened the door of the hall bathroom, and a man in a hat was sitting on the toilet; when she gasped, he smiled and said, "Peekaboo")—that she felt wonderful for days, just knowing she loved them and they loved her. Since she could not imagine anything better than being related to the Mannings, she was not intimidated at all by this fancy boarding school or the other girls she met.

She took English, French, geometry, biology, and ancient his- tory. Whereas her roommate, Cecelia, groaned every time she hefted a textbook, Janet set hers on the left side of her desk and worked through all her lessons one by one, the minutes ticking by, and in every single one counting out her pleasure that she had left her father, mother, and two numbskull brothers behind. She was not the smart- est girl in any of her classes, but she was the most methodical, the most grateful. Likewise on the hockey field: if a girl on the other team was dribbling toward the goal, or passing to another girl, Janet never took her eye off the ball—she was so effective that the goalie got bored and started yawning. By October, the teachers would not call on her anymore. Was she ambitious? Did she want to get to Rad- cliffe, or even Vassar? Not at all. If you took a string and a pin and poked the pin into Englewood Cliffs, New Jersey, where her parents and the twins were, the farthest college from the pin that was still in the United States was the University of Hawaii, which was fine with Janet.

She was friendly to everyone, even to Cecelia, whose heart had been set on Chatham Hall, where her best friend had gone. Cecelia was making herself disagreeable so that they would send her home; she refused to bathe or wash her hair. When Janet told this story at Aunt Lillian's, everyone laughed and said bring her over and we'll throw her in the pool. And, Janet knew, Cecelia would enjoy every minute of it. Madeira, like every high school, was fraught with cliques and gossip, but Janet didn't care. She did not dread being ignored; she did not dread being talked about; she did not dread having the wrong hair or braces; she did not dread breaking the rules and being punished, though this was unlikely. The only thing she dreaded was Christmas vacation at home.

She began her campaign at Halloween. As she wrapped Tina's head in her mummy costume (careful to leave openings for her nose and eyes), she said, "What day does your Christmas vacation start, honey?" Tina went to public school.

Tina had insisted that Janet wrap her mouth. She mumbled, "We onry hab a wik."

"Really? We have three."

"Luggy dug! You shud tay her."

"Well," said Janet. "Ask your mom. We can do lots of things together. I'll take you Christmas shopping."

The next thing was to write a note to her mom. It began, "Dear Mom and Daddy, I am doing really well, I got an A on the geometry test and I have to write a report about cells for biology. It isn't due till next week, but it is almost done. If I turn it in early, I will get 10% extra credit. Guess what? My roommate, Cecelia, is going to take a trip with her family at Christmas. They are going to"—Florida? Too close. Paris? Mom would like that but Dad wouldn't. Australia? Perfect, except that Richie and Michael might blow up the plane before they got there. Caracas? Texas? Her parents went there all the time. She thought of something—"Disneyland. I guess she and her brothers have been there three times, and they love to go back. There is so much to do that"—she thought again—"they can barely keep their eyes open for dinner. Her dad just drops the kids off, and then he and her mom go do things in Hollywood." She read it over. It was perfect. She signed, "Love, Janny," with a little heart next to the "y," sealed it up, and sent it.

Her mom was good about corresponding. She wrote back, "Darling, Thanks for your letter. So glad you are doing well. And enjoying yourself. Know you are being a good girl, as always. Wish the same could be said for you-know-who. Back to the principal's office yesterday. Nothing very bad, though. Knew it was a mistake to put them in the same class, but now Richie is being put into the other class. Think the teacher, who is a man, can handle Michael if he is the only one. Exhausting! Saw Dr. N. the other day. He asked after you. Said you are happy and not worried. You aren't worried, are you? Can't help feeling sad for the North Vietnamese, but do think that the Vietnam War, and even bombing North Vietnam, makes it LESS likely that there would be nuclear war rather than MORE likely. So DON'T WORRY. Daddy is fine, and says to say love to you. Love, Mom." Nothing about Disneyland.

Janet then wrote a note to Aunt Lillian, on a special note card with flowers, telling her that lots of the girls from far away, like her, were staying through Thanksgiving. Aunt Lillian wrote back, "Janny, I was hoping you would invite yourself! Hope you have time to help Debbie and Tina with the pies. Dean and Uncle Arthur are planning to do something very strange with the turkey, so the pies will be important." When she wrote to say that she was staying for Thanksgiving, and that Aunt Lillian had asked if she could, her mom wrote back, "Maybe we will fly down and join you," but then the weather was bad. They were not missed, at least by Janet. The turkey turned out to be delicious—Uncle Arthur and Dean took turns basting it with a mixture of apple cider, butter, and whiskey, every half-hour, so it took an extra-long time to cook, but they played charades. The pies were also good, apple and pecan, her favorite of Lillian's many and always delicious pies.

The day after Thanksgiving, she tried the Disneyland gambit again, by postcard, to Richie: "Hi, Richie! Guess where my roommate is going for Christmas! Disneyland! She says that Tomorrowland is really great!" To Michael, she wrote, "Dear Michael, Get Nedra to tell Mom to take us to Disneyland! You would love Frontierland."

A few days later, she thought she had done it: "Dear Janny, Must say, the constant whining about Disneyland is driving me crazy. Though hear it is a nice place. Daddy should visit his friends out there in Los Angeles and take us along. Christmas is not a favorite holiday!

Everyone in the world should spend it traveling, the way they do in France." However, no plans were made, and Christmas vacation approached.

Janet managed to get Cecelia up for classes, but not much else. Sometimes she went for days with the same clothes on, rolled in her bedclothes, her mattress showing. Janet tried to set a good example by making her own bed very carefully—hospital corners, the way Nedra had shown her—everything smooth and fresh, desk neat, closet straight. Cecelia didn't take the hint. Janet woke up in the night and heard soft noises, but they were so soft that she couldn't tell if it was crying or not.

On December 10, she received her train ticket, leaving December 17, returning January 10. She put it under her mattress and turned over in her mind the idea of saying that it had never arrived, or that she had lost it, but school would be closed, so someone, probably Aunt Lillian, would just buy her another ticket. On the night of December 16, after the Christmas pageant and party, she cried once, and then gave up. The next morning, she left Cecelia still bundled in her bed and went in a taxi with the two other girls who were taking the train. When she came back in January, her roommate was Martha, who was in advanced math classes. She never saw Cecelia again.

1965

~

ANDY SAID, "Well, don't you think it's mysterious?" It was three
months since the murder; Lillian was still upset, and Arthur
seemed beside himself. "I've never seen Arthur so . . . so . . . I don't
know."

"Who was murdered again?" said Dr. Smith.

"A friend of theirs, named Mary Meyer. She was shot in the head
and in the heart, walking down the towpath in Georgetown in the
middle of the day."

"Have you ever met this woman?"

"I don't think so, but it horrified me. I had nightmares about it,
and we had to come home two days early." Andy was lying on the
mat, staring at the ceiling. She didn't often avail herself of the mat,
but Dr. Smith's facial expressions could be unpleasant. His bushy eyebrows lowered over his eyes until they seemed to disappear. Sometimes he tapped the lead of his pencil on his teeth while she talked,
which she found so distracting that she fell silent. What really horrified her was a thing that she was not comfortable telling: that Lillian
and Arthur seemed to be falling apart. The injustice of this disturbed
her. She said, "May I change the subject?"

"There is only one subject."

"I went to Bendel's to get a dress for a cocktail party at the
Upjohns' next week. Frank said it had to be Dior or Chanel, but I

hated the Chanel, and the Dior looked very girlish to me, though brown. Brown is so dull. It was two o'clock in the afternoon."

He coughed as if losing patience.

"Anyway, as I came into the vestibule, but before I opened the outside door, I saw Frank pass with a woman on his arm—rather a plain thing, I must say. I stopped in my tracks. I knew it was Frank—he was wearing his gray Brooks Brothers overcoat that I picked up at the cleaners' the day before. And he was smiling. I registered that right away."

"You didn't recognize the woman?"

"Never saw her before."

"Did you go out into the street?"

"I did. I watched them, and when they turned the corner, I followed them down Fifty-seventh Street."

"Can you tell me their exact demeanor and posture?"

Andy's hip began to hurt, so she crossed her ankles. Dr. Smith would be taking note of this, she knew. She said, "She looked upright and self-contained. Her elbows were at her sides, and her head was straight. Her shoulders were straight."

"And your husband?"

"First he was holding her elbow, and then he put his arm across her shoulders."

"Was he leaning toward her?"

"Yes."

Dr. Smith wrote busily, then sniffed.

Andy said, "She didn't look like a prostitute."

"Is there any reason that she should look like a prostitute?"

Andy crossed her ankles the other way. "This young man where he works, one of the sons, he asked me at a party last summer, when we were staying in Southampton, if I knew that Frank frequented prostitutes downtown."

"What did you say?"

"I said yes."

"You haven't mentioned this to me before, Andy. Were you telling the truth?"

"I didn't *know* it."

It hadn't been as difficult as she'd thought it would be to tell about seeing them, the couple, Frank and the woman he loved. She said,

"I did go to Bonwit's and buy a dress. Navy-blue shantung, with a matching coat. It was last season, but on sale."

"So the sight of your husband and another woman who was rather dowdily attired motivated you in some way?"

Andy nodded.

"Let me ask you this. Which of your physical assets do you feel that this new outfit makes the most of?"

Andy lifted her chin, almost unconsciously, then put her hand on her neck. Dr. Smith said, "Your neck. Your chin."

"My waist. My legs and ankles. I'll put my hair up, of course."

"So—you plan to accentuate your slenderness, your paleness in contrast to the dark color of the dress, your, let me say, androgynous qualities, as if to say to all, once again, that sexuality isn't your business? And so your husband falling in love, if that is what it is, with a dowdy but, let's say, womanly rival makes perfect sense."

Andy said, "I suppose it does, from his point of view." She said this in a reasonable tone of voice, and was just about to say something else when Dr. Smith was right there, nose to nose with her, and apparently in a rage. Andy recoiled. Dr. Smith exclaimed, "Andrea Langdon, are you so flat and small that you have no reaction to this? Is there nothing inside you, no mote of emotion or resistance? No ego? No identity? No being? You come here to me, three days a week, faithfully. As far as I can discern, you are a wraith, floating through your own life not only with no affect, but with no response. I ask you if you drink, you say yes. I ask you if you ever get drunk, you say yes. I ask you if you embarrass yourself when you get drunk, and you say no, you just doze off or go sit in a corner. Sometimes you say you laugh at nothing. That's the extent of your transgression."

"I thought I was supposed to behave myself if I had too much. Frank says—"

"Your husband is cheating on you! He loves another woman! He's been to prostitutes! But your voice trembles only when you describe the murder of a stranger."

"She was JFK's mistress! At least that's the rumor!" Andy coughed, thinking of how many times Dr. Grossman had explained the concept of displacement to her. She leveled her voice, then said, "I don't think she loves him. She wasn't leaning toward him in any way. Her body language said that she was—"

"Are you using my own terms to show me up?" Now Dr. Smith seemed really angry. Andy slid to the right, and put her left hand lightly on his arm, to prevent his moving toward her again. He said, "I am yelling at you! I am berating you! How does that make you feel?"

"I think you must be having a bad day."

"You think this has nothing to do with you?"

Andy stared at Dr. Smith, and decided that he must have been a headstrong child, which was possibly why he had become a psychiatrist. Then she said, "Ragnarök."

"What is that, please?" He sounded both surprised and contemptuous.

"The end of the world, in Norsk."

"Gotterdämmerung. The Apocalypse?"

She nodded.

He said, "Please describe this to me."

Andy closed her eyes, remembering. It was still very clear. "First, I thought, the dogs would begin to howl, and then the wolves in the forests would gather in town, Decorah, where I grew up, and join them. The howling would get so loud that you could not hear, no matter how hard you listened, that the snakes were slithering out of the river. We lived on Winneshiek, which was just south of the river. Anyway, the snakes were big as pythons, but they were cottonmouths, more poisonous than rattlesnakes, and they would slither through the front door and up the stairs, and first they would go into my parents' room and smother them and bite them all over, but you couldn't hear my parents' screams because of the howling. Then the snakes would wait in the hall for me to open my door. I could stay in my room for days, but eventually they would slither around me and bite me. They would be as cold as ice. Then the house would burn down." This was a true memory, from when she was about seven.

"What would cause the house to burn down?"

"I don't know." Andy shivered.

Dr. Smith stared at her, then said, "Perhaps we are getting somewhere."

WHEN CLAIRE WOKE UP from what seemed to her to be a childbirth-induced state of catatonia, Gray was three months old, and it was the first of May. Forsythia was done, dogwood was done, daffodils were done, and she saw that she no longer had an excuse for not visiting Rosanna, something that ordinarily she hated to do. She woke up in a bad mood, even though the sun was shining and Paul was jolly and Gray could not have been cuter, and after she kissed Paul goodbye and he wished her a safe trip, she laid Gray carefully in his car basket, bought by Paul from someone he knew in Europe, and made sure he was properly strapped. The hour that it took them to head up the 330 was far too short, and then there was Rosanna—looking out the window, standing on the porch, her arms open wide. Claire felt her teeth grinding, but only for a moment. She held out the baby.

"Oh, what a peachy peach!" exclaimed Rosanna, but she hardly said a word to Claire. On the other hand, Claire could walk around the yard with Gray in her arms (and him only in a sweater) and smell the apple blossoms and the grass and the chamomile that she trod upon as she made her way. Yes, now Rosanna was peering at her through the kitchen window, supposedly making lunch, though really cataloguing what Claire was doing wrong, but Claire didn't care. It was so evident, looking at Gray, that she was doing everything right. She pulled down an apple branch and inhaled the fragrance of the blossoms. Gray's smile was the thing about him that was not like Paul—it was big and so merry that sometimes Claire wondered what Paul might have been like if he'd had a father who let him get dirty once in a while.

Rosanna had heated up frozen chicken potpies, and Claire did not say a thing about it as she stuck her fork into the crust with her left hand—Gray was cradled in her right arm, staring and making little noises.

Rosanna held out a spoon. Gray waved his hand. Rosanna said, "The only toy Frank ever had was a spoon."

"Oh, Mama! And the only toy you ever had was a mud pie."

"No, I had lots of toys, because your granny Mary loved to crochet puppets and tie rags into dolls. Both your grandmothers were much more fun than I was. But I was too busy looking for black widows in the dresser drawers and starvation in the cupboard."

"Lillian is like Granny Mary."

"She certainly is," said Rosanna. "I spoiled her rotten, and learned a lesson."

"What?" said Claire.

Rosanna patted Gray on the head. She said, "You can't spoil a good one."

"Are there any bad ones?"

"You don't find that out until later," Rosanna said.

Claire knew she was talking about Frank.

Once she had broken through the crust and eaten most of that, the potpie was pretty bad, Claire thought. The pieces of chicken and carrot were tiny and flavorless, and the peas were strange, too. Suddenly, almost surprising herself, Claire said, "Lillian told me that Elizabeth—"

"Mary Elizabeth."

"Mary Elizabeth was struck by lightning."

"Oh goodness!" said Rosanna, setting down her fork with a ding on the plate. "Does she think that? Heavens, no. Lightning did strike. But she fell. Maybe the thunder startled her. It was bang-bang, like that, the lightning so close. The back of her head hit the corner of an egg crate. She died without a mark on her." Rosanna shook her head. "I'm amazed to this day I can say any of that aloud. What is today?"

"May 1."

"You know, she was born forty-one years ago. January 28. And she was no trouble, just like this one."

But Claire didn't want there to be any resemblance between that ill-fated child and this one, destined for greatness. Rosanna offered Gray the spoon again, and this time he curled his fist around it. Rosanna said, "I think that's advanced."

"Of course it is!" Claire laughed.

It was the ice cream that was good—it had been made by Lois, who was going through an ice-cream phase. It was peppermint, sweet and sharp. They ate it while Claire nursed Gray, and then Rosanna quietly washed the dishes (including the aluminum pie holders, for some reason). Then she went into the living room and turned her show on low. Sitting in the kitchen, gently rocking back and forth in her chair, feeling Gray draw the milk out of her and the ache subsiding, Claire thought that maybe, maybe she would forgive Rosanna, but she couldn't remember what for.

LILLIAN TOOK the Mustang. Tim didn't know she was coming, but she knew where he lived, and she could wait for him if she had to. She left a note for Arthur in the middle of his desk, where he might see it if he was not too distracted, and as she drove away—got farther and farther from the note—she began to feel freer and less anxious. She would have expected it to be different—closer to Tim, more worried. But there it was—farther from Arthur, less worried.

The road was one of the most beautiful Lillian knew of, much more romantic and rolling than any road in Iowa. As Arthur invariably pointed out when they went for a drive, the Land Ordinance of 1785 was way too late for Virginia, and so it was not laid out in a grid, but according to chance and convenience. This meant that Lillian drove through this town and that town, around this curve and over that hill, in the shadow of mountains, past farms and fences and thick stands of trees. Horses and cows grazed in green pastures and there weren't many houses. Once she was past Culpeper, the few she saw looked like ones she knew back home—the plantations seemed to have been hidden away. Lillian liked the sweep of it, and the names of towns like Haymarket and Ruckersville.

When Bundy got back from Vietnam (and Arthur had almost gone with him, only kept home at the last minute by a bout of the flu), Bundy was a different man. The sight of the bodies at Pleiku had literally changed his appearance—whereas before he had been sharp but a tad removed, as if always calculating, when he got back he was sure of one thing—the Viet Cong had to be repaid. Sure, he phrased this in terms of strategy—yes, it could be done, a harder push, more bombs, take off the brakes and apply the gas, if they feel our resolve they will back off—but really his blood had boiled, his wrath had burned. At first, Arthur laughed and said, "Well, if they'd let me belt him in a nice straitjacket for a few days, just take him to a suite at the Hay-Adams and give him a shower ten times a day, I might have saved him." But then Bundy had convinced Arthur, and the spring had been calm with conviction—the bombing was unfortunate, but necessary; it would soon be over; sometimes a wound had to be cauterized. The calm had been pleasant. Arthur had been more his old, pre-JFK self, bringing home flowers and lingerie, eating, going to Dean's baseball games, not only admiring Tina's paintings but discussing them with her. JFK had driven everyone crazy—he said this, then he said that, and never the twain should meet, but that was over, had been over for a year and a half. Thinking of JFK made her think of Mary Meyer, gunned down by the canal. (Had she really been his mistress? These days, the rumor mill was strangely silent.) Lillian shook that thought out of her mind and made herself pay attention to the scenery.

She drove through Gordonsville, and soon after that turned off 29 and onto Ivy Road, gazing over the fields to her right in hopes that she would see Tim. Two F's! The lowest grade he had ever gotten before (though there had been several of them) was a C. She did a careful U-turn and headed toward the center of town, to find a Coke and maybe a sandwich.

Straight A's were such a habit with Debbie that Arthur considered them almost a character flaw. When she brought home her report cards, Arthur would lower his brows and growl, "How much extra credit did you do, missy?" Debbie's job was to grin and say, "Hardly any, Daddy!" He didn't mind 800s on her SAT Aptitude tests, but 800s on the Achievements were a sign of a misspent youth. Tim had scored in the low 600s on his SATs, and when those scores came in the same week he crumpled the bumper of the Comet, Arthur was a little relieved. A boy had to be a boy had to be a boy.

But he didn't have to flunk out of college. Lillian parked in a space in front of a drugstore and went in. The soda fountain was all the way in the back, and the girl working there was blond. Lillian perched on a stool and put her elbows on the counter, vowing not to tell the girl that she had worked a soda counter once herself. The few college students perched on the other stools did not remind her of the ones she'd seen protesting the war at the Capitol in April. Eloise had called her from California and said she had to go to the protest—with a hat and dark glasses so no one would recognize her, so that her picture would not cross Arthur's desk. So she did. Eloise had participated in the Oakland protest in February, bringing along Rosa, the baby, and even the strange gambler husband, who was otherwise "apolitical" according to Rosa. Lillian didn't believe there were twenty-five thousand protesters, as Eloise insisted from her vantage point in Berkeley—maybe half that number. But the D.C. protest had been exhilarating. If Arthur, Debbie, Dean, or Tina suspected she had gone, none of them had said a word.

The sandwich was good. She ate it slowly, because once she was done, had eaten every crumb, had drunk her soda, had wiped her mouth and gone into the ladies' room to comb her hair, she would have to find Tim and figure that boy out.

She had been to his room twice before, and knew the number— 215. She knocked on the door, at first lightly, and then more sharply. There was a groan, a pause, then Tim's voice, irritable, "Who *is* it?"

Lillian said, "It's me." She looked at her watch. It was a quarter after one.

"What!"

A little louder. "It's me. It's your mother."

Then, "Oh jeez!" Footsteps. Then the door opened. Tim was leaning on it. He was dressed in a white undershirt and dirty jeans. He stared at her and said, "Oh God." He left the door open and went over and fell on the bed. Lillian followed him.

She said, "Are you hung over?"

"Oh God."

The evidence was under the bed—empty beer bottles.

"You didn't tell me you were coming." He groaned again.

"It was a last-minute thing, and I thought you'd be at work, so how would I reach you?" She looked around, glad to see at least some evidence of a party in the general mess—records lying around, a girl's shoe, two glasses and two plates, a sweater she didn't recognize that maybe someone left behind. She said, "Did you have a party?"

"In a way."

Lillian opened her bag and pulled out the letter. When she handed it to him, he glanced at it and said, "I know that."

"What are you going to do about it?"

"Take the courses over."

"You aren't worried?"

He shook his head, then groaned.

"Are you okay? Is everything okay?" He looked like himself, tall and supple, unshaven, his hair a ragged mess, but handsome anyway. She realized that this was a question he could not answer, at least to her. If everything was not okay, then had she and Arthur failed? If everything was okay, would her concern push Tim into everything's not being okay? And maybe everything that she was seeing now was just the way Tim had been for years, on his own, doing what he wanted, and letting them think that everything was okay. Lillian began to feel dizzy. She said, "You want lunch or something?"

"Can't eat."

"Tell me this is a hangover."

"This is a hangover."

"What time did you go to bed?"

"Stop asking, Mom."

She stopped asking. She got up and walked around the room, picking up this shirt and that sweater, folding them, setting them on the dresser. Tim rolled over onto his stomach. She stood regarding him for a minute or two, and then walked out. By the time she got to the car, she was too dizzy to drive, so she sat in the front seat of the Mustang for a long time, and only pulled away when a man in a uniform peered at her through the window. She drove back, as she had thought she would, seeing nothing but Tim in her mind, sacked out and empty in his messy room, and got home before Arthur did. When he came in, he barely said a word. She fed Dean and Tina hamburgers and baked potatoes; Debbie was going out for the evening, and Lillian was too sad to eat. Arthur stayed in his office.

IT WAS TRUE that Dave Courtland had a nose for oil—even if he didn't know what he was smelling, he couldn't stay away from it. He had bought the one field that Fremont had been developing carefully now for eight years, six of those with Frank's and Jim Upjohn's help. But he had bought another field, too, three years before that, and only on a whim. They hadn't developed it, because a geologist had said, "Well, cattle might do well on it." Dave didn't know why he'd bought it. But now the geologists found oil there, too, and plenty of it, light crude.

Jim Upjohn said that what he and Frank had to do with Dave was shake their heads in a thoughtfully negative way, as if there were simply too many things undecided about the whole Venezuelan venture. Sun was if possible even more avid than Getty for what they'd found in the new field, because of their numerous grades of gasoline. The Sun rep wooed Frank by taking him to the Tabac Club, on the Upper West Side. They went in, stripped down in the locker room, and then discussed Dave's oil field while lying on tables being hosed with hot water, strapped with fibrous whips, hosed again; then they were off to the steam room. The guy never stopped asking questions. The Humble Oil rep only took him to lunch. Jim Upjohn thought that if Frank played this properly, Dave Courtland could walk away with three or four times what he had put into Fremont. Sun had it right: hundred-octane gasoline? If you were driving a Ford Thunderbolt, quarter-mile in eleven and three-quarters seconds, that's what you needed. And the stock market was inexplicably shooting upward—Frank had to laugh when he read the article in the *Times* on his way to work: "The market has proved once again that it can behave just as mysteriously as a woman." (Of course he pictured Lydia, but he thought of Andy, too.) "Everybody tries to figure out what it is going to do, but, heeding some inexplicable inner logic, it goes right ahead and pulls a surprise." The Dow, which had bottomed out at around 840 in May, had hit 942.65 on Monday. Now it was Wednesday, and it had retreated a hair, to just over 940, and nineteen million shares traded. No one had ever seen such a thing before. He read on. " 'Columbus would have been amazed,' one broker declared yesterday." Frank said, "Hey, Tony, looks like we're rich."

"Maybe so, boss," said Tony.

Frank continued reading the article, and decided to take some of Uncle Jens's money out of color TVs and Pan Am and put it back into steel and utilities. The article said that the solider stocks were going to follow the glamour stocks upward, and Frank believed that to be the case. Then he read that LBJ's gallbladder operation was considered a thing of beauty.

At the office, there were four calls from Jim Upjohn already. Jim wasn't impatient—he never was—he just told Frank exactly what to do. Call Hal first, and get him out of bed. Jim had seen him at a party the night before, at the Public Library, and he was so blitzed he couldn't find his shoes—"Or his feet," said Jim Upjohn. "He needs to get up early and ponder his sins." Then call Friskie. Friskie would have been up all night. Friskie read four newspapers, which affected his mood, always for the worse. The stock market was higher than it had ever been? Well, then, it could only fall. "He'll want to sell before ten a.m.," said Jim Upjohn. Jim himself, with the backing of the board, would be phoning Dave. Frank should call a meeting in the head office, and do a lot of frowning and worrying, and then, within a day or two, Jim said, "Everyone will be dragged, kicking and screaming, feet first, into nirvana."

"What's that?" said Frank.

"A version of heaven on earth where money is no object."

Frank was looking at a nice severance package and yet another mysterious new job. Jim Upjohn said it was in weapons manufacture. Weapons were booming now. Frank felt a little nostalgia for his life at Iowa State, that job he'd had for three years, those fruitless attempts to make gunpowder out of cornstalks. He expected to enjoy weapons, and he did truly wonder what all those weapons manufacturers had learned from the trove of German papers and patents he had spent two years after the war sorting and translating. Perhaps weapons had always been his destiny.

Frank went into his private bathroom and looked in the mirror. He was forty-five. He looked a little like Grandpa Otto, though taller, thinner, and colder. He kept his hair short, and because he was graying, there was no distinct contrast between his hairline and his hair; anyway, he knew how to buy a hat and how to wear one. His jawline had sharpened, and his cheekbones, too. All he had left were the blue eyes. Lydia, whose own eyes were brown, often stared at them as if they amazed her. Frank straightened his tie.

The deal, so long in the making, was done by Friday, and Frank was out of his office by five. He felt a little startled by the speed of it. All he carried out was his briefcase, and that was nearly empty. The Sun people told him to leave his files and his secretary. His secretary, happy to still have a job, promised to send his other things home in a box—a picture of Andy and the kids, a raincoat, an umbrella. That was all.

Frank got in a taxi and went straight to the Belvedere Hotel. He hadn't seen Lydia in a month. Of course, he hadn't called her or warned her. They did not communicate in that way. Once in a while, they left messages for one another at the Belvedere, but what Frank really counted on was walking into the bar there and seeing her across the room. They had gone a month before—most recently when Olivier took her to France in August. One of the pleasures of their romance, for Frank, was treating these unexpected separations as if they were disappearances, replays of that first disappearance followed by the exhilarating, predestined reunion. She was not at the Belvedere, and there was no message. The bartender offered, without being asked, that he hadn't seen her in two, three weeks.

Frank hailed another cab and went to 158 Front Street, her apartment building. When he got out, he looked up immediately; he knew which windows were hers, though he had never been inside. The windows were dark, and they stayed that way all evening. Frank didn't head home until ten, and didn't get home until after eleven. He had no driver anymore—he had to make his own way. It didn't escape his notice that his own windows were dark, too. Not even the front-porch light was on.

He made his way in through the garage. Nedra's door was closed; the kitchen was dark; the family room and the living room were dark. Richie's door was cracked—Frank closed it. Michael's door was closed. Janny's door was open because she was away at school. Andy's hall door was closed. He went into his own room. The connecting door to Andy's room was also closed. This was the way rich people lived, and Frank liked it. Jim Upjohn told him that he and Frances both had their own suites—his modern and hers more Art Nouveau.

But he was lonely, and he was quite certain already of what on Monday he discovered had indeed come to pass—Olivier and Lydia had moved, leaving no forwarding address with the building superintendent. Nor could Information find their phone number—not in Manhattan, Brooklyn, Queens, or the Bronx. For two weeks after that, he left home as usual, pretending that he was going to work (yes, he told Andy, the deal had gone through; he'd been given two weeks' notice) and roamed New York City in widening circles, knowing that if Lydia was there he would see her. His eyesight was as good as or better than ever, since he was getting farsighted and had had to buy reading glasses. But he didn't see her, not even once.

CLAIRE PERSUADED Joe and Lois to bring Minnie, Rosanna, and the kids to their house in West Des Moines for Christmas dinner. Henry agreed to come, too, and spend the night, since it was a six-hour drive from Chicago. Rosanna hadn't gone anywhere for Christmas in her entire life, if you didn't count Joe's house. She would bring a green-bean casserole, and Lois was going to bring the fruitcake and the Parkerhouse rolls. That meant that Claire was responsible for the turkey and dressing, the mashed potatoes, the salad, and, Paul insisted that morning, the eggnog. Claire said, "Mama is going to ask if there's liquor in it."

"Say yes."

"If there is, she won't let Joe drive home, even if he doesn't have any."

"Minnie will drive home. Minnie is the biggest stick-in-the-mud I ever met."

"I love Minnie," said Claire.

"That doesn't mean I don't love her. It means she can drive home."

Paul sat down next to the Christmas tree with the morning paper, and she went into the kitchen.

At two, when she was peeling the potatoes, Henry walked in the back door. He was carrying boxes wrapped in Rudolph the Red-Nosed Reindeer paper, and behind him was Jacob Palmer, and the first thought that came into her mind was an expression of her father's, "black as the ace of spades"; then she blushed and said, "Hello, Jacob! Do you remember me?"

"Of course I do," said Jacob in his almost British accent, very musical, and Claire saw that they were in for an interesting Christmas dinner. Henry gave her a hug and a kiss and a Merry Christmas and walked through to the living room. He came back a second later, saying, "Where's that boy?"

"He's napping."

"Poor thing."

"He's not a poor thing. He's a good boy, and we will all be glad he's had a nice nap. Are you two hungry?"

Henry said, "Jacob decided not to go home for Christmas, so I invited him; is that okay?"

"Of course," said Claire. "It's a twenty-pounder. You look nice." Henry had on a gray suit with narrow pants, pointy-toed shoes, a white shirt, and a narrow dark tie. Claire looked him up and down and said, "You look like a Beatle now."

"Which one?"

"Stuart Sutcliffe."

"The sexy one!" said Henry.

Jacob was in a medium-brown glen plaid, blue shirt, regular shoes.

He looked better, and richer, than Henry. He said, "Who do I look like?"

Claire said, "No one in Des Moines."

He laughed.

Paul came in. Claire saw his eyebrows shoot up and then down; then he smiled and said, "Jacob! Didn't know you were in this country."

"I'm at Wisconsin."

"Go, Badgers," said Paul.

Joe, Lois, Minnie, and the kids bustled in ten minutes later, followed by Rosanna, who was already talking as she came through the door. "Well, after all that wet weather the last few days, I was sure the roads would be frozen solid with the cold snap, but Joe—" She caught sight of Jacob and stopped dead. Then she looked around to make sure she was in the right house.

Henry stepped in, put his arms around her, and said, "Hi, Mom. Merry Christmas." He kissed her firmly on both cheeks, and, Claire saw, he held her rather tightly, as if restraining her. She said, "My goodness."

Henry spoke smoothly and brightly. "I want you to meet Jacob Palmer. He's a friend of mine from England. Remember when I worked on that dig in Yorkshire? Now he's getting his doctorate at Wisconsin."

Jacob smiled and held out his hand. They all saw Rosanna hesitate, and they all saw Henry lean toward her slightly. She held out her hand rather limply, and Jacob grasped it. As he said, "I've heard all about you, Mrs. Langdon," in a crisp and jolly way, Rosanna seemed to remember herself, and participate in the hand shaking. But when it was over, she stepped back, went around everyone, and said to Claire, "How's the turkey?"

It was Minnie, of course, who engaged Jacob in conversation, while Joe undressed the kids and Lois took the food into the kitchen. When Claire followed her, Rosanna was closing the oven door. She stood up and said, "What accent is that?"

"He's Jamaican."

"You've met him before?"

"In England, when we visited Henry last year."

"He and Henry are friends?"

"Looks that way," said Lois, neutrally.

Rosanna pursed her lips, then said, "Well, we have to be hospitable."

Claire felt a sudden flush of anger.

Rosanna put her hands on her hips. "But I thought those riots in Watts last summer were just terrible. A hundred people were killed."

Henry appeared in the doorway. He said, "That's not true."

"Well—" said Rosanna.

Henry stared at her. Claire had never seen Henry look so strict. Usually, he looked agreeably distant, as if he didn't quite speak their language. Lois was pouring brandy over the fruitcake. Then Henry said, "And Jacob has never been to Los Angeles. So he knows just about as much about those riots as you do. His specialty is the Caribbean slave trade."

Rosanna said, "They don't have that anymore. . . ."

"You need to talk to Jacob about that."

"Well!" said Rosanna, as if she was about to lose her temper. She plopped down in a chair. But then she looked up at Henry, who was staring at her as if she were a misbehaving student who had better straighten up and fly right. Claire looked at the kitchen clock and said, "Do you think we really have to turn this turkey on its back?"

Rosanna snapped, "I don't understand why you cooked it on its side in the first place. I never heard of such a thing."

"Craig Claiborne—"

"Oh," exclaimed Rosanna, "some man!"

But that was the end of it. Once she had mashed the potatoes and made the gravy, Rosanna settled down, and by the time she and Claire carried the food into the dining room, everyone was seated around the table. Gray was already in his high chair, laughing and receiving a piece of roll from Jesse, who was also laughing. Jacob was seated between Joe and Minnie; they were deep into a discussion of everyone's favorite topic, the weather. Terrible in Madison, said Jacob. He smiled. "Last year, when I first got there, I had never been anywhere that cold in the winter before. I was walking across the campus on a day when it was, oh, twenty below zero, and one of my teachers came running up to me and asked if I had a hat. I said no, and she gave me hers, right off her head. She told me that you lose sixty percent of your body heat through the top of your head. No one had bothered to tell me that."

Everyone agreed that it was much colder in Wisconsin than in Iowa, and snowier and windier, too, and then the conversation turned to Minneapolis, and Rosanna asked, if you had to live somewhere "up there," well, which would be the lesser evil, Milwaukee or Minneapolis? And someone knew someone who lived in Fargo—who was that again? Claire and Henry exchanged a smile.

1966

∽

AFTERWARD, when Tim thought back to those weeks before he went into the army, all he remembered was sleeping. He could have also remembered drinking, but it seemed in retrospect as though he were drunk with sleep, not asleep with drink. His roommates studied (he sometimes opened his eyes and saw them huddled over their desks, trapped in a circle of light). They took their exams (he sometimes rolled over as they came back into the room). Brian even made his bed for him and picked stuff up off the floor. But then he had flunked out, and there he was, finally awake, sitting in the living room at home, and his dad was staring at him. His dad was also talking, but he barely heard that. What he really paid attention to was the disbelieving stare. Yes, he had signed up, since he was going to be drafted anyway, and, no, he could not think of a single other way to occupy his time. Boot camp, a training school, deployment—no, he could not imagine Vietnam. He didn't read the papers, he didn't know what he was "getting himself into," but who was his dad to say a word against it? Didn't he, Arthur Brinks Manning, promote the war all the time? Hadn't he hit the roof when he found out that Mom went to that big antiwar protest in Washington? Hadn't his own father been a career military officer?

Then Dad said, "I want some sense of purpose, Tim. Some idea that you know what you are doing instead of just putting one foot in front of the other!"

Tim gave what he considered a perfectly logical reply: "Enlisting rather than waiting to be drafted has a sense of purpose."

"What do you want to do over there?"

"Don't they always tell you what to do?"

Dad blew out some air, trying, in his usual way, not to lose his temper completely; Dean walked past out in the hall and shouted, "You're an idiot!"

"Fuck you!" yelled Tim. Then he jumped up, felt in his pocket for his keys, and headed out the door. After that, the days were a blur of snow and rain, until he got to Fort Bliss, where the weather was hot all day and cold all night and the landscape was as flat as a frying pan except where it was mountainous, dry, and crumbly. No rain. One kid on the bus, from Dallas, said that it only rained in El Paso if the temperature was over a hundred, and Tim couldn't tell whether he was joking or not.

The screaming began immediately. Uniformed drill sergeants in hats leaned into them, and screamed in their ears to run, run, move it. Tim ran, while trying to carry his duffel bag. He who had never been scared before was, he had to admit, a little scared, especially when the duffel bag fell off his shoulder and hit Sergeant Wheeler, who then chased him nearly across the parking lot, screaming at the top of his lungs.

They were chased into the barracks and told to claim their beds. Tim claimed one of the upper bunks. The kid below him was named Harry Pine, from Waterloo, Iowa. Tim did not mention the farm in Denby. The barracks was shaped like a giant H. A squad of ten or twelve recruits lived in each leg of the H. The latrine and the showers were in the crossbar—no curtains, no walls. The platoon, which was what the four squads were called, had kids of all kinds—black, Mexican, white, even Chinese, one guy named Jim Song.

Tim had his head shaved. He was yelled at by drill sergeants. They ran, they marched, they shot weapons (never guns) at targets, they ran some more, they carried packs, they ate, they yelled (but only *"Yes! Sir!"* and *"No! Sir!"*). They were yelled at, they spoke when spoken to, and looked where they were told to look. One night, when

Tim was sound asleep, he heard just the fragment of a shout, and then found himself pummeled from below and launched out of his bunk by the long legs of Harry Pine, who was having a nightmare. He landed on his ass, and it hurt to run, run, move it the next day, but he ran anyway.

Sergeant Wheeler leaned over the recruits. Every time a recruit opened his mouth or shifted his weight, Sergeant Wheeler asked him who the hell he thought he was, and if he thought he was someone, well, he, Sergeant Wheeler, was there to fucking teach him a lesson. Where was that soldier from? From Texas? Well, all they had here in Texas was steers and queers, and Sergeant Wheeler didn't see any horns on that soldier! Was he from California? Well, all they had in California was homos and strip shows, and he didn't see a G-string on that soldier! And then that soldier (sometimes but not often Tim) would be sent to do two or four laps at top speed around the training field, and he had better not pass out. Sergeant George stood in front of a recruit, practically on the guy's toes, staring into his face, and screaming until it seemed like he was going to knock the kid over, but he never did—they weren't allowed to actually touch you, Tim realized. Twenty-five push-ups, shouting what kind of pansy are you? the whole time. Sergeant George asked him where the fuck had he learned to make a bed like that, and ripped off the covers and told him to do it over. Sergeant Wheeler told him to present his weapon, and peered down the barrel and asked him who the fuck he thought he was, that he didn't clean every last trace of powder out of that fucking barrel? Twenty-five push-ups right now!

Soldiers fell down. Soldiers passed out. Soldiers cried. Soldiers got concussions, broke arms and legs and noses. A kid from Omaha broke his jaw. Soldiers disappeared. Tim, who had climbed to the top of the bookcase when he was two years old and then gotten himself down again; who had ridden his bicycle for miles when he was six; Tim, who had thought nothing of running the whole five blocks to second grade as fast as he could go—didn't mind the regimen. He enjoyed how the other recruits, in spite of wearing the same clothes and having the same haircuts and being told to do the same things over and over again, persisted in remaining intransigently themselves: Harry Pine was slow; no matter how they yelled at him, he could not make his limbs or his reflexes move faster. Eddie Briggs was hotheaded—

Sergeant George could make him do fifty push-ups, and he still couldn't learn not to tell Sergeant George to fuck off. Everything made Jack Saylor, a black guy from Chicago, laugh, even Sergeant George leaping into his face and shouting, "What the fuck you laughing at, soldier?" As for Tim, when he did push-ups or ran around the field, he thought music—Tell him that you're always gonna love him, / Tell him, tell him, tell him right now.

He took tests. He had to answer problems about if you had four gallons of gas in the tank and the truck got seven miles to the gallon, could you get to Kansas City if it was thirty-five miles away, and if you had seventeen apples and twelve pears, how many men could you feed if half of the men wanted two apples and half wanted a pear and an apple? What he would do if three men in a jeep went over a ten-foot cliff, and what he would do if he saw someone in water of unknown depth screaming for help? He listened to recordings of tapping and thought of the tapping as a kind of rhythm that reminded him of playing in the Colts with Steve and Stanley Sloan. He turned out to have some commo talent, along with three other white guys and six black guys.

Sometime in week six—still no rain, but the weather was heating up—Private Wagner from Camden, South Carolina, went around asking everyone for money. Private Wagner was a tall, pasty guy, an inch taller than Tim, who was six two, with round blue eyes, glasses, and a self-confident manner that Tim at first respected—although he never actually said anything to a drill sergeant, he had been known to roll his eyes without being caught. He was going to sneak out, get a ride over to Juárez and pick up some weed. How a kid from South Carolina knew a dealer in Juárez, Tim could not imagine, but Private Wagner intimated that he knew just about everything there was to know. And, sure enough, on the designated night, after lights out, Private Wagner disappeared with fifty bucks. There was some whispering, but then Tim fell asleep. When he woke up at reveille, he glanced down the row of bunks, and there was Private Wagner, sliding out of bed as if he'd been there all night. The buzz went around that he had the stuff, and that night they smoked it. Tim, who had smoked a fair amount of dope with the Sloan boys and with Fiona, didn't feel a thing, and thought the weed had an odd smell. Sure enough, the whisper went round two days later that the junk was weed—tumbleweed. After that, Private Wagner didn't act quite as cocky, and Tim saw him for what he was, an eighteen-year-old kid who didn't know his head from his ass. Tim didn't mind basic training. The only time he was routed to KP, he didn't have to peel potatoes—he had to get up early and smooth the frosting on the coffee cakes that had been baked the night before; every cake on the rack was covered with cockroach tracks.

THE BUS RIDE, sailing through the hot landscape with the windows open, seemed to Tim to go on for days instead of hours. Most of the soldiers were heading for commo, like Tim, but some (the fat ones) were looking at cooking detail. They were calmer and sat up front. Someone was in charge, and that might have been Tim himself, who had been made platoon leader for an unknown reason that probably had to do with the fact that he was over eighteen, did have some college (apparently, passing English and history was not critical to leadership abilities), and had tolerated the drilling well. They all wore their uniforms, including their helmets. They stopped here and there to drop off a few soldiers. Late in the afternoon, the bus pulled through the gates of Fort Huachuca, a much smaller complex than Fort Bliss, set in a blanker and more barren landscape. It was the beginning of April; there were wildflowers here and there—long branches of orange and red blooms struck his eye, and fields of something simple and also orange. These were, of course, interspersed with cactuses. He had seen Road Runner cartoons, he knew what a cactus was, but no pictures prepared you for what a cactus really looked like. Or Arizona, for that matter.

There was a stiff dry breeze when they got off the bus. It didn't feel hot—it felt hot shading into cool. It was fragrant. Tim was told to report to an office across the road. He ordered his platoon to wait for him.

Whether he was tired or just disoriented, he couldn't have said, but when he went into the designated office, he made a mistake— almost his first mistake in the army. He knew perfectly well that you didn't have to salute indoors, and he was holding his helmet in his right hand, so when the lieutenant saluted him, he saluted him back—but it was his left hand that moved toward his forehead. You would have thought that he had raised a pistol and shot the lieutenant, who lunged across his desk, what is the matter with you, soldier, you been through basic or not? Don't you know the first thing about the military? Tim stood there, his face straight and his eyes a little hooded, until the lieutenant's top finished being blown. Then he said, "Private Manning reporting, sir." He had switched his helmet to his left hand, and now he saluted with his right. Lieutenant Canette saluted him back and sat down again, as if nothing at all had taken place. That was the last time he was yelled at.

The barracks was a long building with the latrine at the end. Tim had a top bunk about a third of the way into his platoon. Below him was Private Rowan. Reveille was at six, which these days was after sunrise. Tim's first job of the day was to assemble his men after they had been told to drop their cocks and grab their socks by the sergeant, then dressed and made their bunks (though no one came around anymore to throw their bedclothes on the floor and berate them for wrinkles). He marched his formation from the barracks to the mess hall—a quarter-mile, he thought. "Right, left, right, left! Ain't no use in feelin' down!" (A chorus of "Ain't no use in feelin' down!") "Jody's got your girl in town!" ("Jody's got your girl in town!") "Ain't no use in feelin' blue!" ("Ain't no use in feelin' blue!") "Jody's got your sister, too!" ("Jody's got your sister, too!") Or there might be "Dress it right and cover down!" ("Dress it right and cover down!") "Thirty inches all around!" ("Thirty inches all around!") Tim always scowled as he yelled, in order to make his voice even more resonant in the wind. He hadn't realized, when he was singing with the Sloan boys, how loud his voice was, or how musical.

A few of his soldiers sat at the skinny table, where they had to eat double helpings and clean their plates, no matter whether the eggs were green or not. Two or three sat at the fat table, and Tim, who ate shit on a shingle every single day without once asking himself what was really in it, ate at the regular table. There was plenty of food—none of it good, but Tim ate up. Food was fuel.

After breakfast, he marched a somewhat smaller formation to the commo training building. It was hotter now, but he kept them going, bellowing out, "Left, right, left, right! Jody saw your girl today!" ("Jody saw your girl today!") "How's he gonna stay away!" ("How's he gonna stay away!") "She turned your picture to the wall!"

("Turned your picture to the wall!") "Left his boots out in the hall!"
("Left his boots out in the hall!")

The next four or five hours were spent learning alpha, bravo,
charlie, delta, echo, foxtrot. There were several radios, including the
prick 10, which was about ten inches by twelve inches, looked like a
school notebook, and weighed ten or fifteen pounds. They would be
carrying those. The angry 19 was more of a console radio, maybe the
size of a suitcase. It must have weighed sixty pounds and had a longer
range. It had glowing black dials, and the operator used either a head-
set or a desk mike. Tim imagined himself yelling into it just before an
enemy soldier burst into the room and shot him in the chest.

Thirty recruits sat in the classroom with pencils and pieces of
paper. Their instructor, who had been drafted from a minor-league
baseball team, lolled at the front desk like a domesticated tiger. It
wasn't only his biceps and triceps and shoulders, which rippled with
muscle, or his pecs, which narrowed to a thirty-inch waist; it was his
supple grace. He was waiting for one thing—to be put on the Fort
Huachuca baseball team. His job was to turn on the tape. The tape
ran a series of beeps, and the kids wrote as fast as they could, trying to
understand and write down the letters in groups of five. What came
out never meant anything, or, rather, each set meant one thing, and
one thing only: Dit dit dit—S. Dit dit—O. Dit—E. Dah—T. Dah
dit dit dah dah—Tim. They had to write down letters, and do so
faster each week. Tim was a little bit faster than the others—it took
him about a week to make sense of the letters. Private Rowan never
made sense of the letters, so he was sent over to learn to cook. When
the tape ran out, the kids shouted at the baseball player, "Hey, Bobby,
wake up!" The tiger stretched himself and woke up, reached over,
and flipped the switch.

After another meal, Tim marched everyone to more classes—
army rules, army chain of command, commo etiquette—"You heard
'over and out.' Well, this ain't Hollywood, this is the real thing. 'Over'
means 'now you talk,' and 'out' means 'goodbye,' and 'over and out'
means dogshit!" Another thing that he learned early on was "Diddy
dum dum diddy": "Repeat what you just said."

....

AFTER FORT GORDON (teletype), Tim got two weeks' leave before deployment. He spent a week at home, but he couldn't settle down to eat or to talk or to look at his father. He was so restless that he couldn't wait at the airport for a plane to San Francisco, where he planned to stay with Aunt Eloise for a few days. He took the plane to Los Angeles, squirming in his seat the whole way. When he got off the plane, he decided that he couldn't take a bus, or even another plane, up the coast. He had to hitchhike, and the most direct route looked to be the 101.

Texas and Arizona had not prepared him for California. The sunshine was brilliant but refreshing, and even when the ocean was invisible, Tim could sense that it was out there—not the flat, warm, green-blue ocean he knew from Maryland and New Jersey, but something colder, more beautiful, and more endless, lit by the sun to a burnished hyacinth color hour after hour for the whole long day. And hitchhiking was easy, especially in uniform. The first car took him to Venice; that guy offered him a hamburger. The second couple, about his parents' age, took him to Morro Bay, where they invited him to stay the night. The next one to stop was a girl, maybe seventeen, who seemed unafraid, and took him up and down a steep grade—maybe the steepest he'd ever seen—to Atascadero. A Mexican fellow got him to Salinas, and another guy dropped him near the San Jose airport. The weather was perfect, and the hills to either side of the road were pale velvety green. At San Jose, he made his way to a different highway, one that headed to Oakland, and he waited. It was almost dusk when a pickup truck—a beat-up Ford—stopped maybe a hundred feet past him, and an arm waved to him out of the passenger's window. He shouldered his duffel bag and ran.

A guy in a sharkskin suit opened the door and got out, throwing a large package into the bed of the truck, and gesturing to Tim to throw his duffel in there. A woman was driving, maybe Tim's age. She had on a revealing beige cotton dress and high-heeled sandals. Both the man and the woman wore sunglasses, even though the sun was about down. He got between them, and at once began to regret it. "You in the army?" said the guy, as if that wasn't obvious, but before Tim could speak, he said, "I was a marine myself. Out of Camp Pendleton. You know where that is? Down south. We're coming from around

there now." He looked Tim up and down, then said, "We should feed
this guy to the horses." The girl laughed. "I was in the marines for
eight years. You believe that?" Tim opened his mouth, and the girl
laughed and said, "No!"

"Eight fucking years," said the guy. "Thought I was a big shot.
Who did Wayne get?"

The girl said, "A sailor."

"Yeah."

"He said."

"Anyway, I'm out now. Never got to 'Nam. I don't look that old,
but I'm forty."

"You look forty," said the girl.

"Shut the fuck up," said the guy.

"Well, you dress like someone's dad."

"I dress like *your* dad. That's why you fuck me."

Tim shifted his weight. They passed a sign that said "Fremont."
Tim looked at the speedometer—eighty-seven. The girl said, "Keep
telling yourself that, asshole."

There was a pause, and then the guy turned suddenly to Tim.
"Where you headed, soldier?"

Without thinking, Tim gave Eloise's address. The two exchanged
a glance across him, and the glance clearly said, Nice neighborhood.
As if to underline this thought, the guy said, "We can take you right
there. No trouble."

Tim's skin was practically prickling, he was so sure that this man
was dangerous. Here it was, 1966, and he was dressed like an old-
time gangster from New Jersey: the sharkskin suit, right down to
the flashy tie, and his hair had marks from being combed that you
only got with plenty of Vitalis. He offered Tim a cigarette, which
Tim took, and then the three of them smoked in the darkness with a
thoughtful air as they sped toward Oakland.

The girl knew right where to go, as if she was from Oakland, and
the girl and the man exchanged two more significant glances as they
turned corners. Eloise's neighborhood hadn't started out nice—the
houses were modest wooden ones, similar to one another and probably built from kits. But the yards were large, the trees and gardens
had grown up nicely, and now it was a little on the prestigious side,
or so Eloise had told his mother. You could see under the streetlights

that nice cars were parked in front of them, too: T-birds, a couple of Chryslers, an Oldsmobile, a Cadillac. When the man peered up through the windshield, let his gaze drift along the block with a whistle, Tim became convinced that he planned to kill Tim, and maybe Eloise and whoever was there at the moment—his cousin Rosa, her baby. He maybe outweighed Tim by fifteen pounds, but a lot of that was belly. If he had to, Tim could take him.

The man read out the addresses in the dark, and the girl pulled up in front of Eloise's place, now dimly visible, the porch light bright. The girl turned off the engine. The three of them sat there. Then the man shifted deliberately and stared at him. He said, "I like this place. I like this whole neighborhood. Why don't you introduce me to your friends?"

After a moment, in the toughest voice he could come up with, Tim said, "Well, get out, then." His plan was to grab his duffel bag and hit this guy behind the knees as he was heading up the walk. If the guy had a gun, and made Tim go in front, then Tim would stop suddenly and throw the duffel at the guy's head. His heart started to pound. The guy opened his door and stepped onto the curb—not right under the streetlight, but well lit all the same. Tim eased out behind him. The guy's hand slipped into his pocket, and Tim stepped backward, his hand on the rim of the truck bed, until he was out of the light. He reached for his duffel and pulled it toward him, then moved around the corner of the truck bed. He bent his knees and straightened them, bent them again, poised to spring. The man banged suddenly on the hood of the truck with both hands, and Tim jumped. The man laughed derisively. He jerked himself back into the cab of the truck and shouted, "Just putting you on, kid!" The girl sped away, leaving Tim standing in the street with his duffel in his arms. He trembled for two solid minutes, maybe from fear and maybe from readiness. Afterward, he remembered it as the first time he had ever been afraid for his life.

FOR SOME REASON, Tim thought there would be fighting as soon as the plane landed in Vietnam. It would be like that movie he'd seen years ago, *Pork Chop Hill*—lines of armed men in helmets, crawling from one ditch to another, only straightening up for half a second to fire their weapons at the unseen enemy. But the first thing he saw was air-force guys with their shirts off, walking around in the sunshine. The first thing he smelled, since it was morning, was shit disposal, a powerful combination of what was in the latrines and the diesel fuel they lit to burn it. The air was hot and humid, like Virginia on the worst day of the summer, but the light was bright and oceanic. There was sand everywhere. He realized he had landed at a tropical beach. The second thing he smelled was something sharp, yet floral: incense. That was the smell that told him he was far from home.

He handed in his paperwork, and twenty-four hours later, still foggy from the long trip, he was sent to the 101st, at Phu Bai, a flat, humid spot near the ocean, though no breeze seemed to blow—it was more like Maryland than California.

Their hootch was sixteen feet wide and thirty-two long, with a plywood floor. The walls were one sheet of plywood high, and above that, screen. The corrugated tin roof was weighted down with sandbags, and sandbags were also piled around the walls. Every time a rocket hit outside the hootch, shrapnel flew into the sandbags or over where Tim was lying in his cot, which was eighteen inches off the floor. The other principal feature of his hootch was clouds of mosquitoes.

Two weeks after Tim arrived, a rocket managed to make its way through the open door of another hootch. The roof was blown off, and five soldiers were killed. About ten days after that, a rocket hit a fully loaded helicopter on the airfield in just the right spot to blow up all the armaments it was carrying, in a spectacular explosion that jolted the helicopter into a nearby JP-4 that was holding five thousand gallons of rocket fuel. When that went up, the ground shook. Ten soldiers were medevaced out that evening, but then it was quiet. As the units pushed, day by day, farther into the hills, unbearably hot and much more humid even than Virginia, rocket attacks got less frequent.

He got used to his job, which had two parts. One was to drive his captain in the jeep out of the base to check on the signalmen. Some of these men were no more than ten minutes away but, depending on circumstances, could seem to be on the other side of the world. His other job was to get in a helicopter and fly out to the firebases.

Tim was to make sure his guys had supplies, but the mortician's job was to take the body bags and pick up the bodies. At first, Tim could not help watching. There weren't too many casualties—a body every few days at the most. The creepiest part was not death, even gruesome rocket-attack death—it was the way the mortician took the dead soldier's dog tags from around his neck, slipped them between the corpse's two front teeth, then whacked them with the butt of his weapon to jam them into the gums.

When he drove Captain Bloom, they made their way sometimes in relative solitude and sometimes through droves of people—women, children, old men, all with the sun beating down on their heads. These people would be transporting whatever they could carry or push in what looked more or less like wheelbarrows. Captain Bloom babbled as they drove: Watch this, watch that, careful, do you see the child running there, stop for a minute. You could say boo to Captain Bloom and he would jump out of the seat of the jeep. Captain Bloom was a square-shaped West Pointer originally from Washington State, at the base since January. The object of their drives was to get to the spot where they could make as much contact as possible with each of their guys at the firebases in the jungle. At this spot, Tim would turn on the radio behind him in the jeep and call up each base to get a report. If they could not reach the base, they had to drive even closer to the edge of the impenetrable green vegetation, and figure out what had happened.

The scariest thing that happened to Tim himself was also his best story—he told it for days afterward. He was out at a firebase to the north, on a flat hill just above a rice paddy. The helicopter lowered itself and picked up the body bag and the mortician; then Tim jumped in. The copter started to lift off, and right then there was shooting from the perimeter. The helicopter jerked upward, and he fell right out. He must have been sixty feet in the air. Without even thinking, he rolled himself as if for a cannonball off the diving board. He dropped into the rice paddy, plopped right down into it like a tulip bulb. He was tall enough to get his nose out to breathe and his arm out to wave. He shook his head back and forth to toss the water out of his eyes, and saw the helicopter lower toward him. When the ladder dropped, he somehow grabbed it, and it yanked him right up and out, covered with mud and soaking wet. When he told the story, he said that there had been a loud sucking sound as he was pulled from the paddy.

They had been mostly inside their hootches for about two days, waiting out what was expected to be a typhoon. The rain stopped in the night—Tim woke to the silence. The air was still hot and wet. In the morning, right after breakfast, Captain Bloom was on him first thing—these storms meant havoc at the bases. They needed to communicate with them right away, find out what was going on. By the time they had the jeep ready and the radio stashed behind Tim's seat, the sky was clear and the air merely damp. Tim drove slowly, creeping along the road out of the base. The parade of families had diminished but not halted; everyone was dripping wet.

The road hooked left, and Tim had to slow down. He turned the wheel. Captain Bloom had his weapon across his lap, and he was leaning forward, looking down the road. As Tim pressed the brake pedal, he just happened to glance to the right, and he saw a boy with thin arms and thick black hair staring at him, and then a grenade flew into the back of the jeep. It landed just behind the radio and rattled around. Tim yelled something, and the last thing he saw was Captain Bloom's face turning toward him, and then fragmenting into the wet air.

LILLIAN RECEIVED Tim's last letter the day after the telegram. It was wedged benignly between the electric bill and a letter from her mother. His handwriting, always nearly illegible, now looked terrifyingly meaningful. It took Lillian several seconds to make herself touch the letter, and then she could not help putting it to her nose and sniffing it. It smelled, like all of his letters from Vietnam, faintly of sandalwood. She stared at it for a long time before walking back to the house and placing it on the dining-room table, next to yesterday's *New York Times,* which Arthur had been reading when the telegram arrived. He had left it open to an article about Nixon addressing the American Legion at the Hilton. Arthur had been supposed to attend, but had not done so. Now Lillian looked away from the letter and stared at the article. Nixon had declared, "Those who predict the Vietnam War will end in a year or two are smoking opium or taking LSD." Lillian looked at the letter again.

Arthur had pulled a string, and would be driving out to Andrews AFB to watch them bring the casket. He was taking Dean. Debbie, who had already left for Mount Holyoke, would be home for the funeral. Tina had been in her room for twenty-four hours, working on a memorial painting. As Lillian stared at the letter, she had to put both her hands on the table to prevent herself from passing out and falling out of her chair. The letter was addressed to her—that's what he had done since heading off to boot camp, address letters to her, not Arthur, knowing that she would read them aloud. She and Arthur had discussed this quirk, and they agreed that addressing the letters to her let Tim more easily reassure everyone that he was fine, that he had simply embarked upon a classic masculine adventure. Letters to his father might have consisted of only the fewest words—"Okay here. The colonel is an asshole. Shot two Cong yesterday."

It was dated a week previously.

Dear Mom,

It's been raining again, pretty hard. It's such a swamp here, I don't know how they stand it. Thanks for the books. I started the one *Cat's Cradle*. It is pretty good. I loaned the one *Dune* to another guy in my hootch who was reading *Atlas Shrugged* so many times that his book fell apart, but when he started reading *Dune,* he finally shut up about it. I bought this Vietnamese guitar. It is pretty bad, and because of the rain, even worse, but I can get some sound out of it. I play it with one of the other guys who is from North Carolina and really good. His guitar is better than mine. Another guy, who is from Austin, Texas, plays the drum, which is really a mermite can, but he gets great sounds out of it. If I had a band again, I would definitely include a mermite can or two. Also thanks for the cookies. I think I had one. As soon as the guys saw them, they passed them around and they were gone. Captain Bloom says, "More more more." I suppose you could say that that's an order, Mom. Otherwise, things are pretty quiet, I guess the infantry is doing their job, which is called Operation Byrd, though I call it Operation The Byrds just for a joke. I guess we talk a lot about music here, because Billy Copps was in a band, too, before he came here. Austin, Texas, sounds like a pretty neat town.

Okay, well, I am going to wind this up, because I have to do some stuff for Captain Bloom. Don't worry. Nobody gets killed anymore around here. The civilians always smile at us. Love to Dad and the kids. A message for Dean: Bite me.

Love, Tim

Lillian left the letter open on the table. She didn't think she was going to be able to read it aloud. After a moment, she got up from the chair and walked out the French door to the pool, where she picked up the skimmer and walked around, removing leaves and unrecognizable bits from the surface of the water. She looked out, down the hillside, toward the tree line. She had the strongest feeling that she had foreseen this, that a voice had spoken to her in the night, three nights ago, and said, It's time. But she knew that this feeling was wrong, that nothing of the sort had happened. If it had happened like that, then all of this would be part of a pattern. But it wasn't. Tim had vanished; that was all. He had escaped her long ago—as soon as they moved to this house. It was not that she had seen him more and more intermittently (at first a few times a day, then every few days, then every few weeks, then every few months, then hardly at all); it was that he had gotten less and less corporeal, at first visible from time to time, then almost always invisible, only manifesting very rarely in unexpected spots—at the bottom of the pool, in her shower, in the attic looking for something. It was quite likely, she thought, that he would manifest again. But this conviction was not something she planned to confide to Arthur.

1967

∽

THEY WERE NAKED on his fold-out couch. The treatment room was warm enough (he turned up the heat to eighty) so that they required no covers, even though the windows were uncurtained and the weather outside was frigid. Andy remained positioned as he had instructed her, on her back, her arms above her head, her hands beneath her neck, her knees bent, and her feet flat on the mattress. Dr. Smith was sitting up. His body was much hairier than Frank's— the first time, she had stared. The hair was gray over his shoulders and got darker over his chest. His very thick pubic hair was black. Andy said, "You told me you worked with shell-shocked soldiers in the war. Did you notice a connection?"

"Between . . ." said Dr. Smith.

"Between, I don't know, between being a little wild and being a casualty? Frank came home without a mark on him, and he was over there the whole time—North Africa, Italy, Germany. He didn't even get a hangnail."

"He was—"

"He was a sniper. Why didn't you serve, again?"

"I did serve, though not in a combat capacity. I had asthma. However, psychiatric work was service." Now that his treatment plan had proceeded to greater intimacy, Dr. Smith sometimes offered little nuggets of personal information. Andy knew that they were supposed to help her see him as more human—a man with an inner life and a history, vulnerable and worthy of compassion. His mother, for example, had been an exceptionally cold woman, heavyset and determined; one of his earliest memories was of helping her unlace her corset. But this old fact was not dramatic. Though it had been frightening at the time to see her flesh billow forth, with therapy he now pondered all of his memories with equal disinterest, which was not lack of interest, but a state of emotional remove. What was there to learn from these episodes? If he had persisted in endowing them with the emotions that they aroused at the time, then he could learn nothing from them. Such was his goal for her, too. "You keep coming back to this topic, Mrs. Langdon. The young man was killed months ago."

"Janet wrote me about it again. I guess she told one of the girls at her school that she would rather it was her who died, and the girl told one of the teachers."

"Are you worried?"

"I'm not worried that she's going to do anything, but . . ."

Now he stood up and went to his mat, where he assumed his cross-legged position. He had made it absolutely clear that he did not love her—love was neither his purpose nor his aim (he was, after all, a married man), and if she were to fall in love with him (impossible, Andy thought), then it would be his job to deflect and analyze those feelings as a variety of transference. For now it was sufficient that she almost always had an orgasm, and, with increasing frequency, they had simultaneous orgasms. Simultaneous orgasms were a learned behavior, just like any other. So, indeed, was love.

"But what?"

"But I think her reaction is extreme. I've always thought she was rather remote."

"We see in others what we feel in ourselves, Mrs. Langdon. When you've tapped your own passions, perhaps you will understand your daughter's."

He waited for a moment, then said, "Now, in series of tens, I want you to tighten your pubococcygeus muscle." He began to count, and Andy, still lying on her back, did her best, though he went a little fast for her. He counted three sets, and then said, "You may rest." Next he had her straighten and bend her left leg ten times, then her right leg, then her left leg, then her right leg again. He said, "Turn over." She turned over. He said, "Now tighten your gluteals." He counted to ten three times. This was easy for her—she had been improving her posture since she was ten years old and first heard the word "posture." When he finished counting, she sat up. "I don't know what to say to comfort her. If I say nothing, she says I don't care, and if I say something, whatever it is, she says I don't know what I'm talking about."

He was still cross-legged, still hairy, still self-possessed. He said, "What have you said?"

"My sister-in-law and her husband let those children run wild. It seems to me that, if they had exerted a little control, he might have had more direction, and this wouldn't have happened. I guess that was exactly the wrong thing to say to Janet. I mean, I actually criticized her aunt Lillian and uncle Arthur, which is *not* to be done." Andy knew she sounded a little incensed.

"I thought you were a believer in fate, Mrs. Langdon."

"Yes, but—" Andy fell silent, momentarily startled. And it was true: a year ago, she would have viewed such a thing quite differently. Even as recently as September, she had told Janet that Tim's death was meant to be. Now, five months deeper into her treatment, she couldn't help seeing cause and effect, paths not taken, things that could have turned out in another way.

Dr. Smith looked at his watch, then rose to his feet without his hands touching the floor. It was this act that held her whenever she wavered in her dedication to her treatment. He went to his book and said, "We can take up this topic again."

Andy sat up and reached for her clothes and her handbag. She said, "Friday." He gazed at her expectantly while she put on her brassiere and underpants. She rummaged her bag for her checkbook. He handed her a pen. She wrote him a check for five hundred dollars. About this, as about everything else, he was very strict. He often said, "It may have seemed to you when you were a child that your father was a kind man, but his kindness, so called, had no direction, did it? And so, as a woman, you are untrained and adrift." As she handed him the check, Andy couldn't help agreeing.

DEBBIE'S ROOMMATE WENT STEADY, and her best friend dated three guys at Amherst in a round-robin arrangement, but Debbie maintained that she had set her sights on real intellectual achievement: she was not going to graduate school at Harvard, she was headed for Oxford. Uncle Henry said this was possible. Debbie knew that if she had gone to U.Va. or even UMass, her late nights at the library could have turned into dates with boys also spending time in the library, but if you were at a Seven Sisters, at Mount Holyoke, this was not the case.

So now she was at a mixer, standing in the corner, dabbing her eyes with a paper napkin, because every boy reminded her of Tim— not because they looked like Tim, but because they filled spaces that her brother should have filled. One gawky kid after another walked across the dance floor, dribbling his beer, his Adam's apple poking out, and his mouth half open. Always, Debbie had known that Tim was better-looking than she was, because the eyes of strangers slid past her and rested on him. Always, she had known that he got away with murder and so she had to do everything right. Always, she had been petty and irritable. Well, now she had taken Psychology 101, and Family Dynamics, and Elementary Freudian Theory, and she had identified herself as the wicked stepsister whose foot was too big for the glass slipper no matter what size the glass slipper was. In other words, she was a realist, surrounded by fantasists.

One of the gawky boys, this one at least six four, came to a halt in front of her and said, "You dance?"

"I have danced," said Debbie.

"I danced, I have danced, I had danced, I might have danced, I could have danced, I should have danced."

"English major," said Debbie.

"Might you dance in the near future?" said the boy.

Debbie stepped away from the wall. The song was "Ruby Tuesday." Debbie moved around, and the kid moved around near her, but not too near her. The song changed to "Georgy Girl," which Debbie didn't like, so she stood still for a moment, then backed away. Unfortunately, he followed her.

After ten the same evening, Debbie was still talking to this guy, whose name was David (not Dave) Kissell, a junior at Wesleyan. He already knew her entire name, Debbie Manning, and he also knew that her brother Tim had been killed in Vietnam, something only her best friend and her roommate knew. David Kissell's eyebrows had not risen. He had not backed away from her in either horror or disapproval, and when the tears came, he had supplied her with a clean paper napkin and a fresh beer. He said, easy as you please, "Come with me to the march. Someone in my dorm has a car. Three of us are going, and you can come along." Debbie said, "I don't know. Maybe." And then they went back into the dining hall and danced to "You Keep Me Hangin' On," and David said he was from Long Island and had seen Vanilla Fudge live. When he walked her back to her dorm in time for midnight curfew, he kissed her not on the lips but on the forehead.

He met her at the corner where her ride to Middletown dropped her off. She saw the three other girls stare at him for a moment and then dismiss him—he was wearing jeans and a sweatshirt, and his hair was below his collar (though clean—he smelled good). He took her little bag, and they walked to a pizza parlor. There were two guys he knew there, about halfway through a sausage pizza with mushrooms. Debbie sat down. She had the shortest hair at the table, and the most boring color, plain brown. The guy across from her was wearing a long wool army-surplus coat with a belt, even though it was April, and he had a carefully trimmed mustache. He was clearly the leader. David introduced her to him first—Jeff MacDonald.

They went back to Jeff's room, and pretty soon the boys were passing her a slender cigarettelike object which she knew was a joint. She took it, but when she sat staring at it, David gently removed it from her fingers and passed it to Jeff, who nodded thoughtfully and took another "hit." He had a nice stereo, and they were listening to the Electric Prunes.

The plan was to leave for New York by six, so she slept in David's single bed with him, which, in spite of years of slumber parties, she could not say she was used to. But he was nice, and anyway, he took a sleeping pill.

Jeff MacDonald knew somebody on East Seventy-third Street, so they left the Falcon there and walked to the park. Even by 9:00 a.m., Manhattan was so busy that Debbie had to grab David's hand so as not to lose him. When they got to the Seventy-ninth Street entrance, a small sign directed them to gather with other students, but it looked to Debbie as though everyone was milling around together. The official signs were large and white—Debbie thought the one that read "Children were not born to burn!" was more effective than "Stop the Bombing!" Other signs were homemade: a pair of twins had two signs, "Hey Hay LBJ How" and "Many kids U KILL 2DAY?" They marched shoulder to shoulder through the crowd, deadly sober and carefully holding the signs so that they could be read together. There were families, too—couples with babies in carriages, old ladies, even some men in old army uniforms from the war. Just before eleven, she and David followed Jeff to the rocks near the bottom of the Sheep Meadow. There Jeff climbed on a rock and burned his draft card with a lighter, while she, David, and the other boy, Nathan, formed part of the human chain protecting the small group of draft-card burners. Debbie looked over her shoulder to see if they were going to be rammed by police, but she could see no police, only more protesters lining up behind her, shouting, as the cards burned. When his card was a blackened ash falling into a can, Jeff raised both his arms in a salute, and everyone shouted "Hell, no! We won't go! Hell, no! We won't go!" Then everyone got organized and headed downtown.

On Park Avenue right before Forty-eighth Street, Jeff MacDonald got an egg right on the forehead. The egg broke and splattered over his glasses, and David almost laughed but didn't. Debbie ducked—another egg hit the ground in front of her feet. Then they all started looking up and hurrying a little bit, but there was no panic. Jeff just put his glasses in his pocket and kept shouting. They passed three guys with short hair, holding a sign that read "Hang the potesters!" "Protesters," Debbie wanted to stop and point out, was spelled with an "r." But the march pressed forward, so she just raised her fist and gave them the finger.

Debbie didn't start crying until Phil Ochs started singing. Debbie was not a screamer. She had one Beatles album, and she liked to listen to the acoustic Bob Dylan. Her sole pop-music memory was from three years ago, her freshman year, at a Peter, Paul and Mary concert, when she had gone up afterward to get an autograph from Paul. She was six people back in the line; it was late; she yawned, and Paul saw her. He looked right at her and sang, "On a Desert Island." But Phil Ochs was handsome and graceful, and he had a rich voice, even in this crowd. And when he looked out at them and sang "Is

there anybody here who'd like to wrap a flag around an early grave?"
she decided that he was singing to her, for Tim, and she burst out—
wa-wa-wa—very embarrassing, so upsetting that David Kissell put
his arms around her. And he followed that with "I Ain't Marching
Anymore." She heard David whisper the words "Her brother was
killed," and then there were a few tentative pats on her shoulder.
Would Tim have come to this march? Debbie had no idea. But maybe
his ghost would, knowing what it knew now.

JANET, TOO, was at the march. The week before, she had gotten a
letter from Aunt Eloise. Aunt Eloise was interesting to Janet, if only
because every time her name came up Dad laughed and Mom said,
"Oh, Frank," then laughed, too. They thought Aunt Eloise was an
embarrassment, but she wrote more faithfully than either Dad or
Mom.

Dear Janet—
    Thanks for your letter! I'm always happy to read anything
you have to say, and no, I am not at all tired of you talking
about your cousin Tim or telling me how much you miss him!
You should miss him. I consider him a murder victim, not
murdered by the Viet Cong, but by Lyndon Johnson and the
rest of the imperialist pigs who are perpetrating an illegal war
that they will never win. I know that you don't hear such things
at THE MADEIRA SCHOOL, but you are old enough to
know the truth. When I was your age, I was walking around
the farmhouse, staring out the windows, and wondering what
was out there. Now I know, and I can't say that it has made
me happy, but it has made me strong. There have been many
things that we have not been able to do anything about, but
the Vietnam War is something that we can do something
about. There is going to be a march in New York on April 15,
a Saturday (here in San Fran, too). You should think about
how you might get to that march. I don't know the rules at
your school. But there is never anything wrong with breaking
rules, and in fact, you should practice as soon as you can. You
are a good girl, which is a convenient cover story for you. No

one expects you to misbehave, so, at least for a while, you can judiciously misbehave (not sex and drugs, if you know what I am getting at and I hope you do not).

Then there was stuff about Rosa and her daughter, Lacey.

By midnight that night, Janet had forged a brief note from her mother: "Back from Florida the other day. See your Dad is still in Palm Springs. Guess the hotel is a mess, and he needs to stay for at least another week. By the way, Nedra is very ill, and she asked to see you. A Surprise. Don't know what is going to happen, but you should come home this weekend, Love, Mom." She'd stuck it in the envelope from an earlier letter, careful to tear off the postmark in a ragged way, as if she had ripped open the letter. When she took it to Miss Green, her housemother, the next day, she saw instantly what Aunt Eloise had been getting at. Miss Green barely glanced at the letter, just gave Janet a big smile and said, "Of course. Do you have train fare?" And, yes, she did.

The most adventurous part of Janet's trip to New York was something she would not be telling Aunt Eloise: that she spent Friday night on a bench in Penn Station. She did fall asleep, but only for an hour or so, with her purse between her chest and the back of the bench and her arms through its handles. She was awake by the time the crowds began to trickle through the building, and when she saw two girls in pigtails walking with two guys in army-surplus jackets, with long hair, she followed them as they headed uptown.

When the protesters began to head out of Central Park to Fifty-ninth Street, Janet was toward the front. She didn't dare speak to anyone, but she smiled several times and got smiles back. When they passed in front of the Plaza Hotel, where her mom had taken her for tea a couple of times, Janet looked east down Fifty-ninth Street; it hadn't occurred to her until right then that there were lots of people she knew who might see her, even if everyone in her family was out of town. The barriers were jammed with old people gaping. The only shouting was coming from the protesters, who were screaming "End the war! Stop the bombing!" Janet screamed that, too. Aunt Lillian had said that Tim was killed by a grenade—a piece of shrapnel had entered the back of his head, and he died right away—and that was all Janet needed to know. She screamed until she was hoarse, thinking

of Tim pitching balls to her when she was eight, and of herself striking out over and over until, finally, he tossed it right at the sweet spot
where her bat was headed, and her bat hit it.

At some point, Janet realized that the tall white man and the
shorter black man that she was right behind were Dr. Spock and Dr.
King. There was a way in which Janet had not quite believed that
Dr. Spock existed, like Betty Crocker or Aunt Jemima, but here he
was, smiling and laughing, even when they passed a sign that read
"Traitors!" And then she looked back. Because there was a little dip
in the road, she saw the most thrilling sight she had ever seen, which
was miles of people extending as far as it was possible to extend, into
the buildings, into the clouds. They marched toward the East River,
to the UN. The last time she was here was a field trip in sixth grade.
She found herself a spot.

Janet was sure that Tim's ghost was right there with her, practically
touchable, a figure in the crowd, maybe standing behind the Vietnam
Veterans Against the War's placard. Tim had written her only one
postcard from Vietnam, postmarked Nha Trang, and all it said on the
back was "Hey, kiddo! Everything is fine here! Send me some more
Hershey bars! Love you, Tim. xxx." Aunt Lillian had let her read his
last letter after she asked three times. Both she and Aunt Lillian knew
that she would cry for days afterward, but that was good, according
to her mom. As Phil Ochs sang "I Ain't Marching Anymore," Janet
closed her eyes and mouthed the words, and imagined that it was Tim
singing. Just as he had sung all those songs with the Colts.

THE APARTMENT WHERE Henry was staying for a long weekend, at
Eighty-fourth Street and Broadway, had one window that faced east,
and maybe Henry and Basil Skipworth heard the noise of shouting
wafting on the breeze from the park, and maybe they didn't. As the
crow might fly, they were only a mile or so from where the protesters were gathering. They had talked about joining the march but had
indulged themselves in not doing so. Thinking of Tim, Henry felt
a little guilty. But when he came to New York, he'd somehow not
put two and two together about the protest; he had been thinking of
this weekend as a break from everything about Tim that was putting
his mother and Claire and Paul and Lillian—and himself, for that

matter—at loggerheads. Basil taught German at Yale. Even though he often said "my dear boy," he was two years younger than Henry and about six times more sophisticated, if by that you meant that he read Balzac in French and Boccaccio in Italian as well as Goethe in German (and Kafka, too). On the other hand, he had only the most rudimentary grasp of the etymology of "foot" (*fot, fōt, pes* (Latin), *pod* (Greek), *pada* (Sanskrit), *-ped* (Indo-European), much less that of "penis," which meant "tail" in Latin and was almost unchanged from earlier forms. Basil, who had gone to Cambridge, was much more sophisticated than Henry in many ways, but, they both knew, not nearly as good-looking. He had started subtly pursuing Henry at the Modern Language Association meeting in December. Henry had allowed capture in March, intrigued by Basil's courage, since he himself had never been bold enough to push any pursuit to its logical end. They were using an apartment belonging to some friend of Basil's, who was back in England for a month.

Basil was completely up to date on sodomy laws: In England, still illegal, penalty, no longer death, but imprisonment, as for Oscar Wilde. Wilde, according to Basil, had been convicted under the same law that made the age of consent for females twelve; "however, my dear boy, for us, no consent is possible. I guess it is a sign of progress that, as of a hundred years ago, a man could be jailed for fucking a girl who wasn't quite ten yet, but the wheel of progress moveth exceeding slow." Nor could they meet in Connecticut, where homosexuality meant prison if the judge felt like it. Illinois—didn't Henry know this?—was the most progressive. As for New York, well, buggery was only a misdemeanor, and with all of these draft dodgers in town, the police had their hands full.

"Buggery," "balls-up," "bollocks," "git," "ponce," "poofter," "rodger," "wanker," "stiffy," "todger," "stonker." Listening to the words Basil enunciated in his layered accent (West Country underneath Received Pronunciation—he almost always pronounced his "r"s, for example, and sometimes joked around, saying, "Where ye be goin' to?"), Henry got used to them as if they were jokes, as if what Basil was showing him wasn't a little scary ("Oh, my dear boy, we've not got to that part yet"). Henry knew that Basil sometimes put on the West Country pretty thick just for him, because that was where the purest Anglo-Saxon still resided. Basil laughed at him for caring about such elementary linguistic motes and crumbs, compared with *Death in Venice,* or at least *Doktor Faustus,* which had universal appeal. Henry's standard riposte was, had *Doktor Faustus,* finished only twenty years ago, really stood the test of time? He was willing to admit that Christopher Marlowe's *The Tragicall History of the Life and Death of Doctor Faustus* had features of interest that might prove lasting, but . . .

And then they started laughing. Basil said, "My God, you are a stuffy fellow, for all that length of leg."

Henry was naked. The windows of the bedroom looked south, onto a tiny little square of green surrounded by cats and flowerpots. The apartment was on the third floor, and there were blinds; Basil had drawn them but not closed them. Henry supposed that north-facing windows across the alley had a view of their misdemeanors. They had kissed. They had stroked. Basil had warmed some baby oil and started at his shoulders, then moved farther down, linger-ing over Henry's arse, admiring the fact that Henry's body hair was fine and blond. Henry had rubbed Basil down, also, linger-ing a little around his shoulder blades before descending to the arse (hairy, not like any girl Henry had known). Until now that was all they had done, besides sleep side by side, though Henry wore shorts and a shirt and Basil wore pajamas (a word that was, indeed, related to "penis"). Basil had buggered and been buggered by, but he was patient. When Henry visited in March, Basil had walked around the apartment naked, sometimes with an erection, and he had done noth-ing with it except touch it from time to time, letting Henry get used to it. Watching him, without saying anything, Henry had imagined Jacob Palmer doing the same thing. Jacob had finished his doctor-ate at Wisconsin—highly motivated by the cold, he said—and was now married to one of his fellow graduate students, a Yeats scholar from St. Paul. They had a six-month-old baby boy. Jacob had gotten a good job at UCLA.

They were going slowly. Maybe Henry should be embarrassed, at his age, but they both knew that Henry had offered himself up for an education, and that Basil was perfectly agreeable to the terms, whatever they were.

The question was whether to walk over to Amsterdam and up a couple of blocks to Barney Greengrass, or down Broadway a few blocks to Zabar's, and the answer was—did you want the best bagel or did you want the best lox? Henry let Basil decide, and it was always Barney Greengrass, where they were even ruder than at Zabar's. ("My dear boy, manners are the key. If he ejaculates, 'Whaddaya havin', bud?' then the bagels will be just a little chewier and the lox just a little loxier.") As they walked up the street, Henry thought, they revealed nothing about misdemeanors they might have committed or be about to commit. Basil changed his posture slightly, slouching his hips and straightening his shoulders. He could feel himself do the same thing. Did they know each other? Only slightly—colleagues who happened to meet and were catching a bite.

At Barney Greengrass, there was a lot of talk about the protesters, crazy hippies, what was wrong with those people, wasn't LBJ doing the best he could, these kids didn't know from trouble if they thought the draft was trouble. Henry and Basil exchanged a glance, even though Henry hadn't yet told Basil about Tim, or, indeed, anything at all about his family. Onion bagel, toasted, cooled, easy on the cream cheese, no capers, a little onion. Black coffee, two sugars. They took their plates to a table by the window.

CLAIRE DREADED the hot weather and the muggy noise she would have to endure at the state fair, but since Paul had informed her that irritability was a classic symptom of pregnancy, she didn't say a word. Paul might not be pregnant himself, but when, on his thirty-eighth birthday, he burned the manuscripts of his partly written plays in the backyard, he had done in his mood for the rest of the summer. It didn't matter that his practice was booming so that he'd had to take on a new partner. He considered his new partner merely the best of a bad bunch—Cornell University undergraduate and Wake Forest Medical School. He was great with kids, but Paul didn't like him. Martin Sadler, his name was. He thought going to the doctor should be fun for a kid, or at least not terrifying.

Dr. Sadler was friendly. When he asked if he could tag along, Claire said yes, and began to think going to the fair might not be so bad after all in spite of the belly. He was there when they pulled into their parking spot. Paul snapped, "Well, I'm still not in favor of closing the office on a Friday," but then, because it was cool and the weather looked like it was going to be unusually pleasant, he said, "But we did pick a nice day."

Joe and Lois arrived in the pickup with Annie and Jesse; Minnie followed, with Rosanna, who was carrying Lois's competition pie on her lap. Claire thought her mother looked terrible. She had not seemed to take the news of Tim's death very hard: How many chickens did they think she had killed in her day? What did they think it was like, finding her own husband, ten years younger than she was now, curled up under that damned Osage-orange tree? Death was a fact, and no one knew that better than an old lady on a farm. Why discuss it? But today she looked as if she had given up on her hair in the middle of putting it up, as if she had given up on her sweater in the middle of buttoning it, as if she had dabbed two spots of lipstick on her lips and given up on that. Claire kissed her and asked her how she was.

"Just getting old. Gout in my toe. My hip. What all." She tossed her hand dismissively in the air. "The question is, how are you?" Claire suspected her mother thought she was too far along to show herself in public. She said, "I feel terrific, actually." Dr. Sadler walked right up to them, held out his hand to Rosanna, and said, "I understand you're Claire's mom. I'm Martin Sadler. I'm pleased to meet you." His smile was as big as could be. Rosanna put her hand on his arm and asked him if he was engaged or dating anyone.

Paul strapped Gray carefully into his expensive Maclaren baby stroller, tied his hat onto his head, then pulled his socks up and his overalls down. If one ray of sunshine got on the child's skin, Paul would take him inside. Paul refused absolutely to have a dog, and even though Claire was always saying that a boy needed a dog, it was she herself who needed the dog. But Paul's favorite words were "I don't think so."

Annie had changed overnight—breasts (suddenly large ones), though not much of a waist. Jesse wore exactly what Joe wore, right down to the ill-fitting white shirt and the too-short khakis and the flattop. And he stayed right in Joe's shadow. When Dr. Sadler asked him what grade he was in, Jesse looked up at Joe before he answered. Lois, as always, looked as if she was minding her own business. She opened the door and received the pie before Minnie turned off the engine.

Claire's hand went to her own hair. She had sprouted thirty gray ones, all at the cowlick on the left side of her hairline, right up front for everyone to see. She was twenty-eight years old! It was very unjust, she thought. Paul ran the stroller right over her toes.

Lois said, "I'm going to check in to the Machine Shed. I'll meet you at the crafts," so they followed Rosanna into the hall. Purple cable knit with long sleeves, regular Aran patterned vest, Fair Isle, hand-knitted Iowa Hawkeyes football jersey, including the number and the player's name, "Murphy." After the knitwear, they wandered past the canned goods to the piles of fleece, then tomatoes, longest green bean, biggest onion, heaviest ear of sweet corn. Claire had a little exchange of hard stares with Paul about taking Gray among the livestock, but Claire won—Paul picked him up, and Claire folded the stroller and carried it. It was important not to stand up straight, not to ask for help, and not to pat your belly. There were breeds of hogs here that she would not have recognized without a sign—Old Spots, Mulefoot, Tamworth (these were red)—and cows (Red Poll, Randal Lineback, Belted Galloway). She liked the horses, which were mostly draft and ponies. Paul actually got interested in the chickens. Rosanna took hold of the sleeve of Dr. Sadler's jacket. "Goodness, we had those Chanticleers. Good birds. Smart. I always heard of those Dominiques, never saw one before. Who was that who had a whole flock of those red Russian Orloffs? Claire, do you remember? Those could stay out in any weather, but they weren't good layers. Chickens got us through the Depression. And cream!" Dr. Sadler continued to nod. Goats, sheep. Joe lingered at the sheep, his hand affectionately on Jesse's shoulder, pointing out the Southdowns, like the one he had brought to the fair—oh goodness, was it thirty-three years ago now? Emily, that ewe's name was. And then he met a girl named Emily, too.

The Southdowns were the prettiest, Claire thought. When Jesse asked for one, Joe said, "We'll see." Which was better than "I don't think so." Claire knew she was grumpy.

They came out onto the midway, and she felt a breeze. It was almost noon, quite pleasant—not even eighty, she would bet. Paul said, "We could have chickens. The backyard is big enough." Quite typical of Paul to reject a dog out of hand, but get suddenly enthusiastic about chickens. Dr. Sadler and Rosanna were at the corn-dog stand. Claire waddled away from Paul and joined them there. Dr. Sadler gave her a comfortable smile. She said, "You know the recipe for grilled corn?"

"I shudder to think," said Dr. Sadler.

"Twelve ears of corn, a cup of melted butter, salt."

Paul made her cook with margarine.

Rosanna held out her hand, and Dr. Sadler put the corn dog into it. Claire was beginning to feel a little jealous.

Paul insisted that they go to the replica of the first church ever built in Iowa. "Catholic!" exclaimed Rosanna. "Built in Dubuque." She turned to Dr. Sadler. "Were you raised a Catholic, by any chance?"

Dr. Sadler shook his head, and Claire felt her ears get bigger, but he didn't say anything except "Nice woodworking."

The pies, set out neatly on the display table, were judged at four. Claire thought Lois's did look delicious, but she came in second. After the judging, she went up to the judges and smiled and shook their hands and thanked them for judging. Claire thought that Lois was always excessively polite. You never knew what she was really thinking.

And so they forgot about Tim for eight hours, and Rosanna was, indeed, perked up. As for Claire, she was so exhausted she let Paul put Gray to bed, which he did with better grace than he had all summer. She was lying on her side, and she could feel the baby moving around; she imagined her (him) doing backflips. After Gray was down, Paul came into their room and sat on the edge of the bed, took Claire's hand, and pushed her bangs gently out of her face. He said, "That was a good idea, enjoying plant, animal, and human variety for a day. Let's do that every year." He was patting her hand, and she fell asleep right there, deep as a well and twice as dark—who used to say that?

1968

~

THEIR CHRISTMAS HAD BEEN bittersweet. Debbie invited her
boyfriend, an awkward kid but kind. He helped with the dishes,
and he noticed things like rug corners turned up or stove burners left
on. Lillian liked him. Tina had taken a class in printmaking and made
their Christmas cards. After years of encouraging her because that's
what a mother was supposed to do, Lillian had loved the cards Tina
made, two sheep, a goat, and three chickens peering through a door
into a shed, and the Star of Bethlehem shining above them. Dean
brought home an early admission to Dartmouth, which everyone
imagined to be surrounded by acres of smooth ice. Arthur seemed
energetic and almost happy, and maybe only Lillian noticed that his
hair was nearly all gray now. They hung Tim's favorite ornaments on
the tree and drank to him at the table, and told a few of the funnier
stories, just so the boyfriend would know that they had handled their
loss.

Yes, when McNamara had turned in his resignation, Arthur was
irritated watching it on the news, muttering, "Frank Wisner shot
himself. What's stopping you, Mr. Secretary?," then retreated to his
office as he had so many times before. This was the first thing Lillian
thought of when she found Arthur under the bed.

He was canny about it. Dean took swimming practice before
school, and Tina liked to go in with him and study in the library, so

Lillian was up by six, making breakfast. She ironed Tina's blouse and found Dean a pair of socks, did the dishes, had a second cup of coffee. She thought Arthur had left—he said he was going to sneak out of the house early and not to worry about him. She even went in and out of the bedroom once, noticing only that the bed was made. When she was putting away her robe, she saw a wrinkle in the lower hem of the bedspread. First she touched the wrinkle; then she felt his shoe. There was no blood; he had no wounds, but he was out cold, and she knew he had done it at last. She threw the bedspread onto the floor and called an ambulance.

He was wearing trousers, a pressed shirt, a jacket, socks, and loafers. The ambulance people had to pull him out feet-first, which mussed his hair. One guy took the note out of Arthur's fist and handed it to her. She unfolded it. It read, "Don't call the office unless I'm dead."

She said, "Is he—?," shaking her head and starting to cry. As they rolled him onto the stretcher, the medic said, "Not yet." She didn't call the office. She got into the back of the ambulance with him, and stared at him as they careened toward the hospital, maybe a twenty-minute trip. Every so often, the medic took his pulse and listened to his heart and nodded. Lillian herself kept her hand on his chest. His breathing was shallow, but he kept breathing. It was cold. The landscape was white and the sky was gray, and she knew that he had planned it and had intended to succeed. The unhappy ending, as far as Arthur Manning was concerned, was life.

When the doctor came to her in the waiting room, she was shivering in spite of still having her coat on, and she shook the whole time he talked. It was Seconal, was your husband suffering from insomnia, did he have a prescription for barbiturates, was he showing strange signs of drowsiness or disorientation, could he have fallen down and rolled under the bed. Lillian said, "Didn't they tell you about the note?"

"No. No note." He licked his lips and said, "Has Mr. Manning been treated for depression, or manic-depressive illness? Has he shown—"

"Our son was killed in Vietnam."

The doctor for the first time looked into her eyes, said, "I am sorry. May I ask—"

"Almost a year and a half ago."

"Has your husband shown signs . . ."

It went on.

He was to stay in the hospital for three days, for observation. Lillian said, "May I see him?"

"It's going to take a couple of hours for him to wake up. I guess he'll be surprised to find himself here."

"Very disappointed."

"Oh, maybe not. Second thoughts—"

Lillian shook her head.

It wasn't until she was home to get the car that she threw the bedspread back onto the bed and saw the other note, the one written in a neat hand folded into Tina's Christmas card. It read:

Dear Lily Pons—

I am doing a bad thing to you, my darling. I know even more clearly than you do that this is the ultimate betrayal, and the only way on earth that I could or would betray you is exactly this way. But you know I've been waiting for the chance. You know I've been putting my affairs in order— not my financial affairs, but my domestic affairs. I have been waiting for each of you to recover somehow from Tim's death, and now we have reached the crossroads where everyone has a path to the future. I saw all the paths at Christmas. Even Debbie is in good hands. You are the only one. Why can't I take you with me? I ask myself that. And I ask myself that again, feeling you beside me in the night, feeling your hand in mine, hearing you breathe. But I can't do it, nor can I stay. Why is that? Because I literally and truly see no future. Blank. Empty. Nothing. At last. And I am glad of it. You are perfect. I love you.

Arthur

The first thing he asked her when she saw him in his room, and he was groggy when he asked it, was whether she had told anyone at the office. She said no, and it was true—she had not told anyone at the office. Who had she told? Minnie. She had to talk to someone; she had called the farthest-away person that she could think of, in her office at the high school, and cried to her for ten minutes. Minnie might or might not tell Rosanna, but Minnie did want to tell Joe—Joe wouldn't say anything. Arthur swallowed several times, closed his eyes, and patted her hand as best he could. Finally, he said, "Well, I guess we'll soon find out once and for all."

"What?" said Lillian.

"Whether the phone is tapped."

It was.

Wilbur and Finn appeared after dinner. They took Lillian into the living room, turned on the lights, and offered her a drink from her own liquor cabinet. No, not even one sip of the Rémy Martin. Wilbur poured himself a Scotch and soda. Finn, a shot of crème de menthe over ice. Sheppard Pratt was where he would be going, up in Towson; men like Arthur had walked its halls for years; nervous breakdowns were part of the job, Arthur knew that. Arthur had always taken everything very seriously. That had its good and bad aspects. Electroshock was of course a possibility.

She told the children he was in the hospital with pneumonia. He would be fine; but, no, they couldn't go see him, it was too dangerous. She should have said something else, but Arthur hadn't told her what to say. The two doctors met her as soon as she arrived at Sheppard Pratt the next morning: Dr. Rockford, who was tall and impatient, and Dr. Kristal, who was younger, shorter, and more charming. What had Arthur been doing and saying for the last few months, for the last year, whatever stood out in her mind? Dr. Rockford sat to her left and Dr. Kristal sat to her right. Dr. Rockford would ask a question: Has Mr. Manning shown signs of depression? And then Dr. Kristal would translate it: Did he seem to have a disrupted sleep pattern? Was he eating sufficiently and with enjoyment? Had his drinking habits changed? In half an hour they had elicited most of what she remembered about Arthur staring out the window of his office, about Arthur wandering the house, about Arthur pushing his food around his plate. Yes, he did drink a little, still, but he'd stopped drinking as much as he had been.

Then it was on to his history—the death of his first wife and child in childbirth, his proposal to Lillian not a year after that, the immediate pregnancy, his "manic" (Dr. Rockford's word) reaction to fatherhood, his "excessive sexual importunities" (Dr. Kristal). His habits of secrecy. "He has to keep secrets," said Lillian. "That's part of his job." They both nodded. Finally, feeling that she had been led step by step into this but not knowing any way out, she told the story of his mother, the death of the older sister in the flu epidemic, the hanging. Dr. Kristal wrote industriously on his clipboard, and Dr. Rockford nodded as if he had expected as much. Lillian at once had the sensation that there was nothing about her marriage or Arthur that was at all unusual or admirable. Everything she cherished was, if not a symptom of pathology, then an item of utter triviality. She fell silent.

Well, they would keep him up there for a few months. The staff was highly competent and extremely effective; she would be amazed at the change; best she not visit very often, if at all; a whole new scene, a whole, in some sense, reassessment of oneself, of life itself; in many cases, the effects were amazing, even when the condition was chronic, as it seemed to be in this case. Utter privacy worked wonders, no television or newspapers, concentration on the here and now.

Then they took her to Arthur's room. He had been given something. When he took Lillian's hand, he did so from deep inside a pharmaceutical distance. Dr. Rockford explained what would be done, in no way asking permission or seeking agreement. Arthur stared at the ceiling, and Lillian signed the papers that Dr. Kristal set before her. When she had finished and handed back the pen, he whispered in her ear, "Just wait! He'll be a new man! These things are always hard!" She kissed Arthur on the lips. As she drove home, she wondered if he would ever forgive her.

IT DIDN'T TAKE LONG for Charlie to make out the thing on his chest in the mirror. It was a piece of paper with writing on it, which read:

> My name is:
> Charlie Wickett
> I live at:
> 400 Tuxedo Blvd.
> W02-4659

It was pinned to his shirt with two large safety pins. He could not go outside without this piece of paper. Every day, Mommy knelt down beside him several times and said, "Stay with me, Charlie. You know what that means. Right beside me. And if I call your name, I expect you to answer." Charlie nodded and said yes, that he would stay with Mommy, that he would answer to the sound of his name, that he would not ever run away again so that the police had to be called and find him after dark and bring him home. The police were tall and wore blue and did not like looking for lost children.

Nursery school was at the gray church on the corner, and it was a long walk, but by the time Charlie got there each morning, his legs weren't jiggling and jumping anymore, the way they did at breakfast. For the first part of nursery school, where they sat in a circle on the red rug and Miss Ellery read a story, Charlie could be quiet and not move if they had walked, though not if they drove. Mommy put his hand right into Miss Ellery's hand and said, "Goodbye, Charlie. Be a cooperative boy." Charlie nodded and put his finger on the paper. "That's your sign," said Miss Ellery. Charlie Wickett. "You're a lucky boy to have a sign, so don't touch it, okay?"

The book today was about a fox who wore sox. On the cover, the fox was bright red. Charlie sat quietly and stared at the book, some-times at the red fox and sometimes at the sox and the FOX. He won-dered if they could be xos and xOF, and touched his sign. It wasn't until Miss Ellery came to ticks and tocks that Charlie stood up and started running around the red rug—first one way, as fast as he could go, and then the other way. Miss Ellery didn't say anything. She kept reading. Charlie was careful not to step on anyone's fingers or to fall over anyone. The room was very bright when he was running, and the colors swam around him.

Miss Ellery put the book down and said; "Charlie, do you think you can sit down and listen?"

Charlie came to a halt and stared at Miss Ellery; then he sat down for one more page. When he stood up again, Miss Plesch came into the room and took his hand. They went outside to the playground, and Charlie ran around the swings and the jungle gym. When he was tired and sat down, Miss Plesch said, "A."

Charlie said, "Antenna. B."

"Banana. C."

"Corvette. D."

Miss Plesch grinned. She said, "Dog. E."

Charlie was stumped, so he jumped up and ran the other way around the swing set, then said, "Ethyl. F."

"Flower. G."

"Gas. H."

Now the door opened and the other kids came running into the playground. The girls went one way, and the boys—Davie, Herbie, Barry, and Petey—came toward Charlie. Charlie put his hand on Miss Plesch's knee and said, "Herbie."

"Very good," said Miss Plesch. Charlie took off, and Herbie and Barry ran after him. They ran and ran. It was a sunny day. When Mommy picked him up for lunch, Miss Ellery said, "He knows every car word."

"His first sentence was 'Dere go a Muttang.' He was almost two. Before that we never heard him say a word."

"Sometimes adopted children are a little late talking. That is my experience. But they catch up." She bent down and said, "Charlie, do you still have your sign?"

Charlie touched his sign with his finger.

They walked home the long way, down Greeley. When he got home, he sat quietly and ate his peanut-butter-and-pickle sandwich. Mommy said he was a good boy.

FRANK WAS SUPPOSED TO be in Palm Springs, looking at the renovations Rubino had authorized at the hotel, but he had stayed late in Malibu, at Hughes, so he was driving along Wilshire, past the Ambassador Hotel, about nine. The traffic was a nightmare, and Frank could feel his temper rising, but then he remembered Jim Upjohn's stories about going to the Cocoanut Grove there in the forties, with Howard Hughes. Hughes was on his mind even though he, Frank, would never meet him (wasn't the guy holed up in Las Vegas somewhere now?). He turned off Wilshire onto Mariposa, drove up two blocks, and walked back. The hotel was seething with people, and almost as soon as he walked through the door, Frank felt himself get edgy. As a man with nothing to lose, Frank was almost never edgy. What offended him was not the crowd, but some acoustic quality of the hotel lobby. The chaos was not of a uniform loudness and incomprehensibility—words popped out of the noise and impressed themselves upon his consciousness: "red," "fountain," *"hola,"* "I said," "Nixon," "Pittsburgh." He went into the bar, but he got the same feeling there—he could not hear the man standing next to him saying to the bartender, "Gimme a highball," but he could hear an unknown female voice saying very clearly, "Don't touch that." The word that rose on the din was "Bobby, Bobby, Bobby."

Frank didn't care who won the nomination or the election. Kennedy was of interest to him as a young man still, a man the age of Lillian, a man who had lost many things and had plenty to lose. Bobby Kennedy had been transforming before his eyes lately—getting younger and younger, even as Frank and everyone he knew was getting older and older. Maybe that's why Arthur's colleagues hated him. Look at his recent pictures: he had never been as handsome, as tousled, as brilliant. Every so often, when an old picture popped up of Bobby and JFK, JFK looked exhausted in comparison.

Jim Upjohn liked Bobby Kennedy, both politically and personally. Jim had come around since JFK's assassination, mostly because he thought Johnson was a Texas roughneck and Eugene McCarthy was wheels within wheels. Within wheels. He said that RFK might be too short to win the election, but he kept urging Frank to contribute—it would be good moral experience for Frank, such a tightwad. The thing Frank didn't like about Kennedy was that he didn't seem to be able to keep his feelings to himself, no matter what he actually said. When he worked for Joe McCarthy, when he went after Hoffa, when he walked beside his brother Jack, you could see him almost trembling with intention that was eating him alive. Several times over the years, Arthur and Frank had talked about Bobby the way you did about strange younger men, and not only because the Kennedys also lived in McLean and seemed to follow the Arthur Manning laissez-faire child-rearing program (once, Arthur heard through the grapevine that the daughter Kathleen had hired her own nanny when she was walking down the beach in Hyannis Port, and Ethel had interviewed her through the door while she, Ethel, was going to the bathroom). Arthur's co-workers hated Kennedy, said that he made their skin crawl, that they recoiled from him as from anything small and poisonous.

In the crowded lobby, Frank felt edgy. His eye could not help going to the anomalous figures in the busy roomscape—a man here and a man across the room who were utterly still and utterly observant, who seemed unhappy amidst the rising zest of the crowd. They wore suits as if they were used to wearing suits; they were Frank's age, and they knew too much to be swept up in the enthusiasm around them. Their eyes flickered sideways before they turned their heads, as if they were waiting for something. The crowd, by contrast, was moving in a kind of coordinated exuberance, heads tossed backward, mouths wide open in talk or in smiles, arms lifted, bodies lifted. Just the sort of crowd that thought it knew what was coming. Frank shivered and moved away from the bar. Probably, he thought, he would always be that kid he'd been in college, living in a tent beside the river, shooting rabbits to make a little money, that kid he'd been in the army, comfortable on a quiet morning, focusing his telescopic sight on a figure in the distance, watching it come to a halt, waiting for the quarry to stretch a little bit and yawn. That was when Frank had liked best to make a kill, at that moment of confidence and comfort. It was a mercy killing, in a way, and he'd done it carefully, so that a single shot finished the deed. The sniper units were trained never to fire a second time, never to give away their position, so Frank had made sure that no second shots were needed. He hadn't thought about that in years.

Now Bobby appeared, surrounded by larger men—Frank recognized Rafer Johnson—and headed toward the podium. Frank's edginess peaked in a kind of uncomfortable tingle. He finished his beer and turned away. Outside of the hotel, Wilshire was pretty empty. Even the whores were there, trying to get a glimpse of the next president. Frank found the car and drove around for an hour or two, still a man with nothing to lose, but newly aware of what he had lost— not only Lydia, but Andy, Janet, Eunice, Lawrence (who would have loved Bobby Kennedy).

It was at least three when he got to the Beverly Hills Hotel, where he had stayed for the last three nights and always did stay. The desk clerk was distracted; Frank didn't understand why until he got to his room and turned on the TV. He sat on the corner of the bed in his shorts, watching the black-and-white panic. Was he the only person in America who was not surprised at the assassination of Bobby Kennedy—or, rather, surprised only that the shooter was that kid, who looked as dumbfounded and harmless as a fawn in the headlights?

WHEN SHE GOT HOME from Mount Holyoke in June, Debbie saw that her real summer job was organizing her mother and, once he got home, watching her dad, who was finishing up five months at Sheppard Pratt. She had to press her mother, even bully her, into naming his diagnosis—well, depression, yes, pretty severe, and, well, paranoia, too, though that was not something her mother had noticed, or maybe it was not something that her father had expressed. Apparently, there were people who seemed perfectly normal on the surface, and then you read their diaries or their letters and it was one long description after another of plots and plans. There had been shock treatments. Debbie quailed and didn't ask how many. Lillian at last told Debbie about the suicide attempt, and then she told her about her grandmother, and then she told her about the first wife, during the war, and Debbie cried, but all of this was so new and strange that her grief was more or less like crying when a book was sad. She wrote about it to David.

When he got home, though, her father seemed fine enough. He wasn't ready to go back to work, so he bought and read something called *The Gourmet Cookbook,* which was about five hundred pages long, and he went to the nursery for plants and bushes, which he and Mom discussed as if they were new puppies, and he oversaw the crew that came to trim some of the trees. At the bottom of the property, he broadcast some wildflower seeds that he got at a natural-history museum. He washed both cars. Debbie found herself counting jokes. If he made five jokes in a day or fewer, he wasn't feeling very good, and if he made up to ten, he was okay, but if he made more than ten, he was acting "manic," which was cause for worry. He didn't watch the news or read the paper. Debbie wondered if he was the only person in the world who did not know about the assassination of Bobby Kennedy or the assassination of Martin Luther King. Her father would have been the perfect person to talk to about these events, but she couldn't find a way. Her mother never said a word.

To David, who was caddying for the summer at a golf course in Middletown, she wrote, "It's like a tomb around here. That's the saddest thing. When we were kids, no one had as much fun as we did. We had the first television, we had the sandbox, and both a swing set and a rope hanging from a tree limb. We had more bikes than kids, because if my dad saw a bike for sale cheap, he would buy it in case some neighborhood kid didn't have one. We had so many balls, neighborhood dogs would come over to play even when their kids didn't. Dean keeps telling me to leave Dad alone and stop staring at him, that that's what makes you paranoid!"

She thought she was handling everything pretty well, until she took a weekend and went up to Middletown Friday night, with a return ticket for Sunday afternoon. Mom had been willing to make her a reservation at a hotel. She said, "You're almost twenty-one. When I was your age, Timmy was a year old and you were on the way. What you do is your business. I am not going to ask you how serious you are about him, or anything. Which is not something your grandmother said to me. Which is why I ran off with your father without telling her a word about it." She smiled, but she still looked worn out. Debbie wasn't in fact sure how serious she was about David, since he was more comforting than exciting, but she was eager to go.

David hugged her like he was really glad to see her, and he looked tanned and fit from working at the golf course. He'd had to cut his hair, but it was growing out.

The argument was not with David, but with Jeff MacDonald, whose job was at an "underground newspaper," a bunch of typed articles that they dittoed, stapled together, and handed out on street corners. The argument started when David admitted that he had hit some balls at a driving range earlier in the week. Jeff said, not joking, but in that teachery way he had, "I told you you weren't reliable, and anyway, have you given me twenty-five percent of your tips?"

David scowled, and Debbie said, "Why is he giving you twenty-five percent of his tips?"

"The ruling class has to fund its own overthrow."

"Are you talking about the ruling-class players on a public course, like old Italian guys and people who work in factories?"

David said, "Deb—"

She went back to picking the olives off her pizza. In the nine months or so that she and David had been dating, Debbie had gotten used to Jeff MacDonald and didn't take him very seriously anymore. But she did not want to overthrow the ruling class; she wanted to end the war in Vietnam.

The three boys continued to talk about tips. Nathan, who was waiting tables at a diner on Main Street, was making twenty-eight dollars a week plus forty in tips. His share of the rent was fifty dollars. David was making fifty a week plus caddying, which could be another fifty, but could also be another ten, and that didn't take rainy days into consideration. Jeff, of course, was not putting in his share of the rent, because the paper was too radical to have a large paying audience, but they had handed out fifty copies last week and fifty-three this week. Jeff and the editor had debated about whether they should carry advertising—there was a head shop on Pearl Street that would pay for an ad, and that guy knew a tarot-card reader.

Debbie stifled a smile. Jeff saw it, because he said, irritably, "So I guess your old man was taken out by his fellow spooks."

As soon as he said this, she knew David had told her secret. She said, "I don't know what you're talking about."

"Yeah," said Jeff. "You do. But I don't think you should take it personally. There are more important things in the struggle than the fate of individuals."

"I'm surprised you think that," said Debbie, "when the most important thing to you always seems to be that you have the last word."

"If I consider my analysis to be more correct, then I have to make sure it's understood."

"You have an analysis of my father's . . . illness when you aren't a psychiatrist and you haven't met him and you've never even talked to me about it?"

"I don't have to know particular individuals in order to understand that the ruling class will do anything to retain control of the means of production and of the organs of indoctrination."

"Yeah," said Debbie, "Like *1984*."

"Mistakes have been made." He shrugged. "Look what they did to Bobby Kennedy. I'm not saying I liked Bobby Kennedy. He remained pretty reactionary, but that's the key. He got just a little out of line and they shot him."

Nathan said, "They haven't shot Eugene McCarthy."

"He has no charisma and no chance," said Jeff. "They know that. You know there's five hundred thousand American soldiers in Vietnam? Why do you think they're there? Culling! We have a big generation. Once everyone is drafted, they cull us. What do you think friendly fire is? When we've been trained to toe the line, then they'll bring everyone home and put them to work, and you'll never hear a peep out of our generation again. JFK was the first warning shot, MLK the second, and RFK the third."

"That was in your paper," said David.

"Yes, it was."

"You're 'Kropotkin'?" said David.

Debbie laughed out loud, but it was an angry laugh. Jeff looked right at her. She said, "Everyone in the world knows that communism doesn't work. Even my aunt Eloise knows that."

"Peter Kropotkin was an anarchist."

"Party of one," said Debbie.

Jeff pushed his glasses up his nose. David was staring at his half-eaten slice of pizza. Debbie expected Jeff to start in about Tim somehow. Her fingers were trembling. But Jeff said, in his most superior voice, "What happens after the third warning shot? Well, the revolution begins, and it's about to. Clearly, you think that everyone was upset when Martin Luther King was put out of his misery by a CIA hit man. Don't you recognize crocodile tears when you see them? Ask Eldridge. Whites hated him, even though King didn't really realize that until the very last moment, and blacks with any sense had come to hate him, too, because he didn't understand whites. He thought, if black people were just good boys and girls, then the folks up at the big house would let them grow up. Bobby Seale and Eldridge know better. They're glad he's dead. And, for the same reason, I'm glad RFK is dead. Everybody has to die eventually. But if you are standing in the way, if people think you're going to change everything but really you aren't, you can't, and you don't even want to, because your idea is that if poor people need houses they just need to suck up to big business even harder than they already do, then better to die sooner rather than later." He pushed his glasses up again and looked around the restaurant. His voice had risen. Now he lowered it. He said, "That's what I think."

Debbie said, "That is just a bunch of bullshit."

"You ask your dad the spook. You ask him what is really going on. Go ahead, I dare you."

Debbie said, "Do you think I would want to live under a government that you ran or set up? It's all very nice to say you're an anarchist, but you only want anarchy for yourself. For the rest of us, you want to make sure we do what you say, think how you think, and remember you're the boss. You ask me why you wear that jacket or give away that piece of crap on the street, even though you know that when people take it they just throw it in the next trash can, or why you wear those glasses right out of *Doctor Zhivago*? You just want to get laid, like every guy. My brother, Dean, thinks playing hockey is going to get him laid. You think pretending you are some Russian is going to get you laid—big fucking difference." She tossed her head. "You wouldn't mind running General Motors. You hate big business just because you're not the boss. If, by some magic trick, you got to be the president of . . . of . . . of Dow, you'd do it, and you would be happy to make napalm, too, because if you don't care about one person getting killed, then you don't care about any person getting killed. You're just a heartless asshole."

David had already stood up, and now he said, "I think we should leave."

"I'm not leaving with him," said Debbie.

"We don't have to," said David. He took her hand, and pulled her toward the door. Outside, it was hot and very sunny. When they had gotten about halfway down the block, David said, "I guess his dad is in the Teamsters Union in Pittsburgh. They've always been pretty militant. And his grandfather knew Big Bill Haywood."

"He doesn't—"

"I mean, it's not like he speaks to his dad. I don't think they've spoken since Jeff was fifteen or something. He doesn't agree with his dad, and he always says, 'If you work in the factory, even if you are in a union, then you are still agreeing that the factory should exist.'"

"Well, the factory should exist. Is your mom going to make your clothes, and are your sisters going to dip candles and carry buckets of water up from the river?"

"Are you mad at me?" he asked.

"I told you not to tell."

"It slipped out. Are you mad at me?"

"I don't know."

They came to a cemetery. In Middletown, it seemed, you were always coming to a cemetery. She said, "Let's look at the gravestones, and I'll figure it out."

Afterward, she said she wasn't mad, and they did go to a movie, and he did stay in her room that night, and the next day he put her on the train. His first letter came Wednesday. She wrote right back, and neither of them even mentioned the fight, but she said yes to a date with a guy who went to Vanderbilt, and when the riots broke out in Chicago at the Democratic Convention, she assumed that the revolution had begun.

RICHIE WAS IN Alpha Barracks and Michael was in Gamma Barracks. The one other set of twins, John and Clay Simpson, were in Delta Barracks. Everyone, including the Simpson twins, thought Richie and Michael got along great, though their jokes and tricks sometimes went too far. That was why Richie was in the major's office right now, waiting for the major to come back with his file— Richie had pointed one of the old Springfield rifles right at Michael's head and pulled the trigger; everyone knew the firing pins had been removed. Michael even laughed. And he had pushed Michael off the high dive at the swimming pool. Michael had spread his arms and legs and shouted "Yahoo!" as he was going down.

They were "getting out of hand" once again.

Out the window, it was starting to sleet. That was all they ever had here, sleet. No real snow. The door opened, and the major came in. The major was pretty short—last year, Richie had been about his height, but this year, he had grown six inches (Michael had grown seven), and even without his cap on, he was way taller than the major. He looked down.

The major said, "Corporal Langdon."

Everyone in his class was a corporal. Then you got to be a sergeant junior year, and an officer senior year. Richie saluted. "Yes, sir."

The major started shaking his head. "I've been watching you."

"Yes, sir."

"You may not know this, but I was at the swimming pool the other day, and I happened to witness you pushing your brother off the diving board."

"Yes, sir."

"He made the best of it, but you took him by surprise, and, Corporal Langdon, I don't think you were joking."

"I was, sir. He knew I was right there. He was ready for me. It may have looked like I surprised him, but that's because he made a big deal of it. He was—"

"Are you contradicting the evidence of my own eyes, boy?"

"Yes, sir." Richie said this snappily, his eyes straight ahead and his chin up.

"Finish what you were saying, then."

"He was going to push me off. He knew it, I knew it. I was just quicker. For once."

"You two like the rough stuff, then."

"Yes, sir."

"How would you feel if one of you got hurt?"

"I don't know, sir."

"You don't know?"

"We've never gotten hurt." In the sense that someone had to go to the doctor, Richie thought.

"Well, think about it."

"I will, sir."

"No, think about it now."

Richie thought about it, staring out at the sleet, which was making the windows of the major's office look wet and cloudy. He often imagined Michael getting hurt. For instance, maybe the major would say that one of them would have to leave the school. This would be Michael, and on the day he was supposed to leave, Richie would take him somewhere and stab him to death. He said, "That would be bad, sir. I know that."

"Boys can be heedless."

Richie contemplated the roof of the building across the way. The roof was metal, and steep. If he and Michael were on the roof, Michael might look the other direction, just for a moment, and Richie could give him a push. It was three stories, and Michael would hit the pavement. He imagined that, headfirst.

"I have to punish you, Corporal Langdon. The rules say that, whether your behavior is intentional or out of carelessness, the suitable punishment will bring home to you the gravity of your actions."

"Yes, sir."

"I am not breaking you back to private, but I am warning you that that is a possibility."

"Yes, sir."

"Tomorrow, and for each of the next three days, you will run six laps around the drill field, carrying your weapon and your pack."

"Yes, sir."

"At the completion of the six laps, you will do twenty-five push-ups. You will perform these exercises while the others are drilling, as an example to your fellow cadets."

"Yes, sir." Then this would lead to shouts and laughing back in the barracks. Michael always said, "Shit, you run like a girl!" Richie pressed his lips together.

"If that doesn't do you some good, Corporal, I don't know what will. But I have faith in you." The major reached up and patted Richie on the shoulder. Richie guessed this was supposed to be a fatherly gesture. He stared straight ahead and practiced what he always practiced, which was being a blank brick wall and never letting on.

"All right, Corporal Langdon, that'll do. You are dismissed."

"Yes, sir." Richie saluted again.

1969

∾

MINNIE HAD INSTIGATED a spring-vacation trip to the East
Coast for junior and senior honors students—first New York,
Empire State Building, Metropolitan Museum of Art, Statue of Liberty; then the train to Washington, D.C., where they would go to the
Congress, have a tour of the White House, a trip to the monuments,
and a day at the Smithsonian. Only two of the fourteen kids had ever
been on a plane before. Minnie herself had flown once, to Dallas, for a
conference. She said to Joe, "Do we pin the 'Country Bumpkin' signs
to our chests or our behinds?" Joe laughed. Annie, who was sixteen
but had the demeanor of a fourteen-year-old, was an honors student;
she and Minnie were going ahead of time and staying two nights
with Frank and Andy. Janet, now a freshman at Sweet Briar, would
be driving up for the weekend. Rosanna maintained, "Janet has
adopted herself into Lillian's family, though she acknowledges Frank
and Andy in a distant sort of way." That was kids, if you asked Minnie.

When the plane took off, Annie put her two books obediently
into the pocket of the seat back in front of her. When they were flying, she read them like clockwork, half an hour for *The Mill on the
Floss,* half an hour for *Love to the Rescue.* Barbara Cartland. Well, better than television, Minnie thought. Minnie smoothed her wool skirt
over her knees. That, too, was new—orange. Minnie could never
have imagined herself in an orange skirt with an orange-and-green

matching sweater. Annie had gone to Younkers and come out with a new brown dress; Minnie sometimes wondered what Annie would be like if she hadn't lived all her life with the assistant principal (and now, as of next year, principal, the first-ever female principal in Usher County). Annie was soft and affectionate, a bit of a mouth breather, not much like Lois, who did everything right, including sleep in the same room with her husband and show kindness to her children. Lois acted toward Minnie with total correctness, but gave off no warmth that Minnie could see. Annie, Minnie thought, was, as the kids at school would say, clueless, though appealingly so. Minnie knew it was her job to prod her niece, to give her a little spine so that she might make something of her life. The stewardess announced that they were about to land; Minnie realized that she was not going to be able to distract herself from the marriage of Frank Langdon and Andrea Langdon for much longer.

Andy was waiting at the gate. Minnie saw her gaze take in Annie and then switch to her as she stepped forward and held out her arms. Minnie gave her a brief hug, and Andy said, "What a bright and cheerful outfit you have on."

Andy herself was wearing slender high-heeled boots, black stockings, and a black belted wool coat, way beyond cheerful. Minnie began to see the humorous side of this visit.

Andy said, "Arthur and Lillian should be here by dinner. Nedra is making a leg of lamb. Is that all right? So many of Janet's friends nearly pass out at the idea of eating a poor little lamb. Annie, you look so much like your aunt Claire. Are these your bags? I've parked right out front. So easy. Newark is much more accessible than LaGuardia. Frank should be home when we get there. I thought when he got out of the oil business he would be home more. I thought weapons would have a more relaxed schedule." She took the keys out of her purse and left Minnie and Annie to wrestle their bags into the trunk of the Cadillac, yellow with a black convertible top.

The trip from the airport was a lesson in the steepness of the socioeconomic slope on the Eastern Seaboard. Seventeen miles, according to the odometer, that began in industrial wasteland, ended in pastures of heaven. The driveway was long, and heavily shaded. Andy pulled up in front of a sprawling contemporary house with overhanging eaves and tall, narrow windows. It looked like the Frank Lloyd Wright house in Mason City, though not quite as dark and heavy. Andy and Annie tromped right in, but Minnie stopped to gaze at the blooming forsythia. She saw over the hedge that the neighbors had both a tennis court and a swimming pool. She vowed not to look impressed. Nedra came out of the kitchen and said, "How are you, Miss Frederick? I put you in the upstairs guest room."

Minnie's outfit clashed with every item of furniture in the whole house, so she changed into plain old black trousers and a navy-blue sweater. She was coming down the staircase when Frank walked in. She hadn't seen him since Claire's wedding. He looked gaunt, she thought. When he took off his hat, he was bald over the top. She had only time to think that the shape of his head was quite attractive before he glanced her way and smiled.

He said, "I sense a lurker in the bushes."

"Just an old nanny goat chewing a few leaves."

He gave her a warm hug. Andy appeared with a glass in one hand and a cigarette in the other. She said, "She made Baked Alaska."

"Oh, I love that," said Minnie.

"The Bergstroms invented Baked Alaska back in Eidsvoll, in 1234," said Andy.

"Really?" exclaimed Minnie.

"No. But they called it a Norski omelette. My aunt always spread the sponge cake with lingonberry jam." She sipped her drink. Frank kissed her on the forehead and went to the back of the house.

Andy said, "Bourbon, Scotch, vodka, gin, Burgundy, beer?"

"What are you having?"

"Old Fashioned. Only one. Only one. Only one." Andy smiled.

Minnie said, "Maybe later."

Andy turned the ice in her glass with her finger, then said, "How is everyone?"

"Fine," said Minnie. "How do the boys like their military school?"

"Oh, they don't. That's the point. They had to go somewhere where the adults are one step ahead of them."

"But they're doing all right? That place has a good reputation for keeping the kids active and organized."

"I would have sent them to Summerhill, in England—"

"Good heavens," said Minnie.

"My psychiatrist knows A. S. Neill and respects him. He's withstood lots of unfair criticism. Frank wouldn't hear of it, though."

Minnie was glad of that.

Now Frank came in from the back of the house, just as the door opened to reveal Tina and, behind her, Janet. Tina was wearing black trousers and a shirt dyed black with woodcut flowers in blue and green. Over this, a cape, also in black, that fell to her knees. She was a petite version of Arthur—brown hair, brown eyes—but serious, not playful. Janet had all of a sudden matured. She was Joe as a girl—blue eyes, serious face, full lips, gentle mouth. She was wearing navy-surplus pants with bell bottoms and thirteen buttons, a black turtleneck sweater, and a navy-surplus peacoat. Her hair was nearly to her waist, dark blond now. Janet glanced around, and the look on her face said, as clear as a shout, "Oh, this place again. What a dump." It was the most beautiful house Minnie had ever seen.

Lillian bustled in, her hand on Arthur's arm, then came right over and put her arms around Minnie as if Minnie had weathered blizzards to get here. No one in Iowa knew quite what had happened to Arthur—some sort of nervous breakdown, some famous hospital, out for the summer, back in for a month in the late fall, out now. Always "not bad, improving," according to Rosanna, according to Lillian. Timmy's death, it would have been. Rosanna said, "I saw this coming," and Joe said, "Funny you never said a word about it." But when he gave Minnie a hug and Andy a peck on the cheek, Arthur was grinning in his usual way, pulling off his hat and gloves, already talking about a VW bus they had seen on the highway, painted like a landscape, green with flowers around the bottom, blue along the roof, faces painted on the windows. "When it passed us, the face in the back window was screaming," said Arthur. His hair was completely gray.

"Dad wanted to follow it into the Joyce Kilmer Plaza and trade the station wagon for it," said Tina.

"Straight up," said Arthur. "Kids thrown in, if need be."

Everyone laughed.

The lamb was delicious, and so were the au-gratin potatoes and the asparagus with Mornay sauce. Minnie and Annie had wolfed theirs down before Minnie noticed that everyone else was picking politely.

Janet took no lamb at all. Andy seemed to have begun another Old Fashioned.

Arthur and Lillian kept up the conversation, with occasional assists from Tina, who otherwise sat by Annie and whispered to her about rock bands. Annie preferred Creedence Clearwater Revival, but Tina was still loyal to the Stones. Annie said, "I really like your T-shirt." Tina said, "I made four of them. I can send you one." Please do, thought Minnie.

"Where are you girls going to college?" said Andy. Minnie wondered if she was mixed up—the kids were only sophomores.

"Rhode Island School of Design," said Tina.

"She's already working on her portfolio," said Lillian. "She's been working on her portfolio for ten years."

Annie didn't say anything.

Minnie said, "It's so funny that all of you were born within a couple of months of one another."

Andy said, "It's like a genetic experiment."

Frank said, "Boys take a while, no matter what."

Lillian said, "How tall are Richie and Michael now? Dean is six four. I don't know where that comes from."

Frank said, "I was six feet by the time I was their age. I think Richie is five ten and Michael is a little taller. Michael outweighs Richie by fifteen pounds, and it's all muscle. He's a true mesomorph. Richie's a bit of an ectomorph." He seemed to disapprove of that. Nedra appeared from the kitchen, saw all the food left on the platters, and put her hands on her hips. Minnie said, "My goodness, that was delicious. Thank you, Nedra." Nedra gave a nod.

Andy said, "She always makes an effort when Frank is going to be home."

Yikes, thought Minnie.

A tiny muscle beside Frank's right eye twitched.

Arthur said, "Yes, delicious." He had his arm across the back of Lillian's chair in a relaxed but possessive way, and, maybe without even knowing it, he glanced fondly at her. Well, everyone could see which marriage the old maid should envy.

But Minnie didn't envy any marriages at all. She still loved Frank in the way that ghosts inhabited abandoned houses, but if your job was to monitor the products of all sorts of marriages as they paraded through your office between September and June, then the whole institution of marriage became suspect, didn't it? Minnie, fifty, could see that little Billy Crocker resembled Mom's brother, who had come to no good, but the parents themselves were stunned, still had hope, still thought Minnie could turn the kid around by talking to him, giving him Saturday detention, making him do some extra work, or agreeing that more beatings might be the ticket. To Minnie, they were all bent twigs, for good or ill.

The Baked Alaska was more successful than the lamb. Nedra had piped the meringue in a neat spiral, then dusted it with brown sugar and burned it with real conviction. Inside, the strawberry ice cream was hard and delicious, and the chocolate cake was steeped in some sharp but tasty liqueur. They all cleaned their plates. In absolute desperation, Minnie got up from the table and went into the kitchen, where she insisted upon helping Nedra with the dishes.

When the dishes were done, the kitchen had been sterilized, and Nedra finally shooed her away, Minnie went back into the living room. The girls had gone upstairs; Andy had switched from whiskey to brandy. Frank's hands were on his knees, and he was gazing steadily at his wife, who was holding her drink in one hand and her cigarette in the other. The ash was an inch long and ready to fall on the carpet. Lillian and Arthur were sitting on the couch, thigh to thigh, arm to arm, shoulder to shoulder. When Minnie came in, they looked up at the same time. Andy was saying, "I'm talking general principles only. Nothing personal. But now that we know how chimps operate, we could structure our families like chimp families. Lillian, Lois, and I would have a group house, and we'd stay in there with the children. It would be warm, so we could go everywhere without shirts or bras, and the babies would cling to us, and take breast milk whenever they wanted to, until they were three years old, and then we would allow Frank, Joe, and Arthur, who had been displaying themselves and hunting together, to impregnate us, and then, when those babies were born, the earlier ones would give us a hand with them. That maybe could solve all of civilization's problems." She was slurring her "s"s and her "t"s. Frank glanced at Minnie. Minnie sat down and said, "What's the control?"

"Everyone else is the control," said Andy. "The whole fucking civilization."

Minnie didn't think she had ever heard that word in a living room before.

Arthur turned to Lillian and said, "I thought we did rear the kids like that. We were certainly trying to." Lillian smiled. Andy tossed off what was left in her glass, and let her head drop against the back of the chair. Arthur said, "At least Rosanna believes that we stuck to those principles."

"I'm for nature over nurture, myself," said Minnie. "You see that line of Dugans pass through your office, and you never believe in nurture again."

Frank smiled. "My first triumph."

"Bobby Dugan has not stinted himself on the reproductive side. Closest thing to a litter I ever saw in a homo sapiens."

Frank said, "Bobby Dugan used to bully us. I set a mousetrap for him in the school outhouse when I was two and a half."

"Oh, you were seven," said Minnie. "But it was enterprising. Anyway, he has eleven kids with two wives, and it's like they're stamped out by a press. They all have the same dimple in the chin and the same lopsided grin. And they all think they're going to get away with smoking in exactly the same spot on the high-school grounds."

"Nothing wrong with smoking." Andy's head was still resting on the back of the chair. "A pack of cigarettes is a little treasure, is what I think."

Frank got up and walked out the front door.

It was Lillian who took her up to bed, laughing and cajoling and talking about plans for tomorrow. Minnie sat with Arthur and waited, even though she would have liked to turn in. She said to Arthur, "You don't think this is a real Frank Lloyd Wright, do you?"

"Good imitation," said Arthur. "Wright, but you can actually live in it." He glanced up the stairs. Minnie saw that Lillian was in charge now. It was a poignant thought.

When Lillian came down, she said, "Minnie, you must be tired."

"I could go to bed. I suppose the girls are all right?"

Arthur said, "Tina may be giving Annie a tattoo."

"A tattoo!"

"Oh, you know. With markers. I have one." He pulled up his trouser leg to reveal a psychedelic snowflake on his knee. "This is from an earlier collection—say, two weeks ago. Now she's into snails."

Lillian said, "I'm waiting for flowers, but she says they're too 'static.'"

Both parents smiled fondly. Lillian said, "You should see her room. San Francisco by way of the French Riviera."

"How's Debbie?"

"Strict," said Arthur.

"She will graduate cum laude, I am sure. You know she is at Mount Holyoke, right?" said Lillian. "The boyfriend disappeared."

"As he was destined to do," said Arthur. "You could tell that he wasn't quite formed yet. I think she's going to go for an older man myself, preferably married."

Lillian shook her head, but affectionately.

"It's the Freudian thing to do," said Arthur.

"Speaking of that," said Lillian, leaning forward, "this psychiatrist of Andy's has a terrible reputation. Frank is beside himself. They have spent tens of thousands of dollars on this guy, and as you can see . . ."

Minnie knew that back home, at just about this point, someone would say, "I just don't understand those Easterners."

THERE WAS A balcony off Minnie's bedroom that she hadn't noticed earlier. Since she had her robe and slippers with her (in case she had to deal with some problem among the touring honors students after curfew), she bundled up and went outside to look at the view. She had been out there only a minute or so when another balcony door opened, and Frank appeared, still dressed. Minnie put her hand on her door, but Frank said, "Did you look to the right there?"

Minnie looked to the right. Nothing but trees. She said, "Is there a view?"

"No."

"Then why look to the right?"

"Just to start the conversation."

Minnie laughed.

"How are you?"

Minnie wrapped her robe a little more tightly, then said, "Could be worse."

"Wish I could say the same."

"Oh goodness, Frankie. You have a beautiful house, and I read

about you and your innovative weapons company, was that it, in the
paper, and Richie and Michael—"

"Are safely confined for the moment."

"Rosanna showed me their school pictures. They are very handsome boys."

"Worse news."

"You were a very handsome boy."

"You told me so."

"Me and everyone else."

Frank leaned his elbows on the railing and stared out over the
greenery. As always, he didn't seem to feel the cold. Finally, he said,
"Did your dad whip you?"

"No. My dad was reserved, as they say, and he didn't even drink in
the old days, hard as that is to believe. My mother used the flat of her
hand every so often, but only on our behinds. My grandfather had a
riding crop for all his boys. I know Walter whipped you."

"By the time the others came along, he realized it was ineffective.
I never whipped the boys, but now I wonder if I should have. I was
in Caracas once when Richie nailed Michael on the head with a hammer. Knocked him out cold. I found out a year later."

"What would you have done?"

"I have no idea. I was kind of glad not to be involved."

Minnie didn't say anything. Frank put his arm around her shoulders. She had only time to be surprised before he kissed her smack on
the lips, and then, when she could not help sort of softening through
her whole body, he put his arms around her. She felt her scalp prickle,
and she had a profound sense of being taken by surprise, but that was
all. She bent her knees and slipped out of his embrace.

FRANK HAD NOT EXPECTED her to be receptive—the last time he
kissed her was forty years ago, in the cloakroom at the school, as she
was hanging her plaid coat on her hook. He had taken her by surprise then, too. Probably that was the point, since Minnie had always
seemed to be a half-step ahead of him. He said, "I'm sorry." It was the
appropriate thing to say.

" 'I apologize,' or 'I regret'?"

"Apologize. I won't regret unless you hold it against me."

"I don't hold it against you."

But she stepped out of reach. Frank said, "You can say it's chilly and go back inside." He was being quite a nice person, he thought.

"I might. But not if you want to talk."

Why would this suggestion take him aback? But, then, who did he ever talk to, and what about? Lately, shooting differently shaped bullets into water and calculating how quickly they lost forward motion. The men he talked to about this had no names and no personalities. He said, "I don't believe I know how to talk."

Minnie said, "Frankie, you seem sad."

"Already? I've hardly said anything."

"Well, I was watching you at dinner and afterward."

"I thought all eyes were on my wife."

"Yours were."

He said, "You know what she needs? She needs to drive a prairie schooner with a team of oxen across Colorado and into the Rockies, where she needs to save the party of settlers from three grizzly bears and a long winter." He laughed at the thought.

"This is a lovely neighborhood."

"I told Andy to find something around here. She did. One hundred percent class. Then she had it decorated and redid the grounds. But it's done. What now? Her brother is the same way—born to own a large farm on the North Dakota prairie, but he missed his moment, so he trains every child he meets for the Winter Olympics. She goes to her therapist." He was talking pretty well now, he thought.

There was a silence; then Minnie said, "Maybe that's not working."

He pivoted toward her. "Well, damn me, Min, it's not working. The shrink is a creep who puts it to her every time she decides maybe she needs some other form of treatment."

"Puts it to her?"

"Fucks her."

Minnie looked shocked.

Frank said, "I believe he's calling it Kama therapy. It's not very common in New Jersey. What are they reading these days? Oh, *Nature, Man and Woman*. They finished *The Psychedelic Experience*."

"She took LSD?"

"She says that he took LSD; she just pretended. It was a tiny yellow pill, and she pushed it under the radiator for any passing mouse.

Arthur told me his agency is crawling with people who took LSD and lived to tell the tale. No one is impressed by LSD anymore, Minnie." Then he said, "But that's what I mean! Look at her. She's healthy as an ox, and looks about thirty-five! She has no vocation and no outlet, and the house has central heating, so what's there to do with her-self?" Frank had expressed none of this stuff, ever, especially not to Andy. Of course, he was hardly ever alone with Andy, since the door between their rooms was always locked.

"She said that you play golf."

"Golf is infinitely boring." He reached out and took her hand. It was cold. He said, "What do you do?"

"For fun?"

"Of course."

"I can't think of anything."

"Oh, Min!"

She said, "Now I feel backward. Let's see. Lois and I have a lot of flowers in the garden. They're all perennials, though. We ponder them and discuss them. And we smell them—jonquils, lilies of the valley. Your mother's lilacs are amazing. I guess you never come out during lilac season, but it's like a canopy. You can smell them at our house. I clean things. Take stuff to the church and the Salvation Army. I listen to kids talk. Kids are funny. These days, my student teachers are like kids to me, so they're funny, too. I read books. Joe and your mom watch TV, but Lois doesn't have time, and I'm not that inter-ested." Her eyebrows lifted. She said, "Listen to me. I do nothing for fun!"

And then he kissed her again. This time he kissed for real, because he suddenly, after all these years—was it forty-five now?—appreciated her. And she felt it. She didn't slip away. There was no alarm. It was a nice kiss, an appreciative kiss. When it was over, she put her arm around his waist and laid her head briefly on his shoulder; then she kissed him on the cheek and went into her room.

FRANK SAT UP and looked at the clock. It was almost three. He had dropped off once, and dreamt of, not the real Lydia, but a short woman in heels whom he identified as Lydia. She was walking down the street—a street in London, not New York. That was all he could remember. He was hot. He threw off the covers, then got up to take a piss.

Wide awake. There was something disquieting about having Minnie, Andy, and Lydia in the same house. He reached for a Kleenex from the box on the lower shelf of his bedside table and blew his nose.

Frank sensed a presence when he pushed on the swinging door, but whoever was sitting at the kitchen table hadn't even turned on the light above the range. Frank paused. It was Arthur. His chair pushed back from the table, Arthur was resting his forearms on his thighs and looking straight ahead, neither up nor down. His head didn't turn when Frank came in. Frank assumed he was on some sort of drug. He said, "Arthur." Frank's eyes now adjusted completely to the darkness. He said, "Can I do something for you?"

"Not that I know of," murmured Arthur.

"Are you all right? Is Lillian all right?"

Arthur didn't answer. Frank pulled out a chair and sat down. The fact was, he almost never came into his own kitchen; Nedra served every meal, in either the dining room or the breakfast room. If Arthur were to ask him for something, he would be hard put to find it. Frank cleared his throat, then said, "You'll like what I did all last week. I watched a couple of guys shoot projectiles of various shapes into tanks of water. They were testing their calculations of how quickly the projectiles slowed and stopped. I enjoyed it. They asked me to estimate, and I was always wrong. Water is a brick wall, if you're a projectile."

Arthur said nothing.

Frank got comfortable, and said, "Theoretically, they told me that you could shape the tip of the projectile so that it created a vacuum just in front of it as it moved. Theoretically, it could get faster and faster." He didn't ask whether Arthur already knew this. The rumor was that the Soviets were quite advanced on this very project; he half expected Arthur to nod, or to let his gaze flicker some acknowledgment, but again there was nothing. He said, "Supersonic."

Finally, Arthur yawned and looked at Frank. In the day he looked fine, but right now, in this light, he looked cadaverous. How old was he? thought Frank. Frank said, "Arthur, you're making me think about dead people."

And Arthur laughed.

As always, his laugh was contagious, and so Frank laughed, too.

"Sorry," said Arthur. "I was half asleep. I know it didn't look like it. It never does, but I cultivated that skill in boarding school. It's been a valuable trick."

"Spoken like a bureaucrat," said Frank, "but why did you get up?"

"Why did you get up?"

"Too many women in the house. Makes me nervous."

"Six women under one roof is fine with me," said Arthur. "By the way, I like what you've done with the entry. The slate floor. It's appropriate to the style of the house. The chandelier is interesting."

"Eighteen bulbs," said Frank.

"Who changes them? It must be twelve feet off the floor."

"It's on a pulley. It lowers."

"I like that," said Arthur.

For years, Frank had cultivated indifference to personal concerns. If someone had a complaint, Frank thought, it was that person's job to express it, but, maybe because of the influence of Minnie, he now said, "How are you? Are you all right?"

"That's an interesting question," said Arthur. "I'm probably better than I've ever been."

"What have they got you doing?"

"Divulging top-secret information."

"Pardon me?" said Frank.

"Well, I was so secretive for so long that now, when I talk to news reporters, they think I've actually told them something, because, of course, we only do it in long walks in Rock Creek Park, or in garages, where whatever we say is broken up by the sound of revving engines."

"Are you teasing me?"

"No. Even the KGB does PR. You can only say 'no comment' so many times, because 'no comment' means 'yes.'"

Frank leaned forward. "But why you?"

Arthur shrugged. "What do I know?"

"You've been there since the beginning. You knew about everything."

"I thought I knew a few things," said Arthur. "But I don't know them anymore."

Shock treatments. A chill ran up Frank's spine.

HENRY OPENED the door of his office on the second knock. In his first office hours of the fall, he expected kids either wanting in or wanting out of one of the three classes he was teaching. Instead, there was a pleasant-looking young man carrying a briefcase, smiling and holding out an envelope. The envelope had Henry's name on it in Gothic letters. He took it, and opened it.

> My dear boy,
>   Please note the bearer of this missive. He is a brilliant student of mine named Philip Cross who has taken it into his head, now that your poofters have decided to riot and make their presence felt, to try his luck in the U.S. He is about to enroll in that monument to capitalism, the University of Chicago, in literary criticism. Please do not discuss any work of literature with him, as you will not understand a word he says, and it will lower your estimation of our educational system. He is, however, a young man of exceptional grace and intelligence, and I told him that you will introduce him to the mid-continental wilderness, as you so ably introduced me. I have cultivated him assiduously and I defy you to uncover his dialect roots. In addition, he is an excellent chef. Suet is his middle name.
>   I am, as always, your devoted,
>   Basil

Henry said, "Philip. Do come in." He stepped back, and this young man (Henry thought, no more than twenty-one, no taller than five nine, but neatly made) stepped across the threshold. Henry said, "U of Chicago. Good Lord. It's a jungle down there."

Philip smiled, opened his mouth, and came out with the most beautiful speaking voice Henry had ever heard, as vibrant, deep, and rounded as a human voice could be. Henry said, "I'm sorry. What did you say?"

Philip said, "It does seem a different world than this campus, which is very open."

"Northwestern is a little bit of Iowa right beside Lake Michigan. It came first, you know, before the town. We take an Iowa approach in many things—for example, we approach student unrest by wondering why the students are unhappy. Down there, they just expel you."

"Is that a warning?" said Philip.

"Are you restless?" said Henry.

"Basil would say so," said Philip. He sat down on the windowsill.

So—the young man called his professor "Basil." Henry said, "His letter indicates that I am not to discuss literature with you, so what else are you interested in?"

"How do you feel about these bouts of campus—"

Henry waited to hear what word he would use—"unrest"? "silliness"? "brutality"? Henry had heard dozens of words applied. His aunt Eloise, who knew the U of Chicago catalyst, Marlene Dixon, slightly and said that she was "well meaning but doctrinaire," always talked about "campus preliminaries." Philip said—"rebellions."

That was nicely limiting, but respectful. He said, "Ask me in ten years. I have no idea. I suppose I am sympathetic, but from a distance. As a medievalist, I am not asked to do teach-ins, but I would if I could think of something to teach. The fate of the Cathars is not a heartening precedent. I think the military draft has been God's gift to the left."

Philip smiled. "I didn't realize God gave gifts to the left, or that those gifts were accepted."

Oh, he is a charming boy, thought Henry, and Basil was right—he might have been born at the BBC, his pronunciation was so perfect and smooth.

Just then there was a knock, and when he opened the door, Henry saw Marcy Grant, his tallest student, decked out as usual in her giant army-surplus pants held up by a string, her glasses sporting a piece of masking tape, her hair a tangle. She peered at Henry and said, "Oh, Professor Langdon," then looked around. She smiled her brilliant smile. Someday she would stand up straight and discover that she was a lovely woman. "That's me," said Henry.

"I forgot to sign up for the history-of-the-language course, but I thought I had. I already wrote my first paper over the summer." She held out some typed pages. Henry knew they would be excellent. He took them, set them on the bookcase beside the door, and said, "Come in, I'll give you a note."

She squinted at him, then walked through the door. Philip's response to Marcy wasn't even curiosity, though whether that was because Marcy was female or because she was a mess, Henry couldn't tell. Marcy's response to Philip, though, was gratifying. Her mouth dropped open, and she kept glancing at him while Henry wrote the note to the registrar. Henry said, "Marcy, this is Philip Cross. He's come over from England to do grad work at Chicago. Philip, my excellent but disorganized student Marcy Grant."

Marcy exhibited the good manners her Wisconsin mother had impressed upon her—how very nice to meet you, hope you have a good time—but she could go no further. Philip gave her his fingertips and said, "You are very kind," as if Marcy could now be quietly executed and removed from the company of the civilized. Henry handed her the note and herded her toward the corridor. Henry eased back into the office and closed the door.

Philip had picked up Henry's monograph, which was sitting on the windowsill, *Dialectical Variations in Anglo-Saxon Epic Poetry,* Yale University Press, unreviewed in any American publication, but embraced by two scholars at Cambridge, one at Oxford, and his mother, Rosanna Vogel Langdon. Henry said, "It could keep you up at night."

Now the expected knock came, and then Rick Kingsford pushed the door open, calling, "You here, Doc? Oh, hi. How are ya?"

Henry said, "I'm fine, Rick. How are you?"

"Well, I had this cough, but it's not so bad today. I thought I was gonna havta go to the infirmary, but not yet." Rick was an enthusiastic student of Old English. He planned to do a translation of "The Seafarer," with notes, as his thesis. He also carried a thermometer with him at all times and refused to shake hands. When he saw Philip, he recoiled slightly.

"What can I do for you, Rick?" Out of the corner of his eye, he saw that Philip was getting bored.

"I need a form you got, for the thesis credit."

"Oh, I do have that," said Henry. "Let's see."

Philip stood up and stretched, then looked out the window. Henry opened the top drawer of his filing cabinet and began to go through the folders.

Rick, looking over his shoulder, said, "That's it, Doc."

"Oh, good. Is that all you—"

"Hell, no! I mean, I was thinking I was going to do something like free verse; then, the other night, I thought obviously iambic pentameter, but now I'm not so sure. We could have echoes of Ibsen or something."

Philip was at the door, his hand on the knob. Rick sat down in the chair beside the desk and wiggled around, making himself comfortable. "The words would be English, but the meter would evoke the North, you know? I'm thinking of my guy—let's say his name is Thor—sailing almost to the Arctic Circle. It's dark, it's cold. No Latin-derived words, or, God, Norman French—you don't want that. Well, maybe a few, but carefully se—"

"Just a minute, Rick, okay?"

As a known campus bachelor, Henry had to be careful, but he did step one step toward Philip.

Their gazes locked. Henry said, "Let me know if you need anything." Then, "And give my best to Basil if you write."

"Ta-ta!" said Philip.

The door closed behind him.

"Ta-ta?" exclaimed Rick.

"A bit of slang that could come from Swahili, oddly enough. Now, let's get on with it, what do you say?" He sounded put out, and Rick looked alarmed.

At dusk, when he was walking home from the university, feeling not quite down but not quite up, thinking that the sixteen weeks of classes just now commencing was a long stretch of talking and reading, he sneezed and put his hand into his jacket pocket for his handkerchief. Instead of his handkerchief, which he now remembered leaving on the corner of his desk, he pulled out a slip of paper. It read, "Philip +, 312-678-3456." Henry immediately felt much better.

"YOU LOOK SO GREAT," said Ruth.

"Don't say that," said Claire. They were having breakfast at the pancake house, which they did every Monday morning. She had her turkey and a dozen eggs in the car, but the temperature was in the forties—she didn't think the eggs would freeze. Paul wanted a "private Thanksgiving, just us," but the smallest turkey she'd found was eighteen pounds. She and Ruth didn't have much in common anymore, but they still referred to each other as "best friends." Bradley was sitting quietly on the seat between Claire and the wall. He was holding his blueberry muffin, staring at it, turning it, and taking bites. He was concentrating. Claire smoothed his hair.

"Why not?"

"Because whenever Paul says that it's because I'm pregnant again."

Ruth laughed, but then said, "You don't look . . ."

"No." Then, "Not yet." Claire knew this was a sensitive subject, and was sorry she hadn't thought before saying what she did. She'd been taking the Pill for two months now, and she knew she had put on at least five pounds. She was also wearing contact lenses—she told everyone (including Paul) that that was Paul's idea. It had been, at one point, but he had sort of forgotten about it. Brad looked up at her. Claire said, "That's good, BB. You keep eating that. You need that."

Brad nodded.

"He looks healthy," said Ruth. "He ate the piece of sausage."

"My mother says *she* never produced a picky eater."

"I wish I'd been a picky eater," said Ruth. "We heard so much about the starving Armenians that we had the clean-platter club, not the clean-plate club. You have such cute boys," said Ruth.

"I do," said Claire. This was how she was to be punished for veering toward a topic that had become taboo between them, the fact that Ruth had been married now for two years to Carl and still had no children. Not even a miscarriage. She would soon be thirty-one; ten years ago, she had planned to have had her own two by this time. Nor was she a member of the Wakonda Country Club, which Paul had joined the previous summer—three-thousand-dollar initiation fee, one-thousand-a-year membership. Claire took Ruth there as often as she wanted, but Carl, a builder, wouldn't go. Carl was good-looking, as nice as pie, and could fix anything (Claire hired him whenever she could get him), but playing golf and tennis, swimming in a pool, and eating in a formal dining room with a tie on were not for Carl.

Ruth sighed. "I always wanted three."

Ruth had a way of recasting her old ideas, making them more ambitious rather than less as they got more unattainable. "Sweetie," said Claire firmly, "it can still happen."

Ruth's eyebrows dipped, and she put her fingers over her mouth. Brad got onto his knees and set the remains of his muffin on his plate, then gazed at the orange slice. Claire picked it up, tasted it, put it back on the plate, and said, "You can eat it. It's a sweet one."

Brad shook his head.

Ruth said, "Does he like French toast? I haven't touched this piece." She turned her plate toward Claire, and Claire picked up the yellow triangle with Brad's fork, set it on his plate, then cut it into pieces. She handed the fork to Brad. He said, "Wile Ting."

Claire said, "The book is in the car. We'll read it later. In the car is where the wild things are." Brad grinned.

But it was she who was the wild thing, wasn't it? thought Claire. There were four stages of wildness: Stage one was being married and falling silently in love with a young and charming man, but doing nothing. Stage two was doing something in the hope of trading your bossy, dissatisfied husband for the beloved young charmer; stage three was allowing the lithe physique and the merry nature of the charmer to occupy your every thought. Stage four was not caring, just acting. She was at stage three. If her analysis was correct, then she was a wild thing, but she didn't feel wild, only that she was sitting inside the cage with the door open, and that was enough for now.

Brad successfully forked the first bit of French toast into his mouth, and Ruth said, "Good boy. Yummy." He stabbed at the second.

"You are a good boy," said Claire. She glanced at her watch. "Time to pick up Gray at nursery school. I've got fifteen minutes."

"The streets are pretty clear. But it's only a few blocks from here. Why don't I stay with Brad, and you can bring Gray back here?"

Claire guided Brad's fork just a bit, and he got the third piece. He seemed to be enjoying it. She said, "I'll do that. Do you mind?"

Ruth shook her head. Her look was so sad, though, that Claire felt tears coming when she stood up from the booth. Yes, thought Claire, I deserve to have it all blow up, because obviously I do not value what I should. Why this was, she did not know. It was right out of *Madame Bovary.*

1970

IT WAS ONE THING to break your foot when you were expecting
things to continue to disintegrate, as she did in her own house,
where she now held both stair railings when she went up and down,
but how could you stumble on a single step at Younkers when you
were returning a tablecloth your daughter-in-law had given you for
Christmas, and fall down so that they practically carried you out, and
you went to the hospital, and your foot was broken? So Rosanna was
staying with Claire until she could get around.

Her room was off the kitchen. She was stuck there, either in her
bed (very comfortable) or in the easy chair Claire moved in for her. It
took her three days to start covering her ears every time Paul talked.
If she could have gotten up and closed the door, she would have.

"These eggs are overdone. Did you boil them by the timer? Are
you sure? Oh, I'll eat them anyway. Don't worry about it. It's fine. I'll
just have toast. The underside of the toast is too dark. Just one more
piece, and watch it this time. Only a little butter. Yes, that's enough.
Well, just a smidgen more. I guess I'm not hungry after all." How
Paul could have possibly reminded Claire of Walter, Rosanna could
not imagine.

Then: "What's the temperature again? No, the outside temperature. Sixteen! Okay, I think Brad needs both the hat and the scarf,
and be sure his mittens are pulled up *under* his sleeves, and then his

sleeves pulled down. There was a child Herb Barker saw last week, his feet were frostbitten. Grayson, is your sweater buttoned? Show me! That's a good boy. Sixteen degrees is sixteen below freezing. Can you count to sixteen? No, don't use your fingers. Good boy."

Rosanna could have ascended on billows of rage at the sound of his voice, so she scrunched down under the covers and put her fingers in her ears; she must have dozed off, because, the next thing she knew, Claire was standing over her, saying, "Are you hungry, Mama? I have your breakfast."

Claire looked neat and clean, and she stood there like one of those maids no one in Iowa had, ready to obey orders.

It was as bad at supper—dinner, Paul called it. Claire was sent to get this and that: Gray dropped his fork, he needed a clean one; Brad's bib was dirty from lunch; could she heat up the green beans, they were cold; this was butter; really, margarine was better. Chew each bite twenty times, Gray; don't talk while eating, you could choke; you know what "choke" means? Get something caught in your throat and not be able to breathe—very dangerous. Brad, this is a bean. Say "bean"! A bean is very nutritious. Gray, say "nutritious"! That means "good for you." Sit straight up in your chair. If you loll back, you are more likely to choke. That's a good boy.

Claire said nothing. Rosanna imagined her sitting at her end of the table, eating between trips to the kitchen (Rosanna could hear her footsteps), smiling like she didn't have a thought in her head, and so, the next day, Rosanna called Minnie and said, "Anything is better than this." Minnie came and picked her up and took her home, where Joe set a bed up in the living room right across from the television. But she didn't turn it on—she was grateful for every single moment of silence.

ANDY THOUGHT she had had a good session with Dr. Smith—just talking, very calm, a few fake dreams. They hadn't practiced any Kama therapy in several weeks, because Dr. Smith was too busy with what he was writing to concentrate. And then the drive home was quite pleasant. When she pulled into the garage, she saw that both Frank's and Nedra's cars were gone, and she would be alone—also something to look forward to. She went up to her room, changed into shorts (it was quite warm for May), and entered the kitchen as the phone rang.

Normally, she would not have picked up, but she wasn't thinking, and she was all the more sorry that she had when she heard Janet's breathless voice. "I wanted to tell you before you heard on the news."

"Heard what on the news?"

"We're striking," said Janet. "We're not going to any classes, and I'm taking incompletes in all my courses. But also we're marching on Washington. That's the part you might see on the news. I could end up in jail. You don't have to bail me out. I would rather stay."

Andy felt her good mood slip away. She almost hung up right there, but then she said, sharply, "I don't understand this at all. What are you protesting, Janet?"

"The murders at Kent State. Those kids were nowhere near the National Guard, and they were completely unarmed."

Andy never watched the news, and she had tossed the morning paper on the hall table without looking at it. It wasn't the first time she was maybe the last person in the United States to know about something—Dr. Smith never discussed "ephemeralities." But Frank and Janet found her ignorance annoying, so Andy said, "Such a sad thing."

"It's worse than sad, Mom! Though Eileen told me her mom said those kids deserved what they got. Can you believe that? She's a terrible Nixon-supporter. Eileen might disinherit herself."

Andy didn't know who Eileen was, either. She said, "Unarmed people who get shot never deserve it." However, Andy thought, if they had any sense, they would expect it.

"Will you let me stay in jail if they arrest me?"

"Well, of course. But try not to get arrested."

"I don't know what to try," said Janet. "Where's Dad?"

"He's in Frankfurt." That, she made up.

There was a pause, and Andy began, "Are you—" But Janet had hung up. She'd meant to ask what Janet intended to do for the summer.

She washed her hands at the kitchen sink and plugged in the coffeemaker. She came upon Nedra's doughnut stash, and she looked at the doughnuts—pink, chocolate, maple—for three or four moments before putting them back where she found them. She looked out the back door at the lawn, which needed cutting. On the hall table, the paper was folded together. She carried it into the kitchen. There was the boy, flat on his stomach, his head turned away, his feet flopped to one side, his arm folded under his chest. It could be any boy, any boy at all. Andy put her hand over the picture and then took it away. There was the girl, her arms out, kneeling over the boy, her mouth open in a scream. Andy put her hand over the picture again. There was no reason in the world for this picture to affect her, Andy. It was not her business, and anyway, she was inured to death, was she not? Dr. Smith said she was the least in touch with her feelings of anyone he had ever met; just look at the way she kept coming back to the murder of the woman she had never met, but skated over Tim's death, the death of the darling boy, as if she didn't care. Perhaps she had no feelings beyond nerve endings. Was that possible? But this picture . . . She took her hand away again, and stared. Moments before, that boy had been alive. Now he was dead. Someone his own age had shot him. Andy stared at the picture. She did not read the article—no need for that.

THE FIRST TIME, Claire was at Hy-Vee, beginning her Saturday's shopping. She ran into Dr. Sadler in cereal (he was buying Frosted Flakes, which Paul wouldn't allow in the house). Yes, he had been lightly flirting with her for years by now, but maybe he had never expected to get beyond that. He gave her a kiss on the cheek, which, by turning her head, she transformed into a kiss on the lips, and a passionate one. They left their carts in cereal and went straight to his house, four blocks away. She was home two hours later with her groceries and the news that she hadn't been able to find any lamps to match the new couch—she'd looked everywhere. Paul related all the things he had done with Gray and Brad in her absence, not a flicker of suspicion, and it went like that for seven weeks, as if a slot had opened up in the normal progression of time that was dedicated to the advancement of their affair.

Claire had no shame, no remorse, no fear. Dr. Sadler was in charge of those emotions. Week by week, date by date, he got more tormented and more handsome. The first time seemed like a game they were both playing—hide and seek, don't let the grown-ups know.

They laughed most of the time—that he climaxed within a minute was hilarious, that they did it again and the corner of the contour sheet popped off with the violence of their lovemaking was wonderful. He admired Claire, her patience and her good nature, and her eyes, especially since she'd gotten the contacts—they were beautiful, riveting, such a strange color, not exactly brown, a cat's eyes; he wanted her to keep them open while they were making love. He was wonderful to look at also—the sunlight flickering over his triceps, the shadows of his ribs, the indentation along the side of his gluteal muscles. When they were finished making love, he gave her treats in bed—leftover mu-shu pork, Popsicles, once a mai tai, which she'd never had before (Paul didn't allow food out of the kitchen, he was suspicious of leftovers, and he would not go to a Chinese restaurant). What did Claire want to do? Dr. Sadler did it. Just kiss? He would kiss her a thousand times. Just let her touch it and look at it? He smiled while she explored. He had no inhibitions—he thought getting rid of those was what medical school was for—but, more than that, he was curious, curious about her. In her dating life, she had never met a man who was curious about her, and over the seven years of their marriage, Paul had grown suspicious of her inner life, not curious about it. If she said what she wanted for breakfast, for example, he met every response with an objection: if she wanted pancakes, eggs were more nutritious; if she wanted eggs, waffles would be a change.

After a couple of weeks, he said how could this go on, but of course it had to, he was only joking. He began to embrace her very tightly, as if they were about to part, but they did not part. Each lovemaking after that was more frantic. He never said, "I love you," but he did say, "You're adorable," "I've never met anyone like you," "I can't stay away from you," "I had no idea just looking at you," "You're killing me." Claire floated along, every desire satisfied before she imagined it. Week six, he told Paul he was leaving in a month—going into practice with his younger brother in Kansas City. Dr. William Sadler specialized in podiatry, had served his internship at the University of Texas. Paul sat his partner down and told him frankly that ENT and podiatry made no sense together, and that starting from nothing in a place they didn't know was insane—what in the world was he thinking? A week after that, he was gone from his house, from the office, from Hy-Vee, his telephone disconnected, his front step piled with newspapers and grocery-store flyers. She knew this because she drove by no matter where she was intending to go. She even parked and went into the house—the door was unlocked. A week later, a "For Sale" sign appeared on the lawn, and then she kept her eye out for the listing—"Two bedroom bungalow, single story, 1½ baths, very good condition, $36,000."

He didn't have to write or call. There was no mystery: he had informed her of every shift in his state of mind, every new level of anxiety, every conviction that he had committed an impossible betrayal that could not go on. Claire was not unhappy; he was so present in her mind that he hardly seemed gone at all. Another two weeks passed; she was not pregnant. And so that was that.

RICHIE FIGURED they were looking for him by now. He had maybe one day, and so he was going to make the best of it by joining the army. Once you were in the army, they couldn't get you back. He was seventeen. He had been to military school for years now. Whatever that thing was about parental consent, well, he would deal with that if they realized the letter he'd given them was a forgery.

And he looked eighteen. Michael was still bigger than he was, but not much: six three, 170 versus six three and a half, 175. If he caught Michael unawares, he could still knock him down, but he hadn't done that in a year. Now they mostly ignored each other. Michael liked the Kinks; Richie liked Black Sabbath. That was all a person needed to know. Anyway, now he was in Boston, and here was the bus that was taking him to where he would go through the physical and the tests, whatever they were. He was the first to get on, and he walked to the back and sat down.

It was a nice July day, sunny but damp, a Boston day, not like that armpit in the Midwest where they sweated all day and night. It was a week since he'd walked out of the job that his dad got him, painting at a "Country Club," though it didn't look very exclusive to Richie. They painted green some days, and they painted white other days, and the painters talked about whorehouses and tattoos. Now Richie stared out the window at guys in uniforms telling the recruits to move it, get going. Finally, the sergeant followed the last guy onto the bus, and the door started to close. One of the draftees jumped out of his seat and said, "We need to vote on that."

The sergeant said, "Sit down!"

The kid didn't sit down. In fact, Richie saw, the kid was older than the sergeant. He said, "America is still a democracy. This bus will move when the people have decided it will move. Men!" He turned toward the guys in the seats. "Everyone who wants the door to close, say aye!"

Richie shouted, "Aye!" There were maybe five or six ayes.

"No?"

"*Noo!*" the whole bus erupted.

The kid said, "I think we need to debate this! Parliamentary procedures apply!"

The sergeant said, "Sit down."

The kid went right up to him and put his arm around the sergeant's waist and pushed into him slightly. He maybe outweighed the sergeant by twenty pounds. He said in a calm voice, "Let's have a debate, all right?" He kept his arm around the sergeant, kept pushing into him, until the sergeant backed toward the driver and shrugged. The debate about closing the door, and then about driving away, lasted twenty minutes. Richie participated. He made the case against blocking traffic.

When the sergeant sat down, the kid sat down right beside him. It was clear who was the boss. When the bus pulled up at the facility, the door opened, and an older man got on, also a sergeant, but a lifer. The bus went dead quiet. This sergeant handed out cards and pencils—they had to write down their names, birth dates, and some other information. When everyone just sat there, the sergeant pretended to get mad and said, "Move it!"

The kid stood up.

"Sit down!" shouted the sergeant.

The kid said, "It is moved by the sergeant here that I sit down. Second the motion?"

A hand went up.

"What the—"

"All in favor?"

A few ayes. Not Richie—Richie wanted to see what might happen.

"All opposed?"

The bus roared.

The sergeant shouted, "Son, if you don't sit down, I'll sit you down!"

The kid said, "Motion made to sit me down by force. Second?"

A hand went up.

"All in favor?"

As everyone in the bus shouted "Aye!" the sergeant pushed the kid into his seat. But he popped up to exclaim, "Motion carried!" Everyone laughed.

Now they scribbled, but when the sergeant told them to pass their pencils forward, they all threw their pencils right at him—he had to duck. By the time they had debated and voted for getting off the bus, even he looked a little intimidated, though red-faced and angry. Richie didn't know what to think.

Once inside the building, they were told to line up. Richie suspected that he was between two guys who knew each other, though they didn't look at or talk to each other. For a while, things went along—no debates or votes. The "chairman" of the bus was five guys ahead of Richie, and the only thing he did was try to engage every doctor or orderly he met in conversation. Was Dr. So-and-So aware that 68 percent of American voters no longer favored the war in Vietnam? How did Dr. This-and-That personally feel about the invasion of Cambodia? Had Dr. Up-and-Down known Lieutenant Calley personally, and was he present for the My Lai massacre? (This last was said in a smooth and friendly voice.) "Keep it moving!" was all the army people said. But it moved very slowly, because it seemed like it took everyone in the line at least a minute to unlace each shoe and unbutton each button. Richie thought that the army personnel were pretty patient.

They came to a large room and were told to strip down to their underwear, put their clothes into a basket, and stay in line. It was then that he saw that the kid in front of him had painted black skulls with red eyes on his chest and his back, with the words "US Army" across his collarbones. The kid behind him had a bomb blast on his back.

The line moved, and the doctors kept their eyes down. The "chairman," still five ahead, had a map of Cambodia on his back and the words "Next stop, Peking." They shuffled along very slowly. At one point, the front group paused. Richie could see the first guy come to a doctor sitting on a stool. He turned his head to the right and coughed, then to the left and coughed. He stood there. A few minutes later, when Richie got a better view, he saw that each kid was dropping his pants, and the doctor was sticking his finger up into the kid's scrotum. They shuffled forward.

Finally, the "chairman" came to the doctor sitting on the stool. The doctor's assistant muttered something, and the chairman said, "Please repeat your request."

"Take your pants down!"

"Pardon? Je ne comprends pas."

The doctor and his assistant exchanged a glance, and then the doctor said, *"Baissez votre slip. Tout de suite."* And the kid dropped his pants. Everyone crowded close to have a look. Painted on his chest was an arrow pointing downward, and affixed to the tip of his cock was a photograph cut from a magazine, of President Nixon. Everyone laughed, and even the doctor cracked a tiny smile.

Richie had been told that processing would take a couple of hours, but it was midafternoon by the time they were back on the bus—so it had taken six hours and fifteen minutes. He was tired, and he was glad that the Yippies, because that's what they were, let the bus go back into town. It dropped them at the recruiting office. Richie didn't quite know what to do next. He had thought, somehow, that the back door of the facility would open onto a platform, and all the ones who'd passed their physicals would get on a train or a bus to Fort Dix. From there he would call home and tell them what he'd done. But now he was in Boston, not far from Kenmore Square, with some change in his pocket, and he was seventeen years old, and he didn't know what to do.

DEBBIE DIDN'T GO to Kenmore Square very often. Normally she shopped at Coolidge Corner and enjoyed herself in Cambridge—her new boyfriend went to Harvard Business School, and he did seem to remember her last name and to think she was pretty and fun. He respected her principles. He was from Lincoln, Nebraska, where, apparently, they also had principles, and thought Iowans were a little untrustworthy. He made Debbie laugh.

But Debbie's dentist's office was right across from those shops on Beacon Street. She was standing in front of the case, looking at the sausage, when a guy bumped her, and she looked up to scowl at him. She could have sworn it was her cousin Richie, though taller and without Michael, which never happened. She put aside the thought, but then he ordered a ham sandwich, and the voice was Richie's, too. Richie's and Uncle Frank's. When he took his sandwich and went to pay, she followed him. He couldn't have walked more like Uncle Frank, so, when he was out on the street, she said, "Richie!" and he spun around.

He hugged her. He had never hugged her since he was about four years old and told to do so. He had a beautiful grin, and Debbie had to admit she was a little dazzled. It was when he shoved the whole second half of his sandwich into his mouth at once that she realized he was starving, and not in Boston on a school trip or something. She adopted her best teacherly demeanor (at least, it worked with the eighth-graders she was teaching now) and said, "Okay, Richie, what is going on here?" and as they hiked up Beacon Street toward Coolidge Corner, he told her the whole story about walking away from his job, coming to Boston, joining the army, falling into a whirlpool of Yippies.

"No one has any idea where you are?"

"I don't know."

This sounded sullen.

"Where have you been staying?"

"I had some money, because I got paid Friday. It was a hotel on Copley Square. But I ran out of money, so I checked out of that hotel. I thought I'd be in the army by now, but they just let us all go, even the non-Yippies, because I guess they were fed up."

At her place, she called her mom first, but there was no answer—it was five-thirty; maybe they were outside. Then, with Richie's permission, she called Aunt Andy, but no answer there, either. Richie said, "What day is it?"

"Tuesday."

"Nedra's day off."

"Do you want me to call your dad's office?"

"They've gone home."

"If they are looking for you, you have no idea where they are or what they're doing."

"I'm sure Michael told them some story."

"What story could he tell them?"

"I fell in the river, and there's no point in dredging because I was washed out to sea?"

Debbie said, "You guys! Everyone would know he was joking, right?"

"He can be pretty convincing," said Richie.

Richie went into the bathroom. She felt a little protective of Richie—without Michael, even at six three or whatever he was, he seemed vulnerable. When he came out of the bathroom, she asked him if he wanted to go out for a pizza.

She had two pieces; he had six, and two Cokes. And she didn't have to pry. He was not like Tim had been, secretive about every little thing. He told her about school—he had been busted down to corporal twice for fighting with Michael, but then he had made a friend of his own, from Little Rock, Greg, who was a swimmer. Richie turned out to be a better swimmer than a runner, and he had gotten on the varsity swim team. He and Greg practiced all the time, and his butterfly was really fast—he'd won six races over the winter. Greg was also good at math, and helped Richie bring up his grade to an A+, so he'd been promoted back to sergeant by the end of the year. The kids who hung around with Michael stopped teasing Greg when Richie punched one of them so hard he fell flat down, and Michael refused to punch Richie out, saying that if a guy couldn't take care of himself it wasn't Michael's job to take care of him. So a truce for most of the spring, ready to be promoted in the fall, and supposedly off to West Point or the Naval Academy or something like that—but why wait? thought Richie.

"You can't be in favor of the Vietnam War?" said Debbie. The undercurrent of their conversation, for her, was Tim Tim Tim, but maybe Richie didn't perceive this. He would have been—what?—thirteen when Tim was killed. She knew from her job that thirteen-year-olds were lost in outer space.

"Why not?" said Richie. "The President was elected. He's the commander-in-chief; he knows more about it than I do. His job is to know stuff that I don't know. That's why he ordered the invasion of Cambodia. Those college kids who're shutting down campuses and rioting and stuff are just lazy and don't want to fight."

Debbie felt a pop of anger, but pressed her lips closed around that reference to Tim that she was about to make, reminding herself that Richie had been in military school for three years. She only said, "I guess they feel differently about it at military schools than at liberal-arts colleges."

"My dad fought in World War II. He's not sorry."

"What does he think about the war in Vietnam?"

"He thinks it's us or them."

"Oh," said Debbie. "I didn't know that."

"What does your dad think?"

Debbie shook her head. "I don't think anyone will ever know." And then she must have looked sad, because Richie—Richie!—actually reached across the table and patted her on the shoulder, then said, "Uncle Arthur is the most fun of any grown-up that ever lived." After that, he said, "I thought Tim was our family's version of Superman."

Back at her apartment, she still could not reach Aunt Andy, and so she made up her mind. "Okay. Richie, I am going to give you train fare back to New York, and then you get yourself to Englewood and just walk in the door. Do you have a key?"

He nodded.

"The best thing to do is show up, and see what they say. Answer their questions honestly, but don't offer any extra information. My bet is, they'll be so glad to see you that they'll lay off after a day or so. Also, give your mom a hug every so often, and tell her you missed her, and leave it at that. Did you give the army your home address?"

"Yes. There were cards and stuff."

"Well, my boyfriend says that the Yippies are really successful here because there are so many kids who can be drafted. If you give them trouble, they just cross you off the list and go on to someone else."

"I don't want to be crossed off the list."

"Yes, you do; at least finish high school."

He nodded. She got him off early the next morning, dragging his suitcase, which he had left in a locker at the station the morning he went for the physical. She made him take a shower, so only his clothes stank, but, really, it was amazing what seventeen-year-old boys did not notice. Of course he didn't write, but a week later she got a letter from her mother:

Dear Debbie—

It's been terribly hot here. I hope you are getting some sea breezes! When you come home for Labor Day Weekend, you can revive us, if you feel like it. Listen to this! Richie was gone for six days! He showed up Wednesday evening, and he said NOTHING. Well, your aunt Andy was very upset, so she went into his room and got all over him, and he said, didn't she get his note? And, of course not. Apparently, a friend of his from school had come East for a week, and they had decided to drive around and look at colleges, since the boy had never been in the East before. They went to Annapolis and West Point and Penn, just to have a look. I guess Richie had money from his job. Then he showed her the note he'd left for her, taped it to the BAR in their family room, but now she's stopped drinking, so she never even opened the bar and never saw it. Frank thought it was a sign of manly independence that they did this, so he isn't mad. Wonders never cease (and I'm talking about the fact that she didn't look into the bar for six days). She's a very mysterious person, and your dad wonders if, now that she is no longer pickled, she will start to age like the rest of us.

Too hot to go on any longer,

We love you!
Mom

ANDY LOOKED AROUND the table. Twenty-four people, all smiling. She had been here twenty times now, and she had never once stood up and said, "Hi, I'm Andy, and I am an alcoholic." She had the book, and she had read most of it. She left it on the coffee table, and sometimes she saw that Frank or Nedra had opened it, or at least moved it. Already this evening, Bob had stood up and related how he went off the wagon on Thanksgiving, and fell down in the kitchen and hit his head. Roman had related how he was supposed to go to his mother's house, and he knew there would be liquor there. So Roman had turned it over to his Higher Power and tried to forget about it. When he went out to get into his car Thursday, his battery was dead, and at the very moment he was wondering which restaurant, his neighbor two doors down came out onto his porch and asked him what he was doing, because there were only the four of them, and so Roman contributed the pecan pie he'd been planning to take to his mother's, and it turned out that the neighbor needed new kitchen counters and had the money to pay, and wanted this new surface that was coming out called Corian, God knew what that was, but expensive, so Roman was smiling. And then Mary said that she had gotten through Thanksgiving fine, but yesterday, the 29th, was the fifth anniversary of the death of her daughter from falling out of the window of their old apartment on Ninety-first Street, and even though they now lived in the Village, she had had to go up there and stand on the very spot where her daughter landed, she had had to, but she didn't drink anything, though she came close. A shocking story, but you were not supposed to make drama, which was maybe why Andy never said a word.

Before coming, she practiced saying, "I am fifty years old and, however pointless your life is, mine is more pointless," but comparisons were not allowed. Maybe "I am said to exist, but I doubt it"? When she had said that to Dr. Smith, whom she hadn't seen now in ten weeks, he told her she was acting "grandiose." As far as she could tell, you were supposed to talk about specific incidents—"I lay in bed yesterday morning, after my sons left, on my back, staring at the ceiling, and thought of nothing"? Not even a drink. "Last week, I overheard a woman say she had stopped drinking, no problem, but then she was up in the middle of the night making popcorn, and so she gave up corn, and it was killing her." Maybe the others, she thought, should know this? Next to her, Jean stood up and said, "Hi, I'm Jean, and I am an alcoholic. I just want to thank my sponsor, Mary here, for answering the phone at two-thirty-five a.m. Sunday morning. I was upset, and she talked to me for fifteen minutes, and then I went to sleep. Mary, you are a saint and a half; I am very grateful." Everyone smiled and nodded. Andy stared across the table at Mary, who did have a very kind face, and Mary made eye contact, and then, almost without even thinking about it, Andy stood up and introduced herself, and what she said was "I haven't had a drink since the Kent State massacre, which I think is when I started to wake up from a twenty-year walking coma, and I absolutely do not know why or what is going on. But I do know that my son disappeared in July for six days, and then he returned, and even though I do not believe in God or magic or anything, really, I am deathly afraid to touch the bottles, even to throw them away." She fell silent. The others looked at her, and Bob said, "Any reason is good enough, as long as it works."

1971

WHEN FRANK SUGGESTED that he, Andy, and the boys spend two weeks in Paris, staying at the George V and having Christmas with Janet, who was on her junior year abroad from Sweet Briar, he had consciously fixed things so that there would be no time to go to Calais; anyway, who would want to go to Calais at the end of December? Better to stick to the Eighth Arrondissement, or the First or the Third, even to wander the catacombs, than to think that Lydia and her husband had returned to Calais, and she was sitting in a bistro somewhere, watching the door for Frank. In his mind, Lydia had entirely replaced "Joan Fontaine." Mote by mote, he had come around to the possibility that the two women were different—maybe sisters or cousins or relatives, but not the same woman. And if he had to choose, he would choose Calais over Corsica, his mature self over his youthful self, because, as "Joan Fontaine" was gone from this earth, so "Errol Flynn" was, too, and in the leathery, hard-looking person who inhabited the house in Englewood Cliffs he saw nothing of the boy he had been.

Even so, he found himself watching the crowds along the Champs-Élysées, outside the Louvre, along the Boulevard Haussmann, even in the lobby of the George V, for that characteristic movement—from the front, the lift of the chin and the turn of the head; from the back, the sway of the hips. Her hair would be mostly gray now, but maybe, being French, she would dye it. Would the husband allow that? But maybe she had gotten rid of him somehow, left him in Calais and moved to Paris. What would she be doing? Something orderly— keeping books for a wealthy politician, performing services like making discreet calls to his mistress and paying his child support.

In the meantime, since they had come in the winter, they were surrounded by French people, not tourists, and though Janet's French was good, and people smiled at her and were helpful, Frank was a little nettled by Janet's loud voice, Richie's and Michael's exaggerated movements, Andy's endless observations. It was this last that was a revelation—Andy had always kept her thoughts to herself, except when she had been drinking, and she only drank at home. But now that she wasn't drinking, she talked all the time—what an elegant building, is that really Napoleon, I thought he was short, oh, there were more Napoleons than the one, look at those horse statues on that pillar. The French didn't stare at her, the kids didn't seem to care (though Janet answered a lot of her questions), but it drove Frank crazy. The thing he couldn't stop noticing was the way her mouth worked. All around him, Parisians hardly moved their lips, and their words issued forth in a liquid stream. Andy's mouth was like the mouth of a puppet flapping, revealing the empty cavern within. For ten days, he felt as though his glance was shifting between her mouth and momentary glimpses of Lydia disappearing around corners, up steps, and over bridges. By that time, too, all five of them were expressing the opinion that two weeks was too long—you could only go to the Galeries Lafayette so many times, only appreciate so many paintings of the long, pale body of Jesus, his eyes closed, being taken down from the cross, or of a short man in a fancy outfit sitting on a small, bouncy horse. Janet thought they could have spent the second week in Nice; Frank wondered why he had forgotten about Rome; the boys wished they had gone skiing; and Andy wondered when she would ever get to Madrid.

The evening of the tenth day, Janet talked them into going over to the Rive Gauche and trying her favorite Vietnamese restaurant, a cheap place where she and some of her fellow students went every couple of weeks. Richie and Michael hated the food, Andy hated the *toilette,* which was a hole in the ground in a room with the lightbulb burned out. Frank thought that Janet used her chopsticks in a superior way after showing off about the menu. Then she wanted to take the Métro rather than a taxi, and Richie and Michael thought they would use the map and walk—either down the Quai d'Orsay and across the Pont de l'Alma, or over the Pont Neuf and then down the street where the tumbrels had rolled, taking the condemned to the guillotine. Janet said, "That would be the only thing you two know about Paris," and Andy said, "Isn't it a little dangerous?," as if the two of them could not take on any muggers in the city of Paris. Look at them—they even looked threatening. So they ended up walking, freezing to death. Back at the hotel, Frank went to bed, and got up a couple of hours later, and there was Janet in the living room of the suite, wrapped in a blanket and hunched over a book. When he came in, she glanced up and then turned her whole body away.

"That's nice," he said.

"Don't take it personally, all right?" But she sounded irritated that he had even walked into a room he was paying three hundred a night for.

"I think I will," he said.

"Fine, be my guest." She lifted her book slightly. It was a Proust, in French, *Sodome et Gomorrhe,* which he thought was both shocking and pretentious. He must have harrumphed, because she looked up and scowled, and he reflected that she had always preferred Lillian and Arthur. In their family, she was a boarder who deigned to be supported in luxury, but she gave back nothing except a sort of I-told-you-so perfection of academic performance that was showing off rather than pleasing. He said, "What's eating you?"

"Well, since you ask, I can't stand how you elbow Mom out of the way every time you are walking along. It's very rude. Men here actually have manners."

"Oh, do they?" said Frank. "I didn't notice."

"No," said Janet, "you didn't." She slammed her book shut. "But they notice you. I watch their heads turn."

"Your mother has been talking a lot."

"So what? She's interested. Not all disdainful, like you, or just completely heedless, like Michael and Richie, though I admit Richie looks around every so often."

Frank said, "When did you turn into such a little bitch?"

Janet's face registered shock, and it was true that Frank had never called her a name before—he mostly left the discipline to Nedra and maintained his distance. But she was not intimidated. She said, "About the time I realized that you spend every single minute of your working day stoking the war machine and trying to figure out how to slaughter Vietnamese peasants more quickly and efficiently." Her mouth snapped shut, but then she had another thought, and said, "And profitably."

"Thank you, Joan Baez, for your input."

"I take that as a compliment."

Frank said, "We don't call it the defense industry for no reason, you know. You get to sit around day after day, whining about how you don't like this and you don't like that, and you're safe to do it. Do you think that the Vietnamese don't want to defend themselves? You think they want to be communists and a client state of the Red Chinese? You think Ho Chi Minh is a nice, liberal person who is going to say to those who fought him, 'Oh, honey, so sorry we didn't agree, just go home and plant some rice'? This is what happens when one group of people wants to conquer the other—they move in, they slaughter the chieftains of the village, or whatever they're called, and they put the young boys into the army. I won't say what they do to the girls. Then they go on to the next village to do it again. That's how human beings operate. Right here in France, they've done it more than once, in spite of the crème Chantilly"—he pronounced this quite nicely—"and the haute couture. Maybe because of it."

"That's not our business," said Janet. "Anyway, they were chased out of Vietnam, and it wasn't our business to take over from them."

"So, I take it, you would drive past a family being lined up and shot, and just step on the gas because it isn't your business?" He thought he had her.

But she said, "When did you ever stop to help anyone? Remember that couple by the side of the Turnpike outside of Newark ten years ago? She looked eight months pregnant, and he was struggling with the tire. Remember that?"

Frank must have looked blank. She said, "I don't think you even noticed. I did. Mom did, but you just stepped on the gas."

"Your mother noticed?"

"She put her hand on your arm, and she pointed, and you just shook her off."

Frank stared at her. She was not a pretty girl, but she was worth looking at—what the French called *jolie laide,* in fact. How much credit could he take that she had developed character? But he said, "I don't believe you."

"Why not?"

"Because I am more observant than both of you."

"I'm not saying that you didn't see them."

Frank walked over to the bar, opened it, and took out a beer. The door to the corridor was to the left, and he had his robe and slippers on. He could walk out and put this argument to an end right now. But he snapped the lid off the beer and turned around. He said, "Who got me started in my career? Who set me up reading documents seized from the Germans after the war? Who taught me how things work? Do you know?" She opened her mouth, but he interrupted her. "Your divine uncle Arthur, that's who. What do you think Mr. Perfect Love thinks of imperialism? Of breaking a few eggs for the omelette? Of putting a few peasants through the meat grinder if the sausage belongs to us?"

Her scowl was deep and furious, and about twenty years old— the same scowl she had produced as a baby. He stepped up to her and grabbed her hands. When she tried to pull them away, he opened them out flat and said, "You look, Miss Priss. You take a look at his hands when you visit next, and you take a whiff, because there's plenty of blood on them."

She jerked away from his grasp and said, "Why would I believe you? I've known you were an asshole my whole life."

But her face was white. And what that meant was that she would never trust her instincts again, and if she encountered love, she wouldn't know it. And then he thought, Well, why should she be any different from anyone else?

WHEN THEY HAD TORN DOWN Rolf's house years ago—seven, to be exact—Rosanna had not objected or said a word about her brother besides "Well, he took after the Vogels, but the rest of us were Augsbergers to the core" (Austrian rather than Prussian). Joe put off telling her that he and John had sold the property until she began to press him about what he was going to plant in that field—and why would she care? He always planted either soybeans or corn these days. But one Saturday in March, he took Jesse over to her place for lunch, and she said, "Jesse, you know how your grandpa and I knew that your father was going to be a great farmer?"

Jesse shook his head.

"When he was sixteen years old, he grew his own hybrid seed, and the next year he planted it, and he got, oh, I think ten bushels per acre more than your grandfather. Well, your grandfather was fit to be tied." She turned to Joe. "You don't experiment much anymore."

"They do that at the ag stations, Ma."

"You could try something with Rolf's old field. Just anything. Perk you up."

Did he need perking up? He took a sip of his coffee, looked at her, and honestly, in front of his son, he said, "I sold that place."

"You sold Rolf's farm? My grandfather's farm that's been in the family since Opa came to America?"

"John and I sold it. Mama, between us, we were working over eleven hundred acres. John—"

"John has not taken good care of himself. Only fifty-six, and his rheumatism is so bad he can hardly walk! If he'd started taking chamomile tea twice a day with a tablespoon of honey and a tablespoon of cider vinegar, he would be fine."

"That may be true . . ."

"You should be, too. You're old enough. It would do you no harm."

"We got a good price, and we put it into the new harvester."

"How much did you get?"

Joe glanced pointedly at Jesse, and Rosanna said, "He's fifteen. He's old enough to know."

Joe coughed twice. He just could not quite get it out. But then he said, "Eleven hundred an acre."

Rosanna stared at him.

Jesse said, calmly, "That's a hundred and seventy-six thousand dollars."

"You did not!" exclaimed Rosanna.

"We did," said Joe.

"You could sell this whole farm for a million dollars?"

"That's what they say. Well, more than that. Some of the fields, fifteen hundred or sixteen hundred an acre."

"You did not spend a hundred and sixty thousand dollars on a harvester."

"About ten," said Joe.

"What did you do with the rest of it?"

"John and I put fifteen away for college for Annie, Jess, and Gary Jr. and used the rest to pay off loans."

"Are we free and clear?"

"Just about," said Joe.

Rosanna stared at him again, for a long moment, and put her hand slowly to her mouth; then the tears started running down her cheeks. Joe said, "Oh, Mama."

"I don't know what in the world I was thinking when we moved in here, but I certainly did not expect it to take fifty years to pay off the farm. What was it Walter bought, two hundred acres? I can't even remember anymore, that's how bad my memory has gotten, or maybe I put it out of my mind. But, my goodness, I guess I expected to be owned by the bank until the day I died."

But after a bit Rosanna sat up, wiped her eyes, and said to Jesse, "You know, when your dad lived in that old house, he had four rabbits. They were named Eenie, Meenie, Miney, and Moe. And he had two cats and sheep and cattle and chickens and I don't know what all. His sheep was named Emily. He told me that when he was grown up he was going to have animals in every room in the house, and bring the horses in through the back door." Jesse glanced at his father, who said, "I did always want a flock of Cheviots. They have bare faces."

"Jesse," Rosanna said, "when we took that sheep Emily to the fair, I remember your grandfather told me something you should remember."

"What?" said Jesse.

"This farm was worth eleven dollars an acre." She leaned toward him. "Eleven! Nothing! Didn't matter what we put into it. He bought it right after the first war—paid a hundred, he said. I always thought maybe a hundred and ten. Exorbitant! But he was bound and determined to get out of his parents' house, mortgage or no." She slapped her hands on her knees and looked at Joe. "Well," she said, "glory be! What now?"

"Worry," said Joe.

"Oh, for goodness' sake, yes. Just like always. But buy yourself something. At least a couple of Cheviots. You can build a little pen out behind the Osage-orange hedge. Jesse, wouldn't you like some sheep?"

"Ma," said Joe, "I think you must be losing your mind. I never heard you say a good word about animals."

"Well," said Rosanna, "it's dull around here. Minnie's the principal, Lois is running Crest's, Annie and Jesse are in school all day, and you wear earmuffs from the noise. Sheep would be a little company."

Joe laughed, and then wondered, where would you even get sheep these days? No one had sheep. He did look around when he headed out to the barn before supper. He did say to himself the words "a million dollars." But he knew enough at his age to know that dollars were like drops of mist—they fluttered around you and then dissipated. The real mystery was how your farm bound you to it, so tightly that you would pay any price (literally, in interest) or make any sacrifice just to take these steps across this familiar undulating ground time and time again.

AS BASIL HAD SUSPECTED, Henry and Philip (never "Phil") were quite compatible, though if Basil cared about things like how the corners of the pillows on the couch were turned, or whether sweaters were arranged by color right to left ("Always red!" exclaimed Philip as he was rearranging. "How could you make such a basic error?"), or how much garlic was in the spaghetti, Henry would be surprised. As for other matters, Basil had cultivated Philip quite nicely. He thought sex was a lovely game. Like Henry, he had been a magnet for the women and always wondered what they saw in him. He said to Henry, "Then Basil came along and explained to me what was going on. I was thunderstruck."

"He explained it to you?" said Henry. They were eating from a box of the first strawberries of the season.

"Well, darling, I might as well have been a detached head, I was so cerebral. Don't you remember the girl I told you about, the one in my class who only realized she was preggers when the infant dropped preparatory to delivery? I mean, she said afterwards that she wondered what that strange sensation was, the kicking, don't you know, but it never occurred to her to ask anyone." He helped himself to another strawberry, sucked it between his lips, and pulled out the hull. Henry took the opportunity to smooth the hair back from Philip's very lovely forehead. "All the other graduate students said, well, only in America, so I didn't tell them about the time I went swimming and emerged with a leech attached to my bum and never noticed it until it swelled and dropped at my feet while I was chatting up two girls from Sydney." For Philip was born not in England but in Australia—Brisbane to be exact—though never once had Henry caught him out, pronunciation-wise. He did it like an actor—BBC most of the time, yes, but he would also do Johannesburg, New Orleans, Minnesota (which made Henry laugh), and Parisian-*homme*-speaking-broken-*anglais,* which came in handy for his literary-critical studies.

And then the door opened, and here they were, stark naked on the couch in the middle of the afternoon, and as soon as he saw Claire, Henry remembered that she'd told him she and Paul were coming for the weekend, a getaway, and he had sent her a key in case he was at school. But that was three weeks ago; it had slipped his mind completely. Claire looked at Philip, then at Henry. Her hand was still on the doorknob, and Henry thought for a moment that she would back out the door and disappear, but she said, "Yoohoo! We're here! Did you remember?" And behind her was Paul—and even though he had on a beautiful Harris-tweed sport jacket, he was so stiff and pale that he might as well have been wearing his white coat. Philip said, "I say, you must be Claire. What a spiffing frock, darling. The color is perfect for you. I'm Philip. We're almost finished with the strawberries, but the best ones are left."

Henry got up, went to his room, and returned with his jeans and Philip's khakis. Claire was on the phone. Philip made a gesture to him to keep silent as Claire was saying, "Yes, Sarah. We got here just fine. I left the snacks in the refrigerator. Did you find them? And no TV until after they eat supper. We are so looking forward to the play. Yes. Kiss the boys for us, and thanks so much for helping us take the weekend." Paul held out his hand for the phone, but Henry saw that she turned away, as if not noticing. In the quiet after she hung up, Paul stepped up to Philip and said, "I'm Paul Darnell."

CLAIRE WHISPERED, "I don't think my mother knows that such a thing exists."

"They're very open about it."

"Henry always acted like he's never found the right girl."

"Your mother told me that no one is boring enough."

"How wrong she is," said Claire.

It was only about nine o'clock; the ceiling of the bedroom was still flowing with light, like the surface of a pond. Paul shifted her head on his shoulder, and she said, "I feel like my whole life is being readjusted."

"He's thirty-eight years old. I can't believe no one thought of this possibility before now."

"Remember when he brought Jacob to our house for Christmas?"

"Jacob has kids. Whatever he was thinking about Jacob, Jacob wasn't thinking that about him."

"But he was gorgeous, I must say."

"Now we know," said Paul.

Claire hoisted herself onto her elbow and stared at her husband. She would have expected him to be more outraged and to say something about how maybe Henry shouldn't spend time with their boys anymore. She would have expected him not even to shake Philip's hand, or to put on a rubber glove before doing so. But he had been in a good mood all the way over from Des Moines, enjoying the drive and not complaining. She wondered if she was going to have to change her perception of Paul as well as to continue her marriage to him. She said, "You don't want to go to a hotel?"

"Oh, I don't know," said Paul.

But he made no move toward her. They both lay quietly, and then he said, in his doctory voice, "You know what they're doing, right?"

She hated to admit, "Not exactly."

Paul shifted against her, and said, "Well, I do, and being near it doesn't turn me on."

Claire said, "Okay." The room was now almost dark, which had a way of magnifying the significance of the silence from the other end of the hall.

Paul's voice rose a bit. He said, "I mean, you really didn't know about this?"

"I really didn't. Did you?"

He moved away from her slightly, not as if he did so knowingly, more as if he suddenly felt uncomfortable. She said, "It's only ten after nine. Let's go to a hotel. We can afford it."

But at the hotel they had a fight—not about Henry, or the boys, or what Paul called "her behavior"; it was about where they had eaten dinner with Henry and Philip. Why would you come to Chicago and not eat Italian? Or at least go for a steak? Why had she just smiled and agreed when Philip suggested Greek food? Paul hated Greek food— too many olives and strange-tasting cheeses, and what was the meat in a gyro? It tasted repellent, and smelled worse.

Claire said, mildly, "You could have said something."

"Why do I always have to sound like the spoilsport? You just leave it to me, and you agree with me—you picked at yours and only ate bread."

Claire tried to keep her voice down. "Can't we try something new every so often?" Since the departure of Dr. Martin Sadler, almost a year ago now, she had cultivated a soothing manner.

"I'm over forty years old. I'm from Philadelphia. I've tried everything I intend to try. If you come to Chicago, you do so for a reason. You know that. You said you were looking forward to a steak. You betray me. I'm always the bad guy."

Claire apologized.

Paul said, "Don't apologize. That makes it worse."

Claire put her pillow over her face and lay silently on her back while Paul prepared again for bed, as he had done earlier at Henry's— brushing his teeth, washing and drying his feet, lubricating his eyes, adjusting the covers so that they wouldn't weigh too heavily on him, setting his pillows carefully against his body. Since the end of her affair with Dr. Sadler, she had thought over and over of telling Paul, who still didn't seem to have found out about it, even though he mentioned Dr. Sadler and his brother every so often ("They're doing well enough; I guess pediatric foot problems are commoner than I realized"). Times like these, she thought it would be a kindness to tell him, so that he could understand who was the real bad guy. Or gal.

IT WAS COLD—first of May and hardly above freezing—in fact, there had been a frost the day before yesterday, and Joe expected another one. He was walking along the grass verge he had planted above the creek. It was thick and tough in spite of the bad weather, and the creek was high, too, up to thirty feet across and five to seven feet deep, muddy and a little foamy. He had sprayed this field with atrazine on March 30, and expected the whole thing to be planted in corn by now, but it had been too wet. He had fourteen days left to get his planting done, and he was fretful.

If you farmed nine hundred acres, leaving about two hundred fallow every year (and there weren't all that many farmers Joe knew who still did that), you had to love atrazine. It was cheap, it was safe, it did a wonderful job. You sprayed the field before you planted, and the foxtail and the plantain and the dockweed just didn't come up. No one had to walk down the rows with a hoe, whacking at the stems of the weeds, using the corner of the hoe to drag out as much of the root as possible. When they'd had Jake and Elsa (admittedly, long, long ago) cultivating had been fun, at least for the youthful him, sitting on Jake's back, his fingers twined in the harness as the two horses pulled the cultivator. But riding a tractor was not fun, and it did disturb the soil much more than the horse-drawn cultivator had done. And then along came atrazine, and the manufacturer sent out a rep, and everyone from all around gathered at the feed store and watched the fellow drink a glass of the stuff, burp, laugh, and say, "Mmmm." Of course Joe knew he was drinking water, but the demonstration was somehow effective. And then there were the magic words "no till," words he'd never expected to hear in farm country. Lois was careful about the well—for weeks after he applied the stuff, she brought water home from the market. He didn't object, just as he didn't object when she started saying grace before every meal (the first time, he and Minnie had exchanged a glance, but soon they got used to the "dear Lord" and the "amen").

He had given in on the sheep idea and found Jesse four Suffolks—

black faces, black legs, curious and frisky. Jesse cared for them respon-
sibly, though without much interest, but Joe himself went out to
see them ten times a day and laughed at their antics. He'd bought
them from an ambitious 4-H'er down in Burlington whose brother
was dedicated to Berkshire hogs. Walter had preferred Berkshires;
Joe didn't remember them as being so graceful, ears pricked, belly
tucked up, feet dainty white in spite of their massive size. Thinking
of them and frustrated about planting, Joe was almost ready to build
a confinement barn and go into the hog business—breed them, far-
row them, feed them for six weeks, and sell them to someone else to
finish. Forty-two days equaled fifty pounds each, and off they went,
still rather cute. Ten sows might produce three or four litters each in
the course of a year and a half. It made him smile to think of it.

The habit of worrying was a hard one to break. His corn yield had
been as high as he'd ever seen it—a hundred bushels an acre, with the
soybeans almost forty-five—that was almost thirty thousand bushels
of corn and about eighteen thousand bushels of beans he had carted
to the grain elevator. And somehow, against all probability and history, there had been a market. Minnie had said to him, "Well, if land
is up to fifteen hundred an acre"—and it seemed to be, according to
all the farmers sitting around the café in Denby—"there must be a
reason." Walter would have shaken his head and said, "No, no reason.
Never made sense and never will," but Joe was beginning to believe
that there was a reason and there was a market. Maybe it was true,
as many farmers said, that the middlemen—the grain companies
and the traders on the exchanges—were getting the longer end of
the stick, but the stick was getting fatter, too. What was the world
population now? More than three and a half billion, and no sign of
slowing down—some book Lois had seen called *The Population Bomb*
or *The Population Explosion* predicted widespread famine. Or, Joe
thought, the arrival of an era when farmers might get paid for what
they produced.

Oh well, four lambs was a good start. And a dog, maybe. When
Nat died, and then Poppy, he hadn't replaced them. The wind picked
up as he headed back toward the barn. He hunched his head into his
shoulders. Not much hair to keep him warm anymore, and his feed
cap was worthless. He stopped, though, just to watch a goshawk dive
straight down at the bare field, walk about for a minute, peck quickly

at something, and then rise into the air with a snake in its talons, long and slender. Joe had never seen that before—in fact, it was maybe two or three years since he'd seen any hawk, longer than that since he'd seen a goshawk. He stood and watched as it rose higher, the snake writhing at first and then drooping. Soon, they disappeared into the clouds, and Joe headed back to the barn. What he would do there, he didn't know—one thing a long cold spring was good for was making sure that every gear was greased, every joint was oiled, every belt on every piece of farm machinery was tight.

Standing in the doorway of the barn, looking at the four lambs and the rest of the empty, chilly landscape, a bright sky (though not sunny) arching over the spreading dark and waiting fields, Joe didn't see a soul. The earth, in his experience, was a bigger place than most people could imagine. Sheep made him think of breeding, how the strain of Walter and the strain of Rosanna mixed with the strain of Roland and the strain of Lorena (a little inbreeding there, he knew). He shook his head—breeding was about profit, not love. He fiddled around the barn until late morning, so idle that he began to contemplate dogs. A pointer. A pointer arrowing across the fields after a pheasant or even a rabbit would be a beautiful sight, a luxury, and a friend. And, after all, a man whose land was now worth almost a million and a half dollars maybe deserved a pointer.

ON MONDAY, which was a nice day, Rosanna put on her socks and boots and a sweater over her housedress and walked out to the newly painted barn, where she knew she would find Joe. The corn ran in a long towering barrier on the south side of the barn, and the Osage-orange hedge, hardy as ever, hid everything to the east (though Rosanna could hear the ewe Joe had decided to keep and breed—Hasta her name was, for *hasta la vista*, Joe's idea of a joke). The puppy was cute, too, a purebred golden retriever named Dory, or D'Ory, which meant "golden" somehow. When she opened the door, the puppy ran over and sat right down, because Joe had taught her that she only got petted if she sat. Rosanna leaned down and scratched her ears, thinking she had turned into a softy for sure, then straightened up and declared, "I want to learn to drive a car."

Joe stared at her.

She said, "I mean it. I've been sitting inside my house for forty-five years. I can't even remember why I didn't want to go out. Something to do with looks, I'm sure—I was a very vain young woman."

"Where would you go?"

Rosanna put her hands on her hips. "Wherever I feel like." That must have been the right answer, because Joe smiled. "You could drive Lois's car to start with—that's an automatic." Then he said, "Want to try it right now? She hasn't left for work yet."

Rosanna took the dare and followed him to his house, where he told Lois, "My mother wants to borrow your car," and Lois, who was deep into making something complicated and French, must not have heard, because she only waved her hand. "The keys are in it." They walked out the front door before Lois could come to and stop them.

Rosanna had been in Lois's car a few times. It was a new Volkswagen, a small blue station wagon. Joe backed it around, drove it out onto the road, and parked it. Rosanna got behind the wheel, and Joe got into the passenger's seat. He pointed to the ignition, the brake, and the accelerator. He showed her where drive was, where park was, and where reverse was, then said, "Still want to do this?"

Rosanna said, "Since we're heading down the road toward Usherton, more than ever."

"Well, wait until tomorrow to go there."

"You're not letting me do this because you want to get rid of me, are you?"

Joe laughed. "I have no hope on that score."

She thought she might get to the corner, but in the end, she got them all the way around the section (admittedly, only four turns, but all left turns). She sat up, stared through the windshield, and drove past the boarded-up old school, past the road to John's farm, past Rolf's old farm with the house gone, past her own driveway, over the creek, left again. She was careful about the deep ditches to either side of the road (maybe she did stick too close to the center, but no one came along), and she eased slowly up to the stop signs, using her left-turn signal (no putting your arm out the window these days). Joe seemed relaxed—at least, he didn't startle or gasp at anything she did. The panorama through the windshield was a strange new perspective for someone who usually rode in the backseat. When she stopped in front of Joe's house, she said, "That's not so different from driving old Jake to town."

"I always wanted to do that."

"I know you did. I wish I'd let you."

It had taken half an hour. She left the keys swaying back and forth in the ignition (lovely word!), gave Joe a hug, and got out. Without daring to encounter Lois, she went around their house, then clomped through the corn back to her place, where she straightened the living room, did the breakfast dishes, and headed upstairs to look in her closet. If she was going to start driving into town, she realized, she would have to do something about her hair and her wardrobe.

1972

Lillian thought it was funny that, after forty years or so, what pushed her aunt Eloise out of the Communist Party was Chairman Mao shaking hands with Richard Nixon. Janet told her about it when she came back to Virginia from her spring break in California. She was sitting at the table in the breakfast room. Lillian, who wasn't at all hungry, set the scrambled eggs and toast on the table in front of her niece, then pulled the shades. It was a bright morning for the end of March, and Janet had flown into Dulles late the night before. Lillian had promised to take her down to Sweet Briar, and the weather was perfect for it—there would be magnolias all the way, she thought. Janet said, "I was there for five days, and we spent all of one of them taking boxes and boxes of literature to the dump. I suggested a used-book store, but Eloise didn't want anyone falling for all the crap. As she said." She picked up her fork.

"Otherwise, she seems fine?" Lillian could not imagine walking away from one's entire life in that way—Eloise's version of divorce.

"As in, does she have a brain tumor or has she lost her mind? I don't think so, she seems great. She took me to a wonderful rose garden not far from her house. You can't believe she's only seven years younger than Grandma, or that she ever lived on a farm. She's so lean and muscly, she dyes her hair faithfully, she walks or jogs several miles every day. I was impressed. And I think there might be some kind of boyfriend. He called her, but I didn't meet him."

They laughed together.

Lillian said, "What is she doing for money?"

Janet shrugged. "Who knows? I mean, when did she buy her house? She told me it's paid for. She works at a cheese collective in Berkeley. She's maybe thirty years older than everyone else, but she wears her sandals and her braid down her back, and she fits right in. She said to me, 'Spender left, and I stayed. Koestler left, and I stayed. Mitford left, and I stayed. Then Sartre left, and I stayed, but I am leaving now. Did you see the look on Mao's face? He might as well have been giving Tricky Dick a big kiss on the lips!' She sounded personally insulted."

Lillian didn't mention that Arthur, too, had reacted strongly to the picture of Nixon and Mao. They'd been watching the news, and he said, "I'm amazed he hasn't been shot." Lillian was well trained not to ask questions, but she knew he meant Nixon, not Mao. Now she said, "Is Rosa still married to the gambler? Gosh." Lillian shook her head. "Little Rosa will be forty next year."

"I guess Rosa and Lacey live with some new boyfriend so far back into the Big Sur mountains that it takes Lacey an hour or more each way to school on the bus, but they have enough money. Rosa sells glycerin soap she makes with herbs she grows, like lavender or tarragon, and the boyfriend makes violin bows that violinists all over the world are waiting to buy for sky-high prices. They don't have a television or a radio. Eloise gave me some of the soap—it's in my suitcase. I brought some for you. It smells delicious. You can take your pick, except for the lemon." She pushed her plate away and said, "That was good."

"You're welcome."

"You're thanked."

Lillian carried the plate to the sink, where she rinsed it and put it in the dishwasher. Janet rose from the table and did what she always did, which was to walk over to the bank of Tim's pictures—Tim as a newborn, cross-eyed; Tim walking the back of the couch, laughing, with Debbie off to the side, furious; Tim smiling in front of a broken window, the offending tennis ball in his hand (Arthur had labeled that one

"Bull's-eye!"); Tim walking on his hands; Tim dressed as Elvis Presley for Halloween; a picture Steve Sloan had sent her, of Tim onstage at a dance, flicking his cigarette ash into the nest of some unsuspecting older boy's duck tail—grinning, fourteen, already smoking with expertise; Tim playing his guitar; Tim's senior portrait, so smooth and innocent-looking. Janet surveyed them for the hundredth, the thousandth time. Since the big argument with Frank that Lillian had heard no details about, Janet was more scarce than she had been, though she still came around every so often to look at pictures of Tim. Debbie said only that Janet swore she would never speak to Frank again. Debbie also said that Janet had never had a boyfriend; Lillian hoped that her devotion to these pictures wasn't the reason.

She said, "I think maybe your grandmother isn't quite the old lady she used to be. You heard that Joe taught Rosanna to drive and then bought her a car after she passed the test. She had to take the vision test twice, because they thought she was cheating the first time."

Janet turned toward her. She looked sad, but she sounded normal: "You're kidding!"

"Well, they didn't say that, but they did say that her results were unusual for a woman of her age. Twenty/twenty or just about."

"What did Joe buy her?"

"She learned in Lois's car, so I guess they decided that the safest thing was to get her the same model. Two thousand dollars. Minnie told me that Lois was fit to be tied, in her way."

"What way is that?"

"She wrote a thousand-dollar check to the Methodist church for the new roof. So what was Joe going to say?"

"Uncle Joe is always nice."

Lillian heard a step behind her, and before she even registered that it was Arthur, Janet's face hardened, and then went blank. Arthur put his arm around Lillian's waist and kissed her on the side of the head, then said, "Janny! I didn't know you were here!" He moved to give her his customary hug, and she stiffened, then backed away, but she did eventually smile and say, "Hi, Uncle Arthur. How are you?"

"Upside down and backwards." But he didn't get a laugh.

Lillian said, "I think she prefers 'Janet,' darling."

"I don't care," said Janet.

Arthur stared into the toaster at his muffin. When it popped up, he pushed it down again, and then, when it was just right, he popped it and juggled it to the counter, where he buttered it. All of this made Lillian strangely self-conscious, but she had no idea why.

Arthur said, "How do your brothers like Cornell?"

"I guess they're pretty busy. Cornell still has ROTC, so they joined that."

Lillian said, "Your dad made gunpowder all through college. They were trying to make it out of cornstalks for the war effort. I guess one time it worked, but only once. Did he tell you that he lived in a tent?"

"I didn't believe that. You really think it's true? He also told me he didn't graduate," said Janet.

"Pearl Harbor," said Lillian.

Janet was staring at Arthur, who seemed not to notice. Suddenly she tossed her head and said, "I have to go. I have to turn in my senior thesis in a week, and I'm supposed to be typing all day today."

"What's your subject?" said Arthur.

It was then that Janet finally met his gaze completely. "The CIA," she said.

But Arthur said only, "I thought you were a French major."

Janet said, "I was going to do it on Violette Lecoq, but there wasn't enough material, so I am doing it on André Malraux."

There was a long silence; then Lillian said, "Well, it's almost noon. I guess we'd better go. Arthur, I'll be home for dinner. With dinner."

IN THE CAR, Janet felt more comfortable. She had given Aunt Lillian the lavender bar, which was her second favorite. She thought of it as the last piece of herself that she was leaving behind in a place she had loved but was finished with. She no longer yearned to have the snapshot of Tim on his bike squinting into the sun that had been taken the summer she spent with them. She was almost in that picture—just as Uncle Arthur lifted the camera, a bee buzzed by, and Janet ducked to the left. If you looked closely, her shadow was there in the bottom corner. Whenever any of her teachers at Sweet Briar had used the word "paradox," Janet thought of that picture—her shadow in his picture, his shadow in her life.

They drove along. Aunt Lillian always held the wheel as though the car could leap out of her hands at any moment—Tim had said that once.

Aunt Lillian asked, "What are you doing after graduation?"

"I'm moving to California." It was the first time Janet had uttered this aloud. She spoke with confidence, she thought. "I met some kids who have a house in Oakland. One guy is a mailman and one works for Safeway, and two of the girls are at Berkeley. I met them all." The one who worked at Safeway was a black guy. The mailman lived in the attic, where, he said, it was easier to dematerialize and evaporate through the roof, especially since there was no insulation. The third girl (also black) worked as a nude model for local artists, who paid twenty-five dollars an hour, or more. You didn't have to look like Marisa Berenson to be an artist's model—better not to, in fact.

"Must be a big house," said Lillian.

"Three stories. The rent is forty dollars a month per person, plus a little more in the winter for heat. Someone is moving to Hawaii, so I get that room. One of the girls is going to help me find a job. All I need is a hundred dollars, so I've been saving from my allowance every month. I should have it."

"How are you getting out there?" Aunt Lillian made this sound easygoing, as if she weren't prying. Janet said, "A bus ticket is fifty-two dollars." She did not say that a guy she knew from U.Va. had suggested they hitchhike. It all depended on the next two months, and how much she could save from the last two allowances her mother was ever going to give her. There might be a graduation present, too. If her father gave her anything, she would view it as ransom money. And take it, she thought.

She glanced over at Aunt Lillian, thinking, "I am twenty-one years old," but saying only, "It's a bad time to get a job. And a good time to try stuff out."

Then Aunt Lillian surprised her; she said, "I think you'll have fun." Of course, Aunt Lillian was thinking that she would be seeing Janet again; Janet wasn't so sure about that. Even Aunt Eloise didn't know she was coming back to California—Aunt Eloise thought she was taking a job in Chicago.

ON THE DAY after the end of second grade, Charlie put a dollar and one of the Rice Krispie treats that Mom had made for him on Sunday in his pocket, and set out for the swimming pool. Charlie knew north, south, east, and west, and he knew that the swimming pool was south, but he also knew that he could catch the bus right by his school, which was now out for the summer, although in a week Charlie was going to go to summer school to learn some more about writing. Charlie was left-handed—he knew this because the pointing finger on one hand was longer than it was on the other hand; the longer finger was on his left hand, and to tell right from left, he had to look at his fingers.

Mom had said that he would go to summer school from ten-thirty until noon. Today was a hot day, and Charlie needed a swim. He had taken lessons all last summer and all winter at the Y, and he could do crawl and breast stroke. He had gotten his trunks out of his drawer, and a towel from the hall closet, and rolled it around his trunks. Now he opened the front door and closed it quietly behind himself. Mom was taking a shower.

All through second grade, he had walked to school, at first with Mom, then with Barry Clayton, who was in third grade, and, a few times when Barry was sick, by himself. He went out the front walk to Tuxedo, then walked north on Glen Road. There were six dogs on the way to school. Only one of them was scary, a large brown dog with black on his face who was inside a fence, but as Charlie walked along, the dog ran beside him behind the fence, with his nose to the ground, growling and barking. Charlie said, in his bossiest voice, "Shh, shh, shh, shh," as he walked along, and he didn't run. If you ran, that made the dog more ready to jump the fence. Glen Road went along the railroad tracks, and he was not allowed to climb the hill to the railroad tracks, though sometimes he did. He passed Clark, where Ricky Horner lived on the corner (Mom always laughed at this rhyme), then passed Atalanta, and came to Marshall. No cars. It was a quiet morning. He had no idea what time it was. If you walked all the way to Marshall and turned right, you could get penny candy at that store. Charlie liked Mary Janes, Pixy Stix, and candy buttons. If you turned left and crossed Glen Road (which he was not allowed to do), you could walk under the tracks and down to Deer Creek, which was deep and had steep sides, but

Ricky Horner said there were fossils in the banks if you looked hard enough. He had shown Charlie two he'd found. Several kids in his class lived on the other side of the tracks, and they walked to school every day, so Charlie didn't understand why he wasn't allowed to go there.

The bus stop to the swimming pool was across from the playground. There was nobody standing there, but it was in the shade. He decided it was too risky to stop for candy—besides, he had his Rice Krispie treat—so he went and stood right next to the pole that said "Bus Stop"; those words he could read, though they could also be "suB potS" if you wanted them to be. He was in the lowest reading group, and had been all year. Miss Lewis was not happy when he told her all the words he saw on the page. She wanted him to see "words" when he might really be seeing "sword." And she always wanted him to read the words in order, from the left side to the right side, even when it might be more fun to read them from the right side to the left side. That was why he had to go to summer school. But, as Mom said, there was no reason to get mad, and so he never did, and so Miss Lewis liked him anyway, more than she liked John King, who was also in his reading group and spent a lot of time snapping his fingers and drawing pictures of men parachuting out of airplanes, and more than she liked Billy Swenson, who just stared at the book and picked his nose. No girls were in their group.

The bus came, and halted, and the door opened. The driver, who was a fat man, leaned forward and looked around Charlie to see if there was a grown-up with him, but when Charlie handed him the dollar, he took it and gave him three quarters, two dimes, and a nickel. Charlie reached up and put his dime and his nickel in the machine, where they rattled down through the glass part, and then he put the rest in his pocket and went and sat down. Five other people were on the bus; two of them were Negroes, one was a very old lady, and two looked like high-school kids. When Charlie was sitting in his seat, the bus pulled away, and his mom's car went by, going the other direction. Charlie sat back in his seat and arranged the rolled-up towel on his lap. It was very important not to forget it or lose it. He thought he was doing a good job.

DEBBIE, indulging herself by going for the first time in her life to the National Horse Show in Madison Square Garden, was sitting maybe eight rows up and toward the middle of the arena. She was watching the "Gambler's Choice" class, in which the horse and rider had a minute to get over as many jumps as they could. The jumps were assigned points—most points for most challenging jumps. She hadn't looked at the program, but she recognized Fiona as soon as she trotted into the ring. What was it now—eight years—since she'd spent the night at Fiona's house before Fiona left for college out in Missouri, and they'd gotten into a little argument, though any argument was unusual for them. Fiona was riding a wiry chestnut; she cut the turn and headed for the triple bar (a big one, too). Debbie nearly stood up and shouted with glee. How terrific she looked, how light her hands and how straight her back as the horse jumped perfectly, landed on his left lead, did a flying change, and galloped for one of the high-point fences, a hogback heading away from the gate. Debbie looked at the scoreboard, and maybe Fiona did, too—she had ten seconds, so she sat deep, pulled the horse sharply around, and raced for the Liverpool, a water jump at least fourteen feet wide. As the bell rang, signaling the end of Fiona's minute, the horse landed, never touching the water with even his back toe. Debbie stood up clapping, and so did a few around her, but then Kathy Kusner, who had been on three Olympic teams, came in on a gray, and everyone was looking at her. Debbie watched Fiona leave the ring on a loose rein, nodding at Kathy as she went out. She looked at her program. Fiona's horse's name was Torch. Fiona Cannon, the girl who would do anything, was now Fiona McCorkle, and her barn was called Ranlegh Stables. If she was in the "Gambler's Choice," then probably she would still do anything. Her trainer had ridden in some Olympics. Debbie couldn't remember which one, though 1952 stuck in her mind. Debbie picked up her handbag.

At the aisle, she made her way along the barrier until she came to the gate. Then she waited, looking at the standings. Fiona was third, but there were six more riders. Debbie sat down and watched. Of the last six, four had knockdowns, which lopped four points off your total, and one had a refusal, which was a loss of three and wrecked his time. Fiona had jumped seven jumps in a minute; this guy got over two. When the class ended, Kathy Kusner was first and Fiona was third. She was beaten for second by a single point. Debbie wondered whether Kathy had ever galloped straight downhill, standing on her horse's back. All the winners entered the arena and received their ribbons and their applause. The "Gambler's Choice" was not an Olympic-type class, but the audience appreciated it. Debbie made sure that she was visible when Fiona led her horse past, smiling and holding up her ribbon. Fiona glanced in her direction, smiled an impersonal smile, and then, after she had passed, looked back. Debbie saw that she was recognized—the impersonal smile changed to a look of surprise and then seriousness. Debbie jumped the barrier. There were a few "Hey!"s but she hurried away from them.

Torch's hindquarters were disappearing into the tunnel that must have led to the stabling, and Debbie went after him as smoothly and calmly as possible—she knew how to act around horses. A moment later, a short man—the groom, no doubt—appeared and held out his hand. Fiona, who had taken off her hard hat and her hairnet, gave him the reins. As he led the horse away, Debbie called out. Fiona looked around, took off her gloves, made a little fake smile, but kept walking, though more slowly. When Debbie caught up with her, she said, "Debbie! How nice to see you! I had no idea . . ."

"You did so well! I loved how you went for that water jump! You really—"

"It's a fun class." Then she said, "Well, wonderful to see you. I have to get ready for the next class." And she turned and walked away.

Debbie ran after Fiona and grabbed her by the arm. Fiona spun around and shook her off. She was strong—Debbie could feel the tension of her biceps through her jacket. Debbie said, "I am glad to see you! I wish you were glad to see me!"

They stood staring at one another for what seemed like a long time, and then Fiona said, "I am. I really am. You look grown up."

Debbie laughed, and said, "Is that a compliment?"

"I don't know." But she did smile. She did at last smile. Then she said, "Do I look grown up?"

"No," said Debbie. "You look like a boy."

"Dreams do come true, then." She was back to being serious. Then she said, "I am sorry, Deb. I was very wound up about that class. We've never come all the way to the Garden before. You know me. I was never very nice."

Without meaning to, Debbie said, "I loved you."

Fiona smiled again, leaned toward her, and kissed her on the cheek. She said, "You were very patient. What are you doing now?"

"I teach eighth grade at a private school."

"Do you ride anymore?"

Debbie shook her head.

"You should. You were so game, and I made you do lots of things that most girls would have been scared shitless to do. I am scared shitless just thinking about them."

Debbie laughed.

"So what is your cute brother doing?"

At first Debbie thought she meant Dean, and she said, "He graduated from Dartmouth in the spring, and he's—" But then she realized, and she said, "Oh. Do you mean Tim? I didn't realize you knew him."

Fiona said, "How could I not know the cutest boy in school?" She looked blank, innocent. Debbie licked her lips, and her eyes filled with tears. "He was killed in Vietnam six years ago."

Fiona went white.

It was funny how it all rolled back through you, how you relied on everyone you knew knowing that your brother had been killed, had had his skull pierced by a grenade fragment, and so you never had to say the words or think the thought, because every time you did, it was too fresh to tolerate, if only for a minute.

Fiona twisted her gloves in her hands and said, "I didn't know that. I'm sorry." She looked down. "Did he ever tell you that he used to"—she paused—"he used to give me rides sometimes in his car?"

"I never knew what Tim did." But had Tim somehow been Fiona's boyfriend? This idea was so impossible that Debbie couldn't process it, and therefore decided not to.

But the tears now in Fiona's eyes spilled down her face. She brushed them away with her hand, and then she said, "I do have to get ready for the next class. The horse is pretty green and takes a lot of warming up."

"I'm glad I saw you."

"Me, too," said Fiona.

She turned and walked down the tunnel toward wherever they kept the horses.

Debbie made her way back to her seat and sat quietly for the next two classes, but she didn't see Fiona again, even though she was in the program, on a horse named Restless. There was no explanation or announcement. With the traffic, Debbie was home by midnight, and she lay awake in her bed until four, wondering if they had ever really been friends, she and Fiona, or if it had always been the way she sometimes saw among her students—the one girl, Fiona, the dedicated, oblivious rocket heading into the future as fast as she possibly could, and the other girls milling about her, locked in the day-to-day contest for position and love. Which would you rather be? Debbie thought. And yet there was the picture in her mind of that chestnut horse, airborne over the Liverpool, his forelegs folded, his neck stretched, his ears pricked, Fiona crouched on his back. As with every arc, she knew, there was a moment of weightlessness in there. Once you felt it, you were doomed always to long for that feeling again.

1973

JANET THOUGHT that Marla Cook, who moved into their house after Liza went to live with her boyfriend, looked exactly like Cicely Tyson, but she knew perfectly well that you weren't supposed to talk to black people about how they looked or discuss how they looked with others. There were a lot of land mines there, because, even if you came from a family where only your grandparents ever used the word "Negro" (no one in Iowa that she had ever heard used the other "n" word), there were plenty of words that you had to be careful of, like "boy." When she was (and it was rare) feeling fond of Richie or Michael, she would say, "You are a cute boy!" And then, one day in Oakland, when she was talking to Hunter Morrison, who was about the same age as the twins and worked with her at Lasagna Paradise, she laughed and said, "Oh, you are a cute boy!" and that was that. They were both so embarrassed for her that they never joked around again, and yet she couldn't apologize.

Marla's room was next to hers, and they shared a bathroom—she had moved in because she knew Bobby at Safeway and also knew Cat, who had gone from nude modeling to being in a movie—admittedly, a short movie, but nevertheless a movie. Maybe because Marla was so beautiful, she and Cat were rather formal with each other. After about four days, Marla got more relaxed with Janet, and invited her into her room. It was important in a house like theirs not to form teams or gossip about one another, and so neither of them talked about anything that was going on (including food storage, which was an issue). They talked about French plays and movies. Whereas Janet had seen two Alain Delon films, Marla had seen eight—if there was a tiny little theater somewhere playing something obscure, Marla made an effort to get there. As beautiful as she was, she did not want to be a movie star; she wanted to be a director. She was saving the money she made working two jobs so that she could go to France— she wanted Janet to talk French to her. Marla knew two things about France: a beautiful woman, black or white, could get ahead there, and a play in France could be about anything; it could be about four people sitting on a stage, crossing and uncrossing their legs and occasionally coughing.

Marla was from Los Angeles—not Hollywood, but Crenshaw. Nothing about Los Angeles impressed her. When Janet asked her about it (especially on rainy days), she turned her feet edgewise and wiped them on the rug. Her father worked for the city and her mother for the costume department at Paramount, sewing.

Marla was impressed only by Paris—all Janet had to do was say words like "Tuileries" and "Montparnasse" and Marla would smile. After a week, she got Janet to read plays to her in French. The first one was *Rhinocéros,* by Ionesco, then *Antigone,* by Jean Anouilh. They each had a copy; Janet would translate a line, then read it in French, and then Marla would read the line. If her pronunciation was wrong, even a little bit, Janet was supposed to stop her and correct her. Marla was absolutely dedicated to this, and since she had a sense of her own future that was built of stone, Janet thought of this as her vocation more than her job at Lasagna Paradise. She told Marla that her father was a farmer in Usherton, Iowa, and that she had gone to the University of Iowa. Marla didn't ask if the University of Iowa had a junior-year-abroad program. Anyway, in a just world, Uncle Joe would be her father and Aunt Minnie would be her mother. It was a good thing to lie about.

Cat was nice, too. In the ongoing tensions about food, Cat was the only one who didn't care if one of the boys drank her milk, as long as they didn't drink directly from the carton, and she was the only one who brought popcorn into the living room when everyone was watching television and passed it around. The source of the food problem was really Louis, the mailman. He was always hungry. He bought a lot of food, but if he had eaten it all and it was late at night and there was leftover spaghetti Bolognese in the refrigerator, he would eat it. As for Janet herself, she got a free lunch at Lasagna Paradise, so she didn't care about anything except dried apricots, and she kept them in her room. She was white, she was bland, she had no stories to tell. She was glad they let her stay and were nice to her.

ITHACA WAS farther north than Richie had lived before—already in May it was light into the evening. He looked at his watch, wondering what he was going to eat. He was half a block from the Haunt, and it was a Sunday night. He'd been studying most of the day, which he had to do in order to make up almost the whole semester's work in his American Twentieth Century History course before his final exam in a week. He liked the Haunt—just the night before, he'd taken Alicia there for a Roscos set and she had gotten pretty wild. Back at his dorm, she had left while he was still sleeping. Since then he hadn't heard from her. Balch Hall was a good walk from his dorm, and the weather had been cold.

But today was sunny. As Richie came around the curve on Willow, he saw the door open, and a couple come out of the Haunt, laughing. The couple was Alicia and himself. They turned left and headed toward the golf course. He slowed down, because they weren't walking very fast, and followed them.

Even though he hadn't seen Michael in a week, the two of them were wearing about the same clothes—jeans, leather jacket. Michael's hair was longer than his, but only by half an inch or so. Alicia was wearing what he'd last seen her in—a long green skirt, brown boots, and a coat she made herself out of old jeans cut up and sewn together in a star pattern. She had her big canvas bag over her shoulder. Clothing design was her thing; she was a freshman, intending to major in art. Michael had his arm around Alicia's waist. Richie thought, in a sort of brainless way, "How alike do we look? Does she think she's with me?" He had never introduced her to Michael.

Michael and Alicia came to the T in the road, where Willow turned left along the inlet where the boat docks were, and Pier Road went right, around the golf course. Since it was May, the golf course was quite green. The sky was clear, too, which was a change. If Michael had decided to take Richie's girlfriend out to the golf course and fuck her in a sand trap the day before, he would have been out of luck because of rain.

Richie and Alicia had been dating a couple of months. She was from Indianapolis—Alicia Tomassi. She talked a lot, so he knew a lot about her. Her dad worked for a big supermarket chain. Her brother had gone to work there, too, after graduating from Indiana University. Alicia had gone on a hunger strike to get her dad to let her go as far away as Cornell, but that was okay—she'd lost ten pounds and looked a lot better in her designs. She had dark hair to her waist, usually pinned up, and a wiry, serious body, evidently destined for professional success. She never minded a hunger strike, though at Cornell they were called "fasts." Her hair was already going gray— she plucked a hair or two every day, but she had plenty to spare. She had a great ass, pretty good tits, and great lips. She had a temper, and she hated any kind of tardiness. He'd met her walking across campus: she slipped on some ice, and he caught her. He had not told her that he had a twin.

They passed the green and walked along between the boats and the fairway. He was still maybe twenty-five yards behind them. One foursome was on the green, and he could see another in the distance, getting ready to tee off, waiting for the first foursome to putt. Michael pinched Alicia on the ass. She jumped and yelped, then pushed him away. He laughed a laugh that Richie recognized with his whole body—good-natured on the surface, but vengeful underneath. If there was anything Michael was sure of, it was getting even. Richie's steps were making sounds on the pavement; he was surprised that Michael hadn't looked around, because Michael was as jumpy as a cat, a lot like their dad in that way. And if he did look around? Well, that would save Richie a little trouble.

Michael and Alicia paused to watch the foursome at the tee hit their balls. The fairway was long and narrow, but no balls went into the water, and one got most of the way to the green. Michael, Alicia, and of course Richie resumed walking. Ahead, beyond the golf course, was a little park, with plenty of trees. Richie sped up. The breeze was blowing in his direction, and he could just hear what they were saying to each other—Michael had a naturally resonant voice, and Alicia's was high and piping. Michael was saying, ". . . should stay around here for the summer. You never know what might happen if you go home."

"Anything might happen, right?"

"Right."

They both laughed in a conspiratorial way, and then she said, "You could come to my Dairy Queen. I would serve you."

"I bet you would."

They laughed again. Now they came to the woods, and as they stepped from the road onto the path, Alicia took off her coat and handed it to Michael to carry. She was wearing a different shirt from last night—one she had tie-dyed to look like sunbursts were popping out of a blue sky. Last night she'd been wearing whitish lace, also homemade. Richie followed them into the woods, and when they were all three pretty deep in the shadows, he scraped his feet in the dirt and leaves, and the other two spun around. Really, he was no more than fifteen feet behind them at this point.

Michael grinned, and said, "Shit, man! What the hell?"

Alicia's mouth opened in a little O, but then she smiled, too. She swayed her hips and let her eyelids drift half shut. She moved away from Michael just a centimeter, but he pulled her to him and made her keep walking. He said, "How'd you do that, man? You popped out of nowhere."

Richie didn't say anything, just went up on the other side of Alicia and put his arm around her, though her bag bounced between them. Three Musketeers. They kept walking.

Richie couldn't have said that they were both going to have sex with her. He didn't know if his mind proposed the idea or received the idea, and though he often received ideas from Michael, he also didn't know if this idea was Michael's or Alicia's. Alicia seemed to like rough sex—she fought him off a little bit, and then laughed when he pushed her. She picked fights about other things, too, like whether a compliment he gave her was sincere or not, and then she made up quite enthusiastically, so he had come to realize that arguing was a bit of a game with her. He'd thought she was beyond him in some ways, but now Michael was looking down at her and laughing at her as if she were funny.

At a clearing, not grassy but soft with leaves and mulch, Michael said, "Lie down, bitch," and Alicia said, "Fuck you, asshole." Richie couldn't tell if they were joking. He held back for half a second, and then stepped over the tree root. He said, "You two been seeing each other long?"

"Couple of weeks," said Michael. "Long enough."

Picking her bag up and setting it beside her, Alicia said, "How about you guys?"

Michael said, "Never saw this little fucker in my life before," and laughed.

Alicia said, "Looks like two against one."

But which two against which one? thought Richie.

In their two years at Cornell, Richie had made it a point to wait a split second before Michael said what he was going to do, and then say that he was going to do a different thing. Their paths had not diverged; they had run parallel. Some people knew that they were twins—they did still look very much alike—and some people had been fooled. One professor the previous spring had told Richie he'd taken that class already. The first thing Richie said was "How'd I do?" and the professor looked at him like he was crazy while saying, "You got a B+. You could have worked harder." Richie said, "Must have been my twin brother. I'm sure to get a B-." Then the teacher looked at the roster of students and laughed, as if this were a joke. A girl who had met both of them at mixers but was able to tell them apart said, "I met your brother last week." Richie said, "How do you know?" She said, "Your left eyelid is a little droopy, and his right one is." Richie had been impressed. He'd told her she ought to be a private investigator. They'd danced a few times and had a beer. But he was not going to ask how Michael met Alicia, or whether Michael knew Alicia was his girlfriend. Then it occurred to him that maybe Michael had met her first.

Alicia scooted over so that her back was against one of the trees, pulling her bag with her, and when Michael came near her, she kicked him in the shins with her boots, then laughed again. Richie recognized her laugh; it was an I-dare-you sort of laugh. When Michael leaned toward her, she ducked to one side, grabbed his wrist, and pulled him down. He bumped his knee on something. Richie knew in his body that Michael was beginning to get mad. It could easily be Richie and Alicia against Michael, so he said, "Why did you leave last night? I woke up around four and you were gone."

Michael glanced at him.

Alicia said, "I got my period, and I didn't have any tampons in my bag."

Richie hadn't seen any blood, but, fine, as good a reason as any. He said, "You should leave some in the same little box as your toothbrush and your hairbrush and your deodorant." Michael, kneeling, now put his hand under Alicia's chin and kissed her long and hard. Alicia's arms stayed limp, and her eyes rolled in Richie's direction. He could not read their expression—was she scared, was she appealing to him, was she saying two are better than one? Why would a girl secretly date a pair of identical twins? And yet, he saw, Alicia was just the girl to do it. She was always trying stuff—never a Daiquiri, better a Hurricane; not a joint, better a bong; not marijuana, better kif; not mescaline, better LSD; not *Last Tango in Paris,* better *Deep Throat.* Suddenly her hand came up and smacked Michael in the balls, and then she popped away from the tree and scrambled to her feet. Michael doubled over for a second, jumped up, and went after her. Richie stepped to the side and knocked into him. Michael spun toward him, but Richie put his arm up and deflected the blow. "Oh yeah?" barked Michael, and Alicia said, mockingly, "So I get it: you're the bad twin, huh, Mike?" But she was backing away.

Richie said, "Alicia, you should get out of here. I know when he's mad, and he's mad."

Alicia said, "I can take care of myself, thanks."

Just then, Michael punched her, not him, right on the jaw. Having been the recipient of one of these on several occasions, Richie flinched. "Leave her the fuck alone, Michael!" he shouted. "Just mind your own business!" He stepped toward them.

Alicia opened the flap of her bag. She had a pair of scissors in her hand, holding them like a knife. Richie had the swirling feeling that things had gotten out of control. He shouted again, in a kind of strangled voice, "Why did you start in with him? You were dating me! We were having fun!"

But she was staring at Michael, and then she stabbed him in the arm, the wrong arm—the left arm was the wrong arm, since he was right-handed. He swung his right, knocked her to the ground, knelt down over her, and began slapping her. Blood was soaking the sleeve of his shirt, but he didn't seem to feel anything other than fury; Richie had seen this many times, too. The scissors had been knocked away. Richie picked them up out of the leaves and tossed them deeper into the woods. Alicia was squirming, kicking, but Michael, straddling her, was pinning her hands with his legs and slapping. Richie did the only thing he could think to do, which was aim a kick right at him, right at his bleeding shoulder. He kicked him off her, and as Michael went down, he said, "Shit, whose side are you on, anyway?"

Alicia got up, grabbed her bag and her coat, and ran. She was crying. By now it was nearly dark. Michael lay on his back, quiet, and Richie stood next to a tree. They could hear Alicia running, and then they couldn't. Then all they could hear was the sounds of birds. When it was really dark, Richie said, "When did you meet her?" and Michael said, "What do you care?"

At the infirmary, they gave Michael a bunch of shots and said that the wound was serious but not dangerous, as long as he kept it clean and didn't use that arm—the "weapon" (the boys had said it was a knife) had pierced the triceps brachii muscle fairly deeply. Richie went back and forth about calling Alicia, but then was too cowardly to do it. On the last day of exams, two weeks later, he ran into her friend Eileen, who scowled at him and said, "Alicia told me you and your brother attacked her." Eileen wanted him to explain or contradict this—Eileen had thought he was a nice guy. But he could think of nothing to say.

EVERYONE KNEW that the Russians had bought four or five hundred thousand tons of corn right after Nixon was elected in 1968, and everyone knew that Nixon had turned a blind eye to it. And why not? Joe said to John. They need it, we've got it. Clarence Palmby, the guy in the Nixon Ag Department who ran the deal, was about Joe's age, from Minnesota. If you squinted, you could see him sitting in the Denby Café, sprinkling sugar in his coffee and making his case, just the way Dave Crest did, or Ralph Thorn. Everyone also said that the Russkies were paying cash—that's what gangsters always did, wasn't it?—and of course this was just the tip of the iceberg. Then everyone forgot about it, because the longshoremen said they wouldn't load it and the Russkies said they wouldn't pay for American ships to transport it, so that was that. What with Vietnam and then Watergate, there was nothing in the paper about grain deals, and the ag report you heard on the radio every morning was about the same as what you heard in town.

Earl Butz, the actual secretary of agriculture, everyone in Denby did not know. He was from Indiana somewhere, and wherever he was from, they did not do what Iowans did, which was to leave unpleasant thoughts unspoken. Joe agreed with that remark, though—"Adapt or die," even if dying was the most likely outcome. As Rosanna said, "You know what he's thinking, which is a welcome change." When Butz and Palmby trotted off to Russia and came back, there were no rumors about what they had found out. Palmby disappeared, but Butz was right out there, saying this and saying that about how great for the average farmer this deal was going to be. Then Palmby reappeared, working for Continental Grain, so of course there was conflict of interest, and then Continental put through the biggest grain deal in the history of the world, and the Russians walked away with millions of tons of corn, wheat, and beans at a very good price— hardly a penny of which filtered down to the farmers sitting around the Denby Café. What did filter down was the conviction that it was time to get out of the hog business. All at once, corn was as golden as it looked, meaning expensive, and a farmer had to decide if he should send the hogs to slaughter and sell the gold itself. Some of the farmers at the café thought Palmby had made a typical Minnesota hash of his appearance before Congress. Had the sale to the Russkies driven up prices of wheat, flour, bread? Yes. Had the sale of corn driven up the price of meat and eggs? Yes. A fellow from Chicago would have said, "Maybe," or "We can't demonstrate that," but a fellow from Blue Earth, Minnesota—what could you expect? The lesson Joe took from the whole thing was that people in the cities had no idea where their bread and steaks came from, and no one in the government was planning to tell them.

ANDY LOOKED AROUND and smiled. Only about ten members here today; quite a storm brewing—cold, blustery, dark, and you could see your breath—but the church basement was probably warmer than her house. It was at least better populated. Frank was in— Well, Frank was somewhere. There had been a breakthrough with his supersonic underwater missile. She could say he was in Hollywood, selling it to the movies. This was her joke, and it made her smile even more cheerfully. Then, when Roman was finished talking about his birthday (he had written notes of apology to both his ex-wives), she stood up. She said, "I'm Andy and I am an alcoholic. I just want to list a few things that I am grateful for today, not including the weather, of course." She cleared her throat. "The first thing is that my son Richard flunked out of Cornell and is now at Rutgers. The reason I am grateful is that I can see how this might be the best thing for him, because his twin brother, Michael, is still at Cornell, and this is the first time they've been separated. I was at Rutgers over the weekend to take him some things, and a girl called him, and he smiled when he was talking to her, which made him look very handsome. I know both my sons were drinking at Cornell, but enough said about that. Anyway, I am grateful to have Richard closer now, less than fifty miles away.

"Another thing I'm grateful for," said Andy, "is that I finally got a letter from my daughter, Janet, and it included a return address. She left home in the summer, and the only thing she's sent us up till now was a postcard, telling us that if there were an emergency we could call her at a certain number, and when I tried that number, a voice said it was a restaurant, and when I asked for my daughter, the voice said, was it an emergency, and I had to say it wasn't, because, since coming to meetings, I don't lie anymore. So the person who answered the phone hung up, and I was pretty sure that it was her. But now I've written her a letter, and I did apologize and try to make amends for neglect.

"And, finally," said Andy, "speaking of lying, I am grateful that I don't lie anymore. I have to say that my lies did not get me into trouble, at least as far as I know, but, between the lies and the alcohol, I did absolutely get lost, so that I didn't know which way was up half the time. When you are growing up and the last thing you want to do is make trouble, then lying seems like the easier thing, but so quickly you lose your way." She looked around, and everyone nodded. They had all had the same experience, hadn't they?

JANET DIDN'T SEE HIM before he squeezed into the pew right beside her and stepped on her foot. Janet pushed over into Cat, and Cat pushed over into Marla, who said, "Ouch." He said, "Oh, sorry," and gave Janet a smile, and then he kept looking at her, and smiled again. Janet, Cat, and Marla were at the Temple in San Francisco. The weather was wet—they had taken the ferry, since none of them had a car, and then the bus out to Geary. It was a long trip. Reverend Jones was getting to be an important man, and you could tell that he knew it and that it just made him more enthusiastic. The Temple had been pretty run-down, but the members had gotten together and fixed it up. Marla said that it was an old Scottish Rite building, "Oh, no black folks in those days. Ha!" One of the reasons for going was to fill that building with black folks and drive out the ghosts of the Masons, and every time they went, they saw that Reverend Jones was able to do that very thing. Reverend Jones was not unknown to Aunt Eloise—according to her, he had started out as a commie, and had told someone when he moved from Indiana to Eureka, up north, that the only way to bring socialism to America was through the back door of a church. Aunt Eloise heard that he had faced up to the bigots in Indiana without flinching. Marla, who did not have any religious background, saw the whole thing as a show, but Cat said if she wanted a show Cat would send her to her AME church back in Texas.

Reverend Jones was going on and on about the nature of heaven, which was, indeed, somewhere over the rainbow, and it was a rainbow made up of all the people in the world. The way you got into heaven was to turn to your brother and your sister and welcome him or her into your heart and your life, and there was heaven, right beside you. Reverend Jones's sermons didn't vary much, but they were nice to hear, and harmless, Marla, Cat, and Janet agreed. But Janet wasn't listening to him as much as she was watching the young man beside her. Because there was such a crush, he was bumped up against her. His leg ran along hers, warming it up. Her dearest wish, right at that moment, was to sneak under his arm and cuddle up to him. And then he glanced around and caught her eye again.

It turned out that his name was Lucas Jordan; he lived in Oakland, too, only about three blocks from their house. He worked as a house-painter and was also in a band—he played drums. Janet told him, "I knew a guy once who was in a band. He said that the drummer had to be the most boring and reliable guy in the band, the only one who never smoked dope." Lucas Jordan said, "Did this guy know me?" He invited her to come the next night to the bar where they played, and she did, taking Marla with her. The bar was a dive, but the sound system was good, and she fell right in love with Lucas Jordan, who sat on his stool behind the bass drum and never let up, never lost the tempo, never stopped driving everyone in the bar forward into the future, beat by beat.

1974

HENRY CALLED the number at the restaurant where Janet worked and said it was an emergency. The voice on the other end of the line said, "Oh, God! You're kidding, what?" and Henry said, "Janet, the emergency is that I'll be staying at the Mark Hopkins Hotel from June 3 to June 8, and I want you to come have lunch with me one of those days." And the voice said, "Oh, for God's sake, Uncle Henry!" But she said yes, and then he slipped in, "Bring the boyfriend," and she giggled but didn't say no. Philip had never been to California, and as a summer adventure, he wanted to drive down the coast in a rented car. Philip and Henry would spend a week in San Francisco and Napa before Henry flew back for summer school and Philip embarked upon his journey, which was to end at Grauman's Chinese Theatre.

Their room overlooked the drop of Mason Street toward the flatter, more relaxing areas. Earthquakes? They might imagine the hotel swaying back and forth like a sapling in a storm, but it wasn't going to do that—even the fourteenth floor was original. Philip thought it was exciting, just the way he thought a tornado in Chicago might be exciting.

At noon, Henry positioned himself in sight of the hotel entry, in an overstuffed chair with a tall back. He had sent Philip away with instructions to meet them across the street at the Fairmont at one.

The surprise when Janet came in was not that she was nicely dressed in a respectable outfit—a V-necked green jersey dress with a white jacket and darker-green heels—or that her boyfriend (he had his hand on her ass) was wearing a button-down shirt and a tweed jacket, but that the boyfriend was a black guy with a moderate-sized Afro. They came in together, stopped short, and looked around. Janet's hair was thick and blond, and her cheekbones had emerged, giving her face more character—she looked more like Joni Mitchell than Linda Ronstadt, but she still looked less like a show-business personality than a lifelong bookworm. He stood up and said, "Janny!" She turned, and the boyfriend smiled. He was really quite good-looking, thought Henry. Janet hurried over, put her arms around Henry. The boyfriend's name was Lucas Jordan; close up, he looked younger than Janet. His eyes moved around the hotel lobby, unimpressed but observant, as if it were a matter of survival to take in every little thing. In spite of himself, Henry's spirits rose—he was no longer just checking up on the wayward niece. He held out his hand. "Any trouble getting here?"

"Just a nosebleed," said Janet. Lucas laughed, and so Henry realized that Janet had acquired some wit, too.

They were seated at their table at the Fairmont when Philip appeared in the doorway. He had bought himself the widest and most outrageous pair of glen-plaid bell-bottoms that Henry had ever seen, as well as a pair of platform oxfords that added two inches or more to his height. Philip greeted Janet and Lucas in his plummiest accent, sat down, and said to Henry, "What do you think? Very Louis Quatorze?"

Henry said, "I think, if the front edge of your trousers gets caught under the toe of your boot, you're going to fall flat on your face."

Philip ordered the lamb shank, Janet crab cakes. Henry ordered grilled salmon, and tried not to appear too curious about what Lucas would order. He hemmed and he hawed, said, "I can't decide what looks good." Janet said, "I almost got the cioppino." Lucas nodded, and ordered the cioppino. Meaningless. Henry consciously recalled and put away all the feelers he knew he was sending out toward this young young man, this kid that his niece was evidently mad about. He said, "The city looks wonderful from up here. I hated going to Berkeley. Now I don't understand why."

Their food was set before them. The sunlight from the window nearby sparkled across it, making each dish look uniquely irresistible. They ate in silence for a while until Philip said, "Do you two have any words of wisdom concerning my peregrination?"

"Where are you going?" said Janet.

"Down the Big Sur coastline," said Philip.

Henry said, "I got to Carmel one time, but never farther south." He did not add that he had not wanted to. What a strange boy he had been. He squeezed Philip's knee under the table.

"Well, you won't be able to look at anything if you go alone, because you cannot take your eyes off the road," said Janet.

"Best way is to hitch," said Lucas. "It's more likely that the person driving you knows what he's doing."

"I hadn't thought of that," said Philip. "Am I dressed appropriately?"

"Not if you didn't raise your own sheep, card and spin your own wool, weave your own fabric, and sew your own outfit," said Janet.

"You do that in Iowa, right?" said Lucas.

Janet and Lucas looked at Henry. Really, Henry thought, this kid had unusual charisma. He said, "Haven't sewn an outfit since elementary school. I believe the fabric I chose was mattress ticking. It was very avant-garde." Everyone laughed. "But, speaking of Iowa, you know who has shown up as the savior of Chuck Colson?" Henry sincerely hoped that these young people knew that Chuck Colson was Nixon's satanic lawyer, the author of the enemies list that had included, for goodness' sake, Carol Channing!

"Who?" said Lucas.

Gratified, Henry said, "Harold Hughes."

Philip, who viewed it as his personal obligation to ignore Watergate, kept on with his lamb.

"That millionaire recluse?" said Janet. "I thought he lived in Florida or Vegas or somewhere."

"No," said Henry, "*Harold* Hughes. He was governor of Iowa and now he's a senator. I guess he converted Colson to Christianity, and now he's vouching for him."

Janet said, "I saw about John Dean. He said he talked to Nixon about the cover-up thirty times or something like that."

Henry said, "When was that? I didn't see that."

"A couple of days ago." Janet ate another bite of her crab cake, then poked her fork into the last piece, dipped it in the sauce, and lifted it toward Lucas. He opened his mouth, ate the forkful, and smiled. The comfort of this interaction gave Janet a different look from anything Henry had seen before—grace rather than carefulness.

Henry said, "I guess Mom was talking to Lillian about all of this, and she said that Arthur doesn't believe Nixon did it. He thinks the whole Watergate thing is a frame-up."

"No shit," said Lucas. "Tricky Dick is sure letting it happen."

Henry finished his salmon and said, "According to Arthur, there were two break-ins, and they got away with the first one. The second one, they blocked the lock with a piece of tape. The tape went around the edge of the door rather than up and down it, which would be the normal way. Since it went around, and was white, the security guard was sure to see it. Was meant to see it."

"Why would they do that?" said Janet.

"Trip to China," said Henry.

Janet was staring at him. She said, "Did Uncle Arthur say that?"

"That's my guess. If I saw Arthur, I would ask questions, and if he didn't shake his head no, I would take that as a yes."

"Who is Arthur?" said Lucas.

Janet was staring at her empty plate. Henry said, "My sister's husband. He's in the know. Whatever the know is, he's in it." Lucas and Philip laughed. Janet didn't. Henry said, "Since Nixon's a Republican, they're allowing him not to be shot."

Silence fell around the table.

Henry said, "I'm joking. Sorry."

After another pause, Janet asked Philip what his plans were.

"Cross the Golden Gate Bridge and sightsee. Hunt for Patty Hearst," said Philip. "I have to get used to driving on the right side of the road at some point."

"Oh God!" exclaimed Janet. looking truly alarmed. "When was the last time you drove a car?"

"The last time I was in England. They say—"

Janet and Lucas exchanged a glance. Ten minutes later, the two of them had agreed to drive Philip to L.A. and back, then to put him safely on the plane to Chicago. Part of Henry welcomed this—the part that had any sense and had not really focused on the potential dangers of sending Philip down Highway 1. But part of Henry did not welcome this at all—the part that felt old and fifth-wheelish as the young people agreed on where to meet, where to go, where to stay, and how much it would probably cost. Janet could move her shifts around, Lucas would be finished with the house he was painting late today, but they had to leave tomorrow to be back by Friday night for his regular gig. Here Henry was, left out once again. Someday, perhaps, he would figure out why he had set himself outside of every social group he had ever known.

JOHN WAS ABOUT USELESS now, so Joe was glad to have Jesse around, no two ways about that—they had done all the plowing, spraying, and planting. Maybe because of Rosanna, Jesse had also persuaded Joe to let Pioneer plant the fallow field in seed corn—Jesse promised to run the detasseling and oversee the whole field through harvest. He also had gotten comfortable with the sheep; he held them when Joe clipped them in March, and even though there wasn't the least little market for the wool, he said he wanted a couple more, so now they had six ewes. A ram at Iowa State could cover the ewes, and Joe was ready to do that. But the last thing Joe wanted was for Jesse to ease into being a farmer only because it was the next step. In fact, the last thing he wanted Jesse to do was to continue being a good boy, and why he didn't want that was hard to explain to Lois and Minnie without also explaining that maybe he himself might once have thought about what there was in the world to do besides planting, plowing, and harvesting.

The strange thing was that everything was taken care of— Annie had decided on nursing school, and Lois was thrilled. Lois had decided she was going to open a small antiques store in Denby, two doors down from Crest's. She spent her spare time looking for "pieces." She had found plenty of chairs, a hand-turned rope bed, and three secretaries with ornamented drawers and lids. Rosanna was much occupied with her Volkswagen. She spent her days driving in widening circles around Denby, exploring. Joe would not have said that any circle you could make around Denby in a single day had much to offer in the way of exotic landscape, but Rosanna came back full of excitement—Vinton, Waterloo, Clarion, Fort Dodge, Ogden, Ankeny, Montezuma, Vinton, back to Denby. Over five hundred miles in something like twelve hours. Next stop, Chicago, where she would stay with Henry, or so she said, but she was still "practicing." Minnie had up and taken off for a trip to Europe. It turned out she had been saving her money for ten years, and now she was ready—France, Italy, Sicily. Sicily was where Frank had gone during the war, and she'd always wanted to see it. She'd left June 5 and wouldn't be back until August 16. Joe felt like his house had exploded and dispersed all the inhabitants over the landscape. He was the heavy chunk of metal that ended up in the basement, more fixed in place than ever.

When Jesse came in for lunch, they heated up the stew from the night before, and they were just setting the table when the phone rang. Joe held it against his shoulder while he served up the food. Jesse was rummaging through the silverware drawer. The voice on the other end of the line was Frank's. Joe nearly dropped the phone, maybe because Frank said, "I'm heading your way. I've got a new plane—a Learjet. I'm going to fly into Des Moines and drive up."

Joe almost said, "Why?"

Jesse said, "Who's that?"

Frank said, "I can spend a couple of days with you, right?"

"Sure," said Joe. He could not think of a single thing they would talk about.

Jesse said, "Is that Grandma? Did she have an accident?"

Joe shook his head.

Jesse said, "She's a very weird driver."

Frank said, "Let's see, I think I can get out of here by eight. Flight time is supposed to be three hours. Don't know if that's true. I guess we'll find out."

Joe said, "Are you bringing anyone?"

"The pilot, but he'll stay in Des Moines," said Frank.

Jesse said, "But at least she uses her seat belt all the time."

"What about Andy?" said Joe, but Frank had already hung up.

"Who was that?" said Jesse.

"Your uncle Frank is flying out in his new Learjet."

They attacked their food as if this were at least reasonably routine news, on a par with the tornado that touched down out by County Road 27 a month before—not the one that killed two people the same day and cut a swath of destruction from Ankeny to Carlisle, right through East Des Moines, convincing Paul Darnell to expand his bomb shelter from one room the size of a closet to three rooms.

That afternoon, Joe called Rosanna. She said she would be happy to eat supper the next night with Frank, but the morning after that, she was leaving for Minneapolis, planning to spend the night at a Holiday Inn in Bloomington.

"By yourself?"

"You want to come along?"

"Why are you going?"

"I figure Interstate Thirty-five is a better road to practice going seventy on than Interstate Eighty."

In other words, after that first supper, he was on his own with his brother. Joe wondered if that had ever happened on a voluntary basis—yes, they had slept together as boys, but Frank had hated it. If Joe had a bad dream, Frank shook him awake and told him to roll over and shut up. If Joe had to go to the outhouse, Frank sometimes wouldn't let him back in until he had said various "magic words," which could be anything. Frank had tossed water on him, slapped him, poked him with sticks, tickled him, hidden his nightshirts. They laughed about these antics once they were grown up, but there was that residual reluctance to be alone with Frank, wasn't there?

He tried to talk his mother into going to Minneapolis over the weekend. ("Roads too busy," she said. Didn't she want to see Frank? She said, "I've seen Frank.")

Frank showed up in khakis and a short-sleeved pink shirt, a little sweaty from the hot day, carrying a suspiciously large suitcase, and hugged everyone, including Joe. He hugged Joe rather tightly, actually, as if he meant it.

When he went out for a walk after supper—"just to look around"—Rosanna said, "I guarantee you, he's getting a divorce." But when he came in after an hour, he didn't offer any news, and he didn't seem tense or upset. They talked about Watergate. That's what everyone talked about these days. Frank, of course, had already read *All the President's Men,* which had only been out a couple of weeks, and he wasn't buying it, not really. Didn't trust Woodward. *Arthur* didn't trust Woodward. And he thought Bernstein was the beard. "What's that?" said Rosanna.

"Oh, when a homosexual gets married, you know. His wife is the 'beard.'"

Rosanna tossed her hands in the air and said, "Good heavens!"

Joe and Lois exchanged a glance.

Frank said, "Anyway, you ask me, Bernstein thinks all this is on the up-and-up, and he wrote the book. Woodward knows better. He just shaped the corners. I mean, it's a good story, and people seem to be buying it. Anyway, I figured Nixon would be out of there once Agnew was gone, but he's hung on this long, so maybe he'll stick it out."

Lois started going on about what her new best friend, Pastor Campbell of the Harvest Home Light of Day Church, thought, evidence of the sinful nature of human beings, and powerful human beings in particular, while Jesse sat near Rosanna, holding out his hands so she could roll skeins of yarn into balls. Joe watched Jesse watch Frank, both at supper and afterward. But he couldn't tell anything. He guessed maybe Jesse just saw an old man, fifty-four now, and his gaze passed over him as over every old man. But Joe saw a hunter, lean and avid. Though what Frank might be hunting, Joe had no idea.

Frank was gone before breakfast, and out all day. Joe and Jesse were sitting on the front porch, waiting for an evening breeze, when Frank pulled up. He threw open the door and jumped out, clearly in a good mood, then trotted up the steps and sat down in the empty chair. He said, "I wonder where my old shotgun is."

Joe said, "There's a rifle in the gun cupboard at Mom's."

"I do wonder if I've still got the eye." He said to Jesse, "You shoot?"

Jesse shook his head.

"You want to learn?"

"What's in season?" said Jesse.

"Targets, anyway. Tin cans."

The next morning, Joe heard them through the open front window, talking as they went out the door. He was still lying in bed, planning to feed the ewes at about seven. All he heard was Frank's voice saying, "Fox was all I hunted back then. Twenty dollars a hide, which is a hundred dollars today, or more. Had to shoot it in the head, though, so you didn't damage the pelt. I knew a guy in New York, when I first moved there, who fed himself by shooting ducks in Central Park early Sunday mornings, which was fine, because they are a terrible nuisance."

Jesse said, "Where is Central Park?"

Frank laughed and said, "You come visit me and I'll show you."

Joe's heart sank, not because he had never visited Central Park, but because he had never even thought to visit Central Park.

They were back by noon. It was ninety-six degrees, and they set their guns down, splashed their faces with water from the outside pump, and flopped in the shade of the back stoop. Joe said, "How'd you do?"

Jesse was grinning. He wiped his face with the sleeve of his shirt and said, "I did get a squirrel. Uncle Frank got two jays and a crow."

"That crow was sitting on the branch, screaming at me, daring me to shoot him, so I did. We killed about a hundred bottles, too. I'm surprised there was that much ammo around."

Jesse said, "Do Richie and Michael hunt?"

"They learned to shoot at school, but they aren't fond of it."

"Did you ever kill a person?"

Frank looked at Jesse with a steady gaze, but didn't say anything. Jesse looked at Joe. Joe could not help his eyebrows lifting. But he said, "You two hungry? There's plenty of that rolled roast left."

Frank said, "Where's Lois?"

"Getting her shop ready. She wants to open in two weeks. She called and told me she found a perforated veneer rocking chair. Out in someone's barn, right beside an old Pierce-Arrow."

"Say . . ." said Frank.

Joe stiffened.

"Can I borrow a couple of things?"

"Like what?"

"Pair of overalls, your truck."

"You're up to no good," said Joe, but he said it jovially.

"Always," said Frank.

"That's what Pop said."

Jesse looked back and forth between them.

The truth came out at supper—Frank was looking for farms to buy. He had a friend named Jim someone who had decided that farmland was going to appreciate now that grain prices were up. Jim was

thinking of buying himself a farm in the south of France, growing
lavender and poppies.

"Staples," said Joe.

"There are farms in France that only grow plums. Or sunflow-
ers. Or blond cows. You need a couple of those. Blonde d'Aquitaine.
Beautiful cattle. Quiet as mice; bigger than Angus, too."

"Now you tell me," said Joe. His overalls were roomy on Frank.
When Frank brought the truck back, he had put two hundred miles
on it.

He left three days later. Joe thought they'd gotten along pretty
well. They were certainly too old to wrestle, and maybe even to argue,
and they had nothing to argue about. Frank had walked through the
fields and looked in the barn. It wouldn't be Joe telling him what the
price of land was these days, it would be some appraiser in Usherton,
or even in Des Moines. What made him sad was Jesse's reaction. The
first thing Jesse did was take the rifle out and shoot things—targets,
jays, barn swallows, rabbits, squirrels—and the second thing he did
was quiz Joe and Rosanna about all of Frank's adventures. What did
he do in the army? Was it true he shot some people? Where did he go
besides Italy? Did he really live in a tent over in Ames? Did he really
invent gunpowder? Did he really steal German documents at the end
of the war? Joe could not set him straight, so Jesse started writing
Frank letters, and Frank started writing back, and, sure enough, Jesse
asked in August if it was too late to go to Iowa State. Minnie said no,
it wasn't, and that she was proud of him. To Joe she said, "I always
thought he was a self-starter. That's why I didn't say a word about
college. I wanted it to be his idea." Joe just said, "Well, I'll miss him."

HENRY HAD NEVER ASKED himself where he got his methodical
ways, but as the fall progressed and Rosanna crept toward Chicago
bit by bit, he saw that she must have been the source. Her goal was
to come in early October, when the trees would be at their peak—
she wanted nothing fancy in the way of food or sightseeing, but she
did want to go to the Sears Tower and look out at the lake, to walk
around the campus and look at the changing leaves. Henry made a
reservation at an inexpensive Italian place famous for meatballs, gave

her a map with clear instructions for getting from 80 to 55 to Lake Shore Drive and then to his duplex. He scrubbed his kitchen sink, his bathtub, and his baseboards, and he laundered not only the sheets in the second bedroom, but also the bedspread. He walked around sniffing—he could smell nothing untoward. He bought some chrysanthemums (chrysanthema, really) for the hall table, and a nice coffee cake from the bakery. He pretended to himself that all of this was a pain in the neck, but it wasn't. At what point would he decide that Rosanna had been forced off Lake Shore Drive into Lake Michigan and he needed to call the State Police?

But she was early; she knocked rather than rang the bell, and when he opened the door and saw her neat bun and happy face framed against his neighbors' maple trees, he was pleased. She had a paper sack with her. She put it under her arm and carried it in. When Henry realized that her change of clothes was in that paper sack, he felt a slight pang that, even though they all knew she was extending her range, no one had bothered to buy her an overnight bag.

She came in talking. "You look thin. But that's a nice haircut. Oh, look at your couch; I saw that same fabric in Younkers and I liked it. I even said, 'Henry would like that,' I really did. So bright. Good for a place like Chicago. Have you talked to Claire? Just call her—I'm not saying a word. Well, I will say one word. Insanity. But you'll hear all about it. Those boys! Well, they do fine in school, and why wouldn't they? It's worth their lives to get A's. Of course, I'm exaggerating. Jesse shot a starling right off the roof of my house; I nearly jumped out of my skin. It fell with a giant thud onto the top of the TV room—you know, where you all used to sleep. Jesse is taking it back to Ames, or somewhere down there, to be stuffed. I'm glad he's going to college. He's doing fine, I must say, for a boy who never opened a book in his life. How you children got to be all so different I'll never know, but he made a thousand dollars with that field Pioneer planted between my place and theirs, he had those detasselers practically running. He was very good about making sure they had plenty of water—that was a real hot spell. But—"

Henry offered her a glass of the lightest Riesling he had been able to find, and she sat in the oat-colored armchair and sipped it, looking around. Finally, she said the magic words: "This is a nice place. Small, but clean."

Henry laughed. He said, "How was your trip?"

"My land, until I got to Chicago, it was fine, but there was a car in flames right beside the highway. I never saw such a thing. No one around it. I nearly drove off the road, staring."

"You could have taken a plane, Ma."

"Now, why do that when I have a perfectly good car? I did pass the airport, I believe." Pause. "Chicago is not at all like Minneapolis."

"Not at all," said Henry.

Rosanna took a sip of her wine and looked around again. Henry let the silence fill the room as she stared at his bookcases, as ordered as the stacks in a library. She took another sip, then smiled and said, "Well, that scar has almost disappeared." The tip of Henry's finger went to the spot just beneath his lip. Rosanna shook her head. "Tsh! What days those were! To think I had to sew that up myself, with you lying in Lillian's lap and screaming your head off. Good thing I had a spool of silk thread. My goodness!" Then, "I think I'm a little tired. I should wash up, too."

"You can lie down for an hour or so. I made the supper reservation for six."

He helped her out of the chair, which was deep, and held her elbow lightly—not offensively—into the bedroom. Then he carried in the paper sack. She was sitting on the bed, looking around. She said, "Now, this is a lovely pattern—we used to call it Wild Goose Chase. I don't know what they call it now." She ran her hand over the quilt. "Black and white with the red is very modern." She lay back, and he covered her with the extra blanket. He lowered the shades, even though it was darkening toward twilight by five now. After that, he went out and checked to see whether she had parked the car safely; then he sorted through the tests he had to grade by Monday, went into the kitchen, closed the door, and called Philip. They had started laughing about something when Henry felt a surge of alarm and dropped the phone. What was it? Nothing audible, and yet, when he entered the bedroom and turned on the light, his mother was collapsed on the floor, maybe three feet from the bed, between the bed and the door.

Henry exclaimed, "Oh shit!" and Rosanna moved, opened her eyes. Henry knelt down and smoothed her skirt over her legs. When Rosanna spoke, Henry could barely understand her, which provoked more alarm. There was no phone in this bedroom, so he nearly jumped up to call an ambulance. Instead, he contained himself, and lifted her, eased her onto the bed. She was not at all heavy. She gave out a long sigh that ended in a cough, and then she said something he did understand: "I thought I was the queen, you know, when I used to drive Jake into town. I would wave and smile. Right, left. I would just lift my hands, and Jake would arch his neck." She lifted her hands maybe an inch off her skirt and smiled. "So silly."

"You weren't silly, Ma, you were beautiful."

"Was I?" she whispered. Then she shook her head. But she was still smiling—at the memory, he hoped. Henry put his hand on her temple, gently. He could feel the dry thinness of the skin of her forehead, and with his fingertip, he could feel the vein quiver in her temple, and then he could not feel it anymore. He waited. After a minute or two, he placed his palm over her eyelids and closed them.

1975

〜

Dear Jesse—

I think I told you about a kid I knew in the army—he was
from Oklahoma, but I met him at Fort Leonard Wood, which
is down in the Ozarks. Now, I was a pretty good shot, but
this kid was a phenom. I had a sergeant there at Fort Leonard
Wood, and he was such a perfect and complete sort of sergeant
that I don't remember his name. Anyway, he'd heard about
snipers in the marines. He wanted to toughen Lyman and me
up, so one day, he took us down to a river that ran through a
remote part of the base, and he got us to strip down, carry our
weapons into the river, and look out for game in the trees or
on the banks. We were supposed to go along for an hour—he
would meet us downstream and see what we got. The key was
to move as quietly as possible. Lyman thought he was going to
shoot himself some catfish, maybe, and he did get a beaver, and
I got a raccoon on the shore. Lyman, who was very observant,
then pointed out that there was a cottonmouth swimming right
along with us, about ten feet away. Now, I'd seen a cottonmouth
or two, and they usually ran maybe three feet, but this one was
nearly five feet long and as big around as your arm—an old

fellow and wily. I thought I would shoot it, but Lyman wanted to watch it, so we slowed down and kept our eyes open. Pretty soon, the snake crossed our path and slithered up on the right-hand shore, where it did something I never saw a snake do before, it slithered over to the carcass of a deer and began to eat it. We didn't kill the snake, in the end—while we were watching the snake feed, Lyman noticed a bobcat peer out at the snake and the deer from behind a tree. We stood in the water and waited, and after a few moments, the bobcat eased out, his teeth bared and his hackles raised. I'm guessing he thought he could scare the snake away from what might have been his kill. But as soon as it emerged and slid two steps toward the deer, Lyman pulled the trigger and shot the bobcat. The snake coiled up quick and started looking around and opening his mouth—that's why it's called a cottonmouth, it's got white inside its mouth. Lyman, I know, could have shot it in the head. But he didn't, and he wouldn't let me. I guess he sympathized with it, and respected it for getting so big and old. Lyman was the soldier who stepped on a mine in Italy—it took us four hours to carry him down the mountain. He lost his leg in the end, but he came home, which many others did not.

Got to go,
Uncle Frank

IN THE SPRING, almost six months after the funeral, Lillian drove from McLean to Denby to clean out the house. She could see concern flicker across their features as she said to Arthur, and then to Debbie (who was four months' pregnant), that she didn't want any company—such a long trip, was it safe, where would she stop—but she shook her head decisively. She had already written Minnie, Lois, and Claire, using the words "Don't touch anything," and they had not, though Claire wrote back, "It is such a black hole of stuff, are you sure?"

"Don't touch anything."

But it was a way of preserving the house for a few months, because Joe and Frank were clear: the house had to come down. Two of the basement walls were bowing inward, and the TV room was separating from the main structure. The stairs had never been up to code—like climbing a ladder, how Walter, or Rosanna at her age, had . . .

"Don't touch anything."

So they didn't touch anything, and though it was dusk and a long way from South Bend, where she had spent the previous night, Lillian drove into the old driveway and parked. She had forgotten the house would be dark; Joe had, of course, shut off the electricity. She was a little struck by its air of being a solid object. Joe had made sure that nothing happened to it. Wasn't that a frightening thing from her childhood in the Depression—abandoned houses with the windows smashed, and then the birds got in and built nests, and the wasps and bees. But Joe would never allow anything like that.

She opened her car door and put her foot in a rut in the driveway. Running along the east end of the house was the bed of daffodils, now finished, and among them the first green spears of tulip leaves thrusting upward. Back in Virginia, they were already through tulips, and even the irises were tall, though they hadn't blossomed. Magnolias. Her mother had never gotten a magnolia tree to grow here. She got out of the car and closed the door and waited in the silence for a few more seconds, though what she was waiting for, she had no idea.

Henry said only that Rosanna seemed more than fine when she arrived in Chicago: talkative, and pleased with herself. Went in to take a rest, which was certainly understandable—it was a long drive—and then he had heard something but he didn't know what. At the funeral, everyone had agreed, what a good death, you had to go sometime, she had retained her faculties to the end, and she had eaten whatever she pleased whenever she pleased. In short, life was doing what you wanted to do in the way you wanted to do it, and may she rest in peace. Even this new Pastor Campbell, supposedly quite strict, had stood there at the pulpit and talked about Rosanna's showing evidence of God's grace in her generosity of spirit. Then they laid her next to Walter, and soon they would tear down the house, fill in the foundation, plow the field, and plant the beans; there was a completeness to it that Lillian knew her mother would have considered right and just. No one, not even the dead person herself, minded this death as much as Lillian did. She went up the stairs and opened the door (when had it ever been locked?).

Lillian's eyes adjusted, and she saw how Rosanna had left the room, the afghan folded over the back of the sofa, the September issue of *McCall's* on the side table, the *TV Guide* on top of it, dated the week of September 30. Beside the sofa, Rosanna's basket of yarn, half-skeins and balled-up remnants in pinks and blues on the top. Thrust among them was a pattern book open to a pineapple-lace pattern. Lillian couldn't knit a twenty-stitch row without dropping five stitches, but Debbie had already knitted the baby two hats, a pair of booties, and a blanket. And her husband, Hugh, the only handy intellectual Lillian had ever seen, was building a cradle based on a model from Amish country. Hugh's specialty was the history of Dutch Reformed settlement in America, which was why, Lillian thought, he could build and think at the same time. But he was systematic and literal-minded, and though he loved Debbie very much, Lillian had hoped her daughter would end up with someone handsomer and more romantic, someone, in fact, more like Arthur. Tina had a boyfriend, too—another art student, who specialized in giant paintings of galaxies, where each dot of paint represented a star. Tina had explained to Lillian that impossibility was the sign of art. She herself was doing collages of torn food packaging made to look like animals.

The darkness wasn't dark anymore. Lillian sat down in the rocking chair and gazed around the room. She suddenly remembered Rosanna sitting in this very chair, also at twilight, softly singing the song that Lillian knew from her earliest days was "her" song—"God Sees the Little Sparrow Fall." "He paints the lily of the field, / Perfumes each lily bell; / If He so loves the little flow'rs, / I know He loves me well." In those days, Rosanna had had a light, tuneful voice, and Lillian had asked for it over and over, as children do. Now she hummed it, and realized that she had lived an unusual life for only one reason, and that reason was that she'd known true love from the day she was born. Then she handed herself off, as if by instinct, to Arthur, passing through town, and he had also loved her truly and faithfully.

Looking around the room, though, tired and sad that this space was doomed, she understood that Rosanna's love had required a sacrificial victim, and that had been Mary Elizabeth. No one knew how

Mary Elizabeth had come to fall backward and hit her head on the corner of the egg crate. Rosanna said that there had been a simultaneous flash of lightning and clap of thunder—Mary Elizabeth, who was dancing about, was startled, slipped, and fell. Andy, though, had said years ago, in that questioning way she had, that Frank took the blame—he'd been arguing with Joe about something and scuffing his feet on the rag rug; when it shifted, Mary Elizabeth fell backward. Not daring to ask Frank, Lillian had once asked Joe, who said he didn't think that Frank, at five and a half, would have been able to move the rug—it had been a heavy thing. All he remembered was that, when Rosanna and Walter talked about it to the boys, Rosanna had said that it was the hand of God taking his beloved child to himself, and Walter had nodded in agreement. Joe didn't know what Walter might have said when the boys were older. What had Mary Elizabeth been like? Joe shook his head. He barely remembered her—he was only three and a half when she died.

The ghost of a little girl, Lillian thought, even a toddler, would be completely formed and full of individuality. She would have a way of reaching upward and opening and closing her fist when she wanted something. She would have a rhyme that she asked for again and again—this little piggy went to market—and she would smile and nod when you pronounced it. She would have a characteristic way of balancing herself on her little feet, a precipitous style of walking so that every step was a dare accepted. She would plop down on her little bottom and throw her arms in the air, laughing. She would drag her rag-rabbit around by the ear, and chew meditatively on one of his feet, no matter how often her mother took it gently out of her mouth and said, "No, dirty." The ghost of a little girl would stand by her baby sister's cradle and stare at her, never touching her, but wondering about her, about how she came to be, whom she belonged to. The ghost of a little girl would not necessarily be wise—she might spend her ghostly existence lost in confusion.

Lillian knew that there was no ghost of Mary Elizabeth, but now that she had conceived of her, she closed her eyes and invited her to come closer, step by step. She opened her hand that was resting on the arm of the chair, and she invited the child to take it. Then she said, "Thank you."

It was Jesse who found her. He was home for the weekend, walking back from tracking a flock of turkeys. He was carrying a rifle, but he hadn't fired it—he just wanted to practice getting close to them. He saw the car in the driveway, and the front door ajar. Lillian must have dozed off; she woke up when he said, "Hello?" He was a tall, graceful boy, slender but broad-shouldered. She said, "Jesse, it's me, don't shoot!" and then they laughed. She only thought of Mary Elizabeth again when they were going down the steps. But it was true, she felt calmer, and much more ready to listen to Lois, Joe, and Minnie divvy up the contents of the house. "Are you sure you don't want some of the furniture?" Lois said, "There isn't much of interest. The dishes are so plain. I can put them in the shop. Min, you should ask Henry if you can take his books to the school library. There are some nice ones there." And so on. But, really, Lillian only wanted the yarn remnants for Debbie, the afghan for herself, and the shelf of old books in her pink bedroom for the new baby.

ALREADY BEFORE NOON, it was so hot that you had to tiptoe across the concrete to get to the edge of their swimming pool or you would burn your feet. Claire had put a shirt on Gray even though she had slathered him twice with the sunscreen Paul insisted the boys use. A mist seemed to hang in the air, and the pool wasn't refreshing. Claire took a sip of her Coke. Paul kept glancing at Gray playing with the float in the shallow end. He was a good swimmer, though—they had taken both boys to the Y from the age of five, and Gray, ten, had been on a swim team there all the previous winter. Brad was inside. Claire was thinking she would make sandwiches for lunch from the leftover baked chicken. Paul was sitting up on the chaise longue, watching Gray. He said, "That land is worth twenty-five hundred dollars per acre, which is over two million bucks."

"What does that mean to me?" said Claire, pushing her sunglasses up on her nose and consciously pulling her chin downward so as not to inflame Paul further. She had been half an hour late to pick up Gray and Brad at day camp the previous Tuesday, and, not reaching Claire at home, the school had called Paul's office. He and she had shown up just at the same time, and it didn't help that, upon seeing both of them, Brad burst into tears.

"Some of that is yours. Joe can get a loan and buy you out. The banks are crazy to lend these days. A hundred grand—I could put it in the stock market." He rattled his glass and ate a piece of ice.

"They're crazy to lend? Rusty Burke told me that getting their loan was horrible. Anyway, interest rates are seven and a half percent. Why would I ask Joe to pay five hundred dollars a month or more so that you can play the stock market? Five hundred dollars is more than our mortgage payment." Minnie had told her on Monday that Joe, Frank, and Gary, the last Vogel cousin interested in farming, were already tiptoeing around this issue of who owned what and what would be done with it; Claire did not want to get involved. However, every time Paul thought of that two million bucks, he decided not to investigate where she had been at four o'clock Tuesday afternoon, and why, when he saw her, her hair was uncombed. In fact, she had overslept her nap, but she was too annoyed with him to confess.

He adjusted his hat so that his bald spot was covered, then pressed his finger into the skin of his forearm, checking for sunburn. Claire had to wonder why they had built the swimming pool to begin with. He said, "At the very least, if there is value, it's important to diversify the investment, so as not to lose it all if the market plunges."

"The market? The market for what?"

"Farmland has gone up thirty percent each of the last two years. That's a bubble. Bubbles pop."

She sat up, set her feet on the concrete, then leaned toward Paul and put her face right up to his, which she knew he hated. She said, "Paul, it's not yours."

He pulled back, but he said, "It's ours. It's the boys'. Do you think an Ivy League education is cheap? We have to start saving now. There's no telling what those tuitions are going to be in eight years."

Claire lay back again. Gray had abandoned the float, and was now bouncing up and down on the end of the diving board—another danger. If Paul had had girls, Claire often thought, he would not have had to make men out of them. She said, "There's no telling whether they can get in at this point."

"They can get in," said Paul, evidently aghast that his sons' own mother had so little faith in their intellect.

Claire placed her palms together, bent her legs, and put her hands between her knees, telling herself: Say nothing. Say nothing. That Paul made more than a hundred thousand dollars a year in his practice, and that his father, who was seventy-eight, would certainly leave him a nice portfolio, must remain unsaid. That his parents' six-bedroom English Tudor in Bala Cynwyd, Pennsylvania, was worth $150,000 must remain unsaid (though Paul had said this very thing a few weeks earlier). Their own house, with pool and three-car garage, was worth eighty. She adopted a wheedling tone: "Come on, sweetie. You didn't use to be so interested in money. You knew you weren't marrying into the landed gentry."

Paul smiled, but then he said, "I hadn't met your brother then."

"Joe is a farmer, not landed gentry."

"I mean Frank."

"Frank has plenty of money." Claire meant that he didn't need any more, but she saw immediately that what Paul meant was that Frank was to be simultaneously mistrusted and emulated. She sighed. She had come to think that there was a golden mean for money. Around that mean, which Claire estimated to be about five thousand a month, you worried less than if you had too little, and less than if you had too much. There was space in your inner life for other interests.

She was thinking of this because of Eliot. Eliot was older than Paul—fifty-five, he said—and balder, too—his well-shaped pate had a neatly trimmed pepper-and-salt fringe. He talked more than Paul, but he never talked about money, never talked about his children or his ex-wife, never talked about what people should or could be doing that they were not at present doing (one of Paul's favorite topics). He did not talk about hippies or weather. He talked about books. His favorite phrase was "Did you ever read," as in "Did you ever read Auden's 'Stop All the Clocks'?"; "Did you ever read 'The Rocking Horse Winner,' that's by Lawrence?"; "Say, did you ever read 'Bitter-Sweet'?" And then, " 'Ah, my dear angry Lord, / Since thou dost love, yet strike; / Cast down, yet help afford; / Sure I will do the like.' "

She'd known Eliot now for six weeks, since she'd met him at the car wash on Hickman. He'd been carrying a book then, too, reading while waiting for his car to emerge. She'd gotten his attention by saying she'd read that book—*The Golden Bowl*—though of course she never had. It was by her bed now, however, along with two of his favorites, *The Good Soldier* and *The Plague*. Just last night, Paul had said, "Why are you reading those books?"

"They're supposed to be good."

"Who says?"

She almost told him.

Now he got up and went over to the thermometer. "Ninety-seven in the shade. Gray should come in. I'm going to close down the house. We need to relax and cool off for half an hour before ingesting any food."

She was not going to sleep with Eliot—he was much too old and reminded her of teachers she'd had at North Usherton High. Besides, Dr. Sadler had to remain solitary and pristine in his position as her great love. He would be thirty-six now, and according to Paul was married. Another thing to be grateful for—that he had vanished at the apex of his beauty. But she would keep her date for coffee with Eliot tomorrow at ten. She would have the last chapters of *The Golden Bowl* finished, too, and they would discuss them intelligently, just as if they were in London, or at least in New York City, and not in Des Moines.

Claire picked up her towel. Paul said, "It's all very well to be sentimental about your family and about the farm, but you have to be realistic, too. You understand that, don't you?" And then he stepped closer. "Don't you?" She nodded, the way she always did.

TO SAVE ON heating oil, Janet and Marla had closed the door of her room and wrapped themselves in blankets. Marla was in the chair, Janet on the bed. They were reading *The Madwoman of Chaillot,* their third session, and they were nearing the end of the first act. Two of Marla's plays had been put on, the best one, a one-act called *Cedar Rose Park,* by the Berkeley Rep. She went to the Temple with Janet every Sunday, but she complained about it and swore she was going to write a play about Reverend Jones called *Loudmouth*.

Though she didn't like the Giraudoux play very much, Marla always wanted to finish. She read, *"Dans les trois cent cinquante. Nous n'enverrons qu'aux chefs."* Her pronunciation had gotten better, but it wasn't perfect, so Janet repeated the line slightly more fluently, then waited while Marla pondered it for a moment before translating it as "In the three hundred and fifty. We will not send the heads." This was correct as far as Janet was concerned, so she nodded and Marla read the next line, *"Qui va les distribuer? Surtout pas le sourd-muet! On lui rend en moyenne quatre-vingt-dix-neuf enveloppes sur cent!"* Marla was now twenty-four, and seriously worried that she was getting too old to make her way in France. She was to turn twenty-five at the end of March, so she planned to leave by the first of February, to take advantage of the two months of her remaining youth when she arrived in Paris. She had gotten her passport; her savings amounted to $1,498.76. She planned to put aside another two hundred in the two months before she left, and with luck, she would find a wealthy Frenchman to take her on when she got there. This aspect of the whole thing Janet could not help her with, but she had no doubt that the willing Frenchman would present himself—Marla was as careful of her appearance as any Frenchwoman Janet had ever seen, and much more friendly. She corrected Marla's translation, and Marla went on to the next line. One thing they had done in the summer was to translate *Cedar Rose Park* into French—not writing it down, but saying it aloud. Marla was proud; she did not want to be less than perfect from the moment of her arrival.

The door opened, and Lucas slipped into the room. Marla kept reading, but Janet made a smooch and waved him over to the bed. Then she did what she could never resist doing, which was to press herself into Lucas as tightly as she could. His skin tonight was chilly enough to make her shiver. When Marla finished reading, Janet said, "You are cold, baby." He kissed her, kicked off his shoes, pulled one edge of the blanket around himself, and said, "Keep going. I like to hear it."

Marla read, *"Vous, Fabrice, vous me reconduisez. Si, si, vous allez venir. Vous êtes encore tous pâle. J'ai de la vieille chartreuse. J'en bois un verre tous les ans, et l'année dernière j'ai oublié. Vous le boirez."* Janet corrected her pronunciation of *boirez.* Her translation was excellent. Janet nodded. Lucas took the book out of her hand, stared at it for a moment, then shook his head. "Makes no sense to me." He gave the book back to her.

Marla said, "Really, Lucas, you should act. You look good, you don't give a shit about performing in front of an audience, and you've got style."

Lucas shrugged.

"Start now. You're perfect. Pisses me off, you wasting your talents while the rest of us work our asses flat."

Lucas laughed. "Show me when that happens."

Marla read the next line. Cat and Marla disagreed about how Janet should handle Lucas.

Marla said he had stage presence, which was rare in a drummer, too bad he had to sit at the back, because the lead singer ought to have a bag over his head, he was so ugly. Lucas was way out ahead of all of them, but he didn't have a lick of ambition, "and that seems fine to you now, but give it ten years," she often said.

Cat, who had given up all her acting ambitions and was going to community college in marketing, had a list as long as your arm of musicians who thought they were going to hit the jackpot, and of course never did. She thought Janet should get Lucas to go for his GED and then learn something like accounting or library science. She said, "He smiles, white people aren't afraid of him—he should make the best of what he's got."

Janet turned the page. Almost the end of the first act. Lucas leaned against her while they kept reading, correcting, translating. By the time they were finished, Janet thought he was asleep, but Marla wasn't going to allow that. She tossed down her book and jumped out of her blanket. She went over to the bookcase, stared for a moment, then chose a volume. She dropped it in Lucas's lap, and he sat up a little bit. She said, "Let's try it."

"Let's try what?"

"Let's try you taking a little advice."

Janet did not think that Lucas was looking for someone to tell him what to do. She could see it when he was watching Reverend Jones— when Reverend Jones was saying something he agreed with, his face looked receptive, and when Reverend Jones was saying something he disagreed with, his face looked blank. He was like a radio that could receive only what it wanted to receive. His face went blank now. Janet took a little breath and held it in.

Marla leaned toward him, took the book, and opened it to a page. It was the first page of *Miss Julie,* from a book of one-act plays Janet had studied in college. She said to Janet, "You be Miss Julie, I'll be Kristin, and Lucas can be Jean." Then she read the stage directions in a clear voice and handed the book to Lucas. Lucas stared at it and handed it back. Since she had her hand on his arm, Janet could feel it go tense. "Oh, come on," said Marla. "It's my favorite game. Just a page. Or two."

There was a feeling Janet hated—the feeling of looking back and forth between two people who did not agree. She glanced at Marla, who was smiling, and then down at the blanket, which she smoothed over her knee. The room no longer seemed cold.

Lucas cleared his throat. As far as Janet knew, Lucas didn't have a temper, but she was beginning to get nervous, as if he did have a temper. Marla, however, was never intimidated. She said, "Just say the first line, 'Miss Julie's crazy again tonight; absolutely crazy.'"

He said the line in a natural way.

Marla took the book and said, "'Oh, so you're back, are you?'" She made it sound a little teasing, as if she was glad to see him and would be more glad in a minute or two. She again handed Lucas the book.

Lucas stared at the far wall for a space, then said, "I'm not into this. I hate plays."

"Why is that?" said Marla.

"People keep talking and talking, and if they don't start yelling eventually, the audience falls asleep. I can only take so much talking."

Janet realized that this was true.

Marla was not to be deterred by mere theory. She said, "Just read the speech." The two of them stared at one another for a long moment, Marla looking more and more like a teacher—a French teacher, stylish and haughty, but a teacher nonetheless. And then she shifted, actress that she was—a smile burst out that was both saucy and cheerful, and she said, "You could do me a favor, Mr. Jordan, just this once."

Lucas's gaze went back to the page. After a minute of silence, he looked back at Marla and said the speech, shaping it, giving it warmth. Then he put down the book, took Janet's hand, and set Janet's hand on top of the book. He held it there. Marla said, "My Lord, you are stubborn. But I thought you'd be good, and you are. Just because I'm telling you what to do doesn't mean you can't do it."

Yes, it does, thought Janet.

Lucas smiled his brilliant and charismatic smile. No wonder Marla wanted him to act—if he was in your play, audiences would come back for more and more and more.

There was a long silence, during which Marla sat down again and picked up the French play. She said another line, Janet corrected her, and she said it again. Lucas leaned back against the wall and closed his eyes. With her hand still on the book underneath his, Janet and Marla finished *The Madwoman of Chaillot*. As soon as they had read the last line, Marla stood up, leaned toward Lucas, and said, "I'm going to write a play just for you. A one-act."

Lucas opened his eyes and smiled, then said, "No dialogue, though."

"You think I can't do that?"

"We'll see," said Lucas.

Marla zipped out the door and down the hall as if she was going to get started that very night.

In the eighteen months they had been seeing each other, Janet had been careful of boundaries, as her mother would have said, not because Lucas was touchy, but because she was always careful of boundaries. As a result, though, she knew nothing about his boundaries. She, perhaps, didn't have any, at least where he was concerned. He was three years younger than she was, but six inches taller, five years less educated, but 50 percent better-looking, 20 percent less self-confident, but twice as talented, half as well traveled but half again more experienced. Really, they were equal in no way, and her support of the civil-rights movement told her nothing about how to manage herself or him. She looked at her watch. It was after ten. Usually, they stayed up until midnight, but she said, "It's cold. You want to go to bed?"

"What do you think?"

"About what?"

"You think I'm stupid?"

"Do I think that a person who can recite lines from a play after a single reading is stupid? Or who can do a drum solo that is actually worth listening to without having smoked six joints is stupid?"

He laughed, but then said, "They did use to put that dunce cap on my head. Sit me in the corner."

"What were you doing that was bad?"

"My own thing. Looking out the window and thinking of songs. Refusing to pay attention. When the teacher called on me, I'd pretend not to hear her."

"My cousin Tim really would have liked you."

Lucas stripped down to his shorts and got under the covers. Janet finished straightening the room, then pulled down the two shades and got in with him. He took her in his arms, and that was enough.

1976

D EBBIE AND HUGH AGREED ON everything having to do with
Carlie, who was now four months old, weighed sixteen pounds,
and was twenty-four inches long. She had been born with plenty
of reddish hair, though that had fallen out, and a darker fringe was
growing in. They agreed that she would be breast-fed until she gave it
up on her own; they agreed that, pacifier or thumb, it was her choice;
they agreed no baby food and no table food until she seemed interested; breast milk was a complete nutrient for a baby. They agreed
no hot peppers until she was eight months old. (But this was a joke.
They had taken a visiting historian out for Chinese food, and Debbie,
in her attentive way, had pointed out the dried peppers in the Kung
Pao chicken. The historian, from Ghana, had picked one up and, with
a smile, swallowed it down. Another man in their party, who had
visited Ghana and was eager to demonstrate his worldly savoir-faire,
had done the same thing and burst into tears. The Ghanaian man had
then explained that where he was from, mothers introduced hot peppers at eight months.) They agreed no playpen. They agreed no crying herself to sleep. They agreed no pink or baby blue, and an equal
number of girls' toys and boys' toys—Carlie could choose. They
agreed on this partly because Hugh's mother had taught her three
sons to knit when they were eight or ten, and he had knitted Carlie a
red baby hat with flaps and a pom-pom. If the baby had been a boy,

they would not have agreed on circumcision, but they had avoided that conflict.

However, after four months, Debbie did not like getting up in the night to nurse. She had asked her mother about it, but Lillian, of course, had never nursed. Aunt Andy had—"smoking the whole time, and turning her head to keep the ash from dropping on the baby." When the twins were babies, there were two nurses named Sally and Hallie who brought Richie and Michael to Aunt Andy in bed. What a pleasure that would be, Debbie thought. She lay on her back in the dark, wide awake. Hugh was snoring lightly, facing the wall. Carlie had not started crying yet, but she would any second now. Debbie often awakened before the crying began, and what could be the signal from the next room? Some biological connection? Carlie could move now, which made Debbie a little nervous. Her aunt Claire had always been told to lay the boys on their stomachs, and now you weren't supposed to do that. Backs were worse, in case they threw up and aspirated the vomit. You were supposed to lay them on their sides and prop them with a rolled blanket. Debbie had been propping with extra punctiliousness lately, because what if? And then there was a woman she knew in her feminist reading group who said she had worn a sling over her shoulder with the baby in it for eight months, only putting him down when he was ready to crawl away. She wore long skirts to meetings and said that real feminism was not getting a better job but reclaiming the matriarchy and the Goddess. She was undecided about whether her son was going to be allowed to learn to read and write, because reading and writing privileged ana- lytical, left-brain thinking. Debbie despised this woman, who, when she said the word "Goddess," smiled slightly, as if she was thinking of her ample self.

The screaming commenced. Debbie waited to see if Hugh would react, and somehow rise from his side of the bed and go get Carlie, but he snored again and then again. He didn't even hear her, though to Debbie the crying was loud enough to rouse the neighbors, which, in the end, got her up.

She started on the left, lifting the bottom of her T-shirt and unsnapping the cup of her nursing bra. Her breast was enormous and hard; the nipple jutted forth, dripping milk. Carlie latched on with enthusiasm—she was starving after six hours. Her little hand, her right hand, waved around for a moment, then settled gently and appreciatively on Debbie's breast. Carlie sucked with concentration for a few seconds, her eyes almost crossing with the effort, and then her eyes rolled up and caught Debbie's gaze. She had beautiful big eyes, true blue heading for blue, not baby blue heading for brown. Debbie smoothed her forehead. Carlie sucked three or four more minutes, and then her mouth relaxed around the nipple, and she smiled a friendly smile. She had only just started doing that. Debbie smiled back and said, "Darling, darling, darling." She made a kiss.

Carlie went at the second breast with more enjoyment and less desperation. Debbie had read that there were three milks—cream, milk, and water—but she couldn't remember in which order they came. Carlie was looking at her and grinned again; then her hand slapped Debbie gently on the breast. She sighed a deep sigh, and Debbie did the same thing.

Was this the best part, the soporific effect of either the sucking or the milk or the rocking beginning to take effect? Debbie had to concentrate on the baby's face or on the picture of Black Beauty above the crib so as not to fall asleep and, God forbid, go limp (though she never had). She herself yawned, and yawned again. Now Carlie let go, asleep. Debbie stood up slowly and carefully, leaning forward, placed the baby smoothly in the crib, wedged the rolled blanket behind her back, and covered her with the quilt her mother had given her, her own little quilt from twenty-nine years ago, faded but soft.

Hugh had pushed the covers down; she straightened them and got in next to him. He was lying on his other side now, apparently sound asleep. She settled on her back and closed her eyes, consciously picturing Carlie's gay smile. Everyone she knew who had babies found it impossible to understand how they themselves had managed to survive bottles and formula and playpens and refrigerator mothers. They talked about it all the time. Lillian, Debbie knew, had done her best, given how she herself had been raised. That smile. That smile. Debbie slept.

FRANK WAS SITTING in his office, staring at rain falling on the Chrysler Building and pondering his favorite project, the supercavitating torpedo. It was pretty evident to the navy that the Russians were further along with their something than Frank's company was. Apart from the extreme danger of the something that the Russians were pretty far along with—should they deploy it, a fleet of nuclear subs would become as fish in a barrel—the safest thing to assume was the thing that Frank always assumed, that the Russians would do unto others as they feared others would do unto them. The West was superior in almost every other weapons system, so it was all the more galling that the Russians might have pre-emptively mastered this supersonic underwater missile. Frank suspected they had uncovered a cache of Nazi documents that the Americans had not known about and kept them to themselves. Or perhaps there had been another Wernher von Braun, who disappeared behind the Iron Curtain without the Americans' suspecting. Frank often thought about the war—not himself in it, but how the larger picture had played out. He had written in a letter to Jesse that he could not decide—had the outcome of the war been a close call, because of the V-2 rocket and the atomic bomb, or had it been a foregone conclusion, because of Allied intelligence, American manufacturing, and the overwhelming surge of Stalin's armies from the east? And since you could not decide even now, more than thirty years later, whether the outcome of World War II had been a close call or a foregone conclusion, then you certainly could not foretell the outcome of the Cold War. As a result of these cogitations, Frank was on the verge of authorizing further investment in the torpedo, although his board was getting restive at the expense.

Wendy, his secretary, announced on the intercom that Gary Vogel was here to see him. It took Frank a second to remember who Gary Vogel was.

Gary looked like the long-distance trucker he had become—his hair was short, his paunch was big, and his demeanor was cautious. Frank had last heard that he worked for an outfit out of Omaha. Frank went around his desk, shook Gary's hand, and said, "Sorry to hear about Uncle John, Gary."

"Shit, it wasn't a surprise. He kept arguing with the doc about going on oxygen, and I guess this saved him the trouble. Nice place you got here." He walked over to the window and looked out at the Chrysler Building. Then he said, "You must be on the pricey side, rent-wise."

"We got in early."

Frank understood that this was not a social call, but he sat on the edge of his desk, mimicking informality—in any negotiation, it was better to wait until the other party committed himself. Gary said, "You know why I'm here?"

Frank remained silent.

"I'm no farmer, in case you didn't notice."

"I heard you're driving big rigs now."

"That's what I hated about the farm. The view never changes, except for the worse."

Frank smiled.

"But my dad loved it. So." He walked over to the window again, stared at the triangles and the curves that always reminded Frank of papal headgear. "You know what they say, this acreage is available."

"You mean your part of the land your dad and my brother have been farming."

"That's what I mean. The price of land is way up there now. We didn't even tell my dad what a fellow from Des Moines estimated. Mom thought the shock would kill him."

Frank said, "What did the fellow from Des Moines say?"

"Three grand an acre."

"And you have—"

"Three hundred fifty acres."

"As I remember, some of that is too hilly to cultivate."

"Twenty-nine acres. Pasture and woodlot. Badger Creek cuts off the one corner—another two and a third acres."

"You've had it surveyed?"

Gary nodded.

Frank said, "You want me to buy you out."

"I do," said Gary.

Everyone in Iowa scratched their heads at the pivot between the generations, and if Lois had pushed Roland Frederick down the basement stairs, as Frank sometimes thought she had, well, it was the practical thing to do and Frank respected her for it. He asked, "What have you said to Joe?"

"Ah, Joe doesn't want to talk about it. Why would he? Everything is just the way he likes it now."

"I don't think we can give you three grand an acre. It's not going to produce enough to pay off that kind of investment."

Gary pulled out a handkerchief and blew his nose, then folded it thoughtfully and stuck it back in his pocket. He said, "Frankie, you know that, and I know that, but there's a lot of fellas in Chicago and Omaha who don't seem to know that, and I'm not going to kid you, I plan to get out while the getting out is good."

Frank said, "What's your time frame?"

Gary said, "I don't see myself investing in seed this year."

"All right, then," said Frank.

After that came the usual Iowa discomfort about saying goodbye. Gary and Frank exchanged a few niceties, but the door was conveniently near, and soon Gary was through it. Frank closed it behind him. It appeared as though he was about to invest in farmland. This was not a good idea, but when he caught sight of the Chrysler Building, now wet and shining in the late-afternoon sun, he got an idea, not one that Uncle Jens would have cared for, but one he thought might solve the problem, at least for a few years. He picked up the phone on his desk and dialed Lillian's number.

THERE WAS a rule at the Y that kids ten years old and under could not be in diving classes—or at least real diving classes. They could learn to swan-dive off the low board, and Charlie had gotten the teacher to let him try a jackknife, but off the high board they could only jump, and not even cannonball. Charlie had been grumpy all winter at the rules, but Mom had pointed out more than once that the pool at the Y was only ten feet deep in the diving end, and that was dangerous. The fact that Charlie could swim down and touch the bottom easy as pie worked against him rather than for him. But now it was summer, he was eleven, and enrolled in the diving class at the outdoor pool—that pool was twelve feet deep at the diving end. Charlie felt that the high board was ready for him.

At eight o'clock, he swam laps for an hour, perfecting his backstroke. He had grown an inch in the last year, and though Alex Durkin was faster than he was, Alex was a year older and three inches taller. From nine o'clock, he was supposed to sit around, reading some book that was on his summer reading list, and stay out of the pool until his diving class, but he often took his book up onto the high dive and sat there, dangling his legs and enjoying the view. His teachers—Mr. Jenkins for swimming and Mr. Lutz for diving—let him alone as long as he had his book with him and didn't make any noise. Mr. Lutz taught diving at the high school, and Charlie wanted to keep on his good side forever and ever.

Mom often said, "I have given up on you, Charlie," but she always said it with a smile, and then, "You are bound and determined to go your own way. It's a good thing you're such a handsome and charming boy." Once in a while, Dad sat down with him and had a serious conversation, in which they discussed consequences. Mom and Dad lived in fear of consequences, mostly because Dad's brother, Uncle Urban, whom Charlie had never met, had died when he was sixteen as the consequence of getting drunk and driving his car into a lamppost on a bridge over the Des Peres River. The lamppost had been infested with termites and had fallen over the edge, and the car, which was going a hundred miles an hour (Charlie thought), went right with it. Urban, or "Urbie," had never understood consequences. When Mom and Dad had adopted Charlie from the hospital, they had vowed to our Lord Jesus Christ that Charlie would be properly taught, and so they went to Mass every Sunday at Holy Redeemer. Mom wanted him to be an altar boy, but Charlie could see that the altar boys had to stand very still—their legs never jiggled, and they made no noise that they weren't supposed to make. Also, they had to say things the right way. "And with your spirit" could never be said, "With Dan in Roy's stirrups," for example, which was a phrase Charlie often contemplated during Mass, and if he contemplated it, it was sure to pop out. Now that he was taking diving off the high board (the three-meter board, it was called), Mom was going to Mass every day, but she dropped him off with a smile and a "Have fun!" and so he did. He knew she was praying for him—she prayed for everybody, including Jimmy Carter.

Coach Lutz made them stretch every single morning. "Point your toes, touch your nose, hold your pose, stretching shows" was the rhyme for that way of bending so that your nose touched your knees, and "Stand up tall, show it all, stand up tall, see it all" was the rhyme for making sure that their bodies were straight, from their flat hands to their elbows against their ears to their shoulders, hips, knees, and pointed toes. Once they were allowed on the one-meter board, they spent a long time going straight down the board and into the water, no matter what. Charlie tried to be like Moira, who knew what she was doing every step, and always rode the board perfectly.

Then they had to learn to tuck. Off the low board, a tuck was just a fancy cannonball. If they got to the water without a good, tight tuck (pretty hard off the low board, but not impossible), they lost ten dollars of the hundred the coach said they started the day with. Supposedly, someday he was going to pay them real money, but Charlie knew this was a joke. Every day, as often as he could, Charlie asked Mom and Dad for a trampoline in the backyard. Mom said he must stop pestering her, and Dad said they couldn't afford it, but apparently Mom had lit some candles at the church, and now they were thinking about it. In Charlie's experience, pestering worked fine.

Off the high board, they had to tuck and then lay out and go in feet first with their toes pointed. They got ten more dollars for no splash. Charlie was getting better: if he untucked smoothly rather than jerkily, his splash was good, though not worth money. Today they were going to tuck and lay out in a dive, flat hands first. Charlie had been thinking about it all weekend and all morning, so intently that he'd dropped his book in the pool and had to slip in and get it, then spread it out on the concrete deck and hope that it would dry.

Now was the time. Moira had gone, Emma had gone. Emma's head popped up, and she waved. Charlie climbed the ladder, pulling himself with his hands and pushing himself with his feet, consciously lifting the weight of his body in order to get stronger and bigger. At the top, he took a deep breath and looked around. The blue pool and the green park spread away from him, and he lifted his arms, thinking that this was surely how a bird felt. He took another deep breath—right foot first, three big steps, bend your knees and hips, jump, bounce, tuck, roll, open up, lay out, and wait for the water, with his hands gripping each other and his elbows flat to his ears.

Maybe, Charlie thought later, this was what passing out felt like, because, after he looked at his right foot stepping, he really didn't know what happened. All he knew was that he had never felt anything like it—the world turning upside down and right side up and upside down again, his body unwinding like a string, his hands entering the water as if piercing a hole in a piece of paper. He awakened when he touched the bottom of the pool, shook his head, and swam to the side. Up. Deep breath. Coach Lutz was standing right there. He shouted, "What was that all about, Charlie?"

Charlie said that he didn't know.

"What was that dive?"

Charlie shook his head.

Coach Lutz stared at him, then said, "Don't you realize you did a front one and a half?"

"No, sir." Charlie knew to say "sir" and "ma'am" if he was in trouble.

There was a long pause. Coach Lutz said, "Most kids, I wouldn't believe them, Charlie, but you I believe."

Then he said, "It was a good one, too. But don't do it again."

Only then did he smile.

After that, going to diving class was like putting himself in a box and closing the lid. He did exactly as he was told and just the way he was told to do it. But the day would come, like Christmas, when he would be allowed to open the box, and the rolls and twists would fill him with that sense, again, that he knew everything and nothing at the exact same time, that between the sight of his foot and the feeling of the water there would be an intoxicating mystery, and that was the only thing in this world that he wanted.

MICHAEL GOT IT into his mind that the best place to take girls was down to New Hope, where the queers had these great dance clubs, like the Prelude. Richie didn't object—the sound system was top-of-the-line loud, the mirror lights were flashing, the dance floor was big, and girls could wear great outfits and get plenty of compliments. If you didn't mind queers that much and kept your elbows up in the john, that part was fine, and there were also plenty of poppers, which made for an even better time. Sometimes Michael went without Richie, but they didn't have to go everywhere together, and they weren't living together. Michael worked for Mr. Upjohn as a runner on the trading floor; Richie worked for Mr. Rubino, updating commercial listings and answering the phone. Michael made fifteen hundred dollars a month, and Richie made sixteen hundred.

Their car was the old Chrysler (though Michael was looking at a Jag, and Richie liked Porsches). The number-one girl was Marnie Keller. She worked as an assistant in publishing at Viking, and made about two cents an hour. She lived in an illegal sublet in Chelsea and couldn't answer the phone or the door. If Michael wanted to see her, he had to go to her place and knock, and she would look through the little hole in the door and let him in if she was in the mood. Girl number two was a friend of Marnie's from work, who lived on the Upper East Side, in a dump. The main floor of the apartment was nice enough, but Ivy's room was down a spiral staircase that had been cut into the floor. No window, but there was a double bed and a colorful rug, and it was better than sleeping on couches, which is what Ivy had done for three months after coming to New York after graduating from Bard. Marnie was in publicity, and Ivy was in editorial. They didn't let you hold doors for them, but they did let you pay. Michael said that that was women's liberation for you.

Everyone was waiting for him outside Michael's place on Eighty-fourth Street, also a dump, but in a good neighborhood. Michael had an arm around each girl. He was wearing a tight jacket and boots with heels. A cigarette was dangling from the corner of his mouth. When Richie pulled up, Michael hustled Marnie into the back seat with him and let Ivy open the passenger's door for herself. She got in and gave Richie a kiss on the cheek; Michael said, "Fuck, it's cold. The heat on?"

Richie kissed Ivy in return, then said, "Hi, Marn. Where'd you pick up this asshole?"

"Usual spot," said Marnie, and the two girls laughed.

"Fuck, she loves me, she loves me not," said Michael. He had the expanded quality that indicated to Richie that he'd had a few drinks before the girls arrived. He lay back across most of the seat, and pulled Marnie against him. She said, "How can I fasten my seat belt?"

"No seat belts on you, baby," said Michael.

Ivy fastened her seat belt, put her hand on Richie's knee.

New York was not like college in many ways, and one of them was that the girls he dated in college wanted boyfriends, a ring, and a wedding, but the girls that he dated in New York wanted something more like a wild brother. Michael said that the only thing girls in New York wanted was a decent apartment, and to get that you had to find an older man who (as Richie knew) had purchased his apartment in the early sixties. If that meant kids and an ex-wife, so be it. Boys their own age were for fun, and older men were for membership at MoMA, an account with a car service, access to book parties where Norman Mailer might show up. This system was fine, according to Michael. In the first place, look at their mom and dad, who might as well be living in a hotel as in a house together—a thirty-year-old stepmother would at least buy the old man some cooler suits. In the second place, in ten years, when they themselves had it made, they would have their pick of that crop, the 1963 crop, and who was to say that 1963 wasn't a very good year? Michael planned to sample all the vintages along the way.

Richie felt that he could go either way, depending on the girl. He was a little lonely, so he could imagine himself making something permanent, living in Brooklyn, an upper-floor apartment where the plumbing worked and the cockroaches were more reticent. He could imagine himself talking to this girl and making jokes, and going out to breakfast and seeing movies and taking the subway to work every morning. And not introducing her to Michael. On the other hand, there was nothing wrong with the system they'd come up with, and they could have dated every night if they felt like it. There were that many girls.

New Hope was about an hour and fifteen minutes away. The town was full of restaurants and shops, and all the houses were fixed up, with paint jobs and gardens. Michael said this was mostly because the queers decided they needed a nicer spot than Woodstock, and a closer one, too. This was how New York worked—money went to the Hamptons, hippies and Jews went to the Catskills, queers went to New Hope and Fire Island. In the back seat, Michael was making out with Marnie. They were laughing, and she said, "I should have worn jeans! Keep your hand in your own pants, Michael!"

"You know you don't mean that."

"I do. Shit!" She sounded actually annoyed.

Richie tapped the brake pedal, and the car lurched. There was a moment of silence. When he looked in the rearview mirror, Richie saw Michael hoist himself upright. A moment later, he put on his seat belt (Richie could hear the click), and then Marnie put on hers. He and Ivy exchanged a glance and a smile. Ivy's lips formed the words "Mission accomplished," and the two of them laughed, but softly.

Inside the Prelude, the sight of men with their arms around one another, dancing together and sometimes kissing, sort of shocked him, and when he looked again, there was the even odder sight of very, very tall women with narrow hips in high heels and heavy makeup who he realized after a few minutes were men in drag. Twice, they had seen shows of dance numbers on the stage. The dancers were beautiful and skilled, and when they bowed at the end, they pulled off their wigs and revealed their bristly heads. They got rounds and rounds of applause. The flashing lights and the pounding music made these sights all the more strange; it took him maybe fifteen minutes every time he came to stop staring and start having fun. No matter how well dressed Marnie and Ivy were, he and Michael got the stares. Ivy started laughing as soon as they walked in the door—she loved the outfits the cross-dressers had on that she herself didn't have the figure or the nerve to wear, and she loved the dedication with which some of these guys had taught themselves wonderful old Fred Astaire or Gene Kelly moves. She kept poking him and pointing. The music was disco, but the dancing, often, was *American in Paris*. She got so pleased that she kissed him, saying, "Oh, you are sweet, Richie."

He danced and danced, making sure he partnered with both Ivy and Marnie, until he collapsed at a table and ordered a Heiny. Michael liked Stoli and grapefruit juice. He said it was nutritious.

At one-thirty, Richie was ready to go—after five Heinies, he was still okay to drive, but he didn't want a sixth. Ivy was sleeping against his shoulder, and Marnie was dancing with a tall woman in heels who needed a shave. Right then, the Donna Summer song came on, "Last Dance." He didn't know where Michael was until he heard his voice. Three queers on the dance floor were having an argument Richie had heard before: "He's mine, he's going home with me," followed by "No, Tommy, this is my new friend. I'm leaving with him." Then another voice, saying, "You want to come with us?" Then the first voice, rising, "I brought you! You called me because your transmission is fucked! I paid the cover!" Then Michael's voice, "Yeah!"

Richie eased Ivy's head onto the table and stood up. He was a little off kilter. Michael's voice shouted, "All right." It was Michael's I'm-about-to-punch-somebody voice. Richie made his way through the hugging bodies on the dance floor. They were in the back corner. Michael's jacket was off, and his shirt was unbuttoned, but the three guys (all dressed as guys) were ignoring him. One was shaking his head regretfully, and another was putting his arm around the head shaker's waist. The third was between Michael and his friends; just as he opened his mouth, Michael pushed him toward the other two and exclaimed, "Act like a fucking man, you faggot!" The guy fell forward, and the other two caught him. Michael ran at them and managed to grab one of them before Richie knocked into his twin and bumped him aside; then he closed his fingers around Michael's upper arm and pushed him across the dance floor to where Marnie was petting Ivy's hair. He said, "Let's go to the diner. I need a cup of coffee before we head home."

"Fuck you," said Michael.

"Oh," said Ivy. "Me, too. Me, too. Can we have a pancake?"

"Two pancakes," said Richie. He helped Ivy to her feet and gave his hand to Marnie, who stood up, shook herself like a dog, and said, "Wow, did you see that guy I was dancing with? He was like Cyd Charisse or something. Taller, though." She kept mumbling. Richie put an arm around each girl and steered them toward the door. As planned, Michael stumbled after them, muttering, "Fuck, fuck. Fuck." He almost hit the pavement where the parking lot met Old York Road, but Richie stuck with the girls and put them both in front, only then opening the rear door and kind of pouring Michael into the back seat. Michael curled up and let out a moan. Marnie said, "He really is an alcoholic, you know."

"I know," said Richie. Marnie closed her eyes, but Ivy seemed revived. She took Richie's hand and squeezed it.

At the New Hope Diner, Richie helped the girls up the steps, in the door, then to the second booth, Marnie to the left of him, Ivy to the right of him, himself squeezed cozily in between. Marnie was hungry now, too. The waitress kept yawning into her pad. By the time the food arrived, Michael had staggered in. Through the window, Richie could dimly see that he had left the car door open.

Michael didn't order anything—he ate half of Richie's bun and one of Marnie's slices of bacon. He drank a cup of coffee. He said, "You know what the fuck really pisses me off?"

"What, babe?" said Marnie.

"This faggot sits next to me at that bar there? And I say, Watch your fag, faggot, and he's got this long ash on his cigarette, and he drops it right onto my pants."

Richie laughed.

"Don't laugh! There's a big fucking hole." He scooted out of the seat and stood up. Sure enough, on the front of the right leg of his pants was a blackened hole about a quarter-inch wide. The polyester fibers had burned and melted. "Hurt, too. I shoulda punched the guy out, but I thought I was gonna fall off my stool." He coughed.

Both Ivy and Marnie rolled their eyes.

By the time they got back to Michael's apartment, it was very late, but there was a parking spot in front of the entrance. Richie was fine—not drunk at all. With the girls' help, he heaved Michael out of the car and through the door, into the elevator, up one floor. He was stiff—in its stupor, his body still possessed the tension of finely tuned anger and pride. Richie dropped on the couch, and Marnie took off his shoes. Ivy found a blanket and threw it over him.

When Michael was well and truly taken care of, Richie said, "Okay, sweeties, it's after five. I'm tired. Want to take a nap?" He opened the door to Michael's bedroom. The bed looked inviting—made, at least, no clothes strewn all over it. Marnie yawned, and Ivy said, "I want the left side. I just can only sleep on the left side."

"I get the middle," Richie said.

THE LAWYER, who worked from a walnut-paneled office in his very enormous Gothic pile of a house in North Usherton, was Frank's long-ago chemistry lab partner. He'd always been nervous about what was smoking in the beakers but didn't mind writing up the results. Frank shook his hand heartily, and listened to him yammer on about how proud everyone was of Frank, he'd really made something of himself, a life to be envied, not so narrow as that of a small-town lawyer, six kids, though, and all of them doing fine, the eldest boy down in

South Florida now, first grandchild—he sighed, apparently in spite of himself. And this house, well, it took as much upkeep as any farm. A half-acre front yard—

Joe and Jesse came in—Joseph Walter Langdon; "Jesse," not "Joe, junior." The three of them sat at the table. Jesse gave him a grin, was glad to see him. Joe shook his hand without saying anything. Frank had done a good turn, and everyone was a little surprised at it, including Frank.

The lawyer came back in as they sat down, and spread the papers that they were to sign in front of them. Frank had been right, as usual. Lillian had willingly given her portion of the farm to Joe. Henry had said, "Tell me what a farm is again?" and laughed. He knew they would never sell the place anyway, so why think of it as money? Paul, of course, had nearly knocked Claire over in his rush to put his hands on the $260,000 Uncle Jens had paid for her share (after inheritance taxes). Gary and Aunt Angela had been plenty grateful in the end to take their money, too—Gary was planning on buying his own rig. Andy had made no objection; her Higher Power and her friends in AA thought it was the right thing to do, and besides, she was indifferent to money as long as her charge account at Bergdorf's was free and clear. Frank smiled at Jesse and said, "Got your dollar?"

Jesse pulled a dollar out of his pocket, and Frank frowned, then said, "I've changed my mind. I think I'm going to charge you ten."

Solemnly, Jesse said, "I have that. I was going to—"

But then they all laughed, and Frank shrugged, saying, "Go ahead, buy yourself some lunch."

"I was going to buy gas."

They all signed the deeds, and Frank received his one-dollar "consideration" and put it in his inside jacket pocket. He said, "Okay, I suppose I'll invest this in computers."

Everyone laughed again.

The lawyer swept up the papers and stacked them together. He congratulated Joe and Jesse, now joint owners of a very nice farm, and, as they all left the office, he put his finger on Frank's arm. "I have to tell you, I've seen a lot of grief and fury in this office. Glad to see this one stay together and remain a family farm."

Frank smacked him on the back in a friendly way, then followed his brother and nephew onto the porch and down the long driveway. They paused when they got to the street. It was late afternoon, but the air was still bright and flat with dust. Joe said, "Never thought that would be so easy. When John died, my heart sank, I gotta tell you."

"Who's going to live over in their house?" Only two houses now—the kit house where Joe and Lois lived with Minnie, and this old Vogel-Augsberger place.

"It's in pretty good shape," said Joe. "John told me it was built by a famous bricklayer who'd come over from Bavaria after learning his trade there. I guess he made the bricks himself."

Frank said, "Remember the story Opa used to tell about the brick maker who refused to give the king an extra brick?"

Jesse said, "What was that?"

"Well, every time the brick maker took his bricks from the kiln, he set aside a certain number for the king, and at the end of the year, he pushed them in his wheelbarrow to the castle. They were fine bricks, of an unusual color, and after the king had received them for many years, he decided to build a house with them, with an arched doorway as an entrance. But after the house was built, the builder was one brick shy—the very brick he needed as the keystone of the arch. He wanted all the bricks to match, so he sent his representative to the brick maker to demand one last brick. However, since the brick maker had paid his taxes, he asked that the king pay him one aureus—that's a gold coin—for the brick. The representative sent a messenger to the king, and when the king, who was walking around the new house, heard the message, he became enraged at the arrogance of the brick maker. He sent the messenger back to arrest the brick maker and throw him into the dungeon. He kept walking around and around the new house, and after a while he was so angry at the pride of this mere common brick maker that he decided that he wanted to go and demand the brick himself. And so the king rushed out of the house, and as he did so, his crown hit the top of the arch, and the arch, being unsecured, collapsed on top of him and killed him."

"I don't remember that story," said Joe.

"Is there a moral?" said Jesse.

"Sometimes it's easier to pay," said Frank. "'Do the easier thing' was always Opa's moral. He was a happy man."

Frank did not want to be thanked. What he wanted was just this thing that he was now getting: Jesse laughing at his story, this knowledge that his money had gone for something worthwhile at last, that, against all odds, he was a good man, that happiness could be bought—if not his, then Jesse's and, yes, Joe's. Joe and Jesse got into the same car, Jesse driving, and waved as they drove off. Frank stood for another moment or two, not knowing quite where to go for the evening.

1977

As old as she was and as much as she had seen, Eloise understood politics less and less. How blithely she and Julius had once
discussed whether, in America, class was the most important political divide, or race. Julius held out for class—he was a traditional-
ist, wasn't he?—and Eloise insisted on race. But neither of them had
any idea what they were talking about—they had learned it all from
books. In 1920s Chicago, they had been know-it-all tourists, writing
articles and tracts extrapolated from the theories of Germans living
in England. How was she to think about the Zebra killings, converted Muslim black boys walking around San Francisco, torturing
and shooting random white women and old men because they were
white and white people were devils? She thought several things, and
one of them was, why not, really, given the past and present cruelties
that whites perpetrated on blacks? Another of them was, if women
were equal to men, then why were their murders more affecting? And
another of them was that religion was not just the opiate of the people
but an out-and-out poison; and still another was, I hope I don't get
shot walking down Shattuck, thinking about whether I should wash
the car. And what was she supposed to think about the Symbionese
Liberation Army and Patty Hearst?

Even more current and confusing was Janet and Lucas's growing
attachment to the Peoples Temple. Eloise liked all of these young-

sters. Janet, child of the bourgeoisie; Lucas, child of the working class but with artistic aspirations; Cat, child of the lower middle class with hopes of self-betterment; Marla, a beauty, which was a class of its own no matter what Julius would have said. There was also Jorge, whose father had been a doctor in Mexico City, but who had died when Jorge was two, so Jorge had picked vegetables in the Salinas Valley with his cousins until some kind church group put him in school; it turned out he was good at science and math, and so now he was taking pre-med courses at SF State. Someone whom Eloise had only met once was Lena, a runaway from North Dakota, whom the others knew from the Temple. Maybe she was sixteen. She was, apparently, much appreciated for her blond good looks by Reverend Jones. She might be shaping into a full-fledged member of the Lumpenproletariat, but, then, militant feminism asked you to resist categorizing prostitutes as morally suspect merely because they worked in the sex trade. Truly, Eloise was beyond her depth politically, as she suspected Julius, and even Karl Marx, would have been. What she did was offer advice from time to time and hope for the best. What she also did was worry.

She worried because, one visit to the Temple and one look at "Reverend" Jones, and she knew what she was seeing—Joe Stalin from Indiana, the sort of fellow who sucked down a few ideas and then vomited them forth, now irreparably contaminated by the poisons of his very own body. And soul, for that matter, if you believed in souls, which, as a materialist, Eloise did not. It made no difference at all to her that Willie Brown had called the man "a combination of Martin King, Angela Davis, Albert Einstein, and Chairman Mao"— that was campaign bullshit. Or that this kid Jerry Brown sucked up to the fellow, too. Now that they were in office, she thought, they would be running from the Temple fast enough. Jones was crazy and getting crazier, and you didn't have to be a former member of the CPUSA to perceive that.

Saving Marla was easy: having put off her escape to Paris for a year, in hopes that her two new one-acts would be produced by the Berkeley Rep, Marla just needed a little push. Well, a medium-sized push. She had used most of her savings to produce the two plays at a coffeehouse in Berkeley—no reviews, small audiences, net loss of $487.32. Eloise had liked the plays, both set in a classroom. In the first play, Lucas walked around, drumming on a desk, dancing, drawing, searching here and there, evidently out of control. A teacher's voice-over gave him increasingly impatient instructions, until, finally, he sat down at his desk and read, resentfully, from an old first-grade reader, with Dick, Jane, and Spot on the cover. But he gave up, slumped slowly to the floor of the stage, and lay there for a long moment as the lights got brighter and brighter. The play was only fifteen minutes long, but Lucas was convincing and affecting in his role. In the second, Marla played herself, as a six-year-old child. It took place in the same classroom, and a short woman, maybe five feet tall, played the teacher. But Marla was perfect as a six-year-old—lolling in her chair, asking in a loud voice to go to the bathroom, interrupting the (imaginary) recitations of the (imaginary) other children, making addition mistakes on the board, sitting on a stool in the corner with a dunce cap on her head. She was so beautiful and elegant as she went through this performance that you really were shocked when the teacher caned her. But apparently, no one in Berkeley was interested in the childhoods of black children as portrayed by a woman playwright. This season, the Rep was doing Shakespeare, Noël Coward, *Our Town,* yawn.

And so, when Eloise got her tiny little portion of Gary's sale of her father's farm—twenty thousand dollars it was—she called Marla up and offered to invest in her French career—do *not* tell Janet—and she gave her two grand and bought her a one-way ticket to Paris. Marla was grateful but nervous; the only thing she said that was worrisome was that Reverend Jones thought that when nuclear war came, and you could be sure it would, Paris would go up in, not smoke, but radioactive gases. "No," said Eloise, "it will not. Even Hitler wanted to preserve Paris." And so she put the girl on the plane, and off she went.

Cat was harder. She had grown up in an all-black town in Texas and moved to California against her parents' wishes. She had then done a few things she now regretted. But she was devoted to the Temple, and to Jones. She saw herself as Janet's "sponsor," and Jones had given her some responsibilities that she took very seriously, including looking after his small children two days a week. Cat was vague about who the mothers of these children were—"We are all their mothers" was what she said, "and Reverend Jones is their father, as he is our father." When she wasn't talking about the Temple—who was in and who was out, who was betraying and who was loyal—she loved to talk about cooking and jogging, two of Eloise's hobbies. Cat also liked Janet very much, and did not like Lucas very much. Eloise could not understand why, but she thought it had something to do with the Temple.

Eloise loved Lucas. Of course, she loved Janet, too—Janet reminded her so much of Rosanna, though her hair was dark and she was five seven, not five two. She had some of Rosanna's mannerisms: when she had said something she really meant, she stood up straight and flared her nostrils, and she always sat with her knees together and her feet together, never slouching. Eloise, who had spent years refusing to let Rosanna tell her what to do, but admiring her older sister's looks and self-assurance, was always struck by the resemblance. When Lucas was onstage, she watched the women in the audience staring at him. He was like Cary Grant. There was a being inside of him that was a version of himself; that being was so charming that you could not help being attracted to it, but it had a separate existence from his everyday self. The question Eloise worried about was whether the Stalin from Indiana had noticed the charismatic Lucas, and marked Lucas as a threat or a rival. If so, Eloise thought, Lucas might be in danger, but when she said this aloud to herself, she laughed. Everyone else in town, it seemed, saw Reverend Jones as a powerful force for good in the community. His followers loved him, spoke well of him, reported over and over that their lives had changed under the influence of his loving congregation. They'd found friendship, self-discipline, hope. If they revered him, what was the harm in that? If race was the most important divide in America, then why should Eloise be suspicious of a man who had been more successful than any other in bringing black and white together under one roof, and making them comfortable and accepting of one another?

JANET WAS GLAD in spite of herself that she and Lucas didn't own much, because she saw how difficult it was for some of the Temple members to turn over their possessions to communal ownership. There was one couple she was watching when they donated their house on Potrero Hill. The house was to be set up as a commune. The man had a look on his face like he was happy to get rid of the thing, but the woman cried. Janet watched her; she cried for a long time, and the man just glanced at her every so often, as though he was disappointed in her and waiting for her to stop. When children were turned over to communal care, there was a lot of crying; Janet didn't think she herself would be able to take that so she was glad she and Lucas didn't have children. She also didn't agree with the paddling, but in that she thought she might be wrong, since just about everyone she knew had been spanked or whipped as a child by their own parents, so why not by their caretakers at the church? Reverend Jones was sympathetic but strict—you had to start the new world sometime; eventually, sometime became now. Didn't those who worshipped Jesus suffer for their revelations? No one was asking the members of the Temple to be flayed alive, shot with arrows, or broken on the wheel (Reverend Jones laughed aloud). Only to share. Only to understand that there was plenty to go around, no matter what it was. Only to give up the onerous responsibility that was possession and take up the freedom that was connection.

Janet also knew that right now, for Lucas, giving up what he possessed was more difficult than it was for her. She didn't say a thing about it—she didn't even let a facial expression about it cross her countenance. When he said that the drums were his, they were. When he said that his money was his, it was. When he said that his recordings of his favorite music were his, they were. Whatever pressure Lucas was to feel, it was not going to come from Janet. One night, when they had something of an argument about the Temple, Lucas said that he wasn't going to sign anything and he expected Janet not to sign anything, either, even a blank piece of paper. If she wanted them to attend like all of their friends, then they had to be free to come and go; he had to be free to do his gigs. There would be no signing. Lucas said that one woman, Joyce someone, had told him that the papers were confessions of child molestation that the reverend would then use against you if you were disloyal and tried to leave the Temple, but Janet and Lucas agreed that this was such a ridiculous and paranoid idea that the woman must be making it up. People made a lot of things up about Reverend Jones—that he called himself God, that he said he could cure cancer, that he kept all the money for himself, that he threatened one woman in a service with a poisonous snake—but

Janet had never seen any of this, and neither had Lucas. There was a lot of pressure to go to services more than one day a week, but, after all, her mother sometimes went to AA meetings three or four days a week, and what was the difference, really? The 25 percent tithe was difficult in a way, but when Janet looked around the congregation at the smiling faces of old folks and some others, like Jorge, who had nothing, she could not think of what else to spend her money on, so why not hand it over?

Today she was all right, too. Last night, it had been difficult to stand there and be shouted at by Cat, by Lena, and by Reverend Jones, told that she was vain and foolish and selfish, that she thought only of Janet Langdon and never of others, that she seemed unable to learn any of the lessons the reverend was trying to teach her. She was evasive or stupid, take your pick—which was worse in the end? If she was really looking for the truth, what was she waiting for? Where was her purse? Hand it over. What were these silly things she kept to herself? Just vanity and childishness. No one was asking her to walk down the street naked, just penniless. What would be so bad about that? People all over the world did it all the time, and their souls thrived on it. To give is to receive—how long would it take her to learn that? If her boyfriend, Lucas, was holding her back, get rid of the fellow; it would be better for the both of them. Go ahead and nod and say yes; no one believes you; we all know you; we all know how hard-hearted and selfish you are; you deserve nothing until you have nothing, and then something will come of it. And so on. Until after midnight. Lucas had sat quietly, looking on, and then left at some point. Finally, when she was really crying, down on her knees with her hands over her face, Reverend Jones came over, took her hand, lifted her up, and put his arms around her. He said to cry it out— every tear was a drop of selfishness pouring forth, making room for the humility that was the true grace of God. Surely she didn't want to remain as she had begun, the corrupt child of a corrupt world? No, he could tell that she did not; he loved her; he could see the precious light dawning in her eyes.

It was Cat who led her home in the rain, took off her soaking clothes, helped her dry her hair, put her to bed, and kissed her good night, and though she cried for a while, she was so exhausted that she did fall asleep. Now she was wiped out, almost hungover in a way;

she knew she ought to get up and go to work, but she could not make herself do it.

THE PROBLEM Eloise had when Jorge came by and told her how enemies of the Temple were bent on destroying it was that she believed him. Jorge was twenty-two; he never thought of the Kennedy assassinations, except as ghost stories. Nor, when she asked him, did he know what the CIA did, only what Jones said it did, which was to infiltrate peaceful organizations like his and destroy them from within. Eloise knew that was true, especially if that organization openly—you might say defiantly—professed socialist principles, which Jones did. When Jones said that J. Edgar Hoover had once called him personally and threatened to destroy or kill him, his wife, and his "rainbow children," and told him that he had a dossier on him full of crimes "you and I know you didn't commit, but that I can prove you did," that was the first time Jorge had heard of Hoover, and he believed the reverend, who had been good to him, like a strict but loving father, and allowed him to work as an orderly in the Temple medical clinic. People came in pain and left in joy, because at last they had found treatment, but also love; Jorge was convinced that the latter was more effective than the former. Eloise remembered what Frank had said about that young woman—Judy was her name—that Hoover hated because she knew he was gathering every molecule of shit he could on everyone he knew in order to maintain his hold over them, and how unusual was that? Not at all, in Eloise's experience.

Jorge insisted that there was nothing at all wrong with Cat, Janet, Lucas, and Jorge himself going to Guyana—the piece of property there was beautiful, rather like Marin County, fertile and well watered. The medical clinic was already up and running, and it was no less healthy than family farms in the Midwest had once been.

"That's not a good recommendation to an old farm girl," said Eloise, but Jorge said, "I would rather work in my own communal field than a field owned by United Fruit."

Eloise said that she hadn't known that United Fruit owned fields in the United States. Jorge scowled but pressed on. All they needed was some money for transportation. Janet had let it out that the family farm had been sold somehow, or split up, and there was money.

Just a few hundred dollars was all they needed. No one, not Lucas or Janet, knew he had come over to ask.

"Cat?" said Eloise.

Jorge didn't answer, just smiled and said, "We know that, deep down, you are in sympathy with socialism and with our experiment. You gave Marla money."

Eloise, who was sitting on the sunporch in her favorite rocker, pushing herself back and forth with her toe, said, "Who told you that?"

"Marla is unhappy in Paris. She might join us."

Marla's last letter had been full of news about how she had been taken up by a group of feminists who adored the self-referential profundities of her inscriptions. They wanted to do a street play on the corner of the Boulevard Saint-Michel and Boulevard Saint-Germain, not even translating the plays into French, but acting them out as a reflection of the pedestrians going by, especially, since summer was at hand, of American tourists. Her funds were holding out fairly well, but she was getting tired of hummus and baba ghanouj. Eloise said, "I can't imagine such a thing."

Jorge, who was sitting on the couch, drinking the chamomile tea Eloise had given him, said, "Well, she didn't write to me, but Reverend Jones has the letter."

Eloise said, "If Reverend Jones wants my money, then he'll have to come and ask for it, because I learned long ago never to discuss finances with anyone but the boss."

She expected Jorge to laugh at this, but he shook his head very seriously. He said, "Now that Rupert Murdoch is financing his assassination and the destruction of the Temple, he dare not go anywhere. His life is in too much danger."

"Who is Rupert Murdoch?" said Eloise.

"He's like that Hearst man."

"William Randolph Hearst?"

"Something like that," said Jorge. "Anyway, Rupert Murdoch had one of our members killed last fall, as a warning, and now he has bigger plans, which means that our members are only safe in Guyana. We thought we were safe in California, but that isn't the case. The coming Nazi takeover will happen everywhere, and when it does, people like me and Lucas will be sent to camps. It happens every thirty years or so. We think, for Janet's and Lucas's safety, you should—"

Eloise found herself rocking rather furiously, and made it a point to stop.

"We've already applied for our passports and visas, though Janet's passport is still valid."

Eloise said, coolly, "What don't you know about her?" She thought, Or me, for that matter.

"Janet has been pretty open about her feelings and thoughts."

"And her assets?"

Jorge smiled.

Eloise thought, I used to like this kid. She said, "When are you planning to go?"

"We understand that the visas will come in early August, so we ought to buy the tickets pretty soon." He looked her right in the eye. "Four tickets—Janet, Lucas, Cat, me."

"How much are the tickets?"

"Three fifty apiece. One-way."

Eloise pretended to think for a moment by gazing out the window, but what she really did was note the two men walking down her street; they had been walking the other direction a few minutes before. She said, "You want a check?" She thought that seven hundred dollars, for Janet's and Lucas's tickets, was not too high a price to pay to get Cat and Jorge out of the country. She said, "What about Lena?"

"The reverend is taking care of her. He likes to have her with him."

Eloise thought, I'll bet he does. Then she thought that Lenin may have been a pig but he was not a religious, lecherous pig.

She said, "Let me find my checkbook." Then she said, "Do you know those two guys who keep walking back and forth in front of my house?"

Jorge glanced out the window. He said, "That's Zeb and Vic."

"What are they doing?"

Jorge said, "We are all in danger. It's better to travel in groups."

Eloise, who had lived in Oakland for years without a second thought, had a second thought.

CAT KEPT URGING Janet to up her tithe, especially since "we don't have the reverend's golden tongue to help us raise funds anymore, at least for now." She acted as though Reverend Jones's flight to Guyana and the article in *New West* magazine meant nothing—of course Reverend Jones had made enemies, and those enemies were glad to talk. Cat kept going to the Temple, kept chatting about whom she saw there and what they did. And then, right on schedule, on August 16, she disappeared from her room. When Lucas called the house where Jorge was living, he got no answer. He went over to the house, in the Mission District. It was empty, the back door unlocked. Janet kept taking out her ticket and putting it away again. When she looked at the destinations—Georgetown, Guyana; change at JFK, New York—the very words made her nervous, but she didn't know which affected her more.

Lucas was at first happy. He came over three days in a row, but then it was Friday, he had to play, and he didn't invite her to come watch. After he, too, disappeared—this was the part that she thought she should have noticed—she had watched him onstage so many times, smiling and waving his sticks, leaning into the drums and staring intently as the beat got faster and more complicated, then, when the song ended, throwing his arms in the air and grinning. Would she ever see that again? Not if he had gone to Guyana. Maybe he had changed his ticket, taken a later flight, used this opportunity to leave her behind because he saw that she was a bourgeois materialist after all. It was a mystery. But she pulled herself together. She went to work, she said that she would take the manager's job at the branch her restaurant was opening on Fulton Street, she said that she would move across the bay, find a room in the Castro, or, because she would be making a little more money, maybe a one-bedroom apartment. Maybe communal living was not for her. Maybe she needed some boundaries, and boundaries started with a locked door. Nor did she hear from Marla. Jorge had told her that Marla had gone to the agricultural paradise after all, had decided that Paris was corrupt and shallow, had turned over a new leaf. So they were all there; they had all left her behind.

She did not run out the back of the restaurant when she saw Aunt Eloise in her section. After being prodded by the maître d', she went over and set the menu in front of her aunt and said, "Would you like to hear today's specials?"

Aunt Eloise looked up at her. "I really did wonder whether you had gone."

"I didn't."

"Thank God! I read the article. I was appalled."

Janet was about to say that the article was all lies and everyone was out to get Reverend Jones, but she said, "I was, too." Then, "You should try the risotto. It's rice cooked in broth with mushrooms, garlic, and Parmesan."

"I know what it is."

Eloise stared at the menu as if she couldn't help herself, then said, "What about Lucas?"

"He went."

Janet sat down in the chair beside Eloise at the table and put her head in her hands. Her hair fell in a dirty curtain around her, and that made her all the sadder, somehow. Aunt Eloise gently pushed it back, looked her in the eye, took her hand. Then she whispered, "Honey, do you want to leave here and go back home?"

Janet nodded.

THERE WERE no kids Minnie had ever seen who had been improved by adult influence, and she thought this in spite of all the conferences over the years in which she had said, "Perhaps if you took Billy in hand," or "Perhaps if you helped Janie attend more closely to her homework . . ." Janet, she thought, would have said her parents wrecked her, but Minnie thought she was a strange combination of daring and alert, strong and brittle, overprepared, too smart for her own good, and never ready. Minnie liked her. You could run down the list of what Frank and Andy and Lillian and Arthur and Tim and this mysterious boy Lucas had done to her, and you could imagine how these cruelties (whether intentional or not) had affected her, but she was the same girl she had always been.

When she got to Iowa (she still would not go all the way to New York), she slept one twelve-hour night, and then she was up, her hair washed and combed, her bed made, her bag unpacked, and her clothes put away. Minnie was a week away from starting school, so she sat in the kitchen while Janet fixed herself a hard-boiled egg and a piece of toast, which she ate neatly. She washed up after herself, and then sat down across the table from Minnie. She looked haggard and grief-stricken, but she said, "I should do something."

"Why don't you take some courses?"

"Where?"

"ISU. Iowa. Drake."

"I never applied to graduate school."

"You can still take some courses. Night courses, if you want. Ames and Iowa City are pretty quiet, at least compared to—"

Janet smiled. "That would be a change."

"Do you want to talk about—"

Janet shook her head, and Minnie wondered which thing she didn't want to talk about—what happened after she got to San Francisco, or what drove her to San Francisco in the first place. But that was neither here nor there. Janet was sitting in front of her, as ready as anyone Minnie had ever seen to take advice. Minnie said, "I always say, choose the place, not the school. Then you'll be happier."

"I would choose Iowa City."

"Me, too," said Minnie.

So they did it step by step. The girl would not take a penny from Frank, referred to his wealth as "blood money," but she was willing to take a loan from Minnie of $250.00. This was when she admitted to Minnie that she had given all her savings to the Peoples Temple at the last minute, after everyone she knew was gone, as a kind of desperate gesture. "How much did you have?" said Minnie.

"Eleven hundred dollars. I had a good job. I was making fifty bucks a night in tips."

Minnie asked no more questions, just helped her find a small apartment on Gilbert Street, within walking distance of downtown, and a part-time job at Things, Things, and Things, which was an expensive but cheerful shop on Clinton. She helped her buy a bed and a chest and a lamp and some bedding and a chair. She went with her to the registrar's office, and, yes, there were quite a few courses she could take. She chose an advanced French-conversation class and a class in art history. Minnie paid the fees, which were small, since she would only be getting adult-ed credit. Then she left her there, sitting on her bed, on a very warm, humid, sunny afternoon, with a sad look on her face, and as she drove back to Denby, Minnie wondered if she had diverted Janet to a less self-destructive path, or if she had just supplied her with the setting for more of the same.

1978

IT WAS NINE. Henry was dressed and had eaten a bowl of oatmeal. It had been snowing for fifty-three hours. Henry knew because he remembered getting up in the dark two nights ago to take a piss (from the Old French, *pissier,* twelfth century, origin unknown), looking out the window, thinking that it was snowing again—what was that, the tenth storm since Thanksgiving?—looking at the clock, and going back to sleep. With the howling winds and the sad attempts at plowing, some drifts mounted to second-story windows, covered cars, blocked streets. He had tenaciously kept shoveling and sweeping his little walk—if he hadn't, he would not be able to get out the door. It was fortunate in some ways that he had sold his car and not purchased another: he would have hated to see a new car simply buried in snow for four months on end. And having no car meant that he wouldn't set out hopefully for, say, Milwaukee, only to be stranded, trapped, and frozen to death. On the other hand, if you walked everywhere, as Henry did, being frozen to death or blown away in these winds was also a hazard.

Rosanna had sometimes talked about the storm of '36 or some such year—Henry would have been three; he remembered nothing—when they first sent Frank to Eloise in Chicago because there was no school in Denby. Frank had supposedly gone through a tunnel of snow and nearly died, and two women saved him by buying him a berth in the sleeping car. Maybe, in those days, two women were always saving Frank. That same year, snow outside his future room, the addition where Joe was sleeping alone, had been up to the eaves. After this winter, Henry thought he could go toe to toe with Rosanna; he was in the most prepared-for-snow city in the world, and there was nowhere to put it. All they needed now, Henry thought, would be a nice ice storm to seal them in permanently.

In ordinary circumstances, no one would have said of him that he was a farm kid, not even his parents, but he had a farm kid's plenitude of provisions—bags of flour, bags of rice, bags of dried beans, boxes of spaghetti, cans of tomatoes, a freezer full of chicken breasts and nicely trimmed steaks. He had wine, he had water, he had anchovies and several varieties of Italian cheeses; if he had to make himself pizza for a week, he could do it. He had a kerosene lamp; he had wood for the fireplace (he'd used about half of that, and he was careful to keep the flue clear—his colleague Nina had passed out several times, thinking that it was the dreary nature of her manuscript that was putting her to sleep, but it turned out to be her chimney leaking carbon monoxide into the living room).

He went into the front room and picked up *The Poetry of Jean de La Ceppède: A Study in Text and Context,* which had just arrived from Oxford for his review. Jean de La Ceppède was right up his alley now. In the summer, Henry had visited Aix-en-Provence and decided that medieval France was unbelievably alluring, and why had he not lifted his youthful gaze from Caedmon and Cynewulf and looked farther south, where the weather was better and the literature and history more complex?

But not only had Henry's academic interests shifted toward France, he was also lonely, had been lonely since Philip left, now two years ago. Philip was in New York, and there was no reasonable hope of seeing him until spring break, seven weeks away. And even if he saw him, Philip had moved on. When Henry stayed with him for four days in October, they had gone out to the bathhouses every night, and while Philip ran joyously from room to room, partner to partner, disappearing and coming back, Henry sat at the bar, sipping gin and tonics, frightened, glad of his graying hair, his utterly straight outfits—khakis, sweaters, blue shirts. Though he had appreciated the wildness and color of the scene, though he had been flirted with, he would have grabbed the bar and resisted being taken away from it with all his strength. Philip, irritated and a little offended, had said, as if he meant it, that that emblematic medieval experience Henry had had as a boy, an eyeless white horse exploding in a ditch full of paleolithic refuse, was the key to his whole Weltanschauung: human nature is inherently evil and is never to be trusted. Philip was much more of a Romantic.

Once in a while, he wished he could call Rosanna and pick a fight with her, as he had done so many times in the past. "Ma," she had hated that, but when he called her "Mom," she said, "What are you, twelve years old?" When he called her "Mother," she said, "I am not a nun," and so for a few months he referred to her, only in her hearing, as "Mother Superior," always smiling when she pursed her lips. Ma! Ma! What did you call a finicky maternal figure? She might have liked "Rosanna," but none of them had dared. He'd wept when he saw her in the open casket, neatly dressed in her gray dress, with the pink sweater she had knitted herself and some black pumps. They had fixed her hair anyhow, not in the bun she preferred, and Lois had said, seriously, "Maybe we should fold up all the sweaters she made herself and put them in there. I hate to see them go to the Salvation Army." But it had seemed too strange to do such a thing, and so they had gone to the Salvation Army—they were too small for anyone in the family.

After the funeral, he had come home to the very apartment where she had died, and not thought very often about it. In spite of having picked her up and lifted her and held her hand, he found himself sometimes dialing her number because he hadn't heard from her in a while and felt guilty, and then he would remember. Was this failure to have experienced her death because, in spite of the evidence, he just couldn't believe it, or because she had never accepted that he was gay (though he had never told her, either, leaving that to Lillian or Claire, and it was unlikely that they ever had)? Maybe she knew what a homosexual was, if she dared to think about it, but sexuality of any kind was not something talked about. You wanted to know the facts of life, you went out and watched some sheep. Were there boys in the neighborhood who tried putting it to a sheep once in a while?

My goodness, why are we talking about such a thing? Henry smiled, stopped reading. The windows were flakily white. In the distance, he heard a siren. It had a futile sound.

If he called Philip now, Philip would be short with him, or maybe brusque. Henry wondered if Basil, too, visited him, and made better use of his opportunities than Henry did. In England, it would not be snowing, or if it was it would be mounding silently on the Gothic windowsills of elegant cathedrals.

For fun, he had taken a test that sorted personality types, and he had given it, too—to Beowulf, to Sir Galahad, to Sir Lancelot and King Arthur. All of them—were they sick, sick, sick, or just a certain type? He had come up I N T J—introverted, intuitive, thinking, judging—no surprise, and he had no trouble finding synonyms— stuffed shirt, irrational, persnickety (which was a lovely example of onomatopoeia, a variation on "pernickety," which was in turn a variation on the Scots word "pernicky," origin unknown), snobbish—that he was sure his colleagues thought were equally applicable. But, he had to lament, irrational, persnickety, snobbish (*sine nobilitate*) stuffed shirts had needs and desires, too! It didn't help that, over the years, he had suppressed his sense of humor. When the department had to designate someone to write a gassy, sober report for the administration, Henry was the one. As for being gay, well, he accepted Philip's view that if you were gay you were gay, but he sometimes wondered, did careful come first or did homosexual come first? Those times he had been with women (and, in retrospect, perhaps he had not experienced Rosa as a woman, because of her confidence, the chip on her shoulder, the clothes, the flat chest, the air of sophistication), had been looking at marriage and children, it had seemed as though being gay would be permanent relief from chaos, and this had turned out to be true. Every romantic encounter nicely arranged and self-contained, like a meeting of spies on the street corner, so careful to avoid the notice of MI5 or the KGB—Henry had liked that part. Could you break out of the box of your I N T J, or were you stuck with it? Was it temperament or training, nature or nurture? Maybe it was a little late, at forty-five, to be asking this question. But if you spent forty-four years arranging things to your satisfaction (according to Rosanna, as soon as he could pick up a block, he made sure that it coordinated with the block next to it), then who was to tell you that satisfaction was maybe the deadliest feeling of all? He looked out the window and decided to call Rosa—but when he tried to get her number from Information, none could be found.

ANDY WAS in the bathroom, reading a copy of *Vogue* on the john. She didn't know what she thought about the Madame Grès draped look. Maybe you would have to feel the fabric against your skin to really enjoy the dresses; otherwise, they were rather dull. The phone rang. She had had a phone installed in the bathroom so that she could soak in the tub and talk, but, like—who was that?—LBJ, she often quietly picked up when she was doing her business. Janet's voice said, "Mom?"

Andy closed her magazine. She hadn't heard from Janet in two months, since Christmas. She carefully said, "Hi, honey," as if this call were no big deal.

"How are you?" said Janet.

"Fine." Janet had told her four times since her escape from those people in San Francisco that she really did not care to be reminded of that crap (that crap that Eloise had detailed for Andy with indelible outrage), and so Andy did not dare say, "And how are you?"

"Where's Dad?"

"I'm sure he's at the office."

"It's after eight there."

"Maybe he's getting a bite to eat, then."

There was a silence, during which Andy assumed Janet was choking back some sort of disapproval of their domestic arrangements. But after Nedra retired (and with a nice package, Andy had assured her AA group), no one was interested in cooking. Andy could make her own salad.

"What are Richie and Michael doing?"

"You know they had their twenty-fifth birthdays?"

"I sent them cards."

"Did you? I hope they received them. Michael's apartment is such a mess, no one in their right mind would go in there, and Richie seems to be staying most of the time with a girl he knows on the Upper East Side. She's Jewish."

"Mom!"

"What? She is. I met her parents. They're Jewish, too."

Andy could hear her report this remark to someone. She was getting to that stage that her father had gotten to, where everything he said got laughed at, but if that was the price of conversations with Janet, Andy was willing to pay it. She said, "Her uncle is a furrier. They gave me a hat. It looks good on me. Can you call me back, I have to—"

"Mom."

Andy shifted her position and set the magazine on the floor. She knew she was about to receive some news, felt a moment of dread, but then she sensed what the news would be. As Janet said it, she mouthed the words, "I'm pregnant."

Andy forced herself not to exclaim, "Oh dear."

Janet said, "He's wonderful!"

"You know it's a boy?"

"No, Mom. Jared. Jared Nelson, my beloved. The father of the pregnancy." She laughed. There was a laugh in the background.

There were many questions that Andy did not dare ask: Are you married? Did you meet him in San Francisco? Where's he from? What does he do? Is he divorced (not a bad thing, in Andy's estimation)? Does he get along with his parents? What's his birth order? Does he drink? Does he speak any Scandinavian language fluently ("Nelson" was possibly a bad sign, though "Nilsson" would be worse)? Janet forestalled her by saying, "He's the funniest person I ever met."

Andy smiled.

"Mom?"

"I don't know what to say."

"Say you're happy."

"I'm happy that Jared is the funniest person you ever met."

"Are you happy I'm pregnant?"

Andy let her gaze wander over the pink bathroom tiles, take in a tiny cobweb, then her shoes, which she had kicked off, then the tub and the sink. She shifted position again, and stood up. According to AA, you were not allowed to lie. When was it, sometime recently, she had seen a picture of a sculpture installation—Dad, Mom, six-year-old daughter, one-year-old baby son. All were the same height, six feet tall, but proportioned realistically. The result was that the baby was enormous, the hugest and most dominant member of the family, and the six-year-old came second. Andy thought it was the truest depiction of family life she had ever laid eyes on; all they needed for profounder horror was expanded premature twins. Even so, she said, "Sweetheart, I am happy for you. And I am happy it's you and not me." This was to be their future as mother and daughter, then—the past unmentioned, a fresh start, equals in keeping their feelings to themselves. Quite Nordic, in its way.

Janet turned away from the phone and repeated this. The voice in the background laughed, and then Janet laughed. Andy let out the breath she was holding. Janet turned back to the phone and said, "Oh, I love you, Mom."

She hadn't said that in twenty years. But as if this declaration were routine, Andy said, "Sweetie. I have to get off. But call me tomorrow and tell me more."

Janet said she would.

When she walked into the kitchen half an hour later, Frank was leaning into the open refrigerator. She said, "There's some ravioli from Antonio's in that cardboard box. It was good."

Frank stood up and turned around. Before he could tell her anything at all about work, she said, "Janet is pregnant."

Frank slammed the door of the refrigerator and said, "I didn't know there was a boyfriend."

"Neither did I."

"Are they getting married?"

"I guess we'll find out."

Frank swallowed, and then swallowed again. Eloise's report had frightened him, too, though he had said only, "Doesn't surprise me." Andy walked over to him, put her arms around him, and laid her head on his chest. She could hear his heart beating—loud booms. She'd always wondered how his arteries could take such a powerful current. He remained stiff for a few moments, and then he yielded, put his arms around her. This was the way, so long ago, forty years now, she had first come to love him. You had to get inside his shell to feel sorry for him; if you didn't feel sorry for him, then you couldn't experience love, but if you pressed yourself against him and felt the warm tension of his flesh, you always felt sorry for him, and tender, too, as lonely as he was. He might hate that, but if you were brave, you would feel it anyway. She felt it now.

PAUL HAD INVESTED "their" money from the farm in something called a Money Market Fund, at almost 9 percent, first for six months, then for another six months. He had longed for the money and been happy to get it, but he was preoccupied by it—he made sure that Gray and Brad, thirteen and ten, knew the difference between a Certificate of Deposit and a Treasury Bill, but Claire did not know the difference, and didn't care. All she knew was that her original $240,000 was bubbling up, and the effervescence amounted to about twenty thousand a year. Paul insisted that the wisest thing to do was to let the interest compound, and he taught the boys the Rule of Seventy-two. Even Brad now knew that if you left your money in the bank at 10 percent interest per year, and then divided seventy-two by ten, the resulting figure was how long it would take for your money to double. If you had, say, $240,000, he said to Brad, by the time you were eighteen you would have $480,000, and by the time you were twenty-four or twenty-five, you would have almost a million, but you couldn't touch it. It had to stay in the bank. The great thing was geometric compounding—at thirty, you would have two million; at thirty-seven, four million; etc. Brad could figure it out from there. And Brad did—if retirement age was sixty-five, then at retirement you would have more than sixty-four million dollars!

When Claire brought up the idea of inflation (that sixty-four million dollars wouldn't be the same in fifty-some years as it was today, look at Germany before the war, or . . .), Paul said that they would save that for another time—best not to discourage him at this point.

As for Claire, for the first time in her life, she understood the old phrase "eat, drink, and be merry, for tomorrow we shall die." She thought of that measly little $240,000 (as compared with the future sixty-four million) and she wanted some of it. In fact, she wanted all of it. In fact, she saw it as the door that could open and let her out of Paul's tight, neat, suffocating house. Now that her mother was dead, she had no one she would have to justify this to. All she had to do was make up her mind.

It was not the boys holding her back. Maybe if they had been girls she would have had a second thought (she imagined girls actually talking to her, letting her brush their hair, asking her questions, and taking advice, though she had never done any of these things with Rosanna), but boys, at least her boys, hardly seemed to notice their mothers. At a party, she had heard one woman laugh and say, "Oh, boys! You can be wonderful to them every day of their lives, and this is what they say: 'Mom! I love Mom,' and that's all. They only think about Dad, no matter whether he was a saint or an asshole—'My mom was great, but *Dad*! Blah, blah, blah, blah, blah.'" And it was true of Gray and Brad: their eyes followed Paul wherever he was. Yes, it was partly in fear, since he was demanding, but all three of them treated her more or less as if she weren't really there, or, she might say, weren't importantly there.

JANET OPENED her eyes and noticed two things—the window to her right, across the sleeping (and snoring) body of Jared, was pale but not light, and the apartment was enveloped in silence. Emily Inez (named after Emily Brontë and Jared's mother) was still sleeping, and well she should be, given that Janet had nursed her twice already, once at ten and again at three. Since the apartment had only one bedroom, Jared had taken the doors off the spacious hall closet and fixed it up as a nursery, visible from the kitchen, the bedroom, and the living room, but Janet knew they would have to move eventually. Janet didn't mind waking up every four hours. Emily had such a strong personality that she had inserted herself quite efficiently into Janet and Jared's easygoing existence, and organized everything around herself. Janet faithfully read Penelope Leach (sent to her by Debbie), and did as Emily told her.

She glanced at the clock: six-forty-five. The weather had been nice all fall, and she could tell as the window brightened that it would be another pleasant day; she could put Emily in the Snugli and walk across Burlington, take a stroll down Clinton and Dubuque, and maybe get all the way to the Hamburg Inn for an early lunch— Emily was sucking the pounds off Janet so quickly that she owed herself a cheeseburger, not to mention some French toast for breakfast. She kissed Jared on his bare shoulder (he wore only shorts to bed, nicely exposing his muscular but supple thirty-year-old chest, and wasn't thirty the best age for a husband, especially if you yourself were twenty-eight? And he was a Gemini to her Libra, nothing better than that), eased out of bed, sneaked past Emily, who was sleeping with her mouth slightly open and her lips, which were divinely full, shaped into a sort of a kiss. She half closed the kitchen door and hefted the kettle—full. She turned on the gas, yawned, and decided that it was perfectly acceptable to go quietly down the hall steps in her pajamas, and even to open the front door and get the paper off the stoop. She set a cup and the instant coffee on the counter, and tiptoed once again past the sleeping baby, and then past the door to her room, and down. Six weeks after delivery, going down the steps was practically like flying compared with the last six weeks of her pregnancy, when the pains in her lower belly made her gasp. Tendons? Ligaments? Something in there was screaming in protest at carrying a thirty-five-pound load that it was not designed to handle. She glanced at the Harrisons' closed door, then slowly turned the knob of the front entrance. The paper was lying there. She grabbed it, noticing as well the bare branches and the drift of brown leaves in the gutters—a melancholy sight. She clutched *The Des Moines Register* (they also got the *Press-Citizen* in the afternoon) and tiptoed back up in time for the first cry.

Penelope Leach said that you should answer the first cry—babies only cry for a reason, and to ignore them is to impress upon them the futility of communication—so she threw the paper onto the kitchen table and went to the cradle. After she picked up Emily, she eased over to the bedroom door and drew it shut, letting Jared know that he could keep sleeping if he wanted to. He didn't have to be at work at the U of I computer lab until noon; Mondays, he was on until eight-thirty, advising lost and confused professors how to stack their punch cards and input data. It was a well-paid job, and Jared liked it—he said that every iota of computer competence he introduced into the brains of old men and women was a positive social good, a point in his favor in the mind of the Grand Intelligence that was the universe. Janet had quit her job at Things, Things, and Things when the steps in the shop got too taxing, but they were doing well enough on Jared's salary. She would go back to school in the spring semester, at least at night. Debbie said that teaching fit right into having kids, even two kids, which she now had, so Janet thought she would do that: have two kids, live wherever Jared worked, teach French in high school. This made her think of Marla, who had written from Paris in the summer. She sat down at the kitchen table and, after putting Emily to the breast, flipped open the paper.

The front-page article did not say that they were all dead, only three to four hundred. The article did not say that American soldiers had raided the Guyana compound and mowed everyone down with machine guns, which was Janet's instant thought as her eye raced down the page. When she read it more slowly, she saw that American soldiers were actually nowhere in the vicinity, that everyone was using the words "mass suicide," and Janet's next instant thought was, how did Reverend Jones persuade Lucas to kill himself? Such a thing was not possible. Emily pulled away, and Janet shifted her to the other breast. She read it again. Most of the article was about a congressman killed in Jonestown along with some other people, including a TV cameraman who had been shot while in the act of filming the shooting. The witness to this said he had seen the cameraman's brains "blown out of his head." Janet read that twice and then read the next part again, about the congressman visiting the camp the previous day, about some of the members wanting to leave with him and go back to California. Her body jerked, bumping Emily's head on the edge of the kitchen table. She came to. Emily did not cry, but as Janet looked down at her face, her dark hair and her wide eyes, she felt herself fall into a well of guilt. She smoothed the small head; the baby was fine.

Janet stood up from her chair and walked down the narrow hallway, which was bright now (it had a skylight, the feature that had made Janet like this place in spite of its proximity to the railroad tracks). She made sure she had both arms under and around Emily—she was a big baby. She tried not to stagger, just to balance carefully on each foot as she made her way toward Jared. He would be very surprised to learn about the massacre, and even more surprised to learn that Janet had had anything to do with these people. She had told him a few things about her life in California—that she had a long-term boyfriend who was in a band, that she worked in a wonderful restaurant and learned to love authentic Italian food, that she lived in a communal arrangement. She let him tease her about being a hippie—he was from Rochester, Minnesota. It could be that she was the only person in Iowa who knew any of these people, or who had ever been inside the Peoples Temple. Cat. Jorge. Janet's face was wet, and by the time Jared sat up in bed, she was standing over him coughing and choking with shock. Being Jared, he reached up, ever so tactfully, and took Emily out of her arms.

Jared said, "What's the matter?" Janet intended to reply, but found she couldn't say anything. She went over and collapsed on her side of the bed. Jared sat holding the baby in the bright morning light, staring down at her in alarm; then he said, "Are you okay? Did something hurt you? Did you fall down?" Janet shook her head. She closed her eyes for a moment, but she knew there was only one thing to do, so she got to her feet, went to the kitchen, and brought back the paper. She handed it to Jared, who was sitting up, holding Emily to his shoulder, and took Emily. She lay down, set Emily beside her, and put her to the right breast again. She pressed against Jared; his hand on her hip, he kept reading, then said, "Oh my God."

Lying between the two of them, Janet felt safe enough finally to focus on Lucas. Until right now, she would have said that she had worked through her feelings about Lucas. First off, he had been incredibly attractive, so talented and joyous and good-looking. And, as Aunt Eloise had said, unself-conscious in a strange way. Anyone would be attracted to him, and lots of women and girls were. Second, telling Lucas what to do was the same as telling him what not to do—if he identified something as an order, he resisted. This perversity Janet found to be both daring and sexy. Third, their last year in the Temple had been fraught with conflict, and, she understood now, they both hated conflict. It was as though the Reverend had infused them with alien personalities, and to what end Janet still could not understand. All the things she knew about the Peoples Temple were contradictory—that people were happy and unhappy, that people loved one another and felt tormented by one another, that Jones was a preacher and an atheist, that he loved his followers and hated them. That they had been alive and were now dead. Aunt Eloise had said, in her cynical way, "Sounds like God to me," and maybe, Janet thought, the Temple was just the world, concentrated and sped up so that you gave up understanding it and bowed your head in prayer. But Lucas. Was he dead?

Jared laid the paper on the floor. "Well, that's a piece of news. Amazing. Lots more to come. I guess the CIA got Congressman Ryan after all."

Janet said, "What are you talking about?"

"Oh, you know, Ryan. Didn't you ever see him? He was from San Fran. He authored the Hughes-Ryan Act. Ryan was after Jones for years, and finally made it so they had to report covert ops to Congress. Now they must have—"

"You sound so detached." Jared had a thing about the CIA; another thing Janet had not ever told him was about her uncle Arthur.

"Well, I am detached. I mean, it's shocking, but you had to see it coming. Jones was a nut."

"I did see it coming," said Janet, not quite knowing what she meant. She had told Jared only that she had gone to the Temple a couple of times—everyone did—and had known people who were really into it. Now she looked down at Emily, her savior. She had gotten pregnant the first time they went out, simply because she was too lazy to get up and find her diaphragm, simply because she hadn't expected to end up with Jared Nelson, computer programmer, in her bed. They had gotten married when she was four months along. She had lucked out, or buyer's delight had kicked in—he was right for her, good for her, after wandering in a dark wood, she found the path back to the village. In the village, the streets were clean and straight, gardens were planted, the villagers friendly. Little Red Riding Hood didn't have to say where she had been—they fed her, gave her a job, and laughed about the Big Bad Wolf, what a monster he was, so self-involved and grandiose, just stay away from that guy. And then the bonus—Emily Inez Nelson, perfect baby.

Emily relaxed, fell away from the breast. Janet moved her a little, snapped her bra closed. Jared rubbed his hands over his face. "Looks like another nice day," he said. Just this one, thought Janet, just this one nice day, and then maybe she would tell him more. But she wouldn't think about that now.

1979

Lillian went to the window in the living room, the one that
looked out over the driveway, and watched Arthur. He was
standing with a shovel in his hand just where the driveway curved
down to the road. His back was to the house, and she couldn't tell
whether he was resting, or whether he had stopped shoveling. The
house was utterly silent—she had turned off the TV after watching
The Edge of Night, a show that Arthur thought was ridiculous but that
Lillian watched because Rosanna had, every day. It was getting dark,
and Lillian squinted. Finally, she went to the hall closet, got her coat,
wrapped it around herself, and opened the front door. By the time she
got to Arthur, he was shoveling again, and Lillian thought he looked
all right. She said, "Okay. You want pork chops for dinner? We have
some."

Arthur turned and looked at her for a long moment. Then he said,
"Pork chops are fine." His tone meant that he would pick at them.

"Or I could make spaghetti with clam sauce. You liked that." She
shivered. Arthur took the two sides of her coat and crossed them more
tightly, then turned up her collar. As he did so, he looked brighter. He
kissed her. He said, "I did like that spaghetti. I'm almost finished here.
What time is it?" He no longer wore a watch.

"A little after five."

"Do you feel something?"

"What?"

"Do you feel our estate here, Belly Acres, rising up at every corner to enfold and suffocate us?"

"There is a lot of upkeep," said Lillian, keeping her voice low, neutral. "You should"—but she had suggested that Arthur hire someone to help him before, and he had refused, so she said—"at least find a service to plow the driveway."

"The thin end of the wedge," said Arthur. "Ten years ago, I would have shoveled four inches of snow off this driveway in an hour, running and singing the whole time, and now I had to stop every few minutes and catch my breath."

Lillian shivered again, though it wasn't very cold, and said, "Maybe you should actually see a doctor."

Arthur shook his head, as she knew he would. He hadn't seen a doctor in years. I've had enough of that, he always said.

"What if I, your wife, want you to see a doctor?"

"You're out of luck." Then he turned her toward the house, putting his right arm over her shoulders and carrying the snow shovel in his left hand. They tromped up the driveway. He said, "I do feel sixty today, though. Every minute of it. When Colonel Manning was sixty, he walked thirty miles a day, keeping a list of wildflowers and birds that he saw on his march."

"How old was he when I met him?"

"Sixty-six."

"He had a twinkle in his eye."

"Somehow," said Arthur, "he did. Must have been a trick of the light."

"You have a twinkle in your eye."

"I take that as a compliment."

While she was cooking dinner (green beans, too, with browned butter and almonds), they did their daily worrying about Debbie, Dean, and Tina, a prophylactic. Lillian talked to Debbie every day. Debbie told her about Carlie, Kevvie, Hugh, and the dogs. At the moment, the only thing wrong was that one dog had ear mites. Lillian and Arthur agreed that this was not worth worrying about. Dean had broken his wrist in a game of pickup basketball with eight guys who were taller than he was—he had gone for a rebound and hit his hand on the rim of the basket (pretty impressive), and would be in a cast for four more weeks. Lillian said, "How many broken bones is that over the years now?"

Arthur thought for a minute and said, "Eight, if you count the ribs as two."

"Maybe this will teach him a lesson."

"What lesson, though?"

"That he isn't seventeen anymore?"

"I was hoping Linda was going to teach him that lesson."

"So was she," said Lillian.

Now for Tina. Tina had taken up the blowtorch. She lived in Seattle. She had sent a picture of herself, in her entire protective outfit, blowtorch in her right hand, hair gathered in a neat ponytail, gloves, helmet, standing in front of a slab of glass maybe an inch or more thick, three feet by four feet. She burned beautiful patterns in the glass, sometimes in the shape of animals or plants, but more often in astronomical designs—the solar system, the moons of Jupiter, six galaxies rotating in the distance. Her boyfriend, who still made his own cosmological paintings, then lit these so that the light came in from the edges somehow and illuminated the heavenly bodies. She'd shipped Lillian and Arthur a piece for their thirty-third wedding anniversary called *Virginia Cowslips*. In the note, she had written, "Hope you don't find this too sentimental. I was in a funny mood." Lillian did not find the image of her daughter bent over a blowtorch at all sentimental, but the piece was very pretty, and Lillian had put it on the dresser in their bedroom. Lillian said, "No news is good news for Tina."

"No news is normal for Tina."

"She'll tell us if she gets pregnant. Even Janet told Andy when she got pregnant."

They paused to worry about Janet for a moment. Andy had come back from Iowa City oohing and aahing as if she had never seen a baby before; to Lillian, Emily's pictures looked like those of a normal baby and, indeed, of a Langdon baby, but, having somehow looked past her own babies, Andy was stunned by the new one.

Lillian said, "We could worry about Michael." Michael had wrecked the car he shared with Richie—DWI, girl in the hospital for a week with a broken pelvis, and Michael himself, not wearing a seat belt, ramming his knee into the key in the ignition and painfully damaging the joint.

"Why bother?" said Arthur. "Worrying about Michael would be an existential exercise."

"Jesse? Annie? Gray? Brad?"

"They have their complement of worriers," said Arthur. "I don't see any positions to fill."

"I guess it's time to eat, then."

Arthur set the table, and Lillian dished up the food—always too much. She looked at Arthur out of the corner of her eye. He was the one she worried about: underweight, short of breath, ever alert (now it was the Iranians again). When she woke up to find him staring out the window at three in the morning, he would say that he just couldn't sleep. When she asked what he was thinking about, he would say, "The fact that I can't sleep." Sometimes she thought he might have been awake all night, but he didn't yawn or act tired in the normal way, just more wound up. Was he different or worse than he had always been? Lillian had no idea. Maybe she was the one feeling her age, not Arthur. Maybe he seemed a little strange to her because they were diverging in some way that she couldn't pinpoint. She consciously dragged her gaze away from his plate (he had taken three bites, put down his fork, picked up a piece of bread) to her own, and said, "This turned out nicely."

"Yes, it did."

She didn't ask why he wasn't eating it. She said, "Maybe we should worry about Henry."

"You mean because he took a semester's leave of absence, moved to New York, and is living in the East Village, and no one has heard from him since before Christmas?"

"He's forty-six years old. He shouldn't have to check in if he's going to be out after midnight."

"Even if it's been evident for a year that he is kicking over the traces and making up for lost time?"

"I have principles," said Lillian.

"Name one," said Arthur.

"What, me worry?" said Lillian.

Arthur laughed. When he did so, Lillian put a couple more beans on his plate. He seemed to like those.

JOE WAS HUNGRY after his appointment at the bank, and so he went to the Denby Café, sat down at the counter, and ordered a grilled ham and cheese. He was thinking about the interest he was going to pay on the seed he was about to buy, and whether he should forgo the loan and use most of his savings (but he didn't want to do that). He knew what Lois was going to say, and Minnie, too, but both options made him nervous. How he had gotten to be one of the luckiest farmers in the area was pretty clear, and not only to him—Minnie had a good job, Lois had both a job and a store, the farm was paid off. Their house was like every kit house—strong, solid, and well put together—and Gary's old house, buttoned up for the time being, was built to last, too. Did he need a new tractor? That depended on whether he cared about sitting on a seat or in a cab. On the seat, it was dusty and noisy, but he felt that he was seeing more. A cab would be quiet (not to mention cool), but if you were sitting in a cab, why be a farmer at all?

Then Dickie Dugan bumped into him, and he turned around. Dickie thrust a soiled check under his nose and laughed. Bobby Dugan had died a few months earlier—what had the paper said, that he was something like sixty-four, which didn't seem all that old anymore—and the list of wives (three) and kids (nine) was pretty amazing. Dickie was the oldest boy. The check was for two hundred thousand dollars—not much in some ways, but impressive as a number being handed around the Denby Café. The Dugans had about three hundred acres just off the state highway. The check was signed by Frederick Sanford, CEO, Enterprise Pork Producers. Dickie said, "This is going to be a hog hotel, folks. Air-conditioned suite for every sow."

Farmers at various tables were shaking their heads a little—only a little, because nobody liked there to be a fight. Then Russ Pinckard, who was something of a joker, shouted, "All the Dugans being replaced by Hampshires? What's the difference?"

Dickie flushed, but smiled. He said, "You watch for us on the TV, Pinckard! You heard of *The Partridge Family*? Wait till you see *The Dugan Family*!"

"More like *The Addams Family*!" shouted Russ, and about half the assembled farmers laughed. Marie, who was carrying the coffeepot, shook her head and said, "Shush up, now!"

A hog-confinement setup at the Dugans' made sense in a way, since the place was flat, the soil had never been much good, and the road to Usherton and eastward was right there. The Dugans had made it through the Depression, just barely, and there were so many kids now that they ran wild. On the other hand, Dinky Creek ran right through the back sixty acres, and from there into the river about three miles away, and to the east the landscape flattened and the river started meandering—good spot to deposit any hog detritus. But that was far away from Denby, and Joe had no doubt that the confinement builders would do something about the waste from hundreds of hogs, if not the sights and sounds.

Joe drank his coffee and talked about this new ethanol idea, basically adding corn-based alcohol to gas ("Drink it or drive it, your choice!" joked Russ Pinckard). What was the price of seed, whose ground was ready to plow, who had a new tractor and why, if the world was starving, wasn't the price of corn and beans a little higher, and would a lawyer like Culver in the Senate really do what was best for farmers, or did he care, for that matter, and would Jepsen be any better? After an hour, he went out, got into Rosanna's Volkswagen, and headed home. The weather was still cold and the ground still hard—the way it was in early spring when everything seemed held in place, and ugly, too.

D'Ory and D'Onut were sitting by the gate of the dog pen, staring at him as soon as he got out of the car. They knew not to bark, but they allowed themselves a little bit of a whine as he approached. D'Ory was graying around the muzzle, but D'Onut was young and slender, only two years old. When Joe opened the gate, D'Ory came out and D'Onut went over to her favorite tennis ball and brought it to him. She was such an avid fetcher that she never greeted him without an offering. When Jesse was home, she ran with him everywhere. She was a good gun-dog, and, even when Jesse was gone, lived in the hope that there would be something to fetch.

Joe never minded leaving the café. But now, following the dogs into the lowering steel-gray clouds, he felt lonely again. When he walked through the field behind the house, he could look in all directions and see nothing but his own two barns—the larger one, where he kept the workshop and the tractor at his parents' old place, and the smaller one here, where he kept the seeder and the cultivator and the other implements. Walter and Rosanna had always said that after the Depression, or after the war, after something or other, people would start farming again—it was a healthy life and the best way to raise kids. But in Joe's lifetime, no one had ever come back. That Jesse was taking a fifth year to complete his B.S. might be a sign that he wasn't coming back, either. Joe didn't know if that was bad.

A few days ago, Jesse had called from Ames, supposedly just to say hi, but after Joe talked to him ("Yeah, Dad, I got two A's and two B's, and Professor Holland says I'm doing really well on the scours research") and Lois talked to him, then Minnie talked to him. She was sitting on the couch in the living room, and Joe stood quietly on the landing above her, out of sight, and listened. She said, "Oh, you mentioned her." Then, "I know you did like her." Then, "You hadn't told her you were planning to farm? What did she think you were going to do?" Then, "Well, farm life is hard for some girls. It's isolating. Not like when I was young." Then, "Well, of course you're disappointed, but it's better to find out now." Then, voice lowered, "Well, I'm sorry, Jesse. My heart goes out to you. No, I won't say anything." Joe had tiptoed up the stairs and gone into the bathroom, where he turned on the water and sighed several deep, deep sighs.

Now he stared out over the empty landscape, the fields still dark and frozen, the trees bare and shaking in the wind (a wind that was numbing the tip of his nose). The dogs had their noses to the ground—the ground was endlessly fascinating for a retriever, the tracks of deer, raccoons, mice, rabbits, birds, and even a turkey or two. Opa had raised them on stories of flocks of turkeys, flights of ducks, waves of prairie chickens, and even cougars slinking past the window in the night, heading for the sheep in the pen (always, according to Opa, to have a pleasant conversation about the meaning of life). Joe imagined D'Ory and D'Onut sniffing layers of tracks heading in every direction, from all past eras. But Joe was a man, not a dog, and what he couldn't see, he couldn't perceive. He was lonely, and he knew that his loneliness had nothing to do with Lois or Minnie. He looked at his watch: two-forty-five. He let the dogs lead him on.

························

WHEN MICHAEL DECIDED that he was getting married, Richie could hardly remember who the girl was, even though Michael swore he had met her—Loretta Perroni. She was just about to graduate from Manhattanville College, she was really smart, and her dad owned a hundred-thousand-acre cattle ranch in California. "Dark hair?" he said over the phone.

"Most of the time," said Michael. "It was blond when I met her, but she dyed it back."

"Long?"

"Really dark hair and blue eyes. She's short. When you met her, you pretended to rest your elbow on the top of her head."

Richie said, "You're going to marry her? You've known her, like, three months." Susan, the girl Michael had been in the accident with, had broken up with him once she was back on her feet, and Richie knew that Michael was lucky he wasn't being sued. Michael himself had been shaken enough at the time to go with their mom to AA for a few weeks. It was Richie who had stopped double-dating, because he and Ivy decided to move in together—bed by eleven, because Ivy enjoyed her job at Viking and wanted to succeed. Her goal was eventually to have her own imprint. Richie spent half his day showing office space, and half his day writing ads, finding out the status of new construction, and servicing renters. Mr. Rubino hardly ever came in. He could take a four-hour lunch, or put on his sneakers and go for a run in the park. Sometimes he read two or three newspapers in one day. Michael was now a trader. It was said (by Michael) that Jim Upjohn loved him, that he had great instincts. Obviously, thought Richie, marrying into a hundred thousand acres was another of his great instincts.

The first thing that happened was that Loretta's parents, Ray and Gail Perroni, flew in from California to meet his mom and dad. His mom took Mrs. Perroni to the house. His dad took Mr. Perroni first to the office, then to lunch at the Century Club. That night, Richie and Ivy were to drop by after dinner (the Waldorf), for dessert. Ivy said that the prospect of crème brûlée was her only incentive, since she disapproved of rich people, but Richie knew that she was dying to meet and observe the strange ducks from the West Coast (she had never met Loretta or traveled farther than Philadelphia).

At the Peacock Alley restaurant, Richie could see them all at the table, his parents and Michael sitting across from the three Perronis. It was a bizarre sight, because the older Perronis, slender and weathered as they were, were hardly tall enough for their feet to touch the floor. Ray stood up to greet them; he came to Richie's shoulder and Ivy's eyebrow. But his face was darkly tanned and deeply wrinkled from the middle of his forehead down, and his hands were square and strong and maybe as big as his head. He was wearing cowboy boots. Mrs. Perroni looked just as weathered. She said, "Well, you boys do look alike, don't you? Had a mare foal out a pair of twins just this spring. I went out in the morning, and the mare was standing by the gate with the tiniest little filly at her side, so I went looking around for the placenta, because you have to make sure it's complete, you know, and, oh, I found it, all right. Inside it was another little filly, but she was dead. They must have been identicals, which is rare in horses, because they had the same cowlicks. That foal could barely reach her mama's teats, but she made it. She's going to be a nice animal, I think."

Loretta, staring at her mother, said, "Oh, for God's sake, Mom!"

Mrs. Perroni leapt to her own defense. "Well, it's an interesting story."

"Yes," said his mom, in her usual distracted way, "it is." Richie smiled to himself, pulled out Ivy's chair, which was right beside the minuscule Mrs. Perroni, then went around the table and sat down beside his dad, who seemed to have turned to stone, he was so self-contained.

Things had moved quickly, because the first thing his mom said after they ordered dessert was "Well, what is it today? May 18? I guess Loretta and Michael, of course, want a June wedding, and the only Saturday they can get in June this year is the 23rd, so we have five weeks to put it together." Richie now understood without being told that Loretta was saving herself for marriage, and nothing Michael might have done or said would change her mind.

"Oh goodness. Easy as pie," said Mrs. Perroni.

And it was, because the Perronis had all the money in the world and knew every single person in Carmel and Pebble Beach, California, and it was as if the waves rolled apart, and all Michael and Loretta did was walk between them to the door of the Carmel Mission (the second in California). His dad flew them out: Richie himself, best man; Ivy, one of eight bridesmaids; and his mom. They left at 6:00 a.m., stopped in Des Moines to pick up Uncle Joe, Aunt Lois, Aunt Minnie, Jesse, and Annie, and landed in Monterey at noon. From there, they were driven in a stretch limo to a huge hotel on the ocean. Aunt Lillian, Uncle Arthur, Debbie, Hugh, and the kids had arrived the night before. Janet, with Emily and Jared, showed up in time for lunch beside the pool (the golfers were out in droves), and then Aunt Claire, Gray, and Brad (though Uncle Paul could not get away) in time for dinner, a huge buffet. Uncle Henry had promised to come, but called at the last moment to say he was stuck in Chicago. Aunt Eloise showed up for the rehearsal dinner, having driven down from San Francisco "just to have a look," but she seemed rather at home, especially after Rosa, Lacey, and Rosa's husband, Ross, the violin-bow maker, arrived. Apparently, Ross was very famous; all the Perronis' guests went up to him and threw their arms around him; even the hotel staff smiled at him and shook his hand. The wedding party took up a floor of the hotel, and everyone stayed up talking. Aunt Eloise and Ivy went off in a corner and chatted about John le Carré and Henry Kissinger, and Uncle Arthur said, "Who are they, again?," which caused Aunt Eloise to take Aunt Lillian off into another corner and have a serious talk with her. His mom stayed with Emily, carrying her, kissing her, sitting her in chairs and on beds, bouncing her on her silk-clad knee. Ivy never looked at the baby at all.

The wedding was at four. The mission was a long, pale building set against a hillside not far from the ocean. Richie could smell the garden of flowers through the open doors all through the ceremony. The Langdons sat in four rows of pews on the groom's side of the church, and when everyone had to kneel during parts of the Mass, they gave each other covert glances, leaned forward, and did not make the sign of the cross. Aunt Eloise sat through the whole thing and kept her mouth shut, as did Ivy, but Rosa and Lacey knelt and bowed their heads. After the ceremony, they took a bus along the winding, breezy roads back to the hotel, where the reception, for three hundred guests, was in a golden room with a huge set of windows that looked out onto the bay. Loretta, who Richie now understood was an only child, and therefore spoiled rotten, according to even her own father, wore her mother's dress, updated slightly. It had a huge skirt and a twelve-foot train, and was covered with lace. Ivy kept whispering, "That dress is ridiculous!" All the bridesmaids were required to wear gloves to the middle of their upper arms, and black gowns. Once again, according to Ivy, ridiculous. Most of the men wore cowboy boots. Everyone was friendly. People kept coming up to him and saying, "Oh, you're the twin! Are you the lefty?" There were two congressmen there, four state legislators, the mayor of Carmel-by-the-Sea, as well as Nancy Reagan, Clint Eastwood, Doris Day, and three other actors Richie only sort of recognized. They all stared at his mom, who was wearing a beautiful Chanel suit. But there were lots of other people, too, who weren't dressed any better than Uncle Joe or Aunt Lois, and who ran around dancing and laughing, so much so that Ivy had to go upstairs and change out of her long skirt. The champagne was Veuve Clicquot, and Richie had plenty, but he saw Loretta stop Michael after one glass, and Michael was smiling. So a miracle had happened after all.

The next afternoon, once Michael and Loretta had gone on to Maui, everyone got into a bus that took them to the Angelina Ranch. It was a long ride, even after they entered the gate. A hundred thousand acres was ten times the size of Uncle Joe's farm, 156 square miles, all contiguous, all running up and down hills, over fields, into arroyos. In the seat in front of him, Uncle Joe was staring out the window at the pale-golden hills and the occasional groups of cows and calves. Next to him, Ivy was reading a manuscript. Across the aisle, his mom and Janet were talking about Emily. His dad was sitting in the first row of the bus, hunched forward, listening to little Mr. Perroni and the bus driver. Aunt Eloise and Aunt Lillian had decided to "forgo" the trip to the ranch, Aunt Eloise to go to the beach with Rosa instead, Aunt Lillian because Uncle Arthur seemed very jet-lagged. Lacey's boyfriend had shown up, so they had gone into Monterey, and Ross was sleeping off the party. Richie heard Rosa say to his mom, "No, no booze. But he hasn't seen that many people all in one place since the last Dead concert he went to, in 1969. It sort of freaked him out."

The weather, warm and sunny by the coast, was now hot. All the windows of the bus were open, and everyone's hair was blowing in the breeze. Ivy had to hold her pages flat with two hands. She looked at him and said, "I prefer Central Park." They drove.

At last they turned in past a tall gate, crossing a metal grate in the road. The bus went up a hill through some huge trees that twisted in startling shapes. When they crested the hill, they looked down on the most beautiful house Richie had ever seen. He poked Ivy with his elbow and pointed. She said, "Oh, nice," and went back to reading. Spanish-style, long, two stories, a balcony running most of the length of the second story, painted a pinkish color, with dark beams and a tile roof. The main door, dark wood, was two stories high. An adobe wall extended from each end in a big oval, embracing a courtyard. Water bubbled out of a dish that the hands of a fountain statue were holding aloft, then flowed down its arms, around the laughing face, and over its body, to disappear again into a pool at the figure's feet.

Everyone piled out of the bus and went into the house. Though it was hot outside, maybe ninety-five degrees, it was cool inside—the window openings were a foot deep. The first thing they did was follow Mrs. Perroni into a large dining room, where they were given a Mexican brunch, including all kinds of food with hot sauce and tortillas that Richie had never eaten before, but also plates of peaches and apricots, melon and cantaloupe, blackberries and raspberries in heavy cream. There was also corn, like they had at home and in Iowa in the summer, but it was roasted in the husk, so that the kernels were brown and sweet; Aunt Lois and Uncle Joe ate three of those apiece. His mom carried Emily around the table, picking up bits of things and offering them to her with the tip of her finger. She did this as if she knew what she was doing, something that surprised Richie. He glanced around, but no one else was staring at her—the least motherly woman in the history of the world, fifty-nine years old and still built like a teen-ager.

After that, Mr. Perroni walked them all over the house, up the uneven stairs and down the uneven hallways, opening doors and peeking into rooms, looking at chandeliers and paintings and displays of dried flowers and a broom made of branches. At the end of the downstairs hall was a painting of Jesus gazing upward, and at the end of the upstairs hall was a painting of the Virgin Mary looking downward. Both, according to Mrs. Perroni, were from Spain, and she had seen ones by the same painter in Oaxaca, which was a city in southern Mexico with a cathedral plated in gold. "Alta California could never afford that!" said Mrs. Perroni.

The Angelina Ranch had started out as Angelina Rancho, a mere sixteen thousand acres given to a Mexican soldier in 1835. A battle in the Mexican-American War had taken place right over there—they could see the site from the window of the master bedroom. Three Americans and two Mexicans killed, but the Americans preserved their horses, and managed to get themselves to Colonel Frémont. That family had lost all their money, so, when Mr. Perroni's people came over from Switzerland at the end of the nineteenth century, they bought this rancho, with its old house, and another one, which had never had a house, the Rancho Rojas, just across the river, and that was that. It was a hard life at one time—everyone out rustling cattle at the crack of dawn, including Gail herself, who was from Los Angeles and had never seen a live cow before she married into the Perronis, but it didn't take long to learn if your livelihood depended on it, and in the end it was easier than writing for Hollywood, which was what her father did—had they ever seen *Rubies for Rent*? Or *The Wide River*? Well, no one had. They went for a walk.

For a week after they came home, Ivy was annoyed with Richie for being too impressed with "life in the Old West." She said that she'd half expected there to be a shootout, just for show, and she'd taken four showers to get the dust out of her skin. Anyway, what did it matter? Michael and Loretta were planning to live in New York, just like everyone else, so that Michael could get rich and Loretta could pursue her child-development degree. Everyone had a dramatic history. Ivy's own grandfather had been rescued, as a child, from a pogrom in Odessa, had passed through Ellis Island when he was eight, had his name translated from "Dov Grodno" to "Dave Gordon." And hadn't Richie told her his mother's great-grandfather kept his crazy wife in a tiny little cellar with a trapdoor in the apple orchard, or something like that? Compared with all of this, servicing rentals was rather uninspiring. Or safe, said Ivy. Let's just be glad we're safe.

ON THE DAY Claire filed her written petition for dissolution of marriage and paid her fee, she went from the courthouse to the grocery store, where she bought a chicken and some potatoes for supper. Then she drove home in the chilly dusk, thinking of her new place downtown—in fact, she had been a little late to the courthouse because she was walking around the apartment, enjoying how quiet it was, even during the day. When she got back to West Des Moines, she parked on the street—something she had never done before, because all of a sudden even the garage seemed claustrophobic, and she carried her bag up the walk—no snow yet. Her house—the house—looked like a picture, dark, shiny front door, square panes of light to either side, and an arch of light above. She climbed the three steps to the front stoop, wiped her shoes on the mat, and extended her hand toward the doorknob.

She glanced through the window. Gray, who was fourteen, was sitting on the third step of the staircase, reading a book. As she watched, he wiped his nose with the back of his hand, pushed up his glasses, and turned the page. There was a laugh—Brad's laugh—and here he came, stretched out on his back, sliding down the carpeted stairs. Just then, Claire had her Lot's-wife moment—knowing perfectly well that she should not, could not, look into the past, and yet having the occasion of doing so come upon her like a stroke of lightning. Her hand trembled as she opened the door, and tears came to her eyes. How could this happen, she wondered, after so much preparation? Was mere familiarity that potent?

The boys, of course, greeted her as they always did: Where were the last two Popsicles? Could she sign the note from the teacher right away, before it was forgotten? Did she buy any milk? She nodded, smiled, passed them. When she got to the kitchen, she thought it was only an illusion that Lot's wife was looking backward. Really, she was looking into the future, that strange city empty of herself, and she was thinking, I know nothing else but this.

Putting away the groceries, she did what she always did, which was imagine the boys talking about her someday—out of the blue, no reason of any kind, she must have gone crazy, or, alternatively, good riddance, we never liked her anyway, never understood why he married her in the first place, females are only good for two things and I forget what the second one is. Her hands were still trembling as she smoothed butter over the skin of the chicken and set it in the roasting pan.

But then Paul gave her a wonderful gift. She had just scrubbed the potatoes and was peeling the first one. Brad had the refrigerator door open, and Gray had brought his book into the kitchen. He was saying, "What does this word mean?" and pointing, when the back door flew open and slammed against the wall. Everyone jumped. Paul stormed into the kitchen, yelling, "I ran over a bicycle! Brad, your bicycle was lying right in the driveway, and I ran right over it, and now the—"

Brad jumped away from the refrigerator and closed the door. His mouth had dropped open. Gray moved back toward the doorway to the dining room, ready to flee. Paul yelled, "God *damn* it!"

Claire said, "Are you still on top of the bicycle?"

"No, I am not, for God's sake! I backed off it."

"Then no harm done." She glanced at Brad. "Except to the bike."

"It's dark! I don't know if there's no harm done. There could be oil or gas dripping out of the underside of the car. And the car damaged, too, for Chrissakes. It could be quite a dangerous situation. Not to mention—"

She said, "Why don't you not mention it?"

Brad started for the dining room, and Paul said, "Come back here, young man!" Claire dropped the peeler and the potato and stepped between Paul and Brad, who made it through the door. Paul's voice sharpened. "Did you hear me?"

"How could he not hear you? You sound like an air-raid siren."

And then he gave it to her—he popped her right on the chin and knocked her down.

She was lucky she didn't whack the back of her head on the edge of the table; that was the first thing she thought. She landed sitting. Her neck hurt. Paul stood above her, and she saw his face, which was red with rage, become gradually infused with disbelief. And it was true that he had never hit her before. For Claire, though, there was nothing unbelievable about it. She knew that he had wanted to—that the kicking of a door or the smack of a fist on the table was only a substitute. It could be said, though she would never say it, that her change of tone—a bit of sarcasm for the first time in their lives—had startled him and undone his last mote of self-control. She turned her head. The boys were frozen in the doorway. She said nothing. Paul said, "Your mother fell down."

"You liar," said Claire. It was possible that Gray and Brad had never seen an argument, because it was possible that Claire had never talked back. Claire shook her head, leaned forward, and helped herself up with the chair. Not even the desperate look on Paul's face aroused her pity, and that was how she knew that whatever love she had once felt for him had left no trace.

Finally, Paul said, "I'm s—"

Claire stood right in front of him and said, "I don't care." Then, "Dinner will be ready in an hour." She went back to peeling potatoes.

She served at six-thirty; the chicken was a little dry, the mashed potatoes were good, and cleanup was easy. At eight, they watched *Barney Miller,* and at nine, they watched *Soap.* Brad came in and out with questions about his homework, and at nine-thirty, he was told to go to bed. Gray was, Claire suspected, hiding out in his room. At ten, they watched the news, and then Paul stood up from his easy chair and said, "Well, I'm going to bed. I—" But she must have had a look on her face, so he stopped, and headed up the stairs. She turned off the TV. In the late-night quiet, she glanced around and decided that she hated every piece of furniture, and she was not going to take a single one with her to the apartment. What was that furniture called that those Perronis had in California? Oh, right, Mission style, of course. She would start there. Paul appeared at the bottom of the stairs. She looked at him. His first utterance would be a final test.

He said, irritably, "It's late. I have to be at the hospital by—"

How many times had he said that over the years? He was a very prompt man. But he had failed to pass the test. He had gone on with his life, with their lives, out of habit, not daring to recognize that all was changed.

She said, "I'm getting a divorce."

He said, "I won't allow that."

And then she simply laughed. She saw his fists clench, and she saw him notice and unclench them. She said, "I'll sleep on the couch tonight."

"What will you tell the boys?" Now his lips twisted, and he looked as undecided as Claire had ever seen him, torn between remorse and rage.

"I'll tell them I slept on the couch."

He stared at her, then turned away.

Little had she known what a pleasure it would turn out to be, telling the truth at last.

1980

〜

WHEN JOE GOT the flu after Christmas, he was in bed for a
week, throwing up, lost in a fever of 103 or more, and waking at odd times from dreams about snow. And there was plenty of
snow—Lois and Minnie let D'Ory and D'Onut in the house. After
his fever was gone, he slept for another week, and when he finally
woke up, on January 7, he had lost ten pounds and was as hungry as
a hog. Lois thought this was funny, and made his favorite dishes for
a few days; all in all, Joe was glad that he'd gotten sick in the middle
of winter and that no one else came down with it. Apparently, Annie,
who was home for a few days, oversaw the quarantine and would not
under any circumstances let Lois go to the doctor and get some anti-
biotics, not even to be safe, because flu was a virus and that was that.
She even called a couple of times after she went back to her job at a
hospital in Milwaukee, to make sure that Lois wasn't "going for the
cefaclor behind her back."

"So bossy," exclaimed Lois, but they all knew she was right.

When he managed to get himself into the Volkswagen and go into
town for lunch, he was the only person in the Denby Café who wasn't
up in arms about Carter's grain embargo. Marsh Whitehead had a
paper with him, not *The Des Moines Register* or *The Usherton Post,* but
The Christian Science Monitor, which had an article by two men from
over in Kansas about why the embargo would fail. Joe read it over

while he was drinking his coffee and listening to all the other farmers bitching about it. Here they'd thought Carter—well, peanuts, what kind of a crop was that? But hadn't his sister ridden a tractor back in December of '77, two years ago, when those farmers protested? And Russ Pinckard said, "Well, I didn't see anyone from around here down there at Terrace Hill, driving their John Deeres over the lawn, did I?"

According to the article, you could tell by the thickness of tree rings how much rain there was in the course of a year, which Joe knew, and, furthermore, these rings went in a twelve-year cycle: for six years, the rings were fatter, which meant more rain, and then for the next six years, thinner rings, less rain. Those years when the Russkies needed more grain because of less rain were over, so there was no reason to think they needed to import much this year. In addition, indications were that they had plenty on hand, left over from '78, which they were hiding in brand-new and very enormous grain-storage facilities.

Joe looked up and said, "Why is he having a grain embargo anyway?"

"Oh, you were sick as a dog," said Marie. "Lois told me all about it."

"Well, I guess they invaded Afghanistan," Russ Pinckard said, "wherever that is!"

"Kinda like us invading Mexico," said Marsh Whitehead. "Piece I read said Carter should leave 'em alone, they're gonna regret it soon enough without us lifting a finger."

George, who was manning the register, looked up, and Marie looked over at him. George almost never said anything, but now he said, "You think he wants them to call him a sissy all over again? Those folks in Iran pulled his pants down; now the Russkies are doing the same thing." Everyone shut up at the reference to the Iran hostages—it was something like two months now. The women and some minorities had been released, but there were still fifty-two men stuck there. Forgetting about them had been another privilege of his illness.

"And we got to pay," said Russ Pinckard. No one rose to the bait; everyone knew that Carter's response to the crisis was a ticklish issue. Russ looked at Joe. "You pay any attention to the markets lately? Surely you weren't that sick."

Joe shrugged. "I thought it was the middle of winter."

"Well," said Marsh Whitehead, "don't have a heart attack when you do, because prices are way, way down. He suspended trading for a couple of days right after the embargo, but when they opened again, the price dropped as far as it could go, and it still hasn't recovered. Best thing I think we can do this year is—"

"Shut the place and take off for Florida," said Russ Pinckard.

Everyone laughed, but not cheerfully.

Ricky Carson, who had just come in and sat himself at the counter, said, "That's where Dickie Dugan went. They got themselves a lemon grove down there by Tampa somewhere."

At this, everyone fell silent again. Life surely was unfair if the Dugans were thriving.

A couple of weeks later, Reagan got in trouble for telling a joke that Joe thought was harmless enough—"How do you tell the Polish one at a cockfight? He's the one with the duck. How do you tell the Italian? He's the one who bets on the duck. How do you tell when the Mafia is there? The duck wins." A lot of people went bananas, though no one at the Denby Café. In the New Hampshire debate, which Joe watched on television, Joe wasn't impressed by him until he got to the grain issue—when he said that Carter's move was "for domestic consumption and it actually hurt the American farmer more than the Soviet Union," Joe had to agree, and then when he said that "there could be a confrontation down the road if they continue," he had to agree with that, too. Of course, Reagan wasn't a serious candidate, but he was pleasant—what he said about Carter came out in a genial way, as if he were chatting in your living room or something. Yes, Carter did more or less dare the Russians to cross the Afghan border, and then when they took his dare, he didn't do a thing about it, and how could he? Maybe no one in Iowa, or in Washington, either, was quite sure where Afghanistan was. At any rate, the Russkies took Carter by surprise and everyone knew it.

Of course, this guy John Anderson stood right up to Reagan, and what he said was true—why were we afraid of the Soviets taking over Iran and Saudi Arabia? Well, if they did, where would the oil come from? But Reagan smiled—the camera caught this—as if he expected that sort of talk from a guy like Anderson. (And who had heard of Anderson? Not Joe.) But that was all they said about farming

issues. Mostly it was about taxes and inflation, whether the economy
needed a little shock therapy, and whether the secretary of the treasury should be investigated. Not even much about Iran. None of this
helped Joe decide what to plant when he had to go to the bank a few
days later and apply for his loans to buy seed. The best rate he could
get was 14 percent, and if the ships full of grain were already looking
for places to store the corn, beans, wheat that had been intended for
the Russians, maybe shutting down the farm for a year wasn't a bad
idea. If he were rich, he would plant clover and plow it under in the
fall, just stay out of the market altogether. When he said this to Minnie, she laughed as if he were joking, so he didn't dare say it to Lois.
All he said to Lois was that God would provide, and of course she
nodded, and even quoted a Bible verse, "Therefore they shall come
and sing in the height of Zion, and shall flow together to the goodness
of the Lord, for wheat, and for wine, and for oil, and for the young of
the flock and of the herd: and their soul shall be as a watered garden;
and they shall not sorrow any more at all." Although Joe didn't often
go to church with her, and didn't quite know what he believed, he
found this verse comforting, and asked her to repeat it.

LILLIAN WAS vacuuming. She liked vacuuming more than any other
household task, and she had gone ahead and let the door-to-door
salesman sell her the Kirby, not because she needed a new vacuum
cleaner, but because she liked having two, one at each end of the
house. Now she was pushing it under the bed. It was heavy, it was
loud, it made her feel as though she were sucking every microbe out
of the carpet and smashing it to atoms. When she bent down to push
it farther under the bed, she realized that the phone was ringing in
her ear. She turned off the vacuum cleaner, worried instantly that
someone was calling about Arthur.

But the caller was Janet, long-distance, from Iowa. Lillian looked
at the alarm clock. It was only eight there. She said, "Hi, honey,
everything okay?"

Janet sniffled.

Lillian sat down on the bed. She said, "How's Emily?"

"Fine."

"How's Jared? Are you okay?"

"I'm okay. Jared had to stay at work all night to send some file to somewhere. He's okay." Then she said, in a low voice, "I've been up all night, worrying that there is going to be a nuclear war."

Lillian said, "You have?"

"Well, and so I've done this thing."

Lillian felt a jolt of real fear. She said, "What thing?"

"Is Uncle Arthur there?"

"He went to work already." Arthur was going to retire very, very soon, unless he could persuade them to keep him on against everyone's better judgment.

"Does Uncle Arthur think there is going to be a nuclear war?"

"No, he hasn't mentioned it. But what would cause it?"

"The Iranians."

"But tell me what thing you've done?"

Janet started crying. In the two and a half years since Janet escaped those Temple people, Lillian had been thinking something was going to happen. She and Eloise had talked it over a dozen times. Eloise was more sanguine, especially since this young woman Marla someone had turned up not dead, but first in Paris, and now working in New York, at the Manhattan Theatre Club. Janet seemed to have moved on pretty well; Jared was a straightforward, kind person; Emily had had an amazing effect on Andy, who had then warmed up to Janet— they got along like sisters now. But Lillian trusted nothing, and believed far more than Andy and Eloise that underground poisons could surface unexpectedly. She shifted her position on the bed and adjusted her bra. Janet said, "I keep looking out the window. We have this window that faces west, and I keep looking out the window and imagining a mushroom cloud."

"Why west?" said Lillian.

"Des Moines."

"You are living in Solon, Iowa, and you worry there's going to be a nuclear explosion in Des Moines?"

"The prevailing winds are westerlies."

Lillian didn't dare to smile, even though they were only talking on the phone. She said, "Who is going to bomb us?"

"The Iranians."

"Oh yes, so you said . . . but the Iranians don't have the Bomb."

Silence.

Lillian said, "Did you talk to your mom about this?"

"She said she wouldn't be surprised."

"Oh, for heaven's sake," said Lillian. "That is just like Andy."

"She said I used to have nightmares about nuclear war."

"I never knew that."

"I didn't have them at your house."

"Oh, sweetie."

There was a pause. Janet said, in a lighter tone, "She thought it was a sign that I was precocious."

They both chuckled.

Lillian said, "In 1961, you were right to be worried. Not so much anymore."

"But I can't get it out of my mind. I look at Emily walking around, and I am just terrified something will happen."

Lillian thought of giving her a list of terrible things that were more likely to happen, but refrained. Instead, she said, "Ask your dad about the time he went to Iran." Lillian had gotten to the point in her life where she would talk about almost anything.

Janet said, "What?"

"Arthur sent him. There was disagreement about . . ." She should not have started this. "I think you were three? Anyway—"

"When I was three was when the U.S. reinstalled the Shah and overthrew the democratic election of Mossadegh."

Of course, Lillian thought, Janet would know this. Not Debbie or Dean or Tina or 90 percent of the American population. Ninety-five, maybe. She adjusted her bra again, then said, "Mossadegh was courting the Soviets. We really couldn't take the chance. I could see it at the time. When Frank first came home from the war, he said that the Russians defied the law of probabilities—anything was possible. Arthur seemed to . . ." Her words trailed off.

"What did my dad do there?"

Lillian thought, Well, in for a penny, in for a pound. "He accompanied some money, some bags of money."

"Bribery."

"You need to get over your idealism about how the world works." Lillian hadn't meant to sound so sharp.

"Okay," said Janet. "Okay. So we get what we deserve."

"Oh, honey," said Lillian. Then she said, "We do, but only if we're lucky." She held the phone to her ear for a long time, even though neither of them said anything. Finally, Janet seemed to turn away from the receiver, because her voice got distant. She said, "There's Emily. I have to go get her."

Lillian said, "I love you, Janny."

Janet didn't reciprocate, just said, "Bye, Aunt Lillian."

Lillian hoisted herself off the bed and went back to vacuuming, but her heart was no longer in it. After five minutes, she turned off the Kirby and rolled it down the hall to the closet where it was ensconced with all its many unused accessories. She could not get comfortable. She went back into her room and rummaged in the underwear drawer for a more forgiving bra. It was when she was putting it on that she felt the swelling, low and to the outside of her right breast, not quite painful but unmistakably present. She went into the bathroom and looked into the mirror, something she, a formerly vain young woman, now did as little as possible (and when she did, she made a practice of smiling at herself, so as not to seem judgmental). But there was no smiling now. The swelling was firm and visible, and it was evident that she was not destined to be alive one day and dead the next, Arthur's ideal.

FOR HER PART, Emily Inez Nelson did the best she could with the materials she was given. She did not hold hands if she could help it, and she screamed when Mom put the harness around her. She found it easier to run without a diaper on, or any clothes, for that matter, and she cared nothing about whether she was cold or not, but when her diaper was heavy and her shoes were tight, she ran anyway. She could not yet climb over the side of her crib, or the end panel, but when she awakened at daylight, she got up immediately, gripped the railing, and lifted her feet as best she could, first the one and then the other; some mornings, she managed to hook her big toe, the one that went to market, over the top. She knew she was making progress. It was also important to make marks on flat surfaces. If she had to put her hand in her diaper to get something to mark with, so be it. However, color was better—she liked blue, red, orange, and yellow; she knew the names of all four of them, and could say "boo." Her favorite things could only be done when Mom wasn't in the room.

She knew what a book was, and that pages were for turning. She preferred books she wasn't allowed to touch, with many pages for turning. She put her finger very carefully on the corner of the page, pressed it down, and pushed it back—then it would turn. She liked a certain tub with water in it, and cups. She liked to fill the cups and pour the water out, and she never poured it on the floor—she preferred to see it go into the other water and smooth itself out.

The only things that tasted good to her were breast milk and hard scrambled eggs. She did not like anything that slid through her fingers when she squeezed it; if it could be squeezed, she refused to eat it. She did not care to remain covered up in her crib or to keep a hat on outside or to be strapped into the seat of the grocery cart. She did not like it that Mom was everywhere, all the time. She never had a moment's peace. Mom's face leaned toward her and said, "Are you all right, honey?" Mom picked her up and carried her places when she was right in the middle of something. Mom set her in the high chair, in front of food, when the last thing in the world that she wanted to do was eat. Mom leaned over the bathtub the entire time she was in the bath; Mom held her one arm tightly while washing her, and this happened every day. Every time she said something, no matter to whom, Mom answered her, as if she were talking to Mom. Even when she was lying quietly in her crib, Mom leaned over her and listened to her. Emily tried the doors every single day, more than once. She knew some other people—most notably "Dad," "Grandy," "Eva," who was like herself, Emily, but did nothing but stand and stare, and Eva's "Jackie," but none of them were like Mom. Emily did not know what to make of it all.

BETWEEN THE TIME Lillian made her appointment with the doctor and the appointment itself, she went through all of the five stages of grief, but she went through them on her own—there was nothing in the book about the stage of "telling your worried husband," and so she did not address it. "Denial" was as easy as could be—she got Arthur to take her to see *American Gigolo*; afterward, they went for ice cream, and Arthur had her laughing until her sides hurt every time he mimicked Richard Gere saying, "Helloo, Judy, you are a virry

sexi leddy. Verri good lookn woman. Yu lak mi. Ah giv plejeur."
Then she would say, "How do you do it, Arthur, how do you seduce
all those women? I think you're guilty as sin." Then he would stare
at her very seriously and wiggle his head. It was harder when they
got home, and she had to steer his hand subtly away from her right
breast, but she was good at it, and even as they fell asleep, they were
still giggling.

"Anger" happened the next day, when she chanced to see a woman
she knew at the supermarket, a woman who made a point of gossiping
equally about everyone they knew. She was friendly to Lillian in the
canned-goods aisle, and happened to remark that she had seen "Mary
Jo Canton's new hairdo. Well, darling, hair don't." In the parking lot,
when Lillian was pulling out and this woman was walking behind
the boy pushing her very full cart to her very ample Mercedes-Benz
(and who had one of those? Lillian would like to know), Lillian could
not help reflecting that this woman was six years older than she,
drank heavily, and was poisoned by malice. Surely she should be the
one having a lump in her breast?

Obviously, Sunday was the day for "bargaining." While they sat
up in bed, reading articles in *The Washington Post* and *The New York
Times* about Reagan and Ford being too old for the presidency and
Bush having swiped all of Ford's voters, and now this John Anderson
fellow, whom Arthur rather liked—but at any rate, the Republicans
had overcome the contentiousness between the right wing and the
rest of the Party (they passed sections back and forth)—Lillian did
quietly wonder what she would give up in order to avoid the coming ordeal. Maybe the house? No eggs? No steak? No Brie? No buttery popcorn? She shifted around on the bed, and Arthur offered her
an article about the difference between people who draw the drapes
and people who throw up the blinds: light-house people, dark-house
people. Lillian enjoyed the article, but was there anything she should
have done differently? Detergent? Breast-feeding? She could think
of nothing else that was not human sacrifice, and if you came right
down to it, that did seem to be the bargain that religion dealt in,
didn't it? Someone must die so that others may live. Mary Elizabeth?
Tim? Lillian sighed, and Arthur said, "You okay, honey? You want
another cup of coffee?"

Lillian said, "No, thanks. One's enough today." Really, she did want another cup of coffee, and when Arthur came back into the bedroom with his second, the fragrance was seductive. But giving up coffee was a start. Maybe.

Monday, she pretended to be asleep with her head buried in the pillow, and then, after Arthur left, she sat up and let the tears and sobs flow. It was all too easy to imagine herself dead, and it wasn't good. She herself would be beyond sensation, she was pretty sure, and if not, then she felt she had done nothing to deserve punishment (through no virtue of her own—she had been taught to be a good girl, and she had been a good girl). But what Arthur and Debbie, especially, and maybe Janet and Dean would do without her, she literally could not imagine. Debbie called her every day; Arthur followed her around whenever he was not at work, and when he was at work, he called her in the morning and in the afternoon. Dean called her when he was worried about something, and Tina called her when she was excited about something. There was nothing oppressive about these calls—she loved them. They were the currency of news flowing freely, buoyed with jokes and funny stories, bits from TV, magazines, school. As soon as she thought of something funny or strange, she thought of who might enjoy it more, and called them—they did the same. But they would not as readily call one another. She was the switching station, the spot where information flowed to and from. Claire's situation was shocking, now that Paul had refused to sign the papers and accused her of destroying her children and threatened to find a judge who would make sure she ended up without a penny, but wouldn't Lillian's own departure be even worse in its way, something her family could not make the best of? It seemed like this all day, all the way up to the moment when she mixed the mashed potatoes from the night before with an egg yolk and formed them into little patties, which she then breaded and fried, and then she thought maybe she was making too big a deal of this.

She dreamt all night about a scene she might have seen in a movie, though which one she could not remember. A man is sleeping while his sheepdog is driving his sheep over a cliff. He keeps looking over the cliff at the dead sheep, again and again; how he woke up was not in the dream. She dreamt it, then she dreamt herself telling about it, then she dreamt herself telling herself that it was only a dream. But she kept looking over the cliff at the corpses of the sheep.

When she woke up, she knew there was nothing to be done, and she felt okay all that day. She cooked Arthur's breakfast and kissed him on his bald spot while he was eating and did the dishes and put some laundry into the machine and sorted through packets of flower seed from the year before and exclaimed with Debbie about Carlie's putting together a twelve-piece jigsaw puzzle all by herself. Then she got in the car and drove to the doctor.

Lillian's doctor was an experienced gynecologist—older than she was, and possessed of a competent, reassuring manner, neither forbidding, like Paul (and they should have foreseen how he was going to treat Claire by the way he upbraided parents whose babies got ear infections), nor at death's door, like Dr. Craddock, whose nicotine-stained fingers Lillian still remembered with a shudder—and he hadn't been much of a one for washing, either, Lillian thought. But Dr. Champion was simultaneously clean as a whistle and reassuringly smooth. With his wife and nurse, Kathryn, standing nearby, clucking gently under her breath, he carefully but firmly felt the swelling and also the surrounding tissue, and also the other breast. He looked in her file and quizzed her about a few things, including her mother and grandmother. Then he tapped his pencil on the desk and said, "I am sure this is a fibroadenoma—a harmless and common thing. It feels like that to me. All we have to do, really, is keep an eye on it for three to six months. Try not to think about it, and certainly don't worry. Eileen will make you an appointment for the summer."

So, Lillian thought as she drove home, this was the death-and-resurrection part. She felt nothing for the moment, but she knew that when she got home she would walk out among the tulips, which were brilliant and profuse this year, all colors, but especially the purple ones whose petals came to a slight point and opened outward. Among the tulips, she would take a deep breath, and plan dinner, maybe steak and caramelized sweet potatoes, and she would be very glad when Arthur got home, and probably she would laugh even more at his jokes and kiss him a few more times and hold his hand during *The White Shadow*. But though she might tell Arthur about her visit to Dr. Champion, she would never tell him what she had imagined so vividly these past five days.

IT WAS DEBBIE who arranged the intervention. Looking back, Lillian could see that her daughter had planned it for a while, and Lillian had fallen for it, hook, line, and sinker. First Debbie talked them into renting a house for August on Fire Island; she had gotten Henry to find the place. It would have been expensive, Lillian didn't know how much, but it was near the beach, and certainly cooler in its ocean-swept way than McLean. Then, apparently, on their first evening, Debbie sent Lillian with Hugh and the children out to the beach for a sunset stroll, during which she ambushed Arthur and confronted him. He admitted that he knew that Lillian was supposed to go back to the doctor, but he hadn't pushed her—he hated doctors himself and felt she should be free to choose, just like with anything else. But of course all of his arguments fell to rubble when faced with Debbie's blazing righteousness. That night, in bed, he didn't say a word to Lillian about what was coming. She should have been suspicious when Henry came for the weekend—when had he ever been a fan of family life? If Carlie or Kevvie neared him, he extended a hand and shifted his legs so that they wouldn't touch his perfectly pressed trousers with dirty fingers. For presents, he brought them books—*Oliver Twist* and *The Borrowers,* not entirely suitable for a five-year-old and a two-year-old, however well meant. Then, Sunday night, no one got up after supper except, at a signal from Debbie, Hugh, to put the kids to bed (it was a late supper), and when Lillian made a move to take her plate to the kitchen, Debbie said, "Mom, we all need to talk to you about something."

Lillian could not imagine what this was, given Debbie's high-handed tone, but she did sit down.

Arthur, who was around the corner of the table from her, wouldn't look at her, but he snaked his hand under the table and grabbed hers. Debbie said, "We all have talked about it, and we agree that you have to go back to the doctor."

"Whatever for?" said Lillian; honestly, she didn't right then know what they were talking about. She had gotten used to the lump, in the sense that she never let herself either think about it or touch it, and though Arthur had found it once and asked her about it (which was why she did tell him about her appointment with Dr. Champion), she never let him touch it again. What was withholding sex for, if not abjuring pointless worry?

"You know what for," said Debbie, and of course now she did. This was where Henry took over. "Really, Lillian, I can't believe you've let this go this long, and even though normally I would not consider it any of my business, I do think it's critical that you see someone."

"We've made you an appointment," said Debbie.

"How dare you!" said Lillian, but that was what an intervention was for—the same thing had happened to Betty Ford, though about drinking, not about going to the doctor. Lillian said, "Arthur has to go, too."

"I'll go with you," said Arthur.

"No, I mean, you have to go for a checkup, too." She said, a little self-righteously, "He hasn't had a checkup in a decade."

Then, seeing his downcast face, she was flooded with regret.

The doctor was in the city; they took the ferry the next morning. Hugh was to keep the kids, and Debbie was to wrangle Lillian, as if she were a rogue calf heading for the back pasture. But Lillian gave her no trouble. As long as Arthur was along. And of course the whole experience was torture, starting from the moment they squeezed her left breast and then her right one into that machine, the way the nurse kept pushing her in more tightly until the platform was digging at her ribs, the way she had to hold her breath and stand absolutely still, and the nurse barked at her every time she had a stray thought— stray thoughts apparently caused her to twitch. Her breasts ached— not equally, but equally enough so that Lillian convinced herself for about five minutes that nothing was wrong with the one that wasn't wrong with the other. The nurse wouldn't allow Arthur into the mammography room, and then the doctor came out and invited him into the consulting room, looking him in the eye, but not Lillian. That was the clue right there. Young doctor—Neil Feigenbaum. Maybe forty, maybe not. Debbie remained in the waiting room, as if guarding the door. Yes, there was a large mass; yes, they needed to do a biopsy. Today was Monday. Would she mind coming back the next day? He was associated with NYU; they could have the biopsy done there. Arthur, that old betrayer, kept nodding, and saying they would be there at eight in the morning. Finally, Lillian said, "That means a six a.m. ferry."

Arthur gave her a long, strict, and affectionate look. He said, "We'll think of something."

When they returned to the waiting room, after signing some papers, Debbie was just hanging up the phone the nurse's station had let her use, but Lillian didn't think to ask whom she had been calling—no doubt Hugh. It was not Hugh, though—it was Andy. As soon as they emerged into the heat of First Avenue, here came Andy, and Lillian realized that Dr. Feigenbaum must be Andy's gynecologist. Andy gave her one of her limp hugs and said, "Oh, let's have lunch." She walked them along, chatting the whole time about Emily and Janet and Michael and Loretta ("My goodness, she keeps him in line") and Richie and "that nice Jewish girl." ("So ambitious. I'm sure our bloodlines could stand an invigorating infusion of Jewish blood. But I say nothing. I just bite my tongue.") The restaurant was dark and old-fashioned, with elderly waiters who did everything with a napkin folded over one arm; Lillian half expected their attentive eighty-year-old to wipe her chin. So it was true, she thought, and now she would have to go through the five stages of grief all over again, or maybe only four of them, because she didn't foresee any opportunity for denial, now that Debbie knew, and Andy, and soon Henry and Frank and Claire and Janet and Hugh and Jared. Arthur did not let go of her; even sitting at their table, he was practically on top of her without perhaps realizing it. Andy and Debbie kept talking—Andy about Emily, and Debbie about Carlie and Kevvie. They sang a sort of chorus. Everything Andy said about Emily reminded Debbie of something about Carlie or Kevvie, and so they traded solos. Lillian ordered the crab cakes with aioli, and Arthur (she watched him closely) ordered the scampi, and it was good, so he ate almost all of it. Debbie ordered something and wolfed it down. Andy ate a single artichoke, very delicately grasping each leaf between her fingernails, plucking it off, and dipping it in pure olive oil with just a little sea salt added. For dessert, she did a kind thing, Lillian thought—she ordered two helpings of the crème brûlée and four spoons. Crème brûlée seemed designed to promote denial.

They put Debbie in a cab to Penn Station—she wouldn't get back to Fire Island now until after four. Then Andy said, "Oh, heavens, you should stay at the Waldorf," and Arthur said, "Why not?" and gave her a big smile, and Lillian was already into the grief part by the time they were walking through the lobby.

RICHIE ROLLED OVER and nearly fell out of bed, because Ivy had disappeared. He stopped himself, though—his reflexes were pretty good even when he was mostly asleep. He thought about three things before he thought about the election: He thought that he had to get up right now and take a piss, which he did. He thought that it was already seven-thirty and he was supposed to be at work by nine. He wondered whether Ivy had made coffee. Then it occurred to him to wonder who had won, so he wandered into the living room. Ivy was standing in front of the TV, her robe hanging open, weeping. He said, "Reagan really won, huh?"

Ivy could only nod. After a moment, she said, "I knew I shouldn't have voted for Barry Commoner."

In the kitchen, the last bagel was gone, but there was bread for toast and a piece of apple pie, always good for breakfast. He had adopted the safest course, given the friction between Ivy and Michael—he had not voted at all.

The phone rang—Loretta, who sounded happy, although she said nothing about the election, only, "You guys want to come over for dinner?"

Richie got along pretty well with Loretta, who had a better sense of humor than either Michael or Ivy. He said, "Well, we haven't heard from you guys in a month. You going to rub our faces in the dirt?"

"Not right away."

"When?"

"When you least expect it."

"What are you serving?"

"Humble pie."

"We don't like that."

"Okay. Lasagna."

"Still in the Italian-cooking class?"

"Eighth week."

"I need something more Tuscan than lasagna."

Loretta was silent for a minute, then said, "Tagliolini with new olive oil and fresh herbs? Then some veal medallions with a walnut sauce?"

Richie said, "I'll work on her."

"You should know that I forgive her."

"The question is whether she forgives you—" But then Ivy appeared in the doorway, and he said, "Bye," and hung up. Ivy didn't ask who it was, but he volunteered, "Mom says hi."

"Hi, Andy," said Ivy.

Richie went over and put his arms around her. He gave her a very good hug—she melted into him. He said, "You feel cold. Your feet are freezing."

"I've been up since four. I should have gone to bed before the results were in. I might have at least gotten one last good night's sleep."

"You think he's going to start a war right now? He doesn't get inaugurated for another two months."

"Stop joking."

"Did you talk to your mom?"

"Mom and Dad. At about six."

This was a bad sign. Ivy had met his aunt Eloise, so he did not criticize her parents, who, although very left, had never actually belonged to the CPUSA or been questioned by HUAC, and anyway were twenty years younger than Eloise. But they had both gone to City College, though they now lived on Long Island. They acted as if social programs like food stamps were automatically good and Wall Street was automatically bad. Like Aunt Eloise, they tossed around terms like "working class" and "bourgeoisie" and "capitalism." Their messy house was littered with old copies of *The Nation, Dissent,* and *Mother Jones.* Both Alma and Marcus liked to finish every family dinner with a cigarette and a political discussion; they were aggressive about making everyone at the table, including Richie, define and refine their arguments, and Richie had to admit that, usually, his arguments boiled down to "mere instinct," as Alma put it, shaking her head. They were fervent believers in rationality. Alma was harder on him than Marcus, who most often ended up saying, "Alma! Leave the boy alone! She likes him, then she likes him!"

"How can I leave him alone?" Alma would exclaim. "That's his problem. He's been left alone for all his life!"

He had to admit that, for all her eye rolling, Ivy agreed with her parents' views. The problem was their style—Ivy thought they were loud, messy, and rude. She loved them in private, but would go nowhere with them in public, not even to a deli.

He kissed her on the forehead, then more slowly on the lips, then took the corner of a dish towel and dabbed lightly at her eyes to wipe the tears. He said, "The only reason Reagan got elected was because Carter was such an incompetent. My uncle Joe, who is the nicest guy in the world, thinks this grain embargo is going to bankrupt him. It's like every single thing Carter did was wrong. That was Reagan's point."

"He's too smooth! He's just a mouthpiece for big business, like when he was on that show and then he was a governor! My God, he was awful in California."

Richie said, "Give him a chance. Let him be the best of a bad lot, okay? Just let him be that for a while." But he didn't dare bring up the dinner invitation. For all her good nature, he knew that Loretta would, indeed, demand some humble pie—she was like that. And they couldn't just put it off: Loretta never forgot, and she kept score. The election, say, gave her ten points, but not showing up for dinner and "taking your medicine" would give her a point, too.

When he called Ivy at lunchtime, she said, "Okay, we can go."

He said, "Go where?"

"Their place."

"They invited us?"

"Richie, I know she called you this morning and invited us for dinner. She called me at the office just to make sure you told me."

"She really is like the CIA, isn't she?"

Ivy laughed, which meant she was getting over the election.

Richie said, in a wheedling voice, "What difference does it make who won? They're all the same, really."

"You're hopeless," said Ivy.

"We only see them four or five times a year. It's like a penance. Or maybe like interest payments. We may both hate to visit our families, but we owe something every so often, don't we?"

Ivy said, "Oh, okay. Yeah, yeah, yeah. Four hours. I can take it."

When the argument started (after the veal, before the Sambuca), the girls were like trained debaters, and Richie and Michael kept exchanging looks. Ivy went first: "Whatever you say, just don't start with me about Adam Smith. He did not trust merchants. He thought they would get together and shit on everyone else if they possibly could."

Richie said, "I would rather talk about the hostages in Iran than this." They ignored him.

"Adam Smith?" said Michael. "Was that the guy you slept with last summer?"

Richie kicked him under the table—rather hard, in fact. Michael said, "Ouch."

The girls were used to their shenanigans.

Loretta said, "I don't need a theorist. No one does. I just have to look around and see what a mess all of these agencies I pay for are making of the country. People want to do stuff, and they can't, because there's too much paperwork."

"Like set fire to the Cuyahoga River."

Point for Ivy, thought Richie.

"If people wanted it cleaned up, they would have cleaned it up," said Loretta.

"They did want it cleaned up, and it has been cleaned up," said Ivy, "by EPA regulations. Not by the invisible hand."

At this point, Michael ran his fingertip lightly up the back of Loretta's neck. She laughed, but grabbed his hand. She said, "*You* wanted it cleaned up. But maybe those people living there were willing to make the tradeoff between jobs and a little pollution. There's no proof that pollution is bad. Maybe it's just stuff that's in the wrong place."

Michael said, "When Loretta was little, her room was papered in DDT-impregnated wallpaper. Just for kids. Donald Duck pictures on it."

Loretta spun around. She said, "What was wrong with that? It was a good idea. It killed the mosquitoes that landed on the wall."

Meanwhile, Ivy was staring.

Loretta said, "If you ban DDT, and then millions die from malaria, you haven't done anyone any good."

"Let the market kill them," said Ivy.

"At least it's their choice."

"How about full warnings on the roll of paper, saying what is known about DDT?"

"We *know* it will kill mosquitoes. We don't *know* it will hurt kids. Anyway, I guess the market decided about DDT-impregnated wallpaper, and that was that. I haven't seen it lately. Or lead-based paint, or X-ray machines in shoe stores. Things come and go. If you don't let them come and go, then you get like Russia."

Richie thought maybe she had Ivy there.

But then Ivy said, "Russia isn't the only alternative. Banks in the U.S. used to print all the money, and now the government prints it, because a free market in dollar bills didn't work and was chaos. There are things that the government should do, and things that companies should do. I don't want Russia, but I don't want the Mafia, either."

Michael was beginning to look bored, and Richie sympathized. Michael said, "I loved *The Godfather Part II.* Pow-pow! Let's have the Sambuca. You do this thing—you put a coffee bean in it and set it on fire. Burns off all the alcohol. Pow! Pow! Oh, you got me." Michael fell to the floor.

Loretta said, "Reagan is tough. The Iranians know it, and the hostages will be released."

Ivy said, "We'll see."

Richie thought, "Uncle."

Loretta said, preening just a bit, "Yes, we'll see."

On the way home, Richie and Ivy agreed, no more Michael and Loretta until at least the end of January.

1981

    ᭬

CHARLIE WAS READING a book. He was sitting up in his bed with his back against the headboard, knees drawn up, quilt to his waist. All he had on was a T-shirt from camp that was ripped at the collar, but even though it was zero degrees out and Mom had turned down the heat for the night, he was not cold. It was three-fifteen by the clock, and he was on page 477. There were about 150 pages left to go. Charlie had stayed up over the years to watch movies, drive around, TP Ricky Horan's house, talk to Leslie Gage on the phone, and listen to rock and roll turned very low, but he had never stayed up to read a book. Even while he was following the story with joy and pleasure, he was also rather amazed at himself.

He had found the book lying on the street outside of Kroger's. He took it home, hid it in his room so that Mom would not make a big deal over him finally reading a book, then opened it idly, noted the print was small. The first sentence made no sense at all, but he laughed at the second, "The governess was always getting muddled with her astrolabe, and when she got specially muddled she would take it out on the Wart by rapping his knuckles." He half understood this when he realized that the Wart was a child, not a blemish. It took him half an hour to read the first two pages, they were so strange. But he saw that they were meant to be strange, and he felt like the author was making a puzzle for him—this many words I will give you to understand, this many words I will keep for myself, and then there are these words in the middle, which you can have if you work at it. Things popped out of the page and into his head, and he pictured them. He went on, although he had only the dimmest idea about Arthur and Gawaine from occasionally looking at *Prince Valiant* in the Sunday comics. When he got confused by the words, the story stayed in his head, and drew him back.

He stretched his shoulders a little and turned the page. Now the story had turned to Lancelot and Guenever (which he pronounced in his mind to rhyme with "whenever"). He liked the line "Half the knights had been killed—the best half." He read about the ones that were left, and saw that King Arthur was thinking about how, whenever you set out to do something, you use up the good stuff first, and then you are stuck with the bad stuff, whatever it is. This was kind of like Charlie's experience on both the swim team and the diving team—they always did their best dives first, or swam the backstroke first and the breaststroke last, just to get so far ahead of the other teams that they maybe couldn't catch up. But that meant that you had to do your worst dives when you were more tired, so that you got even lower scores than you might have. The next part he could only sort of picture—stuff about clothes people were wearing and how stupid they looked. But he understood perfectly the part about Guenever. All the good people were gone, and those that were left were like the kids at school—they mostly wanted to see her fuck up, not because they cared, but because they didn't have anything better to do.

Charlie could not say that this section of the book was his favorite, even though he couldn't stop reading. What he had really liked was the part about Merlyn turning the Wart into a fish and a hawk. Even though he had never been farther from St. Louis than Chicago, in one direction, and the Ozarks, in the other, he could read that part and imagine just what England was like—all the birds and castles and hills. There was also a place where he, Charlie, had cried, something that hadn't ever happened before, even in a movie. When the kids—Gawaine and Gareth and the rest of them—killed the unicorn for their mom and dragged it home all dirty and wrecked, and their mom didn't even let it in the house, he thought that was the saddest thing he had ever read or seen. He did not know why. But it looked like even sadder things were to come.

At four-fifteen, the book fell onto the quilt, and his head dropped back onto the edge of the headboard. He was perfectly comfortable—one of his skills was sleeping soundly no matter what his position. When he first went to camp on the Current River, the other campers would test him: Head out of the bunk? No problem. Feet on the floor? Feet tied to the upper bunk? Spread-eagled? If he was asleep, he was asleep, that was Charlie. The other kids came to respect that after he blackened a few eyes for them. And anyway, he was big—six foot three, 165 pounds, too big to dive anymore unless he faithfully lifted weights. But he didn't mind that. He and Coach Lutz both knew he was coming to the end of his talents. Coach Jenkins had told him about a thousand times that Mark Spitz, who was six one, with an arm span of six two, weighed 170. Somehow, Charlie, six three, with an arm span of six four, could arrive at 182 pounds and win seven Olympic gold medals, or maybe only one. "You're the hope!" Coach Jenkins said. But Charlie needed fear to keep him going, and breaststroke was a singularly unscary activity, unless maybe you were swimming to Cuba and there were sharks. He hadn't done that yet.

When his mom came in at ten and woke him up by picking the book off the floor, turning it over in her hands, and then setting it on the bedside table without saying anything, they had a glance—one of those mom glances that said, "Now what?" Charlie smiled. His mom smiled. She knew better than to kiss him anymore, but she ruffled his hair and said, "Oh. *The Once and Future King*. I always wanted to read that."

CLAIRE'S TROUBLE NOW, a year and a half after she first tried to serve Paul the papers, was that no one she had talked to would take on Paul's lawyer. Claire's lawyer was someone she never would have dated. His father had spent the lawyer's entire Chicago childhood at the racetrack, scaring the pants off the kid with big bets that often went wrong and angry language about crooks and gangsters. He was now a brawny, tough-talking specialist in divorce, but every time Paul's lawyer issued some sort of ultimatum, Claire's lawyer would shake his head in despair, and say that they had to abide by it. Claire had no idea if they really did or not. She should have gotten Paul's lawyer, a colder, more genial type, and she would have if she'd had any advice, but she had opened the phone book, run her finger down the column, and decided probably they were all about the same. Oh no, not even in Iowa, one of the first states to grant no-fault divorce. The very words "no fault" enraged Paul.

This did not mean she was unhappy. She had succeeded in confining Paul to a small corner of her world, mostly because, unbeknownst to everyone other than her lawyer and Paul, she had gone to the stockbroker's office the day after Paul punched her and, with the aid of the secretary, a woman about her age, she had transferred $240,000 worth of money-market funds into a different account, which only she had access to. This account was now earning almost 20 percent, so she had plenty of dough. Part of the reason Paul was so bitter was that she had beat him to the draw. When he thought of this strategy as a way of preventing her from departing, he went to the stockbroker himself, and both he and the stockbroker were dumbfounded. The secretary had done a wonderful job, Claire thought, of being unable to imagine why she should have been at all suspicious or failed to cooperate with Mrs. Darnell.

Her apartment was very nice. And her car was running beautifully. Paul had trained her to adopt a strict maintenance schedule for every single aspect of her life, from hair to transmission, no matter how she felt, and it worked just the way he said it would, giving her something to do and preventing unforeseen breakdowns of every kind. She was forty-two now. Same age as Ali MacGraw, Lily Tomlin, and Tina Turner. Sometimes she decided that, while their careers were ending, peaking, or over, hers was just beginning. Other times, she envied them, that they had known what their careers were going to be, whereas she did not. Still did not.

On Tuesdays and Thursdays, she picked the boys up at school, took them to their after-school classes (Gray took German, Brad took Latin and driving). Then she took them out to eat and back to Paul's, where she oversaw their homework. When Paul came in the back door, she went out the front door. At sixteen and thirteen, the boys, she thought, were old enough to stay by themselves, especially since they were both taller than she was, and Gray outweighed her by twenty pounds, but Paul most assuredly did not agree. On Saturdays, Paul dropped them at the skating rink at nine, and Claire picked them up at noon. In the afternoon, she dropped them at a movie or took them shopping, then out to supper again, then she dropped them at home unless Paul had a date, in which case she went in the front door while he went out the back door, and she stayed until he returned (always before midnight). Paul would not allow them to come to her apartment downtown, or even to know the address (which seemed especially absurd, given how old they were). It might have been uncomfortable if they were girls, or if they were not the sons of Dr. Paul Darnell, but following protocol had been so drilled into them over the years that protocols were comfortable if laid out carefully in advance. They were also not in the habit of asking questions, at least of her. She did not know what they asked their father. She was sure that, whatever it was, he lied through his teeth in response.

It was surprising even to her how much she hated him. She had not hated him while they were married, or even after he punched her. She had sympathized with him, recognized that he was doing his best, understood the burden his own childhood placed upon him. She had seen his frustration and his fear. She had glided from day to day, giving him exactly what he asked of her, no more, no less, and agreeing with him that this was a virtue. But after she moved out, and without apparent relationship to his actions, she had come to feel such an aversion to everything about him, from the way he said certain words—like "and" or "drawer"—to the distribution of gray hairs over his temples, to the brown spot in the blue iris of his left eye, that she was amazed at herself. When she chatted with her divorced friends at the gym (there were two of them), she had nothing to say about the odor of his feet or his table manners or his drinking habits. This was how she knew that, compared with them, she really hated him—it was as if for twenty-two years she had been cataloguing the details of her antipathy every time he told her to pay attention. The same traits, when they appeared in the boys, did not bother her, though. Paul was a system unto himself, and it was the system she scorned. Her lawyer said that she should cultivate indifference, but it was hard to do so, because Paul wouldn't let her divorce him.

She had written him a letter—very cajoling in tone—in which she asked him what he imagined their future together would be, since she could not voluntarily return. His letter came back within the week. After the usual passages about marriage as a contract and a sacrament and an obligation, he had continued: "I still can't believe that you meant to do this. It strikes me as some sort of enormous mistake, or cosmic joke that will soon be set right. I sensed nothing. It's like I woke up in a different world. If you do not come to your senses, then I feel that I have to accept that I was crazy then, or I am crazy now, one or the other." Claire could see this, black flashing to white, white flashing to black—her own feeling of sympathy, if not love, converting to antipathy, likewise, his assurance that he knew what was what converting to disorientation. But it had been a year and a half. There was a kind of willfulness to his continuing disbelief that made her hate him more.

Andy thought she should see a psychiatrist, Lois thought she should open a shop, Minnie thought she should travel, Lillian thought she should keep a journal, Henry thought she should go back to school, and Joe said they had plenty of room at the farm, obviously thinking that she might easily find herself homeless in the big world. Someone somewhere, she was sure, thought she should join a convent. The only advice she had taken was keeping a journal. She bought herself an old-fashioned sales log for a business, and wrote about objects, like her set of dry measuring cups that she had gotten for her wedding from some aunt of Paul's whom she never met. There were also four gold-rimmed dessert plates with portraits of fruit that she had never used. She wrote down whatever came to mind about these items, maybe for a page, and then put the book on the shelf next to the toilet. Sometimes she wrote while on the toilet, which gave her a certain satisfaction. She imagined her brain as space like a cave, not very large but expandable—each word she wrote (and her handwriting was quite neat) worked in there like a tiny finger, pushing some edge, some membrane, a little further back, opening up the space and letting light in. Sometimes she wrote down the question "What next?"

But she could never answer it with anything more profound than "grilled cheese" or "a bath" or "*Cosmos*," which was a book she was reading about two pages at a time. She had bought a bunch of best-sellers, including Shelley Winters's autobiography. Shelley Winters was sixty-one. Another book she bought was about investing, *Crisis Investing: Opportunities and Profits in the Coming Great Depression*.

According to this book, she was supposed to take her money out of the money market and put it in gold, which was these days always between \$475 and \$500 an ounce; this would give her about thirty pounds of gold, but no income. She thought this was an investment that would strongly appeal to Dr. Paul Darnell, but it didn't appeal to her. However, she did write a little section in her journal about her wedding ring, which she now kept on a string hanging from the window latch. Writing about it gave her a pleasant sense of understanding gold, even of possessing it, which was close enough to buying some for now.

LILLIAN HAD BEEN SITTING quietly in a corner. She'd never been to this house before, an imposing Colonial on Q Street, and the party was a large one. She had been admiring the paintings, which were realistic, but strange—a donkey standing in a kitchen, a toddler sitting on the crest of a slate roof, holding an apple. When the woman sat down, Lillian struggled to remember her name—Irene—and smiled in her usual friendly way. Irene started in immediately. She leaned toward Lillian and said, "Oh, darling. I have been thinking about you. You'll never guess what happened to me."

"I can't im—"

"So bizarre. I felt a lump right here." She touched the underside of her left breast. "And, of course, I went straight to the doctor, and he felt it, too. So I was terrified! I went home and told Jason." Yes, Irene's husband was Jason. Maybe he worked in the State Department? A rumpled, handsome fellow. "And he was terrified, too. He was so nice to me, all that evening. Very attentive."

Lillian smiled in a sympathetic way.

"I mean, he put me to bed and brought me tea and you name it. The next morning, he took me for the biopsy, and he sat with me in the waiting room until I went in for the procedure, which they said would take an hour and a half."

"It's time-consuming. They have to be very precise," said Lillian.

"Well, of course," said Irene. "Anyway, I came out, and Jason was nowhere to be seen. I was a little—oh, I don't know. So I walked out on the step and was sitting there, sort of dazedly staring around, and here comes this little Toyota, kind of beat up, and it stops at the curb, and out gets Jason, and he goes around to the driver's side and kisses the girl who was driving goodbye!"

"Good heavens!" said Lillian.

"Yes! He had been seeing her for months! I am telling you, it was the turning point of my life!"

Lillian's glance strayed, in spite of herself, to Irene's chest.

Irene said, "Oh well! The biopsy was negative. Everything fine, in spite of all my worries, but I have been thinking of you and your trouble ever since Miriam told me about it all."

Wouldn't want that to happen to anyone, thought Lillian.

"But you're feeling better now. You look lovely. I just wanted to tell you that."

In the course of the eleven months since her operation (radical mastectomy, fourteen lymph nodes, chest muscle, plus radiation, the new miracle drug tamoxifen, everything, it seemed), she had heard more about the breast-cancer adventures of women she barely knew than she had ever thought possible. The mother who had died at thirty-seven. The grandmother who lived to be ninety-eight, and at her age they didn't do operations, because cells divided so slowly anyway. The woman who had something called DCIS in one breast, then lobular ten years later. The lumpectomy during pregnancy (this was the worst one, of course). It was someone new every week or so.

Arthur, who had been talking with a colleague maybe ten feet away from her (he didn't get much farther if he could help it), now went to the buffet and put a few things on a plate. When he sat down next to her, she saw a tiny bacon quiche, a tiny egg roll made of lettuce, and a mushroom stuffed with crabmeat. She ate them one at a time. He said, "Irene must have been telling you about Jason. She gets quite animated when she talks about it."

"What happened with them?"

"He married a twenty-five-year-old. They now have twins, and she's pregnant with a third. If you are ever at the Washington Monument and you see a man with a giant paunch and a perfectly circular bald patch, holding hands with Tweedledee and Tweedledum, that's them."

"Boys."

"Very grumpy girls."

"Not happy-go-lucky like Richie and Michael, huh."

"Well, so far, they haven't been allowed to act out their antipathy toward one another, which would be a joyous experience." He said, "Are you tired?"

All she had to do was sigh, and he helped her up. He put his arm around her. "It's at least a mile to the front door, but on the way, be sure to look at the little painting by the same artist as these. Very elegantly done window box full of violets, plus hand grenade, the pin right beside it." But when they walked past it, Arthur turned her head toward himself, and held her more tightly. On the front stoop, nice weathered brick, he sat her in the glider and went to get the car.

Lillian thought that she should not be tired and she should not be stupid. She had finished the radiation and chemo in the winter. She had hair now, and it wasn't bad hair. She had several fairly comfortable prosthetic bras, and she looked about the same in her clothes. Who saw her naked except Arthur? Certainly not Lillian herself, who brushed her teeth in the kitchen and did not look at the mirror when she passed through the bathroom. She hadn't been in a dressing room at a department store in a year. And, of course, she did not remember the surgery. She remembered lying on the table, and she remembered being lifted into her hospital bed, and she remembered extremely vivid narcotic dreams that gave her second thoughts about the inner lives of heroin addicts. She remembered sleeping a lot for a week, and she remembered Arthur allowing her to lie against him in a half-stupor for hours. It was not, in its way, a frightening experience, not warranting denial, grief, or bargaining. It was stuff. Although she never said this to the women who told her their tales, what she thought was: Just a breast. Still, every day she did two or three crossword puzzles, hoping to wake up some of those slumbering brain cells.

WHEN FRANK GOT TO the Russian Tea Room, where he was to meet Andy, Richie, Michael, and the girls for supper, all he could think about was Jesse. Two years ago now, Frank had offered to bring him to New York, to have a look at the Statue of Liberty, Central Park, the World Trade Center, and the Empire State Building. But there had never been a good time—so much work to do, maybe he could bring his mom and dad along, they might like it. The idea dropped away; Frank avoided mentioning it in his letters, though he was tempted every time. Frank had made this reservation himself, knowing that if Andy had any trouble—for example, a busy signal— she would give up and try somewhere else, because she really wasn't picky. She appeared on the surface to be picky, but she was not. This was one of her more irritating characteristics. But he was not going to be irritable this evening.

Jesse kept up their correspondence. Frank had gotten a letter that very week: maybe he should go to vet school after all. Frank thought Jesse had given up that idea after Frank told him senior year that if he became a farm vet, his main job would be to put the animals down. Frank wondered if Jesse consulted Joe about these things. Sometimes Jesse wrote about religion. Frank said he should do what he felt to be right. He always waited a few days before answering Jesse's letters. Yes, it was like being a girl and having a boyfriend and not wanting to seem too forward.

Richie and Ivy showed up first. Richie needed a haircut, and Ivy's mop was pulled carelessly back in a clip. She was wearing a dark jacket and carrying her usual hefty briefcase. She threw off her coat, sat down, and ordered a martini, just like a guy getting off work. Frank said, "Hard day at the office, Ivy?"

She said, "Not much of a day at the office. We had to go to a memorial service, so I spent most of the day on the train."

Frank asked, "Who died?"

"The guy who started Pocket Books. I never knew him, but my boss wanted me to meet people. It was interesting. He sold two and a half million copies of *Lost Horizon*. Did you ever read that one?"

"Couldn't get through it," said Frank.

"It sold more copies than *The Murder of Roger Ackroyd* but not as many as Dr. Spock."

"How many has that sold?" said Richie.

"Twenty-eight million," said Ivy. Frank smiled to himself. She was a girl with a vocation, nice figure, good legs.

Loretta was upon them before Frank realized it, and when she said, "Hey, Frank," it made him jump. Michael was right behind her. He needed a haircut, too. These girls, he thought, were falling down on the job. Loretta's excuse was that she was five months pregnant, due in early March. She was flourishing in every way—her hair was thick and shining, her ass was huge, her belly stuck out, and her ankles were swelling. He glanced at Ivy, who looked askance at the belly. Frank thought Richie would be lucky to get one offspring out of Ivy. Michael pulled out Loretta's chair, and she grunted as she lowered herself into it. She said, "Michael bought a motorcycle."

"Do not ride that thing," said Ivy.

"What kind?" said Frank, pretending an interest.

Michael exclaimed, "Kawasaki 1000. It's red."

"Why am I not surprised," said Ivy flatly.

Frank looked over at Richie, who was surveying the menu. No response.

Andy floated in, closing the flap of her handbag, glancing around, and only seeming to recognize them at the last moment. Frank cleared his throat in order to get the irritated look that he knew was there off his face, and stood up to kiss her on the cheek. She gave him a vaporous squeeze around the waist. She said, "I forgot how overdone this place is. But the food is nice." Frank, who rather liked the darkness, the extreme red walls, and the samovars, as well as the velvet booths, knew she would order a salad. She looked at her children as if she couldn't quite remember who they were, and sat down. Richie said to her, as if tattletaling, "Michael bought a big motorcycle."

Andy turned her gaze on Michael, and Michael met her look with a challenging stare of his own, but she didn't say anything, leaving that up to Frank. Frank said, "Have you ever ridden a motorcycle?"

"Yesss," said Michael, evidently annoyed. "You sit up, look where you are going, and—"

"Hope for the best," said Loretta, who then rolled her eyes. But she smiled. Frank had noticed that, as long as Michael didn't drink and spoke highly of Ronald Reagan, she didn't criticize him.

"Let's stop talking about the motorcycle," said Michael. Just then the waiter appeared and handed around the menus. Frank said, "The caviar is always good here."

There was an empty chair, as if for Jesse. Frank stared at it, stopped staring at it, then signaled the waiter, who took it away.

Richie grinned, and Michael said, "It is, it is." Even Andy raised her eyebrows in pleasure. "Beluga! So delicious."

The serving of beluga came mounded in a little bowl set in ice, surrounded by other little bowls with blini, hard-boiled eggs, chopped onions, sour cream. Ivy, who considered herself the caviar expert, promptly placed a little dab of each ingredient on one of the thin circular pancakes, folded it, and ate it. She said, "You have to use this spoon. It's mother-of-pearl. You can't use any kind of metal."

Frank watched them—Andy taking maybe two eggs, Loretta patting her belly and shaking her head, Richie topping Ivy, and Michael topping Richie. But there was plenty. One letter Jesse had sent him in the summer mentioned that a guy from over in Muscatine gave him some catfish roe. Lois fried it up. Jesse, he thought, should be here, should be having this once-in-a-lifetime experience. Frank let Ivy make him a serving with everything on it while he pulled himself together—the chair was gone, but there was still a space where it had been—and said, "You know, six months before the Iranian Revolution—when was that, spring of '78—we got invited to the Iranian Consulate; remember that, Andy? That was the only time I've ever seen beluga in bowls like salad."

"I do remember that," said Andy, as if doing so surprised even her. Frank ate his serving. What he remembered about that party, more than the caviar, was standing near one of the windows and being revisited by a feeling from that trip he took for Arthur to Iran; at the sight of buzzards feasting in the moonlight on some carcass, say a goat, he had known all of a sudden how little intervened between the hot breeze on that runway and death itself. Death had shimmered in the air—as close as his next breath—and in that satin-draped consulate, looking out on Sixty-ninth Street, he had felt that once again. Now, he thought, right now, at the Russian Tea Room, it was even closer, if still beyond the boundary. The thought made his hand resting on the table look vivid, still, pale like marble.

Dinner was uneventful, except that, after Richie ate his lobster salad with evident enjoyment, Michael said, "Did you see him lick the plate?" and laughed, joined by Loretta. Ivy said, "Since you picked up your plate and licked the whole surface the last time we were at your place, it must be in the genes."

Richie laughed.

Andy looked at Frank. Frank knew she was thinking that the two girls caused bad blood, or worse blood, between Richie and Michael. Frank did not agree: he thought the boys could not resist egging each other on, and would do it with or without Ivy and Loretta. But look at them, they were doing well. Michael and Loretta had bought a co-op on Seventy-eighth Street, between Madison and Fifth. Rubino said Richie was good at real estate, but he had a plan for something bigger and "more helpful." Income-wise, they were about neck and neck—Michael stopped having Social Security taken out of his paycheck sometime in August, and Richie sometime in September. Loretta, of course, contributed more from her trust fund than Ivy did from her job, but that didn't mean much, given Ivy's dedication.

Jesse. Jesse. Well, he wasn't worth what he had been two years before, but he was worth more than either of the twins—Frank did not look forward to the time when Michael, anyway, and maybe Richie, found that out. But because of that vibrating current that stretched between him, here, and Jesse, there, all of this was fine with him. He was alive and not divorced. Michael was not dead or in prison; Richie had come to terms with Michael by letting Loretta and Ivy take over. Janet had escaped that Peoples Temple psycho apparently unscathed. If someone had told him forty years ago that he could feel relief in all the imperfections of his life, that he could derive some sense of pleasure from a bad marriage, disappointing children, a faltering career, an array of physical aches and pains, and an intermittent correspondence with his brother's son, he would have punched that person in the nose. But here it was again: once he identified a single thing in this world that he actually wanted—Lydia, Jesse—that very thing slipped away. He suspected that Andy would say he had no capacity for love. Only Frank knew that this wasn't true. He swallowed, then said, "Normally, I wouldn't suggest this, but how about some tea? It's worth it here, just to see them make it."

"Mint would be good," said Loretta, patting her belly.

1982

HALF ASLEEP, Janet saw that face again—a black man in a doctor's scrubs, striding down the hospital corridor, tossing off some medical terms as if he knew what they meant. She sat up with a cry that made Jared turn over and ask her what was going on: was Emily okay?

Janet said, "I'll see," and snaked out of bed, wide awake. Emily, of course, was fine. Janet stood in the darkness outside of Emily's room and tried to stop shaking. That it was Lucas was impossible. Lucas was dead; even Marla agreed that he was dead. The worst part was that she could not remember which show it was. She had been clicking through to MTV, hoping for a Pat Benatar or a Blondie video—Emily loved to dance around the living room to "Heart of Glass."

Two days of exploring, and she saw him again—he had a pretty good part on the soap, but not a lead. There was also a black nurse, who would probably end up his girlfriend but wasn't paying much attention to him yet. She gathered that "Dr. Thompson" was a new character.

She wrote to Marla, but Marla knew nothing. In Paris, Marla had thought Janet and Lucas had both gone to Guyana. When she heard from Janet the first time (gosh, two years ago now), she was so happy to hear from her—and that she was alive—but she wrote that she hadn't dared ask about Lucas, because Janet hadn't mentioned him.

Now that she was in New York, they wrote from time to time, but never about Lucas.

What with Emily and day care and her own classes and Jared's schedule, she put it out of her mind, because, thank God, he was alive, and once she got used to his being alive, well, why stir up old business—curiosity killed the cat. That worked for exactly one month.

Right before moving day (Solon to Iowa City), she was packing books to give away, and out of one of them (the Bible, in fact, which was why she had never opened it after leaving San Francisco) fell a note. It read, "Too much is going on. I've got to get out of here. I've got a possible gig at a recording studio in L.A. I'm hitchhiking, and will call you when I can. Lucas." She turned the note over and turned it back. She smoothed it out. Why he had tucked it into the Bible, she had no idea. But she had given in to panic and let Aunt Eloise take her off to Iowa City. She knelt there for a moment, looking at the note, and imagined the phone ringing in her old room after her departure. Or of Lucas getting that message, "The number you are trying to reach is not in service at this time." Not only was he not dead, she turned out to be the betrayer. Did he know that she was alive? It was entirely possible that he assumed she was the one to change her mind and go to Guyana, that he had read the newspapers horrified. Hadn't she, after all, been more accepting of Reverend Jones than Lucas had been? She perused the note several more times. It was dated, too—"Friday," the night he never returned from the gig she thought he had.

She stuck it in her sock drawer and left it there. But as she made scrambled eggs for Emily (it was Jared's late night), she kept jiggling her legs and walking around. When Emily wanted to go out onto the porch and work on the snowman she was building, Janet jumped about as if she were cold, though the weather was pleasant. When it was time for Emily to go to bed, she could hardly read the book. When Emily pointed out letters and even short words she recognized, Janet was too distracted to be enthusiastic. Janet kissed Emily good night, turned out the light, closed the door, and she went straight to her sock drawer, got out the note, read it again. She would do nothing.

Jared rented a truck. Seven of their friends turned out to help with the move. Everyone was a little excited: Janet and Jared were buying a house, a first in their group. It cost $55,000; the sellers were holding the mortgage and letting them pay 12 percent. The house was a brown house on Brown Street, with screened-in porches front and back, three bedrooms upstairs, and a spacious if not modern kitchen. Janet and Jared had, painfully, come up with $10,000, and their mortgage payment would be $450 per month, which seemed huge, especially compared with their $160 rent in Solon. But the price of gas was $1.30 and didn't look like it was going down. Jared thought they could save $120 a month on his commute, not even counting the few occasions where they came into town to go to a movie or to the Mill to listen to music.

Salt crunched under their feet, and Janet kept having to sweep it off the entry floor just inside the front door. Everything was out of the rental in an hour and fifteen minutes. The guys drove off in the truck, and Janet, Leslie, and Gina cleaned. When the girls and Emily got to Brown Street, though, the former owners were sitting glumly on their own boxes. The driver of their moving van, which had the name of a religious organization painted along the side, had gotten lost in Illinois and then again in Iowa City—he and the two movers were too tired from their long trip to do anything. Jared and Janet and the seven friends moved all of the previous owners' furniture and boxes into the van while the movers looked on, and then Janet gave the movers five sandwiches she had made. She knew the look of their faces—the obedient look of people being "given a new life." She wanted them to go away. When the owner thanked her and gave her a hug, Janet said, "Be careful; good luck, and I hope you get there."

She put him out of her mind by focusing intently on everything she was doing, whether it was reading a book, listening to one of her professors, playing Legos with Emily, or chatting with Jared. She could feel herself getting louder, brighter, weirder, the way she always got when she was converting herself. As a result, she could sense Emily withdrawing, Jared looking at her sideways, her Realism and Naturalism professor watching for some other student's raised hand. Finally, one day when Jared was home with Emily, and she was supposed to be going to class, she went to Student Health Services and talked to a Dr. Constance. She talked so fast that Dr. Constance stopped writing things down, had no opportunity to ask questions, just stared at her. She talked for exactly forty-five minutes, thereby giving Dr. Constance five minutes to tell her what to do. The silence was total. Janet waited. Clearly, Dr. Constance had no idea, either. The silence continued. There were three minutes left. Janet shifted her gaze from the woman's gray curls to the window and the brick wall outside, and remembered how her own mother disappeared so often, heading out to see Dr. Somebody. "Dr. Dix," her father had called him. Dr. Constance said, "I think maybe you should consider your marriage and your feelings for your husband."

"I consider my family all the time."

"No, I mean ponder them, not take them into consideration. Whenever we are feeling something strongly, it is related to what is going on in the present."

Janet said, "I guess now you are going to tell me to live in the moment and take things one day at a time."

"That isn't bad advice."

Janet looked at her watch. She really, really didn't want to be rude, so she smiled and said, "Well, anyway, thanks for listening to me, and I think that's a good idea." Then she ran.

Yet another blizzard was in the offing—the snow already on the ground seemed to vaporize upward into the low-hanging clouds. She put on her gloves and pulled the hood of her down jacket over her head, snapped it closed over her chin and mouth. She stepped carefully around the puddles that were slickening as the afternoon cooled and darkened. She had almost done it, almost fallen right into the trap. It didn't matter, Janet thought, who they were or how well meaning they might think they were; as soon as they started talking to you about your problems, their language captured you and put you in a prison of cause and effect, and you had to go along inside that, whether it was Oedipus complex or vitamin deficiency or admitting you were powerless or accepting Jesus, questing for a result that you could feel in yourself. The last thing Janet wanted in this life was to say, Maybe I still love Lucas, he was beautiful, a charismatic and fascinating person—and for the person to whom she was saying this to reply, Tell me about your father. She would of course reply, My father is an asshole, I wouldn't ask him for a penny. And she certainly did not want then to hear, Define what you mean by asshole? She would be thirty-two this year. She had to accept the system that was herself. It had to move forward as well as it could. When she got home—sliding a little as she climbed the hill between Dubuque and Linn—Emily was standing in the middle of the living-room rug, and Jared was sitting on the floor cross-legged in front of her, juggling three of her dolls and saying, "Look at them fly, Emmy. Boom! Up and over! Can I catch it? I can't catch it! Oh, I caught it! There goes another one!" It was Janet who laughed, not Emily. Since they were going to be snowbound for another couple of days, she decided that that was enough for the time being. Then, looking at the daughter who reminded her so much of herself, she thought, If I don't get over this by the first of April, we're getting a dog. She felt better at once.

WHEN RICHIE GOT HOME from work, Ivy told him that Michael and Loretta would be there for dinner in twenty minutes. He put his coat in the closet. The intercom buzzed, and when he pressed the button, Michael's voice said, "This is going to take both of us."

Richie said, aloud, "Isn't she due, like, last week? I can't believe they came." He knew that Michael could hear him. Ivy walked over and removed his hand from proximity to the intercom and said, "Why would you think that she wouldn't rise to the challenge? Just because she, who once weighed a hundred pounds, now weighs a hundred and forty-eight?"

"Why are you so mean to her?"

"It's a fact. She's going crazy waiting. And I don't think inviting them to supper, doing all the cooking and dishes, and giving them a way to twiddle their thumbs in public is mean."

Richie wasn't so sure about that when he got downstairs and discovered that, because their building didn't have an elevator, he and Michael had to get Loretta up the steps. Michael, without seeming to find it strange, came up behind her and pushed, one hand on each cheek. Richie held her arm. It took a long time.

Loretta kept talking: "Don't you think I'm in good shape? I feel absolutely fine. The doctor says he's never really seen anyone sail through a pregnancy like this before. When I went to my appointment yesterday, he estimated at least eight pounds, and that must come from your side, because I weighed six and a half, and my cousins were all six to seven, too. Ungh! There!"

Ivy was standing in the open doorway, wooden spoon in her hand. She said, "Oh, darling. I hope this is worth it, but I did make all your favorite dishes."

This turned out to be rib-eyes, baked potatoes, and broccoli. But, in fact, Richie wasn't as interested in Loretta as he was in Michael, since Michael was being especially nice to Loretta, not teasing her, gazing at her fondly, saying "mmm-hmm" when she spoke. What this meant to Richie was that Michael probably had a girlfriend—he had always been nice as pie for about the first six weeks of any new relationship. Michael knew better than to confide in Richie, but Richie did not snitch any longer, even to Ivy. Knowing was enough. Richie thought of himself as "profiling" Michael.

Part of Michael's profile these days was letting Loretta go on in detail about how they were going to raise their son. There were two larger parts: On a horse by the time he was a year old. (Didn't they know there was a stable in Central Park? The horses went up and down in a freight elevator.) And the other part was structure. A child felt more secure with structure, a boy especially. Girls, you could be a little lazy; Loretta had seen that in her child-development classes, but boys, no meant no. She shifted position and let out an involuntary groan. Ivy said nothing as she placed the platter of steaks on the table. Richie said, "I can't think of a single structure that either of us ever liked."

Loretta looked right at him. She said, "I doubt that was your fault. And anyway, you were in an incubator for weeks. That interferes with the attachment process." As always, Loretta spoke crisply and with conviction; she had never had a doubt in her life. Michael nodded at this as if he had come to some understanding of their upbringing, a subject Richie preferred to ignore.

As if by common agreement, the conversation backed away from these subjects. Michael said that he expected Braniff to shut down, then that the market had closed at 807 ("But not before I sold a lot of GM stock—no one is buying cars anymore"), crude prices were sinking, gold at 345 an ounce, blah, blah, blah, and then Richie felt a splash. As he bent down to look under the table, Loretta half rose out of her chair, and Ivy said, "What?"

Michael said, "Did your waters break, babe?" And he said it calmly. Loretta said, "Worse than that."

"What?"

"I feel like pushing."

"Pushing what?" said Richie.

"Pushing the baby!" shouted Loretta, who then closed her eyes, stood up, and staggered toward the doorway. Ivy went after her. She said, "Have you been in labor?"

"I don't know. I don't know. Maybe. I've had Braxton Hicks for days."

Ivy grabbed her shoulders and steered her toward the bathroom. Richie and Michael followed. Richie felt that he was gaping. He said, "Didn't you guys go to some kind of class?"

"Kind of," said Michael. "We kept forgetting. We went the first time. It was stupid. Hh-hh-hh-hh, a-a-a! We couldn't stop laughing, so they asked us not to come back."

Where had Richie heard this before?

Ivy said, "I worked on a book a couple of years ago about non-violent birth and baby massage. It said the baby should be born into water. Like in a bathtub." She steered Loretta to the tub, and began stripping off her pants. Richie said, "I'm calling an ambulance!" As he left, Ivy shouted, "Don't forget to tell them about the stairs!" Michael followed him, and Ivy slammed the bathroom door.

The whole time Richie was looking for the phone book, then leafing through to the emergency page, then realizing that all he had to do was dial 911, then dialing 911, Michael was practically on top of him, not saying a word. As he gave his address, said "unexpected labor," described the stairs, then repeated, "Okay, maybe ten minutes, thanks," Michael looked unlike Richie had ever seen him, struck dumb. Richie bumped against him, experimentally. No response. He said, "What the fuck is wrong with you?"

"I can't believe she's having a baby."

"What did you think was in there, a pillow?"

"I can't believe it. I have to call the nurse." They had arranged for a nurse for the first six weeks. But Michael made no move. He said, "I don't have her number. Loretta has the number somewhere."

Richie said, "I had no idea you were such a fucking idiot."

Michael gazed at him.

He nudged Michael back toward the bathroom door, but when they got there, he knew in his very being that neither of them wanted to open it. They stood. From inside, Richie could hear the sound of the bathtub faucet as well as Loretta's cries and Ivy's lower, reassuring tones as she said, "Bite this washcloth. It's clean." Then a more muffled grunt, then the sound of the tap being turned off. Richie was used to thinking of Ivy as knowledgeable and competent, but he knew for a fact that she had never assisted in childbirth before. Then a siren sounded in the distance, came closer. Richie bumped Michael gently on the shoulder. "Go downstairs and let them in."

"Where's the freight elevator?"

"There is no freight elevator."

"You're shitting me!" Now Michael looked very white and close to panic. But the howl of the siren retreated and disappeared. Richie said, "Just go. Maybe you can wave down a cop car or something, if the ambulance doesn't get here."

Michael nodded. Loretta gave out a cry. Ivy mumbled something, then said, "It's nice and warm. Just relax. Try to reeeellaaaxxxxx. There you go. Mummble mumble." There was another cry, but softer, less desperate.

"Go down," said Richie.

"Shout if something happens."

"Why should I do that?"

Michael gaped.

"I'm joking! Go!"

Michael sailed out of the apartment, leaving the door wide open. When he had pounded down at least a flight of stairs, Richie gave in to his curiosity and slowly turned the handle. Loretta was sitting naked in the tub, huge and pale, her breasts resting on her belly. She had a washcloth in her mouth and her head was back, but as she cried out again, it tilted forward. Ivy was on her knees, leaning over the rim of the tub. On the toilet lid, she had set several folded towels. Loretta cried out again, a rich, even scary, vibrato howl. Richie looked at his watch. There was no more, and maybe less, than a minute between the cries. According to every movie he had ever seen, that was a bad sign if you were waiting for an ambulance and three guys to carry a stretcher up and a mom down lots and lots of steps. He said, "Can I do anything?"

Ivy turned and looked at him. "Where's Michael?"

"Watching for the ambulance."

"I can feel hair."

He said, "What?"

"I can feel the baby's hair. There's a lot of it. It's right there."

Loretta's head fell back and she groaned. Ivy said, "Oh, shit!" and leaned forward. Richie stepped into the bathroom and stood on his tiptoes. Loretta said, *"Ohhhh Goddddd helppp meee!"* and here it came, dark hair, dark squinched face, little crossed arms, little chest, first slowly and then shooting out, completely under the surface of the water, and therefore ripply and strange. Ivy half rose, leaned way over, and slipped her hands under the baby, back and shoulders and head; then, very carefully, sort of hooking her thumbs under its arm-pits, she lifted it out of the water, hair, forehead, nose, mouth, chin. The water sluiced over closed eyelids, plump cheeks, and full lips; then the mouth opened, silently. Then it let out a cry. Without being asked, Richie opened one of the towels and held it toward the baby. But there was a problem that they hadn't foreseen. Richie and Ivy exchanged a look, and then Ivy leaned forward and bit the umbilical cord in two, spitting out a little blood. Richie wrapped the baby in the towel. It was tiny, much tinier than he had expected. He opened the towel again, just for a look, and said, "Boy."

Now Loretta, who had seemed to pass out, her arms spread over the rim of the tub and her head dropped back, sat up. She said, "Is he okay?"

As if in answer, the baby opened his mouth again and wailed, a healthy and not painful sound. Ivy said, "He seems fine." She pulled the plug. The red, bloody water began to drain away. When it was all gone, she laid another of the towels across Loretta's thighs, and handed her the wrapped-up baby. Richie had to admit that he was sorry to give him up: he wasn't the mother or the father, but somehow that tiny face, with the dark hair and the bowed lips, was imprinted on him. Moments later, Michael burst through the door, saying, "They're here, they're coming up!" And then he stood there, his eyes wide, his arms dangling at his sides. Richie said, "What's his name?"

Michael and Loretta, both now staring at the tiny wrapped thing, said, simultaneously, "Chance."

Ivy said, "You are naming this baby 'Chance'?"

Michael took a deep breath. "Loretta's grandfather was named Chance. Jonathan Chance. He was a cattle rustler."

"He was not!" exclaimed Loretta. "He was a perfectly respectable businessman." But she was grinning from ear to ear. She said, "Chance Markham Langdon. What a boy."

Michael stepped forward, and Richie stepped back to make way. Moments later, a medic appeared in the doorway. He called out, "Looks like we're too late again, Benny!"

IT WAS HOT. The worst winter Henry could remember (worse even than the winter of '78, which drove him out of town), fifty-nine inches of snow, into April—his daffodils had worn snow hats for three days—had given way to the hottest summer. All he was doing lately was sitting around in his shorts, drinking ice water with lime juice and trying not to look at the thermometer. But how could he help himself? He had never seen it hit 108 before, much less for three days running. And at his place, he had a little bit of a breeze off the lake. He was almost ready to keep his air conditioner on all day, though so far he had limited himself to nights, spending at least some of the day at the Lee Street Beach, under an umbrella, where he was now, or in the water. He had also given himself express permission to do absolutely nothing. In his entire life, Henry could not remember doing nothing. His present exile in Chicago was his own fault, since he was the one who had talked Philip (they had resumed their relationship, but only as friends) and Philip's current lover, Yves, who taught at the university in Rennes, into taking their little tour in June, to avoid the August crowds. Two young men escorting a fifty-year-old all over Cathar country, Narbonne to Béziers to Mazamet to Carcassonne, then Tarascon to Montségur, to Foix to Mirepoix, one slaughter after another, rolling fields and vineyards giving way to precipitous mountains and perfectly groomed beaches. Philip, whose specialty was structuralist criticism, and Yves, whose specialty was Baudelaire, had been genuinely shocked at Henry's tales—Simon de Montfort slaughtering all the inhabitants of Béziers, even the Catholics who were seeking sanctuary in the cathedral, which he burned to the ground, saying, "Kill them all, God will recognize His own." Subsequently, Simon's head was smashed to bits by a stone catapulted from inside the walls of Toulouse by "ladies and girls and women." A fitting end, they all thought. It was admittedly strange to drive through such a beautiful landscape and contemplate decades of religiously inspired cruelty and horror, but Henry had enjoyed himself.

He thought that Philip deserved someone like Yves. Philip was thirty-six now, tenured, published, often asked questions about incomprehensible subjects like semiotics and post-structuralism, which he answered with musical good nature. Metacriticism was much more glamorous than etymology, of course. Yves had reservations about Lacan and Saussure and approached Baudelaire with a more generalized perspective, situating him in his historical moment and cultural milieu, writing articles about the various ways in which Baudelaire and his contemporaries had infused this and that. Yves was twenty-nine, but well on his way from Rennes to Paris or Columbia. Henry was like an uncle to them (maybe a great-uncle to Yves), but they put up with him, and moderated the speed of their chatter in French so that Henry could understand most of what they said. The other thing Yves did was live in a large house between Rennes and Fougères. If you wanted medieval, you could hardly ask for anything more wonderful than the former frontier between Bretagne and France—with castles every few leagues—and then on down to Aquitaine, with its fortified hill towns, and below that, of course, Navarre, Ariège, Languedoc. His colleagues vacationed with their families on a continuum between Ottawa and Minneapolis; Henry flew off to Manhattan and Toulouse.

But he felt apocalyptic anyway, and it wasn't only the heat and the contemplation of Pope Innocent III. One thing Philip and Yves had talked about as they drove around was what was happening to friends of theirs, strange lesions in their mouths, weird infections, night sweats, swollen glands. Henry had eavesdropped, only asking a question every so often. He knew, though, that as he talked about Pope Innocent III, who had sicced Simon de Montfort on the Cathars (who held unorthodox Gnostic and Manichean beliefs, didn't give oaths, engage in marriage or reproduction, or eat meat), they were both wondering about curses, about such mysterious and medieval illnesses as the bloody flux, St. Anthony's fire, St. Vitus' dance, the ague, leprosy, the black death. Narbonne, Carcassonne, and Foix put them in the mood—God's curse, bodies piled upon bodies, the sense of one citizen recoiling from another only to flee into the wilds and be eaten by wolves. Henry was sure that Philip's and Yves's residences had seemed as welcoming upon their return as his little duplex had to him.

Now, though, in the midst of all this heat and ennui, there was a name. Not the curse of God, but "acquired immunodeficiency syndrome," every word easily sourced, three from Latin, one from Greek, a stiff, dry phrase, not medieval at all, but right up to date. Henry was falsely soothed by this phrase, somehow. It didn't seem possible, now that he knew it, that he could go into the bathroom to brush his teeth, as he had a day or so after getting home from France, look in the mirror, see a blue lesion on his gum right above his incisors, and nearly jump out of his skin, practically dying of a heart attack before touching the bump and realizing it was a bit of a popcorn husk that he had carelessly missed when brushing his teeth the night before. He felt now that he could somehow review his own immune system, and establish in his own mind whether it was functioning up to capacity: Coughs? Two yesterday, three the day before. Sneezes? Only when confined in the same room with the air conditioner. Skin? No sores, no blemishes. Aches and pains? Nothing mysterious—a filling that needed to be replaced and an occasional migraine (thank God for the telltale flashes and halos). Bowel movements? Regular and consistent in every way.

Henry was not ready to give thanks for his lifelong abstemiousness—even in the last couple of years of comparative excess, he had mostly observed and analyzed rather than partaken, but wasn't his whole life about going to France in June rather than August, dressing neatly rather than beautifully, loving wisely and never too well? Speaking of Baudelaire, the first sight of a *fleur du mal* would have sent Henry quietly out of the room, not once tempted to take a whiff.

His thoughts returned to the Cathars. He wished he remembered what they'd called themselves; perhaps it was "Parfaits," or "Perfected Ones"? In years of eyeballing religion from a greater or lesser distance, which was something you had to do if you read twenty thousand books about the history and culture of Europe, he had never encountered one that drew him at all, but there was something about the Cathars' rejection of earthly filth, their revulsion at the wealth and corruption of the Church, their belief in the equality of the sexes, and their disparagement of the importance of the Crucifixion that appealed to him. He had never been able to imagine himself as a Mercian or a West Saxon—he'd loved them for their strangeness—but he could imagine himself as a chaste vegetarian who considered the God of the Old Testament a satanic usurper who in six days created a Hell on Earth. The evidence of that was everywhere.

JOE DIDN'T GO to church during harvest, but Lois, of course, did. She had incorporated whatever Pastor Campbell wanted into her schedule as smoothly as possible, and Pastor Campbell relied on Lois for everything. Minnie did not agree with Joe that Pastor Campbell was harmless—he had gotten into a brouhaha with the minister at the Lutheran church—Kellogg, his name was—as a result of passing out leaflets outside Kellogg's church and swiping twenty of his members, his justification being that the end was at hand and Kellogg was wasting valuable minutes preaching about the church parking lot and the used-clothing drive. Campbell never asked for money, and he never talked about this world—he talked about the Rapture, which Joe had thought, at first, was a hymn-singing group. It took him a while to realize that the Rapture was more about punishment than reward, but he still saw it as a figure of speech. Only in the last few months had Minnie impressed upon Joe that neither Pastor Campbell nor Lois was kidding—they expected their very bodies to be swept upward, no matter what they were doing, and they did not like any jokes about it. Joe kept his mouth shut, except to complain about the price of corn and beans; at any rate, he was too tired to think about it.

However, when he did get to church after three weeks, the first thing he heard, even before everyone sat down and Pastor Campbell came in, was about Marsh Whitehead's killing himself. That reminded him so totally of his uncle Rolf that Lois had to tell him three times that Marsh had shot himself. Shot himself in the head with his .22, right in the mouth. Hanging had nothing to do with it. Joe came to his senses.

Marsh Whitehead was a good farmer. They knew each other well enough to touch their caps on the street, to compare seed prices at the feed store and to smile indulgently if Sarah Whitehead and Lois happened to get into a conversation about sin. They knew each other well enough so that Joe might be asked to be a coffin bearer—you needed eight of those, and Marsh didn't have any sons. But they did not know each other well enough for Joe to ask probing questions about debtor interest, about that quarter-section Marsh had snapped up the previous year. The best he could do was keep his ears open.

When Pastor Campbell appeared, he didn't say a word about Marsh Whitehead for half an hour—his text was "What do workers gain from their toil? I have seen the burden God has laid on the human race." He then went on to talk about everyone's favorite subject, which was the failure of just about every farm in the neighborhood to make a profit, which meant, of course (and Joe knew he was being cynical), not much money for the church. However, Pastor Campbell focused not on gold but on goodness—the goodness of the toil itself, the tilling of the soil, the richness of the ears of corn, the miracle of soybeans, which "the Israelites would have loved if they had had the chance to grow them." Were we not lucky, in spite of passing weather, nuclear winter followed by scorching summer, still to be here, among friends and relatives, sitting quietly, and contemplating the Lord, in whom there is peace? Why has God laid his burden on the human race? God has laid this burden on us as a reminder, and some days the burden is heavy, but only by feeling the burden at its heaviest can we sense when it lightens. There will come a time when the burden floats away from us of its own accord, and unless we feel our toil, we cannot gain this understanding—nay, pleasure. Pastor Campbell, when he got wound up, did use the word "nay." "You will have heard, my friends in Jesus, of a certain event. I almost said 'sad' event, but I stopped myself. I put before you that I myself do not know if this is a sad event or not a sad event. How we think of this event depends on how we think of the Lord, on whether we truly believe in his mercy and his love. On whether we allow ourselves to ask prideful questions, or whether we simply bow our heads and say, 'So be it.' Our hearts do, indeed, go out to our friend and sister, Sarah Whitehead, and to her children. We are like Sarah in that we must step back and say, 'Father, thy will be done,' but we are not like Sarah in that we do not have to wrestle as immediately as she does with the burden of this event. Sarah is not present this morning. She wished to be, but she was advised to let a day or two pass, so that she might compose her thoughts and look to Jesus for solace. I know, my friends in Jesus, that you will help our sister in all the best ways you know. I have great faith in you."

Joe thought that was a little ham-handed, but he saw that Lois was moved. Her fists were clenched in her lap. After the pastor stepped back, Ethel Roach started playing the organ, and they all stood up— first the usual "What a Friend We Have in Jesus," then one they hadn't sung since last year, which did, in fact, bring tears to his eyes:

> Bringing in the sheaves, bringing in the sheaves,
> We shall come rejoicing, bringing in the sheaves.
> Bringing in the sheaves, bringing in the sheaves,
> We shall come rejoicing, bringing in the sheaves.

Of course, as soon as the service broke up, all anyone talked about was Marsh—how the heat had affected his crops, what prosperous farmers the Whiteheads had always been, to come to this; well, the bank was going after them. Joe walked away. That was all he needed to know, that and the scared looks on the faces of the other farmers, who were probably not in much better shape than Marsh had been. Joe knew that he was the man with the ideal setup, maybe the only one in the county—Minnie had a well-paid job, Lois's shop benefited from being just far enough from Usherton to seem like it was in the country, and Denby had turned out to be picturesque. Not only that, Lois had made herself a network of dealers: if she somehow came up with a picture or a piece of furniture that actually had craft value or rarity, she knew how to estimate its value and get it to a decent market. This year, he and Jesse were living mostly off that bounty, even though they had gotten fifty-four thousand bushels of corn and eighteen thousand bushels of beans. The price of corn was $2.40, and the price of beans was $5.45 (and lucky to get that out of a record harvest). Joe and Jesse had therefore made $228,000 off of the nine hundred acres they planted, but after paying for seed, fuel, tractor repair, herbicide, fertilizer, and the 19 percent interest on their loan to buy the seed and fertilizer, they had cleared only $18,000, which they put away for next year's crop.

Two hundred twenty-eight thousand dollars! Walter would have been speechless, Joe thought. Hadn't there been a year or so when Joe was about ten when their corn yield was thirty-five bushels and they were happy to get it? But the one thing Walter had never stopped saying, so that Joe had had to put his hands over his ears, was: Bigger yields, lower profits. You've got to sell it to someone.

Joe did not understand the purpose of going to church, at least these days. When the farmers talked to one another, they talked about bad times—lately, the way the Reagan administration was doing its best to put that gasohol idea to death, even though processing plants were already being built. When the farmers kept their mouths shut, their wives talked about what in the world they were going to do, and when they all shut up and listened to Pastor Campbell, the only good news he had to offer was about somewhere far away that they might get to or might not, depending not, Joe realized, on following the rules, but on whether God liked you. That's why the pastor had pussyfooted around Marsh Whitehead so carefully—he had committed suicide, but there was no guarantee that God didn't like that, because God worked in mysterious ways and thought mysterious thoughts, and that would be the only thing Pastor Campbell could say in good conscience to Sarah Whitehead and those three girls.

1983

༄

THE WEDDING, everyone knew but no one admitted, was very sudden. Lillian had never even heard that Jesse had a girlfriend, and maybe, Debbie implied, but only by raising her eyebrows, he still didn't. However, the girl (her name was Jennifer Guthrie) wasn't far enough gone to look obvious in her wedding dress, and Lillian was sure that, as the date of parturition approached, there would be some discussion of the eight-pound baby's having been born six weeks prematurely. You had to say for Lois that she put on as good a wedding as if she had been hired by the bride and her parents for the purpose, and you had to say for Jesse that he looked happy, and you had to say for Jennifer that she was local and knew what she was getting herself into. Frank was saying that he remembered her grandfather, who had been six or seven when Frank was five, and who maybe was on the first football team ever fielded by North Usherton High School, and didn't he marry Betty Prince, who was what passed for a cheerleader in those days? Lillian had no idea, but she could see that her brother Joe was more cheerful than she had ever seen him in her life, strolling around the Usherton American Legion Hall in a new suit, grabbing elbows and shaking hands, and laughing.

Jesse was a handsome groom, too—muscular the way a twenty-seven-year-old could be. Best to get married at your physical peak and have a year or so of feeling like you really were Warren Beatty and she really was Natalie Wood, and you could evolve into your humdrum paunchy selves a little at a time. Lillian looked over at Arthur, who was dancing with Andy. Andy had not evolved—she was more like a fly in amber—but she gracefully followed where Arthur led, and every time Arthur swung her around, he looked past her ear, caught Lillian's gaze, and smiled. Lillian said, "Andy is a good dancer."

"She's pliable," said Frank.

Lillian disapproved of the casual disrespect Frank always showed when he talked about Andy, but she had to admit that Andy didn't seem to notice, or else seemed to think she deserved it. Lillian said, "She told me her brother broke his leg."

"His sixty-year-old leg, on a black-diamond slope in Vail. Running the moguls. They had to helicopter him out, and it wasn't easy. But he's getting around. I think he abandoned his crutches after two weeks. Andy said that he doesn't consider pain to be important."

"Emily is cute."

"Isn't she?" said Frank. "She likes to stand there with her hands on her hips, giving you a disapproving stare. She reminds me of Mama."

"She's like Janet. She has high standards."

"Indeed," said Frank.

Lillian decided not to pursue this line of conversation. She said, "I would have loved to see Richie, and I'm sorry Michael and Loretta couldn't come."

"Loretta is calving again, you know," said Frank. "And the yearling isn't even weaned yet."

"That's very traditional."

"Very California. Andy is all in favor. Richie has a new job, and he has to look like he's paying attention for at least three months."

"Our kids seem better prepared than we were."

"Do they?" said Frank. "The older I get, the more amazed I am that parenthood is reserved for the young and foolish. Seems like a recipe for doom, if you ask me."

"You never seemed young and foolish."

Frank turned and regarded her. His suit fit perfectly, and he still had that predatory look. He said, "The less young and foolish you seem, the more young and foolish you are."

"If you could give them one piece of advice, what would it be?"

"Don't do what I did. How about you?"

Lillian looked at Arthur, who was spinning Andy around. She, of course, had a catalogue of worries, but they couldn't be boiled down to a single thing to avoid. In fact, she was taken aback by Frank's remark. Finally, she said, "Don't wait too long to go to Paris?"

Frank laughed out loud in a way she'd hardly ever heard him, and she could not help being ignited into merriment herself. He said, "I think I'll write that down."

Just then, the music ended. Arthur escorted Andy back to the table, where she smiled, picked up her handbag, and wafted toward the ladies' room. Arthur sat down and took a sip of his champagne, then a bite of the wedding cake. He said, "Well, I kept my ears open. You want the news?"

"So much," said Lillian.

"Let's see. They met at a party in Ames when Jesse was down there last fall, visiting his old roommate, who is now in the engineering school, and when they started talking, they realized that they remembered each other from the crèche at Sunday school, lo these twenty years ago, before her family switched to the Foursquare Gospel in Usherton, and she went to South Usherton High, because their house was just inside the boundary between the two districts. She went to Cornell College over in Mount Vernon and studied chemistry."

"Due date?" said Frank.

"Hush-hush. Didn't get that one yet," said Arthur.

"Family income?"

"The farm is paid off," said Arthur.

"Oh, stop," said Lillian, then, "Good."

"She has an aunt by marriage who once knew Frank here."

"Who was that?" said Frank.

"Do you remember a Eunice someone?"

Lillian saw it—Frank turned pale. Then he said, "Maybe."

"She's at the wedding."

"No, she is not," said Frank.

"She is."

Lillian thought Frank almost looked angry. Arthur seemed not to notice. He said, "To the left of the buffet, in the blue dress. Short, a little osteoporotic."

They all stared. Andy, who returned, said, "What are you looking at?" Then, "Oh, Eunice. Poor Eunice. She is unrecognizable."

Frank said, "But you recognized her."

"She recognized me. She's Betty Prince's cousin's second wife. He works for Monsanto. They came up from St. Louis."

And now Lillian saw the really odd thing: Andy, the most dizzy, accepting, hapless woman in the world, drove her gaze into Frank like a knife, daring him to react. Arthur saw it, too. He and Lillian exchanged a glance and dropped their eyes. When they looked up again, normal life had somehow resumed. Frank said, "I should say hi, anyway."

"Yes, you should," said Andy.

It was time to toss the bouquet. There wasn't a stairway in the American Legion Hall, but there was a small stage, so the three brides-maids and two other girls gathered just in front, where the stage bowed out, and Jenny stood above them, now dressed in a green suit with big shoulder pads and white trim. She turned her back and threw the gardenias straight into the air. All the girls in their yellow bridesmaids' dresses threw their arms out and started shouting. It was the youngest who caught them, athletically, as if she were going for a rebound. She laughed and put her face into them, then handed them to someone who looked like her older sister. Now everyone followed Jesse and Jenny out to the car—Rosanna's eleven-year-old Volks-wagen, still running like a champ. They were driving to the airport in Des Moines, then honeymooning at a resort in Arizona.

Lillian, who was holding on to Arthur's arm, caught sight of the Eunice woman making her way up to Frank. It was amazing—they didn't even look like members of the same generation. The woman had blue hair and a frail demeanor. More amazing than that, she gave Frank's arm a familiar little squeeze. Arthur said, "Wouldn't you like to know?"

"I'm not sure I would," said Lillian.

"Just for the drama aspect," said Arthur.

Lillian shook her head.

That night, settling into the very comfortable bed Joe and Lois had vacated for them, Lillian said, "Do you think Frank has a sense of humor?"

"Frank is a terrible romantic, sweetheart. He has always worn his heart on his sleeve."

"Frank? I never noticed that," said Lillian.

"It's a very small heart," said Arthur.

IN THEIR ROOM at the Usherton Best Western, Andy had taken the bed by the window and Frank had taken the bed by the bathroom. It was the first time they'd shared a room in a number of years, and Frank decided his best bet was to pretend to fall right to sleep, thereby avoiding any conversation. Andy said nothing about Eunice in the car; the only thing she said at all was that Arthur acted worried and Lillian looked pale and tired. In fact, she seemed in pain. Frank had thought so, too, but what business was it of theirs? The more interesting one for him was Claire, who'd come into the church flanked by two tall young men who could not be, but were, Gray and Brad. There was plenty of good news about the boys—Gray had gotten early admission to Penn; Brad was a forward on the junior varsity basketball team, and his team was in contention for the league title. Throughout the wedding and reception, they had shadowed their mother—not as if they were shy, but as if they dared not let her out of their sight. Even when two of Jenny's cousins had come up to flirt openly, Gray kept one eye on his mother. Thinking of Jenny made Frank think of Jesse. Jesse had been quietly attentive, had asked him if he had any advice, had seemed to want to be sure that Frank was not just satisfied with Jen, but impressed by her. He wasn't, but she was a Guthrie—Guthries were harmless. And she had hugged him with easy good nature, as if she was expressing affection rather than obligation.

Content with this small pleasure, Frank began his customary going-to-sleep ritual, which was counting backward in fives from a thousand, but around the time he got to 435, he couldn't help coughing, which unfortunately indicated that he was awake, and when he did, Andy said, in a perfectly clear and nonsleepy voice, "Claire has grown into her looks."

He said, "I was thinking about Claire, too."

"I always felt sorry for her." Her tone was even and cool.

"You did?" said Frank. He opened his eyes. The room was hardly dark at all, with the lights from the parking lot blazing on the ceiling. Frank wished they had somehow managed to fly home after the wedding, but the weather was threatening even now. There could be another night in the Best Western.

"She only married Dr. Paul because she was still in mourning for your father. But your mother didn't like her enough to notice."

Frank did not feel that it was his job to defend his mother—she defended herself from the grave perfectly well. However, he didn't disagree with Andy's assessment. Andy said, "But now I think she's lucky."

"Who's lucky?"

"Claire." Then she rustled around in her bed and said, ruminatively, "When your parents don't like you, then you are free."

Frank rolled onto his side and looked at her. There was so much light reflecting off the pale walls that he could see her perfectly. He said, "Your parents liked you."

"Didn't they, though? My father especially. But, you see, there you are."

And he knew right then that she meant that she had never been free. That was not what he had assumed she held against him, not at all. He said, "I am sorry if you never felt free, Andy."

Just then, lying there, staring at her across the little space between the beds, he saw how the architecture of her face remained unchanged by forty years. Her cheekbones and her jawline and her nose were a little more finely modeled, and her blue, blue eyes were a little more deeply set. Her lips were thinner, but not too thin. He laughed at Andy these days, almost as a reflex—but he had not laughed at her at the beginning. He had, in fact, been afraid of her. That was why he had taken refuge in fucking Eunice, in obsessing about Eunice even though he'd hated her, hated her somehow for Lawrence's sake. And now Lawrence had been dead for four decades. Andy smiled, and her smile was still wide and pleasing. She said, "You did your best, Frank." Which wasn't much—Frank finished the thought in his own mind. Then, just to be sure that he knew she was not being ironic, she reached across the space and squeezed his hand, a reassuring, motherly squeeze. She turned away from him. Frank started his counting ritual over but lost interest at 635. After that, he lay there, looking at the lights blaring and rippling across the ceiling. Andy went to sleep, silent and still. He was always surprised at how people thought of him, surprised that they did think of him. He thought of himself as the observer, but really, he was the observed, wasn't he? Maybe he had spent his whole life trying to escape that very thing.

ELOISE WOULD HAVE LIKED to go to the wedding, but she hadn't been able to get out—planes canceled because of the weather. She had finally given up, telling herself that maybe she would go in the late spring. She had a strange desire to see Iowa one last time—she hadn't been there since Rosanna's funeral. She always jokingly called every-thing east of the Sierras "the humid lands." Nothing about Denby or Usherton ever tickled her imagination the way California did. But this year's floods had killed the West Coast romance. San Mateo was a disaster area. Marin was a disaster area. Oakland, always in some sense a disaster area, was cloudy, dark, wet, and threatening, and for the first time in her life, Eloise had had the drapes closed all day—she felt the sense of something encroaching, something like a mudslide, slow and inexorable, not something like a tornado, quick and random.

Maybe her mood came from going through closets and tossing old clothes and shoes. Pink high heels! Could she have bought those? It boggled the mind. Good heavens, as Rosanna would have said, she was seventy-seven! Revolutionaries did not live to be seventy-seven. Buddhists lived to be seventy-seven, and she still knew a few of those, with whom she got along well enough. With three boxes of old clothes to take to the Goodwill, Eloise was wise enough to admit that her life had been a failure, but she didn't exactly mind it. She liked to think of herself as a sport—a branch of a peach tree that had happened to produce nectarines. She had violated her Lysen-koist principles enough to wonder about some of the Vogels and the Augsbergers, both in Iowa and back in Germany—either there were some malcontents hiding back there, or some woman somewhere had imported another genome into the family. However, she knew by her sense of humor, so offensive to every comrade over the years, that she was indeed related to Opa.

Her first mistake today had been to look at the paper even though she hated Reagan. She had been suspicious of Reagan from the beginning. In California, he had extended the right of public work-ers to strike, but he had fired the air-traffic controllers when they struck, showing his true colors—born-again union buster. But more than Reagan, she hated his advisers: James Watt, made secretary of the interior specifically to destroy that very interior. She hated Anne Gorsuch, and she hated Rita Lavelle (now, thank goodness, fired). In her opinion, Rita Lavelle was not the bad apple, she was the open sore that indicates the underlying infection, and the underlying infection, in the Reagan administration, was the drive to suck as much out of the ground as possible and make a few people as rich as they could be. She'd heard that Watt said something about Jesus returning soon, so what did the earth matter—it was there to be put to the use of man, anyway. This was a sentiment people from places like Wyoming often expressed. It was a sentiment the Perronis adhered to, and it was a sentiment profoundly allied to another sentiment—that no one was going to tell a Perroni what to do. If someone tried, that person might get shot. It was not an Iowa sentiment; people in Oakland and Berkeley, who worked, like Eloise did, in co-ops and on local weeklies, laughed at this sentiment, but Eloise did not, having talked to Mrs. Perroni, who was if anything harder around the eyes and more uncompromising than Mr. Perroni. A hundred thousand acres! The hundred thousand acres owed them something, and Mrs. Perroni was going to make it pay. After Eloise looked at the paper, these feelings had rolled around in her head all day, and because the weather was so bad, she couldn't get out and take a walk away from them.

She had sold her car. Even Rosa didn't know she had sold the car. But what happened was, she had fallen into the habit of not turning around to back up—her neck and her shoulders hurt too much when she turned around. She had carefully looked in all three mirrors, left, right, center, and she had done so three times each. She knew that there was nothing behind her. Except that there was something. She hit it, felt it drag, heard the sound of it scraping the pavement. In her panic, she touched the accelerator rather than the brake, and bumped out into the street. Only then had she stopped, turned off the car, leapt out, and rushed around to see one of those plastic tricycles toddlers rode these days—a Big Wheel or something, red and yellow, and fortunately without its toddler. Maybe it had rolled down the street from a neighbor's house, since the toddler was nowhere. But Eloise had been so upset that she'd gone back in the house and lain on the couch for an hour, then called the Ford dealer to find out what she could get for her car, only four years old and with thirty-four thousand miles on it. She would not drive it again; the representative from the dealership came and got it the next day, and she was relieved to see it go.

It was no big deal to be without the car—she could rent her driveway for fifty dollars a month to her neighbor, who had three cars. She was a good walker, good enough to get to the co-op if she took her time and pushed a little trolley. And the co-op was next to the drugstore, and the drugstore was next to the clinic, and so on and so forth. It was manageable. But if she asked someone to drive her one more time to Drakes Bay, a couple of hours, the purest place in California, then could she walk the beach in her own time, and in total solitude make up her mind?

And what was she making up her mind about? And who cared? And why did she still care? Rosa had asked her this question this morning, when she called to report on conditions in Big Sur (Highway 1 was out again, but they were fine). Rosa was Eloise's principal Buddhist, though she didn't call herself that. If you asked in a mild tone of voice that didn't imply a single thing (a tone of voice Eloise could rarely manage) how Rosa viewed her adult life, she would talk about phases, old mistaken desires that had been outgrown or shucked off. She "made no judgments" (except, of course, of Eloise), "had no desires" (except that Eloise stop harassing her), and "took things as they came" (except remarks by Eloise that sometimes caused them to be not on speaking terms for a month or two). But Eloise did make judgments, did have desires, and seemingly could not take things as they came, and she had this feeling that if she could just organize her self-contradictory thoughts she would come up with a program of why care and how to care, and, somehow, she would leave a record of this, and then her life wouldn't be wasted. But she did not want to be someplace like Esalen, and have positive feelings and forgiveness cloud her mind. She wanted to figure out a way to get Rita Lavelle, Anne Gorsuch, and James Watt to denounce themselves, feel shame, feel regret, engage in sincere criticism and self-criticism, and then do penance.

And yet she knew at seventy-seven that it could not be done. And she also knew that James Watt, Anne Gorsuch, and Rita Lavelle would ask her, just as she asked them, was she ready to do penance for the slaughter of the Russian peasantry? For the Gulag? For the Great Leap Forward? For the takeover of Poland? For the Berlin Wall? For the Stasi? For the Khmer Rouge? For, indeed, Reverend Jones? And when they asked her this, she would squirm in her chair and say just what comrades had said year after year, decade after decade—"Mistakes were made."

What if, Eloise thought, they were all nice people, as she herself was a nice person? What if, between gutting the Environmental Protection Agency and allowing PCBs to flood into the rivers, Anne Gorsuch worked in soup kitchens and nursed the poor? What if, between authorizations of the sale of every piece of public land in America, James Watt played with his grandchildren? Hadn't Eloise been shocked at the murder of Lord Mountbatten, imperialist pig, whom she had detested ever since he sent Julius to his death at Dieppe? A few summers ago, when the IRA blew him up with his wife and his grandson and that poor local child, hadn't Eloise thought first of how awful it was? Only later had she wondered whether at the final moment he'd had time for regret.

Was human nature inherently good? Eloise and Julius had disagreed on this one. Eloise had said yes, look at herself, look at her parents—if you showed people the way to do good, they would want to. Julius had said no, look at himself, look at his family—coercion was essential, eggs had to be broken. That was human nature. He thought she was naïve; she thought he was bad-tempered; neither of them saw the other one as the other one saw himself, herself.

Eloise went to the kitchen. Assam? Constant Comment? Mint? She made a cup of each and set them in a row on her coffee table. Finally, finally, finally, when she turned on the show, her show, *Hill Street Blues,* and saw that familiar attractive Sergeant Esterhaus starting the day's shift at the mysterious precinct station (Eloise always imagined Chicago), she forgot, more or less, about Hobbes and Locke and her aches and pains and the rain that had been going on for days. Her brain remained a pleasant blank for the rest of the night—while she put her cups in the sink, while she made sure the doors were locked and checked the windows in the sunporch, while she brushed her teeth and put on her nightgown and straightened her bedclothes, which hadn't been made by anyone that morning after she got up. By her, that was. Her book was by her bed—*Memoirs of Hecate County.*

Hard to believe it had been censored, but it had. She was having a little trouble getting through it, though. She decided not to disturb her blankness by trying again tonight. She got into bed.

Oh, it was comfortable on a rainy day to do nothing. To think of that long beach, so flat, so remote from everything. Eloise sighed and yawned, then yawned again. If it stopped raining and she got to the co-op tomorrow, she had to remember Brie. She had a craving for Brie lately, and every night, she thought, Brie, and every day she forgot it. She had left the light on in the bathroom. No, she hadn't. Brie, she thought, Brie.

EMILY HAD TO eat a bowl of Cheerios and some fruit, and she had to drink milk. Emily didn't mind Cheerios. One of the main things that she held against Mom was that she had to drink four glasses of milk every single day while Mom stood nearby. Mom said, "You are very thin, Emily." Then she shook her head. In order to make herself happy while she was choking down her milk, Emily watched her dog, Eliza. Emily knew everything about Eliza. Eliza was almost two, a black-Lab/golden-retriever mix; she slept in Emily's room, right beside the bed (sometimes she worked her way under the bed, and then, when she wiggled, the bed jiggled, which made Emily laugh). She knew how to sit, stay, come, down, and catch a dog biscuit. When Mom told her to do these things, she did them right away. When Emily told her to do them, she lolled her tongue out of her mouth as if she were smiling, and did them, but a little more slowly. Eliza went to the back door and whined. Mom let her out.

Emily jumped off her chair, showed Mom her bowl, and set it next to the sink. Mom said, "Oh, okay."

Emily walked toward the swings, but really she was watching Eliza, who looked sneaky, the way she looked when she was planning to steal something. Mom always laughed at the stealing—a glove, a shoe, always found in her dogbed.

Emily sat on the swing with her toe on the ground, pushing herself back and forth, her arm hooked around the chain. Eliza went over and lay down under the mulberry tree; Emily bent down and stared at her. In the next yard, Mrs. Gilkisson came out, carrying a bowl; she walked briskly across the yard, and opened the door of the chicken house. A few moments later, she came out, pulled the door, and walked back into her own house.

Now Emily went over to the sandbox and sat down in the middle. She picked up a trowel and began to smooth the sand idly. Eliza got up, walked along the fence, and, when she got to a certain spot in the honeysuckle, slipped through. Emily hadn't realized a hole was there, but when she went over and pushed aside the honeysuckle, she could see it. Emily stood very still and watched Eliza, who crept along the fence line until she came to the chicken house. She pushed on the door with her nose. The first time it didn't move, but the second time it did. Eliza went in.

Emily thought that maybe she should shout for Mom, because someone was about to get in trouble. There was noise in the chicken house—the chickens were squawking. Emily got a little afraid. Just then, here came Eliza, out the door. She did not have a chicken in her mouth, and so Emily felt a little less afraid. Even so, she ran back to the swing set and started to swing, pumping. She held tight to the chains, leaned way back, and stuck her legs out as far as they could go, then whipped them back and fell forward. In four strokes, she was pretty high, but she saw Eliza as she came through the fence and headed toward the back of the yard, where the garage was. Emily stopped pumping, let go, and flew out of the swing. She liked doing that.

Eliza had disappeared. Emily looked at the house. No sign of Mom. Emily went very slowly toward the garage, almost tiptoeing. She went around the corner, and there was Eliza, digging with her claws in the dirt. She was digging carefully, using both front feet. Emily watched. The hole she dug was pretty deep, but the ground was soft, so she didn't have to try very hard. She paused and looked in the hole. Then she went over to something she had set to one side and, very gently, picked it up. She put it in the hole. All this time, Emily had been edging closer and closer, and finally, just before Eliza started filling the hole, Emily was close enough to see what it was. It was an egg, white and perfect. The dirt landed lightly on it and then covered it. When she was finished covering the egg, Eliza turned in a circle and lay down. She stared at Emily with her ears pricked. Emily went over and petted her, and Eliza licked her chin. Emily said, "Okay, Lizie. I won't tell."

1984

O N TUESDAY, Lillian had called Debbie and told her about
driving herself to the doctor—she sneaked out when Arthur
was down at the bottom of the property, digging up bulbs, and went
by herself, and felt fine. Didn't Debbie think that was a good joke?
Debbie did, in a way, but then, on Wednesday, her father called her
and said that she had better come, and bring Carlie and Kevvie, and
Debbie kept saying, almost yelling, that she couldn't believe this, she
couldn't believe this, and her father was horribly patient, and said
that Dean would pick her up at the airport, and Tina was coming
Saturday. But she got herself together by dinnertime—she told Hugh
quietly enough so that he wouldn't think she was going crazy, and
then she sat with the kids on the couch in the living room, and said
that she had something to tell them. Carlie understood—she nodded,
and she tightened her grip on Debbie's hand, but Kevvie just stared
at her, his arm looped around his Funshine Bear and his thumb in his
mouth. Hugh, standing in the doorway, said, "That's why they have
to go, Deb; they have to see it."

And so they did, and because it was Lillian Langdon Manning
who was counting out her last hours, it wasn't that bad, and Debbie
did not have to take over, which was always her instinct. She could
sit in the kitchen and chat with anyone who passed through, give and
accept hugs, offer everyone the food that people brought over because

they couldn't think of anything else to do. The weather was beautiful for January. The kids relaxed and played with the other kids; Carlie was solicitous and maternal with Eric, Dean's two-year-old. She read him an old Raggedy Ann book she found in Tina's room, and she was willing to read it over and over, which made Debbie proud in a melancholy sort of way.

Yes, Lillian had driven herself to the doctor on Tuesday, but then, Tuesday night, something broke, some little membrane or wire or bolt (depending on how you imagined the brain), and the hallucinations began. She woke up Wednesday morning, turned to Arthur, and said, "Have you seen Arthur?" Arthur had patiently reminded her over and over that he was right there, and now, as she lay in her bed, looking at the windows or at the sunlight on the ceiling, she would say, "Is that a lake?" or "Did you hear that Henry my brother died?"

Her father would pat her mother's hand and gently say, "No, darling, that's the ceiling; I'm right here; Henry is fine, you'll see him tomorrow." And her mother would nod and say, "I suppose you're right."

Allegedly, there was little if any pain, and if pain should begin, there were painkillers, but her mother had told her father weeks ago that she wanted to be conscious as long as she could be.

She had greeted Debbie with a kiss and asked if Carlie and Kevvie were hers and what their names were. Debbie had made a strenuous effort not to compare how her mother processed her presence with how she processed Dean's presence, or with the number of times she asked if anyone had seen Tim. Her mother had been precisely and exactly herself for Debbie's entire life, thirty-six years now, and Debbie had found her too disorganized, too yielding, too wrapped up in her husband, too focused on Tim, too affectionate with Janet for most of that time. But since Carlie's birth, she had liked her better (liked her—she had always loved her to pieces) and had talked to her almost daily, sometimes asking advice, but mostly just listening to the soothing sound of her voice. In fact, it was the sound of her own voice that Debbie heard most when she made those phone calls, but she could not help checking in, seeking the how-are-you's, the yes-honey's, the that's-a-good-idea's, the love-you's.

The calls were over, dead as of Tuesday. Now, every couple of hours, Debbie slipped into the bedroom and listened to the strange conversation between her parents, knowing that she would never forget it and maybe she should not let this be her last indelible memory.

The rest of the time, she arranged the funeral, because someone had to. She called the funeral home, chose the dress and the shoes, wrote the notice for *The Washington Post* and the local McLean paper. She went through Lillian's address book, trying to judge who would need to know. She cooked, she washed dishes, washed more dishes.

Her father was perfect—endlessly kind, loving, and reassuring— and her mother seemed to take this for granted (and even as Debbie had this thought, she knew it was stupid). Dean and Linda did the driving-around errands. Linda was nice. Debbie could not object to her in any way, except when she went into Lillian's room, and Lillian said, "Linda. I would know you anywhere. You are very pretty, do you know that?"

She, Debbie, was the girl who had had the perfect mother—kind, indulgent, organized, and capable—and therefore, if you could still feel that spark of resentment toward the perfect mother, then there were no perfect mothers, and best not to try to be one.

Debbie was in the room when it happened. Her father, who was sitting on the bed, had kissed her mother's hand and gotten up to stretch and walk around. When he did, her mother cried out—just "Oh! Oh!"—and then she lay back, and her eyes were open and her jaw was slack. Debbie took a step toward the bed, and her father was just ahead of her. He said, "Lily Pons? Darling?"

Debbie put her head out the door and called in a low but intense voice, "Tina! Dean!" and went back into the room. Tina was there at once. Lillian said, "What is that noise?" And then Dean appeared, and all three of them approached the bed. Lillian lifted her head, then let it fall back, and her last word was "Darling."

It didn't matter whom she was thinking of or talking to, but always afterward, Debbie said that her mother had looked at her father, said "Darling," and passed away.

DEBBIE HAD CALLED maybe seven people, Tina had called four or five, and their father hadn't called anyone, because after their mother died he seemed to collapse. So Debbie was amazed when she finished dressing herself, and then Carlie and Kevvie, to come out to the living room and discover that it was packed to the doors, that there were people chatting in the hall who stopped talking when they saw her and gave her sympathetic looks, that the front door was wide open and there were cars parked all the way down the driveway and out onto the road, and more people, everyone dressed in somber, formal outfits, walking up to the house. They should have had it at the funeral home or at a church of some sort after all—with no one to consult, she had assumed that maybe thirty friends plus Uncle Henry, Uncle Frank, Aunt Andy, and Janet would show up. When she'd called Uncle Joe, he had started crying as soon as she said, "My mom . . ." but he didn't dare come—Lois had some sort of stomach virus, and he had been exposed. Aunt Claire couldn't come, either, because she had just started at Younkers; she and Debbie had agreed they would do a memorial at the farm, maybe at Thanksgiving or Christmas, and then Claire had burst out crying, too, and said, "Oh, sweetie, your mom was my idol. When I was little, I would get her mixed up in my mind with Maureen O'Hara, except that I thought your mom was more glamorous!" The first thing Debbie did when she saw all the people was to go out to the pool area and check that the gate was chained, and the next thing she did was go into her father's office and lock the liquor cabinet. The coffin, closed because her father couldn't stand for it to be open, was in the living room, right out of a nineteenth-century novel, but that hadn't been her intention—her intention had been to keep her mother for as long as she possibly could, not to let her leave home until the very last minute.

Her father was a mess. He kept running his hand back through his hair and standing it on end, and he could not tolerate the feeling of his tie, so he had pulled that off and draped it around his neck. He was wearing a black suit that looked like it had crumpled itself to conform to his state of mind. Debbie watched him. A man would come up to him, shake his hand, mutter something sympathetic, then put his arm around her father's shoulders and walk him a little away from the crowd. There would be earnest words, more head shaking, a pat on the back; then that man would walk him back into the group, and another man would do the same. Her father looked pale and distraught, as though he found all of this attention disconcerting, but Debbie didn't know how to put a stop to it or draw him away.

The weather continued calm and clear. As one o'clock approached, Debbie went through the crowd, handing out the programs that Linda had made at the copy center. Mr. Littlejohn, who was going to play the piano, had to walk half a mile to the house. Debbie thanked him effusively, and saw that he understood—he and she were the only two people in control of this mob. Dean, Linda, and Tina set out the rented chairs—not enough—and every bench, kitchen chair, and stool they could find. At one o'clock, Mr. Littlejohn commenced Pachelbel's "Canon in D." Everyone stopped talking, came into the living room, and sat down where they could. Debbie took her father into custody—she got him to sit beside her, and she tightly held his hand. Aunt Andy was on his other side, and Uncle Frank was leaning against the wall nearby. Janet had come without Emily or Jared, and she was in the back of the room, keeping to herself. Debbie knew from their talk late last night that Janet was barely holding herself together, but she couldn't think about that. Aunt Andy quietly took her father's other hand. When they were all silent, Mr. Littlejohn played the Introit from Mozart's *Requiem,* arranged for piano, and much more somber than the Pachelbel. Faces assumed their proper expressions.

Once the music had stopped, a minister they knew socially—a very liberal and cheerful-looking man—got up and gave the sermon. He did not mention "God," only "our dear Father," and he said the blandest possible prayers that everyone knew. Then Uncle Frank stepped up and talked about the farm, and Lillian with her troops of devoted friends, and then, all of a sudden, she was spirited away by some stranger, and it turned out to be Arthur, and when he met Arthur and saw them together, he knew he had seen true love. Then Janet came forward and talked for a few moments about Tim, and then Tina came forward and talked about watching her mother her whole life and saying to herself, Oh, that's how you do it; and now she had seen her mother die, and she had said once again, Oh, that's how you do it; and she thought of her mother going ahead of her into that unknown kingdom, and somehow felt safer. Then it was Dean's turn, and he started to talk about being allowed to do whatever he wanted when he was a child, and how that was the best—but he couldn't go on, and after a few moments, Linda had to come up and take him back to his chair.

Debbie crumpled her paper in her hand and stared at her strangely moving feet in their black pumps as she stepped to the front of the room. As she passed the coffin, she allowed her fingers to run along the dark-reddish edge. Mahogany? It looked like it; her mother herself had picked it out. When she saw all the faces looking up at her, she crumpled the paper even tighter, then looked at the back wall of the living room and out the windows, at the shine of the pool in the warm air. When she opened her mouth, she said, "I am a know-it-all, and have always been a know-it-all, and all these years I spent telling my mother what to do, and either she did what I told her, or she very kindly went her own way and did it differently and better than I would have done. But even as much of a know-it-all as I have always been"—everyone was smiling—"I always knew that my mother, Lillian Manning, knew all there was to know about being a loving mother and a loving wife and a loving friend. I hate how much we miss her already, and how much we will miss her tomorrow and forever." And then she, like Dean, started to cry, and so she went and sat down, and she could hardly see where she was going through the tears.

Her father got up. Debbie took out her Kleenex and wiped her eyes, of course smearing her mascara. Aunt Andy reached across his empty seat and stroked her arm. Debbie glanced at Uncle Frank, who had gone back to leaning against the wall, and was staring at her father with a kind of hungry curiosity. Yes, they all thought it: How will he survive this?

But her father had pulled himself together, and now he was his usual self. He clasped his hands and said, "I want to tell a little story. Long, long ago, I was driving from Rapid City, South Dakota, to D.C., and when I got to a small town in Iowa, I walked into a bar. Now I say that I walked into a bar, but actually, as I remember, Iowa was dry then, so really, I walked into a drugstore with a soda fountain. And behind the counter there was a very pretty girl. In those days, I, like many of us at the end of the war, considered myself a Big Bad Wolf. Now, thanks to Farley Mowat, we know that the Big Bad Wolf is a wolf who has perhaps lost his female parent, been driven out of the pack at an early age, and may have seen his mate shot by hunters and his single cub die of starvation, but back then, a wolf was a wolf, and if you were a wolf, you had very bad intentions. I chatted up the pretty girl, and I walked her to her car, of course telling her that it was others who had bad intentions, not me. I went to the nearest larger town, and I put myself up for the night.

"The next afternoon, I deployed my very extensive espionage skills to discover that that very same girl showed up to work behind the fountain at noon, and I was at my stool as soon as she put on her apron. I ordered twenty-six cherry Cokes, and have never partaken of a cherry Coke since. I gave her all of my very best Big Bad Wolf speeches, and, sure enough, by the end of the evening, I had her in my clutches. She agreed to accompany me to the wolf den, even though the wolf den was far, far away.

"You know, Little Red Riding Hood always saw herself as the prey of the wolf, but in fact the wolf cared nothing for Little Red—he was after the braised lamb shanks in her bag that she was carrying to her grandmother—and so it was that you should envision that pretty girl, not as Little Red Riding Hood, but as a lamb, frisky and playful, sitting in the front seat of my car. We drove along, and for an hour, the little lamb bleated pleasantly about her job and her family and her brother who had been in the war. I figured that if I drove far enough I could avoid the brother if I had to. I should say that the sun was rather low in the afternoon sky when we departed, and so we stopped for a bite to eat in Cedar Rapids, and then went on. Finally, we got to a town on a big river, and the lamb was getting sleepy, and so I said, 'Would you like to stop for the night?' I was licking my wolfish lips, of course."

Debbie looked around. Everyone was staring at her father, and Debbie thought it was a very good thing most of them knew him quite well. He went on. "Well, I went into the office of a little motel by the river, and I asked for a room, and the old granny there looked at me as if she was afraid she might be eaten, and gave me the key. Then I let the lamb out of the car, and she looked, I must say, just a trifle nervous, so I opened the door of the cottage, gave her the key, and went back to my car. I sat there for a long time, contemplating my wolfish nature. And then I fell asleep. It got very cold, what with the fog rising off the river, and I woke up. I looked around and I was sore afraid. I could not remember where I was, or how I got there, and even my car looked strange to me in the moonlight, because, of course, there was moonlight. And so I opened the door of the car and staggered out. There was a light on in the cottage, and I went to look in the window."

Now he stared around the room for effect, as he had so often stared around the dinner table when they were children, daring them not to believe that a bird had brought him Tim's report card and that, furthermore, the bird had been weeping at the sight of Tim's D's and F's. He said, "The blinds were closed, but just then, two fingers separated two of the slats, and right there, staring at me, was that pretty girl. We both laughed, and I knew right where I was and what I was supposed to be doing, and that, whatever sort of wolf I was, this lamb was on to me, I couldn't keep anything from her." Everyone laughed, and Debbie thought, That's what a funeral is for—laughing. "The next morning, we found a judge, right there in Clinton, and he overlooked a few legal niceties because he was a wise man, and to this day I thank him from the bottom of my heart."

There was silence. Debbie could see that people were, somehow, tempted to clap, but of course they didn't. Her father stared at the coffin, and stepped toward it. He put his hand on it and patted it gently. Debbie bit her lips. He looked at her and smiled. She sniffed. But he didn't sit down. Standing there, one hand on the coffin, he pulled a piece of paper out of his pocket, and stared at it for a moment. Debbie could see what it was—a leaf from her mother's kitchen pad—and maybe, Debbie thought, he was going to do a very Arthurish thing, read her final shopping list. He said, "Early in the summer, after Lillian got her diagnosis, we were talking about this day, and she said that there was something that I had to—well, we had to do—which was to include her aunt Eloise in the memorial service. Some of you may know that Eloise Silber, Lillian's mother's sister, died in San Francisco last spring."

Aunt Eloise had been discovered dead in her bed by the police, who had had to break down the door. They estimated ten days or two weeks. Between Rosa's road's being washed out and the roof's collapsing with all the rain at the co-op where Aunt Eloise worked, no one had put two and two together, and then . . . Well, in Oakland, the cops said, it was not such a rare thing.

"Lillian was very upset by the circumstances of her aunt's death, and the fact that there was only a cremation and no memorial service, so she wrote the following, which I would like to read."

There was some coughing, and Aunt Andy said, "Oh, dear."

" 'Please join me in remembering and giving thanks for the life of Eloise Mary Vogel Silber, who may have been a communist, but never defended Stalin or even Lenin, much less Mao Tse-tung. If she had grown up in one of those countries instead of Iowa, they would have put her to death early on, because she never hesitated to tell the truth, no matter who was listening. She made a lot of people mad, including the California Un-American Activities Committee. When Eloise was asked to testify, she not only admitted holding certain beliefs, she kept saying, "Yes, I thought the German Communist Party was good. Didn't you?" She also was very honest when she said that, even if they threw her in jail, she was not going to talk about anyone except herself and her late husband, and when they asked her about him, she said, "He was shot by the Germans when that scum Mountbatten tested his invasion ideas at Dieppe." I loved my aunt Eloise, and her life is proof that well-meaning people can hold many different ideas. She left the Party, and she saved my niece Janet, and she thought about good and evil for her entire life. Please join me in honoring her memory, whoever you are.' " Her father kissed the piece of paper, folded it, and slipped it into his breast pocket.

And Debbie knew from that last line that her mother knew exactly who would be at her funeral, and did intend to have the last word. Aunt Andy dabbed her eyes, Uncle Frank grinned, and her father patted the coffin again. Then he thanked everyone for coming. The final service at the gravesite would commence in one hour, for those who wished to attend.

1985

❧

THE DAY AFTER Claire's divorce was finalized, the temperature was thirty below zero, and her windows were rimed with frost flowers. The streets of downtown Des Moines were slick and nearly empty, and Younkers was opening an hour late to give the employees time to get in. Paul had agreed to the divorce when he met Veronica, who was twenty-seven and also a doctor. He had always laughed at the idea of women doctors, but Veronica confined herself to the appropriate field of gynecology. Also, she was petite, and she had maintained an A average at Grinnell and at the University of Iowa College of Medicine. In other words, Claire thought, it would take her thirteen to fifteen years to wake up and realize that she couldn't take it. She had considerable debt from college and medical school, and so it was fortunate for her that the family-law judge had decided that half of Claire's inheritance from the sale of the farm should go to Paul. Claire was therefore down to about $150,000. Others were angry on her behalf—most notably Lois and, less passionately, Minnie. But Paul was paying for Gray at Penn and Brad was headed for Haverford, which was, at least, on the East Coast. Brad's acceptance to Johns Hopkins had nearly caused Paul to ejaculate in ecstasy, according to Gray, but Brad adamantly refused to go there, and Paul had had to settle for the nearest thing.

Claire liked to think that he would also be spending a pretty penny of her money on the Valentine's Day wedding to Veronica, which was to take place at the ever-desirable Wakonda Country Club, and who would certainly be there but her former best friend, Ruth. According to Gray, Ruth was bosom buddies with Paul, and she had urged him to let her take Veronica in hand and give her advice on how to cook Paul's favorite dishes. Gray said this in an ironic tone, with his eyebrows raised in amusement. Claire thought that, whatever it was she had done to damage her son's psyche, he seemed to express it in a stream of jokes that were charming and rueful. He could not possibly have gotten his sense of humor from Paul, so she took credit for that. One day, he had said to her, "Do you hate my dad?" She had surprised herself by saying that she didn't—of course she didn't. When he responded, "I do, sometimes," she had said, "He does his best." And that was the tragedy, wasn't it? Just like Hamlet, just like Macbeth, just like Lear, he did his best (Claire thought it was funny that she had read all of those now, on her own, just sitting up in bed). And that was the point—not that they were kings or princes, and therefore grander than you or me, but that they made their own downfall by being who they were (something that, even more tragically, was not set in stone, according to the divorcees and therapists she knew). So she felt sorry for Paul now, and her hatred had left no tangible trace.

She finished her cup of coffee and set the cup in the sink, then started to get ready to go to work: fur-lined boots; her goose-down calf-length hooded and belted coat, which she had bought in Minneapolis; her sheepskin gloves. When she opened the street door of her apartment building, the wind nearly yanked it out of her hand, and she had to clutch her handbag tightly and turn her hooded head to one side. Even then, her eyes teared up. Was this nuclear winter? Three blocks, and because she lived downtown, she was expected to be there. Two cars passed her, going very slowly, and when she stepped outside of the shelter of the tall buildings and had to negotiate the streets, the buffeting crosswinds nearly knocked her down. The sky was clear, which was the reason for the winds, but at least there wouldn't be any more snow. She dipped her chin more deeply into her hood.

When she got to the store, Les, one of the maintenance staff, was waiting. He let her in, and he let in Bev Kinder, who worked in the shoe department. From inside her scarf, Bev said, "You should come over and see my spring styles. You can't believe how high my stilettos are going to be. Scares me to death." Claire laughed, and Les said, "I've given up stilettos myself, ladies, 'cept for hammering stuff." Bev said, "Oh, Les."

Claire unsnapped her coat. "I can't believe there'll be many customers in this weather."

Bev shrugged. "If they make it, they'll buy something, just because they feel so heroic. I love days like today."

The $150,000 at 9 percent interest gave her $13,500 per year—not much. Her job at Younkers was in the housewares department, and most of the time she either made beds or demonstrated KitchenAid mixers. Though she would have given herself up to Nicaraguan revolutionaries before using a dough hook on her own time, the fact was, she looked just like a woman in a Betty Crocker ad, bright and slender, but too domestic to be a threat. At work, she wore a thin gold band that looked like a wedding ring. Her badge read "Claire," though, so she was not actually lying about her postmarital status. Young brides and brides-to-be came up to her every day and asked for advice about what they would need in their new lives. She was a whiz with the bridal registry.

After hanging up her coat and changing into her store shoes— two-inch stacked heels, very matronly—she walked around the bedding displays. The whites and laces in which she had done up the display beds the week before now looked frigid, so she rustled up two livelier ensembles, a nice old-fashioned patchwork quilt in pink and green with four different pillow shams that was springlike and cheerful, and a red, white, and blue set that was always appropriate. She even changed the dust ruffles, because the one for the red, white, and blue set was pleated, which looked really elegant. Her "ensemble" at home was a beige down comforter from Lands' End, plain and thick. Two people could not sleep under it without going into a sweat, which was fine with Claire.

She had thought of moving away from Des Moines, but if she wanted to stay with Younkers, her only choices were Fort Dodge,

Waterloo, Burlington, and Dubuque. She had flirted with moving to Minneapolis and finding a job at Dayton's. She loved downtown Minneapolis, which had turned into a giant mall, with really good food and great shopping, but each of the three times she'd been there, it had been at least twenty degrees colder and 20 percent darker than Des Moines. Claire did not understand quite how a mere 250 miles could make such a difference, but it seemed to. In other words, she was stuck, and clearly the rest of her family thought so, too, because Andy kept inviting her to New York, Minnie said she could accompany her on her trip to Oaxaca or to Maui, the two places she would be going next, and Lois kept inviting her up to Denby to see Guthrie, who was nineteen months old, and Perky, short for "Franklin Perkins," four months old. She had seen the babies. The babies were fine, and nothing more than babies, in Claire's view.

THIS LATEST CRISIS WAS not seen by anyone but Janet herself as a crisis. What had happened was, the weather was terrible, her mother missed Emily, and so, during one of those meandering conversations she did not mind having with her mother these days, but which lulled her into relaxing her vigilance, she agreed that they would meet for a week at the Pinehurst Resort. Before they left, Janet had simply imagined herself wandering around in the humid warmth of North Carolina, maybe going over to Southern Pines for a day or so to watch a horse show. Even though Jared had said to her that he was on the verge of a breakthrough that was going to make them a lot of money, Janet had not sensed the danger.

She watched him on the putting green with her father. She went to one little Wednesday horse show and wondered if having a horse would be possible in Iowa. Emily looked at the horses with fear and distaste, standing at a distance, holding Andy's hand, but Janet got close, stroked equine noses with her fingertips, took in the mesmerizing scent, appreciated the snorts and head tossings, asked mildly intelligent questions of the owners. The closed-in piney warmth of the environment, the ease of the rocking chairs on the veranda, the casual beauty of the place were delightful, but then Jared said that they should buy property—you could buy a square-yard lot on the grounds and get privileges at the club. And they could live in the Research Triangle. Even compared with Iowa City, houses in Raleigh were . . .

"The Research Triangle is more than an hour from Pinehurst—it would be like working in Iowa City and living in Davenport."

Jared blinked, informing her that her voice was sharp, then said, "Your dad says Raleigh is a great place to invest, a real center of education and on the East Coast. . . ."

Janet had been hired just the previous fall as an adjunct assistant professor of technical writing. She taught three sections per week, twenty geeks in each section, many of whom did not speak English as a first language, even though they may have grown up in America and had American parents. They all spoke computer as a first language, and as a computer in-law, it was Janet's job to show them how to reveal their thoughts and ideas to people whose last experience of math concerned the sides of a right triangle. She said, "I like my job." She had to pretend that she understood almost nothing in order to motivate her students to be ever more clear and simple-minded. They thought she was a dope, but she brandished the weapon of grades. Her office mate in EPB, who taught beginning literature courses, had students who sat pensively outside the office door with their legs stuck out in front of them, waiting to discuss their revelations while reading *On the Road* and *1984*. Janet had noticed at parties that when she said she taught technical writing, whoever she was talking to tended to start looking around the room. She said again, "I really like my job."

Jared gave her a flat look, a look that informed her that she was sounding enraged or crazy.

That evening, sitting in the much-bewindowed dining room at the Pinehurst Resort, watching her father and Jared's conversation drop from idle to intense, she understood that the self-protective little pod she had built—staying in Iowa City, avoiding family gatherings as much as possible, never taking money from or talking about her father, pretending Michael and Richie did not really exist—would crack apart. It would soon begin, flights in and out of Cedar Rapids, Jared alight with possibility, her father calling them. And what would she say—"I'll get him," or "I'm fine. Emily is good. I'll get him"? That was the most she could imagine. Of course, Jared could install his own line, just for these calls. All these thoughts came to her within three or four minutes—long enough for her mother to walk with Emily over to the buffet and back. Emily sat in her chair, and Janet saw her father look at the child with interest, maybe for the first time ever, and why was that? Because she was related to Jared, and Jared had a lucrative idea. Janet stood up, said that she had a headache, and went back to her room.

Once there, she thought of phoning Debbie. She had phoned Debbie repeatedly since Aunt Lillian's death. It was not that Debbie was especially sympathetic or even wise—Debbie was not quite three years older than she was, and about that much wiser. But Debbie had Aunt Lillian's voice. It was a warm, good-natured, alto voice, and it pronounced certain words just as Aunt Lillian had. Debbie had let her know that she could not give Janet advice, much less let her go on and on long-distance. She was busy. She had a job and a family and grief of her own. Have I always been like this, Janet thought, so unselfconsciously needy and talkative?

The answer was yes.

So she didn't call Debbie.

Back in Iowa City, Jared didn't speak to her for almost a week, but then his friend Oz suggested they move to San Jose. Jared brought this idea home as if it were a revelation. Janet did not panic, but said, "I've never been to San Jose." She thought, no rain, no Lucas, no Reverend Jones, no Cat. And her dad three thousand miles away. She said, "I hear San Jose is quite sunny." Jared threw his arms around her. She said, "Horses year-round in San Jose."

Jared kissed her.

JESSE HAD GONE to the feed store in North Usherton to do some errands and stopped to buy Pampers. He didn't have much cash—what farmer these days carried much cash? When he went to write out a check for the supplies, thirty-two bucks, Pete at the market said, "I can't take that check, Joe," and that was the first they heard about the Denby and Randolph Bank going under. For Jesse it was a shock and an inconvenience—Pete let him drive away, knowing someone would come in and pay the money—but for Joe himself it was something more. When Jesse found him and told him, Joe gazed into the hot, sunlit dust floating in the barn and felt paralyzed. They had a loan with Denby and Randolph, and they also had accounts there—Lois's shop account, their joint checking account, the farm account, and a savings account. Joe jumped in the truck and drove to Denby, but he didn't have to tell Lois: she was standing in the doorway of the shop, her lips a thin line, staring across the square at the bank, where a couple of guys were already taking down the bank sign. When she saw him, she said, "Good thing I sold that love seat yesterday, and an even better thing that I haven't deposited this week's receipts."

He told her about Jesse's exchange at the market.

"The kids got any cash?"

"I doubt it," said Joe.

"Min always said there was a reason she did her banking in Usherton, but she could never remember what it was. Now we know. I guess she'll take care of them for a few weeks."

And so in spite of the suicides and foreclosures they kept hearing about, it wasn't exactly like the thirties—there was the FDIC—but Joe had no idea how long it would take for their accounts to be repaid, or, indeed, whether there might be some snafu there, too. And the farm, well, in the thirties it had been worth fifteen or was it ten dollars an acre—Rosanna had told him that. Now it was worth maybe a thousand, a third of what Frank had paid Gary, and sliding. Would Walter have considered him a success or a failure? He was getting so many bushels per acre that the government was going to subsidize the farmers to take acreage out of cultivation, but no one in the Denby Café was going to take his best land out of cultivation—only the parts that had some slope or were swampy or ran along the river or were, frankly, exhausted. And that's what Joe was going to do, too, and he expected to get 175 bushels an acre of corn and forty of beans and not to be able to pay his bills and to get a little check in a Christmas card from Frank to cover the shortfall. Dave Crest and Russ Pinckard and Rudy Jenkins always seemed to give him the eyeball, as if they knew he had a rich relative, and of course they did know it. It was an embarrassment to have a rich relative, and Joe knew perfectly well how specific knowledge of the shortfall got to Frank—Jesse's correspondence with him was pretty regular. He probably told Frank all sorts of things he didn't tell Joe or Lois. Wasn't that always the way? Joe felt a stab of jealousy.

He pulled into the drive beside John's old house, which he and Lois had moved into, leaving the big house to Jesse, Jenny, and Minnie. Jesse called it "the Maze"—it was more spacious than it looked, seven rooms. Back in the 1880s, the builder had marked out a forty-two-foot square, divided it into nine parts, designated the two parts across the right front as the parlor, and two parts along the east side in the back as the kitchen, and the other five parts, square rooms, you could do with as you pleased, so it did have a mazelike quality and Joe liked it. But there was none of the elegance of Roland Frederick's kit house, with its oak paneling and sliding French doors and wide-planked floors. The Fredericks' barn was just as rough and simple, but it was big and sturdy. Since they had pulled down Walter's barn, the only trace of the place he'd grown up on was the Osage-orange hedge, which was thriving and, as always, a pain in the neck.

When he turned off the truck and opened the door, he was hit with a blast of heat. He went up the steps of the porch and looked at the thermometer—over a hundred, but the porch faced south. Might be ninety-eight in the shade. The weather had been doomfully good, and you really could hear the corn grow this time of year, if you could stand it. Chest-high by the Fourth of July.

The farm was still peculiar to him from this vantage point: It spread to the south and west of where he was standing, rather than to the north and east. The house was on a long gentle hill with a view, where John had kept cattle until he died, and which Joe had tried in hay and in beans—that was the part he would take out of cultivation. But the house wasn't on the hill. For an Iowa farmer, there was nothing desirable about a long sweeping driveway or a grand vista. John had planted a few apple trees; the apples from one of the trees were red streaked with green, not like any of the others, but they made a wonderful pie. And so, yes, all of his dreams had come true.

Joe crossed the road. The roof of the big house was just visible over the ridge, and inside it were the precious ones, Joseph Guthrie, two years old, and Franklin Perkins, ten months. They were another dream come true—they'd sit on the carpet, stacking colorful blocks, knocking them over, laughing, while across the room Lois and Jenny compared notes on how to bake zwieback. But he could see it, looking south—he could see all the layers lift off—the roof of the house, the second floor, the first floor. He could see the children and Jesse and

Jenny and Lois and Minnie being lifted out on a fountain of debt and scattered to the winds; then he could see the corn and beans scoured away, and the topsoil, once twelve inches thick, now six inches thick, and below that, the silty clay loam, more gray than black, then the subsoil, brownish clay all the way down, down, down to the yellow layer, mostly, again, clay, all of it exposed, all of it flying into the atmosphere like money, burning up in the hot sunshine, disappearing. He shook his head, closed his eyes, took his cap off, and put it back on. The vista re-formed itself: blue sky, green corn, brown roof.

1986

For their wedding, which, Richie was told, would take place at City Hall with Ivy's assistant, Jeanine, as a witness and then would be announced by postcard to all of their friends and relatives, Ivy had required only that they go on a Friday morning, always a slow day at her office, and that it be followed by a cab ride to Katz's Deli just in time for lunch. Her cousin, four years younger, had gotten married in the fall, at their very liberal synagogue in Philly, under a chuppah, with only the two sets of parents present. No one cried, everyone ate blintzes, and, the cousin told Ivy, they'd spent the first night of their honeymoon at a bed-and-breakfast on the Jersey Shore, ripping open envelopes and counting the money. Somehow, for Ivy, this wedding balanced Michael and Loretta's "show-off capitalist bacchanal," and though its effects were slow, they were sure. He had asked her six times if she really wanted to get married, until, finally, she'd taken him to Macy's, where she helped him buy a navy suit and a pink-and-white striped shirt with a white collar.

They got the license before going to work on Thursday. On Friday, Richie left the office at ten and took a cab over to Worth Street, where he saw Ivy and Jeanine climbing the steps, pulling the big gold door open, and disappearing inside. He didn't call out, because the requirements of secrecy meant that he would just happen to encounter her there, and they would just happen to get married. It pleased him to see her from across the street. She was attractive from the front, but she was dynamite from the back, with her square shoulders, slender waist, pert ass, and sassy walk: Oh, how nice to meet you, Mr. Roth, Mr. Updike, Mr. Cheever, Ms. Morrison—who do you think you are? Inside, he saw her down the hall, and followed her. As he watched her open the door to the clerk's office, he got a weird feeling, but it wasn't until he opened the door himself that he understood the reason—Michael and Loretta were standing there, big grins on their faces. As soon as Michael saw him, he whooped and started laughing. Ivy must not have noticed them in the crowd; she spun around. And then Loretta was putting her arms around Ivy and kissing her and exclaiming, "Why would we let you get away with it? Oh, you look great! You must not be pregnant after all!"

Ivy pinched him, hard, on the biceps as she kissed him hello, so he said to Michael, "What an asshole you are. You've been in my stuff."

"Always," said Michael, and Richie knew that this was true.

They hadn't seen Michael and Loretta in months, mostly because of the Donald Manes flap. Back in January, he said he was carjacked, and then it came out that he'd actually tried to commit suicide. In March, he did commit suicide, stabbing himself in the heart while his psychiatrist had him on hold. And then it all came out—bribery, pay-offs, Mayor Koch at the top and who knew at the bottom, maybe Alex Rubino. Richie's boss, Congressman Scheuer, was rich and didn't need to pay any attention to this, and he rather smoothly, Richie thought, eased himself away from the whole thing. Richie explained to donors that, whatever the flamboyant Queens Borough president may have done, his congressman was a war hero, a polio survivor, a harmonica virtuoso, one of the most powerful men in Washington, but Michael went on and on about how corruption was the soul of the Democratic Party, and not only in New York—Loretta could tell you any number of stories about San Francisco, where her parents would not even go anymore. Richie had met Koch. He hadn't met Manes, but, oddly enough, he had met Manes's twin brother when he and Ivy were in Queens, looking at cars. This Manes—Morton, his name was—had the BMW dealership there. "Manes" was an odd name, so Ivy asked him if he knew Donald Manes; Morton said that he was the older twin; then Ivy pointed to Richie and said that he was a twin, also an older one. "Is your twin out of control?" she asked, and Manes rolled his eyes and laughed.

Richie had thought that Loretta, Chance, Tia, and now Binky (also known as Beatrice) were in California for the winter. With a smile, Loretta handed him his boutonniere, a small, fragrant lavender rose. She presented Ivy with bouquet of gardenias and wore a gardenia in her hair. When their names were announced, they went before the officiant, said their vows, and signed their papers; Loretta took pictures with the camera that was in her bag. It wasn't bad; Richie was almost feeling normal, almost feeling, well, positive, until they went back out onto the front steps of the building and saw twenty or thirty of their friends, shouting congratulations and throwing rice. Ivy pressed herself against him and said, "Oh God!" Richie saw at once that Lynne, Michael's newest mistress, was in the group, next to a friend of Loretta's from her cooking-class days. He gripped Ivy's hand and walked her down the steps, and then there were hugs and congratulations, and they were swept over into Foley Square, where, it appeared, the reception was to take place. How Michael and Loretta had gotten all these phone numbers without Xeroxing Ivy's Rolodex, Richie could not imagine, unless . . . He stared at Jeanine—she was smiling, she did not look guilty.

A table, a tablecloth, a cake, champagne, little sandwiches. Richie overheard Loretta telling the woman from her cooking class that she had just gotten in from the ranch three days before; she'd brought the nanny, the nurse, and all three children; they were camped out on top of one another at the place on Fifty-seventh. Michael had done most of the inviting, but of course he'd forgotten the flowers, even the cake—what did he think they were going to eat? She'd done all that. Well, she said, if she ever moved back to New York year-round, she had her eye on Park Avenue in the Sixties, which had a pastoral quality, didn't you think? As she turned away, the cooking-class woman rolled her eyes. Ivy stood beside the cake, staring at it; it looked like white marble encrusted with carved architectural embellishments, two layers. Jewish weddings never had cake. Richie didn't know whether this was true. Michael had not bothered to invite any parents. But, then, neither had Ivy. Michael popped the champagne— Moët & Chandon—and Jeanine went around with small plastic cups. When she came up to Richie, he said, "Were you in on this?"

Jeanine said, "Not till this morning. I got there first, and they were waiting. They asked me not to tell."

"Ivy hates this."

"Only because she didn't arrange it," said Jeanine.

Once everyone had their champagne, the toasts began, and Richie had to stand there smiling—with his arm around Ivy, sometimes gazing at her fondly—while shouts went up. Michael declared himself the best man, raised his glass, and said, "I've spent years looking out for my little brother here, making sure that he stayed out of trouble, or at least didn't get caught, and, finally, here we are, I can pass him over to a better caretaker than I am, knowing he's safe, or safe-ish—let's say that!" Everyone laughed and took a sip. The biggest laugher was Lynne. Just for a moment, Loretta looked at her curiously; then she pulled her gaze away from Lynne and lifted her glass. She said, "I never had a sister or a brother, and as soon as I met Ivy, even before she delivered my boy Chance in a bathtub on the twelfth floor of some rat trap, I knew she was the one I wanted. I don't know if this is their dream, but it is mine, and I'm glad it's a dream come true!" Everyone shouted "Hurray!" and drank again.

It was time to cut the cake. To Lynne, who was now standing next to Michael, Loretta said, "Oh, excuse me," her tone implying that maybe Lynne had strayed over from East Broadway. Lynne looked nothing like Loretta: she was compactly built, with short hair and glasses. Richie felt that he was reading Loretta's mind: Maybe; no; not sexy; not possible. Ivy exclaimed, "It is a beautiful cake. I am so surprised, I'm sort of struck dumb!" and that distracted both Loretta and Lynne. Richie didn't have to look at Michael to sense that he was thrilled out of his tree at the dangers he was courting. Loretta handed Ivy a silver knife tied with a white satin bow. She held the knife, and Richie held her hand, and they cut a piece out of the cake. They had been to enough weddings to know that now they had to feed each other. Richie's hand was trembling, so Ivy had to cock her head a little to receive his offering. After everyone shouted and applauded and Ivy started cutting the cake, he heard Loretta say, "We've never met. I'm Loretta Langdon." She was talking to Lynne. Behind them, off to their right, Michael was practically hugging himself with pleasure.

Lynne said, "I thought we did meet. But, if not, we should." Everyone knew that Michael had mistresses. Everyone knew that, on the very day Binky was born, the reason Loretta hadn't been able to get hold of him (and had had to give him the news through Richie) was that Michael was up in the Catskills, looking at old Victorians with one of them. Perhaps it was Lynne.

"Why is that?" said Loretta.

Having made her way through ten or twelve slices, Ivy set down the knife. She said, "It really is delicious. Infused with some liqueur— Amaretto? Loretta! Pay attention to me! I am the bride! Who made the cake?"

Loretta turned and smiled again, and Lynne, now looking red-faced and very young, slipped away.

Loretta said, "Veniero's. They were the real reason I needed you to have a wedding!"

Richie slipped his arm around Ivy, turned her toward him, and kissed her as he had failed to do after the ceremony, deeply, lovingly, thankfully, appreciatively. Saved again.

CHARLIE WAS a blond now. He had been a blond for fourteen hours, and every time he looked in the rearview mirror and saw his springy hair, he laughed. Riley, his girlfriend, laughed, too, and squeezed his hand. She was now a redhead. First she had done herself, and then they had gone to the drugstore, gotten the dye, and done him. Riley maintained that if you were leaving home in your new Tercel wagon, heading west on the I-70 toward Kansas and Colorado, out of the woods and onto the plains, to Denver, then new hair was the best preparation. After Denver, who knew? But they both had jobs. Charlie would be working for an outdoor outfitter that also ran hiking tours and rafting trips in the Rockies, and Riley had an internship with the Solar Energy Research Institute. If that jerk Reagan hadn't cut 90 percent of the institute's funding ("What did I tell you?" his mom always said, as if anyone she knew had ever voted for Reagan), she might have had a paid job, but an internship could evolve. Rents were cheap; parks were plentiful; guiding raft trips down the Colorado would be fun for Charlie, with his restless temperament. Riley was a great believer in temperament and nature over nurture. Charlie loved Riley. She was never depressed, she could always figure out how to talk people into something (most notably Charlie's mom and dad), and nothing scared her, not even defunding of solar initiatives. As a redhead, she was quite striking.

And so they drove on, past Topeka now, almost to Abilene. The landscape was flat and hot and larded with names that Riley read off the map to him—"Tonganoxie!" "Salina!" "Cawker City!" "Kanopolis!"—that he then said backward to her "Eixonagnot"— which he pronounced in the French manner—"Anilas, Rekwac Ytic, Siloponak." Why did they all sound Slavic? (And then they laughed again.) She threw down the map, got up on her knees, and kissed him while he was driving, all along the side of his face. He was twenty-one; he had a wonderful girlfriend and a new car. He stepped on the gas, and the needle eased toward ninety.

FRANK WAS SITTING across from Loretta at the dinner table when Andy said, "I got a letter from Frances Upjohn today, and Jim isn't joining her, not even for the Arc. I guess that's in three weeks or something."

"What arc?" said Chance.

Loretta said, "The Arc is a horse race."

Chance, who was four, had his own pony in California, which he was required to ride bareback. He nodded knowingly.

"Why not?" said Frank.

"He doesn't want to miss the cranberry harvest, he says, but I—"

"What cranberry harvest?" said Loretta as she sat Binky upright in her lap and hooked the cup of her nursing bra. Frank had to admire the shameless way she nursed Binky wherever she was and whenever Binky crossed her eyes in dissatisfaction. It made for a quiet babyhood. Andy held out her arms, and Loretta gave Binky to her, then went back to eating her own food, which she herself had cooked—veal sca-loppini, good. Frank said, "East of Philadelphia. Near Chatsworth. He's got three thousand acres down there, and the cranberry harvest started a week or so ago."

Loretta's face blossomed into a look both delighted and approving. She said, "Three thousand acres?"

"He's talked about buying a farm for twenty-five years. Horses, plums in France, poppies in France, a vineyard in Sonoma, even wheat there for a while. But he ended up with cranberries."

"Not scenic," said Andy. "Frances says that he won't go to Paris at all anymore. And apparently, it's very hard to find escorts to take her to parties. You can't go without an escort. She's furious."

"She can find an escort," said Frank. "But she's used to standing beside the lightbulb and having the moths flutter around her. He doesn't want to be that anymore."

"Will you take me?" Frank realized that Loretta was speaking to him, and talking about New Jersey, not Paris.

Oddly enough, he said yes.

They started early the next morning. Enough milk for two bottles had to be pumped, and the little bag with the pump and the cooler and another bottle had to be taken along for when Loretta began lactating on the road. Dalla had to be instructed about Chance's and Tia's activities, although she supervised these activities herself every single day. Even so, Loretta ushered Frank out of the house as Michael was sitting at the kitchen table in his robe, taking his first sip of coffee. Andy was still asleep in her room. Frank liked it. It felt strangely surreptitious.

They got into the Mercedes. Loretta said, "This is comfortable. I've never ridden in a Mercedes before."

She was always full of surprises.

Frank said, "What do your parents drive?"

"My dad drives a Chevy truck, and my mom drives an El Camino."

Frank burst out laughing.

"My dad swears that his headstone is going to read, 'Here lies Raymond Perroni, who drove twenty-five Chevy pickups into the ground, 1938 to whenever.' He doesn't want it to include anything insignificant."

"And your mother?"

"Well, she says she's going to be cremated. There's an altar at the house. . . . I guess we'll put her between the Catrina she bought in Oaxaca and Hickock's left front hoof, which she had plated in silver after he colicked and died."

Frank said, "Catrina?"

"Oh, that's a Mexican statue. It's a ceramic skeleton of a woman, all dressed up. Mom's is wearing this red picture hat with yellow flowers sculpted over the crown." She stared out the window. They were approaching the Garden State Parkway. She adjusted her breasts and kicked her feet. It was interesting to Frank how he enjoyed Loretta, Ivy, and Jesse so much more than his own children. Being around his own children was like having sand in his underwear that could not be gotten rid of—the timbre of Janet's voice, the knowledge of Michael's empty brutishness, the sight of Richie's temperature rising and falling in perennial reaction to Michael's slightest move. Such thoughts didn't come up with other people's children; you appreciated them for themselves. Loretta was a one-of-a-kind eccentric who did not seem to know how rare she was; ambitious Ivy was sharp and amusing company; and Jesse was the son he could not have had because he was not his brother. And he didn't at all mind his son-in-law, Jared, who was reserved in his Minnesota way, but knew all there was to know about 1's and 0's and how to string them out until they magically spiraled into some sort of electronic DNA. Janet had talked Jared out of North Carolina and into Silicon Valley, just because, Frank knew, she couldn't stand Frank's presence in their lives, but money was getting more and more disembodied every day, and Jared was no more averse to it than any red-blooded American. Frank drove steadily. The traffic was sparse; the Mercedes had a kind of feral quickness; they were already passing Elizabeth.

Frank said, "Chance is very good-tempered."

"And so he always gets his way. You can deflect him or forbid him or put him to bed, but as long as that idea is in his mind, he keeps at it. This summer, he decided that there was a treasure under one of the flagstones by the driveway. He went into my father's shop and found a big nail, and started scraping out the cement around that flagstone. Every time anyone saw him, they'd say, 'That's enough,' and Chancie would nod and put his nail in his pocket and walk away, and then he'd be back. It took him two weeks. He even figured out how to lever it up with a table knife. There was nothing under there. He didn't care. He just had to know."

"I was like that," said Frank. But, he realized, what he meant was, he'd just had to break it, whatever it was—not see what something was, but feel it fall apart. "Some kids are curious."

"Well, I wore a pair of underpants on my head for a year, because I thought they made a very nice hat. But Chancie isn't opinionated, he's dedicated. Tia doesn't talk much yet. I see her staring at Chancie, making up her mind to do everything exactly opposite to the way he does it."

She went on. They were past Perth Amboy now, not far from Sea Bright. It was too bad, Frank thought, that listening to people talk about their kids was so boring, because there were lessons to be learned. One of them, in this case, was that Loretta was an observant and thoughtful young woman, with a measure of self-knowledge. If so, Frank thought, she was surely aware of Lynne Rochelle, whom, according to Richie, Michael had installed in her own loft in SoHo over the summer. Why Michael wanted two wives, Frank could not imagine. Richie said that it was for their explosive potential—Loretta was the nitro and Lynne was the glycerin.

Frank glanced at Loretta. She was looking out the window at the passing forest. Three children in three years had done no favors to either her figure or her face. She looked forty to Michael's thirty-three. But she also looked like being a wife and a mother was her avowed destiny, and Michael could take it or leave it. If that was the case, then Michael's strategy was maybe the only one.

When they got back to Jim's double-wide after exploring the cranberry bogs, Loretta took her bag from the Mercedes and asked where the bathroom was. Frank and Jim went into the kitchen. The sink was full of coffee cups and soup bowls; the trash bin was piled with Campbell's cans on top of plastic bread bags. Not the diet Frank would have thought Jim Upjohn preferred—or had even experienced, since his ancestors had been obscenely wealthy unto the fourth generation at least. What was he, seventy-one? Five years older than Frank? Over the years, Jim Upjohn had remained far more innocent than Frank had, far more innocent than anyone Frank knew, a nice boy who might cut your head off, but always gently, gracefully, with regret, a rare breed these days. Now he went to a kitchen cabinet and took out some peanuts. He said, "Come on, watch this." Frank followed him onto the back porch of the double-wide. Jim Upjohn trotted down the steps and over to one of the taller cedars, where he slipped out of his loafers and set them side by side at the base of the tree. Then he whistled and called out, "Ronnie! Nancy!" He squatted down and sprinkled peanuts in the heel of each loafer, stood up, and backed away. There was chirping, and within moments, two squirrels, their tails fat and furry, their coats thick, scampered down the tree. Each took a different loafer, as though they knew just what they were doing. They sat upright on their tails, picking up peanuts and putting them in their mouths, all the time expressing various opinions. When the peanuts were gone, they paused a moment, almost bidding adieu before scampering back up the tree. Jim Upjohn said to Frank, "It's surprising how little they cost." He was twinkling.

But then he spun around and said, "Miracle you came, Frankie, because I need a favor. Involves you firing up that plane of yours and heading into the sunset."

"Everyone agrees that I'm semi-retired and have too much time on my hands, so I am at your service."

"I know."

"How do you know? I haven't talked to you in four months, and you don't have a phone."

"You don't think the complaints go only one direction between Paris and Englewood Cliffs, do you?"

"Andy doesn't complain."

"She remarks upon."

This would be true, thought Frank.

"Anyway, I want you to go to Aspen and meet someone. There's a conference there. I was supposed to go and help take over the world, but I can't stand the odor anymore, so I stayed home."

"Do you go anywhere?"

"To the beach over at Barnegat. There's a fellow supposed to be in Aspen, Prechter. He's got a theory about how the market works, and I want you to talk to him about it."

"What is his theory?"

"Well, basically, it's a mathematical version of Yes, uh-oh, well-maybe, or-maybe-not, okay-one-more-time. Large-scale, small-scale, middle-scale. He resurrected it, he's not taking credit for it."

"What do you care? Look at this place. You have it all."

Jim didn't disagree. He said, "I don't have a theory. I would like to have a theory."

The ultimate luxury, thought Frank.

Jim said, "Anyway, you like to fly your plane, you like to get out of the house."

Frank didn't say yes, he didn't say no, but he knew he would do it.

Loretta was charmed by the bogs, the floating cranberries, the mysteriousness of the landscape. She wanted to stay as late as she could, even though she also wanted to get back to Binky. In the end, they watched the men use long booms to push the brilliant berries into one corner, a ground of shining red in the sparkling sunlight. Then, as they left, Jim Upjohn stopped them, ran back in the house, and came out with a pot containing a flowering plant, an upright lavender blossom shading downward to white. "Arethusa," he said. "An orchid." Loretta balanced it on her lap all the way home.

Binky was screaming when they walked in the door, Chance was arguing with Dalla, and Andy was bouncing Tia on her knee. Loretta straightened her shoulders with a military air and handed the orchid to Frank, then said, "You were nice. Thank you."

Frank knew that she hadn't thought such a thing was possible before today.

PRECHTER DID INDEED have a theory, and it was interesting enough. When Frank floated the name "James Upjohn" in the air around them, Prechter turned toward it like a sunflower toward the sun. Prechter seemed to be rich, but that was not the point—the point was to be right. Frank apologetically recorded their conversation for "Mr. Upjohn, who can't make it because of the press of business," but there was no need to apologize: Prechter waxed all the more emphatic and eloquent at the thought of explaining himself to such a deity. Frank said that Mr. Upjohn would be getting in touch, he was sure. Or he was unsure. Prechter had that look when they shook hands goodbye of being stretched on a rack of longing, his goal within sight but out of reach.

Otherwise, Frank nodded to a few men he recognized, ate lunch, eavesdropped, did his best to breathe and not fall asleep. One man was sure that the Dow would hit 2,000 by Christmas (Frank had heard that one before). Another man had heard Maggie Thatcher supported apartheid in South Africa, to which the man across the table from him replied, "Well, you know, the old dear is sending help to Pol Pot, though she would deny it unequivocally."

"She's not the only one," said someone else. Because of the time change, Frank fell asleep in his room at eight-thirty and was up by four. At dawn, he left the Jerome and turned left. Aspen reminded him oddly of Iowa—maybe it was the wide streets and short build-ings—he half expected to see a grain elevator over his shoulder. Even this early, the sunlight was getting ready to be brilliant. It was September 24th, wasn't it? Lillian would have been sixty today. He reminded himself to call Arthur when he got back to the hotel. He stared at his reflection for a moment in the window of a café that was already open, saw kids—hikers, it looked like—lined up at the counter, pointing to the menu overhead, or else sitting in their boots, equipment piled beside them, their hands arced around large yellow cups. When a girl passed him, grabbed the door, opened it, and entered, Frank could smell vanilla, chocolate, and butter. His reflection looked metallic, as if his skin were flaking away to reveal the tin man beneath. He had lost ten pounds in the last year, though his doctor said he was in perfect health. The weight loss seemed to enlarge his hands in an unpleasant way. He looked at them and put them behind his back. When he looked through the window again, his eyes had adjusted. Looking through the window was like look-ing through binoculars, and what he saw, across the room, standing, kissing a girlfriend on her red hair, and then going for another cup of coffee, was himself.

He shaded his eyes, leaned forward. The kid was in his early twenties, blond, broad-shouldered, over six feet. He had teeth, and he showed them—his smile for the waitress was merry, triangular, almost heart-shaped. His eyes were no doubt blue, though Frank couldn't tell that from where he was. The real resemblance was in his walk as he went back to his table, the shape of his hips, the tilt of his torso, and, oddly, the shape of his head. Frank could see his uncle Rolf, but cheerful rather than dogged. Frank turned away and went back across the street. He stood quietly, telling himself that he was getting some air, whatever air there was to get, but really, he was waiting, and when the kid and the redheaded girlfriend exited the café and headed down the block, Frank, on his side of the street, fol-lowed them. Lydia, his long-vanished mistress, must have produced a child. Perhaps that was why she had vanished. She had vanished in '65, which could be right for the age of this kid, but he'd thought she was his own age, so she'd have given birth in her mid-to-late forties. Possible? Not possible? Frank wasn't sure, but he found himself, as he watched them from the other side of the street, doing a thing that he always did, gauging the value of the girlfriend. This one was bulky but strong, carrying a backpack; her legs in her shorts were postlike and sturdy. Her hair was piled on her head. It fell out of its clip once, and flopped forward. She coiled it up without thinking about it, still talking. She was good enough, in her way.

He was carrying a backpack, too, and another bundle, maybe a tent. Frank looked at his watch—nearly eight. He slowed his steps, let his quarry get farther away. At a stoplight, the girl, talking, stepped into the street. The boy's arm went out, automatically preserving her, as he looked both ways. She took his hand, and they obeyed the light, though no cars were nearby. Once across the street, they went along the side of a large brick building and stopped. The boy unlocked the door, pushed it open, and went inside, closing the door behind them. Frank made his way down his side of the street, crossed, took up his position. The building, an outdoor outfitter's store, was in the sunshine now, and he couldn't see much through the windows. He did see lights come on inside, he did see a man in a sweatshirt jerk on the door handle, rare back, look at the hours of operation, and turn and walk away. Nine a.m., probably. Frank went back to the Jerome and reserved his room for another night. His heart was pounding. Why this should be, he had no idea, except that it seemed to him a fixed and permanent truth that this kid was his, the son of Lydia Forêt. He picked up the phone again and dialed Arthur's number.

Arthur lived in Hamilton, New York, now, near where Hugh was teaching at Colgate, in a small apartment above some shops across from a park. Arthur didn't complain. Andy got him down to the city every so often, where she led him around art exhibitions and fed him. He was thin. That he was still alive Frank considered a miracle, but perhaps Arthur considered it a curse. He said he enjoyed his grandchildren.

He answered on the third ring, not "hello" or even "yes," but a cough. Frank said, "How are you?"

"At the moment, vibrating with curiosity."

"That I should call you on Lillian's birthday and wish you well?" That Lillian had been dead almost three years amazed Frank. If you saw someone born, you were not supposed to see them die, an entire life nested within yours.

"Tell me one thing I've always wondered," said Arthur.

"What is that?"

"What was her first word?"

" 'Mama,' I'm sure. Isn't that standard?"

"No, think. I mean after that."

"How old would she have been?"

"Frank, you have three kids and four grandchildren. Debbie's first word was 'up!' Tim's first word was 'kitty.' "

"Or 'titty,' " said Frank.

Arthur produced his first laugh.

Frank said, "I do remember that her dolls were named Lolly, Dula, and Lizzie. She used to pat them on the back, then give a little burp, and then wipe their faces. She treated them very well."

"Of course she did," said Arthur.

"Of course she did," said Frank.

Now came the time to not ask any questions about Arthur's spirits or his mental condition, so Frank said, "If I were to write down a license-plate number here in Aspen, how would I go about finding out the name of the owner of the vehicle?"

"It would take a day or so."

Frank noticed that Arthur didn't say how. He said, "I'll call you. I don't want to send it by mail."

"Are you afraid I'll wad up the letter and choke to death on it? The presence of the KGB in Aspen, Colorado, is intermittent at best." Then, "I await your next communication with interest."

"I'll call you later today."

"Be sure it's from a pay phone, and people are least observant around lunchtime."

At eleven-thirty, he wandered into the shop. He didn't see the kid. The fellow behind the counter was in his forties, balding, cheerful. And doing a good business—he kept ringing up goods, a hundred dollars, $270, is this really the vest you want? Frank moved into the footwear area, less suffocating. He passed the door to the stockroom and glanced in. There he was, shelving boxes of boots. Unencumbered, he was graceful, with a limber gait and a long reach. He was humming to himself. Frank turned an ear and leaned toward him, but he didn't recognize a tune. At that moment, the kid looked his way and said, "Oh, hi! May I help you?" The smile came to his face as if it was second nature.

No, Frank thought. This was not his child. None of his children were this lacking in distrust. He said something about hiking boots. The kid glanced around, reached for a box. He said, "These are my favorites. What are you, about an eleven? These are Timberlands. They last forever."

Frank sat down and let him kneel at his feet, slip on the reddish, heavy boot, and lace it partway up. He said, "I don't lace them all the way unless I'm hiking in pretty rough country, but they're great for stabilizing your step. . . ." The patter went on. "They were eighty-five dollars, but I'm marking them down to seventy-five this week. In Europe, they're twice that. This is the last pair of elevens."

"Okay," said Frank.

"You'll love them," said the kid. "Bob will ring them up for you. May I find you anything else?"

Maybe he was indeed the child of Lydia, kind, generous, who had accepted him, asked nothing from him, might indeed have been "Joan Fontaine," a whore who had not stolen his money, had not had him shot, had not even kicked him out of her room when he fell asleep on the job. His mother had always professed to know where someone "had got that from"—every animal and human was a walking exhibition of traits inherited from Opa or Grandma Mary or, for goodness' sake, Cousin Berta, who ended up in the asylum in Independence, less said about that the better. Frank thanked the kid; got up and walked away from him, not even turning around, over to the cash register, where his boot box was tied with a string. Bob couldn't have been more friendly—was he new to the area, wonderful country, Bob himself came from Georgia, could you imagine that? Frank said, "Your salesman was very helpful."

"Oh, Charlie? He's turned into a good boy. You should see him on a rock face. Yakking the whole time. Scary sight."

"Risk taker," said Frank.

"Good thing his parents live in the Midwest."

"Oh, where?" said Frank.

"Kansas City, I believe. Well, wear 'em in good health. Thank you for your patronage."

It was seven minutes past twelve. Frank stationed himself across the street, in the shadow of an awning, where he could watch both the front door and the side door. Sure enough, at twelve after, Charlie let himself out the side door and walked across the street to the nearby parking lot. When the car drove past Frank, he noted the Colorado license-plate number—FIL 645. Toyota wagon, light green, filled with equipment.

ARTHUR WOKE UP, as he always did, just before dawn, though dawn at the beginning of December in upstate New York was at seven-thirty in the morning. Carlie and Kevvie would be eating their breakfast—no Frosted Flakes for them, not even Cheerios. Then they would be bundled in wool mittens, scarves, and hats, hand-knit by Hugh's mother (and beautifully done, Arthur had to admit). Debbie would walk them to the school-bus stop and wait with them there. Carlie was eleven and in sixth grade, and Kevvie was almost nine and in third grade.

The report was locked in Arthur's desk, even though he knew that the last place you should put something secret was in a locked drawer in your desk. But he wasn't keeping it secret from Debbie and Hugh, who would never investigate his apartment. Nor was he keeping it secret from Frank—he'd told Frank the bare-bones fact that this young man, Charles Morgan Wickett, age twenty-one (birthday June 4, 1965), adopted (through the Our Lady of Mercy Home, St. Charles, Missouri, on June 23 of that year), son of Morgan Feller Wickett and Nina Wickett, née Lewis, of 402 Tuxedo Boulevard, Webster Groves, Missouri, graduate of Webster Groves High School and Washington University (Bachelor of Science), and recipient of one speeding ticket (June 17, 1983, eighty-three miles per hour in a seventy-mile zone), employee of Owl Creek Outfitters, Aspen, Colorado, Social Security Number 499-78-5432, was not related to any woman Frank could have known. He was the son (he hadn't yet told Frank this) of Fiona Cannon, student at the time of the birth, at Stephens College, Columbia, Missouri. Arthur remembered Fiona perfectly well—a short, daring girl, a talented equestrienne, Debbie's great friend. What Arthur saw in the boy's driver's-license photo and the high-school photo included in the report was not Frank, but Tim. The person he wanted to keep the report secret from was himself.

Arthur pushed the covers back, lay there for just another moment, then turned and put his feet on the cold floor. Suddenly he thought of his roommate, freshman year at college. He was from out west somewhere, and he had once told Arthur that his earliest memory was from when he was seven years old—only ten years before. Everything else was a blank. What was it a memory of? Arthur had asked. It was having some hash set before him for some meal, at the orphanage where he lived. Arthur, whose memories at the time were all too precise and abundant, had envied him. He remembered that envy now, and trailing behind it was another memory, of himself in the summertime, he must have been three or four, neatly dressed, sitting on the veranda of their house in Maryland (green mat underneath him, his legs pushed through the white posts, leaning forward, his hands gripping his bare knees). Walking down the street were three older boys. One was pushing a bicycle, another had two baseball bats, and the third was tossing and catching three balls as he walked. They were laughing. Undoubtedly, moments later, little Arthur was removed from the porch, so the memory was pinned into his brain like a photograph, emblematic of the moment he realized what he was missing, predictive of his future embrace of Lillian and Frank and the noisy, wild Langdons, who sometimes did what they were told, but always had something to say about it. Solitude was not good for him, and here he was again.

If Charles, or Charlie, as Frank had referred to him, had been born full-term, then he would have been conceived under Arthur's very nose, around the time Tim was heading off to the University of Virginia. That Tim had had a relationship, romance, one-night stand, episode of intercourse, whatever it might have been, with Debbie's adored—worshipped, he realized—Fiona both surprised Arthur and did not. Also in the report was some information about Fiona: Her name was now Fiona Cannon McCorkle, she ran a riding school with her husband, Jason McCorkle, in Pasadena, California. The McCorkles owed $126,000 on their house, a large sum, but maybe not for California. Jason McCorkle had been an alternate for the show-jumping team at the L.A. Olympics.

Arthur hoisted himself to his feet and walked to the window. The great attraction of upstate New York was bad weather—if not snow, then wind; if not ice, then cold; if not rain, then overcast skies. He had not been party to the negotiations that brought him here. Tina was in Sun Valley, Idaho, now, running a gallery, still making glass sculptures. Dean was in Yardley, Pennsylvania; he and Linda both had their real-estate licenses. Real estate, as everyone knew, was a time-consuming occupation.

Arthur didn't remember much about the fall of '64—that would be the point of his many shock treatments, wouldn't it? If Arthur were to tell Debbie about the report, she would insist on contacting Fiona. If the report stayed locked in his drawer, nothing would be set in motion.

Arthur turned from the window. The brass keyhole of the locked drawer sparkled. He looked away.

Over Thanksgiving, Frank had said again, "The resemblance was uncanny. When I watched Charlie walk down the street, I *felt* his gait in my body. If you saw this kid, you'd agree with me." At some point, Frank would think of Tim, Arthur was sure of that—they had always laughed about how similar Tim was to Frank, especially as an ornery and determined little boy. Arthur shook his head. He had no rights over this young man, none whatsoever.

Coming up on three years now, since his life had ended. After Lillian died, he'd embarrassed himself thoroughly, but it was logical, really—if you would prefer to be dead, why shave, or wash, or sleep, or talk? Why take out the trash? Why eat, especially if you literally could not swallow, if your stomach clenched up and prevented entry, and the smallest items of food felt jammed in your lower esophagus, making you gag? Why not leave the doors of the house open even in the coldest weather, why not empty everything of everything—let the coal burn and the heat fly away and the mice and rats raid the larder, let the water run out of the sink and over the floor, let the lightning strike the trees and the lawn grow and the garden disappear in weeds. Let the fencing collapse. And so he had been taken in hand, and there was not so much pain now. Now there was simply nothing, more convenient for everyone.

But they had returned him to the childhood he'd made every effort to leave behind, including restricting his access to dangerous objects like butcher knives and throw rugs. Was it like this for everyone when they got old? The phone was ringing now. It would be Debbie. Having gotten the kids on the bus, she would be calling to ask how he'd slept, what he was having for breakfast, what he planned to do today—would he like to come with her to the rec center and have a swim? The pool was warm. They could stop at the library on the way home, if he needed a book. She had been reading *Anna Karenina;* had Arthur ever read it? Did he think it was the greatest novel ever written? If Arthur remembered correctly, Tolstoy had written *Anna Karenina* in his late forties. Arthur was not interested in a novel someone had written in his late forties, and he suspected that if Tolstoy were beside him or, say, across from him, sitting on the rim of the bathtub, brushing his teeth, his beard to his waist, turning to spit down the bathtub drain, his hair in tangles, then hoisting himself, leaning to stare into the mirror at what he had become, he would agree. This is what they would do, he and Lev, they would creep down the stairs, making sure to hold both of the banisters. They would wince at the squeal of the front door as they opened it. They would stagger onto the street, turn right, and walk along, waving their arms. Passersby would avoid them.

The phone rang again, right on time, ten minutes after the first ring. Arthur picked it up. As usual, he couldn't bring himself to speak. But it wasn't Debbie. A voice on the other end of the line (buzzy— long distance) said, "Is this Arthur Manning?"

Arthur coughed, then forced himself to say, "Yes."

"Oh! Wow! I can't believe . . . Anyway, my name is Charlie Wickett. I hear you're trying to get in touch with me."

Arthur said, "Actually, Mr. Wickett, I am doing my best to not get in touch with you, but I see that I've failed."

Charlie laughed, and it was, indeed, Tim's laugh, full-throated but self-possessed, and Arthur burst into tears.

TWENTY-FOUR HOURS LATER, things had exploded as they always did. Debbie was both offended and dumbstruck, but she couldn't decide precisely which aspect surprised or offended her the most, there were so many. Frank was relieved, disappointed, and curious, ready to fly Arthur out to Aspen to meet the kid. Tina, somehow, felt vindicated—he lived in Aspen, not so far from Sun Valley, where her studio was—something was significant about that. Dean seemed irritated by the whole thing, as if Tim were returning to the spotlight yet again. Frank said that Andy had said, "I'm sure he's not the only one." Arthur focused on the question of how Charlie had found him. He did not expect to be found, ever, unless he presented himself. But when he asked Charlie a few days later, Charlie was forthcoming— Sister Otilia at the adoption agency was tight with his mom, though not officially, of course, and there had been gossip, and his mom had driven up to St. Charles and gone right to the Mother Superior and given her a talking-to, and so had found out who was doing the looking. His mom, of course, had always been perfectly straightforward with him, had told him early on that he was adopted, and if you were five foot two and your husband was five foot eight, and your child was six foot three, the neighbors had to be told, and so they were; as far as Charlie knew, his mom had never kept a secret in her life. Arthur said that the Mannings and the Langdons were a big family, and Charlie said, "You're kidding! Great! I always wanted a big family."

After four days, Debbie settled on Tim's betrayal as the real crime—he'd known Fiona was her friend, what in the world had he been doing, so that was why, when she saw Fiona at Madison Square Garden that time—fourteen years ago—and told her Tim had died, Fiona had turned white, nearly fallen down, and not ridden again that evening. Debbie didn't blame Fiona.

"What do you care?" said Hugh, as her voice rose.

And then she set her fork on her plate and looked around the table. Carlie was staring at her, Kevin looked worried, and Hugh looked as though he'd had it. For once in her life, she said, "I don't know," and then she shook her head at Arthur and put her face in her hands. After he and Hugh did the dishes (not a word spoken other than "I'll start the dishwasher in the morning"), Arthur went to the master bedroom and knocked on the door. She might have said something. He turned the knob and went in.

The master bedroom was a work of art—Hugh the historian had built the headboard out of spalted maple. His mother had knitted the bedspread, moss-green lace. The two bedside tables were etched glass, made by Tina. In one corner, there was an antique rocking chair with a rattan seat. Debbie was sitting cross-legged on the floor, as if she didn't dare touch any of these beautiful things. Arthur sat in the rocking chair and eased it over toward her. Then he did what Lillian would have done: he started rocking and didn't say a word. Lillian always said, "If you don't ask them, they will tell you."

Debbie didn't look at him, but she did say, "Do you remember when you were forty?"

"More or less," said Arthur.

"Did you feel grown up?"

"Only reluctantly."

"Everyone says that!"

"They do?" said Arthur, genuinely surprised.

"Something like it. Everyone wants to be young, everyone wants to be irresponsible."

"Or maybe," said Arthur, "not responsible."

"I always wanted to grow up!"

"I understand that. Our household was chaos."

"And everyone loved it but me! Are you sure I wasn't adopted?"

"I think you were a statistical outlier."

Debbie said, "But I didn't grow up! I didn't! I just left certain feelings behind without realizing it, and they're always coming back."

"I know," said Arthur.

"Don't tell me that."

"But I have to tell you that, sweetheart. I have to. Because that is my experience. Ask your uncle Frank; ask your aunt Andy. Ask her—she's had as much psychoanalysis as anyone; she would know."

"She is a mess," said Debbie.

"But a strangely prescient mess," said Arthur.

"Why did you love Tim for being bad and hate me for being good?" She said this quietly, as if she were only asking, as if no resentment remained.

Arthur leaned forward, took her chin in his hand. He didn't know what to say, but he did want to look into her face. In spite of the fact that Arthur now experienced Debbie more or less as his jailer, he summoned up some appreciation: she was thorough, she was careful, she had premature wrinkles between her eyebrows from years of conscientious worry, and underneath it all, she had a phantomlike air of vulnerability-transformed-into-bravery that perhaps he had never noticed before. He said, "You must know that you don't love children for being good or bad. I know you know that."

"Why do you love them?"

"Because you do," said Arthur. He paused, then said, "Because they don't know what's coming and maybe you do."

"Doesn't that make them tragic figures?" asked Debbie. "I can't think that."

"You do think that," said Arthur, "because you—"

"Because I put them on the bus in the morning and take them off the bus in the afternoon, because I won't feed them sugar, because the house has been childproofed, because they wear helmets when they ride their bikes."

"And so," said Arthur, "we loved you because you made sure the gate to the swimming pool was latched, and we loved Tim because he jumped off the roof of the house into the deep end, and we loved Dean because he was daring enough to get that fourth foul in every game but careful enough not to get the fifth, and we loved Tina because she tie-dyed all the pillowcases when everyone was out one afternoon. Who you are shapes how you are loved."

"You didn't love us equally."

"We loved you individually. How could we not?"

"How could you not," Debbie said.

After he got back to his apartment that evening, Arthur remembered how completely he'd thought he'd solved the problem of his own childhood once he'd claimed Lillian and enveloped her in his dream—no one idle, no one beset by solitude, everyone laughing. The problem he had not solved, or even known existed, was how quickly it passed, every joke, every embrace, every babyhood and childhood, every moment of thinking that he had things figured out for good, and also every moment, just like this one, when his spirits lifted though he hadn't seen the boy, knew next to nothing about him, had only heard his voice and his laugh and his enthusiasm.

If you enjoyed *Early Warning*
don't miss the final book in the
Last Hundred Years trilogy

Golden Age

Coming soon